AT TWILIGHT'S FALL

AT TWILIGHT'S FALL

DEATH WATCH
KILLJOY

ELIZABETH FORREST

DAW BOOKS, INC.

DONALD A. WOLLHEIM, FOUNDER
375 Hudson Street, New York, NY 10014
ELIZABETH R. WOLLHEIM
SHEILA E. GILBERT
PUBLISHERS
http://www.dawbooks.com

DEATH WATCH

To Sheila, for her wonderful perceptions; to Paula, for her infinite patience; and to Elsie and Betsy, for making me part of the family.

Chapter 1

The lighting in the prison's interrogation room was harsh. It was aimed to leave no shadows in any corner, and the passageway beyond it seemed dim in contrast. Angry graffiti scarred the wooden table-top. Chairs were scattered about, only three for the six or seven who stood there. *Seven,* Carter thought. *I always forget to count myself.* But neither Carter nor any of the others sat down.

His fingers moved against the tops of his thighs, not twitching, but typing. Typing out his thoughts and the story he was putting together as he stood in the corner, waiting. The room smelled of Death Row, although few enough had gone to their sentencing in the last several years. It was the waiting which sweated the odor out of the inmates, he decided. It was the waiting, and the anger, and the hatred, and the fear which sank into the stone.

The guard looked at him, a bluff young man, his glance passing over him, catching the finger movement, pausing, then looking away.

He didn't look threatening enough, Carter noted, almost with dis-appointment.

Steps came shuffling down the corridor. The two lawyers, the war-den, two FBI suits, and one guard all turned to the locked gateway. Three guards, one of them the turnkey, the other two doing escort at the prisoner's elbows, brought in the man for whom they all stood waiting.

Heavily shackled, garbed in prison oranges, the man had lost more weight, Carter noticed, since he'd last seen him. His dark brown hair had grown past the sharp edges of a stylish razor cut. He had the tanless complexion of someone who'd spent years incarcerated, but there was something about his face which had always fascinated Carter. Now he could put a finger on it . . . more than one, as he mentally typed it into his memory. The face was virtually unlined. A wrinkle or two about the eyes, from the West Coast sun. But no laugh or smile wrinkles, despite the vaguely pleasant expression the prisoner wore, as though life had never permanently touched him. Carter, a good five years younger, had a face which could double as a road map.

Within that noncommittal face, however, the light hazel eyes were busy, taking in everything as his escorts marched him into the room. They put their backs to the door as the heavy locks clicked into place.

Bauer's glance slid over him as if Carter were of absolutely no consequence. The serial killer examined every square inch of the room deliberately, slowly, until his gaze came back to Carter. He was looking, Carter Wyndall realized suddenly, for a way out or anything he could use as a weapon. Finding nothing, he turned his attention back to those of flesh whom he might manipulate instead. As if he'd suddenly gained consequence, the man looked fully at Carter. Then he smiled.

"Hello, Windy. Nice to see you again."

The warden spoke icily, "We're waiting, Bauer. Shut up and sit down."

Bauer shuffled forward, his hands snugged down in front of him with so little latitude that if he fell, he would fall face first with no way to catch himself. Bauer's falling was the least of their worries. One of the FBI suits, the black man with gray heavily salted through his hair, pulled a chair out. He was Tyrone Baker, and with the execution of the prisoner days hence, he would face his retirement with the murderer's death as a sort of final victory. Bauer, still looking vaguely amused, sat down.

"Just greeting old friends," he said. "Surely there's nothing wrong in that. Can't add a consecutive life sentence for that, now, can you?" A trace of the South lingered in his voice, though Carter knew that Bauer had spent no more than five of his early years there. It was a part of the charming facade, carefully re-created.

The second FBI agent, beefy white but neat, navy-suited with a blue and silver splashed tie, sat down across from Bauer. He had the haircut Bauer had once owned, sharp, defined, every strand blow-dried into place. He was the agent on record, John Nelson, who'd brought Bauer in. He did not look happy now to see his quarry in shackles.

Carter imagined that he, like all of them, would be happier when Bauer was six feet under, and that date was less than two weeks off, all appeals finally exhausted. It had been a long eight years.

Warden Mulhoney tapped his fingers on the table, trying to get Bauer's attention, but Bauer was looking at Carter again. Even white teeth showed slightly as he asked, offhandedly, "Did you find the body?"

Carter found himself loath to answer. He did not like being in the position of making news. He did not understand why Bauer had asked for him, or passed the information to him that he had, but he'd gone looking anyway, with the police, and found a grisly treasure. Now he was in it, somehow, enmeshed with this monster, and he did not like it at all.

Nelson answered sharply for him. "Yes, we did." The FBI agent's eyes flashed hard and bright, as if in response to a challenge.

"There's more," the prisoner said with satisfaction, "where that came from."

That, typed Carter silently. As if the tortured skeletal framework had not once belonged to anything human, let alone a nine-year-old girl. *More where that came from.* He controlled a shudder, in case Bauer was still watching him somehow although the man's attention was now directed at the agent and the warden.

"What do you say, gentlemen?" Bauer prodded a little.

Mulhoney's mouth twisted. The words spilled out. "You've been granted an indefinite stay. As long as you talk, and locations and details pan out, we'll let you keep talking. But the minute we think you're jerking us around—"

Bauer smiled. The expression folded into his unlined face around his mouth, making little impact. Carter saw that when he stopped smiling, evidence of the gesture would be gone as completely as if it had never happened. He dropped one shoulder slightly, and looked over at Carter.

"Thank you, Windy," he said.

He wanted to remain silent. He should remain silent. He wasn't a media journalist, by God, he was a newspaperman, and this monster had chosen him, cut him out of the herd of reporters following the trials for reasons Carter had never understood, but he knew that flashy verbiage wasn't part of it. He'd been given interviews he could not turn down, and, eventually, information he could not withhold. Nelson hated him for that. Goaded, he could not hold his tongue. "Don't thank me. I have my press pass for the execution. But if your staying alive a little longer means one more family doesn't have to wonder why their loved one never came home, then I guess I have to live with it."

Bauer's smile flushed into a grin. "I owe you one," he said, as if he hadn't heard a word Carter said.

Carter could see it written in the body language all around him. No one there but Bauer was grateful to Carter for getting the man a stay of execution, not even his attorneys. He'd gotten the defense he was entitled to. Now the state and his victims deserved justice. For a fleeting moment, Carter wished he'd never published the interviews, the startling new confession. Ted Bundy had tried this in his final hours, too, but he'd jerked too many chains, been too confident they wouldn't fry him if he started talking. He'd been too coy. His ego could not resist the opportunity he'd been given. He'd tried to drag out the confessions, had been vague, thinking to give himself years. The state of Florida had stopped listening almost immediately and fried him anyway. Carter wished the state of Illinois had done the same here.

Mulhoney said flatly, "Don't get your dancing shoes yet. Your movements will be highly restricted. You'll be part of an experimental program, as well, if you agree to this."

Good, thought Carter. *Stick needles and tubes all over him. Make him bleed a little. Get something back.*

Bauer's smile vanished. As Carter had imagined, the smooth, passionless face looked as if it had never pretended the warmth. "What kind of program?"

"Testing. Neurological mapping. Crime scene re-creation."

The lawyers, who'd been absolutely silent all this time, stirred. The younger one, Latino with a thick gold chain and a Hebrew *chai* hanging upon his collar, said, "You don't have to do this. We can negotiate further."

Bauer dismissed him with a wave of one finger. Animation returned to Bauer's face. The eyes warmed, this time. "Memories," he said as if savoring them. "Of course."

Carter concealed a shudder as he turned away. The two attorneys leaned over the warden, brought papers out of their pockets, no paper clips, no staples, one ballpoint for signing, no cap. Bauer was watched very carefully as he used the pen to sign, and returned it.

Amused, Bauer watched his attorneys and the warden sign as well. While their heads dipped low, he traded a last look with Carter.

He smiled. *Thank you,* he mouthed silently.

Carter would have turned his back on him, but even with nine other men in the room and shackled, it would not have been a prudent thing to do.

What had he done?

Seven months later, when word came that Bauer had escaped, Carter tried to commit suicide for the first time.

He tried again when the first body was found, a young woman, with a note pinned to her mutilated chest.

Thank you, it read.

He never had any doubt who the note was for. He lost the will, the need, to live. He did not thank the paramedics who thought they'd restored him. Eventually, he lost his job and drifted westward, still writing, his face still etched with a roadmap of lines, and the light gone from his eyes.

That was what he saw whenever he cared to look into a mirror. He rarely cared to. He bought an electric razor just so he wouldn't have to, anymore.

Chapter 2

McKenzie hustled indoors. Instead of a Seattle late morning after a brisk rain, the house smelled of coffee growing cold in its pot, the fabric softener from laundry in the dryer, and the musky aroma of dog. The kitchen door creaked behind her as she shut it.

The rental house was modest by any standards, but she had done what she could to make it homey. The furnishings were carefully chosen buys from local garage sales, the curtains she'd hand-sewn from decorator sheets bought at close-out stores. She was proud of what she'd been able to accomplish starting from scratch. Fresh paint gleamed on walls displaying pock and spackle marks from previous tenants. Only the Northwestern tendency toward mildew, a never-ending battle, could wilt her. But it was the dog smell, faint but distinguishable, which made McKenzie smile. "Cody! I'm home."

She dropped her backpack to the floor as Cody galloped in from the family room. His golden retriever tail sliced the air vigorously, nails scrabbling across the linoleum for traction. His throat swelled with greeting. The young dog, no longer a puppy but not yet an adult, launched himself at her knees. He butted his head into her hands, filling her fingers with dog kisses and whining his anxiety to her.

"We made it through finals!" she said to him. "And you're famous. Look!" He nosed the slick magazine from her hand as she pulled it from her backpack. It landed cover outward on the linoleum, its woodsy cover photography with tall trees and college logo, proclaiming itself the *North Woods Leavings*. "Hey! I'm a published poet, even if you don't care. Sarah nagged me and nagged me, so I did it." She grabbed the magazine up before he could trample it. "Just give me a bone, huh?"

She ran her hands through his silky fur as he leaned against her denim knees. She loved the feel of him. It was both sensual and comforting. What would she do without Sarah and Cody in her life? What joy would she have? Her marriage was a cage, classwork and her friends a temporary key. And here at home, Cody was her only warmth. "I love you, big pup."

The golden retriever pressed against her, ears down, his voice a soft grumble of anxiety. As her fingertips traced the muscles along his back, she came to his neck and found the hackles raised there, ever so slightly. He wasn't just happy to see her, then. Something scared or bothered him. The budding warmth of the day escaped her, bled away and replaced by a shock of cold. Her head throbbed once, slightly. McKenzie put her hand to the bridge of her nose, and rubbed lightly between her eyebrows.

Somebody was out there.

It was a tingle of that old feeling, the one she could never quite explain to anyone, the feeling that kept her hanging around the house sometimes, just long enough to get that phone call. The feeling that sometimes let her finish Sarah Whiteside's exuberant statements before even fast-talking Sarah could get there.

A feeling that walked up her spine now with icy steps.

Cody whined again, and pushed his cold nose into her palms. His worry chased away her excitement.

McKenzie paused. She grew still, trying to listen over the dog's sounds. Nothing reached her, but fear grazed the back of her neck anyway. Was someone else in the house?

"Who's there?"

Her voice echoed back thinly from the sparsely furnished rooms. No answer. She ought to be alone.

No one but her and the dog, alone for days, and she expected to be alone for days longer. These were her days of peace, the solitary days when her husband was driving a truck on the road. She normally did not mind them, found nothing to fear in them. But today was different. McKenzie swallowed tightly. Something flickered in Cody's eyes, something drawing his attention. Something behind her.

She bent over, reaching for the strap of her backpack to heft its reassuring weight. Cody showed his teeth.

As she bent over, the intruder spoke. "Now that's a pretty sight. I'd like it a lot better if I hadn't been waiting all morning to see it."

The flat, emotionless voice filled the kitchen.

Her heart fluttered. "Jack! You're home early." McKenzie bolted upright, pack in hand, turning. She looked into the flat-cheekboned face of her husband, into dirty-brown eyes that held no welcome in them, and forced a calming smile.

He pushed at the sleeves of his worn flannel shirt. Blue and red plaid had bled into one another, into a faded burgundy. His hips were hollowed inside his jeans as he leaned against the doorjamb. "Days early, and what do I get for the effort? I pulled back deadhead, just to be with you, and I find the house empty."

"I had finals." She shoved the magazine into her backpack, trying not to let her hands shake. She kept her voice evenly modulated, not patronizing, but gentle. Unprovocative, nonaggressive. Dear God, please let nothing she did be the spark that set him off.

His eyes flickered over her. "Thank God for that. Maybe I'll have a real wife, then. Or has Sarah talked you out of that, too?" He moved his lanky body into the kitchen and sat down at the table.

He didn't want an answer, but she felt she had to give him one. "Sarah doesn't tell me what to do." McKenzie bit off each word, to get them all out. Sarah's plain, yet engaging face, perpetually framed by sable hair tucked into braids, interrupted by wire-rimmed glasses, brightened by an everlasting smile gave her momentary strength. "She's just a friend."

"Tell that to my phone bill." Jack stretched an arm over the back of the dinette chair. "She told you to go back to school; you did it. She told you to put your poem in the student magazine; you did it. Maybe if she told you to clean the oven, you'd do that. Maybe I could work this to my advantage."

Cody, pressed against her knees, had begun to tremble. Dogs, she thought, with hearing so much better than hers. Did he hear the same menace in Jack's voice that she heard, only magnified? Her temples pulsed. *Streaks of crimson across the floor. . . .* Mac blinked in confusion, as something slashed its way across her vision, interrupting it. A feeling of dread balled itself in her stomach, threatening to rise, to fill her.

He put his callused hand out. "So let me see it."

"What?"

"Are you stupid? Let me see it."

She gripped her bag. "No. I mean, it's nothing. Just a silly poem about the dog."

"No love song to me, eh?"

"No. Nothing about us. I mean, that would be too personal, wouldn't it?" McKenzie dropped the backpack, moving automatically, woodenly, to the counter and the coffeemaker. "Fresh coffee. That's what you need. It'll just take a minute." Quickly, to hide the shaking of her hands, she opened cabinets to get coffee and a filter, got rid of the old brew to replace it with the new.

The flash of vision had rattled her, along with Jack's mood. He was watching her every second, hawklike. She could feel it drilling between her shoulder blades. More by feel than sight, she measured the coffee into the filter of the coffeemaker and set the timer. She tripped over the dog as she moved to fill the pot with water. Cody flinched, but stayed at her feet the whole time, weaving in and around her ankles, protecting her and seeking her reassurance at the same time.

What was Jack staring at? She pushed a strand of hair behind one ear, feeling the heat in her face in response to being watched.

Calm. Keep calm. Let sleeping dogs lie. Don't wake sleeping dogs. Don't wake your father's fury. Don't . . . The memory of her mother's voice echoed her own thoughts. *Be calm.* She held her breath a moment to slow her heartbeat. She could remember her kitchen, growing up, her father, his volatile temper, her mother saying, *Calm down, just calm down,* before sending McKenzie away to safe exile in the back bedroom.

McKenzie bit her lip, watched the coffeemaker intently, until the clear water began to steam and drizzle through the filter, emerging almost magically into the coffeepot the color of mud, aromatic and enticing. Jack loved coffee. She flashed a smile over her shoulder. "Smells good."

He did not respond immediately, just tilted his head and continued to stare hard at her. He sat with his legs splayed out in front of him, jeans worn, boots the color of rich chamois, watermarked and mud-stained, his faded plaid shirt open at the throat. The coiled hairs mirrored the dark color of his hair, nondescript, with a fleck of premature gray here and there. There was nothing at ease or easy about him. The muscles along his legs and arms reminded her of a cat about to spring. His mouth opened. "You look different, Mac. I don't know what it is yet, but I don't like it."

She paused, her hands in mid-flight bringing down the mugs from the cabinet. "I don't know what you mean." She hated the way he looked at her.

"Sure you do, Mac."

His chair scraped across the floor. Muscles bunching, she swung around to meet him. Cody tangled her feet and she fell, sprawling across the linoleum. The dog scrambled away, frightened. She gasped to catch her breath, feeling horribly foolish and awkward, and twisted around to put her hands under her to get up. The dread knotted in her stomach exploded, possessing her, rendering her helpless.

Jack's shadow crossed her. McKenzie craned her head around to look up at him just as he put his foot down on her throat, pinning her to the floor.

Fear iced through her. "Jack—"

His eyes narrowed, transforming into slits of darkness. "What the hell do you think you're doing?"

His boot smelled of sweat. Its tread ground into the flesh of her neck. But he wasn't angry yet, just annoyed. *Stay calm. Let sleeping dogs lie.* She swallowed carefully. "Making you coffee."

"I can see that. That's not what I'm talking about." He held his penknife, wicked and slender. It caught the light from the kitchen window as he cleaned a fingernail with it. She could remember the Christmas she'd given it to him, and wished she had not thought of it as a gift.

What did he want from her? What had she done wrong this time? McKenzie's thoughts whirled around her. She lay passively on the floor, feeling her sweat pool beneath her. Her neck ached.

She wanted to wriggle out from under his foot, and shoved that feeling down. *Be passive. Stay calm.* "What is it?"

"You know what you did. Did that bitch Sarah recommend this, too?"

But she didn't know what he meant! McKenzie forced down a breath, felt her throat pressing tightly to get it through. "Just tell me what I did wrong. Please. I promise I won't do it again."

Jack trimmed a cuticle neatly with the tip of the knife. She held her breath a second, fearing for him. Afraid he'd slice himself open, and his temper would spurt forth like hot blood. There was a time when she'd mistaken that for vitality, found the current which always ran just under his skin exciting, dynamic. In a community college full of boys wandering around trying to find themselves, she'd met a man who'd seemed hot-wired into his future. Older, wiser, he'd had all the confidence she and all her friends had lacked. Days of classes had melded into a courtship. She'd left her athletic grant and her scholarship behind to marry him. He was all she had ever wanted, she'd thought.

He was all she had. It was the emptiness which had driven her back to school. Not Sarah. Not guilt at what she'd given up, but a desperate search to reclaim herself.

And he knew that, hated it. He must. She clenched her jaw. He wanted to take that away from her!

He showered fingernail parings upon her face. Like thorns, they prickled her skin.

Coffee aroma steamed throughout the kitchen and Jack ignored it. He looked down at her.

"But that's just it, Mac," he said. "You always make these promises, and you keep them. You do. But then you always go *and do something twice as bad.*"

"I'm sorry. I'll try, Jack, honest to God, I'll try—" Another nail paring fell across her eyelid. She tried to blink it away. She stopped as she saw Jack leaning low over her.

She could see the crow's-feet at the corners of his eyes, wrinkles etched in from a lifetime of looking at the bright ribbons of highways over a truck's steering wheel. College had only been a brief detour for him. She could faintly smell beer on his breath. "You know what they say. Those who can, do. Those who can't, try." He mocked her.

He reached out with his left hand and dug his fingers deep into her hair. "I've been watching you, and thinking and thinking about what it is that's bothering me." One eyebrow went up. "*You got your hair cut.* Now you know I told you never to do that."

The pressure of his foot on her windpipe increased as he bent over her. McKenzie could feel her forehead go slick. Her words tumbled out in a few gasped sentences, losing the calm even as she fought for it. "It was just a trim! The ends were broken . . . the hair won't grow if the ends are split, Jack. It wasn't even an inch, I swear to God it wasn't."

"I didn't ask for any excuses." He wound the hair about his hand. "Did I?" The knife flashed in his hand.

Unreasoning panic swept her. "What are you doing?" She shook, the small of her back bouncing off the floor, as she fought the impulse to push him off and run. *Let sleeping dogs lie.* McKenzie closed her eyes.

"Look at me!"

Her eyes flew open. The foot on her throat gave way as he came down on her chest with both knees, pinning her. "You want your hair cut? I'll give you a haircut." The knife came sweeping down.

McKenzie screamed. The sound tore out of her throat, leaving it raw and empty. Jack's eyes went darker, and his face flushed. The sawing of the blade grabbed at her scalp. She felt the skin part, giving way, the hair tearing clear. He shook his fist in her face. Strands of honey-blond hair waved in the air. He threw the fistful aside and clutched at her again. She arched her back and tossed her face aside.

"Come on, bitch," he said. "This is what you want, isn't it? Isn't it? You want to look so butch no one will touch you, right? You want me laughed at, don't you? When I tell you not to do something, by God, that's what I damn well mean!"

"Jack, please! Please!" The knife nicked her ear and she let out a tiny squeak.

He stopped in mid-strike, as though aware he'd drawn blood.

That was all the opening Cody needed.

She'd thought it had been Jack growling, under his breath, under his cursing. She'd forgotten all about the dog.

His red-gold body sailed between them. He hit Jack on the shoulder and went for his hands, snarling. Ivory teeth clashed and snapped. She felt another handful of hair part from her scalp before Jack pulled away.

"SON of a bitch!" He kicked and missed Cody. The dog lay across her, not moving, his eyes leveled on Jack. He began to growl again in warning.

She could feel the dog's heartbeat across her flank. He trembled, just as she did, but he wasn't moving.

"Cody. That's enough. Stay."

She wiggled out from under him, put a hand on the back of his neck. She crouched on her knees beside him. Her scalp stung enough to bring tears to her eyes. She shook them off. The dog's tail moved slightly to acknowledge her touch, but he never took his eyes off Jack.

"He doesn't mean it."

"Sure he does," Jack answered easily. He skinned his lips back from his teeth, uncannily like the dog facing him. "C'mere, Cody."

The dog flinched under her hand. McKenzie relaxed a little as Jack called the dog again to apologize. The golden retriever spasmed, torn between obeying and staying at her feet. "It's all right, Cody," she comforted him. She had to get him under control.

"I said, c'mere, dammit!" Jack grabbed for his collar, anger spiking his voice.

He caught the dog by his soft ear flap instead. Cody did not yelp. He snarled and twisted, snapping at Jack again. She charged as well. Jack clubbed at both of them. He hit her. The side of her head exploded with pain and she fell backward with a sharp sound, crashing into the counter. She slumped to the floor, dazed. Her vision went blurry, doubled, then came back.

Waterfalls of blood obscured it. It curtained all she saw, cascading obscenely from the ceiling and onto the floor, inundating it, like a tsunami hitting the shore.

McKenzie put her hands to her face in fear. Her hands swam wetly through the air. Like drying puddles after a rain, the blood began to fade, except for the streaks across Cody as she looked at him.

"Jack! Don't, please, don't!" She reached for the dog, to pull him in behind her, despite the terrible pain in her skull and the sick fear in the pit of her stomach. She grasped his hide. Loose hairs pulled out, but she could not keep a grip on Cody as the dog danced forward, snarling at the man.

McKenzie saw his anger erupt from reined-in iciness to volcanic fury.

"Get out of here! Mind, you goddamn mangy son of a bitch! Mind me!" His voice spewed outward. Jack's hand clenched on the knife handle, slicing the blade downward. Her dog swung around to meet it. The edge caught him on the shoulder. A jagged, crimson gash opened. Cody cried in pain and defiance. He wheeled, snapping.

He bit at the knife. Steel and fang clashed. She felt rooted to the floor, her voice frozen in her throat. She could feel the agony of it, welling up, convulsing into a lump which cut off all words, all hope of stopping Cody. His blood splattered the linoleum in wet, pulsing drops.

Jack sliced again. The soft golden-red ear hung in a ribbon. Cody barked furiously, nails scrabbling on the floor as he lunged at his tormentor. Man and dog collided.

Jack tried for his throat. A wound flowered, not deep enough. McKenzie found her voice.

"Stop it! Cody! Jack, stop it, please. He won't do it again. I'll give him away. Stop it! Oh, God, please stop it now!"

Jack watched her over the dog, eyes like cold coffee. He reached out, grabbing Cody with his left hand, slashing with his right. Blood splashed his fingers as the dog squirmed and yelped in his hold. Cody tore loose. They circled one another, dog snapped now in pain and agony, trying to protect her, protect himself. He threw blood with every movement. His nails scrabbled on the slick flooring. His tail was tucked between his haunches, and he made a noise—oh, God— like the animal he was, suffering and hurt, low and guttural.

"I've got to finish him," Jack muttered. "Once they go vicious. . . ."

McKenzie put her hands to her ears, unable to bear hearing. The dog hunkered down on the floor. He snapped at the air. She reached for him, hands trembling.

Jack bared his teeth. "C'mon, you son of a bitch! Come and get it!"

He kicked, catching the dog in the side of the head, where his torn earn hung limply. Cody burst upward, charging.

He leaped at Jack. She grasped at empty air, sobbing, as she saw the blade plunging at Cody's soft throat. A fountain of blood opened up, pulsing at her face, her hands, warm and salt-sweet. It splattered her. She closed her eyes, bathing in the warmth, sobbing as though her heart would break.

Blood everywhere. The woman lay in the ruins of her own body, chest laid open, thighs flayed as though someone had skinned and butchered her, hair wild about her head, eyes wide and staring with fear . . . and the blood. Oh, God, the blood.

Dazedly, McKenzie sat on the kitchen floor, vision impaired by another vision, head throbbing, confused, beaten.

Jack looked down at her. "Get me a beer."

She could feel the sourness pushing upward in the back of her throat, her stomach clenching, ready to hurl. . . .

She woke, chest heaving, her face wet. McKenzie put her hands up, touched the wetness, then drew her hands to her nostrils, her lips. *Tears. Not blood. Not the scent, or the taste of blood. Dreaming.* She'd been dreaming again. A nightmare, a terror from the dark, nothing.

She moved to get out of bed, kicked a nightstand and realized, in the dark, she was not in a familiar bed. Disoriented, she put a hand out, fumbling. An ugly, thick-based lamp met her search and she found a light switch.

A thin, pasty glow flooded the room. It fell on a battered television set, a plastic bureau, across blankets, pilled and patched, hotel issue, and a cheap hotel, at that.

Lastly, it fell across her shoes, rusty brown stains splattered across her joggers, laces lying stiffly across the floor.

Cody's blood.

No dream. Memory.

McKenzie felt her throat close up. The tears began to fall again, as quickly and freely as Seattle rain. What had happened to her? What had she let awaken?

What had she done?

Chapter 3

Night and rain hung over the city. The car's headlights picked out her way through slick, unfamiliar streets. She spent her time looking in the rearview mirror as the cheap hotel faded behind her. No one could be back there. No one could possibly be trailing her yet. No one could even know she'd left, but she could not look away, could not bear to stare forward. The hairs on the back of her neck prickled in constant warning.

McKenzie pulled up as close to the pay phone as she could, but she was still drenched by the time she reached the booth. Rain streaked the greasy glass walls. The interior light came on fitfully, as though nearly spent. The pocket of her jeans bulged with her cash, all she had left, $150, but she had to dig deep to find coins. Her hands shaking, she finally retrieved them and jammed them into the slots.

McKenzie clenched her teeth against the cold and the panic. Taking a deep breath, she looked across the Seattle cityscape, blurred by darkness and the storm, to steady herself. The weather was following her down the coast. *Dear God, let that be all.*

Gray, dreary, leaden. The sky mirrored her heart. Before she could lose this spurt of courage, she dropped coins in and dialed quickly. Her head ached dully. She would be there, Mac intuited. She did not anticipate the answering machine, and the voice which answered was welcoming.

"Whiteside residence. Hello?"

"Sarah, it's me."

"Well, hi there. Got your poem framed yet?"

"No. I, ah, ah." Mac jolted to a halt, voice gone.

Sarah knew instantly, from the tone of her voice. "What is it, Mac?"

"I'm going. He, ah, he killed Cody."

A sharp inhalation of breath. "Are you all right? Get over here."

"No." McKenzie shook her head. Moisture sprinkled her face. "I don't want him bothering you."

A pause, then, "Where are you going to go?"

"I don't know. I don't know. Somewhere. I'll call later."

Sarah sighed. McKenzie could picture her breathy expulsion, puffing the fine sable fringe of her bangs off her forehead. "Take care. If you need anything—"

"I know," she answered. "Leave, just for a day or two. Don't let him talk to you."

"I can't do that—"

"You have to! He butchered Cody, Sarah. Limb to limb. Just because . . ." Her voice failed her. She caught it again. "Cody tried to protect me. You can't be there when he comes looking for me." Unable to bear any more, she hung up.

The light drizzle of rain misted around her, barely more than fog. She shivered. Where could she go? McKenzie hunched her shoulders and looked at the phone. A destination surfaced. The number escaped her, gone, numbed by fear and hopelessness. She balled her hand into a fist and punched herself in the forehead, once, twice. "Think, think!"

Where else could she go? She knew of nowhere Jack would not find her. This was the only chance she had. The only one. She dropped her money into the slots, then froze again. What if she were refused?

Afraid of losing the coin she'd deposited, she spread her hand over the buttons. The knuckles of her right hand shone angrily red in the booth's dim lighting. Prayerfully, *Dad, oh, Daddy, let me come home. . . .* Her fingertips found the numbers as if they were the ones with eyes and a memory.

The phone rang. Even accounting for long distance, it did not sound right. Had he gone since her mother died? Maybe he wasn't even there any more. Her heart failed a beat, then doubled up for lost time, chest panging with its desperation. The ring couldn't be right, it didn't sound familiar. It had been so long, so many years. She'd only talked to him once since marrying Jack. She was on the brink of hanging up when the ringing stopped.

"Hell-lo."

She knew the voice, if not the ring. McKenzie sucked in her courage. "Daddy?" She heard an echo of her own sharply caught breath. Before she could hang up, or say something, she blurted out. "I've got to come home."

"Then come."

No hesitation. McKenzie's knees, locked in anger and desperate strength all night, suddenly went weak. Her grip on the pay phone was the only thing keeping her standing.

"Or do you need me to come get you?"

"No. No. I'm driving down. It'll be a day or two."

"All right." He hung up, the line going dead.

No questions. Nothing.

She wanted to call back, to explain the failure, to sob out the story and feel the comfort, but she had no more coins. She hung up the receiver in the cradle and tried to stiffen her legs. Home. *Home.*

The dash of icy rain in her face sharpened her wits as she walked back to the car. She put a hand on its aging frame. She didn't know if it would get her all the way from Seattle to L. A., but it was all she had. McKenzie slid behind the wheel. She laced her fingers around it.

Something tinkled in one of the cardboard boxes behind her seat, one of the few pieces of her mother's china she had left. She hadn't had time to wrap them well. It didn't matter now. Either it would make the trip whole or shattered, just like she would.

If it had broken, she'd simply have to put the pieces back together. She couldn't stop, couldn't look back. *He* would find the car rental receipt. He would begin looking for her through that trail. He did not know she'd bought this car secretly months ago. She'd kept it parked on campus and used the bus to get back and forth to it.

Her ribs ached. The shoulder which had been dislocated enough times before that it popped out now at the slightest movement made a protesting sound as she leaned over the bench seat. There was a towel laid there, slightly soiled, its surface gleaming under the dome light with fine, red-gold hairs. Dog hairs.

McKenzie closed her eyes. The knot which choked her throat threatened to unwind, to explode. Memory of the golden retriever's soft, intelligent brown eyes flooded her. She folded up the towel and pushed it away so that she couldn't see the hairs. Couldn't see the fresh image of trusting eyes, the low whine of uncertainty, the sudden look of betrayal as the other had reached down and grasped him.

She swallowed tightly. No tears. Not yet. She couldn't afford them.

McKenzie started the car and drove it back into the rain, seeking out the road home.

He stood in the driving rain, watching the frantic activity around the Whiteside home. Figures ran back and forth in front of the brightly lit windows. They were carrying suitcases and boxes. Leaving. The adults and two children, bumping into each other, going through the rooms of their home like ants in an anthill that's been stirred up.

He'd done that. Him. Or the lies she'd told about him. He wasn't sure if it was remorse that he felt now, watching it, or power. They were fleeing because of him.

That would make no never mind. He leaned a shoulder against the tree. They'd be gone in minutes. They'd leave stuff behind. Food. Information. He'd get what he wanted from the Whitesides anyway.

Jack Trebolt bared his teeth against the rainy weather and shook himself like an old dog before moving in under the shrubbery, to crouch, waiting.

When the van had been hastily packed, they loaded up the livestock and left, pulling out with a squeal on the damp driveway. He let the street go dim again, free of headlights, before moving to the back door and popping it open with one twist of a heavy-duty screwdriver. Inside, things were more button-down and orderly than he'd expected. He searched around the two main telephone bases, in the kitchen and in the living room, but there were no hastily scrawled notes or hen scratches to tell if Mac had called.

There was an answering machine. He stood over it, looking at the little lighted dots that told him it was functioning. He reached out and switched it off. Then, he made a pass through the refrigerator to see if there was anything left he could eat.

There was the butt-end of a roast, sitting in its juices in a plastic bag. He fished it out with a pot holder. Jack tore open the baggy and sank his teeth into the cold roast. He surveyed the kitchen pensively, could think of nothing else to do here.

He went to the counter and dug out his wallet. A worn photocopy of an even more worn clipping fell out.

It was an obituary for a Jean Ann Smith, of Los Angeles.

He picked at a bit of gristle between his teeth. No matter what McKenzie thought, he knew blood was thicker than water.

She had no place else to go.

The car ran low on gas long before she ran out of adrenaline. Sometime after the third fill-up, when the Oregonian highway patrolman said, "Flying low?" as he took her false ID and began to scratch out a ticket, McKenzie uncurled her fingers stiffly from the steering wheel. Her knuckles, pale across their expanse except for the three with angry, broken skin on her right hand, all hurt. The weather had given on the way south. The sky was a pale blue, scratched by wispy trailing clouds. The car sat, its engine making ticking noises as it cooled, scrunched down on the gravel of the road's shoulder.

Thinking she couldn't do much about the license plate, she sat in stony silence. The sound of her heartbeat filled her ears. She couldn't even hear the static buzz of his radio. Could he hear her pulse? Could he see her palms sweat as she placed her hands back on the wheel? The ID hadn't been that good years ago in college, but at least now the age was accurate. If he didn't look too closely. . . . It was one of the few ways she could think of to obscure her trail from Jack.

He filled out the citation, giving her a lecture on driving the rural roads of his state, and passed it to her through the open window, adding, "At least you're not from California."

She silently took the ticket, thinking, *Oh, but I am, and I'm going back as fast as I can.* Her head throbbed. She looked briefly into the patrolman's eyes. He had brilliantly blue eyes, thickly lashed, making up for the austere sternness of his face. The pain in her skull made her lose her vision momentarily and she gasped.

"Are you all right, miss?"

Mac looked back at him, afraid of what she might see. White

misted him for a second, cut across his shoulder and arm. She put her hand out, touched his uniform.

"Are you all right?" he said again, his voice sharpening.

A sling or a cast. But it wasn't there, she couldn't feel it. Mac drew her hand back. "Your arm. . . ."

He flexed it slightly. "Broke it a couple of months ago. First day out of the cast. It's good to be back to work though." He leaned down closer. "You drive carefully, now."

She stuffed the citation into the purse on the seat of the car beside her and put her hand on the gear shift.

The Oregonian patrolman hesitated. His attention wandered to the front bumpers of the car. What did he suspect? Was he looking for her? Had she given herself away? Her stomach crawled into a knot.

"You were goin' a pretty good clip. Maybe you thought you hit something . . . there's a lot of wildlife on these roads."

"I'm fine, thank you."

He flipped his glasses down from his forehead. "You look upset. I hate to send you away like this." She could see her face in his reflective sunglasses, the strain apparent. "If there's anything wrong, you shouldn't be driving."

Her fingers tightened on the gear shift lever. Of course there was something wrong. McKenzie forced a smile to her lips. "Thank you, officer, I'm just fine."

His hesitation seemed interminable. She did not breathe until he touched a finger to the brim of his hat. "Drive safely, ma'am," and withdrew.

She wanted to peel rubber, get out of there as soon as she could, but McKenzie forced herself to start the car quietly and pull away smoothly. Not until the motorcycle was far, far in the distance did she begin to accelerate again.

Home. *Home.* Home, where, when you went there, they had to take you in, as Robert Frost had once so eloquently said. Robert Frost. Sarah would approve of the poetic reference. McKenzie let out a sigh, and tried to roll her shoulders, relax at the wheel. She was surprised she still knew the poet's works, hadn't had that beaten out of her. Like the old handyman, she wouldn't be turned away. She knew her father well enough to know if he didn't want her, he would simply have hung up. And so, flying on wings of adrenaline, she was heading home.

The plane dropped lower over the L. A. Basin, like a knife hoping to cleave its way through the perpetual haze which curtained the city. John Nelson hugged the window, watching. His eyes felt dull and gummy from the red-eye flight, and he hoped a dose of California sunshine would wake him up, but what he saw as he looked out did not help.

Congressman Nelson, retired from the FBI, relocated and elected from Illinois, was not happy. He shrugged within his signature blue suit, ran his hand through his equally recognizable silver-blue hair, and sighed. Poor dumb bastards actually thought the air quality was getting better. Why not? The management boards said it was. Trotted out statistics from ten, fifteen years ago. Look at the measurements. Dropping, steadily dropping. What the poor dumb bastards who lived in, breathed, hell, even *ate* down below didn't know was that the standards had been revised, were still being revised, so that the numbers *lied*. Any fool who'd spent the last twenty-five years or so in southern California could tell you the air was worse. All you had to do was look. Facts lied, because the yardstick had been recalibrated. His own industry-laced district wasn't much better.

Nelson sighed again. He ought to spill the beans, make it media public. Anyone who wanted to know could, but like a herd of cattle contentedly grazing on the good life, no one had the initiative. He could make it a major point of the next campaign, and would, except that most of the industries which contributed to that layer of haze would eat him alive. Then what would happen to his law and order hopes?

Nelson decided he would wait. After all, reelection was not for another two years for him. Maybe the air quality actually would get better in another year or so. Then he wouldn't be faced with the dilemma of the truth and the apparent truth. If not. . . .

He thought about his scheduled lunch with Carter. Ten years, a lot of water under the bridge, since he'd last seen the congenial newspaperman as a Fed. A lot of time since Bauer had slipped between their fingers and disappeared. He'd kept track of Windy since Chicago. A few years here, a few years there, floating on a tide of . . .

what? Not booze, like some reporters. Depression, perhaps. The Bauer escape had hit them both hard. They'd kept in touch, a ghoulish glue holding them together. Maybe even, in his own inimitable fashion, Carter was still tracking the serial killer. Nelson had, for the first few years, until it became apparent after the first three killings that Bauer had evidently gone underground, or gone six feet under. Nothing had come on the systems which even suggested the type of crime Bauer was infamous for. He'd either switched methods of gratification, highly doubtful, or he'd been permanently satiated. Only death could have brought that about.

For whatever reason, both crossed paths occasionally in L.A. at this time in their lives, although Nelson spent most of his time in Washington. But, yeah, hoisting a beer with Carter sounded good. Committee business could be grueling. He had a few drabbles of information that he'd milked dry, but which the newsman might find interesting. He was too involved in his new life to keep chasing Bauer, but Carter Wyndall was another matter. Better than the rest of his agenda. He'd come here to kick butt, basically, because the party wanted to use L.A. as a symbol of redemption and rebuilding. First, they had to create a reasonable facade of same.

Nelson grunted as he fastened his seat belt in response to the stewardess' request. His ears popped gently as the plane descended. Seeing Carter sounded good. A few hours' sleep in the old hotel room, lunch with a friend, then on to the rigorous schedule a congressman had to keep with lobbyists, constituents, city officials, and whatnot.

Nelson laughed silently at himself. It was the whatnot that could get you killed.

His heavy eyes shuttered themselves and he was almost asleep again when the wheels bumped the landing strip.

Burdened with carry-on luggage like a pack mule, he made his way to the car rental counter, got his keys, and then drove out of LAX. He checked in at his favorite hotel, a quietly middle-class establishment which he'd gotten used to while an agent. It didn't suit his status now that he was a congressman, but he didn't care. He liked it, was comfortable with the security, knew the various wings and floors, the kind of staff they hired and the kind of clientele who stayed there.

The pretty counter clerk, with almond-shaped eyes and wings of blue-black hair, checked him in with slender, flying fingers. Miko smiled at him as she slid a key across the marble counter. "Enjoy your stay, Mr. Nelson."

He allowed himself a grin back. Miko was the best of East and West combined, California style with Pacific Rim beauty. Although she knew him for what he was, she did not fawn on him. She did, however, always order extra towels. He scooped up the key card. "Thank you, Miko. When's the bar open?"

"Four p.m., as always. Your towels should be up in a few minutes." She hid a smile as she returned to her computer terminal, to finish logging in his presence.

When he threw himself on the bed, it was with a relief that postponed everything but sleep . . . even the telephoning of his staff and confirming reservations with Carter.

Miko caught a line of error in a pending reservation as she closed out Nelson's account. From the corner of her eye, she thought she might have seen something in the security camera's screen. She halted, looked at the monitor, saw nothing else, and decided it was security's problem. The hotel only had a second monitor at the front desk as a backup. Wrinkling her smooth forehead in concentration, she looked back down at her terminal, determined to change the honeymoon suite back over to its original designees, thus avoiding a host of problems this coming weekend.

She did not see the dark, lithe figure in the hooded sweatshirt slip down the service hallway and up the back fire stairs. Security was not at his desk, watching. The call of nature had taken precedence. He was an older man, retired from the police force, and his bodily functions were as regular as he could maintain them. He could be clocked by his early morning breaks.

The tape backup to the camera would only record a lengthening shadow, perhaps a wearing on the film, as they were used again and again, if no incidents had been taped. A bin of tapes waiting to be degaussed sat unsteadily next to the monitor, awaiting their fate. On one of them, a similar shadow might be seen, in rehearsal, making its way around a corridor corner and out of camera sight. It had not been spotted then. It did not plan on being spotted now.

The hooded figure wore jogging shoes, leaving no imprint on the worn carpet runners. The sweatpants, matching the hooded shirt, were unremarkable. Worn, comfortable, somewhat faded from washing. An outfit donned every day for a morning run.

Except they had been purchased just two weeks ago, when the congressman's schedule had been released, washed and dried ten times over, quickly, and worn in actuality only twice, the first time for rehearsal. The wearer moved quickly and confidently in them, staying close to the corridor walls, negotiating the rather complicated tunnels and turns from one wing to the next tower without hesitation as though he had a map drawn on the palm of his gloved hand. The drawstring hood was pulled over, half-obscuring the face, even the eyes.

In the last corridor, his head began to thump as though it would explode. Something inside his head began to crawl and scratch restlessly. *I hear you knockin, but you can't come in—* He put his back to the wall and sucked in his breath. Sweat rolled down the back of his neck and he suddenly got queasy.

He had to do this. He *had* to. There was no backing out. The sleeping man wouldn't let him, and even more frightening was the possibility that the sleeping man would rouse and possess him, exploding through his skin—

He had to get back to *her*. She was the only one who could help him, but he did not dare go back to her a failure. He rubbed the back of his hand over his lips and took a deep breath. He knew what he was here for. He shoved the sleeping man back into the corner of his mind, and put a hand on his gun.

Nelson woke enough at the knock on the door to mumble, "Come in." His towels had arrived. He could get up, lock the door, pull a pillow over his head, and go back to sleep until noon. Damn budget-economizing red-eye flights. He let out a yawn as the door pushed open.

He froze. Strings of old training, precautions, stances, strategies ran through his mind, flashes of a past life. He could feel his guts grow cold as he faced the gun-wielding assailant.

His jaw worked. "Who?—what the hell are you?" Fear made his voice go high.

The assassin put the first bullet down his throat and the second between his eyes. Nelson saw the flash from the gun barrel with the first, never saw the second, already dying, catapulted back into the room, wondering.

He flopped back on the pillows and lay, quite dead.

The assassin backed to the wall and waited a few seconds, counting under his breath, one-Mississippi, two-Mississippi, making sure that the life hissed out of his target. He did not like this part of his job, but it had to be done. He had to report back. The corner of his mouth twitched, partially obscured by his equipment and the sweatshirt hood. *She who must be obeyed in all things,* he thought. She would want to know the target was really dead.

When he heard no more gurgling, mere seconds down the Mississippi as he counted, he went back out the hotel room door.

Face still partially hooded, the gunman returned his pistol to his jacket pocket. He made his way down the corridors and halls the way he'd come in, changing direction only once, breaking into a jog as he exited onto the pool deck and trotting on by into the parking lot as if he were one of the guests going for a run.

He did not stop until he reached the environs of a cardboard city, several miles away. He paused by a Dumpster, stripped off the hooded sweatshirt and pants, revealing an unremarkable pair of blue jeans and a denim shirt underneath. He glanced around before removing the headgear and gloves, stuffing them into his shirt. The gun went down a storm drain, where it clattered to a halt somewhere out of sight. Then he broke into a loping stride, an easy, ground-covering walk which took him away swiftly.

Another mile and he found the parked car where he'd left it. He used the plastic key in his pocket—no rattle, no telltale bulge, compliments of the Auto Club for use in emergencies. He pulled away from the curb, already planning ahead, for he had another job to do that evening.

Fuzzy rolled out from behind the Dumpster when he was certain the stranger's footsteps had faded away. Beard growing in tattered scraps shadowed his face. His hands and arms were the color of graphite, grime permanently tattooed into the pigment of his skin. He rubbed his palms together and nervously licked his lips, uncertain what he wanted to do. He'd seen the clothing go in the Dumpster— and worse—he'd seen the horrific face of the being who'd left it. *Nothing human,* he'd thought, before skittering behind the trash bin for safety, like a bug frightened of being squashed. *Somethin' godaw-ful, but nothing human.* It had been long minutes before his pound-ing heart had quieted enough to allow him to stick his head out and look again.

By then the being had retreated down the street. Fuzzy had squat-ted and waited until the thud of his footsteps were long departed. Now he rocked, back and forth, back and forth, hugging himself, in desperate indecision.

Would it be radioactive or somehow contaminated if he took it? He needed the clothing, he craved it, but his fear of the former owner paralyzed him. Could there be anything left inside it to trans-mit to him? He'd seen the thing, for godsakes, three eyes, metal hel-met, and all.

He'd seen it!

Finally, when his stomach clenched and grumbled, reminding him that the day's scavenging had been lean thus far, Fuzzy scrambled out from behind the Dumpster, hiked himself over the rim of the bin, and grabbed out the clothing. Clutching the sweat suit to his chest, he ran away from the area, crablike, sideways and hitched, as crip-pled by old injuries as by a disintegrating mind.

Chapter 4

The gas tank was ticking inexorably down to empty again when she pulled off the freeway. Late afternoon haze edged the valley, smog so thick she could taste it, even inside the car. She'd forgotten about the look of it, like a curtain of brushfire smoke that hung in the air. The afternoon of uninterrupted music pouring out of the radio paused for the news. McKenzie only half-listened as the newsman delivered the news in the same bop-and-rock voice as the deejay presented the music. They might have been clones, except for the different levels of maturity apparent in their tones.

"The exchange for guns program has wrapped up a successful six-month plan here in L.A., and sponsors say they'll be back in the fall with new incentives. The popularity of this approach among the teens particularly made city council members talk with renewed enthusiasm about the future. The Los Angeles Kings and the Mighty Ducks of Anaheim have also reported continued success with their Tickets for Guns program. . . ." The newsman paused and another voice cut in, saying, "Would you really want to sit in a hockey stadium with that kind of crowd? Now, c'mon."

The newsman responded smoothly, "I don't see the difference from the regular crowd."

A tape of phony-sounding yucks followed this exchange. It wrapped up with raucous duck calls. McKenzie wrinkled her nose.

She watched the green signs hanging over the freeway. Two miles to her exit. She moved over a lane. The news break continued.

"Law enforcement officials report that the body of young businesswoman Denise Faberge was found in her condo this morning after being reported missing from work for the last two days. Authorities have released little information about her death, but one source who helped locate the body reports 'the apartment looked as if a butcher had been there.' Autopsy findings are not expected for several days. Faberge's estranged boyfriend, who was questioned by police as a possible suspect, said only that they had been separated for some time and that she had just completed a self-help program."

She had forgotten the death count in Los Angeles. McKenzie shrugged back her uneasiness. One step forward, two back. She found her off-ramp and eased onto it, suddenly out of the tunnel of multilaned freeway and sound walls, and into tract housing. The radio had surged into the latest by Aerosmith, when it suddenly halted.

The rich-voiced anchor boomed, "This just in. A man identified tentatively as Congressman John Nelson of Illinois has been found dead in a Marina del Rey hotel. Authorities have not confirmed the exact cause of death or the identity, but reliable sources say the congressman was evidently alone in his hotel room when he was shot, assassin-style, while resting after flying in from Washington, D.C. this morning." The newsman took a breath. "Stay tuned and we'll bring you further details as we receive them."

The second deejay said breezily, "Or not. Hey, what's another politician or two, right? Anybody going to miss this guy? Send us a fax if you do. We're out of toilet paper, right, Bobb-o?"

She found herself frowning even more deeply.

The jacaranda had begun blooming, purple smoky haze among towering trees, the blossoms erupting on bare, sable branches before the fernlike green leaves. She hadn't thought about the jacarandas in years. They lined her father's street, an archway of spring green and mauve. They would be dropping their nectar-filled blossoms in a deep indigo rain, their season brief but intense. Their showy heads could be seen among the gray and brown asphalt shingled roofs.

She moved slowly into the left lane for a turn. A California car buzzed past her, horn sounding in angry impatience. McKenzie went on through the intersection, feeling as if she were herself caught in a smoky cloud. The adrenaline had gone. Sweat dampened her sports bra uncomfortably. She could smell herself, the faint tinge of perfume, the edgy odor of fear, the sharper scent of onion from that last drive through.

The first thing she would do would be to take a hot shower. Then sleep for two days. Then figure out how to put her life back together.

The old ballpark, when she saw it, surprised her. Mac slowed down, eyes caught by the backstop, chain-link fencing tarnished black with age. It had been graffitied, sprayed white and garish orange on the dark background. She could not read either the names or symbols painted there. The grass in the infield looked threadbare and yellowing. A weathered billboard proclaimed: Little Blue Field. Then, underneath, in letters disintegrating off the wood, it said: We Bleed Dodger Blue.

She could almost feel the wood under her fingertips. They'd jumped to see if they could touch the bottom edge of the board, she and her friends. Then, all of a sudden, she was grown, and when she stood tall, the top of her shoulder hit the rim. How many years had she played here? T-ball with the Bobby Soxers, then softball with the Pony League, regular hardball baseball with her dad.

McKenzie eased her car into a crawl at the curb. She could almost see herself running across the field, spikes sending up little clouds of dust if it was late in the season and the grass battered from the pounding it had taken.

These were the only good times she remembered as a family, the only times when he'd stayed sober on an evening or a Saturday. The only memories worth keeping, and she'd buried them herself, because it was she who'd ruined her softball career in college, who'd failed herself, who'd lost it all—and why?

Because I couldn't stand being a winner, she thought bitterly. *Because I had to go and find someone else to ruin my life.*

A car buzzed angrily past. McKenzie blinked several times, then pulled her eyes away from the old field and edged back onto the road.

The low wall of the housing tract loomed ahead. She saw the graffiti tracks, and patches where oddly colored paint had wiped out previous intrusions. She turned in, houses of stucco, all fenced, all 1950's built, jacarandas in the boulevard, front porches shaded by pepper trees, every yard fenced. She remembered how uneasy she'd first been in Washington, where few yards in the suburbs were fenced at all. Here redwood fences, blockwall, an occasional chain-link, surrounded every home, and an orange tree stood in every back-yard, or had at one time. Theirs had been Valencia, juice oranges, turning color in January, but not really sweet for juicing until after Easter. Fallen purple buds popped under car tires as she drove over them. Celery-green lawns were blanketed under the blooming trees with their fern-feathery branches.

Everything had begun to slow. McKenzie felt as if she were driving through heavy water. Finally the mailbox marked SMITH appeared, and she turned into the cement driveway, with its cracks from various earthquakes giving it wrinkles of age.

Both she and the car came to a halt simultaneously and she sat, too weary to move. Her vision blurred sharply, the images sliding sideways and she froze, waiting for the violent wash of red across her sight, but nothing happened this time. Mac took a deep breath and forced it downward. She wasn't crazy yet. Not entirely.

The chain-link gate across the driveway to the garage began to move. She straightened, surprised, then saw her father. He strode purposely toward the car, not much different than the last time she'd seen him, except that he'd gone silvery-gray, and his hair had receded sharply. He beckoned to her to bring the car on in.

The house shared driveways, side by side, with a ground strip running between them. Mrs. Ethelridge had always kept that strip blossoming with border plants. Run over a leaf with bicycle or car wheel, and she would be out her kitchen door in a second, sharp tongue ready to deliver a lashing. She'd always seemed old to Mac. She was both surprised and comforted seeing the flowers still there, still omnipresent. Mac sat, looking down the strip. Blue lobelia, followed by white alyssum and yellow marigolds. An unending territory line that ran from the sidewalk to the alley behind their garages.

She started up again. The car protested, then caught, and she edged it forward, careful not to cross the flowers. The driveway had been extended in the back, and she pulled over and under a carport. Her father opened the door as she turned the ignition off and took the keys out.

She got out, legs suddenly feeling leaden. Out of habit, she looked at Mrs. Ethelridge's kitchen door, and saw faded ivory curtains wavering at the window as if someone had been observing.

His hazel eyes appraised both her and the automobile. He followed her line of sight. Then he sighed. "She'll be over later, tonight or tomorrow, asking questions. I don't know how your mother put up with it."

McKenzie looked at Walton Smith. "She used to hide," Mac answered frankly. Her father put a hand out. She took it, feeling the hard warmth of his workmanlike hand. It still enveloped hers though he did not seem as tall as she remembered. McKenzie felt herself being peeled away in layers, by events and memories she could not control, as she looked at the house. This was the life she'd fled when she was young. She didn't feel young any longer. She felt old, and used.

There was no mother to come home to. She'd died almost two years ago, yet McKenzie looked past him, almost thinking that she could see her, too. He flinched, as if sharing that same thought, and let go of her hand.

He broke the contact, but not before she felt a pinch of pain thrusting through her temples, slashing bloody streaks across her father's face.

McKenzie went cold. She blinked twice, rapidly, and the double vision faded as the warmth of her father's touch left her palm. She fought to keep an even keel, to get a grip on reality. It was in her head. All in her head. Everything she thought and felt and *saw.*

Walton Smith stood, head cocked slightly to one side, as if waiting for her to say something. His ears had gotten longer, and there were sharp creases through the lobes. She'd forgotten what that meant. Something to do with his health. His jaw moved, pulsing impatiently, a familiar tic that she knew well.

"I'm back," she said. Her voice sounded thin and watery.

"So I see," Walt responded gruffly. He dipped to look into the backseat. "This all you have?"

"All I could bring with me." McKenzie swallowed. Her throat knotted, again. *Not much for ten years gone.*

"Where's the dog?"

Her jaw dropped. "What dog?"

"You've always had a dog." Walt cleared His throat. "Figured you'd bring one with you."

Her hand shook as she ran it through her hair, trying to clear it from her eyes. She hoped her voice was more solid. "No. No dog."

"Well, then. Come on." He started down the driveway. "Leave the keys, I'll unload."

To look at them now, to hear them, there was no common ground between them. How could she stay, and where could she go? "I'm here," she said, not knowing what else to say or think.

He grumbled, "Some sense in you yet." The color had begun coming back into his face, highlighting his cheekbones. "I'll fix some dinner. We need to eat early if I'm going to catch the Dodger game. It's a doubleheader."

He hesitated, then put out his arm and took her in. The moment was stiff and awkward, and she let go, feeling astonished that he had even assayed it to begin with. Her body flinched under the pressure, joints stiff, old bruises still tender, and she could feel the hesitation in him as well. She let go.

She leaned back in and took one of the suitcases, then entered the house she'd left so long ago.

It did not smell the way she remembered. McKenzie could not readily identify what it was that was missing other than her mother. She could smell furniture polish and fresh coffee. Hardwood floors, clean but scuffed and scarred with age, bent under her step and talked back to her as she went down the hallway, softly, creaking. McKenzie decided to stop thinking until she'd at least had a long shower and a hot cup of coffee. The shower would come first.

"You've learned to cook," she noted, as she sat down to dinner. Hot water and fresh clothes had revived her somewhat. He had spaghetti and a green salad on the dinette table. The spaghetti stayed in the pot, a serving spoon plunged into its steaming marinara sauce, but the salad was in the cut crystal salad bowl she remembered from most of her life.

"The sauce is out of a jar," he responded. "But a good jar." He helped himself, then nudged the pot her way. "Eat what you want. I'll freeze the leftovers."

Was that how he got along now? Cooking and then eating the frozen leftovers until time to cook again? She could not imagine him self-sufficient without her mother, yet here he was, alive and well. She felt a faint resentment that he should be. Maybe they should have woken the old sleeping dog. He'd learned new tricks. She made a dry, ironic sound deep in her throat, one that almost, but not quite, washed away the lump of dread which never seemed to dissolve.

He cocked his head, listened to the radio, and said, "Double play. That cools the inning down."

Her throat tightened. This was the only connection she'd ever had with him. The only time she'd never been afraid to go out in public with him, that she knew he'd be sober, was at one of her softball games. Now, at Chavez Ravine, or Anaheim Stadium, that was another matter. He'd always found a way to get around the two beer limit. Professional games to her always stank of spilled beer and crushed peanut shells. She picked at her salad. The greens were fresh, crisp. "How are they doing this year?"

He shrugged. "Who knows? Maybe the Dodgers are getting tired of the game. But the Angels—" he waved a fork. "That's a roller coaster. Up, down. Young talent wasted, traded away. The strike hurt them a lot. They say the old Cowboy has 'em up for sale. But they're playing .500 ball. Maybe they've got a chance. It could come true, a Freeway World Series." That was what the sportswriters would always speculate about, if both the Dodgers and the Angels had winning seasons. A world series connected by southland freeways.

Mac wrinkled her nose, considering, then both of them simultaneously, said, "Nah!"

She laughed, and he gave a low, rusty rumble, as though laughing was something he hadn't done in a while. A warmth crept inside and stayed there. Not all memories were bad. Not all life had been intolerable. She finished her salad.

"You couldn't have driven all that way without stopping," her father noted firmly. There was a lull between innings. He looked up from stirring his coffee and added, "though you look like it."

"I stopped one night." McKenzie wrapped both hands about her mug. She saw a faint disapproval come and go across his face as she dragged the coffee near. "Believe me, this much caffeine isn't going to faze me."

"But something did. TV said this was the Boomerang Generation, that the children came back. Your mother and I thought we'd never see it."

She took a deep swallow. The sugar-and-cream-laced brew went down hotly, settled into a banked fire in her stomach. It felt good.

She could not bear to tell him the whole story, so she doled out what she could handle. "I'm divorcing him."

She was not sure what she wanted to see in his face—but it might have been carved of granite now. "I'm all right," she added. She'd carefully brushed her wet hair dry so that he could not see the patch where Jack had assaulted her with the knife. She did not want him prying further. Not yet. Maybe never.

"No, you're not, or you wouldn't be here. Then what are you going to do?"

How should she know? How could she have any idea, yet? She put a finger into her cup and swirled the cooling coffee around, deciding. "I don't know. I'll get a job. I don't know about the rest. I guess I'll have to do it one day at a time." She drained her cup. The spaghetti still sat on her plate, and she picked up a fork. It was good, better than she expected. He'd set out Parmesan cheese; she sprinkled it over and kept eating.

She stared, wondering what it was he was thinking. For the first time it suddenly struck her that she looked more like him than she did her mother. Both had hazel eyes, sometimes gray, sometimes greenish-brown. His hair had silvered, hers had stayed honey golden. And their faces were somewhat squarish, while McKenzie remembered her mother as having a distinctive heart-shaped face, right down to the hairline dipping in the center of her forehead.

Yes, she definitely looked like her father: broad forehead, a nose best described as stubborn echoed by a definite jawline which could easily be seen if it clenched. Handsome on a man, not even close to pretty in a woman. McKenzie sighed. Their similarity in looks gave her no ability to read his mind. She never could understand him, knew he would never understand her. There was no bridging the gap between them, and there was still that little girl inside of her who was mortally afraid of him, despite the love. Now that she was grown, the love had gone, retracted, curled up in itself, along with the memories.

"Young for a divorce, but at least you don't have any baggage. Your mother wondered if you'd even married him."

His bitterness surprised her. Had they thought her pregnant and desperate? Her mother had never given her the chance to discuss it. She'd told Mac that she'd betrayed them, losing her softball scholarship and dropping out of school. It had been years before Mac had even tried to talk to her again. That, too, had been Sarah's doing. More friend than teacher.

"I told her I did." McKenzie looked down quickly into her coffee cup before speaking again, forcing lightness into her voice. "You raised me to be traditional, didn't you? I never lied to Mom, not even about that." There was no pat answer in the coffee mug. She had not put much cream in her coffee, just enough to mellow the dark java. Now its rich color reminded her of trusting eyes, playful eyes, puppy eyes. What would she have done if Cody had been human? Could she have struck back, finally? What if what she'd seen had been her rage, bubbling over, instead of blood? What if she were like her father, violence bottled up, terrifyingly destructive if it were loosened? How could she live with that, either?

"You won't get anywhere in life by quitting," her father said.

Her head snapped up. McKenzie said, "How can you say that?"

Night had fallen. One of the bulbs in the overhead kitchen light had burned out, giving the illumination a rich, burnished glow. The radio was on in the background, the sound banked to the monotony of the baseball game, only an occasional burst of noise telling that something had happened. She had always liked eating in the kitchen nook, but her mother had insisted on using the dining room. Her father had often not been home for dinner. It had seemed massive with just the two of them. And here he sat now, talking to her about quitting. Just which of them had quit first?

"I can say it because I know." Walt Smith's hands grew white-knuckled around his coffee mug. "You lost your chance at college, now this."

"Well, I didn't 'quit,' " she threw back at him. "I escaped. While I was still—" she stopped, biting back the word, young. A lot of good it had done her. She didn't feel young anymore.

"Still what?"

"You wouldn't understand." She muffled a sigh.

"Damn right I wouldn't. If you're going to come home now, we've got to have an understanding."

"Who says I'm going to stay?"

Walt sniffed. "Where else have you got to go?"

She stayed silent. Nowhere, unless she wanted Jack to follow her.

"I don't mind it," he added. "I'm doing it for her. All I want to know, McKenzie, is why couldn't you have come home while your mother was still alive?"

Why couldn't he have been sober then? But she didn't let herself say it. "I wasn't tired of the Seattle rain, then." She tried to keep her voice light, but she could hear the edge on it. "Do we have to do this now? I'm really tired." She felt stretched and brittle, like a rubber band on the brink of snapping.

He shoved his plate aside. "Yes. I think we need to get some things settled. You. That's the key word. You weren't thinking about her. Once you left here, you never looked back."

"Should I have?"

Walt rubbed his hands together as if they hurt him. "You left me alone with her."

She pushed her own dinner aside, unable to taste it anymore, unable to force it down. Strange, the way it had turned out. She had always thought her father would be the burden on her mother. It had always been that way, and then the sudden turnaround. "She didn't tell me she was . . . she was dying. I didn't know until it was too late." Her eyes filled. She rubbed them dry with a paper napkin smelling of oregano and basil and tomatoes.

"Don't cry in front of me, dammit. You're a tough kid, always were." Her father's chest puffed up. "Why couldn't you have been here watching her cry her eyes out, night after night?"

"Instead of you? She never asked me." She felt her expression grow hard. *Maybe it was just his turn.*

"You should know what you put her through. What kind of coward are you?"

Her diaphragm clenched. For a moment, she couldn't find enough breath with which to answer, but when she did, the words spilled out like water over a dam. "Are we talking about me, or you? What kind of a coward am I? Well, maybe it's genetic, Dad, maybe I got it from you, because I can sure remember her sobbing over you." Her voice rose with every word. "Are we keeping score? Are we? Just like a damn baseball game? If we are, make it twenty years for you, eight for me!"

"Don't you talk like that to me in my house."

His house. That was the smell she'd smelled. A house devoid of her mother's presence. Only two years gone, and yet it was almost as if she'd never been.

McKenzie tried to take a deep breath, suddenly afraid. She had no place else to go. There was nothing left but this tenuous relationship. She had to retreat. *Let sleeping dogs lie.* "I'm sorry, Dad. Nothing about this is easy."

He examined his gnarled hands. "You were a mouthy enough kid when you left. You thought life was easy." He got up, took the coffeepot, and refilled his cup. He waved it in the air, offering it to her, but she shook her head. "We always did argue."

Argue. Their voices used to blast the air, send her skittering to her room where a stack of pillows couldn't muffle the explosions, words she knew she couldn't aim at him, for the hurt, the harm it would cause her mother. Arguing. Her mouth twisted. "If that's what you want to call it. You and Mom, you and me."

"That's what it was, by God. We never fought. And we never hurt each other. Never."

No. McKenzie's gaze slid around the room, across the cabinet doors, where spackle lines marked new paint over old holes. Kicked in, punched in. The dishwasher in the corner was old now, but she could remember the unit it replaced—front door torn off by her father in a rage. They all used to cower when Walt Smith went on a rampage. He must have been following her glance. His face reddened slightly. "I'm not drinking now."

Something broke inside of her. That was the last thing she wanted to hear, to know. Too little, too late. Her poor mother. She couldn't have lived long enough to see that. She found her mug shivering in her hands and set it down firmly on the kitchen table. "Congratulations."

"Is that all you have to say?" A shadow crossed his eyes, a shadow that seemed to settle into the crags of his face. He stared.

"I could say I wish to God you'd done it when Mom was still here. She used to pray for that." She put her feet under her, feeling the kitchen floor, the old hard linoleum with its speckled colors, ready to move quickly if she had to. "Maybe you never hit her, but you beat her down all the time. Too much booze, not enough money, no steady job, no future. You beat on both of us!"

He got to his feet. She could see the kitchen curtains ruffle with the evening breeze. "Don't you blame me for your mother's death!

Don't you say a goddamn word about that! I was here, you weren't. I held her hands when I brought her home after chemo. Tried to coax her to eat. I was the one who held her head when she was too weak to vomit by herself."

"It couldn't have been that hard for you," McKenzie said bitterly. "You had a bottle to hide in afterward." Her throat worked. McKenzie forced herself to take a breath, whistling it inward between her lips.

"You don't like it here, get the hell out! I'm doing this for your mother." His voice thundered through the tiny kitchen. It brought McKenzie to her feet, too.

"Don't do me any favors. I don't want any from you. You should have been the one who died!"

"Goddammit, I'm your father. Don't stand in my kitchen and tell me I should be dead!"

"Why shouldn't I? Do you think I never wished it! I wanted you to die every night we had to drive to some bar and Mom had to drag you out. Had to beg you to come home. Had to leave me sitting in the locked car in some scummy side street while she went in looking for you. Why the hell do you think I left home as soon as I could? *Why?*"

"That was between me and your mother! You had nothing to do with it."

"Didn't I? Didn't I? Well, I've got news for you, Dad. It was my life, too! I couldn't have friends over. Every year I went to school, teachers looked at me with pity and whispered behind my back. I didn't go to the junior prom, because there wasn't enough money for a new dress and your liquor. She went to all the assemblies and meetings and plays. You never showed for anything but the games—and when you did show up, dammit, for graduation, you stank! You were a stinking drunk! So I bailed!"

They faced one another. She could see the purple in his face, the hurt and anger in his eyes. She could see her own face mirrored slightly in them. He blinked.

A mockingbird ran a trill of song from somewhere in the backyard. Though the skies had darkened long ago, she had no idea of the time. It was later than she thought. The mockingbirds always started up after eleven, closer to midnight. The Dodger game droned away on the radio. Her throat ached. Through the kitchen window, through their own curtains, with faded bantam roosters on barnyard fences, across the driveway, she could see the Ethelridge curtains ripple, just a little.

Her father's expression closed. "You were just a kid. There were things you didn't know. Anyway, it couldn't have been too damn bad. You came back!"

She choked down an angry sob, determined not to cry. Not here. Not now. "I'm not a kid anymore! And it's a little late for you to catch up." She brushed her hair back from her hot face, unthinkingly.

His face changed immediately. "Good God, what happened to you?"

Her jaw trembled. "Nothing." She tossed her hair, flopping it back into place.

"That's not nothing!" Her father reached out, caught her with strong fingers, turned her chin.

She pulled back, breathing hard. "Don't touch me! Don't ever touch me! Just leave me alone!" McKenzie bolted for her room, unable to keep it together for another second. She slammed the door behind her and pitched face first onto her bed.

The old chenille spread was worn and dusty, but it muffled her sobs as well as it always used to. The floor creaked outside her door. After long moments, he knocked.

"Mac? Mac, honey, open the door."

Her teeth chattered as she clenched them together. He should have been the one who died. He should have left them alone to live happily ever after.

"Go away!"

A pause, and then her father hit the door with his fist. The paneling boomed under the blow, rocking in the threshold, but it held. "Goddammit! Who the hell do you think you are?"

She froze in fear, waiting, but no other sound came for a long moment. She didn't know what she would do if he came through the door. Didn't know anything except that the lump in her chest felt as though it were swelling until it burst, and when it did, she would. She wasn't going to take this anymore! Not Jack, not her father! She found herself shaking as she tried to hold herself together.

The door boomed again. She jumped and held the pillow to her as if it could muffle the explosion. Suddenly she thought of Jenny Atkins. *God, not Jenny, I haven't thought of her in years.* Jenny, who'd

told her about the terrible things stepfathers, and occasionally fathers, did to their daughters. Who'd made her fear her own father,
already aberrant, made her fear the same kind of twisted, sick things
from him. Every time he drank and they fought, and she took refuge
in her room, she'd feared that it would not keep her safe just as
Jenny's room had never kept her safe.

As she cringed and held tight to the bed, she thought of all the
years she'd spent in fear and humiliation. When had she ever been
free of it? She couldn't remember.

What had ever happened to Jenny? McKenzie bit her lip. The waif-
like girl had disappeared in their junior year. One day at school, the
next not. There'd been rumors. Jenny was pregnant, and gone. Or
worse. Jenny'd been pregnant, and taken her own life. Even worse.
Jenny'd been pregnant, and her own father had killed her. Mac had
vowed to find out. She'd tried to enlist her mother's help but had
been discouraged by her instead. That was the Atkins' family business. Her mother had frowned. Leave it be.

And Mac had, sensing a house of cards that, if it came tumbling
down, might well catch them, too. After all, Jenny's stepfather drank,
too. And inside, privately, she'd been mad at Jenny for making her
fear her father in that way, as well. Hadn't everything else been
enough?

The door banged. "Dammit, Mac, open up!"

"No!" The pillow muffled her voice, but she knew he heard her.
His fist seemed to drum through her aching head. She squeezed her
eyes shut more tightly.

He left, roaring down the hallway like an angry bull. After long
moments, though she did not think it possible, the warmth of the
spread lulled her to sleep.

Chapter 5

The assassin slipped down old alleyways, where asphalt crumbled under the weight of battered trash cans. The streetlights glowing orange on the facing side of the nightborhood cast only a thin glow here, but it was enough for him. Stucco garages opposite him held the ghostly tracings of tagger marks, painted over yet stubbornly remaining, shadowy etchings under new paint. A ginger cat darted across his path and disappeared in tufts of Bermuda grass which had never seen a weed whacker.

He liked the older tracts, with the alleys dissecting their stucco depths. By the sixties, most had disappeared from the newer tracts, as developers realized how much gold existed in California real estate and had found a way to cram square footage into every nook and cranny of a development site. But for him, like the ginger cat and now the drab opossum which froze as he passed it, the alleys remained a quaint and preferred corridor of travel.

He turned to look at the possum. Its scaly, ratlike tail hung over the block-wall fencing, its shoulders under an altar of oleander sprays. The creature skinned black lips back from needlelike teeth as he raised a hand toward it. The stalker paused, and grinned. If he'd had a light, this nocturnal sack of fur would be frozen in submission.

A cat yowl made him turn his face away. When he turned back, the oleander spray shivered over thin air, the possum disappearing while his back had been turned. He put the palm of his hand on the top of the block wall, absorbing the warmth of the creature, feeling the aura it had left behind. A living body was like a fiery torch, fevered with the heat of all its processes. Through his palm he could, if he did not already know, cipher blood flowing hotly through flesh and fur, feel the exhalation of breath, the shiver of fear when it had first sighted him. He held the top of the wall until the masonry went cold.

He withdrew his hand and began to pick his way down the alley again. Crabgrass poked its way under grapestake fences and inched over the corroded alley. He was hunting and, like the ragged-eared ginger cat who leaped across his path, he had little doubt that the hunt would be good.

The aroma of night-blooming star jasmine drifted from a breeze-way. He took an appreciative breath as he crossed, a welcome respite from the lingering smell of garbage cans just a day or two away from being put out for collection. This was a neighborhood of ethnic foods. The cans carried lingering odors of turnip greens and fatback. He heard a swelling of music, then it faded as he moved across the street, from one neighborhood into another, and the smell of jasmine was traded for that of the jacaranda, muskier, sweeter, almost winy as it collected in the alley potholes.

He paused behind a brown garage which had seen better days, the cracked corners of its stucco revealing chicken wire and tar paper. Across his line of sight, he could see a man in his backyard, taking out the trash and listening to the Dodgers' game. The man dunked a sack into a tough plastic can and paused by the side of a tarp-covered vehicle. Radio balanced on his shoulder, he listened as he fussily tugged the car cover into better placement over the bumpers. The stalker also listened. The peppery coach had just livened up the pro-ceedings by getting thrown out, and now his team, as hoped, had ral-lied to tie the game up. The roar and hiss of overworked radio speakers straining to broadcast the excitement reached him.

He reached in his back pocket, drawing out a kitchen match, and lighting it with his thumbnail. The match hissed and flared into being with a smell of sulfur and smoke. He liked matches. He liked calling them lucifers, as they had been called a century ago. Fitting, with the bite and smell of hell itself, ready at the scratch of its chem-ical head to loose the power of chaotic fire. He watched the flame settle into its tear-drop shape and through it, eyed the house as he always liked to do, thinking as he'd been trained to do, looking for the weaknesses where fire could strike. Where the inhabitants could flee, once the flames betrayed their security and shelter. Peering through the match flame as he might through rose-colored glass, he assessed the home. Beyond, for a distracting flicker of a moment, in a back bedroom, he saw a silhouette thrown up against drawn shades, and like a hound which has winded a fox, his nostrils flared.

Prey.

Ta-rah-rah-BOOM-ti-ay, have you had yours today, I had mine yesterday, from the girl across the way. . . . Vulgarities blazed across his mind, his lips moving soundlessly to the words, his attention caught by the beauty of the girl. He dropped the match and ground it out, watching instead the lithe candlestick form of the naked girl, her brush of hair its own flame. Caught by the endless possibilities of all the ways he might kill her, he crouched down to spy.

A thin veil of sweat crept down his face, under the visor of his gear. It was irritating in the sultry night. He could not reach the salty moisture to wipe it away, and the air would not evaporate it. He blinked, rapidly, several times, aware he was losing sight of the girl as he did so. He sucked his breath in through his lips with a deep, inhaling hiss. She aroused him, and because of that, the sleeping man began to awaken also.

Like the sun in eclipse, a magnificent corona of hair stood away from her shadowed head and torso. *Like a Roman candle,* he thought in admiration; then, the moment passed, and the light snapped off. For a long second, like the corona of the sun in eclipse, he retained a vision of her. Then the silhouette disappeared in total darkness.

Business before pleasure. And doing her would be pleasurable. Very, very pleasurable. As he had done with the possum, his instinct was to go after her, put his hand on the windowsill, leech off the warmth of her presence, stand in the shadows outside the house, and listen to her fall into sleep. The need to feel her warmth, to see her again, to trail his fingers down the length of her throat . . . with a great force of will, he stood where he was, aware she had a protector, knowing that he liked to strike the solitary. *Ta-rah-rah-BOOM-ti-ay.* . . . He hadn't had his that day.

Someone else watched through him. He bit his lips, tasting the flat, iron sweet of his blood, driving the sleeping man out of his thoughts. *He* would not treat this woman as she deserved to be treated. *He* would . . .

cut—bite—rip—rape—torment—

Images sheared through his mind. He blinked again, as if to wipe them away, strobe-lit visions of atrocities which fired him even as they disgusted him. The sleeping man's memories. . . . Duct tape. Blades with serrated edges. Violence and desire interchangeable. The sweet flesh of the inside of the thighs being filleted, excising savage tooth marks . . . blood pooling . . . vise grips biting down on rosy areolae. . . .

Death.

He took a deep breath and shook himself like a dog shedding water even as he fought being caught up in the flashing emotions.

His muscles were tensed under his dark sweatshirt. They rippled with subconscious desire. Though compact, he kept himself built up, and he had no doubt he could overpower anyone who stood between himself and his chosen quarry. But this was not a physical foe. The sleeping man lay inside his mind, of him but not him, and the sweat rippled down his face inside his mask, cascading like a waterfall.

Remember who he was. Remember what she told him, she who'd sent him here, she who would be terribly disturbed if he failed in his mission. Think. Reason.

The thing which kept him free to hunt, his will, his intelligence, his ability to come and go without witness or interference, held him back. *She* had imprinted that on him. That, and his mindfulness of his original target. Bound, the sleeping man began to collapse, slumping, then melting away altogether. Gone.

This was business. Pleasure later. He nudged forward to the side of the alley, where a handful of avocado trees hung over weather-beaten wooden fencing, and the house could still be watched from the back window of the car.

The stalker smiled. He sought prey tonight. He would have to gracefully bow out of this hunt. For the moment. The night was still very young.

He wove his fingers together and stretched them until the knuckles popped faintly. *He* had infinite patience. He stepped farther back into the shadows, turning to leave.

Under the leaning branches of an avocado tree, a roof rat raced across the boards, snatched a green fruit, and disappeared over the top of a garage.

The stalker continued down the alleyway until he found the house he searched for, a beige house, different from the others on this block in that a second story had been added. Done in ocher with white trim, it was a house that exuded a quiet kind of class and prosperity that set it off from the rest of the neighborhood, which was teetering between middle and lower economic groups. The man had not left the neighborhood when he'd begun to prosper, but had tried to take the neighborhood with him. Under different circumstances, the assassin might have admired the councilman, a man of color, who'd gone far and worked hard. But this was nothing personal.

The stalker paused in the shadows again. Overgrown oleander shrubs and bottlebrush leaned over him, hiding him, their dust as irritating as the oleander leaves were poisonous, but he held his breath for the moment he huddled in their sanctuary. Briskly, he checked his weapon, secured it, ran his fingers over the odd contours of his face, snugged his hood into place. When he stepped out, it was with business in mind.

It was not conscience which drove MacBeth from his sleep and his wife into a waking nightmare, Ibie decided, as he swung his feet over the bed and slipped them into worn-out, faded plaid slippers. It was a bad prostate. Shakespearean prose not withstanding, it seemed to be the fate of all men, wicked or innocent.

He scrubbed a pink-palmed hand over his face, digging out the sleep, and sighed, looking at his clock. Not even one-thirty. That meant he'd be up again at least one more time before dawn.

He yawned with the realization and then lurched out of bed, the mattress springs creaking. He grabbed for his robe, as comfortably worn and threadbare as the slippers, and shrugged it on. He ought to go in and have the damn thing yanked, or cut, or whatever the surgeons did. He ought to, he knew he ought to, but he couldn't quite bring himself to do it. No, sir. Not when his doctor had explained some of the possible side effects.

No, sir. Ibie grinned at himself as he shuffled down the upstairs hallway. He had no intention of giving up the ladies. Not that he had many, at his age, and with his dignity of being a city councilman, but he had his chances, and he intended to take them. A hallway mirror reflected his passage, grizzle-haired, mahogany-skinned old man, shoulders still straight, face heavily lined, eyes heavy with sleep.

No, sir, Ibie had no intention of getting cut if he didn't have to. He already knew it wasn't cancerous. Just damned inconvenient. But he liked to stroke the sweet, velvety insides of a woman as much as the next man—more, when he'd been young, and he wasn't giving that away. Uh-uh. So, until they could convince him that he wasn't going to lose anything but the discomfort, he would get up in the middle of the night with his prostate feeling like a damn cantaloupe, waddle down the hall, and try to pee standing up. If he was too damn sleepy, then he would just sit down, like an old woman. That's why he wore pajamas and a robe now. It wouldn't do to be scaring anybody if they found him asleep on the toilet in the morning.

He made his way to the bathroom, relieved himself in spits and spurts as much as he was able, found some comfort, and then decided he was hungry. He'd eaten lightly at dinner and now his stomach growled much the way it had in his youth. Ibie grinned at the memory. He'd had a voracious appetite when young, for women, food, and the law. He'd done all right by all three. He straightened his pajamas, and left the bathroom, padding quietly downstairs toward the kitchen.

His aides all slept with a deafness he admired. Of course, he wore them out. But they did not fear the night, he thought, as he put a hand out to turn on the downstairs light, then hesitated. The telltale gleam might wake NaShonda or one of the other aides who lived in his old house. The kitchen light would be good enough for his aged eyes.

Ibie scuffled his slippered feet into the kitchen at the back of the house, wondering what there was he could eat. If Tildie, bless her heart, was still alive, there'd at least have been sweet potato pie, like pumpkin pie, but sweeter, more pungent with clove and nutmeg and the taste of the sweet potatoes themselves. My, he missed that—and her, the only woman who'd been able to tame him. Had it only been thirty-two years they'd had together? Not long enough. He would make a point of telling St. Peter that at the gate, when he met him. Not long enough at all. He would take the time to tell St. Peter that before sprinting through and finding his beloved, sass-filled Tildie.

He turned the corner and reached out again for the kitchen plate switch, eyes already blinking against what would be a white flood of light, when he saw a movement. Heard something twitch even as his fingers flipped the switch, and he looked toward the deep corner, the corner which angled toward the back door and porch.

As the light came on, it struck the thing which waited for him. Ibie staggered back, slammed into the wall, his head smacking solidly. But the pain he felt was in his throat, no—his chest, spearing downward as he tried to gasp and scream at the same time.

Never in his life had he been so terrified, not even decades ago when he'd awakened to find a white-sheeted and hooded man in his living room. Then, young and strong and fearless, he'd thundered out, "This is Los Angeles. Get the hell out of here!"

Now, words failed him. They swelled in his chest and weighted him down like an anchor. He gargled and clawed at his mouth as if he could free a scream.

The thing moved at him, manlike, dressed in sweats, for God's sake, but its face—and Ibie tried to roll away from him, the awful pain in his chest spreading up into his neck and down into his arm.

The last thing he managed to do was to trigger his alarm necklace and send it blasting into the night, waking his aides and, hopefully, the whole damn neighborhood. There was no way in hell Ibie Walker planned to let any alien take his body and keep him from the gates of heaven and his Tildie.

When the assassin dove back into cover, the coolness had evaporated. His hands shook as he disassembled his weapon which had not even been fired. He dropped the hood from his head, ran his fingers over his face, and ripped off the masklike equipment. He breathed hard. Still in a low squat, he made his way to where he could see the angled front of the house and waited.

He crouched under the oleanders as light flooded the target house. Sound and fury woke the neighbors. A low siren sounded. He could see the emergency vehicle slow, stop, the paramedics disembark, their cases in their hands as they ran to the house.

Nothing in the plans or the preparation had gone wrong, except that he had miscalculated the insomnia of the old. He and his target had run into each other in the kitchen hallway, surprising each other. The councilman had fallen back, gasping. The old man had clutched his chest and gone down, rich brown face graying with pain. He'd had enough presence of mind to set off his medic-alert alarm, but had never uttered a word.

Fright might have done the job meant for a bullet, but the assassin couldn't count on it. He could not allow the councilman to regain consciousness, to remember, to live. He stayed crouched in the bushes long enough to hear the paramedics talking to one another as the first returned to the vehicle for more equipment, communicating to the mike clipped to his shoulder. He learned where the councilman was going to be taken, which triage unit had room and staff available to treat him immediately.

The assassin backed out of hiding and bolted down the alley, knowing that all attention was directed elsewhere, to the spectacle of the paramedics on the councilman's front lawn, desperately trying to save a life.

Chapter 6

Light from the backyard flooded her window. It flared into her dreams. McKenzie woke, blinking, her chest heaving while she remembered where she was. She lay still, her pulse thundering in her ears. He'd been chasing, she'd been running. Like Death with his scythe, he'd been after her with a baseball bat, himself faceless, taller, faster, malevolent. Unlike the bloody visions which washed across her from time to time, this had had a reality to it that, even now, pumped adrenaline through her.

She took a deep breath, trying to exorcise the nightmare. She'd slept in her clothes and felt vaguely uncomfortable. The scent of the jacaranda lay heavily on the night air. For some reason, it reminded her of years ago, blocks and blocks away, where the scent of spring was the rich and heavy star jasmine that bloomed at night. Thinking of pajama parties, small escapes from home, she kicked back the covers.

It hadn't all been a nightmare. She could hear the timbre of a rich, male voice rising in anger. Her father's voice. Did she smell Four Roses on the air, the cheap whiskey which used to fuel his alcoholic rages? What had she done, what had she come home to? Or was he just being Walt, arguing with the baseball announcer over some call on the game?

McKenzie turned her head to read the dusty face of the clock radio. After two. It couldn't be the baseball game, now long over, players off the field and out of the showers. The voice continued to swell in belligerence. She lay back uncertainly, wondering if the radio was still on, if she even knew her father's voice.

"Who the hell are you and what are you doing here?" It had to be Walt, bellowing through the house. "Get out of here before I call the cops."

She sat up. Her jeans had twisted and she squirmed around in them for more comfort. A thinner, more distant tenor answered her father.

"I came for my wife."

McKenzie froze, fingers tucking at the hem around her ankle. Her blood went cold. She breathed quick, twice, in and out, then grabbed her ancient baseball bat from the corner. Its weathered wood, old and gray, fit the curve of her hand snugly. She hefted it. The sound of crashing china came from the kitchen.

She opened the door cautiously and put her back to the hallway, crab stepping through the dark tunnel. Only the bat in her hand seemed familiar. She wrapped her hands more tightly about it.

Light from the kitchen spilled out, menacing and sharp to her sleep-darkened eyes. McKenzie stopped as the argument grew louder, took a deep breath, then stepped around the corner.

Floodlights from the yard silhouetted Jack's angular, wiry body as he moved across the kitchen. She could feel him look at her. "McKenzie," he said. "You lying little bitch." Her vision opened. His lips were thin and tight, and his white teeth gleamed. He looked grimly pleased.

Her heart plummeted. It was impossible, there was no way he could have known, she had had it all planned, buried in Los Angeles under thousands of Smiths—how could Jack be *here?* Only Sarah could have located her and she never would have told voluntarily. . . .

Walt flinched. He brought a fist up. "Don't talk to my daughter like that."

The smell of bourbon did fill the air, but now she could tell it did not come from him. But he was between her and Jack, stubbornly set, and the fear she'd felt for Sarah now suddenly transferred to her father.

McKenzie screamed. "Dad, no! Get away from him. Run!" She hefted the bat.

Jack took a confident step forward. His boots crunched on broken dishware. His muddy eyes glinted sharply. "She's my wife, old man. Get out of the way." He shoved her father against the kitchen counter. Walt hit with a grunt. He grabbed for a frying pan left on the stove stop. Jack caught his wrist in midair, twisting it back. His lips twisted scornfully. The pan went clattering to the floor. Her father breathed heavily, sweat across his upper lip.

"Get out of here! Don't you touch us. Leave me alone!" She didn't care who heard. In fact, she hoped the neighbors would hear, and call for help. For once Mrs. Ethelridge's nosiness would be welcome. Her voice tore from her throat, like the roar of a lioness, but it did not move either man.

Light and dark streaked the room starkly. Jack took a stride forward. Her father moved instinctively to block it. She saw Jack reach out and shove her father aside. He hit the rim of the kitchen sink and held on, gasping. She tightened her grip on the baseball bat. "I'll kill you, so help me!"

Jack laughed, answering softly, "You're not going anywhere." He grabbed for her.

Her father lunged between them. McKenzie cocked the bat. She hesitated knowing she couldn't swing without hitting him. "Dad, get away." She hesitated, seeing Cody, blood-laced and torn, then her father again clearly. "Dad, go call 911. Daddy, *please.*"

Jack shoved again, hard, pushing the older man backward. Walton hit the threshold to the back steps. He rolled off the stucco, going to one knee. Jack watched in satisfaction, before turning for McKenzie. She saw her father hook a leg out. Jack stumbled. Irritation replaced the grim pleasure on his face. He wheeled around and grabbed her father up by his shirt collar. The two began to grapple, sliding off the porch and into the backyard.

Jack's fists slapped into her father's ribs. He grunted coarsely, and her father's breath sounded like a steam whistle. She began to shake uncontrollably. Her throat ached. Arms locked, faces going red, the two men wrestled. Jack's lips peeled back in a fierce grin of pleasure.

She screamed again, "Help! Somebody help us!"

Her father let out a sound of pain. He went to one knee, clutching his shoulder. Jack clasped his hands together and clubbed him on his back. Walt put a hand to his chest. He twisted around, gasping. Sweat poured down his purplish face.

"McKenzie . . . get out of here . . . now. . . ."

He started to fold up, like a broken toy. Jack put out a booted foot, paused, then deliberately kicked him over. He left her father writhing on the ground. He shot a look at McKenzie, who stood frozen in the kitchen doorway, and took the porch steps in a single leap. She swung the bat and missed.

They stared eye to eye. Jack reached out and knotted his long fingers around the end of the bat. McKenzie tried to twist it free, and couldn't. She hadn't enough strength to wrestle it back from him, and she didn't have enough nerve to drop it and run. She just stood, rooted to the ground, numb, as he pulled the bat toward him. Like a leash, it drew her with it.

"And just where did you think you were going, little bit? How far did you think you could get without me? What kind of lies have you been telling?" He began to twist the bat. Her wrists burned as she could not let go, and her arms contorted. "Did you forget to tell him you *liked* it rough? That I was the best thing that ever happened to you? What—did you think you could just spit in my face and walk OUT?" He wrenched the bat from her grip and threw her backward.

The concrete edge of the porch smashed against her spine as she landed. The hot streak of agony made her gasp. It stung her eyes, made her think. She could die here, broken just like Cody, if she didn't move! She could hear her father gargling in pain . . . what was happening to her father?

Jack leaned close, grabbed a fistful of hair and yanked her face up to meet his. He bit her lips, teeth tearing sharply. Her flesh ripped as she pulled her head back in pain. McKenzie could feel the blood well up as she let out a strangled sob. She raised a foot and kicked, hard.

Jack staggered back.

McKenzie rolled over and clawed her way up the back porch. She pulled herself up, through the door and into the house. Behind her, she could hear both her father's feeble cries and Jack's pungent curses.

9-1-1. 9-1-1. Her nails, splintered and torn, ached unbearably. She could feel blood running down her chin. Her butt felt as though it had been kicked in. She skidded barefoot over the hardwood floors, trying to find the phone.

A chair crashed behind her. McKenzie didn't look back. Either Jack had fallen over it, or he'd thrown it at her. She didn't want to know. She burst through the swinging doors of the dining room into the small living room, looking frantically through the dark.

There it was! On the side table, near the TV. McKenzie launched herself at it. She grabbed it up, punched in 9-1-1, and without waiting for an answer, threw the phone to the side of the couch, receiver off. She heard Jack behind her.

They screamed at one another as he grabbed for her. She felt the slaps and blows, hair torn from her head, her face go hot with pain and hurt. She fished around for the phone with her left hand. He jumped on her hand, the rough soles of his shoes digging into her, bones crunching. She kicked and yelled back, fighting uselessly. They crashed to the floor and he straddled her. She couldn't breathe as he took his hands and cradled her face. Then, grinning, he began to bash her head into the floor.

Faintly, she could hear herself crying, "Oh, God! Somebody help me!"

Pain ricocheted through her skull. It brought her twisting into exploding darkness.

She was aware of lights stabbing into her eyes. She winced away from them, found her arms tangled and then imprisoned. Voices floated around her, some near, some far, one strident and jarring. They made no sense to her. Words pounded into her, but McKenzie could not understand them. A lance of light seared into her pupils. She flinched from it. Someone cradled her head. Strong fingers imprinted her scalp, holding her steady. Over the turmoil, the dizzying wash of light and sound, she could hear clearly the buzz and static of a police radio—odd, how could she hear that so well? And, beyond that, someone was playing "Stairway to Heaven." Or perhaps she merely imagined it. The riff went on and on. It must be the long version.

"Keep your eyes open."

McKenzie heard that. Her lids fluttered as she looked up. Dark blue uniforms over, around her. A thick collar about her neck. A shunt pricked the tender skin inside her elbow. She felt the sting of alcohol, then the cool smoothness of the needle sliding into place. Quick hands layered tape over and around her arm. *An IV,* they were giving her an IV. Help. Help had come.

The realization sank into her. She could feel herself lying on the grass, the sharp-edged blades of the St. Augustine jabbing her. She felt raw. Someone held her head up slightly, leaning over her. She could see other figures dimly, working a few feet away from her. The red, white, and blue flash of lights illuminated, then shadowed, fire trucks and EMT vehicles, all crowding the street and curb. They dazzled her eyes, and she could not bear to stare at them.

The pinpoint beam of a flashlight stung her eyes again, and a voice said, "Okay, pupils normalizing, I think we've got her back again." A pleasant, tense face leaned over her as she blinked in reaction to the beam.

Footsteps by her other flank. McKenzie shifted slightly. The hands imprisoning her head relaxed, let her look. A thick-bodied man squatted down beside her, all in blue, darker blue, notepad in hand. He smelled faintly of coffee. "Can you tell us what happened?"

Her throat cracked. "Jack" came out like a croak. McKenzie gave a hard swallow, tried again. "He was so mad at me."

"Jack who? This him? And who are you?"

Her hearing buzzed loudly. Everything blurred suddenly, started to go swinging past. She put her free hand out and grabbed for the policeman's trouser cuff as if it were a lifeline and could steady her. The sharply creased fabric filled her hand. "I came home . . . my father. How's my father?"

Material twisted in her fingers. The masculine voices around her paused. There was a rhythm to them, she realized suddenly.

A voice called out, "Five, four, three, two, one. And clear." A sharp buzz followed it.

"Okay, that does it. Sinus rhythm. Get the ringers going, put the mask back in place."

She had this sense she ought to understand what they were talking about, what they were saying, if she could just concentrate. . . .

The policeman answered her then. "Looks like he's going to be okay. Can you tell me what happened? Did he hit you? Was there a fight?"

Her face felt warm. She let go of the officer. She put her hand up, could feel something sticky trickling down it. Blood? Tears? She couldn't tell. She stared at her hand, unable to see in the unsteady lights what coated it. A sob squeezed her throat tight. "I tried to stop him. My father . . . His chest—is it his heart? He fell. Collapsed."

McKenzie squeezed her eyes shut, opened them again quickly as the paramedic touched her forehead, saying, "Keep 'em open. We need you awake right now. Thatta girl."

"What can you tell us?" The policeman persisted.

She swallowed tightly. She tried to remember Jack Trebolt. Everything wavered. Her hearing began to close off, and the vision in her eyes narrowed to a tiny tunnel, at the end of which the paramedic waited. She thought she got out, "He drives a truck."

The paramedic leaning over her picked up her hand, steadying the IV, and remarked, "From the tread marks on her skin, he drove over her."

There was a flurry of motion beyond the officer. Her tunnel of vision widened enough to show her that they were moving her father in concert, a many-legged, multi-armed blur, hoisting him onto a gurney and taking him away. She felt an odd distancing come over her, as if she weren't even involved, just watching. The back doors of the ambulance closed, shutting her out, and then the vehicle left. Another remained at the curb. *For who?* she wondered.

Paramedics surrounded her, hands on her ankles, under her hips, back, and shoulders. "One, two, three!" She was lifted and moved. The scent of crushed grass and dew wafted up. Agony roared through her body as they settled her again and strapped her in place. The buzzing in her ears escalated, and waves of dizziness overwhelmed her.

Someone said, "We're losing her again."

"Where's she going?"

"Mount Mercy. You can follow up there."

"I'm through here, anyway." Faintly, "I'm getting tired of seeing this shit."

Her eyelids fluttered. McKenzie could feel the corners of her mouth turn up slightly. Someone else thought Jack was a son of a bitch. Maybe it wasn't all just her. The gurney bumped over the grass, jostling her. Mrs. Ethelridge leaned over her. "We'll close the house up, dear. Don't you worry."

The gurney thumped past an old woman with silver-gray hair, and many wrinkles, and a crumpled lavender wrap. McKenzie barely recognized her.

"Poor dear . . ." the woman said faintly. "She and her father used to have the worst rows. Wake the whole neighborhood. Just came back yesterday. . . ."

Mac couldn't stay awake any longer, no matter how they urged her. The ocean surged in her head, carrying away the words, sweeping her away with it.

He didn't need the equipment for the hospital. He already knew it like the back of his hand. He tucked the gear inside his shirt, where it clung wetly to his rib cage, sticky from the sweat of his face. No one took any real note of him as he entered through the ambulance corridor, hood up, face down. His mind darted ahead, planning how to finish the job he'd begun earlier, how to take out his target, how to get away unnoticed, unnoticeable. *She* would be extremely displeased if he did not.

The emergency room was mainly filled with the sick, indigent families gathered around a flickering TV set, awaiting their turn, rocking babies who coughed and spit up phlegm intermittently. He strode through without stopping. The schizophrenic nature of an emergency ward was that a good many cases were not emergencies, except that no regular medical care had been or could be sought, and then there was the unit beyond the doors, beyond the EMT entrance where the real traumas were being treated. Some nights the wounded would fill these corridors. Other nights, like tonight, had been quiet up until his arrival. He had never seen a triage unit so galvanized. It suited his purpose in that it became much easier to blend in on the emergency wing, steal greens, and become a part of the scene. It did not suit his purpose in that the energy was mainly devoted to saving the man he intended to kill. He stayed in the corridors, found a clipboard, walked back and forth as though he had a destination.

A second man in cardiac arrest being brought in drew his keen attention, curtains separating one end of the triage from the other as teams worked to stabilize both men.

There were no similarities. One black and fragile elder. The other late middle-aged, stocky and white. Both meeting and finding a fate in the night. Trays and carts of supplies were rolled through hastily, nurses and residents lined up, monitors and leads beeped into frantic service. He watched as, almost simultaneously, the vast needles for cardiac injections were held up, tapped, extraneous fluid squirting into the air to clear air bubbles from the syringes, then doctors bent and injected into the chest cavities of the patients, the synchronization unnoticed by any but he. He observed, wondering if there was a way he could turn the havoc to his advantage. Seeing none, he decided to wait until the delicate moments when the stabilized patient would be left in triage, awaiting transport to ICU.

He cut across the first floor to the blood labs, found a plastic tray with empty vials, labels, and disposable syringes, and lifted it. Blood work was always being done. It gave him an excuse for being anywhere, anytime. He might even find an excuse for the syringes. When he returned, the councilman was lying quietly, a single charge nurse monitoring him. The window of opportunity would shortly open.

He stepped across the hall, behind faintly yellow curtains, to wait. When he turned, he saw that there was an occupant there, her face battered, but still and silent. A clipboard was thrown across the foot of the bed. He picked it up. Head and chest x-rays had been ordered. Her monitor showed her heart rate stabilized, her IV had been taped to the inside of the rail. She would remain there, forgotten until the cardiac cases were resolved.

The curtains were troubled by his entrance, but the young woman did not awaken. He stood to one side, just out of her peripheral view should she come to suddenly, knowing he could be out of the area before she could focus on him. Watching her, he was drawn as much by the bloodstains and bruises on her face as by the kind of plain beauty they marred.

She slept as she would have normally, if her life had not abruptly met with such violence. In the late evening, closer to sunrise than sunset, her breathing matched that of the tides, slow, sure, ebbing. Morning would bring it surging back, along with her soul, and her awareness.

He loved women. They did not understand him, invariably. They turned away when he needed them most. But he loved them. He loved the curve of their eyes, the gentle creases and folds around their expressive orbs, the tangle of their hair, the shell-like cupping of their ears. He had never seen a woman with ugly ears. But it was their hair which he loved most, lustrous and thick.

He reached out and stroked her hair gently. His finger caught briefly in a silken strand. She had good color, young and rich and natural, unbleached . . . he abhorred bleached hair. He plucked a strand of grass out of it, stroking, styling it gently away from her battered cheekbones, tucking it behind the delicate ear. Then he saw the violation, the rough patch where someone had sawed away a lock. Crudely and savagely, her skin was raw, hair torn or hacked from the roots.

He snatched his hand away as if burned by the mockery. He took souvenirs to remind him of the affairs he'd had, curling tresses to press into his hand whenever he wished to summon memories of the passion, the love, the blood. . . . He knew it was his signature, and did not care. It was the portion of his quarry which would never die, which would go into the grave as beautiful as it had been alive, never subject to the putrefaction of the flesh, strands which would perfume and tickle his fingers as long as he dared to hold them. Every woman's mane was different, as individual as she was, scented with her body's aroma and the soft perfumes of shampoos, each strand a road of memory as vibrant to him as a photograph or video.

And if stealing a lock of hair was his signature, then what was this forgery? Who dared to take what was his and his alone?

Voices broke into his fevered thoughts. He stepped back, catching the blood work tray with his elbow, righted it, vials quivering. He could not see beyond the curtains, but he recognized the tenor of the voices. Police.

Casually, he moved to a spot where he could see the stainless steel supply cabinets lining the walls, found an image in the mirrored surface, and watched it. Two men meeting, both uniforms.

"What are you here on?"

"A Domestic. Same old, same old." A heavy sigh. "You waiting for Ibie Walker?"

"Yeah. If he comes to. Once they plant him in ICU, I'll call the sarge and let him know. If he wants me to stay, I'll stay." A shrug.

"Why? Didn't he just drop?"

"Word is he might have surprised an intruder. We treat it lightly, overlook anything, and there'll be racism cries from every corner. Downtown wants a statement as soon as I can get one."

A low whistle. Then, even lower, confidential. "Heard that drive by was in here earlier tonight."

"The kid? Really? What happened?"

"He didn't make it. He's down in the chop shop already."

The image of the conferring officers blurred, as if both shuddered slightly. Then the taller one muttered, "Maybe some good'll come out of it. Lucky you aren't at Bayshore. Place is crawling with Feds."

"Shit. A congressman there, a councilman here. Did somebody call a war and we missed it?"

"Welcome to El Lay. Come on. I know the maze. Let me show you where the coffee is. The charge nurse'll come get you."

Listening to the effects of his handiwork, he felt a certain satisfaction in the chaos.

In a moment, the stainless steel reflection cleared, footsteps leading away. The charge nurse in question had not looked up from her stool, her post, keeping an eye on her patient's monitors. He watched her a moment longer. She wore her hair in one of those curly, curly perms. He disliked the frizzy, chemical feel of it. Whatever attraction she'd held for him quickly faded.

He stepped back behind the curtains softly. Turned and saw the young woman watching him.

Seeing himself in her eyes, he stepped forward, put one hand across her mouth and the other across her throat. Her eyes widened in sudden, conscious fear. She struggled, one arm free, flailing at him, too weak to bother him.

"Bloody hands!" she got out, before he hardened his palm across the sweet plump lips, dampening all sound. She tossed her head, but she could not throw him. She quit fighting suddenly.

He looked at her fondly, his quarry, glad she had fought off her potential harmer, glad she had saved herself for him, for his more skillful hands. Not for her the ignominy of an estranged boyfriend, a drunken husband, a misunderstood suitor. No ordinary battering and death for her. She lay there like a victim, but he knew her better. He knew her heart and soul. He would not abandon her.

No.

His fingertips found the pressure points in her neck. His marks would scarcely be noticeable among all her other bruises. His hand tightened.

Her hair fell across the back of it. Soft, a silken caress.

As her eyes dimmed and her breath stilled, he knew he didn't want her like this. He needed more.

Her lids shuttered. She went limp in sudden submission. He waited another few seconds, deciding, then lifted his hands from her abruptly.

Her chest rose and fell in a sudden gust of breath and awareness. At his back, he heard one nurse call for another.

"Stacy. Come give me a hand with this, will you?"

Remembrance of his purpose flooded back. He turned and put an eye to the slit in the curtain. He saw the nurse leave the councilman's quiet form and walk to the far end of triage, to where the second man still fought for stabilization.

The window of opportunity, however small, had finally opened. He took rubber gloves from the blood work tray and pulled them on, swiftly, efficiently. Four long strides and he was across the unit, standing at the old black man's head, looking down at the creased face, half-hidden by tubing. He reached up, found the connector to the drip bag, took a syringe and injected one, two, three bubbles of air.

He turned and left, thoughts seething. The blood work tray he deposited on a sink in the bathroom. The gloves he stripped off and disposed of in an infectious waste container. The greens he did not shed until he was across the parking lot and in the shadows. He did not slow, but he recognized the glint of a police uniform as he went around the elbow of the parking structure and disappeared.

McKenzie, drowning, struggled to awaken, her throat raw and sore. Dreams of Jack and drowning men trying to take her down, keep her down, filled her. She fought back, clawing and kicking, and came awake, IV tubing snaking across her chest like something alive.

There was a man there, leaning over her. Fear of Jack exploded like shrapnel through her. The color of his white jacket didn't register. As he reached out, she reacted to the grasping hand, determined not to be dragged under again. She balled her fist and swung. He staggered back. A tray went clattering. The triage unit chimed with noise. He grabbed at the curtain. It and the circular rod came down with a vast ripping.

"Nurse. Nurse!"

People came running. She had a blurred and tipping view of the triage ward, filled with white coats and greens. Monitors beeped like brassy car alarms.

Chapter 7

The hour was late, his story was done, and Carter figured he ought to go home, but he lingered at the hospital and finally decided to go to the lounge to get a cup of coffee. The shooting of Nelson unsettled him. That hadn't been his assignment, the news had bled in around the emotional tragedy he'd been covering, but the notion lingered in the back of his mind that he would find a message or voice mail when he got home. *Let's meet for lunch* or, *How about dinner— some good Mexican, and decent margaritas—you buy. I'm a goddamn congressman, for crissakes. You might even get a story out of me.*

The Feds would be all over Nelson's death, as a congressman and formerly one of their own. If John had called, they'd be tracking him down soon enough. Carter didn't mind it, hell, he welcomed it. But he had nothing he could tell them. He didn't know why John was in town. Who he'd planned to meet. Or how he'd met his death.

But he was a reporter. He ought to care enough to find out. As Carter walked along, he scratched the underside of his jaw, where the razor blade had nicked him two or three days before and a small but decidedly itchy scab now rested. He knew before the matter even started that the Feds would freeze him out. He'd have to wait for the news conferences and media releases like anyone else.

So, with nothing else he could do to help change anyone's status in life, coffee sounded good. He could smell it long before he got there, the aroma drifting through the corridor of the back way of Mount Mercy. The hospital was in a state of flux, halfway through renovation and additions, and the corridors were raw, open to their underpinnings. In some areas big sheets of opaque plastic hung down and fluttered in the perpetual drafts. The beams and insulation were laid open, elevator shafts bared and inoperative and cordoned off, and Carter reflected that the hospital resembled one of its own patients, sliced open in surgery for probing and healing.

The reflection suited his shitty mood. John Nelson had come to town and had gotten himself drilled. The day had not improved from there, until sunset when it had really hit the pits, with another innocent victim—and he'd been called in to milk the story.

Back here, beyond Emergency and Triage, away from Billing and Admitting, downstairs from the wards and upstairs from the operating theaters and the morgue, there were only x-ray and lab techs wandering, their scrubs wrinkled and open at the neck, their faces gray under the unflattering light. Their eyes did not meet Carter's. Back here in the bowels, if he knew where he was going, then he probably belonged. Renovation had wiped out all the little courtesy arrows pointing to this region or department or that and only a participant in hospital business could wend his or her way through the labyrinth of hallways without getting lost. Carter wondered if they knew him for himself, or if they thought he was a surgeon, or maybe from the coroner's office.

He turned the corner. A sheet of plastic moved with him, wearily, shifting as though a gray tide followed him. He felt like a piece of driftwood, old, weathered, twisted and beaten, half-skinned by the harshness of the sea which had carried him along and beached him here. He'd been beached a number of times since letting himself be swept out of Chicago. He'd left when he'd been fired—no, that was wrong. He'd left *before* he'd been fired—the certified fax had followed him—in search of Bauer, he'd told himself, but he had not found the killer.

The tide had taken him all over until he'd been cast up in California. He'd worked at the *Sacramento Union* until it had gone belly-up in early '94. Now he was here in L.A., where reality ground at him until he sometimes thought nothing would be left except a tiny pile of fine dust. Which, he supposed, was one way of achieving what he had not been able to do earlier.

He had already let go of life. He no longer clung to it. He ate when he wanted, which was seldom, and smoked if he thought about it, and slept only when he absolutely had to, and did not care what others thought of him. At first, there had been that vague possibility that finding Bauer might save him, might give him the grip he needed to hold on, but he had been unsuccessful. His paper had tolerated his misuse of the information pipeline far longer than he would have guessed. The VICAP hookups, the taps he had put into various systems, ears to the ground, listening for the mortal footfall of Bauer.

It was as if the killer knew that Carter would come after him. The last time Carter had talked to an FBI suit, the unofficial word was that Bauer was considered probably dead, his mind having disintegrated to the point that he could no longer exist. Like Jack the Ripper, the reporter had been told.

Carter didn't buy it. Bauer was not a disorganized killer like Dahmer, so mentally ill that eventually he would be unable to cover his crimes, so disturbed that his fantasies and murders would hang on him like crimson flags. No. Georg Bauer was a student of torture and sexual violence, and he carried his tools with him so that he might always be prepared if an opportunity arose, but he was not careless. Having been caught once, and liberated by chance, he would not be caught again. Unlike Bundy who'd thought himself above catching, Bauer did not have arrogance. He had confidence. He was still out there, had found a quiet way to satisfy his blood lust, and he would not surface if he could help it. He would know Carter just as well as Carter knew him, and he would know Carter was waiting.

If Carter's current existence could be so optimistically described. He shrugged his shoulders which felt as though something incredibly heavy bowed them down, stiffening his neck, and turned the corner, that much nearer to a good cup of coffee.

He should go home; his story had been filed, and there was nothing left for him to do, but he did not want to be alone. The story hadn't been nice, he knew it when he'd been sent out. That didn't matter, but there were times when he wanted it to be nice. He knew his readers needed that pat ending, that Disney flare, that hope for a rainbow-colored fade-out.

A toddler had gone down in a gang shoot-out. Pronounced brain-dead here at Mount Mercy, the family had been talked into donating the youngster's organs so that not all had been lost, but Carter got no satisfaction out of the gesture. He couldn't escape the image of the mother, her dusky skin darkened further around her eyes and mouth from crying. This was one gun the toy exchange hadn't swept up, one life the Rebuild L.A. committee couldn't save, one more death to be mourned as unnecessary. His story would not be exceptional. Ibie Walker would be up on his feet in council and exhort the neighborhoods to come together, to stop children killing children, but even that gentle black giant, that elderly African American statesman would not be able to stem the tide.

He could hear low voices drifting from the lounge, and slowed his step to listen, a newspaperman, a reporter always, an eavesdropper by profession.

"What are you waiting for?"

"Moreno wants a statement if I can get it out of her."

"What about the other one?"

"The old man? In a coma now, ICU's got him. He was muttering when the EMTs got there, but I dunno." A pause. "Looks like they just beat the shit out of each other, but then there's the hair—"

"Oh, yeah? Think it's the Blue Killer?"

Carter stopped in the corridor, turning his head slightly to focus better. He recognized instantly what the cops referred to, for it was cops talking in the lounge, the pitch and tone of their voices unmistakable even in Southern California. No civilian spoke like a cop spoke.

There was another stalker out there, someone as deadly as the Hillside Strangler or the Nightstalker, and this was someone they'd dubbed Mr. Blue. It wasn't Bauer, Carter had determined that early on, unless Bauer had changed his tastes a great deal, but he hadn't been able to determine much else about the killer, and he had yet to be able to access VICAP successfully. L.A.'s finest were sitting on this one, and so was he, until he found out more.

But he did know, as the police did, although none of them were sure the killer himself realized it, that he had a predilection toward slate or blue-gray houses. Just as Ramirez, the Nightstalker, had subconsciously chosen victims who lived in light yellow or beige houses, Mr. Blue was drawn by Wedgewood. Wedgewood and women left home alone, for one reason or another.

The speaker made a slight noise, shifting his weight in the lounge chair no doubt, for it squeaked with a protesting echo a second after.

"Could be," he said. "She had some hair cut, sawed off her scalp, just behind her ear, real recently."

"Thought he didn't like to take souvenirs until *after* they were dead. And I thought the profile had the perp figured as a young man."

There was a pause, a shrug on the conversation, and Carter knew he couldn't stand there in the corridor much longer. Someone was bound to discover him. He backed up a couple of strides, coughed, and then went on in.

The two officers had subsided to idle chitchat when he entered the lounge. He went straight to the coffeepot, and watched the lines of their bodies ease slightly as he passed them. "Gentlemen," he said, as he picked up the pot and poured himself a large styro cup full. "Long day."

He did not know their names, for the L.A. Basin beat was a massive one, but they knew him; hence the silence. He would not get around that tonight or, at least, not easily

"What brings you here, Windy?" the younger cop asked, conversationally. He had put his feet up on a second chair.

The older cop had been hunched over his coffee. He looked up with eyes that reminded Carter of fried eggs. "Jesus Christ," he said. "How much did you hear?"

His partner did a barely perceptible double take, then flushed all the way to the collar of his uniform. He dropped his feet to the floor and hunched up to the table in an unconscious echo of his elder.

Carter stirred the brew around to cool it, because he drank it black, for the aroma and the bitter jolt of it. He shrugged. "Enough." He pulled up a chair and straddled it, not too close to the patrolmen, but not too far away, either. "You can relax. I'm here for the drive by."

"We heard he was in the chop shop."

He controlled his reaction to the term. "Yeah. The family decided to donate everything." He swallowed, felt hot liquid surge down his throat. "Good copy. But it never should have happened." He looked at the morose senior cop. "So what was it—a domestic or Mr. Blue?"

"Can't tell you anything." The cop hid his face behind the two big, calloused hands curled around his cup.

"I know you don't know, but what's your best guess?"

"My best guess," the man said heavily, as he pulled himself to his feet and signaled his partner to get up as well, "is that we wouldn't have serial killers if the media didn't give them so much publicity. Just like shooters and carjackers. News is a billion dollar business, and, God knows, you wouldn't want to miss any. Why don't you go chase the Feds? I heard Nelson and you go back a ways."

Carter felt the corners of his mouth pull back in a humorless smile. "We haven't written word one about this guy yet, but you've still got a string of bodies laid out at the county morgue. And I don't think you have a chance in hell of blaming us for what happened to John Nelson."

The younger cop grunted in agreement, but his fellow officer took a deep breath.

"Maybe you want to bring the copycats out of the woodwork, too. Maybe you'd like to sign up broadcast rights before someone else sells out. Maybe you'd like to get in my way while I try to do my job." The cop's chin jutted out belligerently.

Carter tilted his head back. "Don't worry, boys, I don't intend to muddy the waters. I'm not asking for anything you won't be making public later. But I'll wait a while longer. When the department's ready to let go, just make sure I'm first in line, okay? And if there's any line at all on Nelson, anything, I'd like to know. But right now, I'm letting both you and the Feds do their jobs."

He got no answer as the two men shuffled out of the lounge. The younger man paused a half beat, then threw Carter a look over his shoulder. He gave his hair a tug, scissored it with his fingers just behind the ear, then smoothed it down and put on his hat. Carter watched them disappear down the corridor.

Mr. Blue liked to take souvenirs. He put his coffee cup down and stared into the murk. When he'd drunk as much as he wanted, and the rest had gotten cold, he decided to go see if he could find the domestic, maybe talk to the woman.

The long, cold room tilted. She could see shapes running toward her and then across the room. Her heart pounded in her chest. Everything looked strange and indistinct. Nothing was familiar. Where was she?

McKenzie dropped back onto the bed, shaking. Her teeth rattled in her jaw. She could not stop shaking. Darkness closed in on her like a tunnel swallowing her whole. Her vision went. Her hearing roared, muffled, sensing a drama somewhere beyond her. In the distance, forms bobbed and weaved in a dance she could barely see or hear, but one which sent a chill down her back.

"Clear! Four, three, two, one, Hit! Okay, that's it. Sinus rhythm is back. Change that IV tubing. We nearly had an embolism there— pull the curtains round him and leave him here, they're making room in ICU—"

"What about Sleeping Beauty?"

Ghostly forms seemed to turn and consider her. Mac's head felt as though it were bursting.

"She coldcocked Zucker. She'll be all right. Move her up to Third when you've got a chance. And watch out for that right hook."

They stood in a crimson pool. It splashed across their whites, up to their knees, dripped down from the gurney they had been attending, shed by the gray-haired black man they'd been working to save. It flowed from him, life itself, expiring. She had to tell them, warn them. *Someone had been here. Someone would be returning.*

Her voice caught on the raw edges of her throat. Her arms and legs had lost all strength in the joints. She could move nothing.

She had to tell them what she saw. Bloody hands, coming for her. Handprints on the old man. Evidence. Someone had been there, killing.

She could not breathe properly. Or think.

Mac gave in.

Sharp pain hammered through dully throbbing pain. McKenzie lay very still. If she could become flat enough, the agony lightning its way through her head would miss her. She held her breath, pressing down into the bedding. Lying still did help, some. But then she realized she was in a bed, cool sheets tucked in around her, and she struggled to open her eyes. Her lids wouldn't cooperate. Something heavy sat on her hands, refusing to let them go free. Panic sliced through her. Tied down. She was tied down. Did they doubt her sanity?

Her throat constricted as she tried to cry out, and nothing issued forth. Like a nightmare, she could not call for help or run. She could do nothing but lie passively while the evil thing approached. McKenzie thrashed. The cords on her neck pulsed with her silent scream.

Pain answered, stabbing through her with such intensity that she saw flashing stars through her darkened lids, just before she sank back into oblivion.

She took shreds of consciousness with her this time, dreaming. She was wiping up the kitchen floor, crying, her tears washing across her face like a curtain of rain. She'd wrapped Cody in his blanket, his body cold and stiff, her first realization that there was no hope for him. She couldn't carry him into the backyard, she had to drag him on the blanket, then stand in the mist of early evening with rain just beginning to gather like a breath of heavy fog, and dig a hole for him.

When she was done, she stood over the hole and gazed down at the still form. He seemed so alone and abandoned, like some poor animal thrown by the side of the road, not a pet who'd been loved and cherished. Not someone who'd slept on her sneakered feet while she read or did homework. Not a creature that had ever romped and chased Frisbees or the neighboring cats. Not a companion that had ever been warm and golden and vital.

Now he was something dead. Alone.

Cody had always hated being alone. She stood in the drizzle, thinking it would soon be raining in earnest. She stripped off her T-shirt, spattered with blood and soaked with her sweat, and dropped it into the hole with him. Like the time she'd had to board him for a weekend while she took a trip with Jack, and the vet had had her bring a worn shirt, so the pup would have her smell to comfort him. It was all she could give him now, and it wasn't nearly enough.

The shirt drifted down to settle over the corpse and then, suddenly, it billowed up. Up and up and out of the hole and about her face so that she couldn't see. Couldn't see and she dropped the spade handle and clawed at it as it wrapped itself tightly about her head and face—she couldn't breathe. She couldn't breathe!

Her scream tore her free.

Cold air. It whisked over her. McKenzie felt it rousing her. She put a hand out, felt a metal railing, but could move her arm little beyond that. A soft, cotton tentacle wrapped her wrist. The other arm was shackled by a like tentacle and an IV rigging. Mac made herself lie very still, fighting the panic of being tied down.

The privacy curtains surrounding her bed were a faded buttercup yellow. She pried her eyes open as they wavered, and a fresh draft of air came between them. She saw a man standing there, quietly, watching her.

She thought she should have been afraid of him, but she wasn't. Perhaps she had become so afraid that she had moved beyond it into a kind of numbness. There was something about the way he stood that made her think he didn't know she was awake, and didn't want to disturb her. McKenzie struggled to sit up in the bed. Her hair trailed across her forehead and she found it difficult to focus.

He noticed her then. Softly, he asked, "Would you like a drink of water?"

Her voice, so dry. It rasped out of her throat. Water sounded heavenly. She must have said so, because he was there, holding a cup with a bent straw for her. He brushed the hair from her face. The water, tepid and too little of it, slid down her throat.

She lay back. "Thank you." The image of him split apart, slid back together, split apart fuzzily again. She closed her eyes as the effort to keep him in focus made her ill.

She opened her eyes. The man stood there, patiently, understanding in his soft brown gaze.

"Can you tell me what happened? Who did this to you?

Her mouth twisted. "Where am I?"

"You're at Mount Mercy."

The neighborhood hospital. It had withstood both the 1933 and 1994 earthquakes. The psychiatric ward here was infamous. Was that where she was? "Mount Mercy?" she repeated.

"That's right. You were hurt this evening. Actually, it's almost closer to say yesterday." His brown eyes watched her, coaxing. Warm eyes, like melting caramels.

"My father. . . ." McKenzie felt herself drift. She caught hold of the sound of her words. She had forgotten. Guilt stabbed at her, sharpening her wits. "Where is he?"

"He's in ICU. He's going to be okay, they told me."

Intensive care. Her father was in intensive care. Why didn't they have them together so she could see what was happening to him?

Her mind stumbled. It throbbed with flashes of memory, incomplete, strained. Another elderly gentleman on a gurney, a man of color. Jack's foot upon her throat. His boot pinioning her hand to the floor. His anger. No, not anger, rage. Raw, unadulterated rage. Blood-ied hands.

She wasn't safe. Jack would come. She flexed her wrists. "Don't leave me like this. I'm not safe here."

"Can you tell me what happened?" her visitor asked gently. "Some-times that helps."

He waited patiently, almost religiously, for her reply. She wondered if he was one of the chaplains on staff. At one time, the entire staff of the hospital had been clergy. She knew that number had tailed off, over the years. She remembered visiting her friend Kim from the fourth grade after a tonsillectomy. Her visitor now had the same quiet mannerisms as the padre who'd come in while they were gig-gling. He'd waited solemnly to inquire how the patient was doing, and then given all the girls popsicles in celebration.

Her throat ached abominably, as though in sympathy for that long ago operation. What she wouldn't give for a popsicle now. A popsicle, far, far from here.

Urgent to make him understand her danger, she licked her lips, her throat still parched. "I left my husband in Seattle. He came after me." Her throat closed. She made a noise. He reacted as though knowing she was about to break down, putting a tissue in her hand. He folded her fingers about it. It was useless with the restraints. She sniffled unsuccessfully. "You've got to let me go! I can't stay here! I haven't done anything. Please let me go."

"You're not going anywhere like that," he answered. He reached out, touched her scalp. "Who did this to you?"

"Jack." She crumpled the tissue into a tight, damp wad. Her breath knotted in her chest. "He said he'd never let me leave."

An expression of profound disappointment swept the man's face. "He attacked you at your father's house?"

"Yes. We tried . . . we tried to stop him . . ." *Her father, moving in concert, trying to shield her as he'd never done in their past.* She squeezed shut her eyelids.

As if sensing her extreme emotion, he put a hand on her shoul-der. The hospital gown slid a little under his grip and she could feel his fingers on the curve of her neck. Warm, solid, reassuring. Her initial reaction to flinch away from his touch calmed. He radiated reassurance.

"You're safe. There are security guards in the hallways. You'll be fine."

"But if he comes back—"

"He won't. Not here. It'll be all right."

In shame, Mac turned her face away. If she said anything else, tried to explain the cold intuition which racked her, he would think her crazy. If he did not already. If that was not why they had tied her down. She had not let the sleeping dog lie. She had awakened the furies. "I tried everything," she found herself saying. "Nothing was good enough."

He squeezed her shoulder. "It wasn't you. Now rest." He left, the lingering warmth of his touch still upon her shoulder long after the curtains had fallen into place behind him. She closed her eyes again. She fell into an uneasy sleep, a dream like an old *Star Wars* clip, where everyone but her wore shielded helmets, their faces blank reflectors, nothing of humanity about them. They stared at her.

Chapter 8

It was clearly past dawn when he returned from his nocturnal wanderings and slipped into bed. He had nowhere else to go, in the mornings, but home. Watching the steady stream of traffic with sly amusement, like ants pouring out of a mound, the stalker took side streets and alleys. The paper was waiting on the porch stoop when he locked the car at the curb. He picked it up to bring in with him. It was a personal triumph that, as the houses in this bedroom neighborhood began to empty, like bowels in the morning, he got to come home.

He did not awaken his bedmate, but he knew she would rouse shortly anyway, for she had a work schedule to keep. He did not mind that she lived different hours than he did, and that all they had were fleeting moments now and again. It was better that way. He lay quietly upon his pillow, watching her face in repose, thinking that was how dead people looked, once the eyes were closed. He did not want to do her, for sex between them was a difficult and ponderous thing—not for her, for she seemed to enjoy any contact with him, but for him. His satiation lay elsewhere, in the night.

Also, he was afraid that, if he touched her, she would know of his terrible struggles, of his fear of the sleeping man. She would be contemptuous of him. He could face almost anything but her contempt.

Her eyelids began to flicker as if she knew someone watched and subconsciously began to rouse. Her hair had been artificially curled, and sleep frizzed it a little. It would carry more sheen and beauty when she combed it later. It hung almost all the way to her shoul-

ders, casually chic, its color natural and lustrous. Her hair was probably her best feature, although her breasts weren't bad. She'd never
had children, so the wear and tear had not stretched and sagged
them.

She was already more than half-awake when the alarm went off.
She put out a lily-white hand to slap it quiet. Girlishly, she scrubbed
her face into her pillow, then looked at him.

"Dudley. Just get in?"

He hated the sound of his name except when she said it. Even inside his brain, it rattled around like a dead thing, beslimed and stupid as only the grave could make it. But she said it, and the name
changed. From the Ugly Duckling which had plagued him all his life
from kindergarten through high school, it became a swan. He wondered how she did it.

He caught up her hand as she extended it, trying to snake it about
him, and held it still. He did not feel particularly like being touched.
The scene of the attack, and the later scene at the hospital, still filled
his senses. He did not want them dulled or marred by the mundane.
He smiled as her fingers went still in his hand, acquiescent. She
knew him well.

"You know I worked late." He kissed the tips, where her acrylic
nails crowned them, and she smiled back.

"Kiss me."

She startled him. "Why?"

"Because." Her full lips stretched wider. "I like the way your lips
taste after you've killed someone."

Because it was an order, not a request, she snapped her hand free
from his, grabbed at his hair, and pulled his face across to hers. Her
lips were pillowy warm and sensuous, and her tongue tickled inside
his mouth, teasingly. He felt the pain of her nails raking across his
scalp at the same time their lips met.

It was like an electrical shock, hurtful and intriguing at the same
time. He found something awakening in his groin, and before the
kiss was finished, he flung his leg over her and pulled her toward
him, their thighs meshing, his cock growing harder.

She made a sound of amusement and desire, and pushed against
him. She did not ask if he thought of his prey as his hands began to
tear her nightgown from her shoulders, and she would not have

cared if he told her the girl from the hospital was in his mind's eye, in the heat of his blood, the stirring of his manhood. He grew unbearably hard with the fire in his blood. *Ta-rah-rah-BOOM-ti-ay.* . . .

She would not have cared at all.

McKenzie woke up choking as panic surged through her. Blindness drowned her, suffocated her. It had to be an attack. Something covered her head, her face. McKenzie clawed at her head. She couldn't see, couldn't breathe. "Get it off, get it off!" Her choking voice sounded muffled, as though she had already drowned, and the weight of the ocean lay over her.

"Whoa, whoa! You're going to rip out your IV!" A squeaky voice sawed at her, scarcely louder than her own, but almost more frightened. Cold, dry hands on her. She could feel them touching her, patting her, helping her sit. The restraints were gone. That fact sank in. She put her hands up, felt something hard and slick covering her face.

"Okay, okay. Sit up slowly. Take a deep breath. It's over your head, but your nose and mouth are clear. It's just a helmet. Here now . . . take a breath."

"Who are you? What are you doing?" She still couldn't see. She started to put a hand back up, and had it caught up, and gently put back at her side.

"Wait a minute. I've got to secure the IV." Noise of something ripping, and then a pressure across her left forearm. "I'm a tech." It was both cool and sticky. *Tape,* she realized.

She touched it, felt the lumpy plastic body of the IV shunt inside her elbow, and tubing, now covered with tape. McKenzie struggled to orient herself, to remember, to see. "What are you doing to me?"

"Boy, you had me fooled. You must have been out before." A male voice, light in its youth, stammering with nervousness. "Okay. Don't panic. You're at Mount Mercy. You can't see because you're wearing a helmet device for testing, but you will in a minute when I start the program. I told you this before, thought you were talking to me. I thought you were wide awake." A boyish voice. Flat tones despite the worry she thought must be genuine. "First time this has ever happened to me. I thought the other techs were kidding when they said it had happened to them. You must have been unconscious. I'm supposed to be testing you."

McKenzie repeated. "I'm still in the hospital."

"Yeah. Concussion, probably. I'm going to run a little program. It'll be projected inside the gear you're wearing. I've got to put some gloves on you first—"

He caught up her hands. She fought the impulse to pull back. Material tugged across her knuckles, fit bulkily about her fingers. Gloves, just as he'd said. She thought she could feel cables trailing from them, but that just might be the IV tubing against her skin. McKenzie cleared her throat. It hurt. Her breath rattled and rasped around inside of her. She coughed, once, harshly, and her windpipe felt raw.

"Still with me?" The voice sounded anxious. "They told me you were conscious, to get in here and do the testing. You were talking to a cop. Do you remember that?"

No. She wondered what she'd told them. Had she warned them?

The tech shifted weight impatiently, she could hear the rustle of his lab coat and the soles of his shoes creak. "You're okay?"

McKenzie started to nod. Her head felt like a bowling ball, her neck too weak to hold it, and she stopped the movement. "Yes," she said. Her voice did not sound like herself, muffled and weak. She cleared her throat again, and repeated, "Yes," going for strength.

"Good. Okay, I've got you all hooked up. Now what this is," and she felt an additional weight atop her head as if he'd placed something upon it, "is a helmet, like a motorcycle helmet, with a visor in front, sort of like binoculars. That's why you can't see. This is a testing unit. Something new. In a second, I'm going to turn on the program. It's three-dimensional. You're going to be looking right into it. What I want you to do is reach for and grip the balls. Use whatever hand is normal and best, okay? See how you do with that and then I've got another program to run."

McKenzie felt as though she were listening, without comprehending. Before she could protest, the helmet buzzed slightly and her eyes ached as a curving screen woke up with light, and then refracted into a projected room which seemed to encompass her entire self, not just her vision. The effect startled her. She was there, and yet not there. The room reminded her of a museum: vast open spaces, columns, and arched doorways. The floor was black and white alternating tiles. Objects slid across the space at her. She stood, frozen, inside the room and watched the animation come at her, reality without being real.

An orange ball swung past her right cheekbone. McKenzie realized she should have reached for it when she heard faintly, "Did you see that?" The tech sounded annoyed.

"I . . . saw it. I just forgot." She braced herself. A lime green beach ball bounced along the marble flooring. She reached for it on the bounce, caught and held it. It dissolved between her hands.

A wall in front of her began to birth bubbles, which solidified slowly. She found no difficulty in reaching out and grasping each one before it disappeared, even when the tempo sped up.

Everything went dark. McKenzie stopped. There was that additional weight on her head again, and she realized the tech must be resting his hand on the helmet.

"Good. Okay. Are you left-handed or right?"

"Right."

"Okay. Everything green is for the right hand. Everything red is for the left. It won't be coming at you, you have to go and get it. Okay?"

McKenzie could feel her lip swell between her teeth as she worried at it. Without waiting for her answer, the absurd movie began again. This time she had to reach out and up or down to grasp the object and pull it toward her. The room was filled with red and green geometric shapes.

Then, suddenly, she saw Cody. He came loping across the black and white marbled floor, his magnificent golden coat gleaming with that red overcast. His tongue lolled out of his mouth as he leaped at her hands, trying to snatch the balls away. He wanted to play. His soft brown eyes glistened with doggy joy as he jumped and mouthed at her hands. He kept her from going after the shapes, putting himself between her and them. He wiggled with excitement as though knowing she had been gone and now she was back. She fondled his ears and massaged his ruff, scolding him gently for not letting her catch the balls.

Panting, he lay across her feet at McKenzie's admonishment. Another series began and she put her hands up to reach for them again. Cody got to his feet, stiff-legged, growling. He leaned against her knees, forcing her to back up. He snapped at the shapes bombarding her, his movements growing ever faster and more frantic as if he thought to protect her.

From what?

She kneed him aside. "I have to do this, Cody."

The dog lay down again, quivering, shuddering with fear. She reached for the objects as they swooped down at her from animated space, without rhyme or reason or menace.

Cody moaned with fear. Then, as another wave began, he stood up. She looked down at him, head aching, eyes unfocusing. Like a tide crashing down on both of them, the ruby stream flooded them. He pressed against her, trembling and whining, forcing her back, back, until she was out of the imaginary hall, and the images were too faint to perceive or catch. She felt the terrible pressure of . . . something. Something with a growing awareness of her. Something awakening. Confusion gave way to that gnawing dread which had become familiar over the last few days.

"Where are you?"

She stood in emptiness. Cody made a last, throbbing whine, licked her hand, and disappeared. McKenzie felt his going like a cold chill passing through her. She froze in place, suddenly bereft.

The weight disappeared from her throbbing head. Yellow light glanced across her eyes, and off the hospital bed. She blinked weakly at the sudden flood of sight.

"All done."

She shook herself mentally. "What are you going to tell them?"

The tech was stripping off her gloves. All she could see were lanky strands of hair across a flat head, colorless strands, and when he looked at her, his face wasn't much different. He shrugged. "It's got to be read by the department head. It's the doc's program. But, like, there's no right or wrong answers. It's all perceptual."

"It's all in my mind? What will it show them?" Would it show them the blood? Would they *know* the state of her sanity?

He stuffed the gloves into the helmet and tucked it under his arm. "Neat, huh. Like the ones in the arcade."

McKenzie stared dully. The young man's face wrinkled slightly in disappointment. "Virtual reality," he said. "Like the arcade games."

"Oh." Her voice sounded somewhat muffled to her, as though her ears were stuffed with cotton. "Games."

"But not this stuff. We can tell brain damage, optic damage, nerve pressures, spatial interpretation, all sorts of things with this little goodie. If the program gets passed, we're going to be able to diagnose and treat all sorts of crud." He stroked the helmet. "Sorry I scared you. Listen, there's forms to sign about doing this, but they won't be around until after breakfast." He checked his watch. "I'm early. That'll be a while."

"Will you be back?" Unspoken, her fear. *Will you tell me what they find?*

"If not me, someone else." He cracked a grin. "Good thing I'm doing this now. From the looks of that shiner, your eye'll be too swollen to see from in an hour or so. Well, catch you later."

The railings on the bed were up. She could see the IV tubing coiled about them and reaching to her arm. Wherever she looked, there were livid bruises on either side of the shunt. She put her right hand to her throat, wondering. Before she could ask, the lab tech disappeared out the curtains.

McKenzie lay back. Her eyes fluttered shut, too heavy to keep open. She had questions. It wasn't about Cody. But what . . . what was it she needed to know . . . ?

"I think I'd like a look at the other guy," the nurse said cheerfully as she put the breakfast tray down on the table and swung it efficiently into place.

McKenzie started to shake her head, winced, and stopped. Swelling had nearly closed one eye, and she had an ice pack tied over it now, the soothing coolness making up for the awkwardness of the compact. "No," she said carefully. "You wouldn't."

"Well, he must have looked like something. You were still fighting when the EMTs brought you in last night, they tell me. You nearly knocked out our resident." The woman stood appraising her. "Still water runs deep, eh? Proves what you can do when you snap."

"I hit a doctor?" No wonder they had tied her arms down.

The nurse was California tan, with sharp crow's feet etched at the corner of her neutral blue eyes, her hair streaked with yellow amid the brown and gray. It was pulled back into a curly ponytail, and made her nurses' cap ride high. She made a face. "Don't you remember when they brought you in?"

"Not much."

"Well, you're our hero, girl. You raised such a fuss in triage that you brought everybody running. You saved Councilman Walker. He'd come in earlier, been stabilized, no one was even looking in on him. He threw an embolism, went into cardiac arrest. But you, child, had raised Cain and he got noticed. Then you decked one of our more arrogant interns. When you decide to fight back, it's no holds barred." She shook her head. "Don't feel bad. There isn't a one of us who hasn't wanted to deck Zucker."

She found it hard to believe. "I'm sorry. I don't remember."

The nurse grinned cheerfully. "Don't worry about it. Happens all the time."

Her jaw had become very sore and stiff. She looked at the breakfast tray and realized she'd be chewing on one side. Her mind felt as swollen as her eye, memories puffed up and inaccessible. She did not remember much except for the fear and the anger and the struggling. Her head ached. As much as she would have liked to lie there all day, the need to get out was like a thorn in her side. "How soon can I leave?"

"Not today, hon." The nurse paused, straightening her pillows. "You that anxious?"

No, but she felt cornered. And even if she were released, how could she leave her father behind? "I'd like to see my father—"

The nurse scarcely slowed as she bustled to the bed controls and raised her into position. "You need to take care of you, first." Instead of answering the question, she offered her opinion. "Somebody did a number on you. Too bad you didn't Bobbitt him," she offered. "I think I would have used a knife instead of a baseball bat."

Visions of her old bat flashed through her, its weathered gray wood with the grain standing out like ridges. Sharp stabs chased them from her mind. She put her hand to her brow.

"Am I . . . am I safe here?"

The nurse glanced at her so quickly her ponytail bounced. "If I have anything to do about it." Her elbow bumped a phone receiver tucked into its niche in the railing.

Sarah. She ought to warn Sarah about Jack. "Can I call someone?"

"Not your father, if that's what you had in mind. There's no hookup in his ICU. Anyone else, you'll have to wait until we get the lines open this afternoon. Too many patients, not enough lines."

Without hesitation the nurse swept the covers off the food platter. "Ever been in a hospital before?"

"Not as a patient."

"Well, today you get whatever we felt like ordering you. You'll be in for a couple more days, so you'll get menus this afternoon, order what you want. Doctor didn't want anything too chewy, so you've got scrambled eggs, oatmeal, toast, and juice." The nurse stepped back, making sure that McKenzie was up to feeding herself. She eyed her sharply.

McKenzie stared at the utensils, then picked up the fork. Her hand was swollen, tears across the knuckles and bruises dappled the back of her hand. It looked as if someone had stomped her with heavily rippled soles. Transfixed, she looked at herself, and saw, for a moment, the hiking boot coming down viciously on her hand. Darkness slanted the room in night and grays and she tried to hide among the shadows as she pulled herself along the hardwood floor. The boot descended with a smash and ground into bone, tendon, and nerves. The fork trembled in her hand.

"You going to eat, honey? Because you need to."

Startled, she looked up, found herself in the brightly-lit hospital room, the nurse eyeing her closely. She took a deep breath. "Yes. I . . . I was just thinking." She switched hands and flexed her fingers.

The nurse picked up the chart and flipped through it. "Sore? They x-rayed it last night. Nothing broken. You had some old breaks, though." Mac could feel the nurse observing her, but she did not let herself react. "Tell you what, after breakfast, I'll bring you another ice pack, put it on that hand." She grinned, her crow's feet breaking new ground, fracturing into her tanned face. "We get the pros in here after a game, sometimes, football players and hockey players. You look like you went up against one of them without the padding."

"I feel like it." McKenzie flexed her hand again, decided to eat with her left hand, and awkwardly dug at the scrambled eggs. Whatever warmth they'd had was rapidly fleeing, but they tasted good. She was hungry, she suddenly decided, and it made her feel human.

The nurse slid the chart back into its holder. "My name's Shannon, and I'll be in whenever you need someone. We operate on a total care system here, which means we don't use orderlies unless we have to. I bathe you, mop the floors, change the linens, whatever needs to be done. My shift is over at three, and then you'll probably have Connie." She hesitated. "Your doctor won't be making rounds for another hour or so. You'll have to save your questions for him."

Questions. She should have more questions. The enormity of the situation came tumbling down around her like an avalanche. Her breakfast stuck in her throat suddenly. She coughed and then managed to swallow, but the tears couldn't be dammed back. "Do you know if I can see my father?"

Surprise crossed the woman's face, then she stepped forward and laid a gentle hand across McKenzie's back. "Honey, you look like you've been thrown up against walls and half-scalped. All I know is what's on your chart here. The doctor will have to tell you more." She paused, as something clipped to her lapel chimed. She put a hand to the shoulder pager. "Gotta run. I'll be back to pick up the tray, and don't you try to go to the bathroom by yourself yet. Those legs of yours are bound to be wobbly." She bustled her white-uniformed self out the door and disappeared.

McKenzie managed a nod. She reached for a paper napkin and blew her nose lustily, then sat and looked at the breakfast tray. The oatmeal no longer steamed, it congealed.

She closed her eyes a moment. He'd tried to accost Jack to protect her, hadn't he? He had never been much of a father before. And had she been much of a daughter? What had she brought home to him? Pain throbbed through her skull with every word and thought until she didn't think she could bear it. Surely, if something serious had happened, they'd have come and told her.

McKenzie opened her eyes and rubbed at them. She needed to maintain an even keel. There was a little stainless steel pot of hot water for tea along with several packets of flavors. Constant Comment sounded bracing enough. Mac brewed up a cup, and dunked her cold toast in it to soften. She stirred the oatmeal, found some still hot bites on the bottom, and ate a little. Finally, she pushed the tray away. Pain raked across the back of her shoulders as she did.

Was there no place on her body that did not ache?

Mac stared at the closed door. There was an emptiness inside of her that food, hot or cold, could not fill. How safe was safe? Was there anyone she could depend on if she couldn't depend on herself?

She lowered the railing. The IV tubing caught and tugged a bit.

She freed it. Her feet, when they touched the floor, went from pins and needles to icicles in a flash. The cold sent shivers up her body.

Mac clamped her teeth together and slid out of the bed, holding onto the railing as if it were a lifeline. The, room swung around her in a blurred circle. She put her head down, to the backs of her hands. Sweat broke out on her forehead despite her chill. She took a deep breath to steady herself. The one hand felt hot and puffy, as though its skin were stretched close to breaking. There was pain, but it was an overall pain. *Funny. She hadn't thought about the different kinds of pain there might be. Throbbing, stabbing, fiery, constant. . . .*

McKenzie lifted her head and stood straight. "This is gonna hurt me worse than it's going to hurt you," she murmured, and took a sliding step forward.

Her ribs shouted in cramping complaint, but her legs held her. She pulled the IV pole away from the bedside, wheeling it as she took another step. The unwieldy unit, ironically, seemed ten times more stable than she did as she crossed the room. She pushed it ahead of her into the bathroom and then hung onto the doorway, counting breaths until her head stopped swimming and the roaring pain between her ears subsided.

Using the toilet without help was a major triumph. Afterward, Mac stared at her hands as she washed them, unable to look herself in the face. She did not want to see what damage Jack had done.

She made it back halfway across the room before she collapsed.

McKenzie felt the tape rip from her arm, but the IV stayed in, the tubing stretched to its utmost length. She lay there a moment, tile cool beneath her aching body. She stared at it. Then she closed her eyes, unable to bear the sight of it anymore, seeing it slick with blood, Cody's blood.

All right, Mac, get a grip! She swallowed tightly. Swam like a legless thing, one foot, two feet, closer to the bed. The IV rack reeled and wobbled along with her. Either she'd have to do it on her own, or lie there until the nurse came back with lunch. She wouldn't be helpless, couldn't be. Just another wiggle or two and she'd be able to catch hold of the bed railing.

Weak as a newborn, she pulled her head up and tried again. Her left hand answered with fiery jolts of pain, her skin so tight she thought it would burst. *Local Woman Explodes in Hospital, Film at*

Eleven, Mac thought. She took a deep, gulping breath and made one last heave. The curved lower bar of the railing conked into her head as she arrived.

McKenzie clawed her way back onto her feet and fell into bed, as wet from perspiration as if she'd just come from the shower. *One little hospital stay and I'm shot,* she thought wearily. As she tried to pull the IV rack back into position, she bumped a button on the control panel. The TV roared into life and she was a captive, spent audience.

She got a spattering of local news, laid her head back on the cool taut sheets of the bed, and tried to concentrate on something.

The local morning news team looked incredibly informal. Paper coffee cups from chain doughnut shops, bags of chips, and other scraps of breakfast adorned their consoles as they chatted together, introducing their clips of news. She blinked, drifting, closed her eyes, and listened.

"Yesterday's Board of Education meeting broke up early as members once again failed to gain a majority vote to release additional funds to rebuild quake-damaged schools. Student and faculty safety and educational facility replacement are two factors which remain at the center of the financial crisis."

At the talk of the quakes, she opened one eye. The TV screen showed an impeccably-dressed young man, coal-black hair a contrast to his light eyes, looking disdainfully at the camera lens. She decided automatically that she didn't like him, whoever he was. The shot panned to the local anchor. "Stephen Hotchkiss denied rumors that his was one of the dissenting votes, but noted that the three-hundred-million-dollar availability of funds was there only because of judicious handling in the past." The smug, overdressed man had to be Hotchkiss. He looked tight enough to squeak. "He pointed out that forty million had already been released since the quake last year, and that replacing those spent moneys would not be possible without levying new taxes."

As the voices droned on, McKenzie's eyes began to feel incredibly heavy. Even the banter between segments did nothing to rouse her. She thought of children—all the children—wondering who would help them, who would protect them, keep them safe in the schools, everywhere. The heaviness seemed to overflow into her ears, and the TV became muffled, then far away, and finally it was gone altogether.

*   *   *

Dr. Susan Craig stepped out of the shower, toweling herself briskly, her gaze already fixed on the small, nine-inch color monitor visible through the half-open bathroom door. Her world consisted of information, constantly altering, and her home was full of the medium which transmitted that information continuously, if not always accurately. Every room in the house contained a screen of some kind. Her house would be stark if not for the pervasive televisions. She lived alone; no memento of husband or boyfriends or family adorned the walls or mantles. Her furniture was functional and attractive, yet oddly sterile. Her life was not really here, the home suggested, and she would have been the first to agree with that.

Miller's call from the hospital to get testing authorization had awakened her early. She'd have test results from one new patient to review when she went in. The challenge of another day beckoned her.

The TV flickered its strobelike shadow over her face. The news today was not as good as the news had been yesterday. As she dried her legs, she showed her teeth at the TV screen as if considering biting it. Members of the Board of Education were shown leaving yesterday's meeting. Young Stephen Hotchkiss loomed large before the interviewer's mike. Pompous ass. She knew him well, through her biofeedback stress relieving seminars. *He wouldn't be under constant stress if he weren't so anal,* she thought, running a slim hand down her legs to assess whether she needed to shave before putting on nylons.

How could he treat children that way? Did he not know, did he not understand, that they were the future of the world? All the facilities, all the opportunities of education should blossom to them. That now was the time to put the ideas into their brains which would carry them through a triumphant lifetime—

Thinking she'd like to take Hotchkiss' head in her hands and swivel it around a couple of times like a possession scene from *The Exorcist,* she moved to her bedroom and began to dress. This new monitor, gleaming from the mahogany depths of the built-in cabinet reflected other, more worldly scenes at her from CNN. *Even you,* she frowned at the set, *aren't as informed as you could be.* As she withdrew a stocking from her lingerie drawer and held it in the air to ascertain if its delicate beige color matched that of the other stocking she'd already put on, Bernard Shaw announced the collapse of Los Angeles Councilman Ibrahim Walker, his medical condition thought to be the result of an attack during a break-in.

Susan dropped her hand to her knee. Near death, but not dead. The old coot deserved to be dead. She'd prayed for it on more than one occasion. He'd blocked every funding bill or grant she'd presented for her projects. Shortsighted, stubborn old coot. Someone ought to drop-kick him into the twenty-first century, if he lived. Ibie Walker was said to be recovering at Mount Mercy. A thin smile etched its way into Susan Craig's early morning frown.

She ought to pay him a little visit.

Deftly, she pulled her stocking on, clipped it to the garter belt she'd bought from Victoria's Secret just last weekend, and stood. She flung open her walk-in closet, examining the vast array of clothing awaiting her. *Yes, now that Ibie was held captive by IVs and catheters and monitor leads and shunts, tied down like Gulliver in Lilliput, yes, now might he a good time to talk some sense into the old relic.*

She had to try. Her projects were too important to let go, to lie fallow in the labs, for lack of funding or understanding. Hadn't she proved her worth? It wasn't the money she needed for herself. Hadn't she given unstintingly at the shelters, the halfway houses, the hospital, helping whomever she touched? She paid for the van, for the equipment herself, but she needed more, and technicians for interpretation—she needed to be able to teach her methods, pass them on, research and write to justify them . . . she couldn't do it all alone. Couldn't they see the potential in her work?

She plucked out a pair of linen trousers and a silk blouse, dressing quickly and efficiently, fingers flying at the silk-covered buttons on the blouse, her thoughts a million miles away.

She stopped at the bathroom a last time before leaving the house. She checked the pregnancy kit, her unlined face knotting over the negative results. Susan looked up, caught herself frowning in the mirror. She put her chin up, and stroked her too flat stomach. Why could she not achieve what other women, lesser women, did at the drop of a pair of pants? Why could she not have a tiny bundle to croon to, to diaper, to teach and mold, to watch as it took its first of many steps, to fall, to get up and try again?

Why not her?

She threw the test kit into the wastebasket. It was not her. She'd availed herself of the medical facilities open to her. She knew it could not be her. Nor did she think it could be the man she'd chosen, this time, to be the father.

Susan looked at her hair, and sleeked it into place. She was still young. She still had prospects, potential. She had other things to achieve as well.

She tightened her belt a notch and, with a last, lingering look at herself in the mirror, left for the hospital.

Chapter 9

McKenzie supposed she ought to have been grateful for the sponge bath and clean gown, but the friendliness Shannon had exuded in the early morning seemed to have been swapped for efficiency. Without talking directly to her, the nurse communicated her displeasure at having discovered that Mac had been out of bed.

"Like one of my kids," Shannon muttered. "So who do you think came in and peed in the toilet without flushing while you say you were in bed—'the invisible man'? When we say we want bed rest, that's what we mean. You were under mild sedation, young lady. You could have fallen and hurt yourself severely. Do you want yourself tied down again?" Without waiting for an answer, the nurse replied, "No, I didn't think so. Now I want you clean and tidy and in one place until after the doctor sees you."

Arm up, arm down, leg over, roll on side, there you go. New sheets being put on without McKenzie even being taken out of the way. Sheet and thin yellow blanket folded neatly into position, corners squared.

Shannon stepped back, her eyes harsh in her face, and dried her hands as McKenzie took the clean gown and tried to shrug into it. She helped only when the IV line became entangled in the sleeve. The nurse drew the plastic bag through and repositioned it above the gown, saying, "You should be off this later today. Ready for visitors? You have someone waiting to see you."

McKenzie clawed at her hair, ends sopping from the hasty bath.

Shannon pulled a drawer open in the tray stand. "There's a comb in here." She drew out the courtesy pack and left it on the table.

McKenzie found the cheap plastic comb and was still dragging it through when the nurse paused in the doorway, saying, "She can see you now, officer."

She paused in mid-stroke, her arm in the air, bruises dappling the underflesh, as the policeman entered. His square, compact form amply filled out his uniform blues, even their laundry-creased corners, his dark hair swept back from his forehead, revealing a face to match his body type, squared and looking as though he had nothing to be happy about. The expression on his face made her abruptly drop the comb and brace herself.

"I'm Officer Moreno," he said, as he hooked a foot about a chair leg and pulled it forward so he could sit, drawing his notebook from his shirt pocket as he did. "I'm hoping you'll want to talk to me about the domestic dispute you were involved in last night."

His voice was rich and slightly flavored, and she realized that was one of the things she had missed terribly, the diversity of the Los Angeles Basin. Beyond the sound of his words, however, was a sense of disapproval. What had the hospital told him about her?

Gathering herself, McKenzie asked, "You didn't talk to me last night? Didn't someone?"

"Not at the time."

The hope of having found some sanctuary fled. "Oh, God. I thought I told you, told someone. You should have been looking for him." She wasn't safe from Jack, had never been safe from him.

"Who?"

"My husband." The word was difficult to say. She found there was already an insurmountable chasm between them. Their marital status was already in the past.

Moreno frowned. His eyebrows, like his hair, was iron-colored, thick and luxurious, not gray but not raven black as it must have been once. "Let's get our business done here," he responded. "I need to take your statement."

Puzzled and worried, McKenzie sat back. Too much interest in her. "All right."

Moreno looked at his notebook. "Neighbors called in a domestic at about two a.m. last night, but they told us they had heard loud quarreling earlier, about ten-thirty. Would that be accurate?"

She wondered what Mrs. Ethelridge had told him.

"Miss Smith?"

"Ah." She swallowed tightly. "That would be about right."

"Your residence is 1026 East Anita?"

"My, my father's residence. Yes."

"And we're told your relationship with Walton Smith is that of father, daughter. He's your father?"

She thought she'd said that. "Yes." She wet lips gone dry. "I know you have a report to write, but no one will tell me—how is he?"

Moreno had black coffee eyes and something unreadable flickered through them as he looked up from his notebook. He scratched a thick eyebrow. "Let's stick to this first."

"But—"

"Neighbors also tell me you've been gone from the residence nearly ten years, that you came home—unexpectedly—yesterday, late afternoon."

McKenzie gave in. "Yes."

"Your mother died several years ago. Why didn't you return then?"

"I didn't feel like it."

His big square face twitched a little around the angle of his jaw and ears. "She was dying of cancer, and you didn't feel like it?"

It wouldn't sound right, and there was no way she could make it sound right, but she tried. "We'd talked over the phone. She knew how I felt, that I wouldn't be welcome, that being there was something I didn't think I could do. And she didn't want me to come to the hospital. We'd already said good-bye."

"Why didn't you think you could be there?"

"My father drinks. Drank." McKenzie looked away.

"Would it be accurate to say that you and your father have a combative relationship?"

"I don't see—" McKenzie stopped. "We had a very loud argument last night after dinner, and I'm sure Mrs. Ethelridge heard a lot of it, but I don't see what that has to do with anything."

"You argued."

"Yes."

Moreno moved in his chair as if trying to become a bit more comfortable. His hands flexed around his notebook. "Words or anything more physical?"

"Yelling. We always yell at each other." Her brow throbbed again.

"Do you remember shouting. 'Leave me alone'?"

"Yes." Her head ached and her vision blurred slightly, overlapping one intent Moreno next to another. She blinked rapidly several times. "What does this have to do with Jack?"

"Why don't you tell me? Who's Jack?"

"Jack Trebolt, my ex, my husband."

Moreno paused, before answering carefully. "We have no information on that. Are you saying he's involved?"

"I'm saying he's the one who did all this. Didn't anyone listen to me? You should be looking for him!"

Moreno sighed. "Miss Smith, I'm proceeding on the information we were able to gather earlier. I'm investigating an assault and battery, but from the marks on you, it could be you acted in self-defense."

The blurring of her vision cleared, but now his words seemed to make no sense. "I don't understand."

"The neighbors aren't sure who started the fight, and I haven't been able to get a statement from your father, so I don't know who picked up the bat and hit who first."

"Jack started it." McKenzie clenched her jaw against the flood of emotion rising in her.

"Miss, at this time, we have no report of a third party on the scene. As near as we can tell, this was strictly between you and your father." Moreno sat rigidly, frowning at her.

McKenzie responded in stunned silence. Then, she forced each word out carefully. "You think I—you think Dad and I—you think I hit my father? You think we did this to each other?"

"That appears to be the case. It happens. It sounds to me like one of you just snapped."

The words plunged into her chest like a knife. She had lost it. The furies had woken up. She had crossed over the edge.

She shook her head in denial. "You've got no clue." It had to be Jack. She had to cling to that. Jack had been real, the bloody visions could not be. Jack could be anywhere. McKenzie pointed at Moreno. "You've got to find him!"

"This man you say is your husband."

"Yes." McKenzie peered around the hospital room. "My purse—if I had my purse, I could prove it to you. My driver's license in my wallet—"

"The forged ID we found under the name of Fordham? The same name your vehicle is registered to?"

She found it hard to take a breath. "I had to do that—Jack wouldn't let me have a car of my own. I had to hide it."

"You forged documents in Washington."

"Yes, but you don't understand."

Moreno lowered his notebook to his knee. "Why don't you try explaining it to me, Miss Smith? Your neighbors don't seem to remember you getting married, but they do remember the argument you had with your parents on the day you left. So why don't you talk to me? I'd like to straighten this out."

"My father—"

"Your father is in no condition to give us a statement right now. Even if he recovers, he may have no memory of the events. All I have to go on right now is you, Miss Smith."

And she looked into those coffee-dark eyes and knew he wasn't too happy with what he was hearing from her. They didn't believe her. They didn't want to believe her. This man sat there, looking at her right now, and what he wanted to believe was that they had gone for each other's throats, she and her father, and tried to kill one another. What kind of a world was this where this was the kind of truth they wanted to see? How could she ever hope to change his mind?

"You can call Sarah Whiteside. She's a friend, the only one who knew that Jack—that I left. You can ask him, too, if he'll tell you. I know he's not there. Jack drives a truck. I left because I knew he'd be gone five, seven days." But she gave them her home phone number as well as Sarah's, and added, "I want to see my father, anyway."

"I'm afraid that's not possible." Moreno flipped over his notebook, closing it. "He's under protective custody at the moment. Until we can make a decision as to who assaulted whom, I can't let you see him. He's a very sick man."

"He's my father!"

"I know." Moreno stood. "I'll leave my card at the nurses' station. If you decide later you have anything to add, please call."

"You've got to find Jack. He'll come back, he'll finish what he started."

"Miss Smith," and Office Moreno's voice sounded genuinely regretful. His eyes sagged at the corners. "If you can prove there was a third party involved, I'll be glad to widen the investigation. Right now, we don't have a lot to go on, except for your fingerprints on the bat."

"What's the bat got to do with it?"

He paused in the doorway, filling it, a solid figure in policeman blues. "That's the main weapon which was used on your father, miss. Someone tried to beat the pulp out of him while he lay helpless after suffering a stroke."

Chapter 10

Carter slept until early morning and woke surprisingly easily. The haunt of his messages had not disturbed his rest. Yes, Nelson had called—from the plane, not the hotel. Like a voice rising from the dead, he'd made arrangements for a lunch he'd never make.

"Hey, Windy. Got a life yet? If not, after dinner, there's a little something I want to leave for you. Nothing really, just a tidbit. Something on Bauer I filed away and forgot about. When Bauer killed his psychiatrist and escaped, he left behind a grad student, a young woman who worked in the practice and labs for the good doctor. Not like Bauer to leave easy prey behind, was it? Anyway, I think I've tracked her down to L.A., thought you might be interested. I'll bring the file with me."

The voice was as chilling as watching a videotape of someone he knew was dead. There was a certain disorientation between life and the appearance of life. And if John Nelson had died any other way than he had, Carter might think Bauer was still around, acting in his own interests. But though Bauer had been many things as a killer, a neat and painless assassin he was not.

Still, lying there trying to decide whether or not he wanted to get out of bed, he wondered what might happen to the file Nelson had brought with him. Seeing as it was probably part of a Bureau investigation, and that the Feds were now working on Nelson's death, Carter held little hope he'd ever see it.

Carter ran the back of his hand over his chin as he swung out of bed. The sandpaper sound reminded him that he'd forgotten to buy razors. He'd have to fish the old one out of the trash and scrape it along one more time. As he crossed the bedroom/living room of the apartment, he paused at his computer. He flipped it on, and brought the modem online to the office.

He only had a follow-up assignment posted. The boy's heart had gone to Loma Linda, and was being used immediately. They wanted him to wring out a few more hankies.

Heart transplants being as complicated as they were, Carter knew he had more than enough time for the follow-up. Loma Linda surgeons wouldn't even be available for conference until after one. There was also a small compliment from the editor's desk about the work he'd done on the boy's death and the various donations. Heart, kidneys, liver, corneas, even skin to the USC pediatric burn ward. Only the heart had granted a follow-up request, the rest of the recipients had anonymity.

Carter allowed himself a little shrug of happiness. It wouldn't win a Pulitzer, but it had been a credible job. He tapped a quick acknowledgment and sent it, no need to hold it back until later in the day.

His hours were his. He debated about John Nelson, but decided he would learn more if the Feds came to him. He shut the computer down. The follow-up shouldn't be too hard to get out of the way.

And it gave him an excuse to go back to Mount Mercy, to see the young woman again.

He didn't know why he wanted to go back and see her, but he did. And if he did, he told himself, he didn't need an excuse. He could do that without a long line of bullshit rationalization.

Had it been that she'd been pretty in an unusual way, not the California Barbie Doll girl the state had been turning out for decades, but pretty in an unrealized way? Though, with the bumps and bruises she'd collected from her assailant, she could hardly be called pretty now.

Or had it been because after he'd left her room, he'd run into the resident in the corridor, ice pack to his cheekbone, and the young doctor had cheerfully told him his story of the victim who'd still been fighting in triage.

He didn't think it was only because there was a story in her. The police had the case listed as a domestic, but there was the matter of the hair, of the souvenir scalping. She'd told him her estranged husband had done it. There was no Mr. Blue, no Bauer here. Just the same old, senseless battering that people do to one another. She was no different than any other case he'd pick up and do a story about this week.

He stared at his computer terminal, thought of something he ought to do, and pulled up the address file. His hard disk rattled a little as if rusty and then displayed the file. He couldn't access the number he wanted, though, so Carter shut down the whole machine. He'd been dragged kicking and screaming into the computer age. He didn't trust hard drives anymore than he would a three-time paroled felon. With a tug, he pulled a stuffed drawer open, sorted through floppies, found a real address book and thumbed through it until he got what he wanted.

The phone rang dully and when it was answered, there was a background of children, laughing and screaming.

"Joyce Tompkins, please."

A pause, then, "This is she."

"Joyce, this is Carter Wyndall." He pictured her as he'd last seen her several months ago, one of his background resources on a story. A woman of color, she was as striking as she was forthright. She'd made women's rights her career and her passion. They'd gone out once after the story was done, but she'd laughingly called it a "mercy date" and said that she didn't need it. Told him to call when he was truly interested. Joyce attracted him immensely, but he'd not been interested in a relationship in years. No time.

The background noise was shushed before the woman's wary tones warmed up. "Why, Carter. I didn't think you would call."

Something a little like guilt, or maybe it was hunger pains, moved in his stomach. "Well, actually, this is business."

"Oh. I see." The warmth chilled a little.

"Are you still an advocate?"

"You bet I am. You got someone in trouble?"

"I think so." He picked up his watch and checked it. "Are you free this morning? Can I pick you up in forty-five minutes or so?"

"That depends, Carter. This person in trouble, is this business for you or personal?"

He thought before answering. "Actually, it's personal."

"All right, then. I'll be ready. Be sure to knock loudly, the doorbell's out and the kids . . . well, they're noisy." Joyce hung up without saying good-bye.

He sat for another moment at his computer desk. It shouldn't be personal to him.

But the girl was. He couldn't explain it. As much as Joyce had attracted him, she hadn't moved him to action. This girl had.

And he wondered how he would have explained the girl to Nelson, too. *Got a life yet?*

Maybe it was because he couldn't explain it that he wanted to go back, to talk to her, to see what color her eyes were.

Maybe, Carter thought to himself, it was just a healthy, hormonal response.

He wasn't sure.

He hadn't had one for a long time.

He sighed and slogged his way across the apartment toward the shower.

It took the young woman a few moments to become aware of him standing at the edge of the room. "I remember you from last night. The one with the kind eyes." Irony chipped her words. "But you're not a cop?"

"Ah, no, I'm not." He'd promised her security, but there'd been none on the floor, and he'd come into her room easily. He felt a little guilty. She looked worse than she had last night, but that was the way of bruises and healing. One eye was discolored all around, the cheekbone brilliantly purple, swelling into her lids, what he could see of the eye itself was bloodshot around its green-gray iris. But it was not injured, or it would be covered, bandaged, hiding from him.

But it was his eyes she'd commented on. So he moved through the faded yellow curtains toward the bed and tried what he hoped was a reassuring smile. "I can't take credit for the eyes," he answered. "Genetic nearsightedness."

He thought he saw her relax a little, shoulders dropping back. The whiteness of the sheets surrounding her emphasized her paleness and bruising. She put a hand to the lopsided ice pack to remove it.

He answered, "I was here when you came in last night. Carter Wyndall. I thought perhaps you could use a friend. You look like you've had a rough time." He stumbled over his name, so connected with his usual introduction as a reporter that it didn't come out right when he abbreviated it. But something in her eyes warned him away from telling her what he did for a living.

"Oh." She twitched her jaw lightly as if there might be more words coming out, but none did. He took her to be no older than mid-twenties, possibly not even that old, but it would be hard to tell for sure until the bruises faded. "That's all I need." She looked at him, wariness renewed.

"No, actually, what you need is an apology. I, ah, intruded on your privacy last night. This morning, actually, early, and I don't quite feel right."

"You're apologizing to me?"

He nodded. He felt as though he'd encountered an iceberg, and he had better be careful of what he couldn't see in the depths. He cleared his throat. "I was here last night because of a little boy who got shot, caught between gangs, in the line of fire. The family was trying to decide how to deal with it, if they should turn off the machines, donate the organs."

She looked away, toward the window, which had the shades drawn so that she could not see the view from the fifth floor, but she had not turned away so quickly that he couldn't see the renewed pain in her face. "Must have been some night."

"It seems to have been." His hands felt chill. She turned back to watch him levelly, a spark deep in her eyes. She didn't encourage him, but neither did she turn him away, and it unnerved him a little. He made his living from news, from the events of the day, be they up-lifting or disastrous, and his skin had thickened over the years. She was like a paper cut into that hide, trivial, yet significantly irritating.

She put her right hand in back of her ear, where the raw scalp had been slathered with what might be Mercurochrome or beta-dine. The rest of her hair was long and soft enough to cover the spot and she tried to tweak it into place before dropping her hand back to her covers.

A scuffle of impatience sounded in the hallway. He cleared his throat. "You told me your husband did that."

"Did I? And do you believe me?"

"Yes."

She let out a tremulous sigh, and he realized that he had had no idea just how tense she'd been. The girl plucked at a sheet hem. "The police don't. They seem to think that my father and I—that we just sort of snapped and tried to kill each other. They won't tell me how he is, and they won't let me see him." Her voice stumbled to a halt, and she closed her swollen lips tightly.

She'd given him the opening. "In that case," Carter said smoothly, "I won't have to apologize for this. I, um, brought along someone you should talk to." He stood back.

Joyce came in, dressed in tribal prints colored brightly in ivory, russet, and black. The geometries moved with her lush, firm body, doing a war dance. Her eyes were gleaming. She pulled up a chair and sat down in one movement, saying, "Girl, those police are going to be sorry they didn't call me."

She looked from Joyce to Carter. "Who?"

"I'm Joyce Tompkins. I'm an advocate for battered women, and I'm here for you." Joyce eyed Carter. "Why don't you leave us alone so we can talk?"

Carter hesitated. "Is that all right?"

Mac blinked. "No. I mean, that is, I don't know—"

Joyce looked pointedly around the hospital room, at her bed and the empty one next to the window. "I don't see anyone else here for you. Your mother?"

"Dead. My cousins live here, but it's been ten years. . . ." her voice trailed off. "I don't know."

"Of course you don't. I'll talk, you listen, then you talk and I'll listen. Whatever you need."

The girl sucked in a breath. "Whatever I need," she repeated. Her voice was shaky. "I need to know what's happening."

Carter said, "I'll be back in a little while to check on things." He backed out and before he'd crossed the door and gripped the handle to close it behind him, Joyce was leaning over the hospital bed, talking softly but firmly.

He took his time finishing up the heart donor story, got a cup of coffee, and sauntered back up to the fifth floor. Joyce, file folder in hand, was just coming out of the hospital room. She took the coffee from him and drank it in two gulps.

"You needed that," he observed flatly.

Her mouth twitched. She hugged her note-filled folder to her chest. "You're interested in this one."

He paused. Then, "Yes."

"Why?"

"I don't know."

"Well, she's lucky."

"Lucky?"

Joyce nodded. "She's a little repressed, hurt, battered, but I didn't see the syndrome I usually have to handle. She comes from an alcoholic family, but she didn't decide to be a victim. Her husband sounds fairly domineering, but this is the first, second time he's gotten physical with her. She got out immediately. She's disoriented, bewildered, she hasn't discovered her own strengths yet—but she's done a lot right so far. She decided she wouldn't take it. From her father or her husband."

"The father beat her, too?"

"No. From what she told me, he yelled a lot, broke a few things, punched in cabinet doors. The x-rays show some old breaks, but she told me that she was quite an athlete when she was younger. Broke one arm riding a dirt bike, and the other playing hardball. He didn't touch her, she says. She left because she simply couldn't take the drinking anymore. She had a scholarship, went away to school, and," Joyce smiled thinly, "like so many of us do, she fell in love and got married."

"To the wrong man."

"For her. Maybe for anyone. Anyway, she worked hard to make it a success, but she bailed out when he attacked her."

Carter said dryly, "She can't be that lucky."

"Maybe not. But some support work, self-esteem building, and a little independence will go a long way with her. I don't have to spend years convincing Mac this wasn't something she deserved."

He shuddered in spite of himself.

Joyce added softly, "It's a good thing you brought me here."

He looked at her.

She nodded, emphasizing her words. "Right now, her life is upside down. The concussion is giving her headaches, making her see things—I can help her see clearly, think clearly. She needs that support."

"All right."

"I'll be back to see her tomorrow. I took Officer Moreno's phone and case number from her, I'll talk to him later today. You don't have to drive me home. I'll catch the bus. I need to pick up my car to do rounds anyway. But, Carter—"

He had his hand on the door grip, ready to pull it open.

"She doesn't need involvement right now. She can't handle it."

"I guessed as much."

"Then what are you doing here?"

"I don't know."

Joyce smiled broadly. "Oh, Carter. There's a heart beating under that newsprint hide, after all."

"Don't tell anybody."

"I won't. Just don't scare her away by letting her know it, too. Give it a few months. Once we get her chin up, she'll start looking around for herself."

"Promise?"

She chucked him on the shoulder. "I'll do my damnedest. See you later." She brushed past him with a determined click of her heels.

Chapter 11

Carter entered the hospital room hesitantly. She looked up from a handful of tissues as he did. Emotion blotched her face. It did not detract from what he was beginning to think of as the endearing quality of her face. He wanted to smooth her hair back and kiss her brow. He couldn't think of a way to do it without feeling awkward, so he just stood there.

"Came to say good-bye." He added, "How did you like Joyce?"

"Now I know what they mean when they call someone a breath of fresh air."

"More like a hurricane warning, but I'd trust her with anything."

She pointed at the chair. "You can sit?"

"For a minute." A mid-morning snack had been brought in while he was gone. Four cartons of juice remained among empty muffin wrappers.

She picked out a carton of apple juice and passed it to him, saying, "I can't possibly drink all this." The IV had been removed from her arm.

"I think they want you to hydrate."

She sipped woefully at her pineapple juice. "One major fruit group at a time."

He laughed in spite of himself. That seemed to please her. She said, "Apology accepted. And thank you. You're the only thing that seems real in this whole nightmare."

Carter decided against interrupting, and settled into what he could do best, which was to listen.

The young woman looked across the room, at a smog- and dirt-obscured window. "He didn't like me having my hair cut, so he decided to do the job himself. With a knife." She winced with the memory, as he watched her talk. "So I left. He followed me all the way from the land of rain, manic-depressives, and wife-beaters to the city of smog, quakes, gangs, and serial killers. And last night, he came after me again."

Carter felt himself smile wryly, pierced by both disappointment and relief that she had not been a target for Mr. Blue. "Like you said, it was some night."

"My head feels like they all happened at once." She moved her jaw again tentatively. "So you know what no one else knows or believes. Or even asked," she added bitterly.

"Sounds like you have a beef against L.A.'s finest."

"They think my father did this to me and I—I retaliated." Her voice broke. She did not continue.

"They're not looking for your estranged husband?"

She jerked her head in a negative.

"What's the problem?"

"They say there's no proof of a third party." She squeezed her eyes shut.

"And you're afraid your spouse will come back."

She hesitated long enough that he intuited that she was not afraid of many things, that this was one of them, but there was something else she wasn't telling him. Then she said, "Wouldn't you be? How many stories like that do you read in the paper or see on TV?"

"Enough. It's not a welcome privilege." His gaze wandered across the room, over her chart hanging from the foot of the bed. He ought to go, but he did not want to. He saw the notation penciled in the corner of her paperwork about her father's condition and location. "A talk with Joyce ought to clear up our boys in blue. Or when they depo your father."

"He can't be interviewed, or so they told me." She slumped back on her pillows. The eyes closed in weariness or defeat.

"Let me help."

"Why?"

"Because I don't want to have to read another statistic. If I can keep him from coming after you, if I can make the police believe in

your husband, if I can keep you from stepping into the line of fire,
so much the better."

"All I want to do is see my dad. Can you do that?"

"I can try."

"What do you mean?"

"First, we need transportation." He stepped out of the room and
went to the floor's nursing station. The women were brisk and busy.
He took a wheelchair from under their watch and brought it back to
the room. No one said a word to him.

She was shrugging into another gown, wearing it like a robe. The
soft, worn pale-blue-flowered pattern did nothing to enhance her
looks. He caught a glimpse of one bare hip before she was able to
pull the gowns about her and settle on the edge of the bed, waiting.
That brief look of young and supple flesh was marred by a slashing
bruise across its contour. Carter had been weighing tragedies in his
mind, but the sight of the wound made him realize what the living
suffered. She'd lost a husband, a marriage, and might yet lose her
father—and the police thought there were no victims here.

Carter pushed the wheelchair forward. "Watch your step."

She swayed a little as she essayed the journey from bedside to the
chair, just three halting steps, but he could see from the lack of color
in her face the effort it cost her.

"All right?"

She settled in the seat and caught her breath. "Yes." She looked up.
Her gaze searched his face, and seemed suddenly reassured. Her mouth
twisted. "I keep wanting to get the number of the truck that hit me."

He laughed without thinking, but that pleased her, and a little
pink came back into her cheeks. "That's truer than you know," she
added. "Jack drives trucks."

He bent down to put the footrests into place. "It takes all kinds,"
he commented.

She looked at him reflectively. "Must be awful," she said, "to live
with someone and have absolutely no idea what's going on inside his
head."

"In most cases that's probably a blessing." He was glad she couldn't
read his mind, with the image of her bare flesh still fresh. He pivoted the chair around. "You up to the elevator? ICU's a couple of
floors up."

She nodded, winced, and said, "Yes."

As he wheeled her down the corridor to the elevator bank, he added, "I got your name from your charts. McKenzie Smith. Do they call you McKenzie? Or is that a hyphenated?"

"Hyphenated?"

"Two last names."

"Oh. No, it's McKenzie."

"Family name?"

"It would have to be, wouldn't it?" She made a gusty sound. "I used to have to fight about it when I was a kid. But I got proud of it. At least it kept people from calling me Smitty. Didn't want to change it, not even when Jack and I . . . when we got married. What about you?"

"Wyndall's a southern name." He drawled it slightly so she could get the effect. "Most people call me Windy."

"But you prefer Carter."

"Yeah, I do. I've always liked the sound of it."

The elevator door opened. There was another wheelchair in residence, the woman flushed with life, her stomach fairly palpitating with the kicking child inside her, her hair already sweat-streaked back from her face, and there was no doubt where she, the admittance nurse handling the wheelchair, or the nervous man pacing behind them were going. The pacing husband was counting, the woman's mouth pursed as she "Hee, hee, hoo'd" in time. They fairly charged out of the elevator on the next floor. McKenzie waited until the doors were closed, then said softly, "That was cute."

"Cute? I thought the guy was going to have a coronary. I think giving birth must be easier on the woman."

She tilted her head back to eye him. "Oh, you do, do you?"

"Be nice or I won't tell you what floor ICU is on."

"You don't have to," and she pointed at the board. "It's marked."

He could tell that the bantering had relaxed her a bit, reading her with an ease that came from years of reading interviewees. He wiggled the chair a little, saying, "Don't upset the driver."

She laughed. It pleased him immensely to hear her, though the laugh was raspy and dry. What would she be like to listen to a month from now, when she'd healed and life looked immensely better?

He was relieved when the doors opened again, checking his train of thought.

He said, as he began to push her out, "Don't let it scare you."

She put a hand on the wheelchair arm, gripping it with a hand that was bruised with treadmarks, puffy and discolored, and held on tight until the misshapened knuckles paled.

No inattentive nurses here. A finely-featured East Indian woman looked up, saying, "May I help you?"

"Walton Smith." Her voice was scarcely higher than a whisper. "He came in last night."

"Ah." She turned aside to look at something on her desk, then looked up, with eyes that were, startlingly, green-hazel, with coffee flecks deep in them. "No visitors yet, but you can stand outside the room and watch for a moment. He's in critical, but stable, condition. Cubicle C."

His passenger almost stood up out of the chair. He put his hand on her shoulder, and she relaxed again. He took his hand away to push her to the viewing window, then, casually, dropped it back in place again, lightly, comfortingly. From the stillness of her body, he had no idea at all what she must have been thinking as she looked upon the sheet-shrouded form of her father.

McKenzie looked through the window, and could hardly see her father for the reflection of herself in the glass, and for the bank of equipment that surrounded him, less sophisticated than she imagined, almost menacing. She rubbed her eyes, trying to keep her vision sharp, failing slightly. He could have been dead, for she could see no rise and fall of his chest as he breathed, but she could see the blips and lines across the monitor registering his life force. She had no idea if there were really protective custody, or if they had just slipped through somehow, but she was fiercely grateful for this moment.

For once not the main obstacle in her life, he'd tried to stand between her and disaster. *Don't touch my little girl!* He hadn't done well, but he'd tried. And she'd failed as well, for if she could have dealt with Jack, her father wouldn't be lying there half-dead.

She brought a hand up to her mouth, felt her lip swollen and split, and trembling. She would not cry. Not now, not yet. Stable condition. Critical but stable. What did that mean, exactly? Poised on the brink, but not likely to fall one way or the other, not wobbling, just . . .

balanced? She found herself holding her breath, in case she might be the factor which toppled him over that brink.

She had a weird sense of déjà vu, a memory of her younger self lying quietly on a hospital gurney, head throbbing, to wake and see her father standing and watching her, tears in his eyes. She'd been hit by a pitched ball. She'd seen double for three days, McKenzie suddenly remembered. Her father had been terrified she'd never play ball again. She'd used his wooden bat until she made the high school team, and graduated to aluminum.

There had been good times. McKenzie gripped the windowsill. *There had.*

She'd forgotten all about Carter until he asked softly, "Are you all right?"

It was then she realized he had in his hand on her shoulder, a softly bracing touch. When had he put it there, and why didn't it hurt? When every square inch of her felt as though it had been pounded on, why didn't it hurt where he touched her?

McKenzie swallowed. "I'm okay," she answered. "It's just—"

"Difficult. I know."

He must know better than she did. McKenzie stirred. He lifted his hand away. A nurse passed behind them, on softly creaking shoes, offering, "We'll know more tomorrow."

McKenzie found herself nodding. Carter backed her away, driving her back toward the elevators. She became aware that there were tubed and wired occupants lying quietly in most of the other cubicles. The nurse was busy readying the F cubicle. She had the doors thrown open, banks of monitors being hooked up, when the double elevator doors opened.

A cart came out, two nurses, a man and woman, in attendance. There was no doubt about a police escort here. Two men, faces drawn, one black, one Asian, brought up the rear. McKenzie found herself drawing back in the chair lest they see her.

Carter stopped to move the wheelchair to the corridor's side. She stared in fascination as this new group passed, caught in a drama of their own, unaware of McKenzie and Carter, the elderly black man on the bed with a gray pallor under his dark skin, his eyes shut, his face in many folds, his grizzled hair matted by the tubing and elastic of the oxygen mask.

"That's Ibie," Carter murmured. "Councilman Ibrahim Walker." He did not push her forward until the cubicle doors had swallowed up the emergency team, and they had begun transferring the man to the bed, wiring and cabling him into the new equipment. "Looks like he's been here overnight and nobody informed us."

"How do you know?"

Carter was watching the scene avidly. "I know," he said absently. "It's my job."

Walker lifted an arm wearily and tried to assist in the maneuvers. She watched as they tucked him in and smoothed the cool white sheets around his rich, coffee-colored torso. He mumbled, nearly incoherent, his voice slurred and masked by oxygen feeders. "Animal. Alien. What was that?"

The fear in his voice ran a shiver down McKenzie's spine. The whites of his eyes showed.

The nurse closest to him shushed him gently and put his arm in place.

"McKenzie," Carter said shortly. "I need to take you back, and then find out what's happened."

"Why?"

"I have to." He was looking around, attention riveted on Cubicle F as banks of machines came online. "McKenzie, I'm a reporter."

Her throat tightened. No wonder he'd been interested in her. A paycheck for her grief. Her knuckles went white as she dropped her hands down to the wheels of the chair. She spun them, wrenching the chair from his grip.

"McKenzie—"

"I can take care of myself!"

He stood, feet spread, hands out, torn. But he kept looking away from her, back to the action.

His kindness, even bringing Joyce, had been a sham. She kicked a foot to the floor, pushing the chair away.

"No. I got you this far. It's just that—"

"It's your job," she finished for him. "Let me know how it all comes out. Film at eleven, right?"

"No—the evening edition."

She could hear in his voice the pride that there was a difference, to him. Not to her. "I thought you were a counselor. You talked about the heart donor—I thought you cared. I never thought you were here because it was your *job*." She leaned forward painfully to propel herself toward the bank of elevators. Without a word she rolled through the first door that opened.

"McKenzie!"

The door shut in his face.

She caught her thumb under the rim as she tried to settle the vehicle. It grabbed skin. She snatched her hand away and sat, sucking the injury, verging on tears again. The elevator sank all the way to the basement before she realized she hadn't punched in her floor number. She looked out on colored lines directing her to the morgue and to the surgery theaters. Dumbly, she pounded her hand on the panel to get out of there. Her head began to throb again as the lift dropped, then began to climb.

She studied the floor, praying no one would walk in and see her alone. Toward the corner, a brilliant bubble of red glistened wetly. It caught her attention. She stared, transfixed. *Blood.* She swung about, but this crimson, shivering drop did not follow, did not drown her. Real, then. Vital and, in this day and age, dangerous. Whose? What patient?

The doors slid open on the fifth floor. McKenzie rolled herself out with an effort. No one stood at the nurses' station. There was some luck in that. She didn't feel like facing questions about where she had been, and why. She felt empty, drained. Her rib cage ached as she bent slightly to roll the wheelchair down the corridor. She had only been gone, what, fifteen minutes, but her legs felt like lead. At the corner of the nurses' station, she got out of the chair. Mac tottered, then determinedly caught herself on the edge of the counter.

Behind her, the elevators opened and closed. She pivoted, but saw no one who could have come out. For a moment, she thought Carter might have followed her. Hope and disgust that he might have warred inside her.

Mac pushed away from the counter. One step at a time, she delicately trod the distance to her room. Behind her, from the far side of the nurses' station, on the other side of the U that comprised the floor, she could hear the laundry cart, and women chatting casually. No one would even know she'd been gone.

She leaned her weight wearily on the hospital door, swinging it open.

Streaks of crimson pierced her vision. She blinked, not under-standing. Was it real, or imagined? It was as if she stood on a thresh-old; one step one way or the other could prove disastrous. She put out her hand. She touched the wetness. The curtains that separated the beds had been drawn. In her half of the room, something awful had struck. She stumbled forward.

Scarlet streaked her bedsheets. It dripped down the walls. Then she saw the white teddy bear on the pillows, gutted, its stuffing strewn everywhere, laced with crimson. An ice pick pinned it to her sheets. What might have been a heart or a liver quivered about its shaft.

"Oh, my God." Her voice leaked thinly from her throat.

The bloody streaks led to the mirror above the small console at the room's end where someone had written, in tall, gory letters: BITCH.

McKenzie backed up, feeling her legs start to give out from under her. Someone had been there. Could still be there. The privacy cur-tains rippled as though someone waited behind them. She could feel a cold draft as if the window had been forced open. McKenzie clawed herself along the wall back to the exit.

She turned to run, lifted her hands to the door, saw her fingers glistening with the stuff. It runneled down her skin, wet and still warm.

McKenzie shrieked.

Shadow grew solid beyond the curtains. Her mouth gaped, throat empty of further sound, as a hand reached around and gripped the fabric edge, pulling it back.

Jack stepped out.

Her heart hammered. He smiled thinly. "Is that any way to greet me, honey?"

Her jaw worked, found words. "Why are you doing this?"

"Why, because we're married. You're mine, little bit. And," and the thin smile stretched widely. "As the saying goes, if I can't have you, no one else can, either. I'll make sure of that."

He took a step forward, the narrow hospital bed the only obstacle between them. McKenzie felt her eyes flutter. The room went suddenly atilt. Everything felt as though it were sliding away. Her voice was the one weapon she had left.

"Nooo!" she screamed.

Jack pivoted and charged the windows. He dove headfirst out the open frame.

Chapter 12

Jack fell farther than he thought he would, thudding onto the fourth floor veranda. The hit nearly took his breath away. He rolled and got to his feet quickly. Adrenaline pumped. He looked back overhead, still hearing the echoes of McKenzie's terror. *Damn, it felt good.* Jack hugged it to himself to enjoy later and ran the length of the veranda until he reached the fire escapes at the building's end cap and swung down to the third floor. From there, he returned to the private waiting room window, pulled himself in through the lower vent, and straightened up. Imagining the activity in the vandalized room several floors above, he tucked his shirt back into place and sauntered down the hallway, took the elevator, and was down.

Jack brushed his hand through his hair as he neared the brace of security guards in the hospital lobby. *Lookin' for baby stealers,* he thought. He was no baby stealer. He attracted no more attention than a casual glance. Their demeanor was bored, and their faces were pinched slightly as if their feet hurt. *They haven't heard the news yet. Won't there be some excitement when they do. They ought to pay me for keeping them from being bored to death.* Jack smiled at them as he walked by.

The bulge in his jeans' hip pocket began to ring as he exited the lobby doors. He put a hand to the cellular phone, removing it once he was outside and flipping it open. The parking lot smelled of asphalt, dirt, and smog. His nose wrinkled as he leaned a hip against the fender of his rental car and answered the phone, eyes watching the lobby doors to see if there were any activity.

"This is Jack."

The line was relatively clear, but he could hear the faint crackling of a long-distance transmission. Someone was trying to reach him in Seattle. He'd done well to have his calls forwarded. The corner of Jack's mouth drew back even as the caller responded, "Is this Jack Trebolt?"

"You're talking to him."

"Mr. Trebolt, this is Officer Moreno of the Los Angeles Police Department."

"El Lay, you said?" Jack gave a short laugh. "I know I put the hammer down between home and Des Moines, but I *know* I didn't hit L.A. What's up, officer?"

"Actually, this is about your wife, McKenzie Smith. You are married to a McKenzie Smith?"

"Mac? Damn right. Is she okay? She isn't in trouble, is she? She bolted out of here about three, four days ago, like a scalded cat. I called all her friends, but she'd just taken off. She's not down in L.A., is she?"

The caller cleared his throat. "Actually, Mr. Trebolt, I'd like to ask you a few questions if you don't mind."

A sparrow went by, chirping and singing. Jack watched it before answering, "No, that's fine. You've got me at a good time. I'm just sitting here at a rest stop waiting for my lunch to hunker down."

"And you said you were outside Des Moines?"

"That's right. You've caught me on my roam phone. I carry a cellular in case Mac needs to reach me. I can get calls damn near cross the country. She gets skittish at home alone." He paused, then added, "If she's in trouble, any kind at all, you tell me and I'll fly right over. Just treat her gently, okay? She gets upset easy. I can't figure out what the hell she'd be doin' in L.A., though."

"It appears she left you."

Jack kept his voice smooth. "Officer, she thinks about leaving every time she gets PMS. Hormonus humungous amongus, y'know? I give her as much love and care as I can, but, man, her whole world just goes tilt. I'm glad I'm on the road then, know what I mean?"

"Are you telling me she has an unstable personality?"

"I'm telling you the little lady is like a rubber band. She snaps at least once a month. I can't blame her, though. Bad childhood. Father was an alcoholic. She just gets skittish, y'know? Insecure. I wish I could be more help, but it takes time."

"Does she take medication?"

"Naw. The doc wanted to give her Valium, but she won't touch it. She's always dieting, says it's supposed to help. I can't see the difference." Jack fished a little, "You didn't tell me if she was in trouble."

"A little," Officer Moreno admitted. His voice grew fainter, as though he had shifted the receiver away. "Nothing we can't handle. I'll let you know when we've done a little more investigating, let you know how the case stands."

"Case?"

"I really can't go into details at this time, Mr. Trebolt. I'd like to thank you for your cooperation. Can I reach you on this number later?"

"It'll be kind of patchy once I leave here, but I should be near a transmitter tomorrow sometime. Then you've got a clear channel all the way to Boston. Ah, officer, will you be seeing Mac later?"

"Yes."

"Would you . . . would you ask her what happened to the dog? Don't upset her or anything, but I couldn't find Cody when I got home. Just his dog blanket out in the trash. It was all crusty with what looked like dried blood. I'd hate to think—well, I'd hate to think she'd really done something awful before she left."

"Do you think your wife is capable of something like that?"

Jack said earnestly, "Officer, Mac is an incredible woman. She can do anything she puts her mind to. But it's the mind I'm worried about. Look, I don't know what happened to make her bail. Maybe Cody got out, got hit by a car—she loved that pup. Purely loved him."

"I see. Well, thank you, Mr. Trebolt. I'll be in touch as soon as I can tell you something definite."

The phone line went dead. Jack took the cell phone down and folded it back up. It was warm in his hands. The little light warning of low charge flickered at him. The police had only intended to tell him what they wanted him to know. Well, he knew *all*. And by the time he was through spinning his little tale about Mac, he had had Officer Moreno thoroughly convinced. His lips skinned back from his teeth. The bitch, his beautiful bitch, looked as though she'd seen a ghost. Both times. He could read her like a book. He knew she'd bail after he taught the dog a lesson. Jack rubbed a finger into the corner of his eye. It was still gummy after the red-eye flight. But he was there, and he had her. He had the plans, he had the brains. "I got you, babe," he informed the phone. "Gotcha."

Still grinning, he climbed into the car and pulled out of the hospital parking lot.

She thought her heart had stopped. Then it sputtered. McKenzie put a hand to her chest, feeling its cold thump. She could not look and pinched her eyes shut. *Don't react. Stay calm, quiet. Attract no attention, no predator, no hunter. It couldn't have been Jack. And if it was, he couldn't have survived the fall. Could he?*

The door opened suddenly, spilling McKenzie onto the floor. She landed sprawled across the feet of a figure in ivory and sand, a woman who looked down at her with piercing blue eyes.

"What is going on here?"

Before McKenzie could say anything, the woman stepped back abruptly, disentangling herself from Mac's bloody form. She looked back over her shoulder. "Nurse! I need a nurse in here!"

Then she looked back down at McKenzie, her lips pursed. As if she'd made a decision, she bent down slightly. "Don't move. You're the concussion client, aren't you? There's blood all over you. Are you hurt?"

"No." Barely audible. She could scarcely hear herself, but this brisk woman who wore her doctor's jacket like it was part of a designer suit heard her.

"Good. Don't move. I don't have my gloves on. If you didn't do this—" the blonde head cast about, before looking back down on her. "This could be contaminated. It's best you don't do anything. You're all scraped up, you don't need any of this worked in. Understand?"

Nearly frozen, still in shock, Mac nodded. Her lower lip began to quiver. "Jack," she said. "Out the window. He can't be alive."

"Someone was in here?" The woman eyed the open window sharply. "Are you certain?"

"He can't be alive," Mac repeated numbly.

The doctor began to pat her jacket pockets as if searching for something. Her name tag bounced on her left breast: Dr. Susan Craig. CyberImago. She pulled out a tissue, took a step toward the bed. She probed at what had been pinned to the gutted bear. "After-birth," she said. "Fairly fresh." She let out her breath. "Possibly not contaminated, after all. Somebody's been into the medical waste."

Running footsteps interrupted the doctor. Shannon halted in the doorway. "Good lord."

"We need to get her cleaned up and out of here as soon as possible." Susan Craig turned back to the gory teddy bear.

Shannon looked down at McKenzie in amazement. Cold authority rang in her voice. "What on earth did you have in mind?"

"I didn't—" McKenzie put out her hand beseechingly, then pulled it back when she saw the blood covering her fingers. She kept her other hand gripped tightly. She looked up to the wall, where her palm-print dotted the streaks. "Oh, God. You don't believe me." Her voice rose tightly.

Susan Craig looked down at her, before locking eyes with the nurse. "Is this the one who snapped last night?"

"Yes."

Her jawline softened. Still out of clear range of McKenzie, she bent down. "It happens," she said gently. "That's what we're here for." Directed at Shannon again, "She's going to be put in my wing, isn't she?"

"Tomorrow."

"Good. I came in to set her up for retesting. The program run this morning came back glitched. Miller called me." Dr. Craig gave a satisfied nod. "This will all work out."

"I didn't do anything," McKenzie begged of both women. "Why won't you believe me? Just look out the window. He—his body—it has to be there!"

Craig straightened and edged past Shannon. "There's a ledge of balconies down there. They run the length of the floor. I doubt if the fall would kill anyone. If anyone had been here to jump. But, then, someone had to do this, didn't they? The world is full of depravity." She checked her watch. "I'll see you again after breakfast tomorrow."

"Let's get you out of here," Shannon said tightly, "while I clean up. I'm putting you in the nurses' lounge. Nobody will bother you there. Then I'm calling Security. After which, I'm getting a mop." She pulled Mac to her feet and put her on the foot of the bed which was relatively clean. "Can you sit up?"

Feeling dizzy and disoriented, McKenzie opened her eyes. "He was here." The words forced themselves from her throat. "He was here!" This was hell, and she was trapped in it.

Shannon repeated in a firmer, but slightly warmer voice, "McKenzie. Can you sit up? I've got to get a disinfectant wash for you. I don't want you falling off and hitting your head again."

"I can sit," Mac said wearily. Her shoulders slumped as Shannon left in a white blur. She was back almost before Mac could even realize she'd gone, hands filled with a basin and a squeeze bottle.

She watched dispassionately as Shannon sponge-bathed her again. Blood. *Ironic,* she thought, *that anyone who works in a hospital should be so afraid of blood. Ironic and terrible.*

She inched out of her gown, and pulled on clean clothing while Shannon left again for a wheelchair.

As she sat and Shannon wheeled her around, Mac said, "I didn't. Honest to God, I didn't do this."

"Well, whoever did it is going to be sorry," the nurse responded. "We'll get Security here in a jiffy. That bear was just delivered for you. I brought it in and found you missing. I've been looking for you."

"Shannon."

The nurse looked down as McKenzie twisted around. "Did Officer Moreno talk to you?"

The other's mouth got very small and tight.

"Call him, too. Tell him what happened. He didn't—he doesn't believe me that my husband's here, that my husband did this."

"It's not my business—"

"Look what he's doing to me! To my father. No one believes me." McKenzie put her hand on the other's wrist. "Please."

Shannon shoved open a door, and guided the wheelchair into a small, but efficient lounge, with a woodgrain plastic table and four chairs. The kitchenette was tidy, but clothes hung helter-skelter in the open closet, shoes scattered below them. There were street clothes and freshly laundered uniforms, and even a pair of panty hose dangling from a hanger.

One beat-up recliner in the corner held an occupant, her feet up, reading *People* magazine. She dropped the periodical to her lap, looking slightly put out. She was young and Latino, her dark hair an ebony cloud under her starched cap.

"Company, Shannon?"

"Someone just did a number on her room. Keep an eye on her while I call Security, will you?"

The recliner foot went down with a bang. "Of course I will."

"McKenzie, this is Nita. I'll be back in a while." The hard look on her face promised nothing before she went out the door.

They eyed each other. Nita pulled a lipstick case from her pocket and outlined her wide, generous mouth with another layer of coral. She got up and went to the small refrigerator in the corner. Popping out a carton of apple juice, she found a straw and with a push and a twist, made the drink ready. She put it in McKenzie's hands.

"You look like you could use a drink," she said, and smiled widely.

"Thanks." As McKenzie lifted the carton to sip, her hand shook slightly. The juice went down icily, tasting only marginally of apples, but good nonetheless. It seemed to etch a path down her dry and paralyzed throat.

Nita wore a white pantsuit. She hiked up a leg and perched on the edge of the dinette table. "What's the problem?"

"Someone decorated my room."

"Well, don't you worry. Shannon will have Security all over his ass, and if he comes back, she'll probably put her mop handle up it."

McKenzie found her lips curling about the straw as she bent her head to take another drink.

Nita leaned back a little, folding her arms over her ample bosom. "Yes, indeed, Mount Mercy nurses are better than guard dogs." She raised a penciled brow. "And prettier, too."

"Definitely," McKenzie conceded. Sitting in the lounge talking with Nita, she almost felt human.

"This the same someone as took some pretty good shots at you? You came in last night?"

"Yeah."

"I thought you were the one. Punched out our best resident."

"I'm so sorry," McKenzie got out.

"Don't worry. He got a free beer for it when his shift went off this morning. Our residents live for the tales they swap. Now he gets to tell a better one than the doc who was held up two weeks ago." Nita swung her leg. "Maybe you shouldn't be so good with your fists. Make the policia wonder, eh?"

"No." McKenzie shook her head, feeling her cheeks still flushed from embarrassment. Everyone on the floor must know of the suspicion. "I'm not like that."

"Practice being invisible, huh? Well, pardon me, but it don't look like it works." Nita stood up. She looked at her watch. "I gotta get back on shift." She walked over to the microwave, leaned down, and bared her smile at her reflection, checking her teeth. She found a lipstick mark and began to rub it off with her finger.

Shannon appeared at the lounge doorway. A wisp of hair had escaped her cap and hung down the side of her face. She said cheerily, "All ready to go back?"

McKenzie hesitated. The nurse added, "I've put you across the hall. Janitorial's going to have to come in and paint the room—I can't get all the bloodstains off the walls and your Officer Moreno told me not to touch it. So Security advised me to switch you. I doubt if you'll mind that one bit, right?" Without waiting for an answer, she took charge of the wheelchair and McKenzie.

Joyce Tompkins was waiting for her in the new room. The woman tilted her head, high cheekbones arching as they looked at one another.

"What happened? I popped back in to check on you, and they sent me here. Who trashed the room?"

McKenzie sagged. Shannon told the advocate, her words like her uniform, crisp, clean, efficient. McKenzie crawled into the hospital bed, the nurse holding her by the elbow for support. Joyce's face showed little emotion as she looked from one face to another.

"And yet no one believes her."

Shannon's mouth moved into a thin, pink line. "We had occasion—"

"I don't want to hear it." Joyce surged to her feet. "I've seen a parade of battered women. I know what I'm lookin' at. And so do you. Now, the question is, what are we going to do about it?"

"She's being moved to psychiatric tomorrow morning."

Joyce bent over and pulled the clipboard off the foot railing of the bed. She scanned it quickly.

McKenzie lay still for a moment, as another siege of dizziness and double vision hit her. It passed quickly, and she swallowed down two breaths as if she could keep it locked away. "I'm not crazy," she managed.

Joyce patted her knee. "No. I know you're not and after a few tests tomorrow," she shot an angry dark-eyed look at Shannon, "they'll know it, too. But, in the meantime, you'll be safer there. Everything is monitored. No one gets in or out easily."

McKenzie felt herself relax a little under Joyce's touch. There was something both formidable and maternal about the African American woman.

"All right?"

She nodded.

Joyce looked to Shannon. "What's for now?"

"A light sedative. A quiet evening."

"Good. Sounds like just what the doctor ordered." Joyce returned the chart to the nurse. "And I'll see you tomorrow. Late morning. Okay?"

McKenzie nodded again.

Shannon patted the pockets of her tunic, found them empty, and said, "I'll be back with your meds." The two left together.

McKenzie rolled in her bed. There was a small but pretty floral arrangement on the side table. Her name was on the card. Carter, trying to apologize? It scarcely mattered now.

She reached for the envelope. Something bulky lay inside. She shook it out onto her palm. Something soft and silken, yet hard and crusty, fell out. She recognized it after a moment.

McKenzie closed her fingers about it. Her chest heaved. She began to sob, violently, without sound, tears cascading. She retreated into the bed, pulling the sheets up around her, cocooning, and did not even notice when the nurse returned and injected her.

Hotchkiss pushed himself away from his desk, leaned over to grasp the remote, and clicked his set off. All in all, the interview had gone well enough, despite the tendency of the media to condense everything down to sound bites. He'd taped all the major channels and feeds. A quick skim had proved they'd all pretty much handled the story the same way. He hadn't been the hero, but neither had he come off villainous. He was saving the taxpayer, not depriving schoolchildren of the facilities so desperately needed to develop their growing minds.

The sudden tragedy of Ibie Walker's condition had almost displaced him on the news altogether. Ironic and fitting, that Stephen had been biding his time, waiting for the old man to falter, because he intended to replace Walker. Everything works out. Hotchkiss had great faith in the balance of the universe.

He swiveled his chair around, facing his computer. Out of habit, he checked to make sure that he was alone. His secretary had blocked all incoming calls, he was at his home office, the part-time housekeeper was not scheduled for the day.

He'd worked hard the past few months, indeed, the year and more since the San Fernando quake, and the days of solitude and rest had been few. But the upcoming election year should see him reap the rewards, following in the sweep of the gubernatorial election. He was in a good position to vault into place for the off-year elections, and his backers knew it. He had the drive, the confidence, the training to do it. Even his youth and bachelorhood could not be held against him—not in California. No. He should go as far as he wanted. Then he could come forward in the next gubernatorial election and try for a statewide position. Ten years or so, maybe even the governorship.

He'd been born into the best of times, Hotchkiss decided, as he ran a stroking hand across the keyboard. Secrets could unmake the man or woman, secrets tried in the media without benefit of court or justice, secrets which would not be understood or condoned. Everybody had dirty laundry, he thought. Who grew up prepared to be examined microscopically? The recent rash of nominees on both state and federal levels who could not stand up to the scrutiny of the media-fed public was not surprising, although lamentable. But who knew, then, twenty, thirty years ago, what might later come back to haunt them?

It made Stephen uncomfortable to think that the next generation of appointees and office holders might be holier than thou prisses whose sole career was not based on achievements, but on the avoidance of secrets, of offending anyone and everyone. What a sorry lot of wusses those candidates would be.

But for now, he could afford to ride the tide of righteousness. He had managed himself well. He had done *all right*.

He could reward himself.

He booted up the computer and took a disk out of a plain paper bag. Its three-inch surface was beautiful in a clinically technological way, shining with opalescent color. Its beauty had little to do with its use. It was unmarked, unlabeled, totally unremarkable in any way.

And unidentifiable.

Hotchkiss held it between his index and thumb fingers, looking at the striking colors that shimmered off the silvery surface. He did not play games. If he had another fault in his personality, it was the lack of gamesmanship. He was a poor loser, and an even worse winner. He had managed to groom himself for the game of politics, but that was different. It was real life. Real power. For that, he could learn to smile convincingly, to give and take and be humble.

It wasn't worth the effort for a mere board game or a deck of cards.

But this was different. He slipped the disk into his computer and booted it up. The color monitor came to life, displaying its brand name and then, as the drive whirled, the logo faded away as the memory gathered the new material. Sitting on top of the monitor rested a full-visored helmet. Like modified motorcycle gear, the front shield was smoked ebony. The fiberglass helmet itself had been custom painted a deep, electric blue, with black striping. It looked ordinary, until one saw the network of cables cascading from the nape of the equipment. Next to it, gloves lay nested, one atop the other, thick and bulky, studded with connectors and more cables, their image sexually powerful and stirring.

The helmet and gloves were his passport from reality into virtual reality, an antiseptic environment where nearly anything could happen—and carry no consequences.

Before settling the helmet over his head, Hotchkiss checked out the room again. The fine, custom-built oak paneling and library shelving. His hand-routed desk. There was a Chagall on the wall, not an original, but a very low number lithograph. Baccarat crystal gleamed on the wet bar. The Persian carpet upon the floor, vibrant in its red and blue weave. These were the trappings of his office, but they did not feed the soul.

It was reward time.

He *deserved* it.

The helmet slipped down. Its wiry cables snaked about Hotchkiss's shoulders and down his arms as he pulled on the massive gloves. He flexed them, feeling the potential power in them, dormant, waiting for him to complete the connection. With crisp, precise movements, he clipped the cable ends together and let the computer power flood them.

His visor exploded with color. Hotchkiss sat back in his swivel chair as sound issued from the helmet's interior, soaking in the experience flooding his senses. He closed his eyes a moment as the virtual reality graphics came on, a beach, golden with sunshine, and young bodies, naked, unblemished by puberty or experience. He stood, braced, within it. He existed here, and only here, for the moment.

It filled his senses. He could hear it, touch it, see it, even taste it, by God. It came roaring in on him like the sea in flood tide, sweeping over him. He threw his head back, a laugh fountaining from his throat.

The rhythmic surge of ocean water upon sand sang in his ears. Sunlight broke into diamonds on the crystal blue water. Towels striped the beach. Surfboards and body boards lay dormant, their colors like the rainbow. He had every sense but smell inundated as the title, *Surfer Boys,* played across his line of sight. It played across him like a banner trailed by a plane. He put a hand up and pushed it away.

Gone was his constricting business suit uniform. Jams and a tropical shirt open at his chest replaced it. He stood barefoot on the beach. He swore he could feel the very warm grains cushioning him. Crossing the sand, he could feel the salt breeze in his face, see the boys waiting for him. Only boys, and only him.

Bare skin met the glowing sunlight. Clothing optional, the young ran past, into the splashing waves. They laughed and shouted to one another, carrying surfboards and boogie boards, or simply racing one another into the water.

Flesh, everywhere he looked. In all hues from the untouched to the bronzed. Buttocks rounded and firm. Shoulders lean, not yet bulked by the hormonal rampage of puberty. Bodies still coltish, some still rounded with baby fat, romped upon the sands.

His gloved hands curved to caress and possess.

There would be no one to tell.

Hotchkiss took a deep breath and let himself stride forward into the scenario. He let it wash over him, bathe him in its sunlight, drawn by the silhouette of a boy laying facedown on his beach towel. The hair, like winter wheat, upon his head, the skin just beginning to acquire a sun-drenched hue, fine hairs upon his legs like wisps of spun gold.

So young, so pure, the skin unmarked by the coarsening of hair and stubble, no pustules of acne scarring, no shaving scars, no marks of adolescence, the youth so clean and innocent. He could not resist the touch.

The boy on the beach towel stirred. He could feel the warmth of the skin under his palm, the ripple of muscles as the child turned over and smiled, white teeth showing, his wheat-colored hair dipping down into his eyes. Stephen could get lost in those eyes, echoing pools of the blue water behind him. They warmed as they beheld him. A smile of welcome.

Then the boy said, "We know who you are, Hotchkiss."

The words catapulted him backward, slamming him back into the reality of the embrace of his office chair.

He sat back in shock. Set off by his trembling, cables rippled around him like electric eels.

Chapter 13

"The nurse says you'll corroborate McKenzie's whereabouts."

Carter looked at the growing crowd of reporters, gathering for the official press release on Ibrahim Walker's condition. He'd already made the early edition with the news break on Ibie when he'd called into the city desk. Now, with the update imminent, he no more wanted to be escorted off hospital property for improper conduct than he wanted an extra hole in the head, but neither did he want to lie outright. Moreno had shown up moments before, hot and rumpled as though the staff car he drove had no air-conditioning. Face growing more and more dotted with perspiration, the policeman had filled Carter in on the destruction downstairs. Without seeing the scene for himself, he couldn't imagine McKenzie having done it, or taken the initiative to do it. He looked at Moreno.

"I can't tell you that I was with her every single second and that she couldn't have done it herself. I stayed up here when I saw Ibie brought in. She could have been alone, fifteen, twenty minutes, an hour. I lost track of time."

"Then what can you tell me?"

"The room was clean when we left it. I didn't bring her back, so I don't know what it looked like later. She mourned her father. I can tell you that she's worried about her husband finding her. From what you tell me, it looks like he did." Carter pulled at his collar a little. "I don't think it makes much sense that she would come home all the way from Seattle just to duke it out with her father. And I don't think I need to point out to you that this town is beginning to have a big problem with the way ordinary people are treated, compared with celebrities."

Moreno had been jotting in his notebook. He met Carter's stare. "The neighbors remember a very combative relationship. Stranger things have happened. If we can lift a print from the room, prove someone else's involvement, we can turn the investigation around. As far as her status, be glad she's not somebody. If she were, this place would be filled with the news media from stem to stern . . . and she would already be judged and sentenced."

"What about taking her word for it? I wasn't aware spousal abuse was getting rare."

Moreno's eyes glittered. His mouth worked as though he was choking back what he wanted to say and he ended with, "Wouldn't that make a headline?" Carter sighed and he put his pen away in his shirt pocket. He nodded toward the makeshift podium, awaiting a doctor and a press rep. "What's the word about Ibie?"

"He may or may not have surprised an intruder, but it's his old age that took him down. Recovery, if he makes it, will be slow."

Moreno made a *tch*ing noise through his teeth. "Hate to see him retire. There's a lot of work left to do."

Carter grinned. "Retire? He'll be ordering his aides and secretaries in here tomorrow. The joint will be filled with fax machines and cell phones."

"Cell phones," the policeman repeated. Then he laughed. "Yeah, I guess so." He started to turn away as the crowd around them grew, making their conversation even more difficult to keep private, then turned back. "Too bad about your friend Nelson. Any idea why he was in town?"

Carter paused. "Officially or unofficially?"

"Either way."

"We never had a chance to talk. I might have an idea if I could find out what the suits are saying. Any leads?"

Moreno's color deepened slightly. "Nothing I could do about it if I wanted to," he returned. "The Feds are crawling all over that one."

"Wouldn't hurt to nudge them in the right direction, though. No, I don't know what he was doing here. We were supposed to have lunch when he called . . . but he didn't get a chance to." He saw the corridor beyond the room fill with personnel. Time to cut this conversation short, and he thought he knew just the stopper. "Now, you want to trade some real information, let's talk about Mr. Blue."

Moreno shook his head. "Now you've reached my limit," he said, smiling, and began to move off.

Carter watched him go for a few feet, then turned his attention back to the doctors who were filing in. He found his fingers twitching as if he already sat at the keyboard. A portly neurosurgeon at the front of the room tapped a microphone and cleared his throat. Instantly, the room became deathly quiet.

There was a light at the end of the black tunnel. Hotchkiss groaned, seeing it, and shifted again in his chair. His life had been passing before him, he knew it, he could taste its bitterness in his mouth. He coughed. His neck creaked stiffly and the helmet, which had been sloughing off, fell farther off his forehead. The pinpoint of light became a blazing sun. Hotchkiss stared and blinked at it, until he realized he was looking at the room's ceiling light, not at God.

He sat bolt upright in the chair and snatched the helmet from his skull. One of the cables ripped loose and fell to the desktop with a clank of its metallic head. Hotchkiss brushed it aside with a trembling hand as he might a snake. He threw the helmet as far from him as he could.

Leaning heavily on his elbows across the desk, as if he were pulling himself free from a drowning sea, he gasped and trembled. What was happening to him?

He looked down at his hands, now swollen and puffy, fingernails bitten to the quick. The mark of an overcritical, anxious, and analytical person, he told himself.

A person who could feel life grinding him down, bit by bit.

What could he do?

He reached for the phone, but his trembling hand went astray and, instead, he punched the radio news line button on his intercom. Voices flooded the office, overriding the thunder of his heartbeat and the tortured, sobbing gasps of his breathing.

". . . extent of the damage to Walker is unknown at this time. His doctors say it will be another day or two before neurological tests can be conducted to determine if the stroke will leave him permanently incapacitated. No interim replacement for Mr. Walker has been named to the council yet, but committees are scheduled to meet tomorrow to discuss this latest development. To recap, news at eleven-thirty reports, from the wires and hospital sources, that Councilman Ibrahim Walker has suffered a major stroke during the night and is now resting comfortably at Mount Mercy Hospital. . . ."

Hotchkiss jabbed a finger hastily at the radio line, deadening it. He reeled back in his chair, struck by the news. He could feel the heat of the overhead light, beating down on the back of his neck as if it were the sun. He could smell the coconut tanning oil, hear the swish of the waves, feel the ache in his throat for a beauty few understood. . . .

We know who you are. You will be called, and you will serve, and you will remember that we know who you are. . . .

All the years of discretion and service, none of that availed him now. They knew that he and his party had been hoping to quietly jockey him into position for Walker's post in a year or two, when surely the old man would be precipitously close to retirement anyway. They knew that Walker had been struck down.

He put the back of his hand to his mouth. His lips, salty with perspiration, were swollen.

He had to get out, even if just for a day or two. Get away and think. Out of town, out of the heat and smog, somewhere where he could just think. *Destroy the disk. . . .*

He stiffened his back. Destroying the software would be a start. He picked up his phone, left a message on his secretary's voice mail. "Cancel my appointments for the next few days. I've been called out of town. Put everything on hold. You're not to give out the information, but I'll be at my condo at Lake Arrowhead. Do not forward any calls or messages to me, no matter how urgent they appear to be."

He hung up and took a deep breath. There. He was gaining control again. Thoughts, which had started to fall like dominoes, began to stack up neatly. He would be in charge again.

He shoved himself away from the desk and chair and stood. His knees wobbled, then caught. His suit, horribly wrinkled at the knees, fell away from his legs. He had been sitting in a daze for, what, hours? No more time to waste.

A sudden thought furrowed his brow. He leaned over and made one last phone call, then left his office to pack.

*   *   *

Moreno looked in on the girl before he left the hospital. After talking to the husband, he wouldn't normally have made a trip back, but something pulled him. As Carter had reminded him, he was all too familiar with domestic violence. She lay with her eyes to the window, lids hooded, unresponsive as he toed open the door. The nurse behind him, the same one who'd let him interview her earlier, leaned close. She wore Jean Naté splash, like his Margo used to, and he found the citrus scent overwhelming. He cleared his throat heavily. The young woman lying supine in the hospital bed flinched, but otherwise seemed totally unaware of him.

"She's sedated," the nurse said.

"Thought you didn't do that with possible concussions."

"We don't. Preliminary tests show that her head injury is mild. The sedation is light, should wear off in an hour or two. Dr. Craig in psychiatric thought it advisable. Once the case physician concurs, we'll be moving her there for observation." The blonde's face smoothed slightly, sympathetically. "Sometimes anyone can just snap, y'know?"

Moreno pushed on into the room, to get away from the perfume as much as anything. He looked at the bank of windows. "This go down to the same verandas?"

"Where she said her husband jumped? No. That's on the other side of the building. If he'd been here, if he'd jumped from here, you'd have found him smashed like a ripe watermelon down in the courtyard."

Moreno's stomach clenched slightly, not at the imagery but because he'd seen scenes like that before, and did not like the memory. He ran his tongue over his teeth, wondering if he had indeed talked to Jack Trebolt or not. After all, who was to say?

Her right hand rested on top of the sheets, fisted over something. He looked down, saw a corner, golden and fuzzy. He picked up her hand, turned it over, and carefully loosened the fingers. A scrap of something rested on her palm. He looked at it thoughtfully, then took an evidence baggie from his pants' pocket and slid the object into it.

"Find something?"

Nurses. Bossy and curious, like surrogate mothers. Moreno cleared his throat of the perfume again. "Probably not," he answered. His voice had gone gravelly.

"Catching a cold?" She smiled cheerfully at him, one patient forgotten, her attention quickly transferred to another. "I can get you something for that?"

"No." He scratched the corner of his mouth. "It's the smog. Give my office a call when she's transferred over, will you? I'll be needing to speak with her again."

The ponytail bobbed as the woman nodded. Moreno brushed past her as he pocketed the baggie. He did not take it out to look at it more carefully until he was alone in the elevator, doors closed after him. There he pulled it out and opened it, running a fingertip curiously over. At first, he had thought it a scrap of material, a patch of mohair from a teddy bear or some such. Women, young women, were as crazy about stuffed animals as they were about flowers. He couldn't figure it, but Margo had told him that when the two of them first started dating. Anything, she'd said, any little sentimental gift. A card, a rose, a little stuffed bear. . . .

But this was not fabric. For one thing, it had a definite odor which he could now smell in the confines of the elevator, an odor of rotting. Moreno pinched the piece gently between his thumb and index finger, getting a real feel for it. Soft, silken on both sides, fine golden hairs, ragged edges. . . .

And then, suddenly, he knew what it was, and the thought sickened him so much that he nearly vomited. He bit off the gorge behind his throat, resealed the baggie and thrust it back into his pocket. When the elevator doors opened, he left them as though he had been launched.

What in God's name was she doing with part of a dead dog's ear in her hand?

Chapter 14

Susan sat going over the new patient's chart again, looking at the synaptic anomalies. She had already highlighted them with a dry pen, so that the paper would not bleed, and she sat now with the same pen in hand like a weapon, as if she might find another spike or curve to color. Miller had long since gone home, but it wouldn't help even if he were there. He didn't know the virtual reality program, he hadn't helped design it, he barely knew how to utilize and score it.

She rested the tip of her pen upon the paper. The ink bled immediately into the fiber, glowing apple green in response, like a dot at the base of an exclamation point. She couldn't fault Miller there, for all his shortcomings. He had done almost as well at scoring as she would have.

So the anomalies weren't his fault.

She dropped her pen and shoved her chair back. The noise screeched in the quiet lab, and the boy in the far corner, head helmeted, avid in front of a colorful monitor, jumped as if the sound had gotten through to him. Dr. Craig watched him for a moment to see if he made any more disruptive responses, but the boy did not, and so she pushed the chair back a little more, softly, and stood up.

The spare helmets, there were only two others besides the one currently in use, sat on a Formica counter, cables neatly wrapped beside them. Miller's obsession for orderliness superseded almost any other work drive he had. Craig smiled thinly in response as she reached up and took down the equipment. He had marked the patient as being tested in helmet C. She grasped it between her hands, turning it over and over. The leads seemed fine. The 64K processor would have to be removed, and the chip tested elsewhere, but she was willing to bet it was all right as well. With the kind of usage she gave it, what could have gone wrong?

Only the software and the patient herself could be suspect. Craig turned the helmet over again, teeth nibbling against her lower lip as she thought. It was a given that her program was experimental. Yet, although she had not offered it up to FDA testing because she was still compiling her own results, she knew that it could not have produced the synaptic responses graphed from the patient.

Therefore, it was the patient herself who was responsible for the aberrant reading.

Susan would have to test her again to confirm that, of course. Tomorrow morning, when the young woman was transferred over, she would have ample opportunity.

She tossed the helmet back on the shelf, loosening the clip which held the neatly coiled cable, and watched it snake loose, striking at her, like a moray eel from the depths of the ocean. Absentmindedly, Craig pushed the cable back as well, and returned to her table and report. Before she could sit, there was a sound from the corner.

Brandon had finished the program and was calling for her, his thin eleven-year-old voice muffled by the helmet. She'd almost forgotten she'd planted him there earlier. The wiry wrists were both bandaged lightly, hiding the newly healing scars of a suicide attempt. As she stood up, she noted the body language, the vulnerable and uncertain way he sat at the console.

Some people should never be allowed to have children. Licenses for bearing and rearing offspring ought to be more important than fishing licenses. Susan shrugged into her lab coat, then put her chin up.

Briskly, she joined him, and began to unclip the various leads. His freckled face, when it emerged from the visor's cover, was pale but excited.

"Did you see my score?"

"Why, no." Craig bent over and examined the monitor, trying to muster enthusiasm.

He had his hand on the monitor screen, ignoring the faint static crackle, saying, "All the way to level nine!"

"That's good. That's very good. But remember what you promised me. An hour of game, a half hour of biofeedback, right?"

His face went slack, hazel eyes deadening.

"It's important," she told him. "Or I wouldn't ask you. You need to know how to handle all those knots that tighten up inside you. This will help. Besides, we made a deal, right?"

Then, he nodded. "I promised."

"Right." Susan wrapped the helmet up. "But you don't have to do it now. I'll wheel you back to your room, you can have afternoon snack, and maybe I'll see you after dinner. Okay?"

Some of the enthusiasm and color returned to the boy's face. "Okay!"

She toed the brake off the wheelchair and brought the boy around, but her mind, as she took him out of the lab, was somewhere else entirely. When she returned, she sat down at one of the several computers.

Her fingers played elegantly over the keyboard, as if awakening a piano. She watched herself type, not because she did not know the keys, but because she liked to watch the interplay of her hands. She thought of Holly Hunter in her award-winning role, her hands so elegant, so work-strong, so emotive.

>>HELLO.<<

After a moment, the screen responded. There was no real reply, there could not be, but a synaptic grid came on. She watched the grid avidly.

A spike jumped. Susan caught her breath, watched it closely. A second spurt followed. Awareness. A stirring of awareness, flaring into kinetic thought. She responded without thinking, coaxing.

>>I'M HERE.<<

The screen exploded into a frenzy, spikes and valleys. She watched the grid as whatever it measured fought its containment.

>>DREAM.<< She rested her hands on the wrist board, watching the lines oscillate, REM patterns like that of sleep. Always dreaming. The matrix could not do otherwise until she awakened it.

But it seemed fitful, and that worried her.

She hastily switched on a second computer. The hard drive whirred into lazy life. "Come on, come on!" In the corner of her eye, the first monitor continued its starburst of activity.

She opened up the modem line and began to type a rapid string of commands, her hard acrylic nails staccato on the keyboard, leaning over from her chair to reach it. Fine beads of sweat dotted her upper lip. She licked them away, tasting salt and makeup.

After long moments, the activity on the first monitor began to soften, to slacken, to lapse back into somnolent readings. There was one last hiccup of a spike.

Susan Craig sat back in her chair. She found herself breathing, spent, as if she'd just run a 5K. After long moments, she felt confident enough to shut down the second terminal.

What had she done?

Susan flung herself back in her chair, face hard for a moment. Then she forced herself to lean forward, out of the morass of self-doubt which threatened to envelop her.

"Soon," she said soothingly, her fingertips brushing the terminal as if she stroked a patient's hand. "Soon."

The phone rang. Susan answered it and listened, and felt her face grow cool. She put a fingertip to the corner of her mouth, as close to chewing a nail as she ever got now, her tongue tickling the hard acrylic edge. For a second, she felt her teeth bare as if she would not be able to resist a bite.

She cleared her throat gently to intone, "That's no problem. Thank you for calling."

Her hand tightened about the receiver as she hung it upon, her fair, pale skin going to dead white about the knuckles.

She punched out a number quickly and, when the party answered, said without preliminaries, "Hotchkiss thinks he's going to run. He's canceled all his appointments. But I know where he's going. We've discussed it before. I want you to drive up to Arrowhead and let him know just how serious we are." She paused. "No, I don't want him hurt badly. I just want his attention."

She smiled tightly at the response.

Carter returned home, filed a backup story, and was signing off when Dolan caught him online. The editorial assistant "sounded" much the same on a computer screen as he did in person.

>>HEY, KIDDO! SOME STORY<<

Carter leaned back toward the terminal with some regrets.

>>THANKS. RIGHT PLACE AT THE RIGHT TIME.<<

>>SOME PEOPLE HAVE ALL THE LUCK. HOW'S IT LOOK FOR IBIE???<<

>>NOBODY'S SAYING. GUESS IT DEPENDS ON HIM.<<

>>WOW. THE BOSS SAYS TO CHECK YOUR VOICE MAIL ONCE IN A WHILE. AND THE FEDS CAME BY TO SAY HELLO.<<

>>THANKS FOR THE WARNING. DID I MISS ANYTHING IMPORTANT?<<

>>THERE'S A GIF FOR YOU TO DOWNLOAD. WANT ME TO STAND BY IN CASE YOU NEED HELP?(G)<<

Dolan needn't have shorthanded a grin at the end of his query. Carter could pick up voice mail, download and upload files on his computer, but graphics were another matter. >>GUESS YOU'D BETTER.<<

>>I KEEP TELLING YOU, IT'S JUST POINT AND CLICK.<<

"Ha," Carter muttered. He pulled down his message menu and located the flag which told him there was a file waiting. The mouse did not seem to want to run smoothly as he tried to position the cursor to download the file. Then, when he thought he finally had it, his drive rattled at him, reminding him that he hadn't put in a disk. Finally, he had it.

The phone rang. Eyes fixed on the screen, as he now tried to load the GIF from his floppy, he answered the phone one-handed.

"Yeah."

"It's me, Windy. I had to get off the net. How's it goin'?"

"Sorry to keep you hanging, Dolan. I've got it now. It's just coming up . . . ." Carter paused, watching the screen as the pixels began to give him an incredibly clear picture.

"Don't need my help?"

"No, I, ah. . . ." Distracted, Carter fell into incoherence.

"Good goin', big guy. See you around." Dolan hung up with scarcely any reaction.

Carter sat in front of his screen for a good five minutes, telephone receiver in hand, staring at what he had. As the phone began to beep at him, he set it back in its cradle without tearing his eyes away from the monitor.

Nelson must have uploaded it for him. Maybe he knew he wouldn't make it with the file, or maybe he was just farther along in computer technology than Carter was, or maybe it was his best way of sneaking the information out of the Bureau.

He'd never know, now.

He stared at the newspaper photo, with its Bureau stamp on the corner, knowing it was out of Bauer's files, that it had to have come from Nelson because no one else would have left it for Carter.

It showed Nelson escorting Bauer to the psychiatrist who would work with him. But that wasn't the focal point of Carter's interest. Nelson had circled another figure, almost out of the camera's range of focus and illumination. He had penned there, neatly so as not to obscure the photo in any way, "still alive."

Still alive.

A grad student, Carter thought. *Too young to be anything else. I know her, or rather, I knew her. Who the hell is she?*

Because he had to remember. He had to.

If for no other reason than the intense look on the young woman's face, naked expression, unaware the camera was catching her, unaware of anything but the serial killer being brought into the lab. The lens had caught her, immortalized in its stare, just as she stared upon the murderer. Sheer, unabashed adoration shone from her face as she looked at Bauer.

Chapter 15

"Shit." Frustration knifed through him. Add ten years onto her and he knew her, he *knew* her. But he didn't recognize her.

Had Nelson thought so, too?

He stared at the monitor, the picture so lifelike, so achingly clear, transfixed by the look upon the young woman's face. Had she known what the camera revealed, would she have veiled the open admiration, the passion she felt? Carter knew the type. He'd run into them before. He could never understand the phenomenon. It was as though they responded to the same raw power that fueled the killer, not sexual, but fantasy and control and violence.

How could he have missed that? And Nelson, too. Or had this one particular photo just surfaced after years, after wads of photos had been studied? Had it even been hidden from John Nelson by other, more ambitious investigators?

Who was she? Where was she now?

Carter found his fingertips moving along the lip of the computer desk as though he were already writing copy. Damn it, he knew her, and that astonished him, too. By all rights, when Bauer killed his doctor and escaped, she should have died, too. Bauer rarely overlooked an opportunity to indulge his capacity for cruelty.

He had to get the photo back to Dolan for computer aging. A newer hairstyle, some maturity to a face so young then it might have been made of marshmallow—he might know it when updated. While Dolan worked on that, he would backtrack to the psychiatrist's estate and records, see if he could find out what grad students from his university classes might have worked with him that fateful spring and summer. He had never concentrated on Bauer before the escape, only after.

Carter stared. Why did Bauer spare her? Or had he been too rushed? That was a possibility. Bauer had always liked to take his deliberate time with his victims. Too long. Carter and the forensic experts had run across victims who'd taken two, three days to die.

He shuddered at the memory.

The computer-generated image began to waver as his screen saver program took over, darkening into a galaxy, with otherworldly transports traveling over them. The program went into effect whenever the monitor stayed on text or an image too long, keeping the screen from being burned with the image permanently. A touch on the keyboard or mouse and the GIF would return. Carter blinked, then rubbed his eyes as the space opera rolled across the screen. Amid the faint sound of warp drives and phasers cutting across space to blast enemy ships, he sat back.

A firm knock sounded on the door.

Carter reacted instinctively. He popped the floppy out of the drive and tossed it in a bottom drawer, where it lay amid a stack of floppies. He put his fingers into the pile and stirred it around a little. Then he got up to answer the door.

No one came to his apartment. There were only a few he might be expecting. Therefore, he was not surprised when he opened it to two suits, both of somber color.

The redhead was perspiring heavily. There was a pallor under his flush and freckles that told Carter he came from back East. Washington, probably, although he could be from the Chicago Bureau. The second man leaned in, his stomach bulging out over his belt buckle, pushing the ends of his tie up toward his chest. The white shirt contrasted violently with the splashed lime green tie. Carter raised his eyes from the fashion statement, meeting a tired gaze framed by crow's feet as deep as any he'd seen etched into a California face. He'd spent a lot of years squinting into L.A. gridlock. This suit was definitely from the L.A. office, although he didn't recall that they'd met.

"Carter Wyndall?"

"I am."

"Agents Sofer and Franklin, Federal Bureau of Investigation. May we come in?"

"Of course. I was expecting you." Carter let them pass, a subtle formality because Franklin, tie and all, was already halfway into the apartment. "Father's Day present?"

"What? Oh." Franklin looked morosely downward. "Yes."

"You'll have a new model in a couple of weeks."

Sofer was grinning ear to ear as he pulled out a handkerchief and mopped his face and the back of his neck. "Let's hope," he agreed. He folded the sodden cloth over, mopped again hopelessly, and then put the handkerchief away.

"Let me turn on the air-conditioning," Carter offered as he shut the door. "I haven't been home all that long. Place still feels shut up."

Sofer's face eased into a grateful half-smile as Carter passed him on the way to the thermostat. The freckles had begun to turn bright red. The apartment let out a couple of creaks as the system cranked up, and air began blowing.

Franklin had parked himself in front of the computer, watching the *Star Wars*ian display. Without turning around, the middle-aged man grunted, "You know why we're here."

"I would guess it's Nelson. I could use a drink. No beer. Mineral water, juice?"

"Water," both men answered. Carter bowed into the kitchen, found a lime and sliced it for the water glasses. He kept water stocked in the refrigerator. Los Angeles water was detestable. He'd grown used to almost everything about the city but that. It was only just better than no water at all.

The outer space display was still twirling planets, spaceships, and tractor beams when he brought the drinks out. Carter avoided looking at it as he settled himself into the wing-backed chair which had become his favorite. Sofer sank onto the couch, Franklin stayed on his feet and pulled out a recorder. He put it on the coffee table and aimed it in Carter's direction.

"Interview, May 16th, Carter Wyndall, agents Sofer and Franklin." He cleared his throat. The lime tie wafted with the motion, then settled. "Mr. Wyndall, would you please explain to us your acquaintanceship with Congressman John Nelson, formerly of the FBI."

Carter knocked back about half his glass of water, then smiled and said, "Before we get too far into this, guys, is there any reason I should have my lawyer present?"

No laughter. They cracked not a smile line between them. Sofer busied himself mopping his face again despite the now chilling air and Franklin fished his lime slice out of his water.

Carter looked back and forth. "Good God. Don't tell me it's been twenty-four hours and you guys don't have the slightest idea who did Nelson."

"How about if we just stay away from speculation and answer the questions, Mr. Wyndall."

"How about if we end this friendly conversation right here and now before I find myself the prime suspect." Carter had been sitting with his legs crossed. He now planted both feet firmly on the floor.

Sofer said reluctantly, "We know it was an expert hit. That's about all the evidence we have. Hotel security cameras show very little. Whoever it was knew how to get in and get out, and exactly where John would be."

"No weapon? No fibers?"

"Everything was clean. The weapon hasn't been found yet."

Carter let out a low whistle while Sofer hastened to add, "This is not for publication."

He shook his head. "I don't step on toes. As long as you two keep in mind the last time I was on a target range, I managed, barely, to hit the broad side of a barn, I'll talk to you. I know John from a case he worked on years ago, when I was a newsman in Chicago."

"Georg Bauer," put in Franklin, flatly.

"That's the one."

"You the newsman the bastard spilled his guts to? Giving up bodies just before he was scheduled to be executed?"

"That's me. No one, not even John, wanted Bauer back on Death Row worse than I did." Carter felt his teeth showing, pulled his lips down. "We crossed paths trying to find him for a couple of years. Then the trail went cold. John says—used to say—I'm still looking. But he retired, then ran for Congress. When he has occasion to be in town, which isn't often, we knock back a cold one, chew on a steak, compare our cholesterol, and wonder what happened."

"So you heard from him this time?"

They suspected already, of course. "He called from the plane. I was out on a story, he put it into my voice mail."

"Could we hear that message?"

Carter shook his head. "Sorry. I dumped it when I retrieved it." Which wasn't strictly true, he'd recorded it, but the message was no longer on the voice mail system.

Sofer said to Franklin, "That's okay. It should be the same message we picked up."

A hackle rose along Carter's back. "You heard it earlier?"

"That's right. Your employer thought, under the circumstances, it was all right to let us access your mail."

Carter felt his jaw tighten. It wasn't all right. Not by a long shot. He bit down on the rim of his glass and took an angry swig of mineral water, felt it hissing down his throat.

Franklin asked mildly, "What was Nelson hoping to pass on to you?"

He was done cooperating. "Damned if I know." A newspaper, of all employers, should know about confidentiality. He found it difficult to believe that his editor would give even with the Feds leaning on him.

"If he was passing anything about Bauer on to you, it would have to be Federal property. We would have to confiscate it." Franklin looked edgy. He kept pacing back and forth. Carter tried not to watch him or the computer monitor across the room.

"I wouldn't want the Feds angry with me." He tried a shadow of a smile. "What makes you think Nelson's death had anything to do with Bauer?"

"Nothing. But, so far, nothing makes us think it doesn't. Nelson hadn't been a congressman long enough to get himself into hot water. There haven't been any terrorist claims, no threats. We don't even have an official reason as to why he was in L.A."

"I have even less of an idea than you do. I had no idea he was coming out before the call."

"According to our records, there was nothing extraordinary about the visit. He liked the hotel, it was quiet, confidential. He usually didn't bring girls in. John was faithful to his wife. He had appointments later in the week to do some politicking, but from all appearances, he came out here specifically to talk to you."

"He did?" That frankly surprised Carter. As diffident as he'd been about the old leads on the Bauer case, his actions were not. Nelson must have thought he had something and wanted Carter's take on it. He'd been casual because he knew the world of voice and e-mail was not a secure one.

Franklin paused by the computer. "This *Star Wars*?"

"Not exactly. A clone, more or less."

"Do you like to play computer games?"

"I enjoy it once in a while. I'd rather meet with an old friend and enjoy good conversation, but my schedule doesn't always allow it."

Carter put down his water glass, edged forward slightly in his chair. The agent's beefy hand waved over the computer as if itching to reach for the mouse or keyboard.

"What's your high score?"

"I don't keep one."

Franklin's hand shot out for the mouse control before Carter could say anything further. At the touch, the screen dissolved away from the galactic scenario, and reassembled in the gray-tone photo clearly marked as FBI evidence.

"Shit." Franklin turned on one heel. "What is this?"

Carter kept his face neutral. "You tell me. I just downloaded that."

"You know as well as I do what that is."

Sofer got to his feet as well. He had stopped sweating, finally, and now fresh beads popped out on his excited face. "Holding out on us?"

"Now do I need my lawyer?"

Franklin brought up an editing menu. He brought the cursor up to "delete." "I don't think so," he answered. "You have this saved yet?"

"Don't touch that!" Carter jumped forward.

Too late. The agent clicked the selection. The hard drive whirred, the picture went dark, and then the light amber screen came up.

"I would hate," Franklin said, "for a friend of John's to be compromised by his indiscretion."

Sofer added, "So would I." He headed to the door. "If you think of anything else you'd like to tell us about Nelson, just call."

Carter felt the corner of his cheek twitch. He let it, before asking, "Anything I should have known about that picture? Since it's possible John died for it?"

"Only that the Freedom of Information Act doesn't apply to it. You shouldn't have seen it. You didn't." Franklin straightened his tie. "Be careful, Wyndall. If John was a target because he was a congressman, you're in the clear. But if he was a target because of the Bauer case, you're next in line."

Carter said dryly, "I guess that gives me an incentive for cooperating with you."

"It should." Franklin scooped up his recorder, shut it off, and slipped it in his pocket. "No one downtown has a clue, for what it's worth. If I find out anything, I'll give you a call."

"So let me ask you one question."

The two suits paused. In the air-conditioning, Sofer's complexion had calmed down to its normal pallor, sprinkled liberally with freckles. He stretched his neck out over his collar.

"Why are you two so worried about Bauer if he's supposed to be dead? We both know he didn't do Nelson. There's a world of difference between a professional killer and a thrill killer. We're not talking about the same man. Is the photo that significant?"

"You think Bauer is dead?" Sofer's voice rose, with an edge.

"Yes, I do."

"Well, I have no information that he's considered dead. His case file is open."

"It's been years since a victim was found matching his . . . methodology. We have networks now that we didn't have then. VICAP or one of the others should pick him up immediately if he's begun killing again." Carter stood his ground.

Franklin sniffed. "We can hope, but we can't confirm anything. I would hate for you to be his comeback." Sofer started to add something, halted as Franklin wagged an index finger at him. "Carter, we don't know that there's anything about that photo or anything else John may have tried to get to you. Our objection is that Nelson is no longer an agent. He had his hands on, and was distributing material that is government private property. We don't know why he did it. We only know that he's dead. We need to find out why, and if his actions had anything to do with it. Was he flushing somebody out? Was he into blackmail? I don't think so, John was a good agent. But it's our job to look and secure whatever loose ends he left behind."

He was silent for a moment, then said, "Point taken."

"Good. We'll be in touch."

Carter let the two of them out. After long moments, he thought he heard car doors close and a car slip away from the curb. He returned to his computer desk and opened the bottom drawer. Dipping his hand in, he pulled out the utility disk with the bright red label.

He popped it into the computer, brought the photo up again, and stared.

Chapter 16

Two hours outside of L.A., the air cleared, the sounds of the highway and the electricity which ran air conditioners, radios, TVs, pool pumps, telephones, refrigerators, hair dryers, you name it, ceased its incessant hum. *Oh,* Stephen thought, *there are lines here, even high-voltage lines, but the traffic they manage, the population they cater to are so thin it scarcely matters.*

One of the eeriest things after the Northridge quake, he remembered, was the total absence of electrical sound. A few car alarms pierced the air, but everything else was dead quiet at first. Then the dogs began to bark. Then, from the shifting dust, people emerged wailing.

But, oh, the heavenly quiet for those first few shocked moments.

That made Arrowhead even better. It took no natural disaster for it to quiet. He sat in the Jag, car door open, and just breathed. The air did not smell quite as fresh, but then it was late May. Even up here in the mountains, the lack of rain was keenly felt. It would be dry, dusty, and even somewhat smog-tinged, though nothing compared to the basin he'd just driven out of. Going back, when he went back, he would hit that dingy brown curtain and, for just a moment, he would wonder if the fires had begun, but there would probably be none. The haze so thick it could be cut with a knife was just the normal air hanging over the basin. It would be sucked all across the continent clear to Denver, under the right atmospheric conditions, as if Denver didn't have its own problems with smog.

Hotchkiss sighed and scrubbed his face with his hand. He blinked several times to clear his eyes, then smiled as the mountain home focused in his sight. He loved his mountain retreat. He called it a condo, to avoid speculation about its worth, but it was a house, all his, all three stories, meandering and stacked and built in a most unconventional way on the sharp hillside overlooking the lake. He'd bought the house in foreclosure several years back when the real estate market had absolutely crashed to a ten year low and interest rates had plummeted afterward, though the second mortgage had been straining. Then his grandmother had died and the strain was gone, and he was eternally grateful he had not missed this window of opportunity.

He reached around back for his duffel and slid out of the car. This was his haven, this was home, this was where no one else could reach him or touch him. He had no phones here, though his cell phone, if he left it on, could function. He didn't think he would even turn it on today. This afternoon, this day, these last rays of sunlight, he intended to enjoy.

Tomorrow morning he would think about what to do.

Hotchkiss threw his keys on the foyer table and locked the door behind him. Through this section of the house, he could see the sunken living room with its fireplace, and beyond, the deck.

Fallen branches and small, rusty piles of needles littered the deck. A few pinecones had eddied to a stop in the deck corners. He could sweep for a while, just enjoying the rhythm of the corn straws across the redwood, or he could go upstairs, fill the spa, and wait for it to heat.

That sounded better.

He took a detour through the kitchen, found some imported beer still cold in the refrigerator, popped the cap, and carried it with him. The mountain air had made his mouth feel like it was full of cotton and the beer tasted great. This would be a premium day after all. Peaks and valleys, peaks and valleys, all life was peaks and valleys. Guess it took a valley to make anyone appreciate a peak.

Upstairs, the wing took a sharp turn, and then wound around. The guest rooms and first set of bathrooms and storage closets were here. He opened a door which looked as though it belonged to a pair of additional closets and, two at a time, took the stairs to the third and master floor. The wood creaked as if welcoming his step. He could

smell the faint scent of the cedar lining the closet even before he
opened the door to the master suite.

It was not opulent, despite the dhurrie carpet and several lamb
rugs scattered over the planked flooring. The massive bed, the dresser,
and armoire were all in Danish modern, spare and clean of line. He
tossed his duffel onto the bed and went straight to the bathroom,
which was a corner of the suite. The cobalt-colored tile bathroom
beckoned, but he stepped past it to another deck, hidden completely
from any other aspect of the house, and began to fill the spa. A squirrel ran along the railing, flipped his tail when spray from the tub
caught it, and ran away chattering. Stephen set the heater as well,
not hot, for he wanted it tepid, then returned to the bedroom to unload his duffel.

He paused when his fingertips came across the software. He took
the laser disk, then Frisbeed it across the room into a shadow-
darkened corner. He would deal with it when he felt like it. Tomorrow. Perhaps later tonight. Maybe he would roast it in the fireplace,
then sink its warped remains in the lake. He stripped down to swimming trunks, finished unpacking and laying out clothes for the next
day. The massive cedar-lined closet filled the room more fully with its
aromatic scent.

The spa shut off when it reached its fill line. Stephen lay down on
the bed and waited for the heater to bring the water up to its preset
temperature. He stared at the ceiling, rough-hewn beams painted a
soft, yet very dark blue, with ivory, amorphous stars splattered here
and there. It was not unlike the sky and cloud-filled ceiling his
mother had painted in his room when he was very young, only this
room held a touch of dark mystery, a brush of the unknown, a hint
of New Age mysticism. He was staring at it when he fell asleep.

The sky's glow had turned to pumpkin when he woke, its harvest
glow slanting over the floorboards and through the window shutters.
Hotchkiss blinked. His tongue felt thick and his throat was dry again.
The room's ceiling had darkened as well, casting long purple shadows into the far end of the room, nearly obliterating the bathroom.
He sat up, massaging the back of his neck, thinking that the spa
would be ready by now. He could almost imagine the surge and pulse
of the water over his aching body. It would soothe away anxieties,
cool his brow. . . .

"Time you were awake, Hotchkiss."

A cramping pain shot through his neck as he swung about in alarm. From the far depths of the bedroom's shadows, a pearlized planet gleamed, a shimmering diskette that rose and tracked through the air as if levitated. He could only see the man-shape that held the disk vaguely, smokelike, in the beyond.

His heart thumped. His voice leaped brashly ahead of his other emotions and fears. This was his territory, his sanctuary! "How'd you get in here?"

"Easy enough. You see—" and the diskette came slinging at him across the room, slicing through the dusk like a pendulum of the Inquisition. He ducked and batted it away.

"We not only know who you are, we know where to put our finger on you any time we want you."

"Who the hell are you?" His voice rose, near to breaking, the cords in his throat aching from the effort to keep it steady.

It moved forward, and the stray column of afternoon light that moved across its face lit up a horror which made Hotchkiss gasp into strangled silence. It was nothing human, not the eyes, not the harshness of its metallic shell, not even the mouth. A hooded sweatshirt was drawn tightly about it and even as Stephen gargled his panic, he thought, *Mask. It's got to be a mask.*

But it looked like no mask he'd ever seen. It took another step forward, back into striped shadow.

"Don't play games with us," the being warned. "We don't want to have to play games with you."

"I'm not—"

"You ran this morning."

"I—I don't like to be pressured. Whatever else you may think of me, I . . . I vote my conscience."

The being shifted. Its massive shoulders shrugged back, the chin of the horrendous face rose, and it began to laugh, as if hugely amused. Stephen felt stung. It pierced through his fear. The thing was laughing at him! It knew his darkest secrets, it thought to manipulate him by them, and now it laughed at him!

Hotchkiss shied the diskette away from himself, back at the intruder, who slapped it down and then stamped a heavy foot upon it, grinding it down into the floor.

"Whatever you want from me, I won't do it."

"Oh, I think you will. After all, Hotchkiss, we both share a love for children. Children are the future, the reason for everything that we do. They are the hope, the potential." The shadowy being shuffled a step closer. The diskette under its feet shattered into a thousand sparkling crystals. It looked down. "What a shame. But there are more where that came from. With your name and self within it. A truly personalized program of porn and perversion." It laughed again, as if amused by its own cleverness.

"It's not as if we're asking so much of you. We're not asking for more air pollution, or money laundering, or contract kickbacks. We're not asking for racial discrimination or union shortchanging. We're asking for some overdue honesty, Hotchkiss."

Hotchkiss tried to swallow. He couldn't quite manage enough spit to do it, and ended up choking. The strange-faced beast waited patiently until he caught his breath.

"This time," he got out.

"Well, of course. We've put too much time and effort into this for a one-shot deal. You're very astute, Hotchkiss. I don't know what we have planned for your future, but I'm sure that we have a future planned for you."

Stephen rubbed his throat. "I can't do it."

"Oh, we think you will. You've worked too hard to upset the apple-cart this far along, haven't you? We're not that unreasonable. We won't ask much of you, in the long run. We've worked too hard, as well." The intruder stepped backward abruptly. Shadows blurred.

Hotchkiss blinked. He jumped off the bed, ran forward, running into . . . nothingness. He found the light switch and flooded the room with yellow-gold illumination.

Nothing.

"Where the hell are you?"

Emptiness answered him.

Hotchkiss stood, breathing raggedly, for long moments. From outside, he thought he heard the faint sound of a car engine starting up and pulling away. Sound traveled far on the quiet mountainside.

"I won't do it!" he screamed. His throat tore with the sound.

A mountain breeze came in off the balcony. It carried a high altitude chill with it. The skin on his forearms prickled with gooseflesh.

Sure he would.

He had too much to lose.

Walking like a broken thing, he shuffled across the room, heading for the spa. Sharp cutting particles ground into the soles of his fish-belly white feet, but he scarcely noticed it. Did not see the faint trail of blood as he stepped into the spa.

He had to think. Had to. Had to.

Hotchkiss lowered himself into the water, oblivious to the red ribbon swirling about him as he turned on the jets. The water churned, late afternoon had become sunset, its own pinks and roses spilling across him, over the foaming water, tinting the side of the deck and house.

The water felt tremendously good. He settled into it, letting it rise up over his shoulders, lap up against his neck. He would relax first, then think.

He never felt the gaping wound in the sole of his right foot, bleeding steadily into the foam. The purpling shadows of the dusk off the lake colored everything.

Hotchkiss sighed and let himself bleed away into the bubbling water.

Jack Trebolt leaned his hip against the worn linoleum corner of the Fat Boy burger counter and knocked off the last of a tepid cup of coffee. The coffee, like the stand's burgers, was best tossed down steaming hot . . . colder, they both tended to congeal. He ran his tongue over the front of his teeth to clean them. The sun was lowering over the smog-tinged cityscape. He eyed the horizon idly, then checked his watch. Dinner must be over. He wondered what McKenzie had had to eat. Something fattening, he supposed, something which would make her hips bulge out like saddlebags and drop her butt down to the back of her knees. Or maybe, since this was California, she'd have gotten sushi and sprouts instead of meat loaf and mashed potatoes.

Grinning at his wit, he pushed away from the food counter and sauntered across the broken asphalt lot to his car. In the privacy of his door-dented vehicle, he pulled out his phone to make a call.

It was answered on the second ring. "Mount Mercy Hospital."

He smoothed his voice. "This is Reverend Michaels. I understand one of my parishioners was admitted last night, poor girl. I don't have her room number, but her name is Smith, McKenzie Smith."

"Just a moment and I'll connect you," the helpful woman offered.

In a moment, there was another ring, muted, softer. He counted them. *A-one ringy dingy, a-two ringy dingy, a-three ringy dingy.* Why McKenzie must be a real little sleepyhead tonight, and the sun not even down.

He recognized her drowsy voice when she picked up.

"Hello?"

"How'd you like your present?"

Blurred, confused, Mac repeated, "Hello?"

"It's me, Mac. How'd you like that little bit of home I brought to you?" He laughed dryly. "Well, there's more where that came from. You see, we miss you, me and Cody. We figure you ought to be back home. We're doin' what we can to bring you back. Of course, Cody has his heart sunk into it."

"Jack!"

"You remember me. Having a nice rest, Mac? I just called to tell you. . . ." His voice dropped involuntarily, dropped to that hard cold place inside of him where he sometimes had to live. . . . "I just called to tell you it'll be a long, cold day in hell before you walk away from me. Hear that? Don't ever think you can walk away from me!"

The cell phone did not give him the intense physical satisfaction of slamming the receiver down, but he did hear a shocked cry from McKenzie before he disconnected. He must have sat in the car grinning like a fool for a good ten minutes before he put the car in gear and headed to Motel 8.

Moreno called from home. He charged it to the office card, but it was late, and he'd put in enough hours, and he sat in the little den of his ranch-style California stucco-sided home and looked at the plastic evidence bag while the phone rang somewhere in rain-soaked Washington. He'd have to refrigerate it and wondered if his wife would put up her usual fuss, then give up and hide it in the back to keep the kids from seeing it. Though, truth to tell, he wasn't sure what kind of evidence this would be. It certainly didn't prove McKenzie Smith or Fordham or Trebolt or whatever she liked to call herself hadn't come to blows with her father. If anything, it might lean toward the "had."

He became aware that the phone had not been answered by the fourth ring. Automatically he checked his watch to verify the time, wondered what time it was in Washington, chastised himself for being so damn stupid about the time zones, reminded himself that, as the thirteen-year-old like to remind him, at his age brain cells were dying by the dozens, and stayed on the line. This was a family phone, and if the Whiteside family were anything like his, a ring-through was a wonder in itself. It ought to be, even with call waiting, terminally busy.

So maybe the family went out for burgers.

In that case, the answering machine ought to be on.

But nothing picked up. *Tsk*ing impatiently, Moreno settled in for the long haul, knowing that if there were an answering machine but it had been turned off absentmindedly, if it was a newer model, it would turn itself on by the twelfth ring or so.

And, if they didn't have an answering machine, the incessant ringing was probably driving the family pet out of its gourd.

Moreno's stubby fingers strayed over the evidence bag again. Trebolt had said his wife had killed the family dog. He didn't buy that. Women very seldom killed anything out of rage, and when they did, unfortunately, it was generally their children. But by far, when it came to domestic violence, the evidence pointed to the man of the house. It was he who rose to the testosterone level of professional athletes during the Super Bowl, World Series, Olympics, World Wrestling Federation, you name it. It was he who could not stand to be disrespected, ignored, hassled, or hampered by family demands.

Ten rings.

So what was she doing with this ghoulish piece of flesh in her hand, clutching it as though it were a teddy bear?

Eleven rings.

Moreno sighed. He'd eaten a big dinner, but he was still hungry, something unsatisfied nibbling at his edges. He ought to go back on his diet. If he had to chase somebody down now, he'd be out of breath in two blocks, hell—

The line clicked. "Hello, this is the Whiteside residence. If you've called for (and the individual's voice spoke each subject's name), John, Sarah, Terry, or Freddie, please leave a message after the beep. Sorry we missed you!"

Good old Washington, where people weren't afraid to say they were gone. Moreno listened to a brief stretch of music, something scratchily sounding like the theme to *Raiders of the Lost Ark,* and then came a faint beep.

He left his message, couched as carefully as he could to not alarm, but to make an impression as to the importance of responding, then hung up.

He wondered when the Whitesides would be home.

Chapter 17

He made a copy of the disk and waited for Dolan to show up to pick it up. Both of them had worried that the Feds might have Carter staked out, but Dolan said he'd taken care of it. Even so, Carter was a little surprised when the doorbell rang and he answered it, to find Dolan dressed as a pizza delivery boy, passing him through a savory smelling pizza box out of the thermal envelope. He looked the part of a delivery boy, spotty face, ill-gotten haircut, his shirt tucked in sideways.

Dolan palmed the disk and a five dollar tip as Carter passed it over. He grinned. "I oughta deliver pizza more often."

Carter pried open the corner of the box. He wrinkled his nose. "Next time, no mushrooms."

"Why not?"

"They're slimy. If God had wanted mushrooms on a pepperoni pizza, He would have put them into the pepperoni along with God knows what else is in it."

Dolan beamed. "Next time, order Chinese. I know this great place up on Hill—"

Carter interrupted, "Don't you think we're carrying this a little too far? If I am being watched by Feds, by now they must think we're exchanging phone numbers."

"Oh. Right." Dolan tucked the thermal envelope under his arm. "I'll have your photo tomorrow afternoon. Early-ish."

"Good-ish," Carter answered, and shut the door in his face.

Hot pizza and cold beer. A near perfect dinner. He sat in his recliner, put the pizza and his beer down on the wooden tray table next to it, and thumbed on the remote.

Three slabs later, he had to admit that picking the mushrooms off was defeating him. His taste buds adjusted to them slowly, or perhaps the beer was overcoming a natural aversion. As he chewed and looked the box over, a certain fact had become self-evident. One, Dolan had brought an extra large pizza and two, he wasn't going to be able to make much more in the way of inroads on it.

Besides which, there was a certain congeniality in eating pizza, a camaraderie lacking when baching it. Carter sucked down the rest of his beer. Eating it alone beat not eating at all. It even beat eating a regular dinner, if hospital food were involved.

He thought of McKenzie Smith. He wondered what it would be like to have her sitting across the table from him, wrapping strings of hot cheese around her fingers and tongue, tucking the triangle of pizza into her mouth and smiling. Wiping off corner dabs of tomato sauce from her mouth. Leaning toward him, smelling slightly of parmesan and oregano and pepperoni. . . .

"Shit." Carter put down his empty. It was a shame to let a good pizza go to waste. He vaulted out of his chair and into the kitchen, where he found a substantial roll of aluminum foil, left over from Thanksgiving and turkey, probably. He covered the pizza box with its silvery sheen and then, somewhat impishly, found an old Christmas bow in the corner of the living room, blew off the dust bunnies, and taped it in the middle of the box.

Smelling redolently of pepperoni pizza, Carter attracted a few stares as he went up in the hospital elevator. A surgeon dressed in greens stared at him intently, before breaking into a smile and saying, "I hope your buddy appreciates that."

"He will if I can do an end run around the nurses."

"If not, bring it to the cardiac lounge on the second. I missed dinner." The heart surgeon got out a floor before he did.

He knew McKenzie had been moved, but Joyce Tompkins had left word for him with the new room number. Almost diagonally across the unit, the door to her room was closed. Dinner had come and gone. The nurses were gathering the carts of empty trays to take back to the kitchen. As visiting hours were still in effect, they paid little or no attention to him, even when he slipped past the door marked "Restricted."

She lay in a clump of sheets, facing away from the door, toward the curtained window bank. The room had a smell to it, a smell that he did not like, and liked even less after he identified it. The last occupant of this room had had a lingering illness, and died here. He wondered if she could sense it, too.

He dropped the pizza box on the portable tray table, the foil bursting open as he did so, filling the room with the smell of pepperoni and cheese. "I don't like eating alone. How about you?"

She stirred and turned about in a tangle of covers, her eyes drooping and weary. The eye which had threatened that morning to swell closed had already begun to heal, going purple with yellowish streaks, the swelling nearly gone. "Already had dinner," she managed, her voice thick.

They'd sedated her. Carter felt disappointment drop into his guts, where it simmered along with other feelings he didn't seem to be responsible for. "Sure, but did you eat?"

"Not . . . much."

"Come on, come on. Besides, I owe you an apology."

"Again?" She gave a humorless smile. "Most people just bring flowers."

Despite the sedation, there was a hard glitter as she focused on him. He felt himself shrink a little under the examination. To her his failure must have been just one of many. He waved the pizza box seductively, wafting the aroma.

"Smells like a peace offering."

"Smart girl."

"You're not doing a story on me? Evening edition or maybe you string for the *National Enquirer?*"

"Ouch." He screwed his face up. "That hurt. No. I'm not doing a story. As a matter of fact, you're wasting my valuable time."

"Oh I am, am I?" A slightly amused look replaced the vulnerable one. "What do reporters do when they have to have dinner?"

"Sit up and pay attention." He leaned over the railing, found the TV control. "The Dodgers are still on the road, but they're broadcasting the Angels tonight. They're still chasing the Rangers for first."

"It's early in the season. Never get excited until after the All-Star break," she said faintly.

"Oh, another baseball fan, huh? Or just a critic?"

She shrugged, winced a little as if it hurt, then sat up, hugging her knees.

The TV set warmed up and the game came on, with the announcer saying earnestly, "The Angels roared out of their hottest spring training ever, slowed down a little, but now they're back in the hunt for first place as June is just around the corner. . . ."

She gave a lopsided smile. "Same old Angels."

He agreed. "Like a house on fire until the All-Star Break."

"My dad . . ." she swallowed carefully. "My dad always wanted to see a Freeway World Series."

"Never happen. It's a conspiracy. The Dodgers win, the Angels lose. The Angels win, the Dodgers lose. It's an unwritten law of the franchise." He passed a decently warm piece of pizza on a napkin to her. "It's a little known fact."

She wrinkled her nose. "Mushrooms on pepperoni?"

He laughed and settled back to watch the game. She managed two slices, he ate three more and the last couple were snagged by the night charge nurse who dropped in to see who was visiting. She recognized Carter from the heart transplant story and backed out quietly, once bribed.

He watched McKenzie neatly lick the last of the pizza juice from her fingers, dainty as a kitten grooming itself.

"That was good," she admitted. "But I expect chocolate if you want me to forgive Moreno."

"Moreno? He giving you a hard time?"

She dried her hands on a cloth napkin. "He doesn't believe me. None of them do."

"Did you trash the room?"

McKenzie shot him a look, almost of betrayal, then shook her head. The meal seemed to have revitalized her slightly. Her speech sharpened, her eyes brightened. "As if I would want to. Jack was here. In fact, he left me something—" She began to search among the blankets. "He sent it in a card with the flowers—" She picked and looked, then gave up with a frustrated sigh. "I can't find it."

"A threatening note?"

"A piece of my dog's ear."

He had been knocking back one of her multiple cartons of apple juice and choked as it went down his windpipe. She sat and watched as he caught his breath. "A . . . what?"

"I had a dog. I've always had dogs, so there's like this big empty hole in here without one," she made a fist over her chest, "so Jack let me get this golden retriever pup. Cody. Biggest feet you've ever seen. A good dog. Jack came home early from a trip. Came home mean. I don't know why, I never knew why. Cody got between us, tried to protect me, so Jack—Jack carved him up. So I cleaned up the kitchen and buried my dog and as soon as Jack left the house, I left, too. I don't know how he found me. I haven't spoken to my father since I left high school. He wasn't someone you'd think I'd come back to. But Jack found me. And he brought a souvenir." She looked at her empty hand. "He told me he had more. Bits and pieces of my dog. . . ." She cleared her throat. "They gave me a sedative, y'know. So I've been just sort of lying here, sleeping, drifting in and out and you know what I keep thinking of, what I think I'll find when I wake up? I think I'm going to find his head on the pillow next to me, just like that guy in *The Godfather* did his racehorse."

He watched her shudder. He hadn't had a dog in a long time. With his lifestyle, a cat was more suitable, but even that was difficult. There was neutering, traveling, adjusting to new apartments and cities every few years. His last cat had gotten disgusted and wandered off, found a new home. He knew because the adopted owner had called the ID tag's number, asked about shots, and refused to return him, saying the cat was obviously happier at his place. He would have liked to dispute that, but knew the finder was probably right.

"Dogs can be like a member of the family," he said, finally, inadequately.

"Yeah." She held her breath for a moment. "I miss him. There are times when—when I still think he's here, close to me." Then, "I never once imagined a pizza box."

She reminded him of the punching clown he'd had as a kid. Knock her clean over and she still bounced up. Looking at her, seeing anew the marks from the past few days, he was struck by the irony of that.

"Look, it doesn't matter if Moreno doesn't believe you as long as Joyce does. She'll fight like a tiger for you."

Mac wrapped a corner of the sheet around her finger. Her gaze strayed to the television screen where Tim Salmon came up to bat and hit a hard line drive that he stretched out to a double for the Angels. "Did she tell you they're sending me to psychiatric tomorrow?"

That would have scared him, and he thought he could tell that it scared her. "How do you feel about that?"

"Joyce says it's okay. Actually, it's probably the best way to prove I didn't flip out. A few tests and I'm out of there, right?"

"Probably."

"And when my father comes out of the coma, he can tell them what happened." Her eyes went to the television screen again, tracking the game.

"Any word on his condition?"

She shook her head. Then she said, "Do you know your fingers twitch when you talk to me?"

He felt his face warm. "Old habit," he answered. "I learned to type the hard way, practice, practice, practice. I still do it, unconsciously. I'm typing our conversation even as we speak."

"That's not good."

"Why?"

"You're not paying full attention to me. Half your mind is directing your fingers what keys to hit."

"Half? Even a chimpanzee can type with only a quarter of his brain."

"Maybe a quarter, then." McKenzie laughed. "It could be worse. Your nose could twitch when you talked."

"My nose?"

"No, seriously." McKenzie waved at him to listen. "I had this girlfriend in high school—she got her nose done for graduation. Done early, actually, so she could enjoy her senior year. And I don't know what they did to it, maybe they made it too short, but every time she spoke, her nose bobbed up and down in time with her upper lip. We stared at it for months, fascinated."

"Another plastic surgery horror tale. This town is full of them." Carter sat back, thinking of older movie queens with faces drawn so tight they looked like Mardi Gras masks.

The phone chimed. McKenzie jumped, rattling the tray table. Carter caught the pizza box as it went sliding. She made no move to answer it. Her face went cold.

"What's wrong?"

"It's Jack," she said. "He's called three times tonight already. I don't know how he gets through. I called downstairs. They said the switchboard closes at ten. So I won't answer any calls until then."

"Let me talk to him. I'd like to aim a shot or two at him." He reached for the receiver.

"No."

"It'll ring forever."

"Why do you care?"

Carter stared at her. There was a unique beauty under her recent wounds. Not Barbie Doll pretty, but strength and intelligence, the way Ingrid Bergman used to be beautiful. God, how he missed seeing movies with Ingrid Bergman in them. "I don't know why I care, I just do," he answered.

Another ring. Then McKenzie reached for the receiver, said, "Hello," and shoved the phone at Carter.

He could hear the man's voice long before bringing the instrument up to his ear, a flat, plain voice, stringing expletives through the air. Carter listened until the first break, then answered, "If the stalking laws don't get you, I will," and broke the connection.

She looked at him, not wide-eyed, she'd been through too much for that, but measuring him. The phone began to ring again, so he unclipped the cord from the end of the handset. It stopped abruptly.

"After ten," he said, "Reconnect it. And give me a call then, okay?"

He stood up. "I know psychiatric sounds scary, but you won't be in the high security ward. They'll put you in the first ward. People will have to sign in and out, and the calls will be screened. In the long run, you'll be safer."

She digested that. "All right." She paused. "Will I get any more pizza deliveries?"

"Chinese next time. I'll see Joyce puts me on the approved visitation list. Okay?"

The baseball crowd erupted in a muted roar. The corner of her mouth curved upward. "Sounds like they approve."

"What about you?"

"I don't have much choice. Hospital food is terrible."

Carter left, his heart, not to mention his stomach, both lighter and fuller than it had been when he came in.

*   *   *

Susan stared at the results from the Smith testing until she thought she would go cross-eyed, then she realized what she saw. From a deeper level of consciousness than she thought possible, the young woman was introducing and directing other stimuli to the program. It was almost as though she'd dropped into REM sleep, but she couldn't have, not even with concussive symptoms. Not and still be receiving the projected program.

What, then, had she done?

And, if she could drop into this state at will, what stimuli could she respond to? Accept. Produce. Interface with.

She tapped the end of the pen on her teeth, as she scanned the readout again. That was one possible explanation for what she saw on the grids. She picked up the phone, called the room to interview her. Someone picked up the line and abruptly disconnected it. Susan stared at the receiver, then redialed. The phone rang interminably, with no one answering it.

Switchboard overload, no doubt. All her questions would have to wait until tomorrow. Tomorrow the subject would be hers. Tomorrow Susan would learn what potential McKenzie Smith had to interface with the subconscious mind . . . and outer stimuli.

She walked across the lab to the sensory deprivation chamber, tapped on the shell, and opened it slowly.

The water inside stirred sluggishly. She could smell its faint chlorine odor from the chemicals which flavored the Los Angeles water supply as the young man within coiled and uncoiled. She checked her watch. "That was an excellent session, Brandon. How do you feel?"

Other than his head, which was kept in a mild restraint (it would be too easy for him to slip down and drown himself, if he wished), he floated effortlessly, surrounded by torpid water, cushioned by the soundless chamber of the egg. He'd screamed the first two times she'd put him in. She hadn't heard it, of course, not once the chamber was closed, but she had heard the telltale hoarseness in his voice when she'd come back for him. She undid the neck restraint, not unlike the pillories used for Puritans.

He didn't like to cooperate with her, this Brandon, and he stared balefully at her now. He liked to be called Brand, as in Brand X, from

Generation X, yet another reflection of his low self-regard. She refused to cooperate with that. "Brandon?"

"Fine," he said.

Actually, if he were into it, she knew the experience could be quite
relaxing. He kept himself bunched up now, and she looked at him
critically, his cheeks turned bright red.

He was at that age, she thought, when personal privacy was at its
utmost premium. She turned away, holding a towel out for him.
Water sloshed as he grabbed it up.

His modesty mattered little to her. The cameras scanning the lab
had already recorded his lithe, naked figure as he'd climbed into the
chamber. She would take the film out before she left that night, take
it home, and ready the video for translation to software, to be digitized and transformed.

The computer age was full of marvels.

From the rustle, she could tell that he was pulling on the soft cotton drawstring pajamas the hospital had issued him. She would tell
him that she had absolutely no interest in his fledgling body, but she
would simply embarrass him more. What did hold an interest for her
was his psyche, wounded and malleable. His fragile ego, his trembling soul. Those she had designs upon. "Ready?" she inquired softly,
before turning around.

He'd barely hissed, "All right," before she was facing him.

He scrubbed a hand across his face defiantly, pushing the hair off
his forehead.

"Good." She checked her watch again, recording the time on her
clipboard. "Ten minutes with the helmet, and then I go home, and
you go back to your room, with control of the remote."

Something sparked deep in Brandon's eyes. "I don't want the
helmet."

He couldn't possibly suspect anything. He was merely being balky.
Susan dropped her clipboard to her hip and reminded him, "We had
an agreement about this."

"I don't like it."

"Brandon, we're here, working for you, but this is like trying to do
a tango with a brick wall. You do want to go home, don't you?"

The intensity in his eyes flickered. Susan realized then that she
had struck at the core of him. He *didn't* want to go home. Not really.

Something there had been so hellish that it had driven him to this desperation in the first place. She softened her voice. "Let me put it this way—you don't want to stay here, do you?"

"No."

"Then you're going to have to work the program. I can't work for you if you don't. Do you want me to leave a note for Dr. Whatley that you're being uncooperative?"

Whatley was the physician who'd committed Brandon to the psychiatric ward.

Sulkily, "No."

"Then let's finish up with ten minutes in the helmet, and we're both off the hook."

She laid her arm gently across his shoulders as she walked him to his room. She could feel the tension in his body as she did.

Brandon had no way of realizing that he was coming along beautifully in her experimentations. No way at all. The ten minutes flew by as if it had wings. Then she secured the software from the helmet in her private safe and got ready to leave.

Humming, she shrugged out of her lab coat and locked her desk. She walked out of the psych ward, the orderly on the front desk smiling at her as she passed through the swinging doors, breaking into song, her voice floating behind her.

"Beautiful dreamer, wake unto me. . . ."

Chapter 18

Brandon waited until he could hear the tuneless humming of the doctor as she left the ward. Then he threw himself out from under the covers of his bed. He ran to the bathroom where he threw up, once, retchingly, so painfully that he hugged his rib cage as his dinner came up. He watched it floating sourly in the toilet before he reached out a shaking hand and flushed it down.

When the water was clear, he kept staring down at it, dizzy and nauseated, afraid that he would have to barf again. *If the guys could see me now, worshiping the porcelain god—Ole Brand X has tossed it again. What'd you lose down there, four eyes?*

He leaned on his wrists and slowly became aware that they did not pain him anymore. They had itched maddeningly for the last few days. He wondered what kind of scars he would have. If he would have to hide them, face all kinds of dorky questions from jerks who should know better than to ask them anyway.

His stomach clenched again. Brand opened his mouth and his throat ached, but nothing came out but strings of drool.

He wiped his mouth and flushed the toilet again anyway. Then he put his head under the sink faucet and rinsed his mouth out, the vomit still bitter tasting. Hospital water wasn't much better. He splashed some on his face and squinted into the bathroom mirror. Strange, to see his face without his glasses. They wouldn't let him have them here. Something about breaking the lenses and using them. He'd told them and told them his lenses were plastic, lighter weight for the thickness, but nobody had paid any attention to him. His right hand balled into a fist and hit the rim of the sink in frustration.

Nobody paid any attention to him at all, except for Dr. Craig, and Brand thought, heck no, he *knew* she was spooky. Oh, she acted like all the other doctors, dressed nice, looked like she didn't know how to sweat, but those eyes of hers. They were like high beams from one of the X-Men. They could see things that other people could only guess at. They sure saw through him.

That was one of the things about her that scared him. He got the feeling she knew everything about him that he knew, and more. All the stuff he didn't know, all the stuff that swam round and round in his skull until he felt like bursting, because he'd never understood any of it, never, but knew it must be awful.

And she seemed to like him anyway, despite the bad stuff, and that bothered him, too, because he didn't know if she liked him because she was a good person and thought he was all right. Or if she liked him because she was some kind of tweaked pervert like he was.

Brand made a face at himself in the mirror. He staggered back to the bed and lay down on top of the covers. He plucked at them nervously. Yeah, Dr. Craig seemed to know everything, even the stuff they never talked about. He'd tried to, once, and she'd just raised her chin and looked him in the eyes, and the words had gone all quiet in him. He not only couldn't get them out anymore, he lost them. He hadn't spoken for most of the rest of the day.

But then he'd realized it didn't matter. She'd known, she must have. And if she didn't, if she'd hadn't, what would she think of him now?

It was those thoughts that kept him awake, made him sick to his stomach, churned everything around worse than a Tornado ride. He'd never had thoughts like that before in his life, not before coming to the hospital, and he didn't know what to do.

He'd never wanted to kill anything before in his life, except possibly for himself, and he'd never thought of what he'd done in that way anyhow. No, he'd done what he'd done because he couldn't stand the pain and emptiness and guilt and hurt anymore. That he'd lived while Grammie and Dad had been taken. He couldn't stand the numb way his mother had begun walking through life, taking care of him, feeding him breakfast, taking him to school, bringing him home, as though it were some kind of joyless life sentence she'd been condemned to.

No, he hadn't tried to *kill* himself. He'd merely tried to cut away the pain. He wasn't trying to hurt anyone. He was just trying to take the hurt away. No one seemed to understand.

What scared him more than anything was that they said they did. That they understood far more than he did, because that was their job. They'd spent years learning it in college and beyond. They understood, and they'd help him. At first, Brand had hoped they couldn't.

Now he was scared stiff one of them could look into his skull and see what kind of monster lived in there. Woke up at night and stirred around. Something that lived in blood and splashed it all over, sloshed through it like he used to do when he was just a kid wading through rain puddles. Something like knives and barbed wire and doing things to soft flesh. . . .

Women.

Brand plucked at the covers again and then yanked them from under him and wrapped them about him. He knew his body was getting older, changing. It was daunting to wake up in the morning with his penis all hard and stiff and hurtful, an ache that took forever to go away. He knew it could happen at school, though it hadn't to him yet. And he knew it had to do with girls, with women, and sex, and fucking. . . .

It was one thing to stare at the girls in his sixth grade class and watch them grow boobs, little buds of soft flesh poking through their T-shirts and blouses until they graduated, finally, to bras. It was always a relief when that happened. It was one thing to stare at the old copy of *Playboy* that he and Mike had picked out of the trash, but this thing that had taken root in his skull like one of the creatures from *Alien*, threatening to burst out. . . .

His stomach roiled again. Brand put his hands to his face, as if he could hold onto everything that way.

All he could dream about was people laid out like so much road kill. It was all getting mixed up together, the throbbing of his growing needs, and the blood, and the violence and torture. . . .

He couldn't tell anyone. He knew they would be horrified. They would shove him away, lock him up for good in some nut hospital, worse than this one.

He grabbed up the remote and turned the TV on, even though the screen was blurry without his glasses. He couldn't go back to sleep, he wouldn't. He tuned in "Nick at Night" where every mom seemed born to the job.

His forearms itched. He scrubbed a hand over the bandages on first one and then the other, faint relief. One thing that he had learned here was that he'd cut wrong. He'd cut across. Next time he'd cut up and down, from the elbow to the palm. That was the way you did it. When you wanted to end the pain. When your head felt like it was going to explode and something terrible was going to come leaping out, when you weren't you anymore.

After dinner hours at Silverado eased slowly from hectic into quietude. Joyce checked her watch and got ready to summarize the points she'd been making to the class of eight who sat and slouched around the living room, listening. They occupied worn-out recliners and sagging sofas and sprawled across pillows thrown on the floor. Their faces were of every color, shaped by every economic sector, and they were universal in that, when she had first begun speaking to them weeks ago, their sole expression had been compounded of fear and fatigue. She normally would not have been out this late without having been home first, but today, as her mama would have said, her plate was full. Full to overflowing.

She thought of blaming Carter Wyndall for her schedule, but she knew better. If not Carter's friend, there would have been someone else for her to take on. There always was. That was the discouraging side of her vocation. There was always another battered spouse, another abused child. She'd like to take a piece of chalk, draw a line, and say, "All right. That's enough. The shit stops *here*." But she knew better.

Her mind working, her mouth on automatic, giving a lecture she gave weekly to five different shelters throughout the county, she finished up, then looked at her watch. "Okay, ladies, what's next?"

"Bathtime," three young mothers said, and slunk out. The rest of her audience checked the wall clock.

"It's Dr. Craig's night."

"Oh? Is it?" Joyce usually didn't overlap with Susan Craig's rounds. "Take a break, then. I don't see her van yet."

She watched the women go, thinking that she might take the opportunity to discuss McKenzie Smith with the doctor before she left. The resistance of the police to treating the case as that of a battered wife frustrated her, though she had to admit that the preliminary investigation gave them little choice. The neighbors had seen no one at the residence but the two of them, and there was a history of family domestic violence.

One of the residents, a lovely dark-haired girl with two small babies under the age of two, came back into the living room with an iced tea for Joyce. Joyce took it, murmuring, "Thank you."

Drucilla would not look up. She shrugged her shoulders and walked away quickly. Joyce watched the young woman as she picked her way through the cluttered, comfortable rooms, never looking up, always looking down as if afraid to see what might be facing her. Joyce sighed and downed the iced tea.

She sat and made notes in her casebook, then looked up and saw the time. She had her own family to think of, Joyce chided herself. Susan Craig was late. A phone call in the morning would have to suffice. She packed her briefcase, drank the last sugary sips of her cold drink, said good-bye to the resident adviser, and left.

As her battered Hyundai pulled around the corner, she did not see the van easing out of a shadowed driveway from the other end of the block.

Susan Craig waited until the advocate's car had rattled out of sight before easing the van into a stop at the curb. Joyce had a lot of savvy. It had been a long day, and Susan did not feel like encountering her. She sat at the curb five long minutes, heat building up inside the van, before opening the door to step out. At the panel doors, she opened both wide, revealing five computer stations, padded chairs, and equipment. At the sound of the panel doors sliding open, there came an echoing whoop of excitement from the house, and the front yard filled with children.

Susan found a smile. The children were not well-dressed, the clothes were hand-me-downs, usually too big and well-worn. WORLD CUP 1994 soccer shirts seemed to be in favor here, the silk-screened letters and designs nearly faded clean away. The biggest boy, with flashing dark eyes and hair pulled back in a slicked-up ponytail, had the *Lion King* shirt, even though it pulled tightly about his armpits and shoulders.

She put a hand up for stillness. The children bustled about, the impacts of their bodies noisy, but their mouths shut.

"Your mothers are first," she said. "I know I'm late, so I can't take too many of you today. But I'll be back. You know I'll be back."

To a chorus of "awwws," she added, "Next time we'll have a kids only day. Okay?"

They screamed approval. Susan reached out, tousled a few heads, slapped palms with the *Lion King,* and turned her attention toward the modest house which bore the ridiculous name of Silverado. She had once asked the resident supervisor, Tricia Gardener, why the name. "If every cloud has a silver lining," the answer had come, "why this place must be a mother lode."

Susan dealt with her clients briskly and efficiently, believing neither in patronizing them nor coddling them. They had made the decision to strike out on their own, changing forever the downward spiral which had been consuming them. She placed each woman at a computer and started the biofeedback program designed to help them combat stress as well as reinforce self-esteem. The lone computer in the corner belonged to the children, and they waited, big eyed, for her to choose the one who would get to play today.

It would be *Lion King,* of course, Donaldo of the flashing eyes, ten years of defiance and sly intelligence, eyes too old inside that cranium. He jumped into the van, avoided the women who were already sinking into beta wave activity, and went straight to his station. He sank into the captain's chair and swiveled it around, waiting for her.

She leaned over, making sure that the station had a full battery pack, and above, her hand brushing across it casually, that the camera was fully focused on the boy. Donnie leaned over the keyboard and picked up the joystick. His shirt bound him.

"Wouldn't you like to take that off? I must have another shirt around here somewhere."

"*Lion King?*" he asked.

"Maybe. Maybe *The Shadow.* Maybe something newer."

He considered it, head tilted, bright eyed like a mockingbird in the garden considering a grub in the grass. The head went from side to side. "Okay," he said, and shrugged out of the shirt.

He had a beautiful body, scarred in only two or three places. The cigarette burns, she recognized, she was uncertain of the cause of the third
scar. Still, they did not matter. The computer which would record and
interpret the data would airbrush those blemishes out. As the camera
scanned his body for later translation into digitization, she took her time
rummaging in a handled shopping bag of old clothing and finally came
up with a *Batman Forever* promo shirt which had never even been worn.

"Wow!" Donnie snatched the bête noire shirt away from her and
pulled it over his head. "This is cool."

"You bet it is. Okay, want to play today?"

His answer was muffled as he strapped on his helmet and slid his
hands into the virtual reality gloves.

Susan smiled widely. "Good." She reached forward and initiated
the program. Frame by frame, layer by layer, she was constructing a
new person from the foundation named Donaldo. When she was
done, she hoped to have learned something extremely important.
Then, she would deconstruct him. Like an onion, she would peel
him back down to his original psyche. Like Brandon at the hospital
ward, this boy was hers, hers as clearly as if she'd birthed him. And
no one, not at Silverado, not at Mount Mercy, had the slightest
inkling of what she was doing, or could do, with the computer terminal, software, and subliminal programming.

She sat back and watched as the boy submerged into his fantasy
world. Children were so important. They were the hidden resource
of the future.

His mother would never enter the van. She leaned inside it now,
her hair a thick burnished brunette, French-braided down her back.
She had done it herself, no doubt, for Susan had often seen her
braiding her hair and that of the others, fingers flashing in intricate
patterns. Graciela had high, delicate cheekbones and wide, dark
eyes. Her lips were not particularly pretty, and she was somewhat
chinless, but her dusky skin had stayed unblemished despite her
youth. She did not look old enough to be Donnie's mother, but
Susan knew that she'd carried him at fourteen, had him at fifteen.

Her ears were pierced up into the cartilage. She wore four studs in
one and six in the other, all tiny gemstones twinkling with a brightness
she would never achieve, not until she tore the veil of shyness from
her face.

"Doctor Craig," she said quietly. "Donnie can't come no more."

Of all the words Susan had expected to hear from her mouth, those astonished her.

"What?"

She frowned. "He can't come no more. I'm leaving. I'm moving out."

This was usually a milestone. "Why, Graciela. That's wonderful."

The young woman would not meet her eyes. She looked around the van. "I've got a place," she said. "For the two of us."

"Are you working?"

Graciela nodded. "I get my license from beauty school next month. I've got work already." She smoothed a wing of soft, lustrous hair from her brow.

"That's wonderful. Have you celebrated yet?"

"No. No one else here knows. I didn't tell nobody." Graciela's tone matched her sullen expression. "So he can't come," she added for the third time.

Susan looked back over her shoulder at Donnie. His face, what could be seen of it under the helmet, was pinched tight in concentration. She'd come so far with him. She took a deep breath and, reaching out, squeezed Graciela's shoulder in encouragement. "You've come a long way. So has Donnie. Tell you what—give me your new address, and I'll try to come by once a week for him."

Graciela's already slim face narrowed. Then, she nodded. "If you don't tell nobody."

She was probably not being released from the program, Susan thought. She was probably leaving to rejoin her ex-boyfriend or a new one. "I can't tell, Graciela," Susan answered brightly. "I'm your doctor, right?"

Graciela took the scrap of paper Susan tore out and handed to her and, screwing her face into lines of concentration that mirrored Donnie's expression, painstakingly wrote out her new address. She shoved it back into Susan's hand. "I'm moving in tomorrow," she said. "Don't tell nobody."

"I won't." Susan watched as the young mother left, shuffling her way across the worn, celery-colored front lawn back toward the shelter house. She put the address into her wallet thoughtfully, wondering how to salvage Donnie from all this.

*   *   *

Hotchkiss felt cold. He sank deeper into the tepid spa so that it became a supreme effort just to keep his jawline above the water. The gentle waves, for the jets had gone off timer long ago—when was it? He had no memory of it—the soft tide left in their wake lapped at his chin. His eyelids had anchors on them. Sunset had left the horizon, and he stared, when he could keep his eyes open, at a velvet shroud sprinkled with crystalline pinpoint of light. The mountain air was so clear, he could even distinguish blue stars from white.

If he cared to.

Stephen Hotchkiss found that he cared less and less, about anything. Even the constant roar of his own pulsing bloodstream in his ears had weakened, leaving him in total peace. There were no worries prickling at him, no nags yelling into his ears, tugging on his arms, images standing in his way. It could only get more peaceful below the water.

His spine sagged and he slipped farther into the tub. He let out a deep sigh, and allowed himself to slide all the way down. The water had a flat iron taste to it, almost bloodlike. He coughed only once as the liquid raced into his mouth and nostrils, a token cough, token of his resistance to the fate awaiting him.

A hand grabbed him by the arm. Water fountained upward with the violence of the attacker. Fingers of steel coiled themselves into his hair and jerked, yanked, pulling him upward, out of the water. Hotchkiss coughed again, weakly, retching wetly down the front of his chest. Night air iced into his face. He blinked numbly, unseeing. Someone muscled him out of the spa and then hefted him over a shoulder. His ears roared as he lay head downward. He heard the floor creak as the man carried him into the bedroom, warm air caressing him, so much warmer than the water had been, and dropped him like a wet sack onto the bed.

"You don't get out of it this easy, Hotchkiss," his rescuer said.

Stephen blinked into the face of the same apparition which had haunted him earlier, but fear had gone. He could not muster any emotion. He rolled over onto his belly, clutching the bedcovers around him for warmth as he began to shiver violently. The hand, skin so hot it felt like it was branding him, grasped an ankle.

"Nasty cut, Hotchkiss."

There was a moment of pain, quite sharp and distinctive, and then the foot was being wrapped.

"We know who you are, and you're not getting away from us this easily."

Hotchkiss retched damply into the corner of the bedspread, moved his face away from it, feeling weak as a mewling kitten. Someone tucked warm and dry covers about his quaking form.

"Don't forget you owe us."

He could not reply.

The floorboards creaked as his tormentor left. He dared not move until the house had grown as still as a mausoleum.

Hotchkiss lay facedown, then realized how close to death he'd come, how close to release and safety, and that he'd been pulled back.

He began weeping. It was not for joy.

Dudley called her from a phone booth. The convenience store lot was busy and he watched the young girls stroll by, seemingly oblivious to his gaze, as the signal rang. She picked up on the car phone, he could hear the difference in transmission.

"Our boy tried to go down for the count," he informed her.

"No." There was a pause which might have been pensive, or simply interference. Then, "I wouldn't have guessed it of him. Before or after your visit?"

"After, I went back because I had my doubts."

"He was not successful."

"No."

"Was there . . . official interference?"

"No. I handled it."

"But you're sure of the attempt?"

"Yes."

"He can't be relied upon, then."

Dudley watched a Vietnamese girl go by, her long dark hair like ravens' wings fluttering almost down to her waist. "I wouldn't think so," he answered, watching her, thinking about her. "I made sure he knew he owed us, but he doesn't have much spine."

"I rely on your judgment. You know that."

The girl turned slightly on one heel, her tanned legs bare to the mid-thigh hem of her miniskirt. She looked at him askance. She knew that he watched her from the phone booth. Dudley turned away then. She would say something to somebody, perhaps. Even if he trailed her home and waited until the darkest hours of the night, someone might remember he'd been watching her earlier. *Ta-rah-rah-boom-ti-ay, you won't stay free that way.* . . . He brought a match out and lit it, concentrating on its beauty. He closed the song out of his mind and found words. "Use him while you can."

"I will. Go home. Have a good dinner. We'll talk later."

She cut the connection without any sentimentality. He hung up, too, and left without giving anyone another glance. She would reward him, she always did. She had taught him patience to go with his cunning.

As for herself, she would have to check into alternate plans. A return to the hospital seemed advisable. She would need the quiet, the relatively laid-back attitude of the night shift to help her decide what to do about Ibie Walker.

McKenzie woke in the darkness of the room. The TV had gone off. Only the light board behind her glowed. She lay in the hospital bed a moment, letting wakefulness chase her dreams away. The night nurse had given her sleeping pills. They had dissolved sourly in her stomach, heartburn creeping up the back of her throat. She got out of bed carefully and made her way to the bathroom, only a little dizzy.

The night-light in the bathroom threw her face into sharp relief. Bruises shadowed it even more starkly, but she could see both eyes were wide open now. She'd always been a quick healer. She could not stand to see herself. Mac ran her hand through her hair. Surely they'd let her shower tomorrow morning. Her skin crawled at the thought of the sweat and dirt ground into her hair, not to mention how the rest of her must smell. Even now she could catch the pungent odor of pizza and sweat.

She leaned over, ran the water until it warmed and shampooed her hair with the hand soap, lathering and rinsing, and lathering again until she felt human. Then she bathed all over again, toweling off carefully with the one small towel allotted her. She felt human for the first time in days.

Once back in the bed, she reconnected the phone and lay down. She thought of calling out and changed her mind, because it was after ten, and she knew Sarah panicked at calls after nine, wondering who'd died.

I did. But I'll be all right soon.

Sarah and Seattle were already a lifetime away. It was as though she'd shed a life, the way a snake does a skin. She wondered if reptiles felt cleansed, as well as raw and new.

For a dizzying, disorienting second, it felt and sounded almost as though something had crossed the room and jumped onto the foot of the bed, settling its comforting weight against her ankles and the back of one calf. Just as Cody had always done, jumping into bed with her. In bed if she was alone, on the floor of the closet among her shoes if Jack was home.

She accepted the phenomenon and then clenched her jaw shut, realizing that nothing was there, nothing could be there. If she sat up and reached down to her toes, she would not encounter any soft, silky hide and ears, wet nose nuzzling her back, paw pads scratching at the covers to get comfortable again.

So she did not sit up. Mac closed her eyes and held tight to the ghostly sensation, knowing it would evaporate with logic. She did not feel like being alone. And whatever it was, it was better than a veil of blood being drawn over anything she looked at.

The phone shrilled. She jumped at its noise in the stillness and grabbed it up.

"How's the dreamin'?"

Her throat closed. She could not speak for a moment.

"Miss me?" Jack laughed.

Her breath squeaked in her chest as she inhaled deeply. "I'm not coming back. Leave me alone."

"You've been watching too many soaps, Mac. This is real life, you and me. I want you to come home with me, where you belong."

Her eyes squeezed shut. She could see the kitchen floor, Cody's life bubbling across it. She could smell it on her hands, her clothes, as she tried to scrub it up. Bile rose in her throat again. She did not know where she belonged, but it wasn't there.

She denied him. "No."

"You liked college. What if you enroll full-time next semester? I could make an extra run or two, pay for the tuition. You'd like that, wouldn't you?"

Her voice husked. "Jack, I can't go back with you."

His tone changed from coaxing to belligerent again. She winced at the volume coming from the phone receiver. "Why not? And who the hell was that who answered the phone last time? You got a policeman sitting up there with you? You got a man in there with you, and you wearing nothing but one of those ass-open flimsy little hospital gowns? Who was that?"

She didn't want to involve Carter. "It was . . . nobody. It wasn't anybody. I don't have anybody up here with me."

"Well, Mr. Nobody got real smart-ass with me. You tell him to mind his own business. Or, better yet, you tell him to watch out for me."

"I don't want to talk about this anymore, Jack. Just go away and leave me alone. I'll forget anything happened. You can go home. But I won't go with you."

"You'll go if I have to drag your carcass. And don't count on your Mr. Nobody to protect you."

He sounded so close. So confident. She felt cold all over.

"How did you—the switchboard's closed. How can you even call me?"

He laughed again, that low and humorless laugh. That mean laugh. "It's closed to outside calls. But not to me. I'm on the inside, babe. I'm right here. I'm watching out for you."

Chapter 19

Rasheed Tompkins struggled out of the garage with a basket of freshly dried laundry. He put a lean, thirteen-year-old shoulder against the door to close it behind him and waited a minute in the breezeway, the smell of clean clothes filling his senses. From his vantage point, he could see his mother as she came up the driveway and went into the house from the front, illuminated by their amber porch light. Her steps had been weary. He counted them to the kitchen counter/desk where she would drop keys, purse, and pager, and then into the family room where his brothers and sisters and aunt were sprawled watching some stupid musical on the Disney channel.

He started into the kitchen from the garage side, banging his way into the house.

"Hey, Mom!"

She was late, really late, but they'd left her some dinner and now he'd have to do the dishes, just when he thought he was off the hook. He balanced the clothes basket on his hip for a moment, long enough to pinch the pager button to the "off" position. Just a few hours, that's all he wanted from his mom. Just that, nothing more. He'd done it once or twice before. When the movie was over, he'd duck back in, get a soda, and turn the pager back on, but for now, their mother belonged to *them*. He was tired of the problems of others taking her away. He had his own crap to deal with.

He took four giant gangling strides out of the kitchen, into the heart of his family, and dropped the laundry basket in front of his sister. "Your turn to fold," he announced. "I got dishes to do."

Joyce turned her face to him. His mom was beautiful, he thought, if old, and that smile of hers could ripen the tomatoes he had growing out back. "Rasheed. You did a good job tonight."

"Thanks. Want your dinner?" He needed to keep her out of the kitchen for a while.

"In a minute. Let Lucy get it for me. How was practice today?"

"I sank forty-two percent from the free throw line."

She nodded. "Getting better."

He wrinkled his face. "I still won't be tall enough. Not no seven foot."

"Not any seven foot," she corrected mildly. She put an arm around his waist and drew him close for a modified teenage hug. "Neither is Jason Kidd, and look what he's doing. Remember, those big guys aren't so agile. You've got quickness. Develop your shots and you'll do anything you want to."

And she pulled him closer to finish the hug. For a second, a tiny second, he felt a prickle of guilt for doing what he'd done to the pager. It didn't last.

Jack said cagily, "You don't know where I'm going to be. So I want you to treat me nice when I call."

Mac closed her eyes tight, unbelieving. She wanted to scream, but knew if she did, no one would be on the phone by the time the nurse came running in. This couldn't be happening to her.

"Do you hear me, darlin'?"

"I hear you," she responded flatly. "You come near me, Jack, and I'll kill you. I don't know how I'll do it, but I will."

That low, raspy laugh. "You just like to fight, sweetheart, so we can kiss and make up. You know you do. Besides, I not only know where you are, I know where your daddy is. You wouldn't want anything to happen to Daddy, would you? Think about it."

Her throat stayed so tight she could barely swallow spit, but she got the words up. "You think about this. I hate you, you son of a bitch. Touch me again, or my father, or anyone else I even *know*, and I'll hunt you down. And that's a promise." She slammed the receiver down and jerked the cord out.

Her heart thumped wildly in her chest like a frightened rabbit. She sat up in the hospital bed and flung her legs over the side. She couldn't stay. She couldn't!

Hands shaking so hard she could barely do it, she plugged the cord back in long enough to dial a number. Her lips felt dry and cracked, but her tongue was just as dry and she put a hand out, searching for a glass of water on the swing-out table. She curled fingers around it just as the phone number answered abruptly. She punched in the beeper number Joyce had given her, and then her number.

Mac drained the glass of water. It trickled down her dusty throat, more irritating than soothing. The phone rang, too soon to be Joyce. She picked it up and disconnected it, but not before she heard a hooting laugh. There was no way she could avoid Jack and still get Joyce's call. She stared at the cord in her hand, then looped it around the rail.

She was a sitting duck. Mac pushed herself out of the bed. The room swung abruptly, then stilled as vertigo throbbed through her skull. Her feet went icy and for a breathtaking moment, she thought it had something to do with her concussion, then she realized the floor was simply cold.

She didn't think anything could be colder than the way she felt. It hadn't seemed cold moments ago when she'd gone in and bathed. Yet now, it iced its way up her joints and into her muscles and nerves until she felt frozen, like some ice queen. No feelings, no life. Dead.

Numb.

What was wrong with her? Why couldn't she move, react, defend herself like a normal person?

Bases loaded, no one out.

She could react to that. She could defend herself against that threat.

Dad coming home drunk, Mom upset.

That she could deal with.

Jack in the hospital. Mac bit her lip. She wished she had her old bat. It was probably lying in Moreno's evidence locker, dusted with soot for fingerprints.

The phone sounded again. The noise made her jump, shattering the icy shroud which had imprisoned her. She stared at the receiver. It had to be Jack again. She wouldn't know if she didn't answer.

Mac reached for it, curled her fingers in midair and snatched her hand back. She didn't want to know. She only knew that if Jack was in the hospital, she couldn't stay.

Her cotton shift drooped off one shoulder. Mac pulled it back up. She wasn't going anywhere dressed in a gown with her tush hanging out the back. The phone rang two more times, then went silent.

He'd guessed she wasn't going to answer it. Either he would leave her alone for a while . . . or he would find his way to her room.

There was no way in hell she intended to be there if he did. Mac ran her fingers through her still damp hair. Clothes. Not hers, they were grass-stained and bloody and they would probably reek. She wouldn't get out of the hospital wearing them. Some security guard would probably tackle her and drag her into the ER.

Mac closed her eyes, trying to think. Clothes. In the nurses' lounge. She'd seen the open closet with a uniform, a couple of sweaters, some dry cleaning, hanging there. And there were shoes below, several pairs. She grabbed up the extra gown she'd been using as a robe and bolted for the door, tugging it on as she went.

The phone began to ring again as she went through the door. *Sorry, bud, strike three. Only two more outs, and I'm out of the inning.*

Shannon's clothes were extravagant on her. The pantsuit fit her with enough room to slip in another escapee. Mac looked at herself critically in the mirror. Only the joggers fit well, but the outfit would have to do. It was infinitely better than the gown with the built-in air-conditioning.

Someone had also left makeup in the small bathroom adjoining the lounge. Mac used the hair dryer, fluffing what body she could into hair that seemed as defeated as she had felt ten minutes ago. Then, she carefully put on foundation, patting it tentatively about her bruised face. She eyed herself. Sunglasses were not an option at ten thirty at night. If they were, she might pass. As it was . . . Mac sighed.

"I ran into a door," she said aloud to her mirror image, and grimaced at the sound of her voice. Maybe it would work, maybe not. It wasn't like she was trying to escape prison.

Not yet, anyway.

No one looked up as she entered the elevator. The doors closed on her before she'd decided where to go.

She didn't know where she could go, but she knew she could not leave without trying one last time to see her father. It might be her last chance to say good-bye. She owed him that much. When the chips were down, 3–2, he'd stepped in between her and Jack.

Just like a father should.

She swallowed down a sudden lump in her throat and punched ICU's floor number.

Susan Craig had long ago found out what most cons knew instinctively, that tones of brisk efficiency and mannerism that echoed automatically broke down bureaucracy. She tucked her clipboard under her elbow as she approached the security guard.

"Little late for a round, isn't it, ma'am?" A tired smile fractured across the man's seamed face.

"Actually, I'm early." She looked over the guard's shoulder at Ibie Walker's shrouded form. "He's coming in for speech therapy on the soundboard tomorrow morning."

"The soundboard?" the guard said, drawling slightly. "That that computer thing which makes the voice for you? Ibie going to have to talk like that now?"

"It's probably temporary, but it's hard to tell with stroke victims." Susan tilted her head slightly, engagingly. "I need to measure him for the headgear. Since I'm still on the floor, I thought I might as well do it. It won't disturb him, I'm sure.

The guard made a noise of agreement in his throat. "Ain't nothing much disturbing these two. It's like a morgue in there. Nothing makes noise but those damn monitors."

She gave him a sympathetic smile. "I know it seems like that, but—" and she consulted the chart she'd picked up on the way across the unit. "He's doing well, actually. He's been sedated for rest this evening, tests and therapy tomorrow. As for the other man—" Susan looked across at Walton Smith. "He's being kept under purposely." The doctor had logged in instructions to keep him down to allow the brain swelling to subside.

"If you say so."

She checked her watch again. "Look, I'm going to be here, ten, fifteen minutes. Why don't you go get a cup of coffee? I smelled a fresh batch as I passed the lounge."

The guard shifted restlessly. "You wouldn't mind?"

"Not at all. And you look like you could use the caffeine."

"That's true. I'm here for the duration, until six a.m." He scratched his brow with a blunt fingernail. "Fresh brew, you say?"

"Nothing smells quite like it." Susan held her smile, though her face felt brittle.

"That's the truth. If you don't mind, Doc. . . ."

"I don't mind at all. Any trouble, and I'll holler. You'll just be a couple of doors down the hall, anyway."

He tipped his hat. "I'll be back in a few, then."

She watched him turn the corner on the U-shaped floor and disappear. Then she slipped into the cubicle. Out of habit, she pulled the privacy curtain out and across the foot of the bed, though the cables from the many monitors warped and dragged at the fabric.

Ibie Walker's mahogany color had grayed a bit. The veins on his left arm looked like they'd collapsed on themselves. A telltale bandage revealed the former position of the IV which was now in the right arm, something not normally done on a right-handed person. It was either there, or on the neck, if the veins in the left arm had given out. But, all in all, the councilman looked as though he was resting in peaceful sleep. Susan checked the monitors, confirming what she had read on the clipboard.

The bastard was a tough old rooster. He was going to make it. The doctors earlier that day had determined there was loss of speech and some mild paralysis, but he was expected to recover from both with time. He was scheduled to go to her lab for biofeedback speech therapy, something relatively new in the field. Though she was technically psychiatric, her computer equipment was the most sophisticated in the hospital, and physical therapy often came up to use her facility when called for. Headgear placed on the face about the cheekbone, temple, and jaw translated the minimal muscle movement of the face, fed the movement into a computer and sound bites resulted. It would never replace speech, and, Susan reflected, the remarkable voice which had come out of Ibie Walker with all its witticisms and idiosyncrasies. But it would enable those partially paralyzed to make their needs known, and accomplish a little beyond that. It was a process which needed to be learned, much as an amputee learns to work with a prosthesis, tightening and loosening muscles to operate some of the artificial limb function.

The diagnosis that had seen Ibie ordered to have computer therapy brought him right into her lap. She needn't even be standing here, now, jeopardizing all that she'd worked for. Still . . . she put her hand into her jacket pocket and then reached toward the oxygen flow monitor. A slight adjustment would ensure the slowness of Ibie's recovery. There might be a chance of minimal brain damage, but that did not matter. She needed time to work with him.

Her fingers grasped the dial, preparing to cut back the oxygen by at least half, when the cubicle door opened. Susan froze. She could not see who entered, except for battered white joggers beyond the privacy curtain. Whoever it was had come in for the other patient.

Susan dropped her hand from the dial and withdrew it from her jacket. She grasped Ibie Walker's bony shoulder and squeezed it slightly. "You're doing fine," she said softly. "Tomorrow I'll be working with you."

She reached for the curtain to draw it back and did not see his eyelids dart open for a fearful moment, then shut again.

The curtain came back with a rattling of the hooks which held it upon the rod. Unveiled, the visitor recoiled.

Susan Craig looked intently at the young woman in the nurse's uniform, instinctively sensing that something was wrong, and then the woman's face appeared out of the dim illumination of the unit. Bruises had streaked through her makeup, confirming Susan's reaction.

"What are you doing here?"

"I had to see him." McKenzie took a cautious step backward, toward the exit of the care unit.

Susan folded her arms loosely across her chest. "I take it you haven't been discharged."

"You don't have to say anything to anybody."

Susan felt a muscle in her jaw twitch slightly. She'd probably already lost Hotchkiss. She had no intention of suffering any more setbacks. "That's right, I don't." She gauged the distance from Walker's bedside to where the young woman stood. "But I don't think walking out would be in your best interests. The police, for one, will be less likely to believe any story you tell them."

"They don't believe me now."

"Then you need to convince them."

A dry laugh. "They're not listening."

Susan shrugged. "They weren't listening this morning, either. Why didn't you bolt then?"

"He was out there. Now he's in here."

The note of desperation in her voice piqued Susan's interest higher. "Your ex-husband? He's still in the hospital?"

"He's been calling."

Susan made a quick decision. "You need protection until the police can substantiate what's happening. You can't go out like that. You look . . . all wrong. The guards will pick you up. Listen. You're due to check into my ward tomorrow morning, but I can put you in tonight. We have a guard at the door, sign in and out . . . he won't be able to get through."

A wary look shone in the young woman's eyes. She stood, her chin up, as skittish as a wild pony.

Susan held out her hand. "You're going to have to trust somebody sooner or later."

"I won't be isolated."

"Isolated?"

"If Joyce wants to see me, or Carter, they can?"

Susan put on her best smile. "Of course they can, within our visiting limits, which are pretty liberal. And once I'm done testing, we'll have a fairly good idea of your overall health." She inched forward. If she talked long enough, the returning guard would handle the problem for both of them.

McKenzie shook her head tentatively. Susan knew that look. She put as much warmth into her smile as she could muster.

"I'm here to help you. We all face the same worries, no one wants to have their insides opened up and looked at, but we don't work that way. Did you ever have one of those gifts as a child, called a surprise ball? It looks like a big ball of yarn, wrapped with streamers, and when you unwrap it, layer by layer, little surprises and toys fall out?"

The young woman stood with a flicker of memory on her face; then, with a shy smile, she gave a slight nod.

"It's just like that," Susan told her. "We don't know what surprises are in there any more than you do. We give you the support to start unwrapping your life, and we help you deal with what comes out, good or bad. We aren't witch doctors and we're not psychics, and we don't enjoy stirring around in the stew of your mind. We do get satisfaction out of helping. That's all." Her hand wavered in the air. She had closed the distance between them. Suddenly, it became very important to Susan to complete the contact between them before the guard came back.

McKenzie teetered.

"There is a guard," the doctor said. "He's on break, but he's due back any minute. It would be well if you made up your mind before then."

"Don't let Jack find me." McKenzie surrendered, collapsing into her arms.

Susan embraced her awkwardly. She smoothed back a strand of hair from Mac's forehead. "Don't worry. I'll take care of you."

Chapter 20

Jack got tired of trying the phone. He bought himself a cheese roll and a cup of coffee in the hospital cafeteria and sat in the corner, half-listening to a group of people wail over some dying old lady. The commotion amused him at first, then annoyed him, and he pushed himself away from the table after wadding up what was left of the sweet roll and throwing it into the ashtray. What the hell did they think happened in a hospital, anyway?

He strolled down the back corridors, where plastisheets flapped instead of walls, and took the stairs. The fire door clanged loudly when he entered the ward, but no one looked up or seemed to hear. The only bright spot of light was the nurses' station in the center of the hallways, but only one woman was there, and she sat, rocked back in her chair, feet propped on the counter, reading a book. Her head nodded in time to the music from her earphones. A head-banging nurse.

Jack boldly pushed open the door to Mac's room and then narrowed his eyes in the dusk light. It only took him a heartbeat or two to see that the room was empty, the mattress stripped of sheets and blankets. The phone receiver had been set back into its niche in the railing console, but no one had noticed that the cord was unplugged. He trailed his fingers over it, wondering where she'd gone now.

He'd been wasting his time. He didn't like wasting his time. No, sir. Not when he had so much to do.

Rolling his bottom lip between his teeth, he backed out of the room. He made his way to the elevator, then halted when he saw the nurses' station was now empty. A red light blinked on the control panel, and the earphones had been thrown hastily next to it.

The edge of Jack's mouth quirked. He strolled up to the chart rack and looked for "Smith, M" and did not see it. Then he saw the aluminum file lying tossed on the counter under a sweater, its end peeking out. Someone had put a Post It note on it. The scrawled message read: Transferred to Psychiatric, 11:19 P.M.

Jack heard a soft footstep and turned away. Scratching his chin thoughtfully, he continued to his original destination of the elevator. So Mac had gotten herself into the loony bin. He grinned. Had he pushed, or had she jumped?

He'd find out in the morning how to deal with the psych ward. He wasn't done with her yet, not by a long shot. When he was done with her, she'd wear her knees to bloody scraps crawling after him, begging him to take her back. Telling him she'd been all wrong, and that she knew nobody loved her more than he did. Nobody. He pushed through the doors. "Sweet dreams, babe."

Dudley found himself sweating profusely in the car. It dribbled down his flanks from his armpits, making his shirt stick uncomfortably. He'd started perspiring once out of the mountains and past San Bernardino, less than an hour from home. It poured down his forehead, making it hard to see. He had the air-conditioning jacked all the way up, until the tip of his nose felt numb from the chill, but he kept blinking the sweat out of his eyes as it cascaded down his forehead and pooled in the palms of his hands. Finally, he pulled off the freeway and just sat, wiping his hands and face on his handkerchief, over and over again.

As he looked out the windshield, it was as though he looked through two pairs of eyes. One, bloodshot and tired from driving, and the other, night-sight keen and relentless, searching, stalking. . . .

Dudley wiped his brow again, hand shaking. He licked his lip, as heavily salted as a pretzel, and took a deep breath.

Not here. Not now.

He knew what he needed, what he wanted, and that Susan would never allow it. He would jeopardize all they'd worked for, all the children, funding for the future, helping all the neglected, channeling precious resources too often abandoned or beaten or molested by the uncaring present. He could never bear the burden of her displeasure.

Yet . . . It stirred in him, the sleeping man did, and brought things up, as a restless rogue tide did from an ocean floor, things thought buried and drowned in the sandy bed. Things that no one wanted exposed to the sunlight. The sun burned. Burned fiercely.

He found himself looking at a 1960s housing tract, wood-shingled roofs, mailboxes sitting at the curb, the stucco sides painted in bland colors, one a pleasant bluish hue that cooled his fever as he watched it in the dark out the passenger side window of the car. Just looking at it gave him peace, like laying a cold compress over a fever blister, calmed the racing beat of his heart and pulse, soothed his throbbing temples. He imagined for a moment the family who might live there, though the lights were all off except one, and from its shape and angle he knew it was the bathroom light. He *knew.* Someone could be slipping out of panties and bra even as he watched, speculating, stepping out of lacy lingerie and stretching, sinuous body, silken skin, hair lying across a bare back like a flame . . .

A white-hot beacon pierced his thoughts. Dudley jumped.

"Something wrong, buddy?"

He blinked into the glare, momentarily blinded, but he knew the style of voice and rolled down the window. "No, officer. Just driving home. The air-conditioning got overheated, so I pulled over. Didn't want to stop traffic on the freeway."

"Everything under control?"

"Oh, yes." He leaned over, reaching for the glove compartment. "Do you want the registration?"

The flashlight wavered. Then the featureless voice behind it said, "No. That's all right. Better get a move on, though, you're still at the edge of the ramp."

Dudley looked about, as if seeing his surroundings for the first time. "I'm sorry, officer." He started the car. He pulled away slowly, to take the cloverleaf back on, doubling back toward the San Bernardino Mountains, not wanting to let the patrolman know his true destination. He would get off and back on again down the road. In the mirror, he could see the officer now, faintly visible in the glow of a streetlight, standing in uniform beside his bike, watching Dudley pull away.

He'd never even heard the motorcycle. The patrolman had either approached him coasting, or he'd been lost in thought so deep—

Never mind. No harm, no foul. Dudley cleared his throat. The profuse sweating had dried, leaving his face and torso feeling flaky and crusty. He looked for the nearest exit, so that he could swing about and head home.

No. Not home. He wanted to look at something beautiful.

He headed toward Mount Mercy Hospital.

"Are you an angel?"

Dudley stood over the shrunken form in the bed, and smiled. "Why, yes, ma'am. You've been calling for me, haven't you?"

The kindly face looking back at him reminded him of an apple doll from a country fair, an apple doll who'd lost her blushed cheeks to the gray of pain and death. The faded blue eyes were nearly lost in the withering of her skin. "I have," the old woman said, breathily, haltingly. "They won't let me go, you know. My cats are home. My plants. No one to take care of them the way they should be. No one who cares the way I do. And my arms—" She tried to hold up her arms, where bruises testified to the difficulty of keeping a good vein for the IV, but she'd been tied with soft rags to keep her from pulling out the shunt yet another time. "They hurt. And I'm so tired."

Dudley put his hand on a monitor. "You need to rest first," he told her. "And then you can go home."

"Rest?"

"Yes, rest." He watched her as her eyes dutifully fluttered shut. Then he put a pillow over her face and held it down until the feeble struggles ceased.

She was not quite dead when he removed the pillow. Dudley turned the oxygen off. He wiped his palm print from the monitor as it began to spike and beep softly in alarm.

Using the tail of the sheet, he pulled the shunt from her arm. Something wet spilled on the mattress. He left swiftly as steps down the hall told him the nurses had reacted to the frantic alarm of the machinery.

The grease pencil schedule board by the station was not more legible than usual, but a quick scan told him the patient he wanted had moved on. The curve of his smile deepened. He was an angel, he told himself, as he followed the trail. The angel of mercy.

Behind him, the intercom bleated, "Code Blue, room 307, *stat.*"

*   *   *

He found her with little trouble, edging the door open. Light from
the corridor fell across her sleeping face like sunbeams from heaven,
illuminating the rises and hollows of her features. Her hair caressed
the pillow slip, a halo about her face. She'd cleansed her hair. It
framed her face in tiny, soft, and unruly fringes, the longer tresses in
waves that made him ache to run his hands through them. The
bruises had already begun to fade, and he was a little relieved to see
he had not left severe ones on her slender throat. She was beautiful,
in a unique way, if marred, and he was glad he was not responsible
for the marring. He stood and watched her, drinking her in like a
feverish man gulps cool water, for a very long time.

McKenzie woke, a splinter of harsh light from the hallway prying
at her eyelids. *Someone was watching.* Her door lay pushed slightly
open and she blinked at the intrusion, her mind fogged by sedatives
which had finally taken hold. The quivery feeling of dread had begun
to build in the pit of her stomach again, but it had dulled this time.
Though her senses seemed blunted, they were still functioning.
Someone was in the room with her, just inside the doorway where
the night lay pooled in shadow. She heard the breathing.
    "Who is it? Who's there?" She shaded her eyes against the beacon.
    "Me."
    She looked to the flow of shadows along the wall. "Who's me?"
    The answer made no immediate sense to her. "You're real."
    A boyish voice. Not Jack's. Tension flowed out of her body.
    She felt real. Like the Velveteen Rabbit, torn and worn hairless
and bruised. Mac pulled herself up in the bed. "I think so. Are you?"
    "Damn right." The young voice, though strained, sounded definite.
    Mac reached back to the light switch on the wall. It clicked on,
flooding the room with its glow.
    A boy sat on the floor by the front door. He wore hospital pajamas,
pullover top and drawstring bottoms, his hair tousled. He had the
coltish look of a boy about to pass that threshold into adolescence,
still innocent, but not very. He blinked furiously against the illumination, put a foot out and closed the door to the room, shutting himself in with her.
    "They'll see that!"

"Well at least I can see you. What are you doing here?"

"I wanted to look at you." His nose wrinkled, and he did not quit squinting even as her eyes adjusted to the light. He must need to wear glasses. "I waited until they all left. They put the temps in here, you know."

"Temps?"

He must be all of, what, eleven or twelve? His chin nodded emphatically. "Temps. The ones who never stay. Sometimes they die in here. Sometimes they just get taken away in the morning." He cocked his head. "You're pretty banged up. What did you do—use the car to try it?"

Mac asked back, baffled, "Try what?"

He held up his arms. The hospital top sleeves slid down a little, revealing bandages wrapped about each wrist. There were seeping rusty stains on his left arm.

Her stomach clenched as she realized he was talking suicide. She did not want to offend him, and swallowed down her reaction. "Not . . . quite like that."

He lowered his hands. "So, do you think you're crazy?"

"Do you?"

His face twitched. "I dunno. I guess so." He got to his feet, back braced against the wall, sliding upward, a game of youthful agility. "I just came to warn you."

"Warn me?"

"Yeah. Don't let *her* touch you." Did he mean Susan Craig? Or were there women techs on the floor? What did he mean? Was her last refuge unsafe, after all? "I don't understand."

"I don't either." He scuffed a bare foot on the linoleum. "Just don't let her touch you."

"Dr. Craig? She hasn't . . . molested you, has she?"

His preadolescent face reddened. "Naw! Nothing like that."

"Then what do you mean?"

He looked back up. "I told you, I don't know. If I did, I'd—" he looked away, across the room. "I'd tell somebody. If they'd let me. Mom or somebody."

"You can't talk to your family?"

He scratched now, behind his ear, like a gangly puppy. "Not yet.

Dr. Whatley says it's too upsetting for me . . . and them. I'd tell Whatley if I could, but he's gone on a seminar. The only one left is her."

"Them?" McKenzie repeated.

"My mom. M'stepdad. The others." His eyes met hers, flicked
away again. "They don't want to hear about it."

The lump she felt for him settled in her throat. "It must be tough."

He crossed his arms across his chest. "It's not so bad. I get ice
cream when I want it. It's just that—it's just there's nobody to talk to.
Everybody in here is crazy."

She thought she knew what he meant. Not crazy, perhaps, but
crazed. Frantic behaviors and thoughts. No one for an eleven-year-
old to talk to. How could she be much better? "There's the telephone. You have buddies . . ."

"I don't have one," he interrupted. "Neither do you."

She thought for a moment he meant friends, and prepared to
argue bitterly with him, then realized what he referred to. Mac ran
her hand across the inside of the railing, along the console board. No
phone was tucked into its niche. Hers lay empty, too. Panic managed
to pierce her benumbed thoughts. No way to reach Joyce. Or Carter.
Or anyone else.

"So," the kid continued. "Do you think you're going to stick
around?"

"I don't know. I have . . . some things to work out." He nodded
wisely. He started edging toward the door.

"Leaving?"

"I get in trouble if they catch me out of my room. Then she," and
his face creased, "finds out."

"But surely they just want to help you."

"I have nightmares," he said abruptly. "No one can help me." He
turned, put a hand on the door. He looked back over his shoulder.
"Do you have dreams?"

She felt a sudden deep kinship with him. Visions and dreams.
"Sure."

He shuddered.

Suddenly afraid, McKenzie said, "I'll see you tomorrow?"

"Maybe."

"If I don't, what's your name? I'll come looking for you."

Prompted, he stood silent for a long moment. Then, "Brandon. But I like it when everyone calls me Brand."

"Brand?"

"Yeah. Like in Brand X, the stuff nobody wants."

Before she could say anything else, he pulled the door open partway and slipped through the crack.

McKenzie sat and watched the door to see if anything else might happen, thinking, *What a strange child.* Yet, she could not help but think of Cody, and what Cody would be like if he'd suddenly been made human.

A half-grown, awkward, lonely eleven-year-old.

Mac reached out and turned the light back off, slumping down into the bed.

The doctor in her made Susan rub carefully, trying not to tear the delicate tissues of her face, but she couldn't refrain from succumbing to the satisfaction of massaging her tired eyes. Elbows on the desk, she rested her head in her hands for a moment. She looked down at the printout on her desk one last time, readying for the setup in the morning. Miller could do it if he came in. She would rather do it herself, but he would think it peculiar if she assigned it to herself only, out of rotation. She did not want any flags.

A shadow fell across the paper. She looked up. She frowned. "What are you doing here?"

Dudley smiled. "It's late," he said. "I came to see you home."

Chapter 21

Susan kept her voice neutral. "I'm not sure if I'm ready to go yet."

"You're tired," he answered. "You can't do it all in one day."

She might need to. Dudley could not read them, but all the signs were there. She might have to close shop here and move on. Move on before anyone became truly aware of who she was and what she was doing.

She made the decision to go with him. With brisk movements, she snapped the file back into place and left the schedule across the desk where Miller would look for it, and pulled her purse out of the desk drawer. "You're right. I should never have come back this evening."

He escorted her out of the lab area and down the hall like a soft-spoken gentleman. The corridor lights were harsh on his face, showing evidence of where the neurosurgeons and plastic surgeons had put him back together, the hairline showing gray along the scarred seams, but the same scarring would barely be visible in softer daylight. The ward tech at the desk looked up, saw them approaching, and went back to her book. She knew Dudley almost as well as she knew the doctors.

Though he looked calm and unruffled now, she could smell the sweat on him and see that his clothes were travel rumpled, and she wondered how close he was to losing it. She talked to him about Brandon, idle chatter, while reading his body language, what he wasn't saying.

He half-paused near the room which she had assigned to McKenzie Smith. His head partially turned as they slowed in passage, and

Susan could feel her brows tighten. He knew she was in there. How? . . . and why?

Especially *why*?

He seemed to realize what he was doing, and quickened his stride, sweeping her past the tech and through the double doors of the ward.

By the time they reached the quiet of the employee parking lot, she knew how he'd cross-connected with the girl, and why he'd come to the hospital, using Susan, using his time on and around the ward to give him access. And she knew she wanted it stopped.

At least until she knew whether the girl was of any value or not.

She swung around at her car door, instead of using the key.

"Stay away from her," she said, without preamble.

They knew each other too well for him to pretend to misunderstand her. A frown rippled across his face. "Why?"

"Because I told you to."

"And if I can't?"

Susan's mouth was dry, but she managed, "Then I'll let him loose, Dudley. I'll let the sleeping man wake, and he'll eat you alive. There won't be a scrap of you left." She watched as he paled under the garage structure's lighting. "Do you understand?"

Rough-voiced. "You wouldn't—"

"I can and I will."

Words failed him entirely. Dudley looked down and nodded.

She put her hand on his shoulder. "We've come too far to lose what we've worked for. I know what you want, and what you need. I won't let you down, either."

"I need . . ." he began and halted.

"I know." She caressed the key chain in her hand. This day had not gone well for her. She faced losing Donnie, Hotchkiss, Brandon, and now the Smith girl. Even Dudley, if he could not obey her. She could recoup her losses, she'd done so before, but such a staggering blow might set her back years. She needed to salvage something from the program. Brandon had family. Donnie had only Graciela, who had strayed down the wrong path before. She found the words. "I've got someone else who might please you as well."

He looked up.

"We'll talk at home."

*   *   *

She knew she was dreaming. That gave Mac only a little comfort as she passed into a corridor which was eerily like and yet unlike the hospital. No cheery paint on the walls here. All was in a gray-green, a color that she thought of as "cadaver green," and it covered the walls and ceilings as far as they stretched. She walked hesitantly through the maze, turning and occasionally trying a door, but none would open to her. She passed empty counters which might, or might not, have been nursing stations. Was she dreaming of Mount Mercy? This was more like a dungeon. She put out her hand, touched her fingertips to the wall. It was cold, as chilled as the inside of a refrigerator. *Morgue,* she thought, as she snatched her hand away.

She came to a halt at the T-section, thinking she had been there before, and wondered which way to go.

She heard him just moments before she saw him: dog claws scrabbling on the hard linoleum flooring in leaps and bounds. Cody burst around the corner, tongue lolling in a happy adolescent doggy grin, his tail waving gaily. He slid to a stop and barked and whirled around, daring her to catch him, coaxing her to follow.

She took a step, he gaily retreated. She put her hand out, he bowed low on his front legs, rear in the air, asking her to play in dog body language. "Cody," she called softly, to hear her voice echo in the cavernous hallways.

His ears pricked. He whined, as though aware he was behaving badly by not coming closer. He shook himself and turned around again, pleading with her to follow.

It was almost as though there were a distance between them he could not cross.

McKenzie looked down the hallway he wanted her to enter. Cloud gray at the mouth, it darkened down its length, ominously, like a growing storm. It frightened her. She did not want to go after the golden retriever. She stepped backward reluctantly.

Cody whined sharply, in warning. A metallic crash sounded behind her. McKenzie jumped at the sharpness of the sound. She wanted to turn around and see what it was, and could not. A second clash shattered the echoes of the first. Cody barked sharply, urgently. He dashed away, then turned and whined, urging her after. Fear raised the hackles of his coat.

Someone was out there.

Her danger rang in her ears. Mac fought to move, but her feet stayed frozen to the corridor floor. She could hear something moving behind her, coming closer, closer . . . she could feel the warmth of another being's breath in the chill corridor touch her, and heard a low, menacing laugh.

Cody threw back his head and let out a bloodcurdling, mournful howling.

McKenzie broke loose and lunged at him. They collided in the intersection of the hallways. Cody yelped once, whirled about, and took off running. She dashed after, heedless of the darkness which loomed. The unknown presence behind her was worse, far worse. The Someone, or Something, followed.

As she sprinted, she could hear her own footfalls, but no others, but she could hear his breath grow as ragged as her own, his low, guttural curse as they skidded around a corner. Cody stopped, incredibly, to raise his leg and mark the wall at a four-way intersection. McKenzie slid past him, crying, "Cody!" and the dog looked at her as if to compel her to remember the area. She looked at the wet puddle on the floor, yellowish stain, and the faint marks dribbling down the wall, like a shadowy fracture. Then Cody took to his heels again, leading her off into an ebony-shadowed tunnel which lightened only as they breached it.

She ran until she got a stitch in her side, and had to gulp for breath. Cody's pink tongue hung from his jaws, throwing droplets of moisture to the floor as he raced. But no matter which way they turned, or how often he marked the passage in his own doggy fashion, they could not lose their pursuer.

Cody reached a last intersection. He lifted his leg in vain and could not urinate. He half-fell, half-sat and whined as she stopped by his side. She reached down to pet him, to run her fingers through his familiar, silken coat. She could feel the heat rising off him in this icy mausoleum.

"It's okay," she murmured softly to him. "You and me against the world, huh, boy?"

Her hand passed through him. He rolled his eyes as if he had felt it, wary of it, a tiny hurt, like the bite of a flea.

"Oh, God!" She pulled her hand back. Warm tears escaped her

eyes, making it difficult to see the dog. There was nothing she wanted more in the world than to hug him, his silken, wiggly dog body, to feel the love in him brimming over, to feel him safe and whole again, to give him back the love.

Cody lurched to his feet, his lips peeling off his teeth, hackles up, growls rumbling through his throat.

McKenzie knew the time had come to turn and face whoever, whatever pursed them. The awful certainty, the dread, the dire sense of wrongness and evil began to rise in her. She braced herself and started to turn around.

She did not make it in time. Something immense and dark hit her with a jolt and—

Gasping, Mac sat up in the hospital bed, grabbing for the railing, the breath knocked out of her, heart racing, eyes wide in the twilight of the room. She hugged herself as the fear ricocheted around inside of her.

Sarah Whiteside sat inside the family minivan, huddled behind the steering wheel, staring at the outside of her home. A thin, Seattle mist trickled down the outside of the windshield and, in a few minutes, she'd have to turn the van on again to defrost the steam fogging up the inside.

She hugged herself, afraid to go in, yet knowing that, in the three hours she'd had the house staked out, she'd seen nothing more than the daring teenagers down the street drive past. The mangy marmalade tom from over the fence had gone strolling through the hedges. The moon had risen and disappeared into the cloud cover.

Sarah gritted her teeth. *Damn that man for making me afraid to enter my own house. Damn him for hurting Mac and driving her off. Damn him, damn him, damn him.*

Her fingers wrapped themselves about the steering wheel until the knuckles pinched chalk-white and ached. After a few long minutes, Sarah noticed the pain and gingerly let go. She winced as tiny aches lightninged through her joints as the circulation returned.

It had been four days. The kids were cranky, her parents and her friends had let her know that she was being overly fearful and cautious and eccentric.

She couldn't help it. Mac had frightened her into fleeing, and only now did she have the nerve to come creeping back. Not much nerve. Enough to park under old lady Rhodes' creeping wisteria and aging carport and stake out her home anxiously. She'd been sitting there until her butt had gone numb and that, Sarah reflected dryly, was an accomplishment in itself.

So. The time had come to either get her nerve up, or tuck her tail between her legs and creep back to her parents' house. And her arrival at three o'clock *in the morning,* as her father would so eloquently put it, would upset everyone.

She sucked in her lower lip and chewed on it as she turned the key, started the van up, and pulled slowly out of the carport. Long, trailing vines of feathery wisteria with their lavender buds pulled across the car like fingers, leaving trails in the damp. She did not turn on the headlights, though, as she drove down the street and into her driveway. As she turned the engine off and pulled her keys out, she sat another moment, debating whether to lock the van doors or not. Quick entrance if she needed it, but what if Jack Trebolt were sitting in the car seat laughing at her when she came back?

Sarah opted for a quick entrance into the van and crossed her fingers, praying no one would take advantage of the unlocked doors. She slid down and outside, shutting the door quietly but solidly behind her.

She loved this house. She had always loved this house from the first day she and her husband had bid on it until this evening when she looked on it in abject cowardice. Had it betrayed her or had she betrayed it?

Doesn't matter, Sarah decided, suddenly realizing she'd chewed her lip into a puffy lump. She stretched her mouth open, trying to soothe it, and pushed her feet up the sidewalk to the back door.

It was closed, but not locked. It gave way to the subtle pressure of her putting the key in, squeaking slightly, as it opened inward to the darkness. Sarah's heart did one of those little pipsqueak jumps and settled into a racy pulse.

This has to be better than aerobics, she thought, as she eased into the storm porch and then into the kitchen.

She felt for the light switch plate, then hesitated again. Light or no light? What if he was sitting here in the dark, waiting for her?

What if he wasn't? Did she really need to break a leg stumbling over something in the darkness?

Damn him. Damn him to hell forever. This was her home, and she knew every square inch of it, even when the kids messed it up and left their junk lying around. She could slink through it in eternal darkness without bucking a shin or stubbing a toe, she knew it so well.

Until tonight.

Impatiently, Sarah turned the lights on and then stood a moment, blinking in the sudden illumination.

The kitchen looked perfectly ordinary. There was some dried grit on the flooring—it had been raining last week, too, when they'd loaded the van to leave. Someone had tracked in mud. Time had dried it. Sarah took a deep breath and passed into the rest of her home, throwing on lights wherever she could touch the switches.

She made her way straight to the answering machine. It blinked sullenly at her. There had been nothing on it for days, because she had checked it by remote. She sat down in the easy chair next to it, casting her glance over the living room, seeing nothing out of place, and triggered the machine.

>>YOU HAVE ONE MESSAGE,<< it told her.

She retrieved it. Listened in amazement to a detective from Los Angeles. The second time around, she had cobbled together a scrap of paper and a pencil so she could write the number down.

She sat back, and decided it wouldn't help Mac to call the police in the middle of the night. She'd go home, wake her husband, tell him they could come back, and then sleep until the kids woke her. Life could ease back into normalcy.

Jack had undoubtedly gone after McKenzie. She had a thing or two she could tell Pete Moreno, but it could wait.

Sarah stood, her throat suddenly dry. She needed a drink. If she remembered correctly, there were still a couple of peach Snapples in the fridge.

She left the living room light on, gained confidence as she passed through the rooms. The hardwood flooring seemed to creak happily under her shoes as she walked. It was lonesome, this huge, old house. It was waiting for her and the family to come home.

Feeling vindicated that she had come back that night, Sarah yanked open the refrigerator door.

The sight hit her full on. She blinked. It took a moment to realize what she saw.

A bloody, severed dog head stared back at her from the milk carton's shelf.

Sarah screamed. Her legs folded under her and she felt herself collapsing to the hard kitchen floor, collapsing like a house of cards.

Chapter 22

Dolan's call woke Carter at an ungodly hour. Eight thirty-two or something to that effect. He squinted his eyes against the harshness of the late May sun creeping through his bedroom shutters as the editorial assistant said, "No artist today, Carter. I can't put her onto it until tomorrow morning."

Carter didn't like the delay, but what could he do? He said as much.

Dolan returned, "Thought you'd see it that way. Anyhow, I'll be by tomorrow for dinner. What do you want?"

"Mu shu pork, but only if the crepes are thin enough to see through. Lo mein. Fried rice. I've already got the Tsing-Tao on ice."

"Gotcha, boss." Dolan clicked off the line.

Carter rolled over in bed and contemplated the ceiling of his bedroom. Tiny spiderweb-like cracks from the various tremors over the years greeted him. Outside the apartment, he could hear the faint, distant sound of heavy equipment working on the nearby segment of the subway system. He had the day off.

He drew his hand up to tuck it under his head, bringing the equally scarred landscape of his wrist into focus. Then he slipped his hand into place, and thought of McKenzie Smith. Even if he didn't have the day off, he'd find a way to go to Mount Mercy and be with her.

Uneasiness crawled around a little, somewhere under his rib cage. Or maybe it was just gas from last night's pizza. He closed his eyes to think and slipped back into restless sleep.

*   *   *

"Well, girl, as they say in my neighborhood, don't you clean up nice."

Mac had been standing at the window, looking through the reinforced glass, determined to stay on her feet as long as possible, building up strength, when Joyce hailed her. She turned around, smiling. "Like the duds?" She was wearing a pullover pajama top and drawstring bottoms, nothing remotely like street wear, but far better than she'd had the past two days.

Joyce, wearing a Monet-inspired print of blues, lavenders, and blue-greens, sat down with a grin. "Hey, I got nothin' against seeing a perky little ass once in a while, but it wasn't *yours* I've been thinkin' about."

McKenzie came over to her bed and perched on it, legs folded Indian-style, laughing in spite of herself. Joyce patted her on the knee briefly. "I came by early to check on you and saw you'd been moved already. I heard you had some problems last night—I wanted to tell you why I wasn't there for you. The batteries went down in my pager. I never even saw the 'lo cell' warning. Mac, I'm sorry."

"It's all right. I just . . . I couldn't stay there. He kept calling. He said he was *inside* the hospital."

Joyce frowned, her ebony brows drawing close. "And you want to know if he could have been."

Mac nodded.

"I won't lie to you. He could have. But heaven knows, he'll have trouble gettin' into Psychiatric. Those double doors lock if the receptionist doesn't like the look of anyone trying to get through. Speaking of which, I better put Carter's name on the guest list or he won't be able to see you, either."

Mac looked up. "He wants to visit?" Faint surprise was in her voice.

Joyce had been fishing through her purse. She met Mac's expression. "What do you think?"

"I don't know anymore." Mac rolled her hand into a soft fist and pushed it into her stomach, just under her ribs. "I don't know what to think. It's gone all numb, and it hurts at the same time, right here."

Joyce answered softly, "You don't have to feel, just now. But you have to think, and keep thinking. The feelings will come along later."

"Have you known Carter long?"

"Not long. He's only been in Los Angeles, three, maybe four years. All I can say is that he's not going to use you to sell newspapers. Not that he isn't a good reporter. He is, one of the best. It's just that he's interested in you, not your story."

Mac looked away then, back at the window, the diamond-shaped screen reinforcement hiding any real view, her fist still in the pit of her stomach. "I'm sorry for all the trouble."

"Trouble? Defending yourself is trouble?" Joyce stood, gathering her belongings. She put a hand to her glossy dark hair, scooping it back from her face. "I get my hands on that spouse of yours and we'll see what trouble is."

"I'm worth it, right?" Mac said dryly.

"Of course you are! I never met a woman who wasn't!"

"I'll bet you haven't." Mac's gaze tracked her to the door. Then, "Joyce—"

"Yes?"

"How long do I have to be in here?"

"Ideally, just a day or two. Long enough for you to feel better, and for us to get our hands on Jack Trebolt."

"Then what do I do? Where do I go?"

"Why, home. If not, I've got a place for you." Joyce's mouth worked a second. "Do you think your father would want you at home?"

"I . . . don't know. He's still not conscious, is he?"

"Not yet, but the good news is, he's not supposed to be. He's been kept in a coma purposely, while the brain swelling goes down. We won't know about injuries or damage until they let him begin to waken. Once they take him off the ventilator, he can talk a little, though he won't be coherent right away. But if you don't want to go home, or we can't find Jack, don't you worry. I've got a place for you."

Mac pointed at the closet. "I've got some money in my jeans. It's not much, but—"

"Girl, don't you talk like that to me." Joyce put her chin up. "I've got a good job, and it pays me well enough. Save it for someone who needs it."

Mac's face flushed deeply. Joyce pointed a finger at her. "Next time I come in, I want to you to be ready to sign legal papers."

"What kind? Not to stay here?" Her eyes widened.

"Are you crazy? Of course not. Petitions for restraining orders. I'm picking them up from my legal offices late this afternoon."

"Against Jack?"

"Unless you've got someone else in mind?"

Legal action would infuriate him. He hated attorneys with a passion. Mac closed her eyes briefly at the thought of the reaction. Then she opened them. "No. He's the one."

"Good girl." Joyce put her hand on the door, saw a hesitation in Mac, and asked, "Anything else?"

"How long . . . how long will they keep me here if I've been seeing things?"

"McKenzie Smith, I'd think you were crazy if you *weren't* seeing things the way you've been knocked around. You just get another day or two of rest under your belt, and stop worrying. You're not in here permanently, okay?"

She let out her breath. "All right."

"Good. Now I've got work to do. And remember—" Joyce was already out the door, and she looked back in, dark eyes sparkling. "Page me. I've got new batteries this time."

"Right."

The door shut.

Too late, Mac remembered she'd forgotten to tell Joyce she had no phone. She put her knees up and hugged them. In a way, it was a welcome relief to be dulled and listless, to have lost the knife edge of terror and dread that had been stalking her for the last few days. The unraveling feeling had gone. Whether it would return, she didn't know.

The door opened tentatively, and she saw a tousled head peak in. The boy had a scattering of freckles and squint lines between his brows as if he needed glasses. She recognized Brand.

"The Nintendo lounge is open. Can you play?"

"I thought the warden didn't let you out."

He flashed a grin. "They haven't built a jail cell yet that can hold me. Anyway, do you play?"

"A little."

"I see you've got your padded cell suit. Come on, let's go before all the good games are gone."

McKenzie swung her feet to the floor. "I'm supposed to have some tests."

Brand shrugged. "They'll come find you. How far can you run?"

Running. Like a slash across her eyes. Cody, weaving his way through a maze of tunnels—

"Mac?"

"Yes." She had herself braced at the foot of the hospital bed.

"You spacing out on me?"

"I . . . must have been."

Brand wrinkled his nose. "Don't take your meds. Pretend to swallow them, then spit them down the toilet or something. Otherwise you'll be so full of dope you'll be a zombie." He made a noise of disgust. "I gotta have somebody around here I can talk to."

"Right." Mac pushed away from the bed. The vision fled, leaving vertigo in its place, a moment of instability when she literally could not tell top from bottom. Then it, too, faded and she was at the door. Brand looked quizzically up at her. She shrugged and made a face of tics and grimaces. "What are you waiting for?"

"You're stupid," he commented with delight and dragged her out into the corridor.

Susan slept late. The lunch trays were already being put away when she entered the lab. Miller sat at his computer terminal, a can of soda at one elbow and a gnawed-on apple at the other. The sounds of Tetris came from the computer as he tapped keys frantically in response to the falling shapes.

Her mouth tensed, but she decided not to scold him for playing games on the work machines. Miller was not an outstanding technician, but he did his work without questions or a second thought, which suited her quite well. She was as certain as she could be that the moment he went home, the day's work disappeared from his skull. When the time came for her to move on, and it would, even if she solved the current crises, that unremarkable memory of Miller's could be worth its weight in gold.

"Did you get the Smith girl retested?"

"Yeah." He tapped a disk sitting on top of the monitor, lost a moment in the frantic pacing of the game, and moaned in frustration.

He cleared the screen to start again, and paused. "I had to look all over for her."

"Look for her? Where could she have gone? I had enough thorazine in her to bring down an elephant. She had a bad night."

"She was in the game room with Brand X."

Susan paused in folding her suit jacket. She laid it carefully over the back of her chair. "With Brandon?"

"Yeah." His attention went avidly back to the game screen. "I've got ten more minutes of lunch."

"That's fine," she answered abstractedly. There was no reason for the uneasiness she felt over the pairing of the boy and the young woman, but she didn't like it, all the same. Until she was finished with Smith, she'd have to find a way to keep the two of them apart. Just in case. "What were the two of them doing?"

"Playing Super Mario."

A game of concentration and reflexes. Susan considered the ramifications and decided to increase the dosage being prescribed. She sat down at her terminal and loaded the new exam disk, sharp blue eyes narrowed. It was the nature of entropy that things would, sooner or later, begin to decay.

But it was much too soon for what she had planned. If she was going to be forced out of here, to cut and run and start over, then she'd do it on her own terms. If a retreat was in order, she'd make certain the enemy had wounds of their own, suffering of their own, to take care of.

First, there was Ibie Walker.

If all went extremely well with Ibie, then perhaps a retreat would not even be necessary.

Secondly, there was Stephen Hotchkiss. She had to determine what his next move would be. He might understand instinctively that he had to follow her suggestions. Or he might need to be nudged further along.

Or he might need to be dealt with altogether.

It might also depend on how much she could count on Dudley. His personality was beginning to show the stress. He needed another overlay, but she was uncertain if that would put him beyond her ability to handle him. He had begun to show the classic signs of disintegration, and they both could ill afford it.

Frowning at the possibilities and alternatives, she did not notice at first the results coming up on the screen. When she did, she sucked in a hissing breath. Miller stopped what he was doing and swung around to look at her.

She raised an eyebrow as she met his dweebish expression. "Lunch hour," she said carefully, "must surely be over by now."

Without hesitation, he shut the computer down. "Right. Who's up next?"

"We'll be working with the speech therapy for Ibie Walker."

"The soundboard?"

She nodded. Miller, of the weak chin and lank hair, flashed a sudden smile. "I'm working a double shift today. I'll go set up the equipment."

"Do that."

As his footsteps faded, Susan turned back to the monitor. She touched the command for the printer. It began to tractor feed paper and print out as she read the screen.

The results were scarcely different from yesterday's readings.

She tapped a thumb on the keyboard, lost in thought. All the work she had done, all the research, all the imprinting, had been done from the aggressor's point of view. Her hopes of finding an empathic match had been dashed time and again, if not by personality disintegration of the subject, then by fear of discovery by the authorities.

But she had never, ever considered trying from the view of the victim.

Until now.

Susan leaned close to read the screen. "Who are you, little woman, and what are you doing to my program? Just what do you think you can get away with?"

As the spikes and grids flashed past her eyes, she began to come to a decision.

Brand crowed as he successfully brought his character through a colorful segment and punched his fist into the air as the Nintendo screen flashed a score in starburst. Then he caught sight of the doctor watching them from the game room door, and he scowled.

"What is it?"

"It's *her*," he answered, putting aside his control pad. He leaned forward and saved their progress in the console, then snapped the television screen off as well.

McKenzie stood up, a little more stiffly than she'd anticipated, not wondering that her adult body had not taken to the floor seating the way Brand's frame had. She watched as the doctor wove her way through the rec room to them.

Dr. Craig folded her arms lightly over her white jacket. "Nurse tells me you didn't eat lunch today, Brand."

He bounded to his feet. "Didn't feel like it."

The silvery-blonde woman inclined her head slightly. "That's not our deal, is it?"

The boy refused to look the doctor in the eye. Finally, he shrugged, saying, "I guess."

Craig brought up a slim wrist to catch the time. "It's not too late. I've had a tray put in your room. You don't have to eat everything, but I want you to make an effort. I asked them not to make it too awful. Okay?"

He shuffled a bare foot. "I guess," he repeated.

"Then I guess you'd better go." She put a hand lightly on his shoulder, urging him.

Brand rolled an eye at McKenzie and went. The doctor waited until he was gone from the room and then turned back. She was smiling.

"Glad he found somebody to relate to. I hate to make him eat, but he needs to."

"Why?"

"He's a manic-depressive. Dr. Whatley treats him with drugs, of course, but nutrition has something to do with it. We're trying to impress on him the importance of what and when he eats. The more stable we can keep his mood swings, the better off he'll be."

"Who's Dr. Whatley?"

"He's the head of Psychiatric, actually. He's been out on seminar. He's not due back until the end of this week. I work with Brand on self-esteem and a new form of therapy which uses rapid eye movement—are you familiar with that?"

McKenzie thought. For a moment, she dizzied and as she looked at Susan Craig, she saw a wet, ruby veil drop across her face and then disappear. She blinked, hard. "No . . . I don't think so. . . ."

"It's relatively new. The therapist trained in it takes a patient who's suffered trauma, recent or even long past—there's been some success with Vietnam vets—anyway, the patient follows a series of hand movements visually. Or watches software, in the helmet, as you were doing this morning. Somehow, and we're still not sure how, the mind gets retrained and focused, and the traumatic memory is reduced so that the patient can handle it."

The doctor had begun to escort her across the game room.

"I thought Brand's problem was psychiatric."

"It is, mainly. But he also witnessed the death of his father when he was very young and that seems to trigger problems. So he gets to wear the helmet, too, twice a day." In the corridor, Susan Craig faced Mac triumphantly. "You wouldn't believe what we can do with that little virtual reality helmet. Or what we can diagnose."

McKenzie felt a pinprick of ice on the back of her neck. It began to spread.

"You've read my results?"

"Yes, I have." The doctor nodded. "Your concussive symptoms are extremely mild, according to the spatial and other results. However. . . ."

She knows. McKenzie felt her whole body go cold. She had to know that Mac was seeing things, terrible, horrific things that were entirely a figment of her imagination. *Crazy*. . . .

"I wanted to suggest to you that you'd be a good candidate for therapy yourself. The trauma of domestic violence is as severe as any wartime experience. It would be voluntary. I can't force you, and since Dr. Whatley isn't here, he can't put it on your orders. But," and the slender woman's smile grew warmer, "I'd like you to consider it." That wrist flashed up again as she consulted her watch.

"In fact, I have someone coming into my lab now for yet another kind of therapy. Why don't you come in, watch, see for yourself? Then when I'm finished, you can sit in for a session, if you like." Susan put her hand on McKenzie's wrist as if sensing her withdraw slightly.

How could she not? She felt as though she were being peeled away. "I don't . . . I'm not. . . ."

"Please consider it," Craig said seriously. "And there's another possibility. With your cooperation, we might be able to re-create the scenario through computer animation."

"The scenario?"

"The attack," amplified Craig, irritation edging her voice. "The violence which brought you here in the first place. The police have just begun using crime scene scenarios to work up cases during the investigation, not just for court presentation. If you cooperate, I think we can present Officer Moreno with some persuasion that you were attacked by your ex-husband. A custom-made program, from your memories."

"In virtual reality?"

"Of course. Interested?"

How could she not be?

Chapter 23

"Don't do it." Brand's tone was sullen. Mac watched the way he pushed his food around his plate, picking rather than eating. It didn't look too bad, actually, the hospital equivalent of chicken nuggets and baby corn, with french fries, and some electric neon blue flavor of gelatin in a cup on the side.

She pinched a fry. It had been oven-baked, but it was edible. Tasty, even. She pinched a second fry and Brand leveled his betrayed expression on her. "They could be drugged."

Mac snipped the fry in two with an even bite and waved the remainder of it. "They're not bad. Wouldn't they have some sort of groady aftertaste if they were drugged?"

He blinked. "Maybe," he said dubiously. He speared a couple and ate them. "Maybe not." He opened his mouth to show the half-chewed food. "My tongue turn some weird color?"

She had to puzzle out the words, muffled as they were by the mulched-up fries. Mac shook her head emphatically. "Not yet." She was betting on the gelatin.

He looked almost disappointed. He pushed his food around some more. "I'm not really hungry. Why don't you eat some more so it'll look like I did."

"I can't do that. Besides, you need it."

His stomach chose that moment to growl loudly, bubbling discontent into the air.

Mac acknowledged the noise. "Even your body says differently. Your system has to stay in balance—"

He shoved the tray away viciously. "Cut the crap, okay? You're not my doctor and not my mom."

She sat on the end of his bed. He dropped his chin, not looking at her, and folded his arms over his stomach as if he could quell the hungry sounds by sheer effort. His face looked pale in the hospital room lighting, and there was a light sweat over his forehead.

"So what's your point?" Mac asked lightly.

"The point is . . . the point is, I have a mom. But she's not here. She's never here."

"She isn't supposed to be, is she?"

Brand looked at her fiercely. "If your kid was in the hospital, would you let some flaky old doctor keep you away? For weeks? Would you?"

Her temple throbbed briefly, but her vision stayed clear. She rapped him on the knee, thinking of Cody and how she'd failed him. "I don't know what I'd do."

Brand picked up a chicken nugget and threw it across the room. It made a moist smack against the beige wall and slid to the floor. "Well, I'd do something. I would. I will!"

Joyce would be back later. Maybe Carter would visit. "Brand."

He looked at her, his eyes sunken, pink-rimmed.

"What if I had a friend call your mother? Tell her you miss her. See what happens."

"Could you?"

She nodded, then added, "I can't guarantee anything."

"I know." He opened the tiny drawer in the tray table. "They won't let me have pencils or pens. Too sharp. But I've got crayons." He pulled them out and began to write furiously on his paper napkin. "Hide it," he ordered as his fingers flew. "Don't let anybody else see it."

"All right." She watched him as he laboriously wrote out a message, choosing different crayons for emphasis, then folded the napkin in half and gave it to her. The tension in his thin body seemed to evaporate as the message changed hands. Mac forced a smile. "Now you finish your lunch for me."

"Deal." He began to stuff the food into his face.

She stood. "I've got to go. I'll see you later. If I get through this lab in time, we can play some more Nintendo before dinner."

He nodded vigorously, the thatch of his uncombed hair bobbing. Mac slipped out of the room.

*   *   *

Councilman Walker brought an entourage with him, a nurse pushing his wheelchair, a proud, beautiful young African American woman with her hair in dreadlocks, and an immaculately suited Hispanic man on her heels. The councilman himself was propped in his chair, one arm lying weakly across the arm of it, IV tubes tangling with oxygen tubes, and a machine on its table being wheeled in tandem with the chair.

The left side of his mahogany, seamed face drooped markedly as he looked about the long laboratory room. His gaze swept Mac, went on and came back, measuring her.

Down but not out, she thought. *Incapacitated but not crippled*. He would, she could see instinctively, do everything in his power to regain what he'd lost. He might even be impatient and querulous in the process. She put a hand to her neckline, suddenly unable to understand why looking at him made her throat tight and hard.

The female aide brought the chair to a halt at Susan Craig's desk, and leaned over to whisper something. He made a feeble wave, dismissing it. She spoke again, more sharply, and this made Ibie Walker sit up straighter. He tried to shake his head but did not complete the gesture, ending up with his head wobbling feebly as he sank back into the wheelchair. Susan sat, fiddling with what looked like a headset, and did not acknowledge any of them.

The nurse straightened him a little. Looking up, she said to both the young woman and the man, "I'll have to ask you to leave."

The young woman's voice rose. "I'm not going anywhere. I'm watching you like a hawk."

The nurse shrugged, her starched whites rustling. "I'm not going to be doing anything." She set the chair brakes with the toe of her shoe. "I'll be back in an hour," she directed at Susan Craig.

Miller sat at a computer console and monitor, leaning back in the chair he'd swiveled around to see the action. A smirk crinkled his features.

The doctor looked up coolly. "Is there a problem?"

"Damn right there's a problem. He needs to be in bed, recovering. You're hauling him around, monitors and all—"

Susan Craig parted her lips slightly, pleasantly, icily. "This is part of his recovery." She looked at Ibrahim Walker. "You've had a stroke,

Mr. Walker, and part of what you've lost is your speech. Therapy session will be short today, working the soundboard takes training. We'll also be asking you to do some exercises to build up the strength you've lost in your left arm and hand, but I'm not going to ask you to do anything beyond your limit. These measures will help, whether your impairment is short-term or long-term."

She looked up then, over Ibie Walker's grayed head and said, "Is that understood?" to the young woman's heated expression.

The male aide put an arm in between them, saying smoothly, "Sounds jus' like what the doctor ordered."

"Since I am a doctor," Susan commented, getting to her feet, "I couldn't agree more. Mr. Walker?"

The young woman's café au lait skin flushed slightly darker. "As you all remarked, he can't speak for himself."

"Of course he can," Susan interjected. "As I saw when you wheeled him in. You've already worked out a few hand signals. Well, is this session yea or nay? If you don't feel strong enough, I can reschedule you for tomorrow." She swung the headset in her hand, cord dangling.

Walker moved his right hand. It trembled, but even Mac could see there was a definite pattern to it.

His aide took a deep breath, then set her jaw. "All right," she said. "But I don't want to leave him."

"You don't need to."

The Hispanic man shifted weight. "I have those faxes—"

"All right, all right, Rafi. Go on. I'll see you after the office shuts down, at six." Still flushed, the young woman looked up angrily, then dropped her hand protectively to Ibie's shoulder.

"Good enough." He turned and left.

Susan shook out the cable to the headset and leaned forward, placing it on Walker. It wrapped over the top of the skull conventionally, but there were three fingerlike arms that lay over his cheek, temple, and jaw. The doctor took a few minutes to satisfy herself with the placement. When she was done, she unlocked the wheelchair's brake, and said to the aide, "Steer the monitor, will you?" as she drove the chair to the computer setup where Miller sat waiting.

"What's going on here?"

Susan fed the cable to Miller, who plugged it into the setup. "Know anything about biofeedback?"

"A little." The muscles along the young woman's jaw worked.

Susan looked amused. It seemed she had noticed the tension as well. "Actually," she said, and pointed to the aide's face with her finger. "That's how it works. This picks up muscle groups as they tense. Even very minor shifts. It converts the tension to sound groups. The computer interprets the sound groups and signals the soundboard to electronically make that sound. That is somewhat simplified, but basically, that's what we're going to be doing." She looked down at Ibie. "Arch an eyebrow and you could be telling them of a personal need. Whatever. Conversations will be basic, but you will be able to voice some of your concerns."

The young woman rocked back on a heel. "Really?"

"Really. It'll take some training. Tomorrow the speech therapist will be up here, doing most of the real work. I'm just introducing it for her today. It's new, but it's been a successful program."

"How limited is the speech?"

"It's expanding every day as we learn more about the technology. Though," and Susan dropped a fond glance down at Walker, "we won't hear any of your oratories from the soundboard. We haven't come that far, yet."

He jerked his hand impatiently.

Mac sat back. The real warmth in Susan Craig's voice was reserved for the technology, not the patient, and she supposed that was what set Brand off about her. Kids were always so much quicker to pick up the phoniness. The doctor set off a certain uneasiness in McKenzie, too, but there was no doubt Craig had been there last night when Mac needed her.

At Ibie Walker's bedside.

Craig stepped back.

"What are you doing?" the aide demanded.

Susan swept an arm at the station.

"All it takes is Miller. We're going to let Mr. Walker see just what kinds of noises certain movements produce."

Across the room, the computer began to grunt and squeal. Then it made a series of "Ta" sounds.

It was not a human voice, but by the time Susan indicated satisfaction, Ibie Walker had learned to make vowel sounds and the consonants T and N. His aide had put one curved hip against the table, body language reading that her judgment, at least for the day, had been suspended.

Under the VR helmet, face partially obscured, the wizened hand Velcroed into its glove, the councilman looked less assured.

His aide stared defiantly at Susan. "What are you doing now?"

"This is a virtual reality program. All we're doing is asking him to react to the simple 3-D exercises he's watching. One hand and then the other. It's strictly repetitive. Tomorrow, again, the program will be more specialized for him."

Walker brought up his right hand, made a gloved fist. The left wobbled, wavered, almost accomplished a like maneuver. After five minutes of raising, opening, and closing, the left could scarcely lift off his robed lap. Susan reached over and tapped Miller on the shoulder.

"That's enough for today."

Her assistant shut down the program and helped strip the helmet and gloves from Walker. The elderly man's color had grayed slightly, but the monitor showed his vitals still strong.

Susan said, "That was a good session."

She leaned down, and looked into Ibie Walker's eyes. "Tomorrow," she added, "we'll have something special for you. We'll make some real progress."

Ibie's hand quivered as though he tried to make a gesture, but fatigue defeated him. He sagged back slightly into the wheelchair.

Susan straightened. "Miller, please help Mr. Walker and his assistant back to ICU."

Miller took the chair, rotating it around, leaving the monitor and IV stands to the aide.

As they passed, the councilman's measuring gaze wavered over McKenzie again. The coffee-dark eyes held hers.

Then Miller leaned into the chair, hurrying it across the lab. Mac wet lips suddenly gone dry. There had been a look in the elderly man's eyes, a plea, a fear that had not been there before. She sat there wondering if she had seen what she had seen.

"You're next."

McKenzie started. Susan had crossed the lab room without her even noticing.

"Already?"

Craig reached for the virtual reality helmet connected to the computer station at Mac's elbow. "You're the one who's going to be getting a real workout."

She settled the helmet over McKenzie's brow and darkness descended.

The doctor's voice, when it reached her, sounded very muffled. "First, I'm going to run a program we have here, it's an architectural program, shows the basic layouts and floor plans of homes. I want you to talk to me, describing the house first, where the doors are, the furniture, and we'll animate it. Let us know when we're close."

Mac looked into the visor, seeing the program as if a projector had been starting—showing nothing. "California tract home, mid-fifties," she said. "Stucco outside, three bedrooms, one bathroom, a living room, kitchen with eating nook. No dining room. About fifteen hundred square feet, built absolutely square."

A 3-D outline of a house played onto the screen, rotating on its axis. It made her ache dully somewhere behind her eyes to watch it. It settled into place.

"Porch?" asked Susan faintly.

"A step up porch, two steps, to the front door. Two column beams on the porch. There's a little rooflike eave over that."

The porch roof came out of nowhere as if a genie had blinked it into being. And, how odd, it looked a little like her home, if her home were only a stick figure of a building, with no solid walls. She looked into the architectural rendering. As she spoke, the bedrooms and kitchen and bathroom realigned themselves, the drawing a virtual carousel until she said, "That's it."

"Close enough?"

If it were any more accurate, she'd say they'd were dead on. "Yes," Mac murmured, intent on the drawing. "Except for the back steps."

"Is that important?"

"Yes. It's where—it's where Jack attacked my father."

"Okay, then we'll work on that. Tell us what you want to see."

She wondered what Miller was doing, if he was punching in numbers, if he saw what she saw, through cables wire thin. The helmet weighed on the bridge of her nose. She felt a drop of perspiration run across her cheek and along her jaw. She put a hand up to wipe it away, and the VR glove stopped her.

"Whoa!" Miller's voice. "What are you doing?"

"Twitching," she said apologetically. "Sorry." Her house had begun to come apart, sliding off its foundation as if sundered by an earthquake. "The kitchen door is here," and she traced an index finger lightly as the house was righted, and Miller focused on the kitchen from the inside out. A door outline appeared. "Three steps down, pipe railing on the left. Then a small sidewalk to the right, to the driveway. The driveway leads back to the garage."

The details became part of the sketch. It wasn't exact here. She couldn't quite figure out what was wrong, but it was close enough. Then, as she looked at the back of the house, she realized the windows were just white outlines. Not the wood-framed, prettily curtained eyes to the world that she'd remembered.

Virtual reality lacked the finesse. Mac took a deep breath, somewhat relieved.

"Now," Susan said softly. "Tell us what happened. We're recorded visually as well as in audio. The computer eye is your viewpoint."

Mac heard the voices. She picked up the baseball bat. She headed out of her bedroom door.

A thin film began to edge downward from the ceiling. It tinged everything blood-red in its wake. She could feel a tightness in her chest, squeezing her voice as she talked. Her jaw ached. She blinked fiercely, trying to dash away the crimson tide which slowly, inexorably, began to obliterate all that she saw.

She went through the line-drawing back door and described the two men she saw there. A simple, stocky line drawing of a man represented her father, but when she focused on the other, Jack grinned at her. "We're the real flesh and blood, babe," he said.

McKenzie gripped her bat tightly as he began to push through toward her.

She remembered screaming.

Running. Furniture crashing, lamps exploding, pain thundering. Someone was right behind her. Someone grunting and cursing, pounding steps, right behind her, sleeping fury, growling like a dog trapped in a nightmare—*Don't let him wake! Don't. Let. Him. Wake!*

Mac sat up, eyes staring, breasts heaving, sweat running off her face, her naked face, as though she stood in a Seattle rain.

"Whoa, whoa!" Carter was there, reaching for her flailing arms. "No wonder your rails are up." He caught her, pinned her, made soothing noises in her ear until she realized that she was in her room, under cool sheets, with strong arms protectively about her. "They'd said you'd had a rough time this afternoon."

The dream so real—

She'd been re-creating it in virtual reality. What had happened? McKenzie swallowed tightly. Her head throbbed, her eardrums felt as though they could burst with the drumming of her heartbeat. She swallowed again and began to pull back, fighting his restraint.

"I'm all right—"

"Actually, I kind of like this." He held her a moment longer, hands patting her shoulder blades in that rhythmic soothing motion mothers use with babies and lovers with each other, a familiar caress. Pat, pat, pat.

Her heart slowed down to match it.

"They told me you were napping." Carter loosed her, letting her sit back in the bed. He fluffed a pillow behind her back. "Nobody told me you came out fighting." He grinned widely. "Actually, I take that back. I heard about the doctor you decked down in triage."

"Carter."

"Yes." He stayed close to her, leaning over the railing, one elbow hooked over it.

Her vision blurred, separated, so that she saw two of him. Kind eyes, two, three, no, four, no, three of them, watching her. She closed her eyes tightly, dizzy. When she opened them, it came with a blinding flash, ruby-red and wet.

His hands and arms dripping with the color.

Mac gasped.

"What is it?"

She backpedaled away from him, pulse shooting sky-high again.

"McKenzie, what is it?" He reached for her.

"Don't touch me!"

"What?"

"Don't!" She shied away, against the other railing, hitting it so hard the bed shook violently.

Carter recoiled. "All right. I won't touch you." He took a step away from the bedside. "Do you want me to call someone? Someone else?"

McKenzie put her hands to her skull, gripping hard, tight, as pain like an ice pick shot through. "No," she got out. "Don't call anyone."

"Then I'll just, ah, go. All right?"

She didn't want him to leave. She peered at him through her fingers. "No. I'll be . . . this will go away." She closed her eyes again and then pounded her forehead onto the railing. "I. Want. It. To. Go. Away."

He came around the other side, catching her up again. "Mac, stop it!"

She refused to look. Refused to open her vision to one of blood. She kept her eyes squeezed tight and just listened to his heartbeat, pacing hers, then quieting, his breath. He smelled faintly, she realized, of his own odor, and a touch of aftershave, and pizza.

"I'm listening," he murmured, running his hand over her hair. He avoided the sore patch behind her ear. McKenzie felt a touch of shame that he knew it was there. "What is it?"

"If I tell you," she said ironically, "they'll never let me out of here."

His stroking movement stuttered, then started again. "In this ward, you mean."

"I see things, Carter."

"You had a head injury. Double vision, dizziness, that's all part of the game. You should hear the sportswriters talk about the jocks—"

"Stop it!" She took a deep breath. "You've got to listen, now, because I don't think I'm going to have the nerve to talk about this again."

She put her head back, and opened her eyes, so close to his face that her nose grazed his chin. Carter said gently, his breath tinged with coffee, "Are you seeing things now?"

"No." The pain in her head had gone, suddenly, inexplicably.

There was that moment when the tension between them thickened and she thought, *How odd, he's going to kiss me,* and Carter pulled back abruptly, letting go of her. He messed about with the pillow again, from this side of the bed.

Then he said simply, "Tell me what it is you see."

McKenzie took a deep breath. "Blood. I see blood."

"Where?"

"Sometimes, everywhere. Sometimes, just . . . in certain places."

"On me?" His face never changed expression. Kind eyes, intent on her.

"Not until just now."

"Where?"

"Your arms. Your wrists. Your hands. Oh, God." And she ducked away, unable to look at him any longer.

He took her right hand in his. His skin was warm, but dry, slightly calloused as if, at one time in his life, he'd done a fair amount of hard labor. She heard a rustle of fabric and then he was taking her hand in his, guiding her fingertips over the inside of his wrist with his other hand. Soft hair interrupted the skin, and then she felt welts, gnarled tracks.

She looked.

Her fingertips rested across scars that were old enough so the pink had gone from them. Carter traced her touch the length of one set, and then the other. He dropped her hand and rolled up his other sleeve.

"Here, too."

Not as evident or as forceful. McKenzie withdrew her hand from his, then looked into his face.

"You saw blood, all right. Mine. All mine."

"What—"

"I tried to commit suicide. Twice."

"Oh, Carter." McKenzie bit her lip. "Why?"

He turned, caught a stool with the toe of his shoe, and pulled it close so he could sit down. "My writing was responsible for getting a convicted man off Death Row."

"Was he guilty?"

"Oh, yes. We all knew it."

She did not know what to ask. "Did you . . . did you lie about it to get him freed?"

"No. But I got involved. You see, he'd killed a number of people. The closer he got to his death sentence, the more he decided to talk. But it was me he talked to. I wanted the story. I made the mistake of listening. Then, when I'd heard what he had to say, it was too late. His sentence got commuted, as long as he kept talking."

"That wasn't your fault."

"No." Carter looked down at his sleeves, rolled them back into place, buttoned the cuffs loosely. He'd gotten used to wearing long-sleeved shirts, even in L.A.'s sometimes hellish summer weather. "No. But some idiot decided he wanted to study Georg Bauer's brain—that was his name—and Bauer took advantage of the possi-bilities. He escaped and started killing again."

She knew the name. Vaguely knew the cold, calculating face from television shots. "Oh, God. Carter, I'm so sorry."

"Yeah. Me, too. It's been years. The first time or two, he," Carter stopped, swallowed. "He sent me a thank you note. So, after these healed, I decided I'd find him. I've been looking ever since."

Mac put a hand to her scalp, remembering. "My hair. Did you think—"

"At first."

She put her hand down. It shook a little, so she covered it with her other hand.

"I don't know why you saw what you did, McKenzie, but that doesn't make you crazy."

"No?"

"No."

"Then what does it make me?"

"Something different, something wonderful."

Carter left, a feeling settling somewhere between the pit of his stomach and the damaged part of his heart he had thought would never heal. He had left her sleeping again, resting lightly, but this time there was a serenity over her features he hadn't seen there before. He did not think he was fooling himself by thinking he'd put it there.

He bumped into a gurney in the hallway. The orderly bringing it out of a room had oversteered and they collided. He and the blonde woman following it stepped aside. She had a doctor's jacket on over her expensive suit. She looked at Carter only slightly more warmly than she might look at a cockroach.

He danced aside a step. "Sorry." He looked down at the gurney. A young boy was wrapped tightly into the sheets and strapped down to the stretcher. His face was slack, the eyes closed, drool stringing from his mouth. "I didn't hurt him—"

"No," the doctor said coolly. "He's catatonic. You wouldn't reach him if you nuked him."

She motioned the orderly to push the gurney down the corridor.

Carter's pleasant mood thinned considerably. "Sorry," he repeated inadequately.

"It was nothing you did," the doctor said. She turned away, following after her patient. She had a crumpled-up napkin in her hand, a drawing he thought, for he could see the multicolors of crayon decorating it. As she walked, she crumpled the napkin up into a tighter and tighter ball until Carter could see nothing of it whatsoever.

He signed out at the reception desk, verifying it with the attendant, and left, telling himself he would leave McKenzie there no longer than necessary. He did not see a lean, hard-jawed man back into a room entrance as he passed, a man who watched him intently.

Jack watched the other man go by. The receptionist had stopped him cold, even in janitorial jumpers, but this jerk had waltzed right in like he owned the place. He leaned on his mop, waiting until the other's footsteps had faded and he could hear elevator doors. Who the hell was this Carter Wyndall and what was he doing here with McKenzie? He could feel his lips thin as though he were sucking out a long-necked bottle of beer without taking a breath. Maybe he'd taken the baseball bat to the wrong man in Mac's life. She hadn't come running home to papa. She'd had another stud waiting for her all along. Maybe she'd met him on the college campus. They were always bringing in some liberal jerk to lecture. Well, she wouldn't get away with it. She might be locked behind closed doors, but Carter Wyndall wasn't. Time to get in a little more practice, Jack decided. He dropped the mop in the alcove. "Batters up!"

Chapter 24

John Whiteside woke to a promising Seattle day. The sky was a brilliant cerulean blue and the few clouds which came through were faint, white tails which drifted by quickly. He showered, shaved, and came out to the kitchen, looking for coffee since Sarah had already been out of bed long enough that her side had been cold when he got up. But the kitchen, when he walked in, was even cooler. He double-checked the coffeemaker, his face twisted in disappointment. The filter unit was clean and ready to go, but that was it. Sarah must have had an early meeting, planning for the summer school session. He decided to rummage through his in-laws' cupboards and make coffee himself.

It was an experience he didn't relish. He didn't like pawing through other people's belongings and damn sure didn't like the idea of somebody going through his. While the coffee began to brew, he found the morning paper at the front door. Sarah didn't read the morning paper, but she at least could have tossed it in, he thought as he tucked it under his elbow. Good thing it was a clear day.

The whole idea of spending the time at the in-laws was not a comfortable one for him, but Sarah had been so emphatic after McKenzie's ordeal that he knew he'd be voted down if he objected, so he hadn't. Last night the kids had spent the evening with their friends to get off to school more easily, so he was able to kick back and read the paper the way he liked to without the various sections being torn out of his hands. He'd call Sarah from the line at lunchtime and see what was up. He finished his coffee with an English muffin, then left for work.

He called early for lunch and got his mother-in-law. "Hey, Betsy. Is Sarah home yet?"

"Oh, John. I'm so glad to hear from you. We were worried about Sarah. No, she's not home."

"She's probably tied up in a meeting. She told me the book budget was murder for the summer session. Well, just tell her I called. I'll be home around five thirty."

Betsy Beckmann hung up and turned to her husband, who'd drifted into the kitchen when the phone rang. She smiled in relief. "That was John. He said Sarah had gone to a meeting at school. You see, we were all worried over nothing. They'll both be home later."

Chester Beckmann warmed up his coffee, nodding. "That's good. I didn't think that could be her I heard leaving last night. Probably the Collins girl next door. I know she's twenty, and all, but they should make her stick to reasonable hours coming and going."

His wife put her hand on her shoulder. "I listen to you talking, and hear your father. Remember when we were dating?"

Chester tilted his head a little. "Do I!" He laughed, and drew his wife closer to him.

At five thirty, John trudged up the sidewalk to his in-laws' house, stomping the factory dirt off his shoes. He came in the kitchen door to find both of them sitting at the table, fixing snap beans for dinner. The family van hadn't been in the drive.

"Sarah still not home?"

"No, John. That meeting must have run over."

"You hear from her?" He poured himself a fresh cup of coffee and tasted it. From the strength of it, it was the same batch he'd brewed that morning. Well, it was better than nothing.

"No, just what you told me, that she'd gone to school."

He blinked, both at the slight bitterness of the drink, and at his mother-in-law. "But she never called you? I mean, I don't know that she went into work. I just assumed . . . she wasn't here this morning when I got up—" Chester Beckmann stood up. "We thought you knew where she was."

John was already fishing out his well-worn leather wallet and taking out the number for the English department. Without saying anything to his father-in-law, he picked up the phone and dialed.

He got one of the department secretaries who giggled a little at the idea that Sarah would be there, adding, "We don't even start work on the summer session until next week. Even teachers get some time off!"

He hung up. "No meeting," he said to Betsy's worried face. "She hasn't been there."

"Then where could she be?"

John Whiteside stood for a moment. His clothes were stiff with metallic dust and dirt from his job as plant manager, and his feet hurt vaguely, and one knuckle stung from when he'd had to take a wrench to a stubborn tool and the setup and the sucker had flipped back on him. He didn't want his wife to be missing. He didn't want to not know where she was or what she was doing.

"I'm going home," he said. "First. I'll call from there."

It made him feel no better to see the van in the driveway, dusk gathering about the house, when he pulled up. House lights were on, blazing out the windows. As he approached the driveway entrance, flies buzzed angrily in and out, a lot of them that sunset hadn't yet driven away, and he could smell the reek of death.

He charged through the door and damn near killed himself tripping over his wife's prone figure. It was the grotesque object in the open refrigerator that smelled, swollen and crawling with flies. He caught himself on the kitchen counter, turned, and looked.

It might have been a dog's head, once, tongue blackened and pushing out of the toothful grimacing mouth. He pushed the refrigerator door shut, trapping flies and the stink inside, thinking that they'd never use that appliance again. Sarah groaned and stirred on the floor, her glasses lopsided on her face, her sable hair feathered about her head.

He wet a kitchen towel and knelt beside her. As he ran a hand over the back of her head, helping her to sit, he could feel a lump the size of a goose egg. She must have fainted and knocked herself cold.

She held onto his hands with hers, chilled. "John—the fridge—"

"I know."

"It was Cody."

He hadn't known McKenzie or her dog that well, though she'd brought him over to play with the kids a couple of times. The carrion object was not recognizable to him. But its significance was.

"He's been here."

Sarah shuddered. "He's been all over here." She groaned. "What time is it?"

"About seven."

"God. I've been here all night."

"And day. Do you want me to call the paramedics?"

She started to shake her head no, then winced. "Later," she amended. "I've got to call someone first."

"Who?"

"On the machine. Some policeman in Los Angeles. McKenzie's in trouble." She groaned again, and licked chapped lips. "John, I'm so scared. She's in real trouble."

Carter was more than ready for mu shu pork and lo mein by the time the knock on the door sounded. He yanked it open eagerly and then slammed it shut.

The brief moment had shown Dolan framed by the two Feds, Franklin and Sofer, an apologetic look on the spotted editorial assistant's face.

Carter had not locked the door and had only moved away a step or two when it opened on its own and the three men edged inside, Dolan whining, "Jeez." A cloud of fragrant smells from the carry-out dinner came with them, scents of plum sauce and garlic and other wonderful aromas.

"I'm sorry, Windy."

"Forget it." Carter watched the Feds shut the front door carefully.

Franklin wore a hideously purple tie this time, like something dyed at the bottom of grape fermentation vats. A pink neon golf club graced its widely flared bottom. Sofer looked like he'd acquired a sunburn since yesterday, and it had already begun to peel down his freckled forehead. Carter felt his nose twitch. He rubbed at it to hide whatever he was really thinking and said, "How did you know?"

Franklin sat down on the edge of the low bookcase which ran the length of the living room wall. "I learned something last year," he said, settling his tie over his belt and navel. "I got to spend a month in London at New Scotland Yard. It's not that they're any better than we are, it's just that they're so damn thorough."

Sofer let go of Dolan's arm and the lanky young man made a bee-line for the dinette table and sat down, bags and all, his face creased in sorrow at his failure. One of the bags had begun to leak a little, and smelled of the brown sauce used with lo mein. Under Dolan's elbow was a tightly clenched file folder, but Carter had no doubt Franklin or Sofer would take it whenever they wanted.

Sofer said, "We asked around about the pizza delivery. Seems you don't get your pizza that way. The neighbors say you like to go down to D'amico's two blocks over for free pitcher night, that you have a fondness for hot pizza and cold beer. The neighbors say last night was the first night in their memory you've ever had pizza delivered. So we wondered who was delivering, and what."

Franklin finished, "So when the same kid showed up tonight with Chinese, we knew you were having something else delivered." He pointed with his chin to the computer. "A little behind in your technology?"

Dolan sniffed. "Told you guys it's all he can do to just turn it on. There's no way I can get him to download a GIF, or modem files."

"Dinosaurs," Franklin interrupted. "We're both dinosaurs, Carter. If you'd stuck to the computer for transmission, we wouldn't be here now. But you had to have hand-to-hand delivery. That's the way of things, isn't it? You're just enough over forty to be slightly out of step. Let's see what you've got in the folder."

Carter came over to the dinette as Dolan, nudged by Agent Sofer, opened the folder and spread it out. Two pictures, one the computer-generated photo he'd had yesterday and the other an aged copy, putting the girl into the womanhood she'd probably achieve today. The two agents looked at the revised photo. Franklin muttered, grudgingly, "Not bad work."

"Thanks." Enthusiasm replaced the misery on Dolan's spotted face. "We didn't have the artist do much here and here—the bone structure suggested she wouldn't age a lot. And it's only been, what, ten, twelve years?"

Carter looked at the woman. The computer had colorized the photo, and the sharp blue eyes glared at him from under a fringe of malt-colored hair. *Mousy brown*, he thought. He didn't know the woman. Still, her image niggled at him as though he ought to. The white lab coat had been replaced by updated clothing. They'd even changed the hairstyle slightly. He knew the artist the newspaper consulted was good at what she did. Her portraits had proven themselves time and again. He knew that when this woman was found, if she was found, she would probably match this rendition. Then, *why* didn't he recognize her as he'd thought he would?

Franklin said, as though he wasn't, really, "Sorry, Carter, but we've got to take this."

Carter sighed. He moved away from the dinette table. Dolan looked up, then away quickly. Sofer added, "And we'll be by tomorrow morning for the originals at your office."

The tension deflated abruptly from Dolan. He nodded, misery again settling on his features. Franklin and Sofer swapped looks.

"Look," added Franklin, smoothing his tie again. "If it's any consolation, whoever did John Nelson probably had nothing to do with the Bauer case. That's the way it's shaping up, anyway. Sources are telling us he came in because of a quiet, low profile investigation on Federal funding of the new subway system, and the problems with the methane gas underground and water seepage, and possible misuse of the money."

Carter felt his eyebrows go up. "He was hit because of the MTA?"

"Subcontractors had some Mafia connections, it appears. Anyway, the funding committee John was on had asked him to look into it, very subtly, but evidently someone knew he was coming."

Not that he'd ever really thought it could have been Bauer, but— Carter sat down at the little dinette opposite Dolan. Nelson shot because of a corruption probe. John always had hated government. He looked up, saw the two watching him.

"Thanks," he said.

Sofer shrugged. "No one's positive yet, but things are shaking down that way." He headed for the door. He looked back over his shoulder. "Don't suppose you could swap us any info?"

"I could try."

"What do you know about Mr. Blue?"

"Only that he isn't Bauer. The sheriff's cooperating pretty closely with the various police departments on this one, and they've kept the lid on. L.A. Basin doesn't even know they've got a serial killer yet and he's done six or seven women so far."

"Ten," Franklin corrected flatly. "That we've been able to identify."

"Shit. That's more than keeping the lid on. That stinks of cover-up." Carter got a hold of himself and continued, "He likes blue houses. And I'm told he takes a scalp lock souvenir. That's all I've been able to dig up."

"And," put in Sofer, "he starts fires."

Carter swiveled on the chair to look at the red-haired man who'd begun to sweat profusely again. "Fires?"

"He gets in and out easily," Sofer told him. "We haven't figured that one out yet, but he seems to know the houses and their weak points like the palm of his hand. Easy entry. But he likes to start fires and not to burn evidence. Drives the victim right into his arms."

"Organized or disorganized?" Carter asked, homing in on the Feds' VICAP profile. An organized killer was much harder to track. He could think on his feet, function despite the fantasies which drove him to violence and murder.

"I'd say very organized, at this juncture."

"What are my chances of getting your profile?"

Sofer pulled the door open for his partner. "First someone has to admit we have a killer to profile. Then we might share it with you. Off the record, of course. As a consultant. Only John put more work in on this than you have. Of course, there are the givens you should know, profile or not. Probably white, male, about twenty-five. A history of aggression toward women, unsuccessful relationships. The usual with a killer of this sort." He held Dolan's file folder in his hands. He looked back, at the sacks of Chinese food. "Wouldn't have enough for four?"

Dolan shook his head quickly. "Sorry, guys."

Franklin nodded, and the two men left. There was a very long moment of silence, during which Carter got to his feet, locked the door, and then stood by the window at an angle, watching the street. Finally he said, "They're gone."

Dolan put his foot up on the table, slid up his jeans leg and pulled a 3½ inch floppy disk out of the top of his white athletic socks.

"What have you got?"

Grinning, Dolan sat down at the computer, sliding the disk into its drive. "Mu shu pork, and Three Flavors lo mein, and chicken fried rice, just like you ordered." The computer beeped faintly as he booted it up.

"I mean, on there."

"Took me all day, but I think I've got a couple of possibilities."

The screen began to compose a color picture. Carter stood, watching intently, as the dots came together, almost like a pointillist picture, until he was looking at a computer-generated image of a newspaper photo.

He shook his head. "No, I don't see her."

Dolan stabbed a broken nail at the screen. "See?"

They studied it together.

Carter shook his head again. "Not her."

"Okay. Well, I stuck to stories you've done in the last couple of years, hoping Nelson had seen a connection between you and her. Try this one."

The screen went blank and then began to compose itself again. Slowly, inexorably. Carter saw the outlines of a platform dais, peopled with images as though a ceremony were taking place, Century City skyscrapers in the backdrop.

Suddenly, there she was. Mousy hair no longer, but a striking blonde, figure no longer in grunge undergraduate clothing, but a designer suit dress. The slender figure, and the avid expression had not aged that much over the years. He looked at the caption under the photo.

"Dr. Susan Craig keynotes expansion of the Women's Shelter center. . . ."

At her elbow was an outdated hospital, damaged by the Northridge quake and closed down, and the whole event taking place had been held to purchase and renovate the hospital into a woman's center. He remembered the story now, with the vague addition that the project had fallen through, budget constraints failing it. The urgency of the school crisis had driven it out of the political spotlight.

"This is social stuff. What's your byline doing on it?"

Carter tried to ease the stiffness of his neck. "They twisted my arm. I'd done a series of pieces on the homeless who'd moved into the hospital after it was abandoned. When it got bought out and fenced off, I had the most background to do the expansion story. The center never happened, though." After two years of wrangling, the hospital was going to be coming down, replaced instead by a neighborhood easement and platform for the MTA subway line. At one time he'd known the hospital like the back of his hand. He sighed. That was a lot of stories ago. He concentrated on the photo in front of him.

He put a finger to the screen, touching the platinum hair. "That's her, by God."

Dolan beamed. "Now all you've got to do is find her."

A sharp stab of concern replaced the joy of recognition.

He knew where she was all right. He'd practically walked right through her at the Mount Mercy psychiatric ward. What suspicions had John Nelson had about the doctor that he'd never lived to voice?

And she had McKenzie Smith.

Chapter 25

Hotchkiss watched the sun dip down over Lake Arrowhead. Blue jays whisked past the deck railing, scolding him. A squirrel ran along it like a gymnast on the balance beam, found the saucer full of peanut hearts he'd set out, stuffed a cheek pouch, and left. All while the sky turned the color of pink lemonade, illuminating mares' tails of clouds. Beautiful. Peaceful.

And if he had any guts at all, he would take this incredibly serene day and make it his last.

Maybe going down the mountain, he could just miss a curve and sail off a cliff into the forest, a glorious, burning statement for personal freedom, like *Thelma and Louise.*

Or he could just crash and burn.

Hotchkiss rubbed his forehead as if he could bury the worries that gnawed through his skull. He'd called his voice mail and gotten an update on Ibie Walker. The councilman had improved, but it would be forty-eight to seventy-two hours before his doctors would hazard a guess about the extent of his recovery. As it was, he had partial paralysis and no speech. The frailty of the mind within the body could not even begin to be ascertained.

His party wanted him to be ready. Ready to leap into a run for the seat which would almost certainly be up for election in September no matter who occupied it now. They wanted him to voice support of Ibie and his policies and indicate that there was a legacy there which needed to be carried on. In his own inimitable way, of course. And they wanted him to come down for a meeting, as soon as possible.

And there was a single, terse last message. *Call us when you're ready to deal.* The number was an unfamiliar one, but he knew who'd called. *They* had.

Even as the pink sky deepened into hues of mauve and indigo, gradually feathering into gray and sooty night, he contemplated the irony of his life. The length to which he'd gone to stay free of entanglements, deals, strings, commitments. As a politician, he'd struggled to remain unfettered so that he could truly vote his conscience. His sexual preferences had nothing to do with his conscience, really. Yet now he could no longer avoid them, for they had changed his life forever. It was no longer a simple matter of gratification.

If he even dared ask what they proposed, they would know they had him. Yet, if he did not ask, begin a negotiation, he would never know if this was something he could, after all, live with. There was no one he could turn to. Even his mother could not be trusted with his confidences.

Hotchkiss rubbed his brow again. The squirrel cleaned out the peanut dish, knocked it rolling to the deck, flicked its tail, and ran off, scolding him for the noise and inconvenience. He got up from his chair and strolled back into his bedroom.

His laptop sat open on the vanity, its modem plugged into the local telephone wires. Hotchkiss pulled up his stool and booted it up.

He dialed a bulletin board. After a moment, the screen showed him online. He typed in his password.

The account was billed through a series of screens and false identities that would lead all the way to the Cayman Islands. It would take, he hoped, a great deal of energy to crack.

>>HELLO. YOU'RE ONLINE.<<

>>HELLO<<, he typed back. >>I'M A VERY, VERY LONELY BOY.<<

Instantly, it seemed, the screen crowded with responses from other, very lonely boys. Stephen's fingers moved over the keys faster and faster as he gained confidence in his conversation. In a short matter of time, they would pair off in private conferences, and begin to exchange intimacies. Perhaps even photos. He had a file just for that, picturing himself as a tall, unmarked twelve-year-old boy with sable hair and sad, turquoise eyes.

A warm glow began in his groin and spread outward, comforting him. He could be loved. He was loved. There was every kind of intimacy here that could be imagined or initiated.

And, if he wished, he could meet the boy at the other end of the phone line.

Stephen's fingers flew.

Perhaps in the morning he would call the anonymous number and see what they wished of him. Perhaps he could deal with it.

Perhaps he would not have to end all of this after all.

>>HELLO, LONELY BOY. I'M A LONELY AND NAUGHTY BOY.<<

Graciela straightened over the last battered cardboard box, put a hand to the small of her neck, *ay, que dolor,* what a pain she had there. Donaldo had stopped unpacking and sat in the room which would be his, bouncing a hard blue handball off the white walls. Thud, thud, thud. The noise echoed in the emptiness. He had nothing but boxes of clothes and a sleeping bag in there. She'd change that, maybe not overnight, but he'd have his bed like a race car, and a dresser, and a boom box, and posters on his wall, just like any other kid. Graciela crossed herself, willing it to be God's will as well as her own.

The handball thudded sullenly again. Thud, thud, thud.

"Donnie! *Callate!* Shut up with that, okay?"

He caught the ball and got to his feet, scowling with the handsome dark looks of his father. "When are we gonna eat?"

She mopped her forehead with the back of her hand. The only utility they had on so far was the electricity—and the stove was gas. The refrigerator hummed, but it stood empty. She had a small amount of money the shelter had advanced her. Tomorrow night the cupboard would have rice and cereal and the refrigerator milk, but now. . . . "How about Mickey D's?"

It brought the first smile she'd seen since that morning when they'd begun packing to leave the shelter. Graciela returned it. "Okay, but you've got to hang up your clothes first."

"What for?"

Her anger flared. "What for? Do I got to tell you over and over again? This place has to look nice. I've got a chance to be the assistant manager here. It's empty now, so you can make noise and stomp around, but next week, in a couple of weeks, it's going to be full of people. Nine apartments like this one. And I'll have a job at the beauty parlor, and I'll have a job here. The manager is a nice man. This is a big opportunity, our big chance. I want this to look nice when Mr. Patel comes back tomorrow."

A sneer flashed across his face. "Some opportunity," he said, adding with a wisdom beyond his age, "All you have to do is to keep humping him."

"Donaldo!" The anger flashed from her head down her arm and into her hand, but she did not swing. She bit her lip until she could taste the blood, but she did not hit him. He knew, and yet he did not know, what he was saying by that. Her face grew hot, and she curled her fingers into a fist until her nails bit into the skin. "Don't talk like that about me, *hijo*. I'm your mother."

"Yeah." He looked around. "Nobody else lives here because the quake ruined it."

"And now it's all fixed," she said firmly. "And it looks brand new, jus' like us. Now get in your room and do what I told you, or it'll be too late to go get dinner."

He turned slowly, deliberately, as if to show her he was still boss. Graciela did not let any more words past her teeth. So much like his father, the bastard, the son was. Yet she loved him, had loved them both. She could not help it.

The apartment manager was not Latino, and he was older, but there had been something quiet about him she had liked from the first moment they met. He had been simpatico about her problems, her need to find a home for Donnie.

So what if her son was right, and wrong, about her relationship with him? It was her life, too.

Graciela squared her shoulders. She had a lot of work to do.

It was barely dusk, and he moved through the quiet alleyways, taking heed of those coming home from work and searching for parking places. He didn't like doing anyone this early, but she had given him his orders, and he did not yet feel like disobeying her. She meant too much to him. She'd anchored him when he'd been set adrift, and he knew she helped him in all the things that he did.

Even things like this.

The apartment unit did not look right to him, set off by an empty lot and across from another, but he could see that it had been restructured extensively, retrofitted after the Northridge quake. The empty lots had probably been other apartment houses which had come down instead of being redone. The isolation of the building both helped and hindered him. It would be difficult to move in close, but there would be less chance any disturbance could be clearly heard.

He did not like the aura the building gave off. Under the gear, little pools of sweat broke through and ran down the cheekbones of his face. He stood in eave-high oleander bushes, and watched his prey, waiting until the sun lowered a bit more.

Ta-rah-rah-BOOM-ti-ay, have you had yours today, I got mine yesterday from the girl across the waa-ay—

"You get the girl, Dudley, and I get the boy. I want that boy brought back. And I don't want any sign that you did that. I don't want anybody looking for the boy. Understand?"

Oh, he understood.

Dudley shifted weight, the industrial strength lawn bag across his shoulders like a Santa's pack filled with a curled limp body still cooling, a cocky kid from off the streets, neck broken like that, *car-rack*, and no one would be looking for the first boy. She had not asked how he intended to cover his tracks, and he knew it was because she had not really cared. She said children were important to her, all children, but he always thought of what she said like what had been written in *Animal Farm*. All animals were equal, only some animals were a lot more equal than others.

She wanted the first boy. She would get him. That was all that counted.

He watched the windows through the gear. Unless he missed his guess, the building was totally empty, as she'd told him it would be. Only a battered silver Corolla hunkered down at the curb. The carports in back stood empty, the windows stayed blank and dark. He swung his head slowly back and forth so that his augmented vision could keep up with him.

The final scan took only a few moments. Dudley analyzed what he saw, picking out the weak spots in the building, the three stories of regular apartments, side by side, with a single, bigger apartment on the basement level, shared with what would be a laundry room and utility basement for the furnace, air, and such. He spotted the accesses and egresses, the fire escape, everything he needed to know. The only thing he could not change was the overall feel of the building.

It was not cool enough. As the killing fever seared its way through his veins, the sweat poured out of him. It pooled under the helmet, plastering his hair to his head slickly. Dudley boosted the sack on his back, as it seemed to grow heavier, and decided he could wait no longer.

He put a hand to his gear, activating the program he needed. He took a long, slow approach to the building, making sure he was not seen. The debris- and weed-laden lots made it easier. By the time he hugged the shadowed, hidden side of the apartment house, the program he wanted played on the visor screen, showing him the building it had identified through the scan and its most logical floor plan. The visor had been designed so that he could see through it, with the virtual reality program an overlay over his own vision.

She would have nowhere to run that he didn't already know about. Nowhere to hide.

Dudley moved into hunting mode.

He stashed the boy's body in the laundry room. He could feel the heat rippling off him. He could feel the fire's brilliance eating through his skin, like a sun about to go nova. He was flame. He was power and destruction let loose. He was . . .

. . . *the sleeping man stirred.*

Dudley stumbled in his tracks, caught himself, flexed his grip around the haft of his knife. *He* liked to do things differently. Dudley ground his teeth. The abrasion made his jaw ache, the cords on his neck stand out.

She had always been disappointed that he was not more like the sleeping man. She had never said so directly to him, but Dudley knew. It scarcely mattered to him now. When the evening was over, he would feel a strange emptiness, a draining, a depression that he had somehow failed her again. It would matter then, because her acceptance of him mattered to Dudley.

He needed it.

It was all he had.

Dudley gritted his teeth again. The movement made him ache

throughout his skull. He let himself burn. The sleeping man liked shadow. He would not stand for the fiery torch Dudley had become. Dudley drove him out, as he had time and time again.

He found himself standing on the back stairs. The building, without occupant or appliance, was preternaturally quiet. Sweat ran off his face, had pooled at his feet. His shoulder, braced against the internal wall, had gone numb as if he had tried to drive it into the newly painted plaster. How long had he stood there, putting demons to rest?

Too long.

There was a sound behind him, a choked noise. Dudley whirled and struck, without thought, all sinuous movement from his chin to his fingers.

The boy sank without a whimper, eyes wide, staring at him, at Dudley's face obscured by the gear, the knife blossoming in the dead center of his childish throat.

Shit!

She would never forgive him this, never. Dudley pulled the knife free. There was a gurgling sound as the boy died, inhaling his own blood. Dudley scooped up the small frame and made his way back to the laundry room, where he dropped his burden on top of the other. A litany of lies ran like wildfire through his brain. The boy wasn't there. The boy was there. The mother had beaten him. Nothing he could do. No. The boy wasn't there, he'd run away. Or the boy was there. He'd tried to protect his mother. Dudley'd had no choice.

Maybe that last would suffice.

He decided it was time to build his fire.

Hands shaking, he searched inside his waistband for the homemade accelerator, a chemical which would ensure the results he wanted, without leaving a telltale trace. He brought the pouch up and shook it out.

Graciela smelled the faintest tinge of smoke. She paused, kitchen cabinet door open, and turned. The smell grew stronger as she did, then faded again.

She frowned and wiped her hands on a paper towel. Donnie was at that age. She decided to see what he was doing so quietly in his new bedroom. Matches were strictly off-limits for him, but she'd had trouble with him playing with them before. Parenting classes at the shelter had taught her it was normal. Not that she should allow it to continue, but that he would be curious.

As she passed through the living room from the kitchen, she noticed the front door ever so slightly ajar. She stopped.

"Donnie?"

No answer.

Her heart felt as if it had lodged somewhere in her throat. She ran to the bedroom. The door flung wide open before her. The room was empty.

"Donaldo!" Graciela tore through the tiny apartment and out the front door. She could smell smoke again, this time very definitely. She hesitated in the hallway. What if he'd set a fire? No phone yet. What could she do? Let it not be a fire. Her whole future hung before her. Her son, her new home. She ran in search of Donnie, praying for the best.

She did not know the building well yet. The hallway took her downstairs and around a corner, then sank into dimness. But she could smell the smoke again, and thought perhaps she could even see a wisp of gray puffing into the air.

"Oh, shit, *hijo*," she cried, and plunged down the basement steps.

She came to a halt as something dark and menacing moved at the foot of the stairwell, shadows coming together and taking shape. Something glinted in its hand.

Almost a man.

Almost a man, but not quite, a mask obscuring its face, a mask staring at her with glittery, shimmering lenses. A deathlike visage, ebony carved and grotesque, watching her.

And it carried a knife.

"I've been waiting for you," the being said.

Dudley had had all sorts of reactions, but he was not quite prepared for what she did. Without a sound, she turned and leaped like a gazelle up the stairwell, taking the steps, two and even three at a time. He thundered up after her, gaining the hall too late to see her slim form disappear.

But he heard the slamming of a door. He swung his head. The VR program overlaid the floor plan. That had to be the door to the interior stairs between floors. If she were returning to her apartment, she'd become confused. She was going the wrong way. And he knew exactly which way he had to go to cut her off.

He peeled his lips back off his teeth and sprinted down the hallway.

They met nearly face-to-face at the next T-intersection. Graciela slid to a stop, scrambling, her sneakered feet nearly slipping out from underneath her, her bosomy chest heaving under its T-shirt. She cursed, in Spanish, then flung herself away as he grabbed for her. He caught the worn sleeve of her shirt. It ripped away in his hand.

She would head back to the basement stairs again. The smoke would drive her away. This time she would be headed in the right direction, toward her apartment.

She would slam and lock the door, hoping to keep him out.

She might even try climbing out the window for help.

He would be there first.

Dudley moved swiftly.

She ran blindly, the smoke stinging her eyes, her shirt sliding off her shoulder. Her sneakers squeaked on the heavily polished floor. There wasn't a thought in her head, not for Donaldo, not even for herself, except to flee. She careened away from the basement stairwell a second time. Thick, black clouds rolled up from below, and she smelled the unmistakable odor of the fire. She veered away, found a turn in the hallway, remembered it, and ran desperately for her apartment.

She slammed the door behind her and slid the two dead bolts into place and then the door lock. It would not hold the beast behind her for long. Graciela looked desperately around the empty rooms. The first floor was not really a ground floor, because of the basement level. She was up, maybe half a story. She had a veranda, a balcony off the living room, instead of ordinary living room windows. The jump wasn't far.

She crossed the living room.

It came out of the kitchen.

Graciela sidestepped her attacker and flung herself at the sliding glass doors, screaming. He dug his free hand into her hair, pulling her back into his hard embrace, and said softly, "I don't think anyone can hear you."

She tore at his hand. The glove stripped away, knife clattering to the floor, and she sank her teeth into his flesh, tearing savagely. Dudley's rage flared white-hot.

The sleeping man roused.

Chapter 26

"All right, so that's her doctor. Who's the buff guy standing with her, this guy here?"

Carter stood at the phone, staring at the editorial assistant, but not seeing him, listening to the drill as he left another page for Joyce. "She's either out of range, or she's got the damn thing turned off." He slammed the phone down. "I can't get in this late without her." He scrubbed at his face in frustration. "What did you want?"

"I just wondered if you knew this guy with her."

Carter perched on his chair as Dolan stabbed a finger at the screen. The picture was slightly out of focus beyond Susan Craig, but he could see the man Dolan asked about. He started to say, "DamnifI-know," and stopped. Because he did know. "That's a firefighter. I can't remember his name, he was some kind of hero or something. Burning building dropped a beam on his head, but not before he got a baby and couple of kids out. They had to put his skull back together. He was working with her on some project. Let me think." Carter paused. So many stories. He never thought he'd forget any of them when he'd first started seeing his byline, but it happened. You couldn't remember them all, no matter how you tried. Memory, like a drowning man, struggled to surface.

Dolan said, "I can always call the morgue, see what they've got on file."

"He wouldn't be listed. He's not part of this story, just an escort." Carter took a swig of the Tsing-Tao, which had begun to warm slightly. The beer seemed to loosen the old synapses. "I've got it. They were working on a virtual reality program for firefighting. Architectural imaging, hooked into high-tech helmet equipment for the firemen. It was like medical imaging—see the tip of the iceberg, project the entire structure."

"I don't get it. I know about the medical programs. They track tumors that way, other surgery. But I've never heard of architectural imaging."

"Neither had anybody else. She didn't get the funding for that, either. They wanted to project an overlay into the helmet visors. The image would give them the floor plan of the building they were about to enter. That way, even with no visibility because of the smoke and flames, the firefighters would have a good idea where they were and where they wanted to go."

Dolan sat back in his chair. He let out a low whistle. "Impressive. It might work."

"Nobody thought so two years ago. Nobody wanted to foot the bill to put blueprints into a database. The thought was that the programming wouldn't be feasible. There was the question of manpower, and also access to the blueprints. If it would even work. You've got to admit," and Carter drained the last of the beer. He rocked back in his chair, balancing it on the back two feet. "Virtual reality has come a long way since then."

"Not that anybody could prove it by you." Dolan put his hands into the air and wiggled his fingers. "You still type by hunt and peck."

"I type a hell of a lot faster than that."

"Sure." Dolan moved back to the screen. "It wasn't a bad idea. Scanning technology today could make building the database a lot easier. . . ." He pursed his lips in thought. "They say going into a burning building is like going into a black hell. To know where you are, at all times, regardless—"

Carter was caught in a swirl of his own thoughts. To pit a killer like Mr. Blue, who liked to break into buildings and start fires and kill, against a man like that firefighter, who rescued lives and put out fires . . . what was a man like that doing paired with Susan Craig, who was clearly, avidly, attracted by Bauer's type?

What would a human predator do with a program which would give him access into any building he wanted? How well could he hunt and stalk then?

A cold chill went down Carter's spine. He set his chair carefully down on all fours.

The phone rang jarringly. He leaped up from the computer desk and snatched it up.

Joyce said testily, "You're beginning to bug me."

"I'm sorry, Joyce, but I had to get hold of you. I want to get Mac out of Psychiatric."

"Why?" Suspicion tinged her rich voice.

He had no proof to offer her. Even Nelson had had no proof of anything, just a nearly intangible lead to a serial killer long gone from the public eye. That did not make her an accessory to anything Bauer had done. It did not make her a suspect in Nelson's killing. He had nothing but a spine that felt as though polar bears had decided to make a slide out of it.

"You're taking too long to think, Carter. That means you're going to tell me a story."

"No. No stories. Honest to God, I can't give you a reason. I just don't think she belongs in the hospital. Can't we get her into protective custody or something?"

"She committed voluntarily for forty-eight hours of observation. Even if I could get Moreno to budge, I couldn't get her out before then. And if I could get her out tomorrow night, where would she go?"

Carter cleared his throat, and Joyce interrupted, "Uh-huh, boyfriend, no way. Don't even say it." She paused. "Come to think of it, I might have a place. New shelter, not open yet, but just about ready to go. I'd have to stay with her, but I think I could get the okay to go in for a couple of days. That's what it's there for. What's this all about, anyway?"

"I don't want anybody messing with her mind."

"Or any other little bit of her, I expect." Joyce chuckled. She stopped. "What's up?"

"Nothing I can pinpoint. What do you know about Susan Craig?"

"*Doctor* Craig? She works there, has her own unit within the unit, called CyberImago or some such. She does a lot with imaging. Self-esteem, biofeedback for nervousness and pain, virtual reality rehab for stroke victims."

"Sounds diverse."

"It's all part of the computer technology. All of it uses virtual reality programming. I've seen her work. She's good. No bedside manner, but she gets results."

"I don't like the result she got from Mac today." Carter briefly described the emotional state in which he'd found McKenzie. "And I don't like the fact that John Nelson came to L.A., hoping to find her."

"Congressman Nelson?"

"The one they just shipped home in a box."

"How do you know he was looking for her?"

"Because," he told her, "John was hoping I might help him find her. Craig was a graduate assistant, working with Georg Bauer when he escaped."

"My, my."

Joyce knew a little of his obsession with Bauer. He said, "John never gave up either."

"I guess not. Well, that doesn't make Dr. Craig poison, either, but I'll see what I can do. Just keep your trigger finger off my beeper. I'll call you when I know something." Joyce hung up.

The polar bears were still doing bobsled runs down his spine, but they'd slowed up some.

Dolan looked at him.

"She said she'd try," Carter repeated.

Dolan nodded morosely.

The only good thing about going home for a late dinner was that the food would be chilled and the traffic thinner. The day had been hot and smoggy, and the roads congested, so Moreno guessed that everything evened out. The first thing he did when he walked in the door was grab the portable phone so he could check his voice mail while he stood in the glow of the open refrigerator door, enjoying the temperature as he decided what to eat. Margo called from the other room, over the television noise of her favorite series, "Don't stand there with the icebox open."

"Anything to eat?"

"It's all to eat," she called back.

Naturally. He punched in the office number and started listening to his mailbox. If he stayed in the office to pick up these messages, he'd never leave. Half of them were just fellow officers passing along grievances of the day or, in some cases, a tip or two. He pulled out a bowl of what looked to be tuna salad. On closer inspection, it was salmon salad, even better. He could tell it was leftovers, because the bowl was less than half full. He couldn't get in too much trouble for finishing it. He would ask, but he was too fond of salmon salad to risk losing it.

He grabbed a fork, a bottle of chilled iced tea, and sat at the kitchen table to eat. The salad must have been dinner because the celery was still crisp. He munched in enjoyment as his messages rolled on.

Then he sat up straight, changed the handset to the other ear, and pulled his notebook and pen out of his shirt pocket. He pushed the bowl aside. Sarah Whiteside of Seattle had finally returned his call.

He copied down the number, and repeated the message to verify it. He used the office charge card to return the call. He went through two or three very worried people before he finally got Sarah on the line.

"Officer Moreno?"

"Yes, Mrs. Whiteside. You returned my call earlier tonight, and I'm getting back to you."

He could hear a breathy sigh of relief on the line. "You're not him. I can hear a faint accent, can't I?"

"Not who, Mrs. Whiteside?"

"Jack Trebolt." She made another breathy sound, and he thought perhaps she had been crying. "But you couldn't really convince me long distance, could you?"

"I don't know how I can try. I can give you my shield number and have you call the desk sergeant, if that would help."

He heard a whispered conference, then she said, "No . . . no, that's okay. Please. Is McKenzie all right?"

"Yes and no. Before I get into that, I'd like to verify some information I have on Ms. Smith. Would you be willing to answer some questions?" He doodled on the page while there was a pause of consideration.

"She gave you my number?"

"Yes."

"I'll help if I can."

"We found ID on her that appears to be false. As far as you know, what name or names does she go under?"

"Oh, Smith. McKenzie Smith. We call her Mac. Jack was always very irritated she didn't take his name, but she didn't want to. She was a star softball player up here the first two years of college before she dropped out, but some of us remembered the name. She was proud of it."

"What about Fordham?"

That brought a little laugh. "Oh, God. She kept that? She bought that fake license when she first went to school. All the kids had 'em. For beer and stuff, y'know. She showed it to me once. It was so bad."

"Then," and he spoke as he made a notation in his book, "she didn't use it as an alias."

"No. Well, she might have used it when she left. At hotels and stuff. I know she was scared to death Jack might follow her."

"Did you know she was heading to the Los Angeles area? Had you told anyone?"

"No. She didn't want me to know. I never would have guessed. She hasn't talked to her father but once or twice since she left home. Listen, if Jack finds her, she's in serious danger. He broke into my home—he left—oh, God—he left their dog's head as a warning."

"He what?"

"She had a dog. Golden retriever. Cody made her so happy. That's what pushed her over the edge. Jack had beaten her a couple of times, and he was always verbally abusive, and sneaky mean, but he just flipped out. Killed the dog. She ran. She loved that dog like a child."

Moreno listened, marking that Trebolt had told him the opposite, that she had killed the dog. "Is there a police report that he broke into your house? Someone I could call?"

"They just took it tonight. I'll have to get back to you on that. Maybe they could fax it down. They told me, there's no proof who did it, but I know. He tracked mud all over. Little things. Then the . . . the other."

"Mrs. Whiteside, why weren't you at home?"

"We left. Just for a couple of days, you understand, but Mac had frightened me. So we moved out for a while. I couldn't get any messages off the machine, and I was worried about Mac, so I came back."

"And my message was the only one."

"Yes." Sarah Whiteside cleared her throat and sniffled slightly. "How did you know"?"

"Did you leave the machine on?"

"It's always on." She sounded as if the question had been ridiculous.

"It wasn't when I called."

"But you left a message—"

"The newer machines will kick on if there are more than a dozen rings or so. If you didn't turn the machine off, there's a possibility the intruder did, and then my call activated it. Call your police in the morning and ask them to fingerprint the answering machine, all right?"

"All right." Another low conference. Then Sarah said, "It had to have been Jack. He loves the telephone. He carries a portable cell phone wherever he goes. He used it to haunt Mac. She'd never know if he was in town or out on the road like he'd told her. He wouldn't let her drive or have her own car. When she finally bought one, we kept it for her. Arranged for permanent parking at school."

"You're a teacher, ma'am?"

"Community college. A professor."

"I see." He made a note as to her probable credibility. Then he brought the pen point up a line or two and circled "cell phone" heavily. Jack Trebolt could have been anywhere when Moreno had called him. Cellular calls could be forwarded easily enough. Anywhere.

Even L.A.

"Officer Moreno, please tell me what's happened to Mac?"

"We're still investigating, but she was involved in a domestic battery. She's been hospitalized for a couple of days, but she'll be all right."

"Oh, God. God," Whiteside repeated. "How bad?"

"Contusions and a mild concussion. Her father had a stroke and was pretty badly beaten. We haven't been able to corroborate that there was a third party involved. The neighbors called us in for a domestic disturbance. You've helped a lot."

There was a heavy silence, broken by, "You mean . . . you think Mac did it? She's a suspect?"

"Yes, ma'am, at the moment. But I have to tell you, you've changed the picture a lot. Can I reach you at this number again if I need to?"

"Yes, this is my parents' home. The Beckmanns. What hospital is she in? Can I call her?"

"She's at Mount Mercy. That's in the 818 area code. I'm sorry, but I don't have the number handy."

"That's all right. And thank you."

"No," said Moreno. "Thank you." He made an exclamation point at the bottom of his notebook as he hung up. There was a lot of crime happening in the Basin, but he made an extra note to call the lab in the morning and hustle their butts over latent prints on that baseball bat. He found himself wanting to prove Jack Trebolt had indeed been in the area.

Mac searched the game lounge a second time, heard the chimes ring softly, announcing that visiting hours were over, and she still had not found Brand. She worried that he might have been sulking, and she had not felt well enough to get up and about until after dinner. She hoped he was still not upset about her working with Dr. Craig.

A teenager, face challenged with acne and the beginning brushes of a beard, sat in a beanbag chair in front of the television, intent on a science fiction program. He looked up, frowning, as she peeked in again.

"What do you want anyway?" he said. His voice had matured far beyond the rest of him. It boomed deeply out of a thin, wiry body, the effect startling.

"I'm sorry," Mac said. "I'm looking for Brand."

The boy took part of his cheek in hand, pinched it between his thumb and forefinger almost absently, popping a pimple. He wiped his hand off on his pajamas and told her, "Won't find him here. He overdosed. Went into a coma. He's in isolation at the other end of the ward. No visitors. Not a pretty sight."

"B–Brand? You're sure?"

"I found him. We were supposed to play Nintendo. We'd talked about it early. He said his other partner was busy kissing up to Dr. Craig, and he bugs me, but not a lot, so I said okay. So when the time came and I went to find him, there he was frothing at the mouth with his eyes rolled back in his head." The boy gave a sharp laugh. "Shoulda seen the staff come running."

"I bet." Mac felt sick to her stomach. She took a step backward out of the lounge. "Is he—"

"They pumped his stomach. Word is, he had a reaction to the meds. He's alive, but his mind is in la-la land."

"But will he be . . . will he be all right? Did you hear anything?"

The boy shrugged. He brought his thumb and finger up to his face again, found a site off his temple, and squeezed again. "They said so. But you never know around here." He wiped his hand again and beckoned. "Want to come in and watch? Pretty cool movie."

She looked at the screen in time to see an alien slurp the skull off someone's head and inhale the brains. Her stomach roiled queasily. "I don't think so."

He shrugged. "Cool." He scrunched around in the chair, gaze fixed avidly on the set.

McKenzie made it back to her room. She closed the door against the noises of the nurses' station and the shuffling footsteps of the ambulatory patients. She sat on the bed and drew her knees up to her chin. Brand had made such a point out of not taking his meds. Could he have been storing them up for a suicide?"

Or had he instinctively known, after the first or second time taking them, that his body had been reacting to them? Was that why he avoided them?

And if he was avoiding them, how did he get enough medication to OD?

Or had someone forcibly given the dosage to him? And if someone had, who?

And why had he disliked Susan Craig so much?

Mac stared across her room. The boy was manic-depressive. He wasn't doing his maintenance. He could have swung low enough to have attempted suicide.

But had he?

She put both her hands to her head as the dull throbbing began again. There were no answers, only questions. She felt as if she walked a tightrope in a high wind and everyone was watching, waiting, watching for that deadly slip. A death watch for McKenzie Smith to finally strike out.

Susan Craig stared at her computer screen and licked her lips, tongue flicking hungrily over them. McKenzie Smith had fainted while they were trying to compile an animated VR tape, but they had a great deal done. That, compiled with the spatial and personality disk retaken had given Susan enough data to work with. She looked at the grids in satisfaction.

All these years of work. She had never thought of trying to match his imprints with those of a victim. All these years, she had done her work from the other side, from the predator's side. The compatibility had never fully been achieved.

Until now.

She bumped the heel of her hand on the desk. The victim! She should have thought of it, should have run across it sooner, she'd spent so many years among victims. The analysis had simply not occurred to her. She had been building an onion, imprint over imprint, subliminal suggestion layer by layer through the appropriate virtual reality program. Only then could she hope to deconstruct Georg Bauer. Only then could she hope to understand, control, cure.

Maybe she would have come to it eventually, instead of accidentally. She put a hand to the back of her neck, rubbing it. Maybe. Start with the victim to learn as much as you can about the perpetrator. That was basic at Quantico. Basic, basic, basic.

But she didn't think she would have believed it until she'd seen it in front of her. The indices and matrices which were McKenzie Smith promised even more. Smith had a talent for incorporating minute suggestions into the reality programming. Given the proper stimulus, she would be able to bridge a communication gap which had been frustrating Susan for the last seven years. The girl was gold.

Satisfied, the doctor snapped off the monitor and shut down the computer. A few days to imprint dependency on her, and then it did not matter if McKenzie stayed in the psych ward or not. She would seek Susan out wherever she was, to get the help she needed.

Just a few days more.

She shrugged off her lab coat and changed into her linen jacket. She looked around. Pity about Brandon. He would recover completely, of course, but he would be of no further use to her. He was too wary now. It was a good thing Susan had been able to separate him from McKenzie before he'd spread his paranoia.

As she left the ward, she paused by the reception desk as was her habit, to check the sign-in book maintained at the desk. She ran her finger swiftly down the signatures, then paused. Carter Wyndall. She had thought he looked familiar.

She clicked her tongue against her teeth. He would not remember her, but she remembered him. He had not bothered her all the years they'd been together in L.A., but that was only because he'd never made the connection between her and Georg Bauer.

She did not intend that he should. She wondered what interest the reporter had in McKenzie Smith.

"Anything wrong, Dr. Craig?"

She smiled at the receptionist. "No. Absolutely nothing that I can't handle." She pushed her way on through the doors. Carter Wyndall was about to find out what a double-edged sword a woman in distress could be.

Yes. That would be appropriate. When the worm turned, as McKenzie Smith could be made to do, it could strike almost anywhere. Susan could dispose of Carter, and bind the Smith girl to her irrevocably, with a single, desperate act. It was the burning bed syndrome, the battered woman defense.

Susan began to hum as she walked through the hospital corridor. *Beautiful dreamer, wake unto me. . . .*

Chapter 27

The phone rang sharply into the darkness. Carter stuck a hand out and pounded the nightstand blindly until he found the receiver and dragged it to his ear. He propped an eyelid open to check the time.

2:22 a.m.

He stifled a groan and managed to get his name out. "Wyndall."

"Good morning, Carter. Rise and shine."

It was not the city desk. It was not the night city editor. Nor was it Joyce Tompkins, from whom he half-expected it. He wiggled a little more upright in bed and, now that he knew he could afford to lose his temper, said, "Son of a bitch. It's the middle of the night."

"Don't we know it. This is Franklin, Carter. You wanted in, you've got it, but you need to get down here before the locals get this one all cleaned up."

"What?"

"Mr. Blue has struck again."

A fresh kill. Carter sat up abruptly and swung his feet out of bed. He reached for the lamp and started searching for paper and pencil. "When?"

"Early this evening."

"They won't let me cross the tape," he told Franklin.

"They will this time. But there are some curious differences. We think you might be able to give us some insight." He gave Carter the address and directions. He added, "Oh, and bring some hot coffee and doughnuts. We'll be here until mid-morning, at least, on this one."

"I'll be there, but don't wait for me."

"Don't worry. We won't."

The line went dead.

Carter hung up. He was half-dressed when he stopped, one leg in his trousers and one leg out. What in hell was he going to do about McKenzie?

He hopped to the phone and, after a moment's hesitation, stabbed a finger down and dialed.

A sleepy voice answered after the fifth ring. "Tompkins residence."

"You don't use an answering machine?"

"Good Lord. Carter, do you know what time of the night this is? Do you have any idea how normal folk sleep?"

He cradled the phone under his chin, still hopping, and put the other leg in his trousers. "Believe me, I know. I've got a story that won't keep. I'm out of here, and I may not be back until after noon. I would have paged you and left a message on voice mail, but you told me not to do that anymore. Something about broken fingers."

"Well, you don't need to worry your pointed little head about that. Now it's your neck! I'll take care of McKenzie. I tol' you that."

He felt relieved despite Joyce's irritation. "Good. I'll hang up now."

"Not until you tell me what's so all fired important."

"Can't." He puffed a little as he tucked in his shirt.

"Carter!"

"Really, I can't. Not even you. Sorry, Joyce."

"So I suppose I'll read all about it in the evening edition."

"No."

"What do you mean, no?"

"I mean that the police have been keeping this one under wraps. My hands are tied. But I've got an invitation for a front row seat, and I can't turn that down."

She made a sound which he could not possibly duplicate, a sound which verified her ethnicity. "I'm goin' back to bed, and don't you even dare, white bread, bother me again tonight."

"I won't. I promise. Honest to God—" She hung up on him. Carter grinned to himself and started looking for his shoes. He eventually found them under the computer desk, and he was out the door.

It hadn't taken him long after moving L.A. to find a decent dough-nut shop, open all hours, which would also lend out thermal pots to hold hot coffee. Carter made a beeline there, took in two empties he'd tossed into the back seat of his car, got two dozen doughnuts and two fresh pots. Then he studied his Thomas Brothers Guide until he found the address.

Twenty-five minutes later, he pulled into the cul-de-sac, notable for its fleet of late model, fully operational police cars, all bulbs blinking on their light bars. Two fire trucks looked like they were wrapping it up, weary men taking off their slickers and folding hoses. There were also several unmarked cars, including a rental car which probably belonged to the Feds. The coroner's van had evidently arrived just before he did. He watched them unload a gurney, body bags neatly folded on the top and wheel it toward the yellow police tape which surrounded an entire nine-apartment complex. It reeked of smoke and ashes and water. From the looks of it, Mr. Blue had gotten carried away with his little fires. He did a quick step to catch up with the gurney and set the coffee and doughnuts on it. The two hauling it never noticed. The corner of Carter's mouth quirked. You didn't get far in this business being unobservant.

Also immediately apparent was the fact that the building was not blue. It was a kind of sickly-looking ocher, thanks to the amber streetlights and the flashing lights from the official vehicles. Empty lots surrounded it and he thought he was looking at a building which had undergone restructuring after the Northridge quake, more than two years ago. Buildings on either side of it had been torn down, beyond repair. This was a common sight the farther north and east of downtown L.A. you got, and the closer to the epicenter.

Two uniforms looked up as he started to duck under the tape after the coroner's gurney. They stepped toward him.

Carter held up his press credential and added, "Franklin and Sofer called me."

The one young cop he recognized from that long night three days ago at Mount Mercy. He said, "They told me you might show. You're here as a consultant." To his partner he added, "It's okay. The suits called him in." Carter passed him a thermal pitcher, a box of doughnuts, and a stack of paper cups. "Throw the empty in the back of my car when you're done."

"Thanks. You're all right."

Carter did not linger to hear more. He followed the gurney attendants who followed the steady stream of investigators and uniforms moving in and out of the doors like ants.

Someone exiting the building took an abrupt right, leaned over, and spewed into the pink hawthorn bushes ringing the complex. She hugged her rib cage tightly. Carter slowed. "That bad, huh?"

The lieutenant nodded and waved him on, her face a cadaverous gray under the poor lighting. She vomited again, finishing with a moan as he stepped past her.

The complex had to be vacant. There were no sleepy-eyed occupants leaning out of the windows or walking the lawn trying to figure out what had happened. He'd seen only one car at the curb which had probably belonged here, and the line of carports to the rear of the complex had looked fairly empty as well. Inside the lobby of the building, which was fairly small and probably only existed for the mailboxes, the gurney attendants were stopped.

Sofer held them up. He wore the same solemn gray suit he'd worn earlier to Carter's apartment, only now he and the suit seemed rumpled. He said quietly, "Take it downstairs to the laundry room, right turn at the bottom of the stairs. Don't touch anything, we're not done there yet. Got a body thermometer?"

They nodded. Sofer grunted. "Good. Get a body temp if you can. Make a note of it on both boys, one for me and one for the police. Got that?"

They nodded.

"Use gloves. Try not to step in anything, it's a little wet down there."

Carter leaned past and into the stairwell. The stink of fire reeked worse here, and he knew it had probably been started down below. There was another smell, too, one that he tentatively identified as burned flesh.

The attendants flashed their hands to show they were already gloved. Carter grabbed up the second box of doughnuts, the coffeepot, and the cups as they steered downward.

Sofer looked at him with gimlet eyes. "You shouldn't have."

"Franklin told me to. You'll have to drink it black though, I only have two hands. Couldn't carry the cream and sugar."

"God. Lewis must have a cast-iron stomach." Nevertheless, Sofer reached for a cup and let Carter pour. He took a glazed twist from the box as Carter set both on the floor.

"I'm here as a consultant?"

"That's right. No story yet. Franklin wants to get your take on the scene before it gets cleaned up."

He poured himself a cup and took a strong hit before asking, "What's downstairs?"

"Two juveniles. He started the fire down there, but the building was retrofitted for sprinklers. They worked down there, not up here. Piping hadn't been connected up here yet. The building's just been readied for new tenants. Go on down and take a look, but don't touch."

He swallowed slowly. He had no desire. Police photos would be bad enough. He shook his head, saying, "I'll wait for Franklin." Then, quietly, he added, "Mr. Blue doesn't do kids."

"Bingo." Sofer finished his doughnut after stirring it around in his coffee. He wiped his wet lips off on the back of his hand, then licked a sticky finger. He picked up the coffeepot. "Walk this way."

Carter bent over and retrieved the doughnuts. The agent waited for him, as they entered the main floor of the building to the left.

He stopped immediately. "Oh, shit."

Sofer paused. He commented, "We've got photos."

Photos would not do the scene justice. The walls had been freshly repaired, freshly painted. There was still a faint odor to them of the drying paint. That odor now was all but drowned by the sweet iron stink of blood. The scent of blood added to the primitive fury of the drawings done on the corridors. Pictographs splashed hastily were of the most basic, the sun, stars, the symbol for infinity, fire, man, woman, the woman prone in death. When freshly done on the cream background, they must have been pulsating with redness. Now, as they dried and the wall absorbed them, they had begun to turn a rusty brown. *Bauer.* Bauer had drawn pictures. They hadn't always been found at first, because he rarely left the bodies where the killing had taken place. When investigators were able to backtrack later, crude drawings had been found at the murder site. It had never been written up publicly, just as many of the actual atrocities done to the victims had never been released. One, to protect the integrity of the crime scene and evidence, two, to protect the families who'd already suffered enough.

Carter felt his heart stutter, thump heavily once or twice, and then stagger back into its rhythm. His eyes shut involuntarily as he realized what he looked at.

"Wyndall."

He looked out. Franklin had joined Sofer in the framed doorway of an apartment the next door down. "In here."

He didn't want to go in. His body knew it, his thumping heart forbade it, his feet dragged, but as the two agents watched him, their stares seemed to draw him along inexorably. Past the crude paintings drawn in a victim's life stream. Past the speckled droppings on the floor. Past the final strokes which showed a woman, her torso cavity opened, gutted as if she'd been venison.

"You told me it was Mr. Blue," he said. He'd gone cold. The hot coffee in his hand threatened to burn him through the cup.

Franklin still wore the current god-awful purple tie. Sofer had splashed a little coffee onto it. It could only be an improvement. He smiled thinly in response to Carter. "Isn't it? You haven't even been inside the apartment yet."

Carter shoved the cardboard box of doughnuts into Franklin's hands and went into the apartment. He stood for a moment and then closed his eyes to avoid abrupt dizziness. The coffee cup dropped from fingers suddenly gone numb.

One of the police lieutenants looking over the scene reacted. "Damnit." He knelt down and marked it off, saying, "Get this blotted up and out of the way." He looked up, unshaven, shirt unbuttoned at the collar. "Don't mess it up or keep out." He gave a hard look at the FBI agents. "I don't care who he is. If he can't stay out of the way, I want him out of the crime scene."

Carter nodded. Words failed him, words that would issue from his mouth. His hands began to twitch as they imagined the words he would type to describe the scene.

Whoever she was, she had just moved in. Her belongings were meager almost beyond belief. Almost no furniture, though they did have a television set, resting on a precarious-looking tray stand. Cardboard boxes had been neatly unfolded and stacked in a corner. Blood splashed across them, all the way from the kitchen, for she had surely died in the kitchen, though it was apparent she'd first been caught at the other end of the living room, at the sliding glass doors.

She'd tried to get out. The first, high spurt of bloodletting had splattered there, blood driven by a heart still beating furiously, through a severed jugular. She'd been dragged, then, into the kitchen. Her heel marks sliced blood into the carpeting, tracks that marked how she'd been taken.

Several investigators milled around in the kitchen. The corpse must be there, just beyond his line of sight. He could only see the congealing pool of blood on the floor through the narrow doorway.

There was a measuring cup lying on its side a hand's span away from the main pool of blood. It held crimson as well. The primitive artist had used it to capture his medium. One of the investigators was stretching into the kitchen, and powdering its surface for prints. He called out, "Somebody go over the corridor closely. The son of a bitch might have used a paintbrush or something. Look for fibers in the blood." He added, "Any luck finding the blade?"

A clammy sweat covered Carter's forehead. "He used a knife?" It was to be expected. Murders of such sexual violence almost always involved a knife.

"Yeah. Bite marks are all excised. Head's nearly been decapitated. Took two cuts from left to right to do it. Seven stab wounds in the frontal area, in the breasts. Uterus has been punctured several times as well. That appears to be postmortem." The investigator never looked up from his careful brushing. "We'll know more after the autopsy."

Carter pivoted around to face Franklin and Sofer. Franklin had been eating a powdered sugar doughnut. The evidence covered his chin.

"Not Bauer," Carter said. "She died fast and furious. This guy was in a real frenzy. Bauer liked to do them slowly. Sometimes he took days. He didn't lose much blood, either, except for the paintings." Nelson and the other caseworkers had never found out what Bauer had done with the blood, either.

Sofer remarked, "She's been partially scalped. Mr. Blue likes to do that."

Franklin said, "So is he or isn't he?"

"What do the kids look like?"

That stopped the agent. He dropped his half-eaten doughnut back into the box. "You sure you want to go down there?"

"I don't want to. But that's the only way to tell if it was Bauer or not."

Sofer ticked his head to follow him. Stepping carefully, Carter started back out of the apartment. He stopped, as a new bloody pattern caught his eye.

Thank you.

It had been splashed extravagantly on the interior living room wall.

He felt his throat close. Sofer caught his elbow. "We saw," he told Carter gently. "We know." He drew him back down the hallway toward the basement stairwell.

His surety that it couldn't have been Bauer fled. He scarcely noticed where the agents led him.

The stench from the laundry room grew worse step by step. He pulled a crumpled handkerchief from his back pocket and held it over his mouth. Sofer and Franklin had left their coffee behind, Sofer's pasty white skin going even paler and Franklin gray under his tan.

Franklin stopped him at the entrance to the room. It looked like a concrete bunker and smelled like a charnel house. Carter knew where the policewoman had come from when she'd charged out of the building to vomit. He raised his handkerchief from his mouth to his forehead, then returned it.

The gurney partially blocked the doorway. Franklin bent over it. He straightened.

"They're taking body temps now." He licked his lips as he faced Carter. "You don't have to go in there. Tell me what you'd look for, if you were looking for Bauer."

He owed the agent one, and could tell from the expression on Franklin's face that the Fed knew it, too. Carter took the handkerchief down. "He liked children best. What do we have down here?"

"Two juveniles, males, age and race indeterminate at this point in time, bodies partially burned. One killed by neck slashing, the other uncertain. One body bound with duct tape, the uncertain not."

"Tortured? Genitals mutilated. Bite marks on the neck, just below the hairline? Possible sexual assault?"

Franklin leaned back in. Then he came out and shook his head. "Not as far as I can tell."

"Not Bauer, then. He wouldn't, he couldn't, change that much."

Not Georg Bauer.

No matter what the message read upstairs.

Franklin said to him apologetically, "I'd like to go back up with you, and go through the evidence line by line. What Bauer might do, what he wouldn't do."

What could he say? "All right." He started back up the stairs. "It's going to be a long night."

"We don't have much choice. This was Mr. Blue, until he lost control. Mr. Blue doesn't do kids, or pictures. He's never done wet work like this before."

"Do you think he's disintegrating, becoming disorganized? Or do you think he's trying to mislead us?"

Both agents shook their head in the negative. "No. But ask yourself . . . what if he'd learned from Bauer? What if he'd been a victim who'd survived? He relieves it, exorcises it, by killing himself and this time lost control . . . flashing back."

"I can't answer that until I know what you know about the perp. As far as I know, no one ever survived an attack by Georg Bauer. We'll have to go back to the victims, to see what draws Mr. Blue, what he's looking for and what he wants and what he finds." Carter braced himself, braced himself for the kind of knowledge that had torn him apart before, driven him to suicide twice.

He prayed he was strong enough to handle it this time.

Chapter 28

Stephen Hotchkiss decided during the dawn of his second morning that he had no way out. It was a rather pitiful life anyway, relegated to a computer screen for sex and companionship. He was a voyeur only because he knew his needs weren't acceptable. He had no other choice. He would prefer to love a warm-skinned being, to love and be loved in return. It was the knowledge that he did not, and could not, that made him decide it was no longer worth living. He had never called the number left for him. His nimble mind had come to the inevitable conclusion that it was his own doctor, his own therapist, who'd betrayed him. Susan Craig had him by the short hairs if that was true. He could never safely hope to impugn her. No one would believe him.

He wrote out his instructions and laid out his clothing. He pulled his dress shoes out of his bag. As was his habit, he'd wrapped them in newspaper to keep them clean and to keep them from soiling anything else. Stephen spread the paper out.

It was the headline section from several days ago. The cover story was a feature on the tragic drive-by shooting of a child, and the heart donor good which had come out of it. He recognized the byline: Carter Wyndall. Carter did not cover politics, but he had a good reputation as a well-researched and honest writer.

Stephen stared down at the newspaper. The more he stared, the more he felt as though a door were opening, a door into the pit which trapped him, a ray of light into the darkness.

He picked up the phone and got information in the Los Angeles area, then the main number for the newspaper. As he dialed the newspaper, preparing to run the gauntlet of the voice mail system, he mentally composed what it was he was going to say.

What he could say that would be compelling enough for Carter Wyndall to want to investigate and open up a can of worms. The phone system cycled him ever closer.

The line clicked. "Hello, you have reached the mailbox of Carter Wyndall. Please leave a message and I'll get back to you."

Hotchkiss began to speak. The words spilled out of him, a dam bursting, and he did not stop until he'd become absolutely breathless. Then he hung up.

If Wyndall did not return his call in forty-eight hours, then he would reconsider his final solution again. Hotchkiss carefully rewrapped his good shoes and set about dressing for breakfast. The lake lodge had a nice restaurant. He felt like comfort food: hash browns and eggs, and freshly squeezed orange juice.

Carter's eyes felt like raw scrapes. It was only a little after nine, but the crime scene had emptied and there were only a scattering of uniforms and two lieutenants left. The air inside the rental car smelled of their sweat and Sofer's occasional cigarette. He decided he wouldn't be much good any longer. He smothered a yawn as he told Franklin and Sofer, "I'm heading for bed." He put his fingers on the car door handle to let himself out.

Sofer smothered a yawn of his own, muttering, "I should be so lucky." His chin rested on top of the steering wheel.

Franklin had been searching for crumbs in the doughnut box. He looked up. "Thanks for coming, Carter. Nelson was right. You're a boy scout. We can use some of them from time to time."

Carter started to slide out of the rental car. He answered, "I liked Nelson, too." He hesitated in the open door. "Since you showed me yours, I guess I should show you mine. Remember that photo you took off me?"

"The one you had updated?"

"That's the one. My assistant ran a search on it. He came up with a match. I think we have the same woman here in L.A. She's a psychiatrist now, Dr. Susan Craig. I put her at the psych ward at Mount Mercy, but she probably has a private practice, too. Her company's called CyberImago."

"Cyber-what?"

"Imago. She uses a lot of virtual reality programming for treatment. Very cutting edge. I think there's a good possibility she's one reason Nelson came here."

Franklin made a noncommittal sound deep in his throat, and Sofer said, "Thanks. We'll look into it."

Carter shrugged. "For whatever it's worth." He hooked a thumb through the now empty thermal coffeepot and headed to his car.

Curious onlookers had already been discouraged away from the site. He looked down at his rear right wheel. The hubcap was missing. Stolen right out from under a fleet of L.A.'s finest. He kicked the black-wall tire in frustration before throwing the coffeepot into the back seat. He did a circuit around the vehicle. All four hubcaps had been ripped off. A crude substitute had been torn out of thin cardboard—a lid to a doughnut box, he noted with irony—and put into place on the left front. Somebody had markered "Sorry" on it.

Carter ripped the cardboard off the wheel and sailed it vigorously into the air. It Frisbeed off across the weed and debris-ridden empty lot before disappearing. He got into his car. He started to laugh as he drove off, weaving in and out between patrol cars.

Pete Moreno came back from an early, early unofficial break to find his phone ringing off the hook. He grabbed it up before the system could rotate it to voice mail. "Moreno here."

"Off-i-cer." The voice, richly and most definitely female, hailed him. "I'm so glad to be talking to you in person. This is Joyce Tompkins."

That confirmed his identification of the caller. Moreno hooked his foot around his chair and drew it to him so he could sit down. "Mz. Tompkins. I'm glad to be talking to you, too. We've been playing phone tag. How may I be of service?" He'd been avoiding her for the last two days, but now he had no need to.

"I'm working as an advocate for McKenzie Smith. Are you familiar with—"

"Most definitely."

"Good." Joyce took a deep breath. "Do I have to read you the riot act on this one, Officer Moreno? You've had this young lady practically under house arrest when you should be out looking for the proverbial estranged spouse."

"I'm aware of that, Mz. Tompkins. Or rather, officially, I should say that we've been able to develop some new information on her case that corroborates past abuse by her husband. I still haven't been able to find witnesses who can confirm that he's here in the area stalking her, but at least we have new leads to follow up."

"I'd like to make arrangements to take her out of Mount Mercy and to a safe house."

"What kind of safe house?"

"Now, Pete. What kind do you think? I have a shelter which has room for her temporarily."

His starched shirt pulled on his armpit and he scratched it uneasily. "Mz. Tompkins, I don't think we'd have a problem with that. Of course, we'd have to know that you were supervising, and we'd like to know where she is if we have to reach her. And I'd have to stipulate that she's still a suspect until we can get a statement from her father. She'd have to stay in the area."

"Back at you, no problem here. Could I impose on you to call Mount Mercy and let them know you've no objection to releasing her to me?"

"Will do."

"Thank you, Officer Moreno. You are, as always, a delight to talk to. How's that diet?"

He puffed. "It could be better."

"It's going on summer. You'll be a lot better off forgettin' red meat and just stocking up on fresh fruit. Why don't you try it and see if that doesn't jump-start your day?"

"I might just do that."

They exchanged one or two more pleasantries and then hung up.

Joyce sat back in her chair and let out a big sigh of relief. The biggest hurdle to getting McKenzie Smith out of harm's way had just been passed. In a few hours she'd be a free woman. She'd barely finished her exhalation when her beeper sounded. She pulled it off her purse. She knew the number immediately when it flashed.

The shelter supervisor answered, voice shot with near hysteria.

Joyce said, "Honey, calm down. I can't understand a word you're saying. What is it?"

"The police just called. It's Graciela. She—she's been murdered. Donnie, too. It's awful, just—" the woman hiccuped. "I can't leave the girls alone. They want somebody to come down and identify the body. I pulled her dental records from the work she had done while she was here. She—oh, God, Joyce. Who would want to kill her?"

Joyce answered calmly, far more calmly than she felt, "What do you need me to do?"

The woman began to sob. Joyce paused a moment and then said, "Listen, something has to be done here. Tell me what you want from me."

"Could you . . . could you go to the coroner's? I just can't do it again. You know her by sight almost as well as I do."

This was the hard part of running a shelter. The girls left, oftentimes before they were ready, and the vindictive ex-boyfriends, spouses, had a habit of catching up. Usually they just saw them come back, just as battered as before. But every now and then, more frequently of late, the next encounter would be the last, fatal one. Joyce did not answer for a moment. She had heard Graciela was leaving. She had never thought disaster would overtake her so quickly. Her and bright-eyed, independent Donaldo. She felt her eyes quicken with tears she didn't have time to shed.

She heard the woman on the other end of the line take a deep, tremulous breath.

Well, shit, Joyce thought briskly, gathering herself together. *This just goes to prove you win some and you lose some.* She'd gotten McKenzie out of hot water, only to lose Graciela. "Leave those charts out where I can pick them up. What time did the coroner's office want someone there?"

"By two o'clock. They told me there was a rush to do the autopsy. Thank you, Joyce. Thank you, thank you."

"Don't thank me. This is what it's all about, girl, and you and I both work damn hard doing it. I'll be by as soon as I can."

Joyce pulled out her appointment book. She wouldn't have time to make her next meeting, free McKenzie, and then get to the morgue. McKenzie would just have to wait a little more. The girl shouldn't mind. At least she was among the living.

He staggered in, thought of coffee, decided against it, because the cups of last night felt like shoe polish against his teeth. The answering machine looked dim and empty and was. With a vague feeling of disappointment, he dropped on the couch, portable in hand, and called the office.

His assignment board was still empty, though Carter knew he was free to pick up a story if anything interested him. What interested him now, he was not free to write about. Bored, he pushed buttons on the handset and went into his voice mail system.

The voice was low, breathy, and slightly feminine, though it was definitely a man's voice. He listened once without hearing everything that was said, then sat up straight and thumbed in the instructions to replay the message.

He listened again, carefully. He forwarded a copy to the city desk, and coded the mail system to make a permanent record of the message. Then he set the phone down and stared at the ceiling for a long moment. He could feel the bags under his eyes, the crust at the corners of them. He could feel a vague pain in his chest, a sympathy pain for the damage the woman had taken. As he shifted, thinking, he saw a tiny smear of rust on his sleeve. He'd touched the walls somewhere, he thought, where the blood hadn't quite dried.

He was too old and experienced, wasn't he, to chase wild geese?

But what if it could make the connection with Susan Craig that he needed? What if suspicion could be countered with proof.

He rubbed his eyes. "Aw, shit."

Carter went to his computer rather than to bed. He booted it up and dialed the office.

>>ONLINE. GOOD MORNING, CARTER WYNDALL.<<
>>DOLAN.<<
>>SEARCHING.<<

Then the screen went quiet and Carter waited. He waited so long that he went to sleep in the tilt back chair. The computer began to beep querulously like a watch alarm and brought him bleary-eyed back to the screen.

>>CARTER. CARTER, CARTER, CARTER, CARTER.<<
>>I'M HERE.<<
>>HEY, YOU CALLED ME. WHAT'S UP?<<
>>SPEND THE NIGHT AT A CRIME SCENE.<<
>>! ANYTHING WE CAN USE?<<
>>NOT YET. ARE YOU STILL HACKING?<<

>>THAT'S LIKE ASKING A SENATOR IF HE'S STILL BEATING HIS WIFE. WHAT HAVE YOU GOT IN MIND?<<

>>I WANT TO KNOW WHAT CYBERIMAGO IS UP TO. I ALSO WANT TO CHECK AND SEE IF CRAIG'S ORGANIZATION IS STILL HOLDING ONTO THE FERNANDINA HOSPITAL.<<

>>WHY NOT JUST ASK?<<

>>I DON'T WANT TO RATTLE HER CAGE YET.<<

>>OKAY. I'M GOING TO MAKE IT A THREE-WAY HOOKUP. YOU JUST HIT "PRINT SCREEN" IF YOU LIKE ANYTHING YOU SEE.<<

It had taken Dolan much diligence to make the print screen button an easy one for Carter to find and use. He typed back, >>WILL DO<< and sat back to let Dolan do his work.

The first was a simple trust deed search. It only took a few minutes to find out that CyberImago still held the paper on the Fernandina Hospital. Carter sat up and stared at the screen closely, though, when Dolan pulled up the fact that the Senate Appropriations Committee had just made a similar search four weeks ago. The user posted was John Nelson. He hit the print screen button and listened as his laser printer awoke into abrupt action.

Dolan broke off the trust deed search. >>HOW'D YOU LIKE THAT ONE? DID I DO GOOD?<<

>>DON'T KNOW YET. LET'S TRY THE CYBERIMAGO OFFICES.<<

>>I'LL GET BACK TO YOU.<<

Carter laid his head back and stared at the ceiling.

CyberImago was an anonymous office in a modest complex building. If anyone were to care to walk in, they would find a receptionist in a lobby, her desk blocking the door to the back, walls paneled in fake walnut, with a ficus growing out of its planter in the corner, steel and plastic desks, beige carpet, and little, if anything, to note what it was they did.

The receptionist, her moon-round Asian face of Korean ancestry, sat there, intently interested in the textbooks at hand. She moved only to do her job, which was basically, simply, to answer the phones and keep anyone from entering the restricted workshops in the back. One belonged to her employer and led to her office and a small lab.

The other was labeled "Research and Development" and was generally full of the most pathetic-looking dweebs she'd ever seen.

Her hand moved to the receiver. "CyberImago."

"Phone company. We're doing some work on the major trunk lines into your building today, and I have a work notice that says you have computers which have to stay online., modems operational."

She snapped to attention, flipping a strand of blue-black hair behind one ear. Losing phone lines could be disastrous. "That's right. You can't shut them down."

"Well, I might be able to reroute the lines. Can you give me the phone numbers they're on and their access codes?"

Jennifer Lee quickly rattled off the information. The pleasant voice thanked her and disconnected. She blinked once or twice, then ducked her chin down and returned her attention to the international business textbook in front of her.

Dolan came back to the computer. >>I'VE GOT IT.<<

Carter had taken another short nap, then gotten up, fixed himself a cold drink, and sat with it held to his forehead. >>NOW WHAT?<<
>>LET'S SEE WHAT I CAN DO.<<

In the rear offices of CyberImago, movable walls divided open space into two areas. The spartan business atmosphere of the front lobby gave way to chaotic disarray. Computers and bits of computers dominated one half, printers and cables and chairs pushed every which way. The other side of the room held huge cork bulletin boards, their surfaces filled with computer art of every size and persuasion. The clutter here was of an entirely different variety, diskettes and light pens, sketching paper, scanners, CAD equipment.

The room looked as if a line had been drawn down the middle. Programmers on one side, animators on the other. Both sides were empty now, and voices could be heard from the small room off the side which doubled as a lunch and storage room.

On the technical side of the office, a computer which had gone into screen saver rest mode suddenly came to life. One of the programmers came out of the lunchroom, laughing, his dark hair rumpled as if he'd just run his fingers through it, glasses sliding down his nose, bright red apple in his hand. He sauntered across the work space toward a huge drink vending machine, popped in a token, and punched in his choice of cola. As the dewy-sided can dropped into the retrieval bin, the programmer paused and looked toward his area.

He saw the computer was active. He snatched up the can, yelling, "Hey, guys, I think we got a hacker trying to break in."

The lunchroom emptied immediately. The first programmer already had his chair pulled up and was trying to keep the system secure. He snapped, "See if you can find out who's logged on."

The second programmer sat and began to work his keyboard. The animators, who could also do this sort of work, but whose talent was that of rendering art out of the medium, watched with interest.

The first man sat back in satisfaction. Whatever downloading had begun had been shut off. "Got 'em," he announced.

"Me, too."

"Who is it?"

"It looks like the newspaper's ID. Let me verify that. . . ." He dialed out a number on his own, the modem responded with its atonal sounds, and the newspaper flashed its online. symbol.

"Verrry interesting. Dr. Craig will want to know this." He checked his watch. "Hey. Ten more minutes for lunch." He picked up his apple and his cola and sauntered back to the lunchroom.

The other three fellows joined him where they sat and speculated if the break-in had been deliberate or accidental and, if deliberate, what the paper could have been trying to do.

Dolan came back online. >>THEY'RE GOOD. THEY SHUT ME DOWN ALMOST IMMEDIATELY.<<

>>GET ANYTHING?<<

>>I THINK I GOT A DOWNLOAD ON ONE OF THE PROGRAMS THEY'RE DEVELOPING. LET ME TAKE A LOOK AT IT AND I'LL GET BACK TO YOU LATER.<<

>>YOU KNOW WHERE TO FIND ME.<< Carter signed off. He rubbed the cold water glass over his forehead again, thinking, *hurry up and wait*. The bedroom looked inviting. He got up and lumbered in that direction.

After lunch, the head programmer opened the door to the lobby and stuck his head through, startling Jennifer Lee, who rarely saw any of them once they passed through the portal.

"Hey, Jen. Give the boss a call and tell her we had someone try to break into the system."

"A hacker?"

"Maybe. Could just have been a wrong number, too."

She was already reaching for the phone. "Do you know who it was?"

"Yeah, we picked up a user number. It was the newspaper."

"The newspaper?"

"Yeah. Probably thought we were AP or something. But Dr. Craig might want to know. She always says there are no coincidences."

"Right," Jennifer answered dryly, familiar with her employer's perfectionism. The programmer popped his head back into the workshop, rather like a chipmunk going back into its hole. She telephoned the hospital, going directly into Susan Craig's private mailbox to leave word, knowing that the doctor rarely liked to be interrupted at the lab during work hours. That done, her attention once again returned to her study.

Chapter 29

In the wee small hours of the morning, Jack discovered that the hospital stirred with a life all its own. He had found shelter more or less in the fourth floor chapel, leaving it only when other people came in, which happened rarely and only for moments. Even the chaplain had yet to stop by. Jack put his feet up on the richly-grained oak pew, finished the cafeteria turpentine that passed for coffee, and decided on his plans for the day. The wardens at the reception desk for the Psych ward changed often. Often enough that the old cow with the pleasant expression on her face who sat there now wouldn't recognize him. Couldn't tell him from Carter Wyndall from a hole in the ground.

He picked a coffee ground from between his teeth. A little too early to visit Mac. Even on a good day, McKenzie was hardly what one would call a morning person, and she'd scarcely had a lot of what Jack would call good days lately. No. Later in the day would suit him just fine. After lunch, maybe, when visitors flowed in and out of the hospital like trash carried on a gol-darn flood tide. That way, if anyone was looking for him, if anyone gave chase, he could disappear a little easier.

Not that the police knew a damn thing yet. He slurped the last of his bitter coffee from the paper cup and then crumpled it viciously in his hand. The police might as well have their heads up their asses. They weren't even making a good game out of this.

Jack swung his feet down. He hiked up his jeans. *Getting a little ripe there, buddy boy.* His pants felt stiff enough to stand on their own. Maybe it was time to get another motel room, shower, change.

Of course, if he did that, if he left the hospital, he'd have no way to watch her, to know what she was doing. She might even walk out this evening when her forty-eight hours were up. Voluntary commitment. They couldn't keep her if she didn't want to stay.

He had no intention of letting her sashay right out of Mount Mercy without him.

Jack's thoughts motivated him to leave the chapel. He took the back stairs which had the carpeting stripped off them now, showing the cement surface, rough with old carpet and tile glue, black with dust. He caught the elevator door just as it was closing and stepped in to the empty conveyance. He punched in the floor number and waited for it to jolt into movement.

He stepped out and took a cautious look around the Intensive Care section. The old black fellow who'd been sharing Walt Smith's room had been moved clear across the unit. With the move had gone the security guard. The ailing councilman now took up a large theater-sized room, filled with machinery other than hospital equipment. Faxes. A computer station. An extra phone line.

Jack wiped the back of his mouth. Shit. Even when the old guy was sick, dying, they couldn't leave him alone. They just kept shoving business in his face. Business, business, business. He put a thumb through a belt loop and casually sauntered over to the room of the man he'd tried to beat to a pulp.

He looked at a sheet of paper taped to the door. It noted that the patient had wakened during the night.

"No shit," Jack murmured. He put his fingers on the handle and eased himself inside.

Walton Smith's eyes looked baggy and bruised, but they flew up when Jack kneed the end of the hospital bed, rocking it sharply.

He grinned. "Hi, Dad."

Susan Craig looked critically at her face in the mirror. The last night had smeared purple shadows under her eyes, deepened the tiny lines at the corners. Her icy fury at Dudley's mistake had thinned her upper lip to mere existence. She outlined it carefully with a lip pencil, then took her brush and filled it in, making it fuller, softer, than it really was. She added a light cover-up under the eyes and reapplied her foundation.

She turned her face from side to side, examining the results. Her silver-blond hair shimmered about her face, a face which did not show the ravages of its forty-some years. Still young. The best of genetics and the best of care. She was still beautiful, sexual, fertile. She would have the child she wanted, and the husband, and the success. A warm genuine smile answered her for the briefest of moments.

She passed the bank of television sets, leaving them on for Dudley to turn off when he woke. She'd kept him up late, debriefing him, making sure she understood the tragedy which had taken Donnie from her plans. Then she had punished Dudley, medicating him with new imprints, hoping to keep him in line. He was the only one of her subjects still active. For now, he was the only hope for her to keep her project viable.

The drive to work occupied her mind only briefly.

A new receptionist greeted her at the ward, a pleasant-looking older woman, silver-blue hair coiffed into gentle waves, a dewlap of a second chin ruining her neckline. Her pin proclaimed her to be Donna and a "Silver Striper." She wore glasses on a cord about her neck and quickly slipped them on to read Susan's name tag.

"Oh, Dr. Craig! Good morning. I'm so pleased to meet you. I've never worked up here before, but I've heard a lot of good things about you."

Susan had no time for small talk. She shifted her briefcase impatiently, murmuring, "Thank you. How's everything this morning?" It was late enough so it scarcely qualified as morning.

"Just wonderful. The nurses said to tell you that Brandon is blinking his eyes and showing some stimulus response. Oh! I have a message for you. It's from the speech department. The therapist called and said she's terribly backed up all day today and wondered if you'd mind doing another session with Mr. Walker?"

Opportunity had come quicker than she'd anticipated. She took the phone slip from the receptionist. "Of course not. Would you call them back and tell them it's fine—just what the doctor ordered?"

Donna, the Silver Striper, giggled. Craig hesitated, then added, "I know Carter Wyndall is on the authorized list of visitors, but if he comes in today, I'd like to know. He's a reporter and I'm not so certain my patient is going to have the privacy she needs."

"Oh, certainly." Donna jotted down the instruction. "Anything else?"

"Just enjoy yourself covering the desk. Have a nice day." Susan left her behind as the buzzer freed the second set of doors.

Working with Ibie Walker again gave her options she needed time to consider. She had checked with her office already. Hotchkiss had not yet called. He could have gone ahead with the suicide Dudley had aborted. Or he could be waiting stubbornly, like the anal retentive ass he was. Or he could be on the precipice, just waiting for another push like Ibie Walker's death.

As for Carter Wyndall, she would have to deal with him expeditiously. Graciela's tragic murder had already made the morning news, but to her surprise, it had not been linked with any of Dudley's previous kills. Either the police did not know they had a serial killer or they had put out a news blackout. A blackout did not mean Carter was unaware of Dudley's presence. Eventually, his obsession with Bauer would be rekindled and could lead to her. She had to wrap up her dealings now and prepare to move on. She almost had enough data to license her therapy software programs through CyberImago that would give her funding to live anywhere she pleased. Someplace where she wouldn't be second-guessed or questioned.

Miller was not in the lab on Wednesdays. She put her briefcase down and put on a fresh lab coat, then repositioned her name tag. Her intercom light went on.

"This is the nurses' station. Ibie Walker is on his way over."

"Good." She liked promptness. She could deal with him and move on.

She stopped at the isolation room where Brandon had been moved and shut the door quietly behind her as she entered, so as not to attract attention.

He lay so still that she considered removing his restraints, his spare form hidden under ghostly white sheets and a paper-thin thermal blanket. Blue veins ran through his eyelids tremoring with the dream movement of the eyes they curtained. His chest rose and fell with shallow breaths. He looked like an alabaster carving of a child, pure and untouched, innocent and full of latent potential, as every child is a seed unplanted, a bud unfurled.

He was not much younger than her own child would have been, if she had kept him. But she had had her residency in medical school to consider and although she was often mistaken then for an under-grad, she was within a few months of finishing when she had joined the project involving Georg Bauer. The pregnancy had been un-planned, unexpected, but not unwanted.

Until her supervisor had discovered it. Dr. Morrissey had been none too pleased with her assignment to the Bauer survey anyway, stating that it was madness and folly to have a female anywhere near the killer, but when she had begun to struggle with morning sickness that lasted day and night, the good doctor decided he had real rea-son to put her off the project. Susan had struggled with Morrissey from the first day, finding the doctor unfamiliar with the computer technology they were using to map Bauer's personality, unfamiliar and hostile. Oddly enough, the subject himself had never been any-thing but courteous and soft-spoken around her.

He had power, reined in. She recognized that in him, though he was relegated to a subservient position, and he seemed to know she recognized it. That power ran through him like a raw sexual core, masked but omnipresent.

Morrissey, for all his years of experience and learning, seemed oblivious. He ran mazes and designed new ones for Bauer, noting the results, and the killer would sit quietly on a stool in his prison or-anges, hands and feet lightly shackled, and his flat hazel eyes would meet hers across the room, shining with humor.

He was a lock to which Morrissey could discover no key.

The doctor decided to vent his frustrations on her. As her preg-nancy became more difficult, and his ineptitude with the study more apparent, Morrissey finally gave her an ultimatum. Have an abortion or resign from the project.

Resigning would not only take her back months in finishing her program, it would mean that she would have to give up the work she'd done on Bauer, all the computer studies and stored informa-tion. She would have to deliver them to Morrissey's hands and see them destroyed, lost, invalidated.

She'd done what she had to and accepted Morrissey's ultimatum.

And found an ally in Bauer, who seemed to understand instinc-tively what she'd gone through and what she struggled with. They formed a bond.

The more she studied him, the more complex a Gordian knot his mind proposed. Violence and power and sex were braided and tied together in layers that would take years to chart, years to unravel. He reminded her sometimes of a caged animal, a light deep in the back of his eyes warning that whenever that lock was left unturned, the bars ineffective, the door unlatched, all hell would break loose.

The more unfathomable Bauer became to Morrissey's methods, the unhappier the doctor was about Susan's continued presence on the project. And the more incompetent Morrissey became, the closer Bauer came to being delivered back to Death Row. A failure in the project would result in Georg Bauer's execution. The FBI was not happy with Bauer's cooperation as he began to drag his feet in the interviews, sensing that only his knowledge now kept him out of the execution chamber.

Susan was let go, being flatly told by Morrissey that the project was being wrapped up. He would handle the final four weeks of interviews on his own. Her sacrifice, her love, her understanding, all for naught.

Except that Bauer understood, and they spoke softly to one another as she prepared to leave, and he told her what he wanted her to do. Not that week or even the next, but soon, before the FBI took him back. He would avenge her abortion and humiliation by Morrissey. He knew what she wanted of him. He told her what he wanted of her.

So she did it. She made a copy of the key for the shackles and left it for him several weeks later in the lab.

She was never a suspect in the breakout. Even the FBI interviews had been shallow, cursory. Only John Nelson had even bothered to take notes. Her involvement in the project had ended.

She finished her residency and waited.

He would come back to her. He had promised. Only, like the beast he was, he needed to be sated. He needed to run free before coming back.

She understood that. A year passed. Then two. Three.

And then, one day, coming home late from the hospital where she'd begun her professional career, she found him waiting.

He was much more dangerous than he had been in the lab.

So was she. Her training, her knowledge, her work had become weapons. If he had come seeking her out, hoping to find yet another victim, he did not. She looked Georg Bauer in the eyes and never looked away.

He let her live. She let him live. Until the realization that he had begun a downward spiral of self-destruction which would ultimately drag her under as well. She'd taken steps then.

Susan Craig put a hand to her face. Her fingers were chill, the tears brimming in the corners of her eyes warm. She carefully patted them away, watching Brandon sleep.

She hoped the medication hadn't damaged him too much. It was a pity she was going to have to leave him behind.

Susan opened her briefcase at her desk. Three-and-a-half-inch diskettes gleamed back at her from their various pockets. She considered her choices, then made a selection. Ibie Walker's demise ought to be short and sweet.

She plucked out a second program, made up especially for McKenzie Smith, and slipped that into her trouser pocket. Then she locked the briefcase, sliding it under her desk. She had come too far, done too much, to change her mind now.

Ibie Walker was wheeled in, minus his IV and monitors, and aides. His granddaughter followed a few moments later, after a loud aside to the nurse in the hallway outside. Her color was high when she came in, taking up a position by her grandfather's wheelchair.

"I thought the speech therapist would be here today."

"They called and asked if I could spend an additional day acquainting Mr. Walker with the soundboard equipment. My schedule was free, so I agreed." Susan put her hand on the back of Ibie's. "How are you today, Mr. Walker?"

He rolled an eye at her unhappily. She smiled. "Making progress, I see. You've left most of your equipment behind."

A pager went off. Both women checked their beltlines. The handsome young African American said, "It's mine." She checked the message, then leaned over her grandfather. "Pops, it's the office. I've got to go call. You'll be all right here. I'll be back for you."

She turned briskly and was gone before Ibie could respond. He managed to lift a hand after her, beseechingly, but only Susan Craig was there to see it.

He turned his gaze back to her and they stared at one another. "Don't trust me, Mr. Walker?" She shook her head. "I'm sorry. Well, let's just get through this session as quickly as possible, and see what happens."

She whirled the wheelchair about and pushed it into place at a computer station. The elderly man reached for the headset, placed it to his cheek and the soundboard began to cry. "Nuh. Nuh. Nuh."

Susan looked up with delight. "Why, Ibie. That's very good. 'No.' Now what is it you don't want?"

His hand was shaking. His eyes teared from the effort of holding the handset. The soundboard stopped making recognizable tones and retreated into melodic garbage. Susan reached out and gently took the headset from her patient.

"I think we'll practice with this later. I've got something special for you."

With quick, skillful movements, she strapped the VR helmet on and slipped his hands into the gloves. Then she took the software disk out of her trouser pocket and slipped it into the computer's drive. She patted Walker on his shoulder. "This shouldn't take long."

She stepped back to watch.

After a few moments, his body began to twitch and shake, doing a Saint Vitus' dance. He moaned softly, helplessly. Spittle dripped out of a jaw dropped slackly. His gloved hands shook wildly upon his lap. His feet kicked out and drummed upon the wheelchair supports. His movements became more and more grotesque and violent as if he sat in an electric chair, current pouring into him.

Susan licked her lips.

Ibie Walker fought, oh, she could see him fighting the "reality" which gripped him. She could see him in hand-to-hand combat with the unthinkable. His narrow chest heaved with the effort, breaths coming faster and faster, gasping—

And then it all stopped.

Susan waited for a long count, then stepped forward to the slumped figure in the wheelchair. She had all the time in the world. Moving slowly, deliberately, she took off the helmet and saw his face, eyes rolled back in their sockets, mahogany skin gone ash-gray. She put her fingers to his throat, searching for a pulse.

"Dr. Craig, I've just got to know about Brand—" McKenzie stopped in the lab doorway. "Dr. Craig!"

Susan reacted instinctively. She took Ibie's still form out of the wheelchair and laid it on the floor, ordering, "Don't just stand there. Get on the intercom. Call a Code Blue. He's gone into cardiac arrest." She balled up a fist and thumped him heavily on the chest and began to administer CPR.

McKenzie lunged for the nearest phone. From the corner of her eye, she saw Craig reach up to the computer, eject the software from the drive, and slip it into her pocket, even as she pumped the dying man's chest and counted.

Mac could hear the defib cart being rolled down the corridor toward the lab even before she got off the com line. Mac stepped back, staring at the doctor bending over the elderly councilman, watching her pump and breathe, as the cardiac team raced toward them.

As they came in, Craig got up off her knees and stepped back, giving them room to work. She looked across the lab at Mac.

If looks could kill, Mac would be lying on the floor next to Ibrahim Walker.

Chapter 30

The proud young woman who was both Ibie's granddaughter and his aide paused by the lab door. The turban scarf which bound her ebony hair and matched her tailor-made skirt had started to come undone as she bent over her grandfather's still form just before the nurses prepared to wheel Walker back to his cubicle in ICU. She reached up now as she faced Susan Craig and McKenzie, unwrapping it, letting down her fall of stylish hair. She tossed it back to keep it from her face, twisting the scarf about one hand.

"Thank you," she said quietly. "I'm told you kept him alive."

"It's my job," Craig answered. "I could do nothing less."

She bent her head in a slight nod, then passed through the doorway, hurrying after the gurney.

She did not seem to have even noticed McKenzie, who stood as still and quiet as she could in the corner behind Craig. Silently observing. Closing and unclosing her hands. Watching.

Let sleeping dogs lie. Don't question, don't stir the pot.

But, oh my God, what she thought she'd seen Susan Craig doing.

As if hearing McKenzie's raging thoughts, the doctor pivoted and looked her way. There was chilly consideration on her face. The piercing blue eyes held none of the warmth of the parting smile she'd given Ms. Walker.

McKenzie involuntarily took a step backward, then froze, knowing she had betrayed herself, ever so slightly.

Susan paused in holding out her hand, then reextended it. "Ready for your session?"

She did not answer the doctor.

Susan put her hand in her trouser pocket. Her lips pursed a little as though she began to speak, then paused. Finally, she said, "What you've just seen must be very upsetting to you. Why don't you come with me a moment? Let the lab get cleaned up. Talk a walk with me."

McKenzie could not control her hesitation. Had she even seen anything? Had she seen the doctor deliberately let a patient lapse into trauma? What would have happened if Mac had never entered the lab?

Ibie Walker would have died. She was almost certain in her heart that Susan Craig never intended CPR or any other lifesaving method. Had been waiting, like a vulture, over Walker's body to ascertain the exact moment of his death, when Mac had interfered.

If the doctor noticed the tension in her body as she took Mac by the elbow and escorted her down the corridor, Craig never said anything. She walked lightly beside McKenzie, guiding her through the hall to the locking double doors and beyond, into the main body of the hospital.

Neither woman said anything as they got onto the elevator and it carried them upstairs. McKenzie recognized the Intensive Care Unit as soon as they stepped out. The activity over Ibrahim Walker quietly took over part of the U-shaped unit, doctors and nurses in attendance, with Walker's granddaughter vigilantly observing. No one noticed them come onto the floor. Susan Craig looked briefly in that direction, then put her hand on McKenzie's elbow again, and steered her the opposite way.

Toward the cubicle which her father had shared with Ibie and in which Walt Smith now lay alone. The number of tubes and cables connected to him had diminished greatly. Susan Craig pulled the chart posted on the door, running her long nail down the cryptic jottings. "Brain swelling has gone down considerably. It says here he's had moments of consciousness."

"He's waking?"

"Yes. Though," and Susan tapped her nail on an immaculate white tooth now, "his condition stabilized, and then regressed sometime during the night. He may have many, many weeks of recuperation ahead of him." She leaned into Mac's face intently and said, "He's not out of the woods yet."

McKenzie turned her face away. She had just been threatened silently, subtly, like the hard look a pitcher gives a batter who's just come up to the plate. Second warning, the brush-back pitch.

Third warning, a straight shot to the head, a duster.

Mac didn't think Susan Craig gave second warnings. She turned back to face her.

"I have a study," the woman prompted. "I would like to see it finished. That's all." McKenzie had not seen what she'd thought she'd seen happen with Ibie Walker. Doubts would never be voiced.

Mac had no proof of anything else and who in the hospital would believe her otherwise? "May I see him?" she asked softly.

Craig opened the door. McKenzie slipped in. The monitors made their soft machine sounds. One of them beeped every six seconds or so. She noticed that it kept time with the IV drip. She approached and took his hand. The flesh felt warm and firm. Life, somewhere, somehow, was banked and kept kindled inside of him.

"Daddy. It's me, Mac. I hope you can hear me. Please, be all right." She squeezed his hand tightly, brought it up to her chin, rubbed it.

A finger moved, knuckling her jaw. Mac started, looked down into her father's face, saw his eyes open and focus weakly on her.

His voice broke into a croak. "Mac-kenzie."

"Daddy!" She swallowed back a lump which made words difficult. "You're going to be okay. You hear me?" His right eye bleared. It watered ferociously and she took the corner of a sheet and wiped it for him.

"Mac-kenzie," he got out again. "I tried. . . ."

She knew that. She'd thought of little else the past few days. How he had tried to keep her safe. The father she had always wanted, at last, then struck down. "I know. I'm here."

"Trouble. Jack."

"I'm okay. You just . . . you just . . ." McKenzie pulled at the sheets and blankets ineffectually as a shudder ran through his form. "You just get well."

"Mac-kenzie." He squeezed her hand tightly. "Circled . . . bases."

Icy blue eyes looked at her from the other side of the hospital room. "Incoherent," Susan Craig said softly.

McKenzie shook her head. No, it meant something to her. Everything to her. She'd circled the bases, she'd come in a winner. He was telling her that in the only language that the two of them shared easily. She leaned close to him. "Home," she confirmed. "I came home. You waited for me, and I came back."

The monitor jumped and began beeping erratically. Her father tried to squeeze her hand again. "Mac—" His voice broke off.

"Cardiac arrest." Susan Craig shouldered her away from the bed abruptly. She hit the intercom and for the second time shouted for a Code Blue team.

Mac stepped back, trembling. She had felt the strength, the warmth, ebb from his hand even as she'd held it. She could not take her eyes from the bed as her father died despite all they tried to do for him. Jack Trebolt, in one way or another, had taken nearly everything from her. Her blood went cold.

Susan Craig stepped away from the bed, pushing past the Blue team wearily, brushing her silver-blonde hair away from her forehead. She focused on McKenzie as though surprised to see her standing in the corner of the room. "You shouldn't have stayed."

"You have a project to finish."

The doctor nodded.

McKenzie said numbly, "Then let's get it over with."

The visor helmet fit snugly. Craig instructed, her voice muffled, "I'm going to be showing you some relaxation programs first. You don't need to react in any way, just sit back and watch."

Her body felt brittle, as though she might snap in two. Let the doctor have whatever brain wave data she needed, let the hours drift by, and then Joyce would come and get her. Carter would be by. The jackal was at the gates, she could not pass without the help of friends, but they had said they were friends. She was alone now without them.

They'd said they would come back to get her.

Mac found herself gritting her jaw until it made her fillings ache. She jumped as Susan slipped a cold hand down her neck and began rubbing her shoulder muscles. The fingers were like iron, the doctor's nails scraping her skin every once in a while. She was so tense, the massage only sickened her.

Mac sensed, rather than felt, the doctor move away. The virtual reality visor lit up, and she looked into a world of water, running water, rocky mountain slopes with tumbling brooks, pink-sanded beaches with foaming tides, bridal veil falls cascading from the heavens. . . .

The knot in her back began to ease. The doctor had said she did not need to do anything, but who could resist the puddling stream that she could almost put her feet into, the tiny fingerling trout darting away as her hand broke the still waters, the dragonfly that knifed through the air past her face—

Mac jerked back. She blinked inside the helmet, the tranquil scene around her interrupted as well, as if the virtual reality sunlight had suddenly become a strobe light.

Flash. A knife blade, dripping red, in midair. Stark in its stainless steel sharpness, black and white background. *Flash.* The image as quickly gone.

Mac breathed through her mouth rapidly. In, out. Had she seen it? Or had its image already been there in her mind, painted in Cody's blood? Was she seeing the program the doctor was feeding her, or had the images she'd begun to see on her own taken over?

What was real and what was not?

And if this was not real, then what was happening to her was what she had always feared. She carried her father's rage inside her, an unwanted gift, a legacy which had always terrified her. *Don't let it wake.*

That rage was a river and in its torrents, she could see the potential consequences of acting on it. Blood. Destruction. Mutilation. *Death.*

Her mother had known. Had sensed it in her. Had always removed her quickly from her father's tantrums as if fearing Mac would ignite as well.

Her head throbbed. Stinging pangs jabbed her eyes.

Flash. Dead children, strewn upon wild grass and brambles, their faces twisted in agony. Rage had killed them. She could not begin to guess whether it had come from within them or from another.

She did not recognize them. But she would not be one of them. She would not be a victim anymore!

Moss-covered boulders led her down to the brookside, and across. The sound of the river pouring over its bed filled her ears. Trees dipped down to the banks, lushly green and heavy-boughed. Their roots cracked the rock beds, sinking deep into the earth, determined to drink freely—

Flash. A woman's breast, the nipple dimpled erect, the mound full and round, bursting open with the slash of a knife—

Mac jerked in the chair. She felt its frame around her, though her senses told her she walked, no, ran, through the woods. Branches slapped at her. Fog rose in white cottony banks, obscuring the pathway to safety. Her footfalls pelted the ground.

The hunter woke. Leaped to its feet, running. The rage came to a life of its own, outside of her skin, yet inside, knowing where she ran. Tracking her. Intent on destroying her.

She could hear the sound of other breathing, other racing steps, other branches cracking and whipping behind her.

Don't stop.

She the prey, the other the hunter, the chase was on, was all, blood-pounding, heart-bursting. She darted to her right. Fog exploded from the tangle of her legs as she hit it. She expected the mist, the coolness of it on her face, but all she felt was the fiery stream of her blood pumping through her body. *Run.*

Susan Craig's voice, hotly whispering in her ear. "What is it, McKenzie? What do you see? What are you afraid of?"

Keep running. Don't look back.

Joyce checked her watch. The limp salad she'd picked up from the fast food joint down the block had picked a corner of her stomach and was filling it like a lead cannonball. That was what she got for being good, uh-huh, and didn't that make her madder than a wet hen, that and being stood up here at the morgue. She clicked a heel on the marble floor. She clutched a brown envelope with Graciela's and Donnie's records between her thumb and her purse. She had other places to go and then Mount Mercy. *God help me, but I've got appointments with the living. I can't do any good here.* She was about to leave when someone plucked at her sleeve.

"Miss Tompkins?"

She whirled, surprising both herself and the attendant, a young college-type, glasses, narrow face, his black hair thatched on top of his head like some scruffy little bird. He blinked. "I'm sorry I'm late. We've been busy." He paused. He wore a lab coat over his jeans and shirt, and sturdy jogging shoes, with the aquamarine paper protectors still over them. The lab coat was clean though spotted with old stains. "We're not the murder capital yet, but we're close. Very close." He rubbed his palms on the coat nervously. "I'm Grady."

Joyce briskly handed him the envelope. "You asked for records."

"Oh, good." He blinked again. "This will make it a little easier." He turned. "Ah. Could you follow me?"

Joyce did so, wondering if it was his first viewing. It certainly wasn't hers. Her ex-husband had been first. Over the years, two or three of the women she'd been an advocate for. Her staccato steps echoed in the building as they approached the elevator. He cleared his throat several times as he held the door for her.

Misinterpreting her look, he said, "This door is a killer. It closes fast, and it hurts. There's supposed to be a safety on it so that if it closes on anything, after so many pounds of pressure, it pops back open. Don't you believe it. It's like a boa constrictor. We call it Crusher."

She entered the elevator. "Grady, I'm not a novice at this, but I'd like to know what I'm expecting."

The watery hazel eyes fluttered rapidly. "Oh. Ah, well, it's not going to be pretty. I, ah, tried to arrange some sheets—and Vicks. I've got some Vicks you can put on your upper lip. The juvenile is a burn victim. It's, ah, pretty gross."

She looked at him, hoping for his sake that he would never face attorney Robert Shapiro in an L.A. courtroom. "I don't think I'll need the Vicks, thank you. I'll be quick."

"Well, ah, with the dental records, we'll know for sure, anyway."

The elevator glided to a halt.

"Grady."

"Yes, ma' am."

"Have you been doing this long?"

"Ah, no. Two weeks."

She nodded. And pointed. "It's this way."

He flushed. The stand-up ends of his dark hair seemed to reach even higher. "Um. Right."

The viewing room felt good, momentarily, after the heat outside which was pushing 90, but it carried a smell with it that even the chill and the antiseptic cleaner couldn't scrub away.

He said, "The young woman first. We're pretty sure who she is, because of the fingerprints and the ID in the apartment the police gave us."

"All right." Joyce braced herself.

He carefully peeled back a corner of sheeting that she realized he must have arranged just as meticulously. She found herself staring into dull eyes, widened into a terrified expression. No one had even taken the time to close her eyes yet. She wondered if they were going to be able to later.

Blood stiffened and matted her hair, her beautiful hair, the hair that she had such skill with and which had led her into what Joyce had hoped would be a successful career for her. There were smears upon her face, and though she could not see her mouth or throat, Joyce could tell from the draping of the sheet that both yawned open in agony. She looked away.

"That is Graciela."

"Thank you," Grady murmured. He quickly reclosed the drawer.

She took a deep breath, telling herself that shedding tears for the dead did nobody any good. Her lungs seemed to fill with the odor of death in the viewing room. The smell worsened considerably as Grady pulled open a second drawer.

From the shape, she knew it had to be Donnie's remains. She had a moment in which to regret not taking the Vicks when the young assistant pulled a corner of the sheet down. There was another second in which she recognized the boy despite the stench of burned flesh, and the hair torched from the scalp, for the upper face was almost clear.

She choked. Tried again. Faintly, "Yes, that's him." Joyce put a hand out to Grady, meaning to ask for the Vicks when a roaring in her ears took away her hearing, and then her vision narrowed down to pinpricks. Everything went dark.

She heard Grady squeak, "I'll catch you." Then the room caved in.

Chapter 31

Susan Craig watched her patient. Virtual reality did not hold its dreamers in the near-catatonic stasis of real sleep. With every flinch McKenzie Smith made, every gasping breath she took, Susan followed her through the world she'd programmed especially for Mac. She could only guess what scenario she might be in at any given moment, but there were actions which tipped her off, things MacKenzie did, like warding her face unconsciously, which placed her within the VR theater.

Craig had put a blood pressure cuff lightly around McKenzie's left arm. Every fifteen minutes or so, she took a reading. The girl's heart rate fluctuated wildly as she reacted to the programming, but nothing had reached dangerous levels. After the Ibrahim Walker incident, Craig could not risk another. She needed the sponsorship of the hospital, for however long she could obtain it. The dosage of drugs had been so light, the girl had not even felt the needle prick when Craig had massaged her neck muscles to ready them. Their hallucinogenic dose even now raced through her body. The faster McKenzie's heart beat, the quicker they spread, bringing her to the state Craig wanted. Vulnerable. Pliable.

The minutes came and went. Susan worked with other patients being brought in, for large segments of McKenzie's software kept her quiet and passive. It was late afternoon before she hit the segment in which Craig had the most invested.

McKenzie's hands shook, even as her fingers curled, and she said in an audible voice. "No. No. I can't. I can't. Let sleeping dogs lie. Don't wake. Don't awaken them. Please."

Susan pumped up the blood pressure cuff to take a reading. The pulse had jumped, though it surged strongly. The doctor smiled with satisfaction.

The moment when McKenzie stopped fighting the image, bent, and took up the basketball bat, came out crystal clear on the tape. She tossed her head from side to side and fought the impulse.

Then the hand curled as if it grasped something firmly. Hefted it. Swung it lightly.

Susan Craig patted her on the knee. "Good. Good girl."

There was no response to her, but the monitor needles began to jump. The doctor watched everything, smiling. "Good girl."

No more beaches, no more sunny glens or shadowy, dew-tipped woods. Pine needles no longer cushioned her burning feet. She walked in an urban jungle now, dilapidated houses, walls layered with graffiti, and the fog which roiled up was a dirty, stinking condensation.

And I am the hunter, Mac thought, and wrapped her fingers tightly around the handle of her bat. She searched the deserted streets for shadows. She listened for footsteps before or after her, chest tight with apprehension, shoulders hunched with anxiety.

She'd known ever since she'd picked up the bat that the tide was turning. That things were changing. All the running, all the throat-lancing panic, changed. Now she had a choice.

A choice to keep running or be a victim no more. There was power in the bat, in the old weathered wood whose feel her hands knew so well. McKenzie had lost her way, but now she was back. The power ran through her fingers, lightninged up her wrists and into her arms, rested in her shoulders, dormant. Dormant but there, reserved, *power.*

Something went skittering away from her. She half-turned to see it go, scaly tail dragging behind it, a moth-eaten rat running from her. She knew that it was she who'd scared it. No one else.

She turned the corner. The neighborhood looked vaguely familiar, in that way that she sometimes dreamed of her home and it would be her home yet not be her home, not really. This was her neighborhood. Mac knew that instinctively. Her neighborhood and she was stepping onto its streets for the first times in years, unafraid.

Flash. Running and hiding in the neighbors hedge.

She took a step past the oleander boundaries. Grapestake fences sagged, weathered and termite-ridden.

Flash. Her father screaming in her face.

She curled her fingers so tightly around the bat handle that she could feel a knuckle pop. She could feel an answering surge of power.

Never again.

Don't let it wake up. Don't. Smother it. Let sleeping dogs lie. Walk away.

Her chest felt tight. The breath seemed to be squeezing in and out of her through a narrow, constricted passageway. Walk softly, but carry a big stick.

The biggest. She looked down at the piece of wood. So faint against the grain: Louisville Slugger. An antique, an icon, among bats.

She saw her house, vaguely recognized it. She turned down the driveway to come in the back, the way she always had when she was growing up. In the back, to the kitchen, to the heartbeat of the house. Before she stepped up, she could see lights going on, as twilight fell, and shadowy figures moving behind the curtains.

Mac watched, torn by the need to run, to hide, and the need to . . . what? She didn't know, couldn't identify it. Not the need to be safe, for it was not a haven she was entering. Confrontation faced her once she crossed the threshold.

She walked into the house.

"Who's there?" Shouted at her from rooms beyond, shadowy rooms, unlit rooms, beyond the bright pulsating heart of the kitchen.

Who do you want it to be? She tapped the bat once lightly against the side of her shoe as if she were knocking off dirt from baseball cleats. *Who am I?*

Flash. Blood dropping in runnels along the floor, golden-red dog's body lying in disarray.

McKenzie blinked. She put up her free hand and waved it through the air, searching, as if cobwebs obscured her vision. The quicker than the eye vision of murdered Cody did not flicker away. He stayed there, in the corner of the kitchen, her kitchen—*no*—*no*—which kitchen? She could not remember. An icy emotion seized her. She walked past the dog's body and kept on going.

"Who the hell is there?" she answered back.

As she passed into the hallway, listening for the familiar creak of the hardwood floors, shadows grew longer, darker, deeper. She turned her face slightly toward them. She would be aware. Alert. Empowered.

Darkness leaped at her, grunting with a man's voice; she swung about. McKenzie planted her feet. Ready. The man charged at her and she swung, swung with all her might, swung from her shoulders and her hips, toeing the plate.

Home run!

The man slumped down to the floor, soundlessly, his face a red ruin. Breathing hard, arms tingling with the release of the power, McKenzie leaned down. She clubbed him one more time to make sure he stayed down. She stared at the features.

Jack? No. It couldn't be . . . her father? Mac leaned closer.

Carter Wyndall.

She straightened. "You killed my dog, you son of a bitch."

He wouldn't do it again.

She would never have to run again.

McKenzie panted. Her head felt heavy, so heavy her neck couldn't hold it up any longer. Heavy and weighted, encompassed.

Flash. Susan Craig's soft voice. *"Who do you want to kill?"*

A man stood behind her. He reached around and took the bat from her.

"Very good," he said.

"Did I do all right, Georg?"

"You did fine." The man smiled, with a warmth that never reached his hard eyes.

McKenzie's hands felt strange, empty.

"Wake up and smell the blood," he said. "Taste it. Enjoy it. He'll never bother you again. Serves the son of a bitch right." He dipped a finger in the blood and traced a sun, a crescent moon, and stars on the wall behind the body. "Immortality," he said. "Neverness. Pain."

Never again.

McKenzie fought to breathe.

"Oh. My. God."

Sweet Jesus, Joyce thought. *I've died and gone to the Valley. There must be some mistake.*

She couldn't be dead. The promise was that all wounds would heal, all spirits would be made whole, all aches and pains and discomforts of the physical world would be gone. She ached as if she'd been dropped from a ten-story building, was as cold as hell, and her stomach burned like it needed a raft of antacids.

She couldn't be dead.

No. She was probably laid out on one of the tables in the morgue since she remembered going down as if Grady had yelled timber—

Joyce let out a shout and got up almost without opening her eyes. The two attendants who'd been leaning over her screamed in panic.

The three of them faced each other, weak-kneed. Grady's face paled to the color of ashes. His companion, a young woman in her late twenties, panted until she swayed from hyperventilation and Joyce braced herself on the pathology table. She felt like Rochester in an old Jack Benny movie.

"You didn't think I was dead, did you?" she asked wildly, looking at them closely.

"Oh. My. God," the girl repeated. She wrapped a blond tress around one finger and tried to breathe normally.

"Ah, no, we knew you weren't dead. But," and Grady put up a hand. "I couldn't catch you. You're, um, heavier than you look and swept me right off my, ah, feet."

"I fainted."

"You fainted."

Joyce straightened up. She pulled her blouse and suit jacket around slightly, untwisting them. "How long have I been out?"

"Um. About . . . a little over an hour. I'd say so, wouldn't you?" Grady looked desperately at the valley girl attendant, who must have been his supervisor.

"Like that," she agreed.

"I didn't want to get in any trouble," Grady said. He gulped. "So we just put you in the empty viewing room to let you rest."

"Your pupils weren't all dilated or like that or anything," the girl added.

Joyce could only thank her stars that they dealt with the already deceased. She checked her watch. Their little over an hour was closer to two hours. Like the White Rabbit, she was late, late, late. "Do you have an office? A phone?"

"Well." They swapped looks. "We're not supposed to let anybody use it. Not the public or anything. There are pay phones upstairs in the lobby. . . ."

"Forget that. You owe me. While you had me laid out here like Sleeping Beauty, I missed a court appearance. I need to make a call." She flashed her eyes at them like she would have one of her kids who was having trouble getting to the homework.

They moved like they'd been jump-started. "Follow me Miss Tompkins." Joyce passed him in the hallway.

Carter slept. He knew he was sleeping, which made it easier to bear the dream, the dream of passing through endless corridors painted with the rusty-red pictographs of a madman's visions. His head began to pound with every footstep he took, every footfall of his shoes a thundering boom upon the hall floors. Boom, boom, boom! His temples throbbed and his neck cramped. He put a hand up to ease it and woke himself up, half-falling from his chair in front of the computer.

Bam, bam, bam! The front door shook with every blow. Sleepily, exhausted, Carter hauled himself to his feet and fumbled at the lock. Dolan, leaning on it, fell over the threshold. Carter blinked. He looked back at the computer. "You were there. Now you're here." He stifled a massive yawn.

"No shit, Sherlock." Dolan's face was flushed from the warm sun, bringing the last two or three pimples, remnants of his expired teenhood, to volcanic proportions. "I thought you might want to see this in person. I didn't know I'd have to raise the dead to do it."

"See what?"

"What we, I, downloaded off CyberImago."

Carter sat back down. "That was hours ago."

"I've been fooling with it off and on all day. I'm not exactly getting paid for this."

"You're not?"

Dolan gave him an exasperated tilt of the head. "Shall we pump caffeine into you, or do you think you can stay awake for this?"

Caffeine sounded good. He sent Dolan to the kitchen for some bottled iced tea. Dolan came back with a couple of long neck bottles and tossed him one. He drained the bottle in three long gulps. Feeling revived, he dragged a second chair over next to his. "Anything in the fax?"

Dolan looked before he came and sat. "No. Expecting something?"

"Yeah. It's FYI, so keep your hands off it."

Dolan held both hands in the air. "I don't touch or read anything I'm not supposed to."

"Right." He sucked the last few drops out of the bottle and tossed it across the room. The Bureau would send him material when they could. He'd grown to trust Franklin and Sofer. "Okay. What have you got?"

"I've never seen anything like it. I've heard about it, rumors, y'know, stuff like that. From the fifties and again in the seventies. Buy popcorn, drink Coke. You know."

Carter looked at Dolan. Words were coming out of his mouth, and Carter was listening, but he hadn't heard anything that made any sense. "What are you talking about?"

"This." Dolan stabbed a finger at the computer monitor as the color screen filled with generated images that were as sharp as any cinematography he'd ever seen.

Carter sat back in his chair, watching a seascape from the rugged but scenic coastline of Northern California, or perhaps it was Oregon. The spray of the incoming tide flurried off the rocks like white feathers, before raining down onto the sand and foaming away. Driftwood logs rocked under the assault. Yet it was peaceful.

"Dolan."

The other's eyes fairly shone. "Great, isn't it? Really good. And then there's this." He stopped the frame with a click of the mouse and the editing file he had brought up from another program.

Carter jumped. "Jesus!"

He looked into the sadistic face of Georg Bauer. Smiling at him. Eyes watching him. "Where did that come from?"

"From the program. It's subliminal, Carter. That frame would float by so quickly you'd never consciously realize you saw it. Software isn't regulated yet like the movies are. And who would even think to look?" Dolan advanced another few frames.

A double-bladed knife, dripping with blood.

Carter gripped the edge of the computer desk. "You would, Dolan. You would. How much are we looking at?"

"Not much more, unfortunately. They shut us down pretty quickly."

"Can we prove it's them?"

"It's CyberImago?" Dolan shook his head. "Not with this. We'd have to get our hands on the original software . . . something packaged with the logo, maybe even copyrighted." He shot a look at Carter. "Worried about legal?"

"Only if I have to make the evening edition." But he didn't. Not this time. He stared at the screen. He had the connection he wanted, between Bauer and Susan Craig, but he had no idea why or what it meant or what it could ultimately lead to.

He only knew he had to get Mac out of there. He pulled back his sleeve cuff. "Almighty. It's after four."

Dolan slapped a hand on his shoulder. "You've been asleep, bro."

He swiveled in his chair. Dolan had no idea how right he was. Carter felt as though he'd been asleep for the last decade. Now this had jolted him awake.

"What is it, Carter?"

He shook his head. "I don't know what she's doing and I'm damn well sure she isn't going to tell me if I walk up and ask."

He might even get killed for his effort, like John Nelson. His fingers twitched. "I've got nothing but a shitload of bad feelings."

Chapter 32

"Incoming," informed Dolan. He stood by the fax machine, his hand wrapped around a slice of pizza. "I hope you've got a lot of paper or a big memory. This looks to be a whale of a transmission. And it looks official, too."

Carter came in from the kitchen, two more bottles of tea between the fingers of his left hand, and a similar piece of pizza folded in his right hand. He'd showered and changed, and his hair was slicked wetly back from his forehead. Barefoot, he walked over to the dinette table and sat, listening to the fax feeding up pages.

"That's got to be the Bureau."

"Franklin and Sofer?"

"The same.

"What did you do to deserve this? These look like copies of an investigation." Dolan joined him. Having emptied his hand, he refilled it with another slice.

"That would be telling."

Dolan pulled a long string of hot cheese from his lips. "As long as you didn't go to bed with 'em."

"Not my type."

"Really? I thought the redhead was kind of cute. In a crawled out from under a rock sort of way."

"They all look like that. Everyone's got a tan, out here." Carter looked over a second piece of pizza critically. "You didn't get anchovies, did you? I thought I told you no anchovies."

"Would I do that to you?"

"A man who would rewrite another man's copy without permission would do anything."

Dolan squirmed. "That was a long time ago. I was just a green intern then."

"You're still green."

"Yeah, but now I'm earning money."

The fax machine made a noise and a red light came on. Dolan jumped.

"It's out of paper. Go put in a new roll. It'll hold everything in memory and start fresh on a new page, then back up when the transmission's ended and print out the memory.

"No kidding." Dolan got up and did what he was told. "I guess all the excuses you're always making about the fax machine screwing up don't hold water."

Carter said, "I may have to kill you, after all." He tossed the crust back into the pizza box.

"I'll keep your secret if you let me help you finish the story."

Carter grew silent. Dolan, busy with the machine, didn't notice at first. Then he became aware and turned around slowly.

"I'm not looking for a byline or anything," he added awkwardly. "I just want to do the gofering and watch you work. Like an apprentice or something."

"Indentured servant."

"Right. Like that."

Carter looked at the spotty young man. Had such earnestness ever oozed from his pores? Such eagerness shone in his eyes? Had he ever been that young and itching to work on a paper?

He vaguely remembered that he had.

In a strange way, Dolan was doing for his career what McKenzie Smith had been doing to his libido. Like the phoenix, he was rising—being pulled—from the ashes. He hid his emotion behind the tea bottle and muttered. "Just don't get in the way."

"No, sir!"

Carter got up and left the room, the fax machine still humming away. He did not return until he heard it stop, then begin again to transmit those pages in its memory. Dolan looked up expectantly.

"Collate the pages," Carter told him. "We've got some work to do."

"What are we doing?"

"We're looking at Mr. Blue."

"It's going to take a while," Dolan responded. "We've got over thirty-two legal-sized pages."

Carter checked his watch. Still no word from Joyce. He didn't want to go to Mount Mercy until he knew he could bring Mac back with him. To go in without Joyce would tip Susan Craig that he suspected her. Of what, exactly, he couldn't prove yet, but if she were doing anything, anything at all, she could spook. He didn't want that. Better to stay here, cool, and work the files until he heard from Joyce. Besides, Franklin and Sofer were waiting to hear from him. "I've got time," he said to Dolan.

Even if every instinct he'd ever honed as a reporter told him otherwise.

The traffic on the freeway crawled. Joyce watched her dashboard clock. Finally, she got out her cell phone to dial Carter to have him meet her at the hospital, but the phone did nothing. No lights, nothing. Dead as a used firecracker after the Fourth of July. "Da-amn," she said and tossed the useless phone onto the passenger seat. There was an adapter somewhere—maybe even in the glove compartment—and wouldn't she look like somethin' weaving in and out of traffic while she tried to fish it out and hook it up? That would be too foolish to even begin to think about.

She wrapped her hands about the steering wheel, trying not to think about what she'd seen in the morgue. Her court appearance had been, thankfully, postponed, so there was no harm, no foul there—but that fool of an attorney could have called her earlier and told her that. She would have marched into that courtroom and found herself in the middle of a whole other problem if she hadn't dropped in the viewing room. Come to think of it, she owed that attorney an earful, yes, she did. Her time was just as valuable as his.

"Lawyers," Joyce snorted to herself, and changed lanes to avoid one who was talking on a car phone *which worked*. "See that, uh-huh," she said to the dead instrument on her car seat. "That one works."

She looked out over the crawling traffic. If she was lucky, she'd be at Mount Mercy by six and before her hair turned gray.

Joyce Tompkins believed she made her own luck. "Girl," she told herself. "Get to it." She put the accelerator down and the turn signal on.

There was a young man at the reception desk of the psych ward. He looked unhappy to be there, and kept jumping every time someone bumped the locked doors from the other side, which happened two or three times while Joyce signed in. He wore expensive, trendy clothes and had his hair designer cut, and she guessed that he was at the desk because he owed some community service work to one of the judges Joyce appeared before regularly. He'd probably been caught using some designer drugs or flyin' the silver highway recreationally.

She smiled widely at him as she pushed the guest register back. "Relax, son," she said. "They're just pulling your chain."

He flinched again and stretched a sensitive hand over the release buzzer. "You won't let anyone come through."

"Honey, I was married to a Raiders fullback. Do I look like anyone can get by me if I don't want them to?"

He opened his mouth to say something, shut it, and then pushed the door buzzer.

Joyce swept through before anyone could do anything else. She looked back at him through the screen-reinforced view window. He looked just as nervous as the doors swung into position and locked shut. That boy was going to think a bit before he got himself into any more trouble.

A young woman and an older woman, both in the half-pajama, half-hospital outfit that was standard issue on the ward, looked at her and laughed.

The young one said, "He's kinda cute."

Joyce laughed gently, answering, "Yes, he is, but he's awful nervous."

They both giggled as she walked by them. She went straight to the nurses' station and told them what paperwork to pull, found no problems, and went on to McKenzie Smith's room. It was almost dinnertime, and she could hear the rattling of the food tray carts and smell the odor of something—meat loaf and potatoes—from down the hallway.

She stuck her head in the room. A still, silent form lay under the sheets, food tray untouched, TV on, but silent, flickering forms mouthing news that could not be heard. Joyce hesitated, sensing something not quite right, unaware of what it might be. Had Mac given up hope? She gathered her energy and bustled in.

"Your forty-eight hours are up. It's time to go home, and let me tell you, I've got the meter running."

Mac turned her head. Joyce smiled genuinely. "Oh, honey, you clean up nice." She'd obviously showered, changed pajamas, and had her hair shampooed and brushed. There was no response. Joyce wasn't even sure whether the young woman had recognized her.

She sat on the edge of the bed. She reached out and took Mac's hand, the one which had been so bruised, and traced it lightly, the colors faded into yellows and greens instead of the deep purples and reds. Joyce thought of her dead ex-husband, the one who'd played pro ball. What he would have given to have been such a quick healer!

McKenzie had obviously been given medication that would calm and quiet her. Joyce could leave instructions, as an advocate, that she was not to be medicated anymore, that she was no longer a patient, and would be released as soon as she was able. But she hated to leave without her tonight. Mac had depended on her. Carter, too. If only she could have made it here earlier. . . .

She threaded her fingers through McKenzie's. "Things will be all right."

The fingers wiggled within her grasp, the tiniest of movements, but the first sign that McKenzie had even noticed she was there.

McKenzie closed her eyes slowly and opened them again, like shuttering a window and then releasing it. "I'm lost," she murmured, licked chapped lips, and added, "I've lost my way. Joyce . . . my father died. I was there, and he . . . he died."

Joyce patted the hand she held. "Oh, honey. I'm so sorry. But that means you've got to come with me. Jack Trebolt won't leave you as a witness. Can you get on your feet? I can't take you with me if I can't get you on your feet."

"Where's . . . Carter?"

"Waiting for us to call. But the best thing to do is get you out of here first."

McKenzie seemed to wince at the mention of his name. Joyce caught hold of Mac's chin. "If you want to go with me, you've got to get serious. Motivate that butt, girl, or I'll have to leave you here to sleep it off."

Mac's attention wandered in spite of Joyce's firm grip on her chin. Joyce looked too, to see what held her attention.

The six o'clock news appeared to be trying to cover Graciela's and Donnie's murders. She'd heard it on the radio. There wasn't much known. Joyce could barely hear the whispering voices at the volume Mac had the set. Mac didn't seem to need to hear the words, though.

There was a blurry, ill-lit few feet of film of which the news team seemed awfully proud. The video camera wavered, showing what appeared to be cave drawings from—Joyce gagged suddenly. These were drawn on the walls from the murder scene, and she could see, even with the poor lighting, that they must have been drawn in blood.

Mac said, "Sun, moon, stars. . . ." She broke down and began to sob. She cried as if her heart had been shattered. Joyce gathered her in, felt the slim shoulders shake within her embrace, listened to her voice grow raw.

She knew. How could she know? Joyce couldn't ask the question, but something uneasy burned in her chest. Finally, she pulled Mac away from her.

"Mac, we have to go."

McKenzie nodded jerkily. "I have to—go." She tried to sit up in the bed. She swung her feet over with all the coordination of a sleep-drunk toddler, and looked up through a veil of golden hair. "Can you help me get dressed?"

Joyce sighed. "I don't think I have much choice." She stood up, thinking that Carter would have paid to be in her place at the moment.

Susan picked at a Cobb salad from the cafeteria, speakerphone on, retrieving her messages. Nothing seemed of much importance until Jennifer Lee from the office came on the line.

Susan listened and quickly flicked off the speakerphone. Why had the newspaper been trying to access CyberImago R & D? How had they even known there was an R & D to turn a hacker loose on?

Was Carter Wyndall involved? He did not seem to have remembered her, from past or present, the last few times they'd been face-to-face. But the coincidence was too convenient. If he was bird-dogging a story on either John Nelson or McKenzie Smith, he was too close to her.

She slammed a fist on the desk. She would be naive and unprepared if she thought he wasn't. Jennifer had dismissed it as a quirk, surmising that the newspaper had probably been trying to send a fax to the wrong modem, or download a file from a wrong number. She reported that nothing appeared to have gotten through.

Susan felt her forehead grow tight and narrow. She doubted that they would tell her much of anything different, knowing how strict she was with secrecy and control.

Jennifer didn't know what kind of software they made in the back room and, to their credit, only two others did. A programmer and an animator. The others were blissfully unaware that their efforts were spliced, diced, and edited to obtain the end result Susan desired. She uncurled her fist and checked her hand carefully to ensure that she had not damaged her nails.

She waved them in front of her face, long, slender, elegant artificial nails to replace the ones she always kept bitten to the quick. Perfectionists did that. But they didn't have to suffer the consequences of their actions.

Susan stood up. Another session or two with McKenzie Smith and not only would the girl be ready to interface the master imprint, but she would handle whatever Carter Wyndall dished out.

She decided to check on Mac one last time.

Joyce had gotten the better part of a hot cup of coffee down McKenzie's gullet. The effects were . . . well, it had always been said that if you gave a drunk enough coffee, what you had was a wide-awake drunk. McKenzie held her eyes open in exaggeration and focused on Joyce.

"I think I can stand now."

"Sweet Jesus, I hope so, because I can't waltz you out of here. They'll stop us before we get out those double doors." Joyce stood up and backed away.

McKenzie got to her feet, holding onto the swing-out tray table. It wobbled, she wobbled. She wore jeans, a size too big for her slender hips, and a short-sleeved blouse which hugged her sculpted torso. Joyce eyed her slippered feet.

"One step at a time," she muttered.

"I'm trying. I can't . . . I can't feel them."

The analogy to a drunk was more appropriate than Joyce would have liked. "Sure you can," she coaxed. "Just slide 'em a little bit. Like skating."

McKenzie had been resting her bottom on the bed's edge. She now stood fully erect and took a deep breath. "Okay."

She shuffled halfway across the room, Joyce backing up like a mother urging her toddler to take her first steps. As they crossed, Mac began to smile.

It was a beautiful expression. Joyce dusted her hands off.

"Girl, we're gettin' out of here." She hooked the door open. "Let's go."

There was no traffic in the ward. Everyone was eating. At the nurses' station, the charge nurse handed her the forms and nodded absently. Joyce ran her eyes over the forms as she kept a hand hooked around McKenzie's elbow, guiding her down the hall. Everything was in order, including Officer Pete Moreno's call to release her.

Joyce felt a glow of satisfaction.

McKenzie halted at the locked doors. "What do I do?" "Knock on the window. He's supposed to look up and identify me." Joyce moved to the window, still looking at the release forms.

McKenzie rapped gently.

"He's not looking."

"He will. He's new at this." Joyce folded back the sheet. Everyone's signature was in place. There was no way Mac was coming back if she didn't want to.

Now all they had to do was keep her out of harm's way from Jack Trebolt.

"Joyce, he's not going to look. And my knees . . . I think my knees are folding up. . . ."

Joyce hit the doors with the flat of her hand. They rattled against the dead bolt.

"What do you think you're doing?"

Joyce swung around. McKenzie made a small sound, and leaned against her. Dr. Susan Craig, mouth shrunken and angry, faced them in the corridor.

"Where do you think you're going with my patient?"

That small noise came from Mac again. It sounded like a whimper.

Joyce smoothed out the forms in her hand. "Voluntary confinement is lifted, and everything else is in order." She gave the doctor a warm smile. "There's nothing wrong with Mac, and I can situate her better elsewhere."

The doctor's jaw worked. "What about the assault?"

"Moreno agrees that Trebolt is in the area and should be apprehended."

"Well, then." Craig's icy blue eyes looked to McKenzie. "Everything appears to be working out." She looked at the forms again. "Good luck to you. Joyce, I'll see you later this week, undoubtedly." She turned and left.

Joyce felt as though she had passed by an iceberg. She turned around. McKenzie's face looked chalk white. Joyce pulled her foot back and booted the door.

Angry words from the psych ward reception desk could be heard all the way down the corridor to the hallowed confines of the chapel. Jack lifted his head from his copy of *Penthouse* and listened. The air thundered with attitude. He heard a black woman give someone sarcasm that could blister the skin, and then a soft, hesitant voice he thought he knew. He dropped the magazine.

He crept to the niche which allowed him to see the corridor without being seen.

The black woman stalked by, McKenzie leaning heavily on her arm. She looked pale, but good. His chest tightened immediately and he bit down hard to keep quiet. What were they doing with his wife now?

"First, we'll get you all settled in that shelter I told you about, and then we'll call Carter. After that, we'll sit down and figure out what to do, you and I."

He knew that Carter well. He'd checked up on him. Jack didn't like the sound of what he heard at all. *Babe, you didn't run near hard and fast enough if you thought you were gonna outrun me.*

"Sounds like you're good at making plans," McKenzie whispered.

"Oh, I am. Don't you doubt it."

Eyes hard, Jack watched them pass. Trailing after, not too close, he followed. He was good at planning, too.

Chapter 33

They barreled out of the hospital and dashed across the parking lot until they reached Joyce's car, and then they collapsed upon it, laughing like maniacs. McKenzie hugged the hood of the car, her face flushed.

"God," Joyce said when she'd caught her breath. "I feel like we just got caught toilet papering someone's house."

McKenzie turned her head, putting her cheek to the cool metal of the car. "Caffeine and adrenaline. What a rush." She laughed again, shakily. "I feel like I'm on *Cops*."

"You look like it, girl." Joyce rattled through her purse for her car keys. "Hurry up. I think I'm going back to sleep."

"Oh, you won't sleep in this car. My son has the radio station button preset to boom box." Joyce found what she was looking for and fished them out. She opened the passenger side door, leaned in to search the glove compartment for a few seconds, and made a sound of triumph. When she stood back to let McKenzie in, her hand was full of black wire and adapters. "Once we get settled, I can give Carter a call to let him know we're there."

McKenzie slid onto the passenger seat. She picked up the cell phone and held it as Joyce entered the car. "Why not now?"

"Because that baby is as dead as a turnip, that's why. But I can use the adapter when we get to Calico House." Joyce snapped her seat belt into place and turned her head to watch herself back the car out. True to her word, the radio had come on, full blast, but she turned the volume down. Still, the music pulsated throughout the car.

McKenzie watched the street slide by. The rush was dissipating. The oddly artificial feeling of tranquillity had begun to catch up with her again, but she did not let it overwhelm her. She had the uneasy feeling she wore it like a mask. Hidden underneath it was what had transpired during the day and in Susan Craig's lab. She had only hazy memories and none she wished to bring back. To distract herself, she asked "Why Calico House?"

"Why not? It's a shelter. It'll be open officially in about two more weeks—"

"No. No, I mean . . . the name. Why Calico?"

"Ah. Well, it's because of the sponsor. She's a retired home ec teacher. She sews quilts. They're authentic and prize-winning. Anyway, when her husband died, she took part of the estate and set up funds for a shelter. But that's not the best part." Joyce steered expertly around a corner. "She bought some equipment from the high school when it was being renovated, and she's donating that: six sewing machines. She'll teach anybody there who wants to learn. Quilt-making to baby clothes, you name it. She uses a lot of calico fabric when she works, hence the name. Anonymity, but not."

"She didn't do it to see her name on the building."

"No. Most of us don't. We do it to see you walk out, and hope you never have to come back." Joyce's mouth tightened abruptly, but her passenger didn't see it.

McKenzie watched the houses, buildings, other cars blur past her window. "Never be a victim again."

"That's right. You've got it, girl. We don't ever want to see your bruised and bleeding body again. And we particularly don't want to see it down at the morgue." Joyce lapsed into silence, a silence which McKenzie let stretch out.

Susan made the call from a pay phone to avoid the trace. It rang nearly half a dozen times before Dudley answered it.

"Where were you?"

"In the shower."

She could hear the resentment in his voice. She had pushed him hard last night and this morning. She softened her tone. "I was worried."

"Don't be. I'm here."

"I need you to do something for me. I have a situation developing. I have faith in you. This is your chance to redeem yourself for last night."

"Tell me what you want me to do."

"We're going to have to pull out. We've discussed this before."

"There's trouble."

"Yes, but nothing you can't handle."

A lengthy pause followed her statement. Then, "They're looking for me. You know that."

"Not tonight. Even with the Bureau's help, they couldn't get their act together by tonight. It will take weeks before they've developed their profile."

Sulkily, he said, "It should have burned."

"But it didn't, and so now we have to take steps, to protect you, to protect me."

"All right. I understand. I'll get ready for a pullout."

"Good. And then, you need to go to these addresses. She has to be at one of them. Take the gear." Susan dropped to a whisper as someone passed by the phone booth. She turned her back to them to avoid being seen and told Dudley what it was she wanted.

Joyce flicked on the lights. "We have water and electricity. No phones yet, they're to be installed the end of this week. No gas, either, but you didn't feel like cooking tonight, right?"

McKenzie rubbed the bridge of her nose, somewhat dazzled by the sudden light. "Right," she agreed sleepily.

"First, I call home. Then, we order pizza. Then, we take care of that friend of yours. Okay?"

McKenzie drifted farther into the house, freshly painted, carpeting still with tufts and clippings from the installation, only odds and ends of furniture in place. "Sure."

"The bedrooms are upstairs. Six in all. Small but they'll do. There're some boxes of donated clothing up there, too. Why don't you see if you can find something?"

McKenzie started upstairs. On the landing, a quilt had been hung, the double wedding ring pattern. It was indeed a work of art. She trailed her fingers over it as she passed it on the stairs.

Flash. The quilt, bloodstained and crumpled, lying at the bottom below her. McKenzie froze on the step.

"What is it?"

What could she say? Thanks for rescuing me from the psycho ward, but I'm still seeing things? She screwed her head slowly around, lips parting, to tell Joyce, but the words that came out were, "I don't like mushrooms on my pizza."

Joyce smiled. "Gotcha."

McKenzie gripped the railing tightly and continued on up.

In the quiet lobby of CyberImago, flames began to flicker, to burn orange and then yellow-white as the accelerant fed them. The plastic plant in the corner melted almost immediately. The receptionist's desk caught fire, Jennifer Lee's textbooks burning like solid lumps of charcoal in the center of the cheap plastic and chrome. Smoke bulged the doors to the office and R & D, pinched its way through the narrow cracks. No alarms or sprinklers went off in the office.

The fire would have burned very brightly and gutted nearly the entire structure before alarms began in the rest of the complex. The accelerant used would leave no trace, except for the nature of the fire itself—unstoppable, incredibly hot and swift and destructive.

"Tums," Dolan pleaded. "Rolaids. Maalox. Anything."

"Take your pizza like a man," Carter returned. "Give me that grid." He reached for the chart they'd been working on the last few hours. The first thing they'd gridded was that Mr. Blue did not always hit blue houses. That seemed to be his preference, but it wasn't a given. What they had found was that his victims were always single women. Until last night, when he'd added two male children.

Dolan belched, a resounding rumble that perfumed the air, and pushed the chart within reach. Nose wrinkled, Carter sat back in his chair to look it over once more. He took a highlighter and marked through two lines carefully.

"What are you doing?"

"These two. They just don't fit. I don't think they're Mr. Blue. For one thing, the fires that were started were much bigger, more ambitious. They were meant to consume the evidence, not drive the victim into the killer's arms."

Dolan belched again, then got up and leaned over. "I can see this one," he agreed and tapped a finger on the grid. "She wasn't even stabbed, though it appeared she'd been beaten. The suspect they pulled in on this one was all wrong."

Carter rubbed the corner of his eye. "Who was that one?"

"The ex-boyfriend. They'd had some problems before." Fax paper made crinkling noises as he shuffled through them. "He's some kind of hero. They let him go finally, admitting their evidence was screwed."

Carter had put his elbows on the tabletop, chin propped in his hands, half listening to Dolan and half thinking that Joyce had yet to call. He put his head up and rolled his shoulders slightly. "Okay, that one stays out. What else?"

"Not a whole lot." Fax paper rustled some more and Dolan belched again. The odor wafted Carter's way.

The reporter got to his feet. "I surrender." He sauntered to the bathroom to search the counter for antacids.

Dolan stayed hunched over the file copies. He wished he had them on disk. He could rearrange them, collate them any way he wanted. This hand-grid method Carter used was beginning to bug—

"Hey, Carter."

"What?" He tossed a crusty roll of chewables at Dolan who ducked and snagged them out of midair.

Dolan quickly emptied half the roll into his mouth, talking around them. "This is interesting. If you include the one done last night, four out of the ten were battered women."

"What do you mean?"

"Well, Graciela had just left a shelter. According to the grid— look—" Dolan's broken fingernail skidded down a column. "This one was waitressing, but I remember the file. She'd gotten chef's training from the shelter she was in, and she was waiting for an opening. And this one, right out of the home. Court had her listed as a runaway. The primary suspect on both were the ex-husbands at first, until the agencies realized they fit the Blue profile."

Carter grabbed for the files. "What about Denise Faberge, the one done last week? Wasn't she just out of a shelter, too?"

Dolan scanned the sheets he held. "Yeah, yeah, here she is. Been out a couple of months. Just took out a temporary restraining order on her ex, though."

Carter was grabbing for everything Dolan wasn't holding. "That makes four. And if you include that one we just eliminated, that makes five. Five out of the ten victims were battered women."

"Sometimes I think the world is a sewer."

"No. No, you're missing the point."

Dolan looked up, still sucking on the multitude of antacid tablets he had stuffed in his cheek. "What point?"

"Mr. Blue does victims. He makes them the ultimate victim. And, conveniently, he's not the suspect. The batterer is the first and automatic suspect." Carter began to lay the files down in order. "But how does he know?"

"Know what?"

"Know their past. What they are? Where to find them? How the hell does he know? Shelters are safe houses. I don't even know the addresses of the places Joyce works with, and I've done stories with her." He sat down. "I've missed something. What is it? Give 'em to me again."

Dolan watched him warily, as if some insanity had just reared its head. "Again? What about the one we eliminated?"

"Throw her back in, too. We've got to go through it again." Carter popped two chewables into the palm of his hand and took them. His teeth ground on the chalky, vaguely pepperminty objects. Dolan's voice droned.

"Shit!" Carter bolted upright.

"What? What?"

"The hero. What kind of hero?"

Dolan's eyes dipped. "A fireman. He's a fireman by the name of Herbert Dudley."

"That's him. That's him." Carter went to the computer and booted up the GIF image of Susan Craig at the women's benefit. "Shit. That's him. That's him standing right behind her."

"And that's a benefit for battered women," Dolan echoed. "Are we looking at Mr. Blue?"

Carter stared closer, at Susan Craig. He wondered if he was staring at someone who'd created Mr. Blue. A firefighter, who could go almost anywhere, anywhere he wanted, and with architectural imaging, any building would be laid open to him, like a surgeon lays open a chest cavity before doing delicate work on the heart. A man who, for one reason or another, kept killing his wife again and again and again.

Had Craig given him those reasons? The software they'd downloaded earlier said she could have tried.

The phone rang sharply.

Dolan watched him as he answered it, said, "That's great," and, "I'll be right there," and jotted down an address.

Carter pulled on loafers. "Write everything down we've just talked about. This is not an article. Just list the grid and the pattern. Give 'em the name. Fax it back to Sofer and Franklin. Tell them I think we've got a prime suspect for Mr. Blue and that it's likely he's taken lessons from Georg Bauer. That'll make 'em jump."

"Where are you going?"

"Mac's out. Joyce has her bedded down in a shelter that hasn't been opened yet."

"Do you think she's a target?"

"She's been around Susan Craig. That's enough to worry me."

"What about Dudley?"

"Let the Bureau pick him up."

Dolan seemed reluctant. "Then what do I do?"

Carter stopped halfway out the door. "You go home," he said, "And take care of your heartburn."

Dolan nodded in disappointment. "Right."

Carter shut the door.

The cloudless California skies finally deepened into night. Jack took his boots off the dashboard of the car, dropping his feet with a thud that rocked the vehicle. He'd been staring at the house so long he was damn near cross-eyed. For amusement, he'd watched a nearby palm tree where the rats skittered in and out of the fronds. Damn things were everywhere. Palm trees *and* rats. He wished he'd brought his .22. Pop! Pop! One less Mickey or Minnie Mouse.

Mac had been in there with her newfound friend long enough for the leftover pizza to get cold. Long enough to hang blankets at the windows, shutting out his view of them walking back and forth upstairs. Long enough that darkness cloaked the neighborhood. Silently, he got out of his car. He reached in the back for his dark, hooded sweatshirt. No sense in letting the whole world know who the hell he was.

The air, when he tried to take a deep breath to steady his nerves, stank. Dirt and smog drifted in the unrain-washed atmosphere. He and Mac would be better off home in Seattle, the quicker he could arrange it. She was probably ready to listen to him now. He'd given his itchy mean streak a long scratch, and now he was ready to talk nice to McKenzie. He'd promise her another dog—hell, he had the name of a breeder with a litter of puppies all ready to go that he'd ripped out of the paper that morning in the hospital and stuck in his pocket. He'd let her go back to school full-time if she wanted. Even have a career. He could use another breadwinner in the house. No sense to the bill-paying burden being all on his shoulders. No wonder the stress drove him crazy sometimes. Things could be worked out. All he had to do was make sure her newfound friends wouldn't change her mind or get in the way.

A bit unsure, Jack wiped the palms of his hands on his hip pockets. He looked into the darkness and stepped out.

It didn't come as a flash. McKenzie paused, as she and Joyce sorted through the boxes of clothes. There were neat piles of items that were in her size range, and neat piles of all the other size ranges, on the floor around them. She stopped folding and paused. The feeling came as a tingle down her spine as though someone had stepped on her grave. At least, that's what her mother used to call it. She scrubbed her arms briskly.

Joyce looked up. "Cold?" It was the first decent weather of the week. The evening had cooled and there were hopeful weather reports of coastal fog and inland low clouds in the morning, shaving maybe ten degrees off the previous forecast. It was getting cooler, but it was a long way from cold.

"No." McKenzie hesitated. "Twitchy." If she were a dog, if Cody were here with her, their hackles would be up.

"Can't blame you." Joyce smoothed down a blouse. "Carter should be here soon. Then I'll head on home."

McKenzie wanted to say, Do you have to? But she knew the advocate did. She had a family, a home life of her own. "Maybe that's Carter now."

"Where? What makes you think so?"

"Well, I . . . I thought I heard a car door. Or something."

Joyce rolled an eye at her. "Don't go trying to spook me."

Mac laughed. "I'm sorry. I was, wasn't I? You know, this is a big place with just the two of us here."

"It won't be long until it's full." Joyce beckoned. "Women and children and mentors. I don't think it's empty. I think it's full of promise."

A thud sounded on the roof above them. McKenzie jerked nervously, staring upward.

"Roof rats," Joyce said. "In the palms all around us. I'll tell the house leader to get a cat." All the same, she stopped drawing out and inspecting clothes.

Another thud, and with it, the house shook. The wooden framed windows, and sliding door closets jumped in their tracks ever so slightly. The overhead swag lamp swayed from its chain. They sat stock-still until the room stopped moving and groaning.

Then Joyce blinked and let out a derisive bark. "Four point oh, if it was anything. Here we sit like dummies. That was an aftershock. Probably from the Northridge quake. It's still dancing."

McKenzie felt her face warm in embarrassment. Of course, she knew what it had been. She'd grown up here, hadn't she? Four point oh was a pretty good shock this long after the primary quake. "Maybe it was on a new fault line."

"As long as it's not *my* fault," Joyce told her. She tossed Mac a pair of acid-washed blue jeans. "That looks like your size."

The label and the size had been sliced off the waistband. McKenzie stood up to measure it to her hips. She modeled it for Joyce. "Looks like they could."

"Kick off your shoes and pull 'em on."

Mac had already found practically new running shoes. She wiggled her toes in them, and opened her mouth to say—

THUD.

She snapped her mouth shut. Joyce got to her feet and charged across the room, grabbing her by the wrist. "Biggest roof rat I've ever heard. Get away from the window."

They heard the glass breaking on the other side of the blanket they'd hung for a curtain, but they took to their heels, not about to stay to see who or what was coming through. Joyce slammed the bedroom door shut and keyed the dead bolt. She looked at Mac. "It works from both sides, but only if you have the key."

Mac wet her lips. "The other rooms!"

They went from door to door, keying the dead bolts. Joyce had kicked off her heels. She made practically no noise on the carpeting. "Phone," she said softly.

She looked downstairs. A loud banging shook the upstairs. Mac nodded and started down.

The upper half of the house grew very quiet.

Joyce came down with her, step by step, eyeing the house. "Whoever they are, they don't seem to care what kind of noise they're making."

Mac became aware of just how much glass was in the front and other rooms as she paused downstairs. She looked back at Joyce, who was framed by the quilt.

The lights flickered and then went out.

"Shit." Joyce's voice, out of the twilight.

The blanket curtains let in only slivers of light from the outside, weak yellow beacons from the streetlights. Not enough to see by.

"Whoever it is, he's still outside."

"I left the cell phone on the kitchen counter."

"I'll get it," said McKenzie. She put a hand out, touched the wall, and, trailing her fingers, went in search of the instrument. It had to be Jack, terrorizing her, but how did he find her? How did he *know*?

How did he always know where to hurt her?

Never again.

Mac stopped in her tracks, put her hand to her chest. Her heart railed there like a wild bird beating itself against a cage. Besides the cell phone on the tiled kitchen counter, there had been a can opener and a flashlight, one of those heavy-duty torches.

Mac stubbed a toe turning too soon. She stopped and could feel her own heat being reflected back at her by the wall. If she squinted, she could almost see the darker wall against the midnight of the house's interior. She put her hands out and felt to her right.

Toward the corner. She wasn't close enough. She took a side step, cautiously, quietly. Stretched out her arm. Slid her palm against the wall's surface again. Reaching out.

She hit air.

McKenzie took a deep breath, knowing she'd found the turn to the kitchen.

Then warm flesh grazed her hand. Someone tried to grab her fingers.

"Christ!" McKenzie jumped and lunged the other way. She ran, unthinking. Words tore out of her mouth. "Joyce! He's *inside!*"

She sprinted. He came after. She could hear his breathing. She collided with Joyce at the stairwell. Her eyes had adjusted to the dark well enough to almost see the hazy lines of the banister. The keys went flying, up the steps.

"Come on!" She charged after them, pulling Joyce up with her.

He leaped and caught them mid-stair. The tackle drove them to their knees. Mac grunted under the weight and put a hand out to the wall, anything, clawing, to get back on her feet.

The quilt met her hand. She wrapped her fist in it and pulled herself out from under Joyce and Jack as they fought. She could hear flesh and bones hitting, the sick thud of contact. Joyce swore fluently and the man stayed silent.

Hanging from the quilt as if it were a strap, McKenzie swiveled round and kicked with all her might.

She struck home. A masculine cry answered her. Jack staggered back, a shapeless shadow among all the other shadows.

McKenzie let go of the quilt and grabbed at Joyce. "Come on!"

She kicked the keys on the step, bent over to grasp at them. The chill metal answered her search. Her position saved her.

Joyce screamed as Jack leaped again. Something flashed in his hand.

There was a monumental struggle. Joyce's voice, raw and urgent. "Run, McKenzie! Run!"

She hesitated.

She could see the two grappling, not well enough to know which was which, as they teetered in the stairwell. Then Joyce let out a sharp cry, and fell back, against the quilt. The wall hanging came down on her. Caught in its folds, she fell. Her weight took the other shadow with her as her body bumped heavily down the steps.

Flash.

McKenzie did not wait for the vision. She turned and ran, gobbling the remaining steps. She hit door frames, counting them, found the one she wanted and tried to plunge the key into the dead bolt lock.

She couldn't find the slot!

She fumbled her fingertips across the metal.

"McKenzie."

A low, somewhat breathless masculine voice from the stairs. She did not turn to see what Jack wanted.

She inserted the key. The lock turned stiffly, and then she fell inside the open door. Wrenching around, she pulled the key out and kicked the door out of her way.

With her entire body, she slammed it shut and locked it from the inside. The key cut into the palm of her hand as she leaned against the door.

What about Joyce?

She didn't know.

Carter was on the way. How long could she hold out?

McKenzie turned to face the window. Saw the skyline, the silhouette of palm trees that framed the houses next door, the window glass like scattered diamonds on the rug.

She'd locked herself in the wrong room.

She couldn't stay. He'd been up this way once before. He'd try it again.

If he could get in, she could get out. Run to the neighbors. No one would let her in, but maybe somebody would get scared enough to let their dogs out. Call 911.

It was better than being cornered.

Mac shoved the keys down into her jeans pocket and crossed the room. Glass slivers ground into the floor under her feet.

No one pounded at the door. She could hear nothing.

He'd already guessed. Was already back outside, looking up.

He had to be.

Mac carefully leaned out. The tiniest of ledges led from one window to the next. And then the roof tiling eaves led to the garage.

She could jump that.

Adrenaline gave her wings.

She picked up something, the blanket, and laid it over the windowsill where jagged glass fragments threatened like teeth. She swung one foot out. Secured it on the ledge. Then the other.

She held onto the corner of the window as long as she could, scooting along the ledge, until she could not help but let go.

She pressed her face against the stucco wall of the house. Hugged with her whole body as intimately as if she were locked in lovemaking. Inched her way along until her searching hand found the next window frame.

Below her, Jack called softly, "McKenzie!"

She did not answer. His voice did not sound close. Mac thought of looking down but did not.

She inched along the minuscule ledge until her sneakers touched the tile roofing she sought.

She jumped off the ledge and slipped, going to her knees.

The noise had to bring him running. McKenzie straightened and fled, her night sight guiding her over the roofing. A black abyss yawned in front of her. Then the flat roof of the garage. From there she could see the neighbor's yard.

Already lights were going on. Dogs began to bark frantically. McKenzie took a deep breath and ran. She took off like a deer over the abyss, hit the garage, and kept going until she reached the other side.

"Mac!"

A slender figure at the edge of the yard, in the lantanas and shrubbery. "Carter!" Hope surged in her. She would be all right. He would save her. She leaped downward.

He moved toward her as she hit awkwardly and toppled. A stab of pain that she knew well from softball went through her right knee. She keeled over, sucking her lip in agony.

There was the solid thud of a collision. She looked up to see two dark figures grappling. Jack and Carter danced with obscene violence. Grass flattened under their feet. Shrubbery branches whipped about. They wrestled with angry intensity. Fists struck, arms flailed. They cried out with thick guttural sounds.

She wanted to scream, but the sound choked in her throat. Doors banged. Dogs kept barking furiously.

Carter let out a low cry of pain. He twisted in his opponent's hold. She still could not see his face as the garage shadowed them.

For a second he broke away. McKenzie took a deep breath. She saw the other coil, like a snake ready to strike. She pushed her warning out, birthing a faintly audible "Carter!"

Then she saw a gleaming streak, a swath of silver cut through the night.

"Noooo!"

Carter doubled over. He went to his knees, then onto his face.

His shadowy attacker turned toward her, hesitated. A beam of light sliced across the driveway and backyard. It outlined him. Her assailant turned and bolted.

McKenzie got to her feet. Her knee tweaked her once, and then she was steady. She could do this. She had to. She approached Carter's still figure. "Oh, God. Oh, God."

Flash. She was to kill Carter.

Flash. She saw love in his kind, gentle eyes.

McKenzie stopped and put the heel of her hands to her sight. When would it stop?

People poured out of surrounding homes. The sudden flood of porch lights and flashlights dazzled her. She put up an arm to shade her face.

"Call 911," she said. Begged. Over and over. "Somebody call 911." Carter couldn't be dead.

Could. Not.

The son of a bitch would never hurt her again.

Confused, McKenzie stared numbly down at the fallen body as if she'd struck Carter Wyndall herself. She leaned over, hand trembling, to turn him.

"Mac."

She looked up. Carter forced his way through the growing crowd. "What's happening?"

Her senses whirled. "Carter?"

He caught her by the arms, then enfolded her in his arms. Could he hear the wild beating of her heart?

"Carter?" she repeated breathlessly, disbelieving.

"I got here as quickly as I could." His breath smelled oddly of pepperoni and peppermints. It was real. She touched his face. He tightened his arm about her. "What's wrong?"

"I thought it was you."

"What happened?"

"Jack broke in. He came after us, all through the house—the lights, he took the lights out. Oh, God, Carter, I think he might have killed Joyce. She fell on the stairs. I got out over the rooftops. You called to me—"

"Not me," Carter interrupted softly.

"They fought after I jumped." She looked down. "Then who saved me?"

Strangers ringed them, flashlight beams cutting the air wildly, excited voices babbling. One of the neighbors put out a foot and nudged the fallen man over. The body flopped about, arms akimbo.

Jack Trebolt stared up at the stars with death-clouded eyes.

Chapter 34

"Knocked cold twice in one day, this girl can take a hint. I'm punching in my time card and goin' home." Joyce stood in the front yard of the Calico House, porch light glowing behind her. Red and blue lights from squad cars cast deeper bruises on her face. She held the quilt wrapped in her front arms, bloodstained from the split lip and battered nose she'd suffered going down the stairs.

She leveled a look at Carter. "Take my advice and take this one home for the evening."

Mac shivered, though the spring evening was still far from cold. The shock of seeing Jack's body had iced through her and she seemed far from thawing.

Carter put an arm over Mac's shoulders and drew her close to his flank for comfort. "I'm considering it."

"I told Moreno what he needs to know. Everything else can be handled in the morning." Joyce took a step away.

"But," said McKenzie. She scrubbed a hand wearily over her face. "What happened here?"

"Jack Trebolt got killed here, and you didn't do it," Carter answered. "We've got an eyewitness next door who heard the commotion and saw the fight. That's all we need to know right now."

"And it wasn't you, because I thought you were the one who . . . the one who. . . ." Her voice failed her. McKenzie put her face to Carter's shoulder and just stood.

Joyce patted her on the back. "We'll sort everything out in the morning." She looked at Carter over McKenzie's head. "I'll page you when I'm ready to get together."

The corner of his mouth quirked slightly. "Fair enough," he agreed.

Joyce kept her hand on McKenzie's back. "The man is a gentleman," she said. "Go home with him. You can't stay here alone tonight, anyway. They'll be crawling all over doing fingerprints and such."

Mac looked up. "All right."

Joyce looked at the quilt. "I sure hope I can cold-water-soak these stains out." She turned and left, walking slowly, obviously in pain.

Moreno came up as Joyce got into her car.

"Well, Mz. Smith. You're keeping me on my toes."

"I'm sorry."

She looked as though she genuinely was. Moreno slipped his notebook into his pocket. "I'll let you know tomorrow what else has to be done. I'll have to talk to you again, go over your story once more."

"I know."

"At least," he said, and his mustache fluffed out a little. "It's in better circumstances this time. I know this is probably not the time to say this, but sometimes this is the only way to deal with a stalker."

"He was my husband." Her mouth worked a moment, then she added, "I ought to have some feelings for him. But I don't." God help her, she didn't. What kind of a monster was she, unless numbness were a feeling all its own.

Carter stirred as if he could buffer her from the reality of the whole ordeal. "I'd like to take her home."

"Fine. Just the usual, don't leave the area. I'll contact her there."

Carter steered her toward his car. She walked steadily with him, as though her mind were a million miles away, and her body on automatic.

He unlocked the apartment door a little apprehensively, but the place was dark and Dolan had gone. The assistant hadn't picked up any before he'd left and the dinette table was strewn with the faxes and the pizza box.

McKenzie smiled faintly. "The universal dinner," she said, as he strode around the small room gathering up the mess. The faxes he did not want her to see, not only because the Bureau's information was confidential, but because there were photos and drawings which were grisly enough even in their reproduced form. She'd had enough blood-letting for one night. Joyce had traded words with him, short and sweet, telling him all that McKenzie had been through. Jack's death would be no balance for her father's. Not now. Not yet.

McKenzie dropped into his recliner, putting the back down and the footrest up.

Carter paused near the kitchen door, hands full of trash. "Can I get you anything?"

"Ice," she replied softly.

"Just ice?"

"For my knee. Put it in a baggie, if you have one. Or a towel. Please."

She spoke as if the effort of putting words together in a sentence were almost too much. He knew the feeling. He went into the kitchen, mashed up the pizza box to get it in the trash, and went about making her an ice pack. He twisted off the cap of a lite beer and brought it out as well.

She took both, tossed back a swig from the beer, and handed it back to him, foam swirled inside the neck. She laid the baggie across her jeans. The denim was scuffed and dirty where she'd gone down. After a moment, she said, "This is no good."

She flipped the recliner upright, got out of it, and reached for her zipper.

Carter watched, baffled.

Mac paused. "Turn around."

"What?"

"I'm taking my pants off so I can put the pack on my knee. So turn around and go get me a robe or bath towel or something."

"Right." He nodded and headed in the general direction of the bedroom and bathroom. While he was in there, he straightened that up, as well. Seat down, lid up, sink cleared.

He came back, tossing her a bath towel from across the room. She settled it across her lap, but not before he got a glimpse of her long legs and slender, firm thighs. Mac leaned the recliner back again, ice pack in place.

She laid her forearm over her eyes. He pulled up a dinette chair and nursed his beer.

After long moments of silence, she peeked an eye at him. "Aren't you supposed to ask me if I want to talk?"

He flexed his lips a little as if he would, then shook his head.

She turned her face toward him. The bruising had retreated to shadows which looked as if perhaps she'd been playing with her mother's makeup and had smeared it about. She had been attractive. She would be more so when those shadows disappeared completely. "You're a reporter. You have to talk."

He shrugged. "This is not an interview."

"Oh." She lifted her arm from her brow. She sighed. "I can't believe it's over."

"Believe it."

"But I—" McKenzie stopped. Her eyes glistened. "I loved my dad once. But there's nothing here," and she thumped her chest. "Nothing. I cry for my damn dog and I can't cry for him. Or Jack."

"But you are."

She sniffled. "No."

"I've been around a lot of stories in the last twenty years." He picked up the beer bottle, rolled the chilled glass between his palms. "I've seen people mourn in every conceivable way. Some yell. Some scream. Some tear their sleeves from their clothes. I've seen them smear ashes on their faces. Heard the women in the Middle East wail." He took a drink. "I've seen them stand with blank faces, immobile, voiceless to express the grief inside of them." He thought of Georg Bauer. "I've even seen them laugh."

"And where does that put me?"

He brought his chair a little closer. "I'd say you're right up there with those who've been through too much to cry right away. Like someone in a war zone." He put his hand out, gently smoothed a fringe of hair from her forehead. "You can't get tears from a stone."

"A stone," she repeated. She took the beer from him and drank again. "Do you think I'll cry later?"

"Probably. When it's right for you. Because, McKenzie, when you came home, you must have been thinking of the life you'd have together. You'll cry for that lost hope. As far as Jack goes, the good and the bad, he stole that from you. When you're ready, you'll weep for everyone."

The corners of her mouth turned up slightly. "Now you sound like a reporter."

"Can't help it. I'm a sentimentalist." He did not take his hand away from her face. She turned to his palm, as if seeking the warmth, and cradled her face into it, molding his hand to her shape.

"I don't remember when I lost my way," she murmured.

"Most of us don't. But you're found now."

"Am I?"

"Oh, yes. Never doubt it. I've got you." The tears began, soft and warm, on his hand. She started to cry in earnest, the tears spilling from her as if flood gates had opened.

"This is no good," he said. He stood up and lifted her from the chair, then sat down and pulled her into his lap, and held her as he would a child, pillowing her face on his shoulder.

She sobbed until she could sob no more.

He found a couple of paper napkins from the pizza company stuffed down the side of the chair. They looked relatively clean and unused, so he gave them to her so she could dry her face and nose. Then she sagged back onto his chest and he listened to, felt, the slow steady beat of her heart. The faint perfume of her skin tantalized him. He studied the arch of her eyebrows, the color of dark honey like her hair. There were light and dark hairs, and even one or two of reddish cast. *No one is ever just one thing, one color. We are all mixtures,* he thought.

She blew her nose a last time and then gave a shaky laugh. "What would we ever do without pizza?"

"Darned if I know."

One or two last tears sparkled as they dropped onto her cheeks. Mac said, "Kiss them away."

He had long since felt himself stirring, but she startled him. "What?"

"Like this," and she pulled his face closer and her lips, like gentle butterflies, journeyed across his cheekbones. Then she let him go.

He looked into her eyes. "Why?"

"I don't want to be stone," she answered. "Anymore."

He did as she asked him. He kissed her lips last, felt her mouth swell and open to him, their kiss long and hard and passionate. When he leaned back for air, he said, "There are some situations in which being as hard as rock is preferable."

McKenzie laughed. She ran a hand through her hair, combing it and letting it cascade down onto her shoulders. "Tell me."

"I think," he replied, bringing her face back down to his. "This can be considered one of them."

She laughed again and when their lips met a second time, it was with a shock, a tingling, an acknowledgment of something happening or going to happen between the two of them. Her mouth tasted faintly of the beer they had shared, and sweet and warm. She tasted him as eagerly as he did her and when they finished that kiss, deep and dark and wet, she leaned her head against his shoulder.

Although he did not feel that way, he knew events could still be stopped. "I didn't bring you here for this."

"I know." Her voice buzzed against his skin. "I'd lost my way, and you came and called for me. Listened to me. Brought Joyce to me. Treated me—"

"No different than I treat anybody else," he interrupted.

"No? Well, then, I understand why people spill their guts to you. Why you're a good reporter."

"This is going beyond research and an interview."

"You're damn straight." McKenzie turned in the chair, laying herself atop him, full length. He could feel the heat of her bare legs as they entwined his. She reached both hands behind his neck, capturing him and when they kissed a third time, it was with every square inch of their bodies, nerves afire.

He came up gasping. ". . . too old. Too old for this kind of activity."

McKenzie looked at him in astonishment. "You?"

"No. The chair, the chair." Even as he protested, the recliner opened up another notch and they were practically prone. When she'd finished laughing, he was able to convince her to move to the bedroom.

He didn't remember undressing. Lying close, she kissed his scars and he kissed hers, incredibly tenderly, knowing she must still be aching and bruised. She whispered soft words in his ear that he almost, but didn't quite hear, but it was enough to catch the tone of her voice. He discovered caressing the backs of her thighs brought her nipples to hard, firm points and that she liked it when he cupped both breasts at the same time and trailed kisses down the curve of her throat.

She ran her fingers over his flanks. He winced out of habit when she hit his lower ribs on the left side.

"What is it?"

"Nothing. It doesn't hurt."

She rolled him over slightly and kneaded the tender area. "What happened?"

"I broke a couple of ribs playing football in high school. I didn't even notice it for weeks, it happened at the end of the season. By the time I had it x-rayed, the ribs had healed crooked."

"Poor ribs," Mac sympathized. She kissed them. "Poor Carter." She trailed her lips downward and across the flat of his stomach.

She moaned when he slipped his hand down to the soft bush of her pubes and massaged her gently, stirring the moist heat of her body. He did not think he could last when she grasped his cock, giving him light, feathery strokes, his skin becoming fiery sensitive with each and every touch.

And when she finally began kissing him again, each kiss a stroke of lovemaking on its own, and they touched chest to chest, he found himself unable to hold back any longer. "McKenzie," he began softly.

"Now," she responded, opening her legs and guiding him inside her.

She was tight and warm and moist. Every stroke sent a thrill through him and he tried to pace himself, but she grabbed his buttocks, kneading her fingers into him, pulling him close, answering by arching her back. Heat ran along their silken skin. Sweat pooled in the small of his back, kissed their stomachs lightly, added fuel to their heat.

The strokes came faster and faster. He couldn't hold back, she didn't want him to, and she came first. He could feel her go rigid as she cried, barely audibly, "Oh!" And she stopped his thrusting for a moment, but it did not matter. He was already deep and answered her orgasm with his own.

She moved her hands back to his shoulders and crushed him to her breasts, and began crying again, softly, ever so softly.

Before they drifted off to sleep, McKenzie smiled into his eyes. She turned on her side, spooning, and wrapped his left arm about her shoulder as if he were the blanket. She was asleep almost before he realized it. He lay very still, not wanting to disturb her, thinking.

Then he, too, drifted off.

McKenzie started awake. "What's that?"

Her jolting movement woke him. The room had plunged into the total darkness of evening and he rubbed his eyes against the blindness. He listened.

"It's the computer."

He took the top sheet with him, wrapped it about his waist, and went in the other room. McKenzie trailed after him. She wore his shirt which almost, but not quite, came down to the tops of her thighs.

"What is it?"

He looked at the machine. It had come alive, though the monitor was off—it was possible Dolan had left it on. But the hard drive was working, chattering to itself, and it shouldn't have been. He flipped the monitor switch and the screen came to life.

He stared for a moment, trying to comprehend what was happening. Then, he answered her. "Someone's trying to access my computer."

Like Dolan had done to CyberImago.

The machine was displaying its directory of its hard disk files and software. The lines scrolled by so quickly, he could scarcely read them.

"What do you mean?"

"Someone's accessing my computer by modem." He could hear the faint atonal whine of that accessory, as well. If Dolan were here, he would know exactly what was happening.

The hard disk whirled, then whirled again. It stopped, then started a third time. As though someone were trying to get something from it, could not, and kept trying in frustration.

Someone trying to read his files.

But he kept nothing other than operational software on the hard disk. His files were on floppies, and there was nothing in the disk drive. Whoever was searching did so in vain.

He stabbed a finger down at the escape button, temporarily freezing the screen.

SEARCH FILE: SUSAN CRAIG.

The good doctor certainly knew more about computers then he did. Carter stood in hesitation another second as the screen wiped clean, then the directory tree began to scroll by rapidly once more.

"It's Dr. Craig, isn't it?"

"I think so."

Mac rubbed her temple wearily. "What does she want from me?"

"You?"

"She's never going to let me go." Mac slipped her arms around his waist, an intimate gesture, but there was more the need for solace in it than passion like that which they had just cooled. "I can't remember it all . . ."

"Joyce told me she found you sedated."

"Before that. I saw her with Ibrahim Walker. He looked so . . . he was frightened of her. The stroke changed him, I know, but . . . I saw his eyes."

Did she know Ibie Walker had suffered a second stroke and even now lay on the brink of death? He turned round in her embrace. "Mac, when was that?"

"Yesterday. Today . . ." she frowned heavily. "Today he was in the lab with Dr. Craig. I saw him." She stopped as a sorrowful expression replaced one of concentration. "She was running a program. He . . . I saw him . . . he tried to fight it. I saw him reacting, and she just stood there, watching. So quiet."

"Are you sure? Ibie Walker was fairly severely incapacitated."

Mac blinked slowly. "He moaned. He jerked as if trying to get away and then—he slumped over."

"And what did Dr. Craig do?"

"Nothing. For the longest time. I don't think she intended to do anything. So I blurted out that I was there, and then she started CPR and told me to call a Code Blue for the lab and . . ." Mac put her hand to her mouth. "Oh, God, Carter. Did I see her try to kill him? And why didn't I do anything?"

"You did do something." And so had Craig. Why Ibie? Was it because he carried most of the votes against her Fernandina project? Would she have eliminated him if Mac hadn't been there? Or had she been running an illegal program on him, and had the elderly man just collapsed on her? What had he and Mac stumbled into?

"Get dressed," he ordered Mac. She looked over his shoulder.
"Why?"

"Just do it. We've got to get out of here."

He'd been too complacent after the death of Mac's husband. He'd
sent faxes and pointed fingers, but he had no way of knowing when
or if the Bureau would act on them. If Susan Craig or someone on
her behalf was breaking into his system, they were still active.

They were still trouble. Perhaps far more trouble than he had
guessed.

He left the computer running, knowing that the hacker would not
find anything, and dressed rapidly. McKenzie met him at the closed
front door.

"Where do we go?"

"Anywhere," he answered, "but here." He pulled the door open.

Something quick and massive hit him in the chest with bone-
cracking strength. A great dark roaring opened in his mind as he fell
forward. His attacker put a shoulder in his gut, hoisting him off the
floor in a fireman's hold and then throwing him across the threshold.
He knew he hit the floor, and that was all for a moment or two, and
he lay there blinking.

He got to the door handle of the open door and used it to pull himself up, to get on his feet. He palmed the light switch, hand shaking,
aching with every breath he attempted to take.

"Mac! Mac!"

He looked around the apartment in desperation.

She was gone.

Chapter 35

A heavy, sweet, and sticky smell hung on the air. It sickened him as he staggered to the phone. He intended to call in the cavalry—Moreno, Sofer, Franklin—whoever it took to get McKenzie back. But the phone vibrated in his hand as he reached for it, the ring sharp and clear until he snatched it up.

Dolan said, "Our friends just went up in smoke."

The smell on the air made his ears pound. Carter answered dully, "What?"

"I'm watching the late news—"

Carter checked the clock readout across the room. "Very late news," he got out.

"Whatever. CyberImago went up earlier tonight, and about an hour ago, Susan Craig's private residence burst into flames. The fire department is calling it a total loss, and of suspicious origin."

"What?"

"Interested?"

"What's the buzz?"

"A former psychiatric patient came back for revenge and torched both addresses. Some schizo."

"Name?"

"Not being released. Word is it's Stephen Hotchkiss. Craig's been treating him for depression and something labeled as 'sexual perversion.' Hotchkiss isn't just any poor schmoo—he's a political up and comer on the school board. He's been out of town since Ibie keeled over, trying to avoid speculation he might run to replace old Walker.

Sounds like a setup to me. It smells. I haven't been able to trace back where the buzz started. Anyway, it's our man who starts fires." Dolan paused. "Do you think it's Mr. Blue?"

Carter took a deep breath. His rib cage answered with stabbing pains and he threw a forearm across his diaphragm, hugging himself for comfort. He remembered the fireman's hoist, the carry which had boosted him up and then thrown him halfway across the room. The assailant had to have been Herbert Dudley. "If it was, he's been awfully busy tonight. He has McKenzie."

"Jesus. When?"

"Just now." Carter told him a little about the assault at the shelter and why he had Mac at his place. "He broke in, trashed me, and took her. I was just getting ready to send the county mounties to Craig's place." He took another experimental breath, sucked in the pain.

"What do you want me to do?"

"Help me to think. If Dudley has her. . . ." Carter stopped in midsentence. Mac had said that Susan Craig would never let her go. If Dudley was out and operating, it was likely on the doctor's behest. Dudley took her for Craig.

"Carter?" Concern was in Dolan's usually breezy tone.

"Yeah. I'm here. Listen, if Dudley's on a rampage, it's because the doctor set it up. Find the doctor, and we'll find McKenzie." But *where?* His thoughts felt as scrambled as his insides.

"She won't go back to Mount Mercy. And there's nothing left but ashes at the other two locations."

He couldn't focus. "I can't think. Listen, Dolan, before I forget, there's a good chance she tried to waste Ibie Walker. I want you to call whoever is in charge of that investigation, and make sure they know he's still a target. She might send somebody."

"What's the connection? That's pretty far out in left field."

"McKenzie saw the good doctor more than hesitate to revive Walker after he collapsed in her lab. As far as motive, it could be payback for Walker's interference on the Fernandina project—"

Fernandina, a hospital, dormant and still. Quiet. Layers of floors, above and below the surface. It wouldn't be a refuge too long, but if all Craig wanted to do was to gather her resources and beat an organized retreat. . . . "Shit," blurted Carter.

"What?"

"I think that's where she might be."

"The old hospital."

"That's the one. Call Moreno. Call or fax Sofer and Franklin. If Susan Craig is there, Dudley may not be far behind. I don't want any loose cannons barging in there."

Dolan said worriedly, "You're going to need some serious firepower."

"You just make sure the troops aren't far behind me." He hung up before Dolan could answer.

Carter retraced his steps across the room to the bedroom closet. There, from the back of the top shelf, he retrieved his .38. He hadn't bothered getting a permit for it here. Georg Bauer's trail had grown cold long before. He slipped it from its holster. The gun smelled faintly of the last oiling he'd given it. He loaded it, and dropped extra ammo in his pocket.

Programmed to kill or not, he'd bet the .38 could drop Dudley in his tracks.

If Carter could see him coming.

If Susan Craig had ever developed her program on architectural imaging, and if Dudley carried that around in his head, he might be facing a killing machine who knew all the loopholes. All the ins and outs of the mazelike building. All Carter had were his hazy memories of years gone by when he'd written a series of stories there.

He could hope they'd underestimated him, and he'd overestimated them.

He could hope McKenzie was still alive.

Dolan put his TV on mute and dialed Moreno's number. He got the voice mail for the department. He almost hung up, knowing Moreno probably would not check the mailbox before morning, but he stayed on the line and left the officer a detailed message that made as much sense as he could collect out of what Carter had told him. He put an urgent flag on it. He also put in a call to Moreno's pager and left the department's own voice mail number on the beeper's message system. Maybe that would do some good.

Then he went to his computer and booted up his fax-modem program and composed a like message for the Bureau. When it came time to transmit, the software hung up, signaling him the transmission couldn't go through.

FBI traffic, coming in at night. Dolan bit his lip. He instructed the program to keep trying transmission, recycling automatically. It was all he could do. When he called, he got a polite recorded message informing him of Bureau hours.

He had only one other person he could try. He pulled up Joyce Tompkins' pager number and dialed it. She would be madder than a wet hen, but Dolan didn't think he had much choice. He sat back in his chair, folded his arms, and waited for callbacks.

Otherwise, Carter was going in alone.

All the coffee in the world couldn't help Sofer combat his jet lag. His body seemed determined to maintain E.S.T. even though his mind had to work three hours later. It was hell in the early mornings and late evenings. So was the heat and smog. He trailed after Franklin, his suit smelling faintly of smoke and char. The call for the CyberImago fire had taken him out of a late dinner and the greasy super taco he held in one hand did not promise a satisfactory substitute.

Franklin sat down at his desk and eyed the clutter as Sofer wearily lowered himself into a chair. Franklin said, for about the twelfth time that week, "You know, if you like Mexican food, this is the town to get it in, not that fast food crap—"

"I know, I know," Sofer muttered around the taco. His teeth chomped down, squirting hot sauce and melted cheese into his mouth.

Franklin picked a slip off his desk. He looked up, California crow's feet deepening around his eyes. "Better hurry. We've got another call to make."

Sofer's free hand went automatically to his tie. "I smell like Smoky the Bear. Should I change jackets?"

"Don't think so. This time Susan Craig's home address burned down. Arson investigators are doing some preliminary work."

"It's after midnight!"

Franklin put up an eyebrow. "No rest for the wicked."

"Only because the very, very wicked won't let them." Sofer stuffed the rest of his taco into his mouth, mopped up the overflowing juices with a napkin, and followed Franklin back out of the office.

Behind them, as the door closed, a single phone began to ring. The automatic phone system cycled it quickly into the phone mail, and Agent Franklin's mailbox got ready to record a message.

"Hello. I—I don't know if I'm speaking to the right agent or not, so I'm trusting that this gets passed along properly. I can't leave my name, but I will leave a pager number—702-5555—and someone needs to call me back. I need to talk to an agent about Dr. Susan Craig. I have reason to believe she may have ordered a hit on Los Angeles Councilman Ibie Walker, and she's trying to blackmail me, as well. Please contact me as soon as possible."

The line went dead after a last, quavering word from Stephen Hotchkiss.

Carter turned off the car lights and pulled in quietly, gliding to a stop. He ached and put his hand to his rib cage again. That sweet, coppery smell was thick in the car. He pulled his hand back wet and warm.

"What the—" He cracked the car door, letting the light come on, and looked at his fingers.

Blood.

He'd been stabbed and hadn't even known it. He skewed around on the seat, swinging his feet outside to the ground, leaned back and pulled up his shirt. Nothing too gory, though the sight of the entry wound made him queasy for a moment. He reached up to his left shoulder and ripped the sleeve down after three or four very vigorous tugs, made a compress, and tucked it inside his shirt.

Dudley had been going for a fatal wound. He'd missed—God knew why—then Carter smiled grimly. God bless those crooked ribs. The knife blade must have slid off them. He was losing blood, but not too rapidly. The compress would have to do.

He retucked his shirt tightly and gathered his thoughts again. Chain-link fencing ran all around the hospital site, though he could see it had been breached in several places. Wild thistles pushed their way up through asphalt, dark purple in the late evening. Lights gleamed from the hospital building, though anyone could tell the building was abandoned. Power had been maintained to keep it from becoming a ghost town, a shooting gallery. At one time, a janitor had even lived in Fernandina, though Carter had no idea if anyone did now. The lights were sporadic and insufficient. Inside, the building would be creaking, dirty, aged, disrupted by the earthquake and abandonment. Still, there were four floors up and two, no, three, Carter corrected himself, three floors down. The surgical theaters and the morgue made for two. File storage and utilities the other one. The floors below were basements in the foundation, basically, not the full size of the stories above although Fernandina was a small facility by anyone's standards.

Mac could be anywhere.

He wanted to wait for reinforcements. Every painful breath told him he should.

But he didn't dare.

He got out of the car and shut the door quietly. He slipped a hand to the small of his back, checking his belt holster and the .38. He was no Lone Ranger, but he could not wait.

Chapter 36

Flash. Looking into a face in which nothing was human except the general outlines, a death mask with eyes that watched her avidly.

Mac came awake with a jolting dread. Her head pounded with a sickly sweet smell and her tongue felt like cotton. Where was Carter? Where was she? She remembered being caught up, of trying to kick free. A man had burst into the apartment, throwing Carter aside like a broken toy, and snatched her up. She had fought, uselessly. Then a rag was pressed to her face, and she had tried not to breathe, but she had to, sending her into a dizzying drop, a downward spiral which seemed never to end, a dreamless unconsciousness.

Her lips tasted horrible. She choked as she tried to lick them clean. Gagging, she nearly fell over, slipping against soft cloth bonds which held her to a chair. The chair scrapped against the linoleum flooring as she managed to right herself. Alone. No sign, human or inhuman, of her captor.

The long, thin room—no, she told herself. A corridor. The corridor was lit in a golden, sepia manner, almost adequate to see, but not quite. The linoleum under her feet was an anonymous brown speckle, heavily waxed over the years, until it had a patina almost as golden as the illumination around her. Her neck felt too weak to hold her head up, so she stared at the flooring.

Remembered it. She'd seen flooring like it before. Was she somewhere she knew?

Mac lifted her chin. Beige baseboards ran a foot or more up the walls, like splash guards or chair rails, then the walls were an indifferent ivory color. The hallway was not totally empty. Here and there an old wooden desk might be pushed against the side, a chair or two sitting beside it. It reminded her for a moment of an old school, when the janitors used to push the furniture into the corridors so they could clean the classrooms. But it had been a long time since any student had been here, if this had been a school.

At the joints where one intersection met another, the plaster was heavily cracked, crevices zigzagging their way from ceiling to bottom. Lights overhead were caged in thick, wire covers. Desiccated insect forms dotted the inside of the lights. Had she been left to die, alone and caged as they had been?

Mac twisted her wrists, felt the soft cloths which held her give. She pulled more vigorously, then stopped as she heard a heavy door open.

Susan Craig and a man came into the corridor. He walked with an easy athletic grace, his shoulders wide inside the dark sweat suit. His head seemed malformed, and it wasn't until he turned to look at her that she could see he wore one of the virtual reality helmets, modified, its visor covering his face. The shiny ebony surface gleamed, reflecting her shocked face back at her, but she could still see through its translucent shield to his hard eyes that watched her back. Hungry eyes. Eyes without a shred of sanity or compassion.

A tiny sound escaped her as he reached up and pulled the garish-looking mask off. Behind it, the face was hard as stone, and warped, as if it had been misshaped. As if someone had taken his face between the palms of gigantic hands and squeezed it under tremendous pressure, offsetting it. A delicate, fine-lined scar ran along the brow, across the temple, and disappeared into the hairline. He had been a handsome man once. It was the eyes which made her look away. Mac could not meet the terrible expression in their depths.

Even as she took a shuddering breath to steel herself, she felt something more. *She could hear the sleeping man stirring.*

As much as she feared Susan Craig and the man with her, Mac was more afraid of what she sensed but could not see.

The sleeping man. He did not stand before her, but his presence filled the air as powerfully as if he did. What was he, what could he be, that she feared him more than she did the two in front of her, the two she could see, the two she knew existed?

The unmasked man plucked at the doctor's elbow to gain her attention. "She's awake," he said flatly.

Susan turned around. "Good. We've no time to waste." She pushed her light blond hair away from her face in a strangely feminine gesture, smiling, though her blue eyes stayed as chill as always. She drew near.

"Who is he?" Mac asked.

Susan looked over her shoulder. "Not that it will matter, but this is Herbert Dudley. The papers have been speculating about him lately. They sometimes call him Mr. Blue."

That would have scared her enough, but she knew that what she dreaded meeting was even more terrible. This was flesh and blood. The other defied her comprehension.

"No," Mac returned. "Not him. The sleeping man."

Dudley went incredibly pale and stepped back against the corridor wall in retreat. Susan's eyebrows flew up, a genuine expression of surprise on her face, and then she composed herself.

"You have depths," she answered, "I hadn't suspected."

"She can't know." His mouth worked a moment before Dudley got the words out.

"Of course she can. That's why I kept her alive." Susan pushed her sleeves up. "Aren't you going to ask how you got here, McKenzie? Or what we did with Carter Wyndall?"

At the newsman's name, the big man let out a short laugh. Her chest tightened, but she would not let them see her respond. She could still smell his scent on her skin, feel his warm hand on her shape, share the look in his gentle eyes.

Nothing like the eyes watching her now.

Mac stared back levelly.

"No? Well, we haven't time for small talk anyway." She said to Dudley, "Boot up the computer. Load the main program. I want the master matrix brought up."

He had not yet fully regained his color, and it seemed to McKenzie that the big man paled even more. He hesitated.

"Do it."

Dudley, holding his helmet by a strap, went back inside the doorway they'd just come out.

She walked around behind Mac and unlocked the chair's casters

with a kick of her toe. "You asked about the sleeping man," Craig told
her, as she wheeled the chair down the corridor. "You share Dudley's
nickname for him. Did he tell or did you sense it? Dudley has a special relationship with him, but nothing, I suspect, like yours will be.
You have a gift, McKenzie, of being able to interface reality with virtual reality. I found it when I was going over the empirical data of
your spatial scans.

"Virtual reality is just, and only that," Craig continued. "To be
sure, the animation and graphic imagery has improved by leaps and
bounds. With certain hallucinogenic drugs and subliminal cues,
you'll even swear you can smell and touch and taste what your eyes
are watching, what your ears are hearing. But you can't. No matter
how much you might wish to, because it isn't real. It is a dream world
which we can train you, to a certain extent, to manipulate. We can
use it for therapy and diagnosis, for recreation, for mind expansion,
behavior modification—" Susan Craig broke off. She turned the
chair sharply into a doorway. "The applications are almost endless.

"But we cannot blend it into reality. One leaves this world to enter
the other. Sometimes knowingly, sometimes not, but there is a
threshold which exists."

"But I can do something you can't."

"Indeed." Susan leaned down. The room they entered was, or had
been, an office. It was empty now. Old, brittle, yellowed paper drifted
across the floor like autumn leaves, skittering away from Dudley's
steps as he came back toward them. Battered and rusting old file
cabinets sagged against the wall. In its midst, several newer chairs
and a computer setup seemed jarringly out of place. A second, spartan monitor and phone line ruled a smaller desk.

But it was the major setup which drew Mac's attention like a magnet. The monitor was alive, and a face filled the screen. His dark
brown hair had been neatly combed back, and the hazel eyes glowed
with life, the flecks of gold and green in those caramel depths gleaming like flames of fire. She knew that face, those eyes. Fingers that
dipped in blood and drew. She wanted to turn away from that stare,
that watcher, a predator waiting for the prey to make the tiniest of
moves, like a cat or a raptor. One small motion and the chase would
begin. The eyes were unblinking, eternal.

Mac stopped breathing as Susan wheeled her around to look at it.

"Meet the sleeping man. McKenzie Smith, this is, or was, Georg Bauer."

She managed to take a breath as the screen did not respond. She looked into a photo, a still picture, as lifelike as any reproduction.

But it was not alive.

Susan Craig touched the monitor screen gently with her fingertips. "Put her in the chair, Dudley," she said absently.

Scowling, Dudley untied Mac's arms and lifted her in his. He dumped her in the contour chair in front of the computer.

Without looking around, Susan ordered, "Secure the feet and left arm only."

"She could get loose."

"Once she's in the program, she won't even try. She needs to wear the glove."

Don't let him waken.

She must have spoke aloud, for the other woman looked back over her shoulder, and her mouth stretched with irony.

"That's what I kept you alive for, McKenzie. You've met with him before. Now you're going to join him, for me. We'll work together, you and I." Susan broke off, humming a few bars of "Beautiful Dreamer."

Dudley carefully secured her to the new chair. The only good thing about him was that his muscular body broke her field of vision, and the deadly stare of the man on the computer screen. When he had finished, she found her voice.

"He's a monster."

The cold blue eyes looked into hers. "You don't know him the way I do. But you will."

"He's dead."

"He's dormant," agreed Susan. She tapped the computer. "But not in here. I have him broken down, fragmentized, everything that he was and could be. The force of his personality—I've been studying the effects of his imprints for years."

"You killed him."

Her mouth tightened a moment. "No," Craig answered. "But Georg and I both knew that he was . . . socially unacceptable. That we could never have a life within the norms. So we did what we had to, and this is what I was left with. His essence. His psychological soul, if you will. Digitized into virtual reality."

"You keep trying to recreate him."

"Yes."

Dudley came toward her with the VR helmet. McKenzie jerked wildly away. "Brand," she said.

"Yes. Only partially successful. He had his own wild personality traits. Dudley here is a far better copy, but then, I had excellent raw material to work with. But, again, he has his own life. He does not wish to live as a copy of another man, and I would not wish him to."

Dudley grabbed Mac harshly by the chin as she tried to snap at him. He began to pull the helmet over her head.

"Why me?" cried McKenzie.

"Because you bring reality into virtual reality. You create and manipulate what is not in the software, the program. I don't want to create a legion of serial killers. I don't know how you interface, I only know that you do. You can meet him face-to-face without my imprinting him over your own matrix. You'll bring him out. You the victim, he the hunter. Two halves of the same equation."

"Why?" screamed Mac again, struggling against Dudley and the chair, afraid as she had never been in her life. All the *flashes* she had ever seen began to careen through her mind.

"To cure Georg Bauer, naturally." Susan's face lit with the first genuine, warm smile Mac had seen from her. "I hope you enjoy meeting him."

Dudley thumped the helmet down, shutting her into twilight.

Flash. Her father placing the bat in her hands. The wood, new and shiny. The weight, heavy. Walton Smith smiling, his eyes bloodshot from a hangover the day before, but his love fresh as the new day. "Just swing when you're comfortable, Mac," he said. "Don't try to hit a home run. Just get on base."

She seemed to hold the bat firmly in her hands. Had she done this before? She moved hesitantly forward into the neighborhood of California tract homes.

Something sharp pinched the inside of her arm. *What are you afraid of, McKenzie? Susan Craig's voice echoed in her head. It must be Carter Wyndall. He knows what's inside of you. He wants to free it. You mustn't let him.*

Rage.

The sleeping man.
Don't. Wake. Mustn't. Rouse.
She tightened her hands around the handle of the bat.
A whine at her ankles.
"Cody!"
His tail waved for her, golden silky hide rippling, his chocolate eyes sparkling with doggish spirit and love. But as she tried to take another step forward, he hugged his body against her legs and lowered his head. He growled in warning.

He pressed heavily against her, forcing her back.

Mac rocked back in the chair. The sudden feel of it around her knocked her from the program momentarily, her senses reeling.

An alarm sounded.

Mac put her gloved hand to the visor, was able to tip it up and partially off.

The small black and white monitor showed a tipped view of a double-door entry in one of its cubed shots. Someone walked through warily.

Susan said to Dudley, "It's Carter. I thought you took care of him."

"He went down."

"He didn't remain down. Handle it. I've got to stay here. I need her if this works; she's expendable if it doesn't."

He hesitated.

"Go on! I just gave you the imprint for the building. You'll be one step ahead of him the whole way."

Dudley leaped into motion like a deadly cat. Craig leaned back over the security monitor.

McKenzie drew one foot out of her cloth shackles and kicked the other free. She slid her right hand out of the VR glove and picked her left hand free. The helmet she drew off her head as she got stealthily out of the contour chair.

Susan must have heard her coming, for she straightened and turned halfway around when Mac faced her. "Don't try anything, McKenzie."

"My father isn't here now."

"I know you better than you know yourself. I've started a process you can't stop this time. There are strings I've pulled. Thoughts that can explode like land mines inside your head—"

"I will not be a victim!" Mac backhanded her with the VR helmet.

The doctor's head shot back and she fell with a sharp sound, and lay very still on the floor. An empty syringe rolled beside her.

In the corridor, McKenzie paused for a moment. Her guts reeled as if she were going to be very, very ill. When she looked up, it was as though she were in two worlds. She had brought the program with her, a waking dream, one that she could not leave.

She looked down at her left forearm and saw the angry spot, the puncture mark, on the inside curve.

With certain hallucinogenic drugs. . . .

Susan Craig had tried to ensure her meshing with the artificial world of her murdering lover.

Mac took another staggering step. The double vision was excruciatingly painful to endure.

She looked up. Cody stood at the intersection. He lifted his head, and gave her a grin, red tongue lolling from between sharp, clean teeth. His ears pricked with happiness.

If not real, then at least Cody came from her, formed by her experiences.

She ran after him.

She sprinted up a story and skidded around a corner. Cody faded, his golden shimmering body growing fainter and fainter until he disappeared. Mac stopped. She held her breath, listening.

A faint scuffle. The corridors here were dark, illuminated only by the faraway glow of fixtures mounted along other pathways. She put her back to the wall and eased toward the intersection.

The darkness seemed to help the war within her senses. She looked with one vision momentarily, heard with one set of ears. Touched with one pair of hands. She came to the right angle corner and stopped.

She crept around the juncture.

He turned as she did, and they stared face-to-face.

"McKenzie!"

Seeing him jolted her. She flung up a hand to stop him as he drew close.

She could not bear to have him within arm's reach. Within harm's way. She warred with herself and did not want to add casualties.

Flash. The bat, in her hand, standing over Carter's body, a crimson wetness splashed around. Her vision or Craig's?

The son of a bitch will never hurt anyone again. Her voice, in her head, low and snarling.

But it was Jack she thought of. Not Carter. Why did she see Carter's body?

It couldn't happen to him.

Not her.

She closed her eyes as visions crowded.

What did she see from within? What did she sense that Susan Craig had implanted there?

"Mac?"

She swallowed it down as if that was all it took to suppress it, and looked at him. The lines in his face deepened with concern as she answered, "I'll be all right."

"Let's get out of here."

"No."

He had her by the hand, but her flesh was so chill and numb she could scarcely feel his touch.

"She has a program," Mac got out. "You have to do something. She has him on disk."

"Who?"

"Georg Bauer."

Chapter 37

He took a step back as if she'd physically hit him. Then he inhaled deeply, though it seemed to pain him. He put a hand to his ribs, bracing himself. "Where?"

"Back this way." She turned to lead him.

He stopped her. "Tell me which way to go. And you stay here."

"Dudley is looking for you. He thought he'd killed you."

"I know who he is." He stared back the way he'd come, then met her eyes again. "She has a program . . . do you know—"

"She said she'd imprinted him with the hospital's layout."

Carter looked grim. "Then he'll find us wherever we are." He put a hand to the small of his back. She gathered he carried a gun there.

Flash. She saw Bauer's face.

The death watch blinked.

The prey had given itself away. The stalker leaped.

The realization set off a flood of adrenaline, a rush. He was in her mind, but she stood, fighting the impulse to attack, that idea that Carter was the enemy.

She had done this to McKenzie. She who loved a computer image, a printout, a personality matrix was trying to come between Mac and Carter.

Mac shaded her eyes from Carter. *It's not real,* she told herself. They had lain together. She had felt the love pooled between them. That was real. She knew what it was now. She'd never had it from Jack, but Carter had touched her, embraced her with it, and she knew what it was. She didn't want to let it go. She didn't want to let him go.

But Susan Craig had taken her father's legacy of rage and turned it back on her. She could feel it mounting inside her, like a volcano ready to blow.

He took her hand. "Mac, what is it?"

She heard a noise beyond the intersection and slipped her hand away quickly. "Hurry."

They ran.

Carter could not catch his breath. Even if they could stay ahead of Dudley, whenever they paused, he sounded like a bellows. His left side grew wetter and slicker. McKenzie seemed to know the way, yet she paused and doubled back once or twice.

He knew he could not go much farther. He caught her sleeve. "Mac!"

She froze in place. He bent over and tried to breathe deep. Had Dudley sliced into a lung? He lost his bearings for a moment and slapped his hand onto the wall to keep himself upright.

He left a bloody palmprint.

Mac grabbed up the edge of her shirt and tried to scrub it away. "He'll know. He'll see it and he'll know."

Carter stared at it dully, trying to think, to remember. Then it came to him. The horrible drawings in the apartment building, like and unlike Georg Bauer.

"Let's give him something to think about," he said. He pushed Mac away. He wiggled his right fingers inside his shirt, dampened them on the compress. Oddly enough, he wondered if he'd bled enough to do anything.

He managed a sun, a sun with corona flames. The original was emblazoned in his memory from the very first murder site he'd stumbled across, a Georg Bauer original.

Mac shuddered. "Why?"

"Because part of him is Bauer, and part of him isn't. Even when he kills, this guy is torn apart. He's going to kill us when he meets us. This is going to stop him in his tracks." Carter wet his lips. He turned around, unable to face the pictograph himself.

"He's afraid of the sleeping man," Mac murmured in agreement. She brushed her hair from her forehead. She seemed to wake. "Come on."

He shook his head, "I'm not going anywhere." He pointed at a shadowy doorway ten yards down. "I'm sitting here, and I'm waiting."

"Carter—"

He looked into her face. "Where does Craig have the computer set up?"

"One more turn and then downstairs."

"The old offices and storage rooms. I know them. You go on. I'll catch up."

She started to argue, but then Carter grabbed her by the arm and dragged her down the corridor to the recessed doorway. She heard then the whisper of running shoes on linoleum. They crouched side by side, and Carter put his hand in his pocket, reaching for his gun. They waited.

He charged them out of the shadows, from in front of them and not behind. He had circled them. A warning scream tore out of Mac's throat. Carter did not even have a chance to pull the gun out or get to his feet in response.

Dudley put his shoulder down, driving a tackle into Carter that threw him across the corridor. Carter hit the wall and slid down limply.

The gun. What had Carter done with the gun? She did not see it in Carter's hand or on the ground.

Dudley picked Carter up by a fistful of shirt. Carter blocked the first blow, then came a crunch of meat and bone. Carter went to his knees and spewed helplessly, painfully.

He rolled aside, scrambling out of Dudley's reach, lunging at the other's ankles. His weight brought Dudley down with a surprise grunt. They grappled while Mac watched in horror. Dudley got to his feet by sheer brute effort and drew Carter with him. He turned, holding Carter at arm's length, and threw him across the corridor again, slamming him into the wall.

Carter's breathing rasped in and out of broken lungs. His nose was a crimson smear. But he stayed on his feet and when Dudley pivoted around to finish him off, the stalker froze in horror.

He stared into the bloody sun signature of Georg Bauer.

Carter reached into his trouser pocket and brought his hand out filled with the .38. He hesitated.

Dudley let out an inhuman roar and charged.

The .38 answered back, knocking him halfway down the corridor.

He landed on his back and jerked once. Then he lay sprawled in a gory pool.

Carter swayed. He returned the gun to his pocket. He looked up, met Mac's eyes. She said nothing. She came over and placed herself under his arm, and braced herself as he leaned on her. They moved crablike into the darkness.

"I think this is it," Mac whispered into his ear. They came to a painful stop.

Carter put his hand behind him, then shook his head. "You stay away from Susan Craig. I'll do what I have to."

Mac nodded. She turned the doorknob slowly, waiting for the click, and pushed it open as soundlessly as she could.

They had entered the wrong room. As they stepped in, the soft beep and chime of monitors filled the air. Hospital equipment of every imaginable kind ringed the room. Old filing cabinets and desks had been shoved aside to accommodate the medical equipment. They stared in disbelief.

Carter said, "Holy shit," softly and limped toward the massive coffin that stood in the center. "It's a hyperbaric chamber."

It looked like an Egyptian sarcophagus. Mac tripped over a heavy cable, one of several crisscrossing the floor. The room hummed with the power and the working of the machines. She looked at a monitor which she recognized from ICU. A slim paper fed in and out. She touched it, read it. The heart rate had been holding steady at 55. Then it had begun to increase and was now approaching 75. She dropped the paper, uncomprehending.

Carter reached the side of the chamber and looked down through the glass lid. "Oh, my God. She's got him on ice."

The sleeping man.

Mac turned toward him. "In suspension. Waiting for a cure."

"There's no cure for what he has." Carter stepped back, his face creased with disbelief and horror. "Find the plug and pull it." He whipped around, started to retrace the cables. "This is why she didn't get out. This is why she hesitated, even when everything started to fall apart."

The chamber drew Mac. She went to it, one shaky step at a time. She reached it just as Carter yelled at her.

"Don't fool with this, Mac. You don't know what you're getting into."

She leaned over the glass lid. Pale in death, yet appearing merely asleep, tucked into loose overalls, he lay, eyes closed, hands palm up, a beatific pose. His dark brown hair waved over a satin pillow. The Father of All Violence, A Bringer of Destruction.

With a grunt of agony and triumph, Carter found a connection and pulled it apart. A bank of machinery went blank and quiet.

The chamber stayed lit. She could see an intricate network of fine lines and wires that crisscrossed his body, as well as tubes. Fluids dripped in and out. The body was remarkably well preserved and she wondered what Susan Craig had done to it.

The door crashed open. Susan screamed, "Get away from him!" She hurled herself at Carter, clawing at his eyes. He fell back into a stand, taking the machine with him.

Sparks flew in blue and orange arcs. They snapped and crackled and Carter, locked in mortal combat with Susan Craig, could only swing around and barge into another bank of equipment. He managed to topple that as well.

The smell of electrical fire filled the room. A thin veil of smoke rose.

Mac froze. The machinery still on at her elbow began to chatter. The stylus danced and drew intense, increasing lines. She looked down into the chamber.

The eyes opened. Hazel orbs with yellow fire licking deep inside them stared into hers.

He was alive and awake.

Mac bolted. As she dashed into the corridor, she heard a massive crash, a thunderous clanging. Its echo filled the hallway and gripped her, freezing her in place. The chamber had overturned. Had to have. She couldn't leave Carter behind—

Flash. Bauer was behind her, awakening, coming. She had to run.

A woman screamed. It was truncated, cut short. Mac's heart pumped faster and faster until she thought it would burst, but she could not move. Could not turn around. Could not scream. Her eyes watered as the stinging smoke of an expanding electrical fire surrounded her.

Cody appeared at the end of the corridor. He barked once, urgently.

She knew this nightmare. Mac leaned forward and her feet followed.

She broke into a shambling run. Something metallic crashed behind her and she could hear hoarse breathing. Blind panic drove her.

The dog led her through the maze. They went up and up and around and around. She could feel him coming after her. The heat of his body was like a smothering cloud, drawing closer and closer.

Mac slipped and went down, sprawling. She sobbed in exhaustion, hugging the floor. Cody's apparition disappeared. She got to her feet.

A thin wailing sounded. Smoke alarms, going off throughout the building. She turned.

She'd left Carter behind.

She could not.

She went back.

Carter crawled painfully across the floor. He caught Susan Craig up as he would a drowning swimmer and crawled back across the room, dragging her limp body with him. She began to kick and fight feebly. Blood matted her silver-blonde hair. The side of her face had swollen purple-red and only one eye could open to look at him. He pulled her over the threshold and into the corridor. There was no sign of either Bauer or McKenzie. Carter and Craig coughed and choked until the fresher air of the corridor revived them. Carter managed to pull himself to his feet. He hauled the doctor up with him.

"What was that thing that came out of the chamber?"

She glared balefully at him. The bruised and swollen shut eye teared blood. "Georg Bauer."

"How do you stop him?"

She coughed again and said hoarsely, "You don't."

"What the hell did you have him in?"

"A medically induced coma. It was the only way to keep him safe while I worked. I gave him everything—" Susan looked in distress down the empty corridor as smoke snaked out across their feet and began to rise, a lethal fog.

He started to limp, pulling her with him.

"My work—"

"Fuck your work. You know him so bloody well. Where's he gone? What's he doing?"

Her chin trembled slightly as she squinted down the abandoned hallway. "He's hunting," she said simply.

Carefully, Mac traced her steps backward. Whenever she halted, could not find her way, she searched for the sign Cody had left. Pools of thin urine upon the floor. Once or twice, the sign had been disturbed. Fading wet footprints led the other way. The pursuer had been outrun.

She began to speed up as the alarms got louder, noisier. The building might smolder for a while, but once it caught, it would go like tinder.

She went downstairs. Her footsteps drummed in the stairwell, echoed up around her and gradually faded away, saying to anyone who listened, *Here I am. Come get me.*

She stood in the lobby. Another stairwell faced her and as she hesitated, she heard them come up out of the depths of the building.

Carter was dragging Susan Craig. Halfway across the lobby he let her drop to the ground and bent over, coughing, retching miserably. Blood dripped from his side as he did so.

He raised his head and spotted her. His jaw worked. "Mac—"

Too late.

A hand dropped on her shoulder. Fingers gripped her like iron.

Susan Craig got to her feet with a sob. Staggered forward, entreating. "Georg," she said in a lover's pleading tone. "Please."

Mac swung free as the hand moved. Bauer came from behind her, crossed the floor in three swift strides, to catch Susan Craig up in his arms. The woman smiled and tilted her battered face upward.

"Georg—"

He bent her backward in his embrace. "For what you did to me." His voice was dry and rusty. Without another word, he put a knee up and cracked her back across it. Then he dropped her on the floor. He looked at McKenzie.

And smiled.

McKenzie's hell burst in her mind. She took a step forward.

Wires trailed from his jumpsuit. He looked as if he had stepped out of an ebony spiderweb. As she looked at him, his image seemed to waver and fade, like a bad television transmission.

Carter begged. "Run, Mac. Get out of here." He squirmed on the flooring and brought his gun out, held it up, tried to keep a steady bead.

Georg Bauer glanced at him. And laughed. He drew closer to McKenzie.

She watched him with vision both real and virtually real. She knew him, and he knew her. Susan Craig had brought them together, tried to meld them.

What are you afraid of?

This was her dark half. This was the rage she had inherited from her father, doubled, trebled, quadrupled by a warping society.

She could let it swallow her or break free.

Bauer held out his hand.

Curling smoke began to pour out of the downstairs well. Carter's hand shook. The barrel of the gun wavered uncontrollably.

"Mac," he said hoarsely. "Run. Get out of the way. Please."

Bauer pivoted and kicked out in one deadly move. The gun flew from Carter's hand as he gave a shocked cry. The .38 disappeared down the stairwell into the fire. Bauer moved to stand over Carter.

"Leave him," she said. "It's me you want."

The killer looked over his shoulder at her. "Actually," and his smile grew wider. "You're a little old for my taste."

Mac took three sharp breaths, closed her eyes, and loosed her rage into the virtual reality plane. Bauer staggered back.

No more.

She stuck her right hand out. A baseball bat immediately filled it. *What are you afraid of?*

She ran her hand over the weathered wood. Her touch renewed it into gleaming freshness. She could feel her father's hands over hers, guiding her into the correct grip. This was their bridge, the span which crossed the gulf between their ages and their genders, his rage and her innocence. It was all he'd had to give her, and McKenzie knew now that Walton Smith had prayed daily that it would be enough. She could feel the puff of a breath across her temple, the warmth of a presence standing behind her to embrace her, as he wrapped his arms around her, enfolded her hands in his. *Circle the bases, McKenzie.*

This was her heritage. Not the rage. The love of a sport. The enthusiasm. The goodwill in playing, and playing well. The fairness and drive of the competition. The lesson and future that athletic success could give her, that he could not. She could feel his hands engulfing hers still, molding her fingers about the wood.

What are you afraid of?

Not this. Not anymore.

Her weapon. Her tool. She gripped it tightly with all her senses and all her heart. Virtually real. She advanced.

Bauer seemed frozen in hesitation; she could see the overlapping realities. Carter gasped at his feet. There was a serious pool of blood growing around the reporter. He couldn't last much longer.

And she could see others as well. Children. Shades of Bauer's victims. Watching her. Their tortured flesh hanging from their bodies. The souls shining through like beacons of angelic light. The suffering. The violence.

Bauer put his hand out. "You're part of me," he said.

"No. Never."

"I know what you feel."

"No. Never!"

Carter felt the heat from the two of them, hotter and more searing than the flames at his back, as his own body grew icier by the second. *So this is what it feels like to die,* he thought. *Like lying down to sleep in the snow.* He ought to get up to help McKenzie, but his legs had stopped obeying him.

Only his heart still responded. Bauer and Mac faced each other like wrestlers waiting for an opening. She denied him, but fear for her resided in Carter's guts like a ball of ice. He leaned over and dug his fingers into the tile, dragging himself across the floor. It was slippery and tried to cling to him, tried to glue him down.

"Mac, don't listen to him. Whatever he wants in you, *she* put in there. It's not you! Don't let him take you!"

There was no sign she heard him as the killer leaned close and placed his hands on her shoulders. She gave a mighty shudder and her face paled to a silvery unearthliness.

She faced Georg Bauer across the planes. He began to draw on her. She could feel herself grow thin, insubstantial. In his way, he was murdering her here.

Just as he planned to do in reality.

"No. Never!" She stepped into the swing with all her might, the bat following through.

Carter saw her take a step into Bauer's embrace. It wrenched an incoherent cry from him and he pulled himself up, grasping, hand outstretched, fingers curled at her ankle as if he had strength enough left to yank her away. He felt a shock through his hand, a levin bolt, a jolt of electricity charged enough to stand his hair on end.

He heard her shout, "No. Never!"

Bauer grunted with the impact and rocked back on his heels. His arms flung into the air, wires trailing, black licorice whips about his body. His lips peeled back from his teeth in a rictus grin. Then he brought his hands in, clutching his chest. Tottering back, the killer went down and did not move again.

Headlights streamed through the night. The wailing of fire engines still pulling into the Fernandina lot was deafening. Behind them, the flames rose hungrily, licking white-orange into the heavens. There was no way the firefighters were going to save the building or anything that might be left in it. Police and Bureau agents busied themselves in the flickering light, pulling yellow crime scene tape into place. Helicopters beat overhead, adding their beams to the effort to light the scene.

Mac walked beside the gurney, holding tightly onto Carter's hand. Dolan trotted on the opposite side, suspending a plastic bag in the air. His other hand held a tape recorder and he was trying to catch all of what Carter was saying.

Sofer and Franklin sat on the bumper of the ambulance, watching as the attendants and paramedics steered the gurney near.

Moreno helped collapse the gurney legs and hoist it into the ambulance. Dolan clicked off the recorder.

Carter coughed once, wetly. He made an effort to keep his eyes open. He said, weakly, "When you call out the cavalry—"

Dolan grinned. "Better late than never, right!"

"Right," softly answered Mac. She climbed into the ambulance next to Carter. She smoothed his tousled hair from his forehead.

He coughed again and winced in pain. Then he told her, "We've got to stop meeting like this."

She only smiled.

Joyce Tompkins leaned into the back of the van before they closed it up. "Carter, just tell me you got that son of a bitch who killed Graciela and Donnie."

Carter lifted his head. He looked back at the outline of the building as the fire consumed it. A corner caved in as they watched, sparks like shooting stars aimed to the skyline.

"We got 'em," he answered. Then he put his head down and closed his eyes peacefully. Mac leaned over and put her face to his chest, listening to his strong, steady heartbeat.

In the depths of the night shift, Brand awoke suddenly from a dream. The lamp in the backboard was on, and in its halo, he could see his mother, drowsing in a chair pulled close to the hospital bed.

Delight burst in him. "Mom!" He reached for her, bandages trailing from his wrists and sheets falling from the bed.

She woke with a smile and reached back. Her face came closer and closer—

and he looked into Susan Craig's ice blue eyes.

Brand screamed.

He bolted upright in his bed, sweating, the sheets falling from him, his room shrouded in night. Steps came swiftly down the hall, the door to his room bursting open.

He sat, panting. "Bad dream, bad dream."

The light came on.

"Brandon. You're awake."

He looked up.

His mother stood in the doorway. Tears began to stream down her face. "Brandon!" she cried joyfully. "My baby." She opened her arms to embrace him.

He was afraid to reach for her.

KILLJOY

Dedicated to Kathy Lewis,
who left this world too soon,
but who leaves good friends
and memories behind.

ACKNOWLEDGMENTS

Anything I did well, I did with the help of those named below, as well as friends and family. Any mistakes I claim as my own.

Special Acknowledgments to:

Lawrence Weber, Emergency Planner of the City of New Orleans, for invaluable time and assistance.

Paul Britton, Jr. (CWA), of Valley Christian High Schol, Cerritos, CA, for tracking Hurricane Opal for me.

Also, Shawn P. Keizer, President of Weather Watchers Online for Compuserve. A special acknowledgment that hurricanes rarely reach the "Y" segment of the alphabet.

USMC, El Toro:

Cpl. Chris Cox, also Lt. Col. Farrell, for information on burial and notification.

Sgt. Todd Keit and wife, Cathy Stone Keit, for further insight on the Marine Corps tradition.

Tom Canfield, pharmacist, for his insight and advice.

Julia C. White, fellow author, for her timely and much needed information on Native Americans.

To the Advanced Eye Care Institute of Newport Beach for answering questions about radial keratomy. And, in particular, to Dennis Hollow and Dr. Sandrowski of the Southern California College of Optometry for their help concerning eye surgery.

With apologies to the lovely city of Brea for rearranging her geography and ignoring her state-of-the-art new police headquarters.

PART ONE

Prologue

Early April

They broke cover at 0530. Wind swept a warm rain across them, boiling dark clouds in a night sky which kept dawn at bay. Equipped in field gear, they moved swiftly across the Haitian foothills, the rotary noises of an idling chopper fading behind them. Jogging in point, William realized what it was he didn't like about the observer they were escorting. He dropped back casually to talk to his sergeant.

"Boss man," he said softly.

"Corporal." Sergeant Christiansen was a smart man, smarter than most, and he answered in the same careful tone of voice which would not carry over the rain.

"That's no UN observer. I don't know what he is, but he ain't what he says he is. I got Nawlins ears, and that's no French accent. Not Canadian French, not Creole, not no Parisian French."

Christiansen looked strange, his white face streaked in commando blackface, and his jaw tightened. "I know, William," he answered shortly. "Just get back and do your job."

"Yessuh." William began to lengthen his stride, but not before he heard Christiansen add gently, "and watch your back."

As he loped back into position, skirting bent grasses and the shrubbery whipping at his legs, Christiansen wondered what else his corporal had noticed. The Gore-Tex boots, maybe, not standard issue, with the haft of a knife barely visible atop the footwear's shaft. Or maybe it was the kevlar armor under the neutral UN vest, definitely not standard issue. There was a ramrod stiffness to the man's back which made Christiansen think that he had a weapon snuggled in the small of it, in addition to the holstered Glock on his hip. Perhaps it was the demeanor of the man himself, running through the countryside like a good coonhound on the scent.

They were just Marines, Christiansen thought, doing their duty. They'd been told to take him in, and bring him out. The chopper should not have been in the air—its crew knew it, and its cargo, a seven-man patrol flown hunkered down on the floor of the craft, knew it. But they had been given a window through which to make this approach and, weather or not, had been told to take it.

They were where they were not supposed to be, about to do that which they were not allowed to do. If he had any qualms at all about his orders, it was over why they were there and not the SEALS. He tried not to think that it might be because they were more expendable.

He wondered who the operative could be, with enough clout that they had been boated in from Puerto Rico, encamped on an uninhabited Caribbean island halfway between Guantanamo and Haiti and then helicoptered out in weather that was damn near unflyable. Christiansen snugged into his field gear. He was not there to question. He was only there to *do*.

And the five-man patrol under him would carry out their orders as well: two African Americans, William Brown and Short Reynolds, and the two *tejanos* Lopez and Aldemar, and Burrows, wiry, nasty, and balding. William was his patrol leader and Christiansen trusted his judgment almost more than his own. So he stopped beside them, one by one, and repeated his advice to the corporal: *watch your back.* All of which made him feel no easier as dawn finally grayed the landscape and they neared the rendezvous area.

The UN observer had given his name as Stark, distinctly un-French even though he was posing as an officer from French troops. Christiansen watched as he paused by a mahogany tree and put up a hand, signaling them to halt. William made a sharp hand signal, and the patrol scattered silently, then flattened. Christiansen, the last to drop into place, did so with pride in his men.

They advanced by increments, one man at a time, at the patrol leader's instruction. Christiansen took the flank, both to protect the vulnerable side of his patrol, and to keep an eye on the observer.

The Haitian foothills were thinly forested, although they moved under a canopy now. He could smell a fragrant cedar as they brushed past, though most of this area seemed to be scrub brush and broad-leafed trees he did not recognize. A poor country, poorly treated by its inhabitants, whose prospects were not likely to improve greatly in the short term. He had not spent time here in the initial occupation, but he anticipated that sometime in his career as a Marine, he was likely to be called back.

The warm rain made his uniform stick to his body like a leech. Although the sun had barely made its presence known behind the cloud layer, this was the tropics. It was warm now, it would be hot and unbearable later. Christiansen hoped to be aboard the chopper headed home by then.

His efforts to stay abreast of the observer brought him almost shoulder to shoulder with William Brown as they entered a clearing. Stark pivoted around, looked at them, and motioned them to stay afoot and fanned out. To their credit, his men did nothing until Christiansen seconded the signal.

As bare as the foliage was, it had mostly kept the rain from the dirt and bruised grass clearing. A small pool of water churned at the basin of a waterfall so insignificant as to barely rate the classification. There was only one major river on this side of the peninsula, its flow made up of a multitude of tiny tributaries, and this most definitely was not it. The bush and mango trees grew more thickly here, and there was a crude wooden lean-to set up among their trunks. Beyond, Christiansen saw a chalk drawing on the ground—a design that was geometric and yet not. A huge post was set deep into the middle of it, and at the foot of the post lay a dead goat, its blood already turning black, and flies beginning to gather despite the rain, their angry buzzing growing louder. Brown said under his breath, "Uh-oh."

Christiansen flicked a glance toward the corporal.

Before he could remark, the brush parted and a man came forward, six others following him. He was obviously a man of the island, sandal-footed, dressed in casual khakis, but there was nothing casual about his demeanor. Hatchet-faced, with sharp black eyes that glanced piercingly over all of them, and when they rested on him, Christiansen felt the hackles of his neck go up. He carried himself with authority that belied the wiry strength of his body. His smooth, dark skin looked ageless, but the shadow of years lay in his eyes.

"I am Delacroix." The six men behind him stood as if oblivious to the outside world, their muscular torsos showing through the rags of their simple cotton shirts. They carried machetes in their belted pants. Flies buzzed about them, too, and landed from time to time, crawling across their skin, even their faces, without prompting response. Their eyes were coffee-black, without expression. Dead eyes.

"You are the man," the Haitian said to Stark, his voice deeply accented with island French. He waved a hand over the slain animal. "I have asked for a blessing on our meeting."

Stark only replied, "We haven't much time." His own words were flatly American.

William Brown shuffled in the dirt uneasily and rolled an eye at Christiansen. The sergeant felt the palms of his hands itch and he shifted in his field gear so that his weapon would be easily accessible.

"Give me the powder," Stark added. "I have the money." He fumbled at his waist, undoing a money belt which had been tucked up under the kevlar vest, and which Christiansen hadn't even noticed. He tossed it at Delacroix's feet.

He made no move to pick it up, only hitched the rolled up sleeves of his shirt a little higher. His face tightened, accentuating the sharp cheekbones. "The deal was not for the powder. The powder is not mine, it belongs to—" and he spoke a name which Christiansen could not decipher. William gave a violent shudder.

"The deal's been changed. We want the powder. We'll do the converting ourselves . . . it will take too long to do it otherwise."

Delacroix looked at Christiansen and his patrol a second time, and again an icy feeling knifed across the back of the sergeant's neck. "The deal was that you would bring me men, and I would give you an army." He turned on his heel and touched the arm of one of the islanders flanking him. "Like mine."

The man made little response other than to take a step forward, aggression in every iota of his body language. The eeriness of his silent power pierced through Christiansen. What kind of soldier was this?

Stark said, "Have it your way." His hand moved, and he dropped a percussion grenade. Delacroix shouted something in French to the man at his side, and fell back.

Christiansen let out a yell, and his men scattered. The grenade erupted. The blast drove him to the ground, ears ringing, and as he rolled, he saw Stark ripping into the lean-to. He grabbed for his rifle. Stark emerged from the crude chapel, stuffing leather bags inside his vest and running face-to-face into one of Delacroix's men.

The islander made no sound, but grinned widely, flashing ivory death in his dark face, and reached for Stark's throat with a massive hand.

Stark dodged to one side, going to his knee, and came up, his hands filled with the assault weapon he'd had secreted at his back. "Delacroix! I have what I came for! Don't make me shoot your man! Take my men and do what you will with them—take the men and the money, and the deal is made! Marines, marine uniforms, and gear— think what you could do with them!"

"Fuck that," grated nasty, balding Burrows and emptied his rifle at the islanders' feet.

Puffs of dirt and grass blew up. Not a round hit them. They moved with blinding, agile speed that left Christiansen gaping. Stark lunged with a shout, out of range of the bullets and Delacroix's man, rolling when he hit. He came up spraying the clearing with the assault rifle and Lopez went down, blood fluming from his astonished mouth.

Delacroix stood impassively in the chaos, calling out in French and his men responded single-mindedly, going after Stark. Stark spit out a clip, and one of the men finally went down with a dull grunt, his shirt bloodied and in shreds. He fumbled at the jammed weapon, trying to insert another clip.

"Damnit," Christiansen said. "Save his hide!" he shouted hoarsely and got to his feet. His rifle bucked in his hands almost before he made the conscious decision to fire. He'd been brought in to escort Stark. The patrol's job was to bring him back alive, regardless, no questions asked.

Once back, Stark's ass would hang if Christiansen had anything to do with it.

"Bring him back alive," Christiansen ordered, and began to flank around Delacroix's men.

Delacroix met him, weaponless, with hands like steel cables. Christiansen grappled with him, looking deep into his obsidian eyes. Sweaty and rain-soaked, they clenched and Delacroix drew close. He snapped at Christiansen's neck, and bit, as they wrestled. Sharp teeth sank snakelike into tender flesh, and Christiansen felt the flick of the man's tongue over the wound.

He let out a howl of both pain and surprise and wrenched back. Delacroix grinned at him, blue-black lips stained with his blood. "I have your taste, now, man."

Burrows clubbed Delacroix across the back of the head, sending him reeling into the dust. Christiansen staggered back onto his heels. The first thing he noticed was that Delacroix's supermen had stopped in their tracks almost as one while Delacroix writhed on the ground, shaking off the pain from the blow.

Reynolds got to Stark first and literally cherry-picked him out of reach of a swinging machete blade.

Christiansen reacted. "Pull back! Pull back! Head for the chopper!"

One of the islanders reached for Burrows and picked him up, rifle spurting aimless fire from its barrel. He screamed, legs flailing, and his scream ended abruptly as the islander took him in both hands and snapped his back.

William Brown charged forward, yelling, his deep voice cracking with the strain. He pulled his fallen patrolman out of the hands of the Haitian, slugging him in the face with the butt of his rifle. As the islander went down, toppled like an oak, Brown took a flare from his pack and set it up. He stuffed it inside Burrows' shirt. The sodden uniform caught fire reluctantly, in spits and spurts.

Delacroix lurched to his feet and, with a curt word or two, sent his men packing after Short Reynolds. He traded a look with Christiansen, smiled slowly, licked his lips and then ran after his prey as well.

"Shit." Christiansen looked at what was left of his patrol.

"Corporal! Get out of here!"

Brown looked desperately at Christiansen. "Burn the bodies! We've got to burn the bodies!"

"Come on, get out of here!"

"Sarge, you don't understand!"

He snapped, "I don't have time to understand! Move out, Corporal, and that's an order!"

Face slick with sweat, Brown took a deep breath and then broke into a run, taking Aldemar with him. Christiansen hesitated long enough to pull Lopez into line with Burrows. He tore a plank off the rugged lean-to and threw it over their bodies, while the flare burned brightly. Maybe the old, dry wood would catch. Maybe it wouldn't.

He didn't like leaving Marines behind, but their open, lifeless eyes did not judge him.

Trampled ground left a wide trail. Christiansen could hear the shouts and grunts and muffled gunfire. They slowed. He sent William and Aldemar wide to the right, circling the clearing, and he went left.

The islanders had taken Short Reynolds down and had his gear. He saw Stark take one in the shoulder and drop. Brown and Aldemar charged in, firing. Of Delacroix, there was no sign. The three remaining islanders took their bullets and kept closing on Stark, as he got to his hands and feet, crawling. Blood and sweat streaked their shirts, glistening on their dark torsos.

"Son of a bitch!" Aldemar sang out. "Nothing stops them." He put in a new clip and kept firing, the spit of his bullets echoing Brown's and Christiansen's.

Christiansen's rifle jammed as the last standing man slowly fell to his knees and then, with the only sound they'd heard him make, grunted and sagged to the ground.

Stark stopped crawling. "Sergeant!"

Christiansen stowed his rifle slowly, closing the ground between them.

"Get me on my feet."

He blinked, looking down at the shoulder and neck wound the kevlar vest had not been able to stop.

"You were going to leave us here."

Stark blinked. "You have your orders."

"You're finished. Whoever you are, you're finished." Christiansen watched the crimson fountain from the other's neck.

"So are you." Stark coughed, and pink foam flew from his lips. He smiled weakly as he put a hand up, wiped his mouth, and saw his fingers.

"Who are you?"

"A representative of the United States government, just like you."

"No. Not like me. Never like me."

"They won't know that. They won't care. Bring the powder back—that's the only chance you've got. You—" He shuddered, making a horrible, guttural sound, a last attempt to breathe, and died.

Christiansen looked down at him. William let out a whistle. "I hear the chopper, boss."

"All right." He leaned over and took the leather bags from inside the other's vest. He stowed them in his gear, unsure of what he intended to do with them, certain he was not about to leave them behind.

Brown and Aldemar got Short Reynolds to his feet, bloodied and dazed. He towered above them. Christiansen taking point, they made their way toward the idling chopper.

Christiansen got his men in. Then he looked around. The tooth-marks on his neck throbbed slightly. He put a hand to them as the chopper pilot said, "Get your ass in, or I'm leaving it behind."

He got in, crouched in the open cargo doorway as the chopper revved up and began to lift off the ground. Greenery moved, and suddenly Delacroix was there, sighting down the barrel of a rifle.

William let out a cry and lunged forward, knocking Christiansen off his heels, as the weapon fired once, twice. The corporal let out a cry, falling face forward out of the open door. Christiansen grabbed at his pack as he went by.

The chopper bucked and rose steadily, twisting and lurching, gravity attempting to pull William out of his hands. Christiansen set his heels and Aldemar crawled on his belly over the floor to anchor him.

Brown twisted in the pack, looking upward, his face creased with pain as his shoulder turned fiery red. "Don't let me go," he pleaded. "Don't leave me here."

Christiansen had no time to answer him. He could feel the cords of his arms stand out as he hauled the corporal's slack weight back into the chopper.

The pilot looked back over his shoulder. "He in?" Without waiting for an answer, he pushed full throttle and took the chopper up and away.

Christiansen looked down as Delacroix lowered the rifle and faded to a smudge on the landscape and then was gone. Brown lay against his legs, and began to shake with the shock of his wound. Christiansen leaned over and took a look. It was clean, not too messy, and already the blood had slowed.

"You'll be fine, Corporal."

William looked at him. "We're dead men," he said. "We're all dead men. You don't know what you're dealing with."

Chapter 1

One April Morning, New Orleans

Heat hung like a curtain over the New Orleans day. Magnolia trees, heavy with fuzzy green buds ripening into creamy petals, framed the sidewalks while neighboring Spanish oaks cracked the cement with determined roots. It was early morning yet, and the only creature stirring in the decaying neighborhood plowed through like a mighty barge traversing the great Mississippi. She walked with no-nonsense, business to be done steps, creating an eddy, a stir of fresh air as she approached the churchyard, her dress swirling about in strong, primary colors that set off the rich brown sheen of her skin. She paused at the churchyard of her destination, but her skirt and hair remained alive, as if she herself were part and parcel of the morning breeze.

Shepherd's Mortuary, old clapboard sides whitewashed like the mausoleum ovens in the cemeteries, gleamed in the sun. Detailed wrought iron, reminiscent of the French Quarter, fenced it in. Gray-green moss trailed from massive oak branches against its chestnut-shingled roof, but the wrought iron cross stood out next to the steeple. The only thing more prominent on the roof was the lightnin' rod.

Mother drew her gaze down from the rooftops and sky.

She could feel the stares of others watching, though if she looked across the street to the cemetery, where the ovens and the worn stone crosses dotted narrow alleyways of grass, Mother knew she would not see who. They weren't looking after her, anyways, not now, not this time. She'd pay them no never mind.

Shepherd's had a front door, but she'd been entering through God's door, the churchyard, for the better part of her adult years. Mother Jubilation put her pink-palmed hand on the gate and stepped onto sacred land.

Pain hit her, sharp as a serpent's tooth, and the sheer force of it drove her to her knees. She bared her teeth and sucked her breath back, stunned by the attack. Anger boiled through her. Who dared to give her attitude on her ground! As Mother tilted her head and opened her eyes wide, she saw darkness boiling about the mortuary like thick molasses syrup. Her nostrils flared as she caught the scent of the evil loa casting the shadow, and Mother cried with a fierce joy as she saw into the sorcerer who'd brought it into this world to be-devil her and her children.

But they didn't know who they were tryin' to take a bite out of this time! Mother threw her hands into the air with a laughing shout. She grabbed at the shadows, ready to bring them down, where she would stomp them into holy ground. Mother Jubilation got to her feet, her whole body trembling with the joy of her own power. "You won't beat me that way, child!" she cried.

Darkness thinned. For a moment, she saw the face of the other mambo, sharp-featured, jawbones and cheekbones like pointed blades, deep angry eyes. She saw the rune-worked knife clenched in his hand, and the carcasses of the sacrificed animals lying in the dirt about his feet. She saw and felt the essence of him and would know him instantly if they ever crossed paths again. The sorcerer faded, but the bitter taste of his loa remained, and Mother knew that she had more work to do inside.

She dusted herself off, patted down the apron of many pockets she wore over her dress to make sure her fetishes, amulets, and charms were all still in place, and headed to the chapel door.

The chapel door stuck in its frame as though locked when she put a hand upon it. There was a child inside needed her, for that was why she'd come that morning. She'd been summoned during the night for a sorrowing. If the loa lay over that child, she'd not be turned away. She let out a rich chuckle, spoke a word, or perhaps it was just a coaxing noise, and the latch clicked in response.

The chapel smelled of lemon-polished wood and of bruised, heavy-scented flowers under the faint odor of disinfectant, the perfume of the dead. The teak hardwood floor creaked as she trod upon it, her ample weight making its boards sing. Its burnished surface reminded her of her grandfather's face, worn and proud, as she made her way along the outer edge of the sanctuary. The teak boards accompanied her journey, sounding, the rows of pews creaking as she passed.

The chapel had been empty, as she knew it would be, but its air was still and heavy with sorrowing. Shepherd's was modest, as one of the oldest Negro mortuaries in the state, carpet runners laid down over teak flooring throughout, an office and four visitation rooms clustered about a small parlor. The furniture was clean, French classical, dark burgundy upholstery dignified against the paneled walls. Below, the more clinical workings of the mortician could not be seen or heard. Slightly worn, slightly outdated, slightly second class, it had all the cachet of a Southern black establishment. Like a treacherous undercurrent in a sleepy river, she could feel the presence of her attacker running deep. She shrugged her purse close to her flank, the family gathered in the corridors beyond as the woman who'd summoned her turned and saw her.

"Mother Jubal!"

They embraced. The black woman who'd called her name was not older than Jubal, but she looked it, with knifelike wrinkles about her mouth and eyes, her hair ironed and coiffed fastidiously, her suit a somber charcoal off the rack from one of New Orleans' better shops. She had long since moved from this neighborhood, but she'd come back to bury her dead. Tears brimmed in her eyes. "I'm so glad you could come." Carla Brown Johnson flushed and touched her handkerchief to her mouth. Through it, muffled, she whispered, "He's in there," and pointed.

Beyond, in the viewing room, Mother could see the casket, the finest the Marine Corps could supply, flag draped over it, and a soldier in uniform standing in the corner guarding it. The room seemed to blend into his navy uniform, the brightness of his buttons and ribbons glittering like stars in a winter sky, echoed by the pallor of his face. The guard looked fine, she thought, real fine. A pity she'd never seen William in his dress blues.

No one sat in the viewing room, though there was a settee and a line of folding chairs which had seen better days. There were two wreaths on stands, and one large urn of flowers, and scattered bouquets. She knew the flowers may or may not have originally been intended for William and that, when the coffin left here for the cemetery, some of them might be passed on to the other viewing rooms, where those less fortunate were mourned. No one at Shepherd's ever had a threadbare funeral.

The soldier's gaze caught hers. He was likely to be the only white boy in Shepherd's that whole long day, and for a moment, she thought they communicated that to one another, and the corner of his solemn mouth pulled just a stitch in wry amusement. He looked fit in his dress uniform, though he had to have been tired, having accompanied the casket throughout its long flight home. She caught the aura on him of the loa, but she could not read it for ill or good, just as a hurricane has no morality. He was no sorcerer, but he might have been the "horse" which the loa rode across the mortal world. She might have trouble with him. It was certain they were going to have a world of trouble from her!

Mother took the grieving mother's elbow. "Now, Carla. It looks like you're doing just fine."

Carla's second husband George, the dead boy's stepfather, stood in the corner, his hands clasped, studying the floor. Gray peppered his thick black hair and mustache. He looked up, as if just sensing Mother's glance.

"Madame Jubal."

She nodded briskly as a child darted behind his trousered legs and refused to come out. This was Carla's last child, William's half-sister, young enough to be George Johnson's granddaughter. Normally Mother's heart would have gone out to the gawky girl hiding behind her father's legs, but this was not her business today. Their eyes met. The child retreated behind the safety of her father. She did not need Mother's comfort.

Besides, Jubilation had come to help the dead.

Lord knows, she had tried to help him hard enough when William was just a flint-eyed boy, too quick to take the easy way, too smart to not know the difference. Carla had done her best by William and marrying George had helped, but William was still a long-legged boy, a boy for whom the night had seemed to have a strong call. He had, however, found his own in the Marine Corps. Carla had shared his letters proudly with her on many an occasion, and he had done well, earning promotions all the way to corporal.

Promoted himself all the way into a casket, hanged by his own hand.

"I never thought it could come to this," Carla said. Her voice choked with emotion.

With just a touch of "no-nonsense" in her voice, Mother reminded her, "We all come to this."

"But so young—"

"And if it hadn't been for all your hard work and caring, you and George, it might have been a lot younger." Jubal folded her hands over Carla's chilled fingers. "You have pride in him. There's no shame in this."

Carla put the handkerchief back to her mouth. It was a beautiful lacy square of fine linen, with lavender embroidery about the edges, and her bright lipstick had already stained it more than once that morning. "It was *suicide*, Jubal. That's what they told me. Suicide! How could he? He was coming home, William knew he was coming home—why? Why?"

Jubal reached up and put her capable hand to the back of Carla's neck and stroked it, gently. Muscles knotted in distress under the damp, dewy skin and she smoothed them away. "Now, girl, in't that why you called me? I'll lay that soul to rest, right in the cradle of Jesus' hands."

"Amen," seconded George Johnson, watching them with eyes patient and saggy, wearing the look of a man who'd married a woman young enough to have been his daughter. He knew when to keep his silence and when not to.

Carla kept her handkerchief pressed to her lips and nodded.

"Then let me be about my business." Mother pinned a small fetish to Carla's jacket lapel. George had to lean down so she could reach his. He put the palm of his hand over it, covering it, as he backed away.

"Georgia Ann."

The girl peered out from behind her dad and received another fetish, which was pinned to her starched white dress collar. She picked at it.

"Now you just leave that there. I want you all to go into the chapel and pray for William's soul."

"Mother—" Carla began.

She shook a finger at her. "Do as I tell you now. And don't come out no matter what you might be hearin' or seein'."

"All right." Carla took a deep breath and then, surprisingly, hugged Jubal again. "God bless," she whispered in her ear before letting go. She stepped back hastily into the shelter of George's arm and looked away as if she could not bear to watch.

Mother crossed into the viewing room. What Carla only sensed with her maternal instinct now spoke to Mother Jubal with a hard, chiseled voice, mean and small. She followed its invisible lines about the compact, square room. They swirled about the Marine in dress uniform in his own island of unease. The coffin rested in the eye of the storm, and she could hear the dead, restless, fearful. "Hush, child," she whispered. "I hear you."

Her eyes met the Marine's again. He blinked in slow acknowledgment and said, "Ma'am."

"You look tired," she suggested. "Perhaps you should go and get a cup of coffee and sit."

"No, thank you, ma'am."

This was his duty, she knew. As William's closest friend in the unit, it was his assignment to bring the body home, see to it through the services, fold the flag, and return it to William's mother. He would do it with honor and, if there were tears in him over the death of his comrade, he would shed them some other time, some other place.

"Lieutenant—"

"Sergeant, ma'am. Sergeant Christiansen."

A good name that. Perhaps an omen.

"I have business here," she tried again.

"I have duty here, ma'am," he answered respectfully. "Corporal Brown was my patrol leader. It is both my honor and my obligation to stand for him now."

No one beyond the room could hear them. It was as if a curtain had dropped between the rest of Shepherd's and the viewing room, a veil between the living and the dead. She had work here and there was the thought at the back of her mind that this white boy just might be part of it. The force which she had discerned had subsided, ebbed, as though part of his life's tide. She could not determine whether Christiansen's soul was colored light or dark, and that bothered her.

"Very well," she answered. "Remember what you have called upon yourself." She shook an amulet out of her pocket store of charms, a black-thonged necklace with a twisted piece of silver upon it, blessed silver recovered from the salt water of the Gulf. Before the Marine could move, she had dropped the amulet around his neck and undone his top button, slipping the silver under his jacket. She did the button back up with a maternal efficiency. "You wear that," she commanded, her tone no less used to being obeyed than that of a drill instructor.

Mother decided, with a twist of her lips, that he would see what he would see. She dipped a hand into her large purse and brought out a triangle of chalk—it had once been a thick square, but usage had worn its fourth side down to next to nothing—and grasping it firmly, bent over and made a series of signs upon the wooden floor. Not a circle of protection, for she did not know whether she wished to contain or repel, but veves of basic protection.

"Ma'am . . ."

"Hush now and let me think. If you're going to be here, you've got to let Mother Jubilation do her work." She paused, and looked up, salt-tasting sweat beading up on her lip. He had not moved from his sentry position, but he looked down at her with fear in his eyes.

Mother smiled. "You tell your mama the next time you see her that she has a good boy. Stubborn, but good. You keep that amulet on, you just might live to see your mama again." She moved away from him, across the creaking floor. "Now don't you move."

"Yes, ma'am."

Then she stepped briskly to the casket and drew the flag from the end even as Christiansen protested.

"Ma'am! It's been sealed and it needs to stay that way." He started out across the wavery chalk edges, looked down and hesitated.

"Not to me, child." Even as she spoke, running her fingers over the lid, it clicked open to her touch, its weight keeping it lowered. She drew more symbols upon the seal and, for an icy second, gathered her power to open the coffin.

"Do you go to church, son?"

"Yes, ma'am. I'm a Methodist."

"Fine church. Fine, fine people." She looked across at him. "You'll be seein' things here you never saw in no Methodist church. Now you just bite your tongue and remember that I asked you to step out and have a cup of coffee. What you see, what you hear, what you feel, you asked to."

He swallowed. She could barely hear his "Yes, ma'am."

She placed her palm on the edge of the casket. It felt alive to her, like a living animal, lying and waiting for her touch. Then she pushed it up.

Chapter 2

"Think they'll have a jazz band, and black umbrellas, and high steppers?" Binoculars obscured the speaker's voice, but not his enthusiasm, as he watched the mortuary. "Captain."

"They don't do that anymore. Besides, the cemetery is right across the street."

"They could strut down to the corner and back. I always wanted to see that." The high-powered binoculars wavered slightly. "They don't do that anymore?"

"Not unless you're a celebrity. One of the old jazz greats." The voice, slightly honeyed with the accents of the region, sounded bored. "Disappointed, Lieutenant?"

"Well, yes."

"Don't be. This is Intelligence, son, not sociology." The man designated as captain moved forward in the van, looking intently at his monitors, the pocked canyons of his face shadowed like the surface of the moon. His name was Rembrandt, and he might have been called handsome, if not for those varied craters, but they did not mar him extensively. It was the coldness of his eyes and the downward slant of his eyebrows that made people turn away. He knew his acquaintances called him a real work of art, though not often to his face.

"Whoa. She just took a fall. No, no, I guess she's all right. She's inside the churchyard. Look at the build on her." The lieutenant paused. "My dad liked big women."

"Did he?" Rembrandt said, not really listening.

"Sure did. Always told me, more cushion for the pushin'. Told me I would never want a dry twig of a woman under me, just waiting to go snap."

Rembrandt redirected him with just a touch of irritation. "Anybody go in after that civilian?"

"No. Looks like William Brown isn't havin' much of a send-off."

"Services aren't for a couple of hours yet. Just keep your eyes glued to that building. I want to know everybody who comes in and out. And I don't want to lose our subject."

"Where's he gonna go? He doesn't even know we've picked up what's left of his patrol." The watcher let out a dry snicker. "One murder and two suicides don't leave him much of a command."

"Just keep your eyes peeled, Lieutenant. Christiansen isn't going anywhere, talking to anyone, doing anything, without us glued to his ass."

"What'd he do, anyway?"

Rembrandt did not answer. That was on a need to know basis, and he did not feel the lieutenant he'd picked up yesterday to aid him with surveillance in New Orleans as long as he had a use for him had any need. Christiansen would be picked up as soon the man in Washington who had assigned Rembrandt to follow him felt he had been followed sufficiently. Privately, Rembrandt felt that the sergeant would be picked up as soon as the funeral proceedings were over, bringing the Marine back for debriefing.

And, also privately, he wondered what it was that had happened on that covert mission in Haiti and how Christiansen had lost his patrol, but he knew better than to ask questions.

The small fiber-optic camera among the flowers in the viewing room gave a restricted angle. He could see Christiansen at stiff attention, the black and white tones of the camera making him appear even more fatigued than Rembrandt had seen him look while escorting the coffin off the flight. The black woman had stepped into range, but with her entrance, they lost audio. "Aw, damn."

Rembrandt adjusted knobs, brought up a static blizzard and quickly dampened it, but although he could see they spoke to one another, the mikes were not picking up anything clearly. He tapped his console, muttering, "We've lost the sound."

"Again?" While still peering through the binoculars, the lieutenant dropped a hand down, found a cold cup of coffee and an even colder beignet and stuffed the powdered sugar delicacy into his mouth, following it with a slurp from the coffee cup. "Ever been over to Cafe du Monde? They've got these homemade doughnuts. Taste just like what my mom used to make Saturday mornings for us kids back home. Make 'em like biscuit dough, then just fry 'em up and roll 'em in confectionery sugar." He popped another one in and added, mouth full, "Won't my mother just shit when I tell her she makes what the great chefs of New Orleans make?" He swallowed. "Check the cables?"

"Yes, I checked the frigging cables." Rembrandt shut his jaw tightly. He preferred to look back to his monitor, searching its eerie green screen as if he might find the secret of life in its depths. The video went berserk and then went south, in the direction of the audio. All he had now was the alarm. He slapped the heel of his hand on the console.

Something pinged.

He straightened. "That's the alarm. Someone's putting the lid up. *Damn.*"

"Thought it was sealed."

"It was. Now it's open." He'd anticipated that, actually, which was why the interior had been wired. He stood, gathering himself to go inside, when all hell broke loose.

The sergeant jumped when Jubal ripped out the wiring and tossed it to the floor at his feet. He bent over and gathered it up, stringing it through his fingers. "What the hell. . . . What's going on here?"

She did not have time for him. She ripped the white silk lining from the inside of the lid. The unpolished wood gleamed rusty brown with symbols already painted there. Mother flinched at the sight. She *tsk*ed loudly as she sketched over them, scarcely glancing at William's body as she did so. She remembered him well as a lanky teenager. She did not want to see him as a corpse.

But she saw. She could not help but do so. He'd hanged himself, and so the face was bloated slightly, puffy, lips blue-black. His thick, rich black hair had been so severely cut that he was nearly bald, giving his face the look of a chocolate moon. There was no peace or serenity in it. His uniform's neckline was tucked high into his chin, hiding the ligature marks, but not the face or the eyes—

"Good God."

She knew the white sergeant was looking at William, too, at the wide open, staring eyes, eyes which were usually always closed compassionately by the preparers of the body even if they had to be glued shut. His were not, were instead stretched wide open in horror. An opalescent film obscured the orbs. It was as though he'd been put in the coffin strangled, but still alive.

"This boy did not hang himself. He was *murdered*."

"No. No, he couldn't have. We made it back. We stood up for each other. No. He was scared. I tried to talk to him. Nothing I could do helped. He knew it was going to happen. He tried to tell me. Christ, he picked the casket out himself. Drew those signs all over the inside of the lid." He paused. "I don't know who in hell wired it."

"Oh, he may have hanged himself, all right. But something else drove him to do it. That something I got to beat out of him now or he'll never have peace." She narrowed her eyes at Christiansen. "Hush, child. You want to help your friend, you stay out of my way."

An aura rose from the casket, ominously, awakening fully that which she had only barely sensed earlier. The palms of her hands tingled. She worked furiously, but not quickly enough, for the cross-barred table which held the coffin began to shake and rattle. It started with a low, quivering moan as the braces trembled. Its vibrations translated upward until the casket itself, heavy and solid as it was, began to dance as if caught in an earthquake.

"Hold it down!" she ordered the Marine.

There was an astonished pause, as if disbelieving of her command, but Jubal could not pay him heed, for she needed to sketch over the other symbols and the wood itself bucked away from her touch.

She could feel the strength of the curse, the stranglehold it had on William, the blood wishes of it sunk deep into the earth. Under her feet, the floor began to shake and sway. The joints of the room creaked as the Marine threw himself onto the coffin and embraced it, attempting to keep it from bouncing to the ground. It rattled against his hold and he grunted with effort.

She could hear Carla's stifled shriek and George's mumbled call upon the Lord as all of Shepherd's began to sway and rattle. The vibrations sounded like a freight train bearing down on the mortuary. The building would come down on their heads and worse, what William had brought back with him would be irrevocably loosed. Whatever had murdered him lay inside him, trapped and entwined with William's tortured soul.

Something crashed against the building from outside. The exterior walls *Boom*ed under the blow. Glass broke, tinkling to a floor. Shepherd's trembled and groaned as if in pain.

"Ma'am—"

"Not now, child!" Jubal flinched despite her concentration as she laid the casket open wider, her drawing moving on its own, chalk dusting her palm as white, as pale as the Marine sergeant's face.

"Damballah! Aido Wedo! Hear me!" The names of the husband and wife of creation filled her mouth, warm and rich. "Listen to my needs!" Under her breath, she added the sacred name of Bon Dieu, the Lord of all Good and all Creation, to aid her.

In a piercing echo through the chapel doors, Carla shrieked, "Dear Jesus, hear us now!"

Leaning over the icy corpse which had once been William and was now a host, she could feel the loa, the evil spirit, rising. It was angry, it had been trapped in the coffin despite its power and it was hungry. So powerful, it had thrown its aura over Shepherd's even when trapped, and struck at her.

She could feel the starvation gnawing at it, rumbling in her own ample stomach, pinching at guts and bowels, aching. It would devour her if it could once she cast it out, that loa would if it could.

Its undervoice hissed like a snake. Mother threw a glance at the Marine, who desperately wrestled the coffin to still its shudders. If he heard it, he gave no sign—but then the whole building spoke and shuddered, complaining and threatening so loudly she could not even hear her own words and her heart beat as loud as a drum.

Concentration ran down her face in hot streams of sweat. The armpits of her dress were heavy with wetness. It rose in vengeful heat as though straight from the pits of hell. Though she fought to cast it out of William, she feared where it would go. Would the amulet be the white boy's proof against it?

The casket gave a terrible heave.

"Shi-it!" The Marine wrestled to keep it from toppling over on them. The movement sent the body inside nearly upright, and then it settled back onto its silken pillow. Christiansen nearly dropped the wooden box with a sound that was half-gasp, half-scream.

"Bon Dieu be with me!" Mother cried aloud for the Good Lord to shield her. Jubal felt the loa go with a snap that was as loud as the cry of the wooden beams in the roof over them.

The coffin ceased its motion though the rest of the building still rattled. She drew her last symbol, fingers nearly numbed.

Shepherd's clattered down upon its foundation where it settled to a kind of percolating.

"Sweet Jesus. What was that?" The Marine stood, panting, eyes locked upon the body of his friend, the body which the loa had nearly brought to its feet. He had wrestled the casket to a halt, but his posture suggested that if he eased his hold, it would begin to jump again.

"Vodun." Mother put her hand to her forehead, mopping up the sweat.

"What?"

"Hush, child," she interrupted, casting her senses about them. The loa was not returning to its master or to the city of loas beyond. She could feel it looming over them, searching. Bon Dieu had laid His Hands over hers, now He was gone, and she was alone, spent. The loa seethed. Its hunger tore at her. She sketched upon thin air, her invisible signs repelling it slightly. She was not finished with it yet.

Then it centered upon Christiansen. The loa circled the Marine, as uncertain about his power as she'd been. A hurricane of force, yet he was the eye of it, the neutral calm. The amulet kept the loa at bay, kept it from possessing the white boy who had no idea of what he was, what his potential could be.

She threw her chalk back into her purse and fished around madly, hurriedly, until she found the small vial of sweet water, holy water, purified not by the Catholics but by her own rituals. She uncorked it with a flick of her thumb.

She sprinkled a little of it over William's body. The staring eyes shut.

"That's enough. Oh, God." The Marine dropped the casket and jumped back. She saw his eyes widen, his jaw clench in disbelief. He did not seem to notice the ever-widening pool of calm which spread away from them. He moved inside his uniform as though it guarded against the harm of a world he no longer found sane. Yet he had become a magnet for the curse. She felt it, knew it was so.

She felt the loa drawn toward him. Jubal tossed holy water over him, sprinkling him from head to toe. Its temporary protection strengthened that of the amulet. Startled, faint drops of water trickling down his face like teardrops, he stared at her. Like a shadow which he had thrown, the loa withdrew behind him. She watched it retreat.

"It'll be all right, child," Mother told him.

With a last groan, Shepherd's hunkered onto its foundation with an almost animal awareness. Mother Jubal shifted away wearily. She tangled a foot in the wiring she'd ripped out of the casket. Whatever had happened here, this was a part of it and yet was not. Vodun had no hand in this. She stooped and held it out to the sergeant.

Dazed, he took it from her. "The casket was wired."

"Whatever happened," she told him, "whatever it was that killed William was of two worlds. I cannot help you with this one," and she tugged at a cable. "This is your problem."

He looked stricken as their gazes met. "I don't—I don't have anything to do with this."

"So you say. Someone else thinks differently." So pale his face, this white boy.

The front doors burst open with a clatter of footsteps echoing throughout the mortuary. Voices shouted, "United States Government! Halt!"

He twisted his head to look back at the coffin, where William's face had now settled into a slumbering expression, eyes shut. The U.S. flag hung canted to the floor. She knew then he was going to run. She could not help this wild one now, if he did, but he would come back.

"I told him, I swore to him, I'd take care of him if anything happened. He was my patrol leader. My *friend*. He took a bullet for me." He looked at her.

"Mayhap. The loa took him. It could have made him take his own life. It don't matter now. William is at peace. What about you?"

"What's happening here?"

"Who thought Marines could fight this voodoo? Who crossed you against this? Where were you? I'll tell you where you were . . . in the heart of the vodun . . . in Haiti."

"You don't know that."

"I know it. And you know it. And whoever wired the coffin knew it, too." Mother pointed at the casket. "Nobody can you trust. No place are you safe. You were sent to die, but you lived. You have one choice left to you." She whispered. "Run."

He blinked. "I'm a Marine."

"They be hunting you. Do you think they don't know you're a Marine?"

Christiansen shook himself. It was like coming out of a bad dream. The loa would be hunting him again. She pressed. "You leave, you straighten yourself out, then you come back to me, you hear? You come back to Mother Jubal."

"Who the hell are you?"

She rapped a knuckle on his brow, where the holy water still glittered like diamonds, not hard, not gentle. "Mind your tongue. Now you listen. This was evil work. I know. I don't know why William died, and I don't know why the fear of it fills you. But you've got to run, boy, because those men out there don't mean you good. I know this in my bones . . . under my skin. I think you know it, too."

"We followed orders . . ."

He was interrupted by shouting from without. "All persons inside the building. The grounds have been secured. Stay calm. Put your hands up as we enter!"

Christiansen turned slightly to the voice booming orders. She could see the tumult within him.

"I can't run—"

"You can't stay."

"They've got the place surrounded—"

"Go through the door of God, child, and no one will be stoppin' you." Mother pointed back through the chapel.

He let out a tortured grunt as if deciding his destiny, then turned and bolted into the chapel, scattering Carla and George and Georgia Ann from the doorway. Beecher, the mortician, had been frightened up his basement stairs and tottered around like a tall, dark grasshopper in his funerary suit.

They turned to her in bewilderment. Mother nodded, counseling, "Let him go."

Government agents and their guns filled the hallway. Carla and George met them in the corridor, hands outstretched and faces grim, innocently blocking their entrance into the mortuary. Their daughter began to cry softly in fear.

Mother Jubal felt the Marine's spirit leap as he reached the sunshine. But the triumph would be fleeting, she knew. He could run, but he couldn't hide forever. She put a hand to her bosom, where the crystal and the cross it was bound to hung on a chain, and clasped her fingers around it.

She could feel the loa, a nasty, oppressive cloud hanging over her, but it would not leave her world. Behind it, she saw the lean, hatchet-faced man, his skin the color of roasted coffee beans, a man whose soul was as black as that of the loa spirit. His vision snapped into hers, and she knew he saw her as well, this counterpart. His lips thinned, purple streaks of dislike. Mother braced herself. The crystal grew hot between her fingers.

She stared into her inner self. She wanted to send the loa flinging back to him, but she no longer had the strength. She could feel her dry lips moving. "Bon Dieu, help yet once again. Help me!"

The breath which formed her words was nearly stillborn, her tone so quiet none but Mother could have heard it, but she knew the greatest God did. Before she could blink, a veil dropped between them, and the sharp visage of the other was gone.

Gone but not forgotten.

She opened her eyes.

A white man stared at her, a man with a once handsome yet pitted face, a man in a uniform with an uncomfortable starched collar, with anger reddening his expression. For a second she was confused, for though he was white, his eyes held the same sharp glare as the black sorcerer's. They might be two sides of the same coin. Mother took a deep breath.

"And who the hell are you, ma'am?" he said wearily, with the air of one used to being obeyed.

Mother drew herself up. "You may call me Madame Jubal, my son," she answered, though he was nearer her age than not.

He looked down at the coils of ripped-out wire on the floor, and the casket which still rested sideways on its stand. The officer held a cell phone in his hand rather than a gun, like the others, and his jaw slid sideways as if he chewed on a fact he did not like. "There was a soldier on guard here. Where is he now?"

"He's gone, Colonel."

"Captain," he corrected absently. "Gone? What do you mean, gone?"

"I mean that he isn't here." His tones were clipped now, military style, but she could hear the echo of the South in them. She smiled knowingly at him.

His knuckles paled even more as he gripped the cell phone and pulled it close to report. "Sergeant Christiansen has gone AWOL, sir. Yes, sir, I intend to do just that. We'll find him."

The captain pointed through the walls to the beyond which he could not see, but evidently knew quite well. "I want a spiral search, bordered by the streets, now, report back in sixty minutes' time," and he rattled off the local avenues.

Captain Rembrandt looked back at Mother. "Am I going to have any trouble with you, ma'am?"

She smiled wider. "Why, no, Captain. Not just yet."

He spun on his heel and stalked through the mortuary, an aide trotting nervously just behind him. She could feel the loa tasting his aura. It lowered over him, a vast dark stingray of evil, drawn to the captain and yet held at bay by the man's unconscious spirit. Mother could feel its aching, smell its fatigue from its battle with her. It shadowed the captain.

Mother loosed the crystal from her grasp. She coiled her fingers around the vial of blessed water and when the captain brushed by her again, the heels of his shoes staccato on the aged creaking floors of Shepherd's Mortuary, she threw her hand out, droplets cascading over the man.

He halted and pivoted around, complexion reddening with anger, running the palm of his hand over his face. "What the hell was that?"

"A blessing, Captain," Mother said. "Holy water. You should thank me."

He gazed into her face a moment, a hard stare which did not make her blink though it drilled into the very back of her skull. Then he relented and gave her a nod. "Well, then, ma'am, I thank you. Come on, let's get everybody out of here." He brushed a rivulet of water from his chin as he turned away and snapped at the aide to keep up.

Mother relaxed a little as the mortuary cleared of the soldiers who'd invaded it.

What had been unleashed upon the world? What had all of them been up to? "Ah, child," she sighed to the now silent William. "You always was a handful."

Rembrandt opened his briefcase. the van seemed too small after what he'd just witnessed and the vehicle occasionally shimmied as though vibrations still ran through it.

He dialed the phone and waited. As a pleasant voice came on the line, he punched in a series of numbers which abruptly rendered the line still. Then, almost reluctantly, the phone rang. Another computerized voice, this time male and brisk, answered. He punched in a second series of numbers and waited.

He was answered immediately.

"Speak."

Rembrandt knew the gravelly voice. He could picture Bayliss sitting behind his huge mahogany desk, knew his fine Cuban cigar, hand rolled upon the thighs of young Cuban girls, would be clenched in his flashing white teeth. "The bird has flown."

"Well, hell, now why aren't I surprised at that?" A dull thunder accompanied Bayliss' response, the high-backed upholstered chair being rolled closer to the desk, its leather complexion so fine-grained that women would weep to have pores so clean and tiny. "He took out Stark. He kept his patrol out of Delacroix's hands. You had him, Rembrandt. You let him go."

"We had no choice, sir. It's Marine Corps tradition. He had to bring the body back or it would have raised flags all over the place. It was dicey enough covering for the covert action. But he's not talking. Not yet, anyway." Rembrandt felt his teeth click into place when he stopped talking. The line was private and secure, but he did not like his name being used on it, all the same. Nor did he like having been caught with his quarry fled.

"And I suppose deserting is just another fine tradition." Bayliss cleared his throat. "I want him found before that crazy, son-of-a-bitch witch doctor does. You hear that?"

"I hear you, sir." Rembrandt flicked a glance out the paneled side, making sure none of the detail approached. "Budget?"

Bayliss rattled off a code, adding, "Get what you need. It won't be traced."

"How long do you want me out?"

"Until one or the other of you finds him. I want our goods, Captain . . . is that clear?"

"Never clearer." Rembrandt had nearly replaced the receiver when Bayliss' voice stopped him. He snatched it back to his ear. "I'm sorry, sir. Would you repeat that?"

"I said, you checked the cadaver, didn't you, Captain? I remember when the body bags coming back from Nam were full of little goodies."

Rembrandt stretched his neck a little at the memory of the black woman's angry stare as they'd gone over the corpse again. "Yes, sir, we checked it. It was clean."

"Then you're to stay out until you find Christiansen and he gives you my shipment. That understood?"

"Understood." This time, Rembrandt did not replace the receiver until he heard the other end go dead. It only stayed silent for a few seconds, then it abruptly clicked onto the previous line, with the dulcet-toned female voice instructing him, "If you wish to return to the menu, please stay on the line. If you wish to speak to customer service, push 2. If you wish—"

Rembrandt severed the link.

He closed up the briefcase and spun the lock out of habit with the ball of his thumb, thinking. Half the detail who'd been in unmarked cars stood outside, talking quietly among themselves, enjoying the game they played in civilian garb, waiting for him to emerge and tell them what to do next.

He would be better at this alone. He fiddled with the corner of his briefcase another moment, then set it down in the middle of the van. He let out a shrill whistle. The lieutenant came running, with the other half of his detail.

"We're pulling back. Transport is waiting for us at the base. We'll debrief in the air."

No one spoke if Rembrandt did not, and he did not feel like initiating conversation en route to the base. His mind worked with the various scenarios of tracking down the deserter. Christiansen might run, but he wouldn't run far. The sergeant had his background in the

Pacific Northwest, states that had been booming for the last half decade, a population easy to hide in. Rembrandt would start there. He carried his briefcase with him as they turned in the rental cars. The van was driving onto the tarmac and left, keys in the ignition, the equipment downloaded and clean, all evidence of their surveillance packed into a second briefcase toted by the lieutenant.

A helicopter waited for them, its blades already twirling in warm-up, the rotor sound cutting the silence with a lazy cadence. Rembrandt stood back and watched the detail board. He had the same pilot and navigator he'd used to take the patrol into Haiti, and the sense of it struck him, like killing two birds with one stone. At the last moment, he leaned in and handed his briefcase to the lieutenant.

"You go with them to Lackland, Lieutenant. I want to check something we may have overlooked. Go ahead and start debriefing."

"Yes, sir."

Rembrandt slammed the door shut. He turned and strode briskly away, got in the van, and drove off base. He heard the copter as it took to the airways overhead, and was still driving when the explosion hit, a shattering boom that rivaled any he'd ever heard. He did not look back to see how total the destruction had been for he had a fairly good idea as the shock wave rocked the van and the sky began to rain debris.

Chapter 3

October, Southern California

"What are you staring at?"

"Nothing."

One teenager had dirty blond hair, the other had tousled light-brown waves, his face nearly obscured behind glasses and accented with a dusting of freckles. They shared the gangliness of their fourteen years, but the brown-haired boy also had an air of wisdom, a maturity in the framing of his shoulders which his friend lacked. The earpieces of his glasses were bowed far apart as if he wore frames meant for a much smaller head. Behind them, the noise of an arcade tinkled, pinged, and boomed as they stood framed in its back doorway. Laser fire exploded with blue-white strobe light frequency.

The first one gargled a noise of discovery deep in his throat. "Oh, I see. You're watching *her*. She catches you, she's going to call the geekazoid patrol." He snatched at the glasses. "Let me handle this for you."

The brown-haired boy slapped his hand away. "Leave me alone." He dodged a second time and then turned, frowning for a second, before reaffixing his gaze.

"Uh-oh. It sounds serious for the X-man. Brandon, she doesn't even know you breathe."

Without moving his stare, the watcher said, " 'Man's reach must exceed his grasp, else what's a heaven for?' " He paused. "Or something like that. Do you think she likes poetry, Curtis?"

"Poetry? Oh, God, you've got it bad." Curtis whipped back his dirty blond hair and waved fingers at him. "Whoop, whoop, whoop, geek patrol, geek patrol."

Brand resumed determinedly ignoring him, watching the young woman emptying trash into the bins behind her store. She was, he reflected, the only spot of beauty in this back alleyway, its corridor of Dumpsters. and stinking trash cans an ugly underbelly of the mall. Her blue-black hair and porcelain skin looked like sculpture against a graffitied and eroded stucco background. Despite the distance and angle of the arcade from the trendy clothing store and espresso bar, he could see the silkiness of her dark hair, the pale glow of her complexion, her slender, long legs set off by her short skirt.

But Curtis was right. She didn't know he existed and why should she? He was Brand X, the stuff nobody wanted. He'd tagged himself proudly, unhappy with the mundane, everydayness of his name, happier to stand alone, aloof. Only, lately, it had begun to matter to him.

Curtis gave up irritating him and settled a shoulder into the doorjamb. "She's never gonna look at you, man."

"She doesn't have to," Brand answered softly.

"She's not so pretty."

"Is too."

"Julia Roberts is prettier."

"Julia Roberts is bowlegged."

"Is not."

Brand flicked a look of disdain at his friend. "She is so bowlegged they had to use a body double on that scene you like so much from *Pretty Woman* where she puts on those boots."

"No way."

"Yes, way. From her ankles to her thighs."

Curtis grinned. "Then I'll take the body double."

"Figured you would." Brand turned his attention back to the leggy young woman. "She's hot. She's like Uma Thurman in *Pulp Fiction*."

"Think so?"

"I know so." Brand sighed. He pushed his glasses back onto the bridge of his nose. "But you're right. She'll never look twice at me."

Someone called from inside the arcade and he swung around, dragging his friend with him. It was a relief not to have to look at her in a way, trying to be himself and yet have the shadow of another in his thoughts, coloring everything he saw. Watching her just now, he was two people, his familiar disgusting nerdy self . . . and the other. He feared the other. He closed his eyes, wrestling images, until he was in control again.

"We're up." He kicked the door shut behind them, plunging them into a netherworld of pinball and computer simulated game machinery.

"So many machines, so few quarters," Curtis lamented.

Brand slit his eyes against the inky lighting of the room. Only the neon blue and white glare of the machine's screens, emblazoned with color graphics, and pinball orange could be seen. A host of players ranged about the room, their faces illuminated by the machines they played, their otherwise ghostly forms inhaled by the darkness. Graphics burst like bombs against their expressions which never changed, intent upon moving the joysticks or palming the ball controls which ran the machines. Brand moved through the obelisks of machines, the one marked NOVA his destiny, a black and white No Fear sticker on its outside panel.

A rangy seventeen-year-old shoved away from the control panel with a reluctant grunt. "I coulda used more time."

Brand squared himself away in front of the game. "Wouldn't do you any good," he answered. He dropped his quarters in as he ran his left palm over the trackball to bring up the latest list of scores.

On the top twenty, his name stood out no less than sixteen times. A tiny crease of pleasure quirked his lips. Then he frowned sharply. His name no longer rode the number one position. "What the—"

"One of the skaters," Curtis said, reading over his shoulder. "They were in here all day yesterday."

Brand's mouth thinned. He didn't like skateboard jocks, cement surfers, with their saggy clothes and breezed hair. "One game," he countered. "Then I'm back on top."

"You'll never do it, man. We'll be here all night."

"One game."

"I've got English homework."

Brand kicked a backpack stowed at the foot of the game machine. "Then take your shit and go."

Curtis wavered. He shifted from one foot to the other. Brandon could feel his Milk-Dud-smelling breath down the back of his neck. "One game?"

"Yeah. Watch me."

So Curtis did.

They squinted into the bright sunlight, backpacks on their shoulders like cowboys of old carried their tack, and swaggered into the late afternoon. Curtis crowed, "One game, man! High five!"

Brand swung his hand up obligingly and let his friend congratulate him again.

"You're *legend,* man. Legend."

"Nothing to it." He looked across the mall lot. It was late. He had to get home before his working parents did, bury his head in a book, pretend he'd forgotten about unloading the dishwasher, play the game with the dweeb. He took a steadying breath. Then, "Oh, man."

"What?"

He pointed across the asphalt. "She's out there again, breaking boxes down. They've got her doing stock." Curtis followed his line of sight and saw the girl again, wrestling with cartons, at the cardboard recycling bin which the mall required. "So?"

"So . . . so . . . she's gonna get all dirty doing that."

"Then go help."

Brand blinked an eye at his friend. "Think so?"

Curtis grinned. "Dare ya, X."

"Take my backpack."

Curtis did so.

They paused.

"What's keeping you?"

"Nothing," answered Brand. He wiped his hands on the thighs of his jeans.

"Then go on. She's almost done."

He licked his lips. "Okay, all right, all right." He put one foot in front of the other. Before he had knowledge of it, they'd carried him across the parking lot alley. When he'd halted, he stood in the bunkered area and could smell the rankness of the trash bins, where frozen yogurt had melted and gone bad, pizza crusts and paper plates rose in mountains, and animals skittered under the iron bottoms.

She looked up. His throat had gone dry and felt tougher than the cardboard she was attempting to flatten. He couldn't hear anything but the thunder of his own pulse. Her dark hair swung forward onto a cheekbone. She tucked it back behind the shell of her ear with a slender finger. He thought she might have spoken to him, but he wasn't sure he could hear. He thought of asking if she remembered him from buying coffee, then thought better of it. What if she didn't?

"I—ah—saw you. Need some help with that?" His voice went thready in the middle of his words, but it came back strong, and he stood, face warming, hoping to God that his glasses wouldn't steam. Or slide down his nose. He looked at her hands and arms. She'd rolled up the silky sleeves of her blouse and he saw the tattoos, living art, move upon her skin. They were crude and yet evocative, primitive black drawings upon the pale canvas of her flesh.

He looked away quickly, after that first stab of awareness that he'd seen a part of her he'd never seen before.

She did not seem to notice his stare. She pushed her hair from her forehead and almost smiled. "Actually, I'm about done, thanks. And I think your friend's waiting for you." She glanced over his head and behind him.

His hearing had come back with a rush. Now he could hear Curtis calling, no, *bellowing*, for him. What the hell? Brand's ears went hotter. "Just thought I'd . . . you know . . . ask . . ." and turned suddenly before she could laugh in his face.

He saw the wave of flesh inundate and part around Curtis, snagging at the backpacks as they came, skateboard wheels humming.

Behind him, the young woman muttered, "Oh, shit."

It didn't sound dirty coming from her lips. He blinked, trying to think of what he should do, watching Curtis bend down, frantically putting textbooks, notebooks and papers back into the various bags. The skaters, five of them in a wedge, began to circle Brandon.

"Get out of here," she demanded.

The lead skater, his hair so far down into his face he looked like a greasy shaggy dog, laughed. "She your bodyguard?" he asked Brand. "Or who's watching who?" He howled at his own wit.

"Leave her alone." He stiffened his spine. He could kick a board out from under them easily enough, but he wasn't sure getting them on his footing would be an advantage. He didn't want a fight, he wanted to avoid one. He wanted them away from her.

The leader waved his buds over to the recycling bins, where they began to haul the bails out. Brand turned around slowly to watch, while the young woman got angry.

"Put that stuff back, you little shits."

None of the boys paid any attention to her. She strode forward, grabbed back a bundle and returned it where it belonged.

"You're going to cost me my job. Leave this stuff alone before I call Security."

"What's wrong with four-eyes here? He not good enough for you?"

"She's gonna have to call Se-cur-ity!"

They began to hoot and play-cry and whistle as they circled, passing bundles back and forth like Houston Rockets players in a basketball court's key. A wiry, dirty-faced skater made kissy noises. "Come get it."

She lunged and caught the cardboard away from him as he slalomed past, daring her. Her movements knocked him off-balance and he and the skateboard went sliding sideways before he hit the ground in a nasty skid. He came up with blood and grime pasted across his legs.

"You're going to get it now, bitch."

"Don't you call her that!" Brandon launched at the youth. He didn't feel the first few blows, striking or struck, but he felt it when one of the others hit him in the back with a skateboard, wheels spinning. The violent bone-crack dropped him to his knees where he fought to breathe. He staggered back to his feet.

Her voice came to him shrilly, "You keep your hands off him! Hang on, I'm getting Security!"

And then he was alone, fists hot and scraped, glasses sliding down his nose, breathing hard and furiously, dancing between jostling bodies. Where the hell was Curtis, he wondered, just before sweaty bodies sandwiched him.

He could feel himself being hefted, his glasses gone, the whole scene blurry, thrown through the air and when he landed, the trash bin lid came thudding down after him, sealing him in darkness.

Then the stink began.

Perfect, Brand thought.

They hammered on the sides of the bin like a gong until his ears rang and his head throbbed.

"Come on out, sheep dip! We'll be waiting for you."

He folded his arms and sat. He could hear the spin of their wheels on the asphalt and their war whoops of victory as they left. The reek and dampness around him began to sink into his clothes. He could feel the blood under his nose congeal as his ragged breathing calmed. What had he just proved, anyway? That he wasn't man enough to protect himself or her?

All he wanted to do was get out of there before she could face him. He put his palms up to the lid, felt the corroded and gritty surface and braced himself.

A door banged.

"Hello? Anybody out here?"

Brandon froze.

"Sweet God. What a mess."

"I'll get somebody to clean it up later." A man's voice, a young man. "You should get your store to cage the recycling bins. Paper's worth a lot now. The mall gets ripped off all the time. You could get hurt by jerks like that."

"It's not me I'm worried about. There was someone else here—"

Her voice, so near the metal, thrummed slightly with the vibration of her tone. Brand held his breath.

"Hello?"

As the sour and rotting odors rose around him, he knew he couldn't face her, not like that. So he made no answer. He folded his arms and sat.

"Look, I'd like to stand out here with you all afternoon, but I can't." Stud muffin sounded slightly impatient.

"Oh. Right. Well . . ."

"He probably split with the rest of them. What say you buy me a cappuccino and we call it even?"

Her voice chilled slightly. "I thought you worked for the mall."

He could hear their steps drawing away. The mall cop was a jerk, too, of a different kind, but that didn't seem to be stopping her from leaving with him. "Actually, that's what I like about this job. There're all kinds of perks."

A fire door banged shut. A moment of stillness before the sudden chirping of birds told him he was alone again. He'd been holding his breath, but now his chest began to tighten and his stomach to clench. He didn't want to be in here, shut in. The confinement closed about him, but he told himself he would be all right. He could get out. He wasn't locked in. Everything would be okay and, short-sighted or not, he fixed his gaze on single beams of light which found their way in under the lid. He waited until he was certain he was alone.

Then he cautiously stood among the plastic bags and the offal and tried to put the lid back up.

It stayed fast.

Brand swallowed hard. *He would not panic.* Could not, even though *she* had done this to him in the psych ward, locked him in metal drum darkness, floating in nothing but his own putrid thoughts. . . . He scratched at the metal, clawing desperately. Flakes of rusting paint rained down on his face. He blinked frantically to keep his eyes clear. His throat tried to close as panic surged through him.

"Oh, God, oh, God, oh, God, let me out, let me out." He tried to scramble up the mountain of garbage, thinking if he could stand taller, he could force the lid open and, bent under it, tried again. It did not budge. He pushed until he could not breathe and halted, crouching. He tried again.

The sweltering heat and rankness of the enclosure rose to greet him.

He was *locked* in. They'd wedged it shut. He'd be in here till some-one else came out to the bins or the collector trucks came.

Sweat poured down his face. He'd be dead by then, alone with his thoughts and fears. He grasped for calmness as it was being shat-tered and blown away, disintegrating like a target in the video arcade, dissolving into brilliant motes that slipped through his fingers.

Yellow Dog. He would concentrate on Yellow Dog, and that would make it all right. He squinted upward, at the lid, at the yellowish light beaming in, making an image. . . .

He didn't know when he first began seeing the Yellow Dog, but it was unmistakable to him that the creature came to guide him. To aid and protect him. It was an unreliable Lassie, he couldn't always sum-mon it, but when it came, Yellow Dog could always bring him back to the edge of sanity.

The psych ward, he'd been told, would help him. It had at first, just being away from home and the screaming fights of his mother and husband number two had helped. And he might have been all right if Dr. Susan Craig hadn't taken a keen interest in him. It did not help now that she was dead and gone, her deeds exposed. She lay in his mind and it was at moments like these, in the dark and alone, when all that she had done gathered itself like a living, breathing beast, and wrestled him for his soul. Yellow Dog sometimes helped him blunt it. Sometimes Brand fought it all alone.

He'd gotten used to it. There was no one he could tell today about the battle for his brain. He knew the buzzwords to give his current therapist, knew how to tell him just enough to be left alone. He trusted no one, least of all his mother and his psychologist. What would they do if they knew there were two of them inside his skull? The scars Susan Craig left behind ensured that he would never have peace.

He'd lived in a metal tank for her, bathed by soothing water, until his mind was as clean and unfolded as a newborn babe's. Then she'd taken him out and put straps and probes about his body, fastening a helmet upon his head, a helmet which beamed its own private theater with its own very private thoughts into him. Yellow Dog, when it came, guided him home. When it did not, Brand would dare the maze himself, always searching for the light, coming out of the dark. . . .

Golden beams dazzled him now. Yellow Dog hunched over him, showing him the way to freedom, if he could just jar the lid. He looked down at Brand, then began to waver and fade.

Brandon swallowed hard. If he stayed inside the bin, Susan Craig would have him for sure. He took a deep breath and began to pound already bruised fists upon the trash bin. Drummed along the lid, the sides, anywhere he could strike, screaming until he grew hoarse.

Suddenly, the lid split open with a creaking groan. Yellow Dog shone fiercely into his eyes like the sun, then began to waver again, change, mutate into a human face, staring down at him with the light at his back. Brandon recoiled, embarrassed and relieved. He blinked and narrowed his eyes as his rescuer peered in.

He knew the face, begrimed and weathered, hair shagged down to his shoulders, hands seamed with everyday dirt as the man leaned in to look at him. Something metal swung forward on his chest and chimed gently as it hit the rim of the bin, metal to metal.

"Shut up," the man said mildly. "I'll get you out of here."

* * *

Brand stood passively as the hose played over him, cold water sludging off the worst of the garbage and smell. It ran down his clothes and pooled at his feet.

"Rough crowd," commented the homeless man who aimed the water at him.

Brandon looked up at him, then away. He could only see the man's face clearly when they moved closer together, but neither of them was particularly interested in that at this point. Curtis had taken the backpacks and run, a fact which had eventually drawn his rescuer's curiosity, and the man had backtracked until he found the trouble. Like a firefighter dousing flames, he aimed the water stream expertly up and down Brand's shivering form.

He turned off the hose. "They'll hear the water running," he said matter-of-factly, "and come check it out. I don't like messing with Security."

Brand cleared his throat before answering. "I don't think I'll get much cleaner without soap anyway."

"Probably not."

Brand watched the other coil up the hose neatly and stow it. He and Curtis had often speculated about this man who lived in the shady environs of the mall and its accompanying plazas. He added, rather lamely, "Thanks."

The other looked up quickly, appraisal in his eyes, then nodded. "All right." He stuck out his hand, unafraid to shake Brandon's, even in its current condition. "I'm Mitch."

"Brand X. You know, like the stuff nobody wants. Not new and improved."

Mitch's face creased slightly under a three-, four-day growth of beard. "Somebody wanted your ass."

"Just long enough to can me." Brand sloughed water off his shirt. "I've gotta go."

"You can't get far without your glasses." Mitch handed something out of a patched shirt pocket.

"You found 'em!"

"Something like that. I saw somebody go by me who didn't look like he should be wearing them."

Brand cleaned them up as well as he could and settled them on his face, thinking that this man was the good guy he'd tried to be, and had failed miserably at. His lenses brought Mitch's face into sharp focus. "Well. Thanks again."

"You're welcome."

It didn't seem enough, but it also seemed like a terrible breach of etiquette to ask his rescuer what had gotten him here, why he had to live the way he did, what Brand could do to help. Maybe he didn't want any help. Maybe he just wanted to be left alone. Brand swallowed his words back. The line of the sun had been lowering on the horizon. It was too late to not get in trouble, but his condition should rate mercy. Brandon took a soggy step toward home.

"Stay out of trouble now," Mitch offered.

"Yeah. Right. You, too." He stopped several paces away. "I owe you one. Cup of coffee and breakfast."

"Sounds good," the man said.

Brand squared his shoulders and walked off. He had the feeling that he'd managed to salvage the day somehow, man to man.

Chapter 4

Late October

The young woman skewed the car around a corner and found the house while the streets were still dark, streetlights burning a dim yellow, swirls of dust kicked up by the Santa Ana winds gritty along the sidewalks. Pulse drumming in her throat, she pulled over and let it hug the curb, watching the rearview mirror warily. The gun under the driver's seat slid forward at the rapid braking and tapped her gently in the ankles.

Kamryn gave it a dazed look. It didn't appear real, looking more like a toy that took caps instead of bullets. She wasn't sure if she should leave it where it was or kick it back under. What if she needed it . . . ? Almost without thought, she shoved it back under the seat where it lay out of sight but burned like a hot coal at the back of her mind.

Kamryn stared out the side window at the street. The winds were quiet now. They'd pick up again when the sun warmed a little. The homes were stucco tract homes from the '50s, looking like they'd been cut out of cardboard and set up like dominoes, like every other home she'd ever seen. Chain-link and grapestake fences sagged. Trash cans, some battered tin, others tattered plastic, tumbled next to garages. Front lawns were only patches between cracked concrete walks and crumbling asphalt driveways.

It was the kind of neighborhood whose corner houses on the fringe of streets with heavier traffic had become businesses. Accountants, a lawyer, an acupuncturist, and across from her, a dermatologist. None of them, from the houses they occupied, extremely successful. Her gaze darted along the streets, watching the traffic to see if she'd been followed. She was chicken, she knew, but she felt better with the gun.

She shut the car off after a few minutes of empty horizon. It dieseled once or twice, then hunkered down. Kamryn kept watch alertly. She would not move from the car until she felt safe.

She left the radio on, heart fluttering wildly inside her chest. She hugged herself tightly to make it stop. No, not stop, to make it *slow.* To keep it regular. She hugged herself so tightly her breasts hurt. The pain made her gasp.

A glimpse of herself in the mirror as she kept a lookout overrode her vision. Sky blue eyes framed by dark lashes, a fringe of dark hair leaving a crescent scar across her brow, skin paler than pale. A comet's tail of gems studded the outer shell of her left ear, a single diamond stud winked in the right. Frowning, she pushed her hair back off her forehead.

The wad of money felt as though it would burn a hole in the pocket of her jeans. She shifted her weight slightly and the hard knot in her pocket dug into her from a different angle. She shouldn't keep the radio on, it would pull the battery down, but Kamryn didn't want to sit there in silence. Her arms itched, as though something small and creepy crawly moved across her skin. She rubbed at them, first one and then the other, but the faint irritation did not fade.

A brilliantly-diamonded orange and black python coiled down her arm, ringed by Old English lettering and swastikas. A skull and cross-bones and several variations of knives and roses decorated the other. Her tattoos rippled, undulating, alive as she chafed her skin. She tugged at the hem of her shirt as though she could pull the short sleeves down over them. Across the knuckles of both slim hands, letters stood out: HATE across the right, LOVE across the left. And, around the ring finger, a tattoo which read Darby, a ring tattoo, instead of a wedding band. She curled the fingers of her right hand about it, obliterating it, and sat tensely, looking down the street, watching.

A late model sedan pulled into the tract from the far side of the intersection and cruised slowly toward her. She watched it keenly until she spotted the driver, a middle-aged man, unaware of her scrutiny, pulling into one of the office-converted houses. He got out of the car, hauling a battered and dull black briefcase with him, lab coat thrown over one arm. He looked like the tract houses, dusty and mediocre, as he opened the locked front door.

Kamryn shot one last glance over traffic, which had begun to emerge and pick up, then bent over, reaching for the gun under the car seat. She hesitated, brushing her fingertips over its cold metal surface, then left it. It wouldn't fit well in her purse anyway. The doctor had been spooky enough about meeting her at this hour. She would scare him out of the appointment altogether if she showed up packing. She took a deep breath to steady herself, then shoved the car door open.

The house creaked as she entered it. Its living room served as the waiting room and its kitchen had been gutted into an office area, file cabinets against the wall, the pass-through bar now a service counter. The doctor swung around, startled, half-shrugged into his lab coat. He was Middle Eastern, and his rich color paled, extravagant dark eyebrows flying up like wild birds. He cleared his throat and settled his arms into the coat and straightened his tie, grooming. *Like a cat,* she thought, *that licks itself to calm down when it's been scared.* He looked as unnerved as she felt.

"Miss Smith? If you'll have a seat. My nurse isn't in yet—"

"No," she answered flatly. "I can't wait. I've got the money. Let's get this over with."

The doctor's nose flared slightly, but he dipped his head. "Exam Room 1. I'll be in shortly."

Kamryn followed the wave of his hand down a short hallway. The commercial carpeting was worn but clean, and the whole office smelled faintly of lemon-scented disinfectant. She stepped into the room, where crisp white paper already lined the exam couch. Panic ticked in her throat and she fought the desire to turn and run. What was she doing here? She could handle this at home, heat a spoon until it glowed molten-hot and jam it against her skin, burn the tattoos away herself, scarring over the ink-stained pigmentation.

Her flesh crawled. It would hurt like hell. Easier, maybe, just to take a knife and skin herself. But here, maybe here, she could find a way to be free.

Kamryn clenched and unclenched her hands, hearing the doctor's footsteps not far behind her. She stepped to the couch and perched on it, one foot outstretched to touch the floor, ready to flee if she had to.

Dr. Amand stepped in, carrying a stainless steel tray. He smiled apologetically. "I am not quite set up yet."

She felt like gritting her teeth. His voice, faintly yet richly accented, bounced around in her head like a pinball. It set off small explosions in her thoughts, thoughts which careened around her skull, hateful things, ethnic slurs, words which she had promised herself she would never say, never *think* again. As hard as one part of her tried to narrow her eyes and stare at this man, stare hatred at him pointed enough that he ought to drop dead, the rest of her scrambled to not stare, not think, not hate.

She had given her promise.

They were all one people, she breathed to herself, forcing the philosophy down her throat and into her chest, where it weighted her like lead. She had to believe it. She had to. To do otherwise would find her down in the cellar again, looking hate and death in the eyes . . . would have her dying again, with no angel and no miracle to rescue her a second time.

Kamryn found herself losing the battle and looked abruptly across the room. Cold liquid splashed onto her arm and she jumped as Dr. Amand took up her wrist. He'd slipped on glasses, wire, round John Lennon glasses, spindly things perching on a strong nose. "Antibiotic wash," he said. He laid a towel across her leg. "Dry yourself." He stepped back and pulled rubber gloves on while she did. When she'd finished, he took up her wrists again. "Boyfriend do these?"

"Something like that."

"Nearly professional. I think perhaps it might take ten, twelve visits to clear them totally. Colored ink is most difficult to remove." He tapped a gloved finger. "The charge will be the same—sixty dollars an inch."

Kamryn swallowed back disappointment. She'd been told six to eight visits over the phone, depending on the tattoo. "I have the money," she repeated. Her vintage Kawasaki was gone, leaving $8,000 cash in its wake. First the tattoos, then she would decide what to do with the rest of the money. "Will it hurt?"

"Most of my patients do not need medication. Did it hurt getting this?" He stroked the Iron Cross symbol. Without waiting for an answer, he reached toward his machinery, turning it on, and checking the settings. "You could be a pretty girl. You'll be glad you decided to do this."

Kamryn found herself blinking rapidly as he removed a thick, pen-like instrument from its holder, coiling cable trailing behind it.

"This is a Yag, a ruby-laser. It burns away the skin, like a sunburn. You'll be tender. I will give you a topical cream, an antibiotic. Use it as per the directions. I have these gauze sleeves, to protect the tender new skin. They are like evening gloves—see? You will feel like Audrey Hepburn in *My Fair Lady*. Buy fresh ones from the pharmacy. Make an appointment for next week whenever you can, although," and Dr. Amand's almond eyes assessed her through his John Lennon glasses, "I would prefer not so early in the morning."

"I had to get away. It's a bitch to—" Kamryn paused. She wanted to tell him she was trying to save his ass, and hers. If Darby or any of the others found out what she was doing, that she was leaving them, that she was already gone, she was dead meat and so was anybody who tried to help her. He seemed to sense it.

"My scheduling nurse will work with you." He appeared to be choosing his words carefully. "I have done tattoos like this before. Sometimes gang members. I know it can be difficult. But it is a new life, is it not? It will be worth it." The machine hummed. "I will start here." The laser tool poised over the lemon python.

"No," Kamryn told him. "Take the ring tattoo off first. I want it off me." Just in case she couldn't take the burning. She wanted that gone, no matter what. She closed her eyes as her skin burned and tingled and the smell of singed hair filled the air, and the laser crackled over her flesh, doing its best to obliterate the past.

"She's dead, man! She's toast. The freaking bitch is dead, man! No one cuts me cold like that. No one!" The speaker paused for air, his white T-shirt stretched so thinly over his heaving chest that it was like a second skin, his tattoos moving like living creatures under it. "She sold the bike!"

His words bounced off the unfinished basement walls and he paused to wipe the spittle from the corner of his mouth, catching sympathetic glances from the broken-down mattresses scattered around the room. Even the bright dawn light could not scour the debris-encrusted atmosphere, though it tried to pierce through ground-level windows where banked dirt from unsuccessful gardens rose like mountains against the glass. Now and then a brindle pit bull put his nose to the window, aggressively leaving slobber and more grime behind as he snuffled at the basement occupants. It was not a basement, really, more of a crawl space, and if the age of the stucco tract home served, it had probably been at one time intended for a bomb shelter. The low ceiling made it far easier to sprawl than to stand, and the young man in the center of the basement had to bow his head slightly. He looked around for a response.

"No one, Darby," echoed a low voice from the corner.

He nodded and ran the palm of his hand over his closely-buzzed skull. "She sold the bike. And no one disses me. No one disses *us*." Having caught his breath, he began again. "She can't drop me because I'm dropping her *first*. First I'm getting my bike back, then I'm dropping *her*. She's going to freakin' *die*."

"How dead do you want her?"

The voice unfurled from the other end of the room, out of the shadows, as its owner stood up. Tattoos rippled up and down his bared torso as he did, like diamondback patterns on reptilian scales. His face and shaved head were as pale as an exposed underbelly in contrast to his arms and torso. Black pants hung tightly on the points of his pelvic bones. Named for his inkings, Snake leaned one hip against a ceiling beam and showed his teeth, waiting for an answer.

Darby looked across, his petulant fury answered and he took in all the ramifications. Snake had been known to kill people. If he said he wanted Kamryn dead, Snake could make her that way. He swallowed, uncertain of what to say next, though his broken heart seemed to pump jaggedly in his chest.

Snake snagged a nail edge between his teeth and dragged it down. He then sucked on the incisor for a moment as if savoring some private pain. His dark-eyed glance flicked about the basement room, and came round to Darby again. " 'Cause it's up to you," he said. "I could kill her just a little, so she'd be like brain-dead. She could still hang with us, and be like your slave or something, and she'd be good enough for that, except later, you might get tired all the time tellin' her what to do. Or I could just kill her all the way. It's up to you. How dead do you want her?"

There was more than just him at stake here. She knew about the group, about what they'd done, what they planned to do. He couldn't just let her walk, all snarky the way she was. Ever since Oklahoma, the Feds were thick as flies, all over everyone. Sooner or later, she might tell, and then it would all come down on them. He didn't have a choice. He sucked in a deep breath, feeling it in his chest like a stab wound, where she'd betrayed him. "I want her *dead,* man," he said, and there was no mistaking his meaning.

Snake grinned. "Cool."

Chapter 5

Furtive sounds woke his dreaming. They were his own, a panting which echoed that of the guide pulling him out of his nightmares. Yellow Dog faded away abruptly into a shimmering glow which became a window beating into his vision. Brandon reached automatically for his glasses, even before he was awake. A hot sun slanted through the venetian blinds of his room and cast zebra shadows. Morning had come too soon. He turned his head and a massive blob bumped just into view. "Jesus!" Eyes squinted nearly shut, he jammed his glasses on over the bridge of his nose and the blurs jumped into startling focus.

"Rats! Mo–om."

She recoiled from view. "Sorry, Brandon." The close-up memory of gray hairs trying to disappear among frosted highlights in her malt brown hair and thick gouges of worry lines deep in her forehead between her eyes remained. More potent expletives crowded his throat, but he dared not loose them. Not in front of her. She would die, he thought, if she heard the average language in a high school corridor. But then, she still had trouble dealing with the vending machines on campus being fenced off to prevent theft. She would be more comfortable among the Amish.

She frowned. "Bad dreams again?"

If she only knew. "No." He started to shove his covers down, then pinched them tightly at his navel. "Will you quit hoovering over me? How about some privacy here?"

She drew back, half-smiling. "Hovering. If I were hoovering, you'd be getting vacuum cleaned."

"Whatever." His glasses slid down. He put a finger square in the middle of the frames and nailed them in place on the bridge of his nose.

"It's time to get up. Now, remember, no water. No breakfast. Nothing until after the procedure."

His stomach rumbled in protest. "Shit." Brand swung his feet out, covers over his lap, and stared darts at her. "I thought I was going to sleep in today."

Her lips pinched as she consulted her watch. "You did. Everybody else left for school forty-five minutes ago." She stood, the palm of her other hand unconsciously cradling the slight bulge of her stomach, proof he thought, that husband number three, the dweeb, had done her at least once. The thought of his mother and the dweeb engaged in sex made him nauseous. That, on top of other concerns, made him want to get her out of his room as quickly as possible.

"Mo–om." If she ever left, he could get dressed.

"What? Oh, right." She got as far as the doorway, then turned again.

Brand hastily threw his blankets back over his lap. "What? What?"

"Aren't you excited?"

"Yeah. Kind of."

"Only kind of?"

He was scared, too, so that took a lot of the edge off the excitement. He shrugged. His mother and the dweeb were doing this for him, he knew that, although the dweeb hadn't pounded it into him the way husband number two would have. But the RK procedure hadn't been his idea, he'd been lobbying for contacts. None of this would have happened if Curtis had stuck by him at the mall, but it had and now he was in the process of getting what he wanted. Sort of.

They wouldn't be calling him owl eyes anymore, and he'd have a better chance of surviving gym class, so maybe all this noble sacrifice stuff from her would be worth it. She'd dug the money up from somewhere, maybe the psych hospital had finally settled after what had happened—anyway, she'd announced what they'd arranged for him like they'd gotten him a car. He'd spent the better part of an afternoon with his eyes dilated while the doctor looked at him like he was a prime specimen for alien abduction, measuring him for surgery.

Anything to get the Coke bottles off his nose, to not look at himself in the mirror and see a freak grinning back. Although, freak or not, he was usually happy to recognize himself. His dreams were worse, but he'd keep them to himself. Anything was better than going back to the psych ward.

His mother let out a little sigh, and shifted weight. "I'll be glad when it's over," he said finally.

"Well, hurry and get dressed."

He tilted his head and looked at her. "Duh."

She left, shutting the door behind her.

Brand waited a beat or two to make sure she was really gone, before pushing his blankets to the floor and standing up. His penis had finally begun to wilt, and he hated that, he really hated it, waking up hard every morning. He'd told a friend about it, who'd snickered and called him a "throbbing, pulsating love machine" until Brand had gotten sick of both his friend and the label. It was part of life, he guessed, but he didn't need his mother fussing over that, too, making him miserable. She'd probably make the dweeb come in to talk things over with him and he *really* didn't need that.

What he needed was not to be a freak anymore.

Brand peed and then looked at himself in the bathroom mirror. He had the only other room in the house with its own bath, but he supposed that would change when the dweeb's kids, both girls, got older. He'd get shuffled around again, maybe even thrown back in the hospital. It could happen. But only if someone got inside his skull and stirred around in there, like a rabid bat in some attic. Only if someone knew what he thought. What he dreamed. What lay behind his eyelids as surely as darkness lay on the far side of the moon.

He found himself gripping the edges of the porcelain sink so hard his hands had turned chalk-white, like the fixture. He forced himself to let go, shaking.

Brand X, the stuff nobody wants.

And his mom wanted to know if he was excited about having surgical knives pointed at his eyeballs.

"Shit," he said, and spat into the sink. He ran enough water to wash it down, combed his hair, and left.

His mom was a morning person, but she knew that he wasn't, so she said little in the car. She'd found a more or less current music station on the radio and left it playing, though if Brand had had his choices, he'd have brought his Cranberries tape and cranked it up until the car boomed with the bass. He stared out the window at the still somewhat unfamiliar neighborhood. Orange County wasn't L.A., by a long shot. More palms and ficus, less graffiti. The schools, bankrupt or not, had fields for soccer and baseball and swimming pools, outside, with a deck, not upstairs in some prehistoric building.

The neighborhoods had dress codes, for crissakes, God forbid somebody should paint their house blue or something instead of white or puke color. There were rules about the fences, how high and whether they could be out of wood or cinder block or bars, which depended mostly on how ritzy the neighborhood was and whether they would "obscure a view" or not. Cars could not be left parked on the streets, the beaches had curfews, and the principals had cows if anyone wore a shirt with a rock band or beer brand name on it. Brand's stepfather could not afford a home in one of those areas, for which Brand daily thanked whatever passed for a God. If the conservative county got any more rigid, it would go into rigor mortis.

He wondered how good the doctor was. How could he be, with his office tacked onto the Brea Mall? Was a mall any place for an eye surgeon, for crying out loud? With any luck, he could roll right out of there and head to the arcade afterward. He could page Curtis to meet him. Brand rested his forehead against the cool glass of the side window, wondering if his high score was still riding supremo in the arcade.

"Hey! Slow down."

She tensed at the wheel, even as she steered into the lot.

He bumped his forehead against the passenger window. "Mom, slow down." The power window slid away from him and he hung over the door frame.

"Brandon, what are you doing!"

"Looking for the homeless guy." It was early enough that Mitch might be out, before the security cop wanna-bes were out on patrol. "The guy that pulled me out of the Dumpster."

His mother's voice came from behind his head, but he knew the expression that went with the tone. "I don't think I want to meet him, even after what he did for you."

"He's a cool guy."

"He doesn't work and he has no home. I don't think so. We talked about this. I told you to stay away from him. It's not just drugs and alcohol—"

Brand thumbed his glasses up the bridge of his nose and twisted around in the car seat. "I wanted you to see him, to see he's an okay guy. All right? And he's got a name. It's Mitch."

"Mitch what? Or should that be, what Mitch?"

He shrugged. "Just Mitch. And you'd like him, really, and not just because he saved my butt."

"There's a hole under your feet and you're the one digging it." Her eyes looked like baked clay.

"Ohhh-kay." He turned back to the window, dropping the Mitch subject of an interesting guy. Brand had already paid him back the breakfast and coffee. Mitch liked McDonald's coffee, scalding hot and pure, not flavored with hazelnuts or amaretto or cinnamon and whipped cream. Curtis was of the opinion that, slipped ten dollars, the guy might even buy them beer or more. He was obviously a Vietnam vet, his friend pointed out, who'd seen better times. Brand pondered the possibilities of playing in cyberspace while blasted. It might add a whole new dimension.

If he played his mother right, he might even get a second get out of school free card to explore the possibilities. He settled back on the car seat. "Glad we're not homeless," he said thoughtfully. "You worked awful hard to keep us that way."

Out of the corner of his eye, he caught the tightening of her lips at his acknowledgment of her sacrifices. Oh, yes, she'd worked hard, and married poorly, too. That was the only reason he could think of for husbands two and three.

Brand turned away again, blinking. His glasses began their usual slide. He pushed them back into place savagely. With his newfound oily skin it was like balancing on a banana peel, forty, fifty times a day.

His mother seemed more nervous than he was when they parked the car. The north end of the mall was dead, he thought, looking around. Parking spaces as far as the eye could see. He looked at the coffee bar next to the ophthalmologist. "How about a cappuccino, Mom? We've got time."

She looked startled as she locked the car, and then fidgeted with her purse. He knew that look. She was trying to remember how much cash she had on her.

Brand finally looked away, knowing the answer before she gave it. "Not today, Brandon."

"Sure." He tossed her a grin. "Just checkin'. You don't have to go in with me. I could just have them, you know, call when it's time to pick me up."

A grateful look washed over his mother's face, and for a moment, he thought he would have killed to have brought her that peace permanently. The realization felt like a kick in the gut. She shook her head quickly, brushing aside the opportunity. "No, they want me here. Just in case."

"Sure," he repeated. They both knew that was only half the reason. She was also afraid that if she turned her back, Brand would be gone. He felt sorry for her, but not terribly. She'd spent most of his years wrecking her life and his, too. Husband number two had convinced her that Brand was the core of their problems and, eventually, they'd had him hospitalized, putting him into the hands of a monster.

They'd all found out just in time.

Maybe.

He shoved his hands into his jeans pockets and followed her across the parking lot.

He heard rapid footsteps to his flank and turned. He saw the girl hurrying across the parking lot, going into the side entrance of the mall. She probably had work to do before the boutiques were open. He stared at her now, but she did not notice, for she wore evening gloves, it looked like, and she was pulling her sleeves down over them, quick-stepping across the asphalt.

"Hi."

She jumped like a shot rabbit, her startled eyes fixing on him. Then she answered, muffled, "Hi."

He thought his heart might sink, but there was no recognition in her eyes. He cleared his throat. "You work at Hot Flash, right?"

"Right." She looked him over and Brand felt himself shrink a little as she measured him. "Your sister shop there?"

Older sister, she meant. Brand cleared his throat again. "No. Ah— I've seen your tattoos. When you were doin' espressos. Cool."

Her face closed and she said icily, "See you," in a tone which meant she wouldn't be looking for him. She angled away, heading for the steel doors just beyond the fire lane.

He bumped into his mother, who had stopped just ahead of him. "A little old for you?"

"Yeah. Probably." He felt his face warm and dodged around her, so as not to discuss it. She kept looking for signs of normalcy in him, as though each stage he reached was a monumental achievement to be celebrated. For crissakes, was she worried that he didn't like girls?

Defensively, he said, "She's nice enough, under all that. It's just flash, y'know? Inside, she's nice."

His mother reached out, gave him a half-hug. "You're a good kid, do you know that, Brand? A little strange, but a good kid."

Her embrace stopped him in his tracks. Instead of radiating warmth, it iced through him, stabbed through the bones of his neck and shoulders like a stiletto, filling him with dread. Because he wasn't a good kid. He tried, but he wasn't, and if she could see into his mind, see into his dreams, she would think that Hannibal Lecter was fit to teach kindergarten compared to him.

Brand shuddered.

His mother let go of him abruptly as if sensing his rejection.

He closed his eyes tightly for a moment. He wasn't a good kid, but he could imitate one. If he tried hard enough. If he walked that tightrope very carefully, no one would ever know.

He could do it. He had done it, and he could keep doing it.

"Come on, we're late," his mother said sharply.

His entrance into the ophthalmologist's office seemed unreal, after that. There was a time where he sat in one of several chairs arranged in a waiting room that was supposed to look like somebody's living room, if that somebody lived with dissections of the human eyeball hung on the walls, and with golfing magazines strewn all over the coffee table. There was a hushed discussion in the corner between his mother and one of the women who worked behind the counter, about money he presumed, because she had that defensive look on her face again.

And then, finally, he was being called in. His mother took his glasses and looked as if she wanted to say something or give him another hug. Brand pushed past her before she could take the opportunity. He felt himself moving mechanically, watching himself out of body go through the drill. Given a backless smock to wear, having his hair put in a matching bonnet, being laid down on a surgical table where a special pillow held his head steady. A nurse smiled down at him. "I've got your eyedrops for you."

Brand felt like saying something smart-ass, but his tongue felt like his comforter from his bedroom and stuck to the roof of his mouth besides. He stared up at her, watching her somewhat pretty face through the floating teardrop as it splashed and stung briefly into his eye. She had to hold his left eyelid open.

"Remember what the doctor talked to you about. Keep your eyes focused on that target and don't move. This won't hurt at all, I promise—" Her bleary image crossed her heart over her uniform. "He'll be right in."

Brand knew better. The drops would take about fifteen minutes to be at their optimal. The doc wouldn't be in before that. He watched the target design which had been tacked to the ceiling overhead. He couldn't see the tacks today, without his glasses, but he'd been shown it two weeks ago when he'd been brought in to have his eyes tested and measured. He thought now, as he'd thought then, if the doc was really all that marvelous—how come he still used knives instead of lasers?

So if he felt that way about it, why did he even agree to it? Brand listened to his inner voice and returned a shrug. *Pull out my fingernails, stick pins in my eyes—just don't send me to school!*

His thoughts wandered and before he knew it, there was a noise at the side of his table and the doctor had come in. The nurse had reappeared with him. She held something shiny in her hands. "I'm going to secure your eyelids. The human eye blinks every five seconds. Even if you tried not to, you probably would, and we can't have that."

"What is that?" His dry throat squeaked on the last word, and he felt his face go warm, but they ignored it.

"Lid speculums." The tips of her fingers were incredibly cold as she pulled his upper eyelid into a steely hold, then positioned the instrument and captured his lower lid.

Strange, but not unbearable. He felt her repeat the sequence on his other eye.

Then they dropped the target rings gently onto his staring eyeball. That, the doctor had warned him about. It would help pinpoint the direction of the scalpel. Brand closed his jaws very tightly.

Brand desperately wanted to change his mind as the scalpel descended toward his eye, but he dared not move. He tried to focus on the target, as the steel-blue edge dove closer and closer.

The nurse, not the doctor, said, "You're going to feel a pressure, like someone pushing a finger into your eye, but it won't hurt. It might even make a small pop, but don't worry."

He had no choice about not moving, or staring upward. What was he doing here, anyway?

The surgeon stood over him, a white cloud, and the steely instrument in his hand arced downward like lightning. Brand could feel his entire body go rigid.

How much, for a moment, the vision looked like Dr. Susan Craig, standing over him. How much at her mercy he still was. She was dead, wasn't she? Dead, but not gone.

And with her, she brought the other, the hunting man, the killer, looking down at him instead of out through him.

He thought for a moment he'd gone to sleep and was immersed in the dream that continually haunted him, but the face behind the knife was different. Awake or asleep, he knew he was dead if he stirred or showed any fear as the blade dipped near.

"Just hold very still."

A dead man. Dead. Dead.

Chapter 6

"Life sucks and then you die. How do you think I feel?"

Brand felt, rather than saw, his mother recoil from his response to her question. He couldn't see her—he couldn't see a damn thing beyond the end of his nose since they'd left the doctor's office, a disposable pair of solar shields resting across his face like a bad pair of 3-D glasses. The car swerved slightly with his mother's movement. He continued looking out the window even though all he could see were dark clouds rushing past him. He felt like a vampire. As dim as everything looked, the daylight made him flinch. Brand sighed and added brutally, "You had to ask."

"But I didn't have to hear that."

"You want me to lie to you? Look, I'm fourteen. I get trash-canned with regularity, leaned on about my grades, my skin prefers to get pimples just before picture days, I've had two stepfathers—and I can't see shit." His shoulders twitched. He did not add that he could not afford the luxury of moods. She watched him like a hawk and if he so much as sneezed, she thought of throwing him back in the psycho ward. But she'd asked. Why would she ask if she didn't want to hear the answer. "What do you expect? What if this doesn't get any better? At least I could see something before."

He knew what she wanted. She wanted another round of thanks for the RK, but he didn't feel like giving it to her. If he'd had his way, it would have been more useful for her to take the settlement money and buy a newer car, and he could have nagged that off her in a couple of years. But, no, she had to make a noble sacrifice.

And what if she'd ruined him . . . left Brand alone in the dark, with *him?*

"Brand, they told us to expect this. Haziness for the first day— that's one of the reasons they told you to go home and go to bed. Keep pressure off the eye, no bending or stooping, just go home and rest. Sleep if you can."

"I hurt."

"I know, honey. And you're swelled up like—" She paused. "Like when you were first born, and they used the forceps on you." Her voice softened into sentimentality.

"Oh, jeez."

The car stopped for a red light. Her fingers played lightly over his hunched left shoulder like a spider crawling on it. He suppressed a shudder to listen to her.

"It'll get better. He told me he was really pleased with the inci- sions. As long as you don't get fluid buildup and those light auras, you'll be fine. I've got the Vicodin and the eyedrops. We'll go home, you'll take your pain prescription and go to bed."

"Right. And when I wake up, everything will be wonderful." It never had been before. His face itched. He put a hand up to scratch and bumped the dark glasses off his nose.

"Don't take your glasses off, honey!"

"I wasn't. They just fell." He maneuvered them back into position.

"Well, you don't want any side effects. Burst, or whatever they called it."

Flare, Brand thought but did not say it aloud. She would never get it right anyhow. He didn't know what it was, except that the doctor said it was a common side effect. Brilliant light, sometimes auras, around objects, disrupting the vision although it would eventually go away, if he developed it. He would welcome that if it happened. What he had now, along with the blurriness, were dark smudges, as though someone had clouded everything over with dirty fingerprints, blind- ing him.

Blind.

He shuddered again, and tasted something bitter at the back of his throat. He made a gagging sound.

The light changed, the car surged forward cautiously. "You just have to be more patient. With the operation, me, your stepfather—"

"Right." Brand cut her off. He didn't want to hear a thousand reasons why he had to be a saint while the dweeb could be a total jerk and get away with it. Although, he had to admit, the dweeb wasn't a jerk. Usually. And even if he was, Brand could deal with him. Brand had experienced worse in his life. Wrestled with it every day.

"Just think positive, all right? Do me that much of a favor."

"All right, Mom." Brand didn't turn around or take his clouded vision off the road. "You want it, you got it, Toyota." Landscape slid by. He wondered how blind he would get. If it didn't get much worse, he might be able to get by with a cane and a dog. Dogs were good. Girls liked dogs. The tattooed girl—

Of course, nobody would look at him twice with these things the doctor gave him hanging off his face.

Brand turned around in the car seat. "Hey, Mom."

"Yes?"

A little cold, but nothing he couldn't handle. "How about hitting the drugstore on the way home? I need some decent shades. I can't wear these things to school tomorrow. Not Ray Bans or anything, maybe just some imitation Quentin Tarantinos or something. If there's enough money left."

He thought he saw her lips tighten slightly. It wasn't as though he asked for much, ever. He waited.

Her jaw loosened. "All right. I think we can do that."

"Thanks." He settled back. Misery could be profitable. Not fun, but profitable.

Nicholas Solis smiled into the vanity over their dresser as his wife put her arms about him. Her shapely arms were in sharp contrast to his police uniform and his own, squarish bulky body, crow's-feet etched heavily about his eyes, and the whitish square above his left eyebrow where someone in south L.A. had once told him exactly what he'd thought about law enforcement.

He felt no small pleasure that, despite their decade's difference in age, his muscle tone was better than hers. That's the way it should be. He worked at it, to protect her. He concentrated on buttoning his uniform shirt and she seemed intent upon distracting him.

"Freeze," her small, muffled voice declared from behind his shoulder. "I've got you surrounded."

"Covered," he corrected.

"No," she insisted, her head nestled between his shoulder blades. She butted him gently to make her point. "Surrounded." She clasped her hands and squeezed her arms tightly around him. The firm rotundness of her six-month pregnancy pressed into the small of his back, and Solis thought he could feel the baby move in protest.

He laughed. "Hey! Both of you. I'm going to be late for roll call."

"Tell them it was a hostage situation." Andrea Solis moved slightly, her heart-shaped face coming into view in the mirror. Soft hair, like waves of chocolate, broke from her forehead and lapped about her shoulders. Her eyes, neither green nor brown, smiled at him with tiny lines echoing those around her generous mouth.

For just a half-beat, his heart responded to both the unconscious sexuality of her beauty and the police situation she described, his pulse beginning to race. He didn't have time for the one, and the likelihood of such a situation in Brea took care of the other. This was most definitely not South Central. He reached back firmly and drew her away from him.

"I've got to go to work."

"I know, I know." Andrea made a fleeting pouty mouth. "Still, I might have had fun with the SWAT team."

He placed his palm over her stomach. Their unseen child swam again under his touch. "You look like you had fun with somebody."

"You should know." Andrea made a sandwich over his hand with hers. "I wish you didn't have to go today."

"I've got a double day off in just three days. We'll do something then. Dinner, a movie—"

"I know, but I feel good today. No nausea, no backache, my ankles are a normal size. Who knows what kind of a wreck I'll be then?"

"I guess I'll just have to take my chances." He slid his hand away, picked up his cap.

"You think I'm spoiled."

"Not half as spoiled as I'd like you to be." Nick brushed his lips across her forehead. He would give her anything he could, this tiny, funny miracle who had, literally, saved his life. He had hoped, two years ago, that someone similar might be in his future, but he had never hoped for someone as wonderful as Andrea.

His dad's birthday was coming up the first of November. Nick would have to call and thank him, one more time. Thank him for the advice which made him change his job and think about picking up the pieces of his life instead of opting out. Thank him for taking him out of the line of fire and putting Nick just around the corner from this heart-shaped face with espresso eyes who would rescue him.

Andrea paused and gave him a look, brow crinkling at his sudden silence. "Nicky . . . what's wrong?"

"Nothing." Heedless of putting wrinkles into a crisp uniform shirt, he wrapped his arms around her and drew her as close as he could. "Absolutely nothing."

"You're sure?"

"Very sure." He released her. "Now remember, I'm not off until eleven."

"I won't worry! I promise." Andrea crossed her fingers. "Breakfast with my mom tomorrow?"

A groan escaped him. Andrea's mouth twitched slightly, but the gleam in her eyes danced. "Just to pick out wallpaper for the baby's room. You promised?"

"I know, I know." Actually, Andrea's mom was a good thing. If the rose didn't have a thorn, he might think he was still at the bottom of a bottle, still in the middle of a bad divorce, still asleep in a living nightmare. He could take Andrea's mom easily, when push came to shove. She just wanted what he wanted, the best for Andrea, although she seemed to enjoy butting heads with him to get it. He could manage. He had a pretty damn thick skull, witness the scar over his brow. "Set the alarm, we'll do breakfast. Just don't ask me to eat chorizo."

Sunshine broke on his wife's face.

He crossed the bedroom and reached into the hat shelf in the closet, where he kept his gun belt and shield, and took it down. He wouldn't put it on in the house, her unspoken request and his quiet compliance. When the baby came, they had agreed to put a lock on the closet. There would be no gunfire accident in this household. No tragic scenario. They had their whole future in front of them.

"Wake me," she said softly at the front door. "When you come in." She quirked an eyebrow to punctuate her request.

Nick grinned, bathed in the light of mid-morning, as he walked to his car. The job wasn't glamorous, it was even dull by his old standards, but it brought him home every night and that was a big plus. He had a life.

Rembrandt stretched his legs as he got out of the rental car. He rubbed his eyes, then dropped his sunglasses back into place, his forehead smoothing after squinting into the glare off the parking lot. The air was dry and gritty. He could smell the smog, and the sound of the 57 freeway just to the east of the mall roared annoyingly in his ears.

Welcome to the good life in Southern California. He retrieved a folder from the front bucket seat and then shut the door, listening to the electronic locks secure the vehicle. He understood only one thing about why Christiansen could be in the area: the weather. Even at its worst, one hardly faced freezing to death while huddling over a heater grate. No, a derelict here was most likely to be clubbed to death by the state's active skinhead groups or maybe run over by a DUI while trying to cross the street . . . but Mother Nature was not likely to be the killer. Not that it didn't get cold and frosty once in a while. It did. But nothing that would pose a threat to his sergeant.

A Marine wasn't a Marine without a thick skin and good survival skills, and Christiansen had shown himself to be one of the best. Rembrandt had trailed him down the coast for the last few months until losing him completely just over the Oregon border. Once in California, his job was damn near a fool's errand. There was a whole civilization of derelicts on the Gold Coast, an underground if you would, and picking a single man out of it was like isolating a particular grain of sand from their ubiquitous beaches.

Finding him in the beginning had merely been a matter of tracing banking transactions, but then Christiansen's father had died, leaving him a considerable wad, and once that had been cashed, the man was gone. Bayliss had talked Rembrandt into setting up circumstances that made that old man's death look suspicious, just to get even, and that had forced Christiansen out of the area entirely. He couldn't go back unless he was willing to discuss with the authorities just how an ailing man had passed on, and if suffocation had been involved.

Beyond his skills at tracing, a little luck had been involved. Among the vets who worked the Santa Monica parks and beaches, he'd found someone who'd met Christiansen. Had to have been the sergeant . . . no one else could have spouted a story of voodoo and military treachery and betrayal like his quarry, drunk or not. At that point, he was only two months behind him.

So what Rembrandt was doing now was searching inland, then coastal, zigzagging all the way down toward San Diego and Baja, California. In late October, even the homeless had moved off the cooling sands, to more sheltered parks and freeway underpasses. It rained even in paradise.

Someone honked behind Rembrandt. He twisted about. A large woman with fashionable silvery hair leaned out of a forest green Jag. "Are you leaving?"

"Leaving?" His train of thought had been momentarily derailed and he was uncertain of her intention.

"Are you leaving the parking space?"

Ah. He shook his head courteously. "No, ma'am, I'm sorry. I just arrived."

Without another word, she pulled her head back in the window and patched out, the speed of her disappearing vehicle expressing her contempt. Rembrandt watched her drive the aisle at a rate of speed which might have qualified for the Indianapolis 500 and then gravely moved toward the bank of stores himself. He had work to do. He would start at the arcade, passing around the most decent photo of Christiansen he could dig up, then show the artist's rendering of what he might look like after months and months of neglect.

Someone might know his face.

Snake came back to the car, climbed in through the open passenger window, and sat, sweat bubbling up through the pores of his head. He gave a wolfish grin. "Found her." He licked his fingers before Darby could see what it was that stained them—slick and pinkish, he thought, but he couldn't be sure.

"That easy?"

Snake rubbed his hand dry on his jeans. "Quick, not necessarily easy." He looked out the window back up the weed-choked sidewalk to the small bungalow-style home. Sheets hung sloppily across picture windows. One of them rippled slightly as if the occupant pulled it aside to look out, then hastily draped back into place. "Kamryn tells Lyndall everything. Always."

"That bitch," Darby muttered and ground the gears of the car as it lurched forward. "Where is she?"

"Working. At the mall in Brea. She's got a place up there, too, somewhere. But it'll be easier to find her at the mall. Place called Hot Flash."

Those were more words than he had ever heard out of Snake at one time, but the information they contained held volumes. "I'm bringing her back," Darby said.

Snake writhed into a more comfortable position in the car seat. "Go by the pad first," he responded. "I need my stuff."

"I want to bring her back."

"And if she don't come, I'll need my stuff." Flat-voiced. Snake turned his head, so his eyes could meet Darby's. Flat eyes.

Darby swallowed hard at what he saw in them. "All right." He swung the car toward Costa Mesa. "If she doesn't come home with me, she's toast."

"She's mine," Snake corrected, his attention gone back to the windows and whatever it was he saw out of them.

Chapter 7

"Ma'am, I'd be pleased to stay with you until Animal Control arrives, but I want you to understand there's nothing I can do." He used the reassuring voice he'd learned to adopt on calls, but the agitated woman did not respond. Nick waited patiently before repeating, "Ma'am?"

A handkerchief, rapidly getting sodden and stained with mascara waved in answer. "Oh, I understand, officer, I do, I really do. But . . ." The plump woman's face collapsed into a moon-round echo of an apple doll. "Tigger wouldn't hurt anyone. Not anyone. How anybody could do something like this . . .?" The handkerchief played over the body—half body—of a beloved cat. Its red-orange furriness lay in extremis on her well-manicured front lawn. There was a tremendous amount of fur, but little blood in what was left of the cat.

Nick squinted down the hillside at the line of brown-and-sand-painted homes which took up territory that had previously only been occupied by the oil company and coyotes. As the foothills had become more urban, the previous occupants had only withdrawn, waiting, as if hoping to reclaim their lands. The oil company had recently announced it was giving up. The coyotes were still there.

"Ma'am, you can't tell a coyote what to eat and what not to eat. We're not allowed to kill or trap and relocate them. We just try to live with them. As I understand it, you let your cat out early this morning and didn't find the, ummm, remains until just now."

She looked at him with eyes bloodhound red and sagging. Her lips thinned. "Officer, I don't need your lectures. Tigger was a longhaired cat, purebred Persian, and he enjoyed the coolness of the morning hours. But I did not shove him out the door. We keep him in the backyard. And I knew he was missing hours before I found this!"

Solis pitched a glare toward the house's backyard. Like all the others on the street, it was restricted to black bar fencing. Small dogs and wily coyotes could easily slip through the railing, although hers did seem to be hedged inside. "Mrs. Davis, ma'am—"

"Oh, for heaven's sake. Do you think I'm an imbecile? Young man, I have my yard fenced from the inside, where the association guard dogs can't see it. I don't want things wandering in and out of my yard all day and night. Come with me."

She pulled up the hem of her violet-flowered muumuu and strode determinedly away, stepping over the body of her late lamented buddy as though he no longer existed, and leading Nick toward the back of her property.

"See? There!"

He followed the pointing finger. Inside pink hawthorn and privet hedges, he could see the cleverly concealed fencing. It should have been, he reflected, effective against even high-jumping coyotes. "Perhaps," he suggested, "a meter reader let your cat out."

"I would be filing a complaint against the company now if I thought that." Mrs. Davis shook her head. "Officer, Tigger was murdered, tortured, and I expect you to take a report."

He smothered a sigh. Sooner or later, he'd been told, he'd run into one of these. Ladies, mostly, who insisted their property bordered on the edge of a satanic coven, miserable people whose sole joy in life consisted of stealing, torturing, and quartering beloved pets. Stu Randall had told him of one of his calls where the woman actually kept the corpses in her deep freezer, hoping one day to prove her claim against her neighbors.

The county, of course, had looked at every corpse and pointed out the signs of coyote kill, but the woman had not listened. Did not to this day.

And Solis had had the luck to run into one of her disciples.

"Officer." Mrs. Davis stared at him with her gimlet eyes.

"I'm listening," he responded dutifully.

"I hope so. At the end of the street, where it leads out of the tract, there's a dirt road that goes into one of the back canyons. It's a fire lane, but there are squatter homes in there." Her faded lipstick mouth made another hard line. "When the oil company moves out, they'll be cleaned out, too, when the developers go in, but until then, we have to deal with them. The bikers are bad enough with their choppers, but then there're the others."

Solis kept his eyes on his pad as he took notes, smoothing down the expression of his face to a careful neutrality. He did not want trouble here. He did not *need* trouble. It was almost dark, and almost time for his dinner break. He found himself thinking about Andrea's promise to wake for him at the end of the long day. "Tell me about the others." He steeled himself for the satanic cult routine. The religious right slept hand in hand with the political conservatives of the county. They suspected everyone of either being anarchists or devil worshipers or gays, and his shift had already consisted of rousting one poor homeless guy from the environs around Brea Mall just because someone was offended he slept in the bushes. The guy would be back, he knew it and Solis knew it, but in the meantime some fat cat in his Mercedes had gotten his taxpayer's worth of his being displaced. Nick readied himself to listen to the woman's complaints.

"Young man, I know you're being civil, but it's written all over you." Mrs. Davis looked down at Tigger's body and pressed her handkerchief to her face, as if all her resolve had suddenly disappeared. She cleared her throat. "I'm not going to tell you it's witchcraft."

His pencil point stopped on the pad. "You're not?"

"No. I wish to be taken seriously. Have you heard of Santeria?"

Only when he'd served in hell. Nick found himself staring quietly at her face while she patiently waited for an answer. He shrugged a shoulder. "I worked in L.A. for a while. It's not unheard of."

"Animal sacrifice. That's what we've got living down in the canyon. I won't say they're evil, but they are opportunists. I think they needed Tigger, so they took him and then they returned what they didn't need. They kept his . . ." she sniffled, "head . . . and . . ."

He saw a white panel truck pull up out of the corner of his eye. Solis interrupted. "Ma'am, here's Animal Control now. Let them examine the remains, dispose of them if you want them to—you can't bury him legally up here, but I understand if you want to—"

"You don't believe me."

"No, ma'am, I do." He snapped the cover over on his notebook and stowed it in his uniform pocket. "Have you got a picture of your cat? An extra one?"

She blinked rapidly, then dipped her hand into the side slit pocket of her muumuu. She brought out a little plastic folder, filled with pictures of grandchildren and several of a magnificent rust-colored cat. She pulled one out.

"If it'll make you feel at ease, ma'am, I'll just drive over. This will help me ID any remains."

"Thank you, officer. Thank you very much."

Nick nodded and started down the sloping driveway. The female Animal Control officer swapped looks with him, and he just dropped his head in a short salute of acknowledgment. He did not think Mrs. Davis would fare so well with the no-nonsense looking woman, who'd probably had it up to her eyebrows with people who let their adored animals outside to become coyote appetizers.

On the other hand, he did have more than a passing familiarity with Santeria, not devil worship, but a religious ritual which did require sacrifices. Out of all the officers in Brea's police department, he was probably the only one who would have understood. So for that, if nothing else, he owed her a side trip down that dusty road. Dinner would have to wait, even though he had a distinctly empty feeling inside.

The sun lowered behind the scrubby, heat-burned hills, casting the canyon in long, purple shadows. It was that eerie time between dusk and night, and Nick found himself looking forward to the not so distant weekend when daylight savings would be repealed. Always around Halloween it seemed nighttime would never come and then the hours changed, and it fell, dropping like a guillotine blade into place with its immense darkness. The changing of the hours was the start of the winter season in southern California, which only really had two seasons, winter and summer. Darkness and light.

His right front tire hit a rut in the dirt road and the car skewed around for just a second, headlights piercing off the road into eucalyptus and brush, and he saw eyes reflecting back at him, eerily, in the twilight. The hair went up on the back of Nick's neck. He wrestled the car back onto the road. He spotted the goat again, eyes shining, and saw the rope around its neck, tethering it. Beyond, the shanty-sided house.

This had to be the Santeria suspect house. He did not recall that bikers had any particular fondness for goats, while the beast was an almost staple for sacrifice in Santeria. In this country, old goats had little other use as goat meat was not often eaten in the United States Some of the immigrants from the south were starting to change that, but it was not a meat, which, barbecued or stewed, had found many converts yet.

So the goat which watched him warily, yellow pupils gleaming like snake eyes from the shadow, probably was not here for its meat which, although it did not prove Mrs. Davis' statement, gave her more immediate credence.

Nick pulled the patrol car into the driveway, noting the mid-80s model Malibu which sat close to the door of the house, its springs broken from the way the frame sagged to one side. He had easy flight blocked with his unit. He pulled up the mike and gave his location. Dispatch didn't respond immediately, then gave him an answer, distracted.

"What's up?"

She gave him the code for a freeway high-speed chase. It meant he wouldn't have backup available, but he didn't really think he needed any. He responded, "Tell 'em good luck."

"I copy that," she said and left again. Nick clicked off, knowing that all attention, including TV network helicopters, would be following the chase drama. Last month some kid had stolen a fire engine and taken it from North County all the way to Laguna Beach, chippies and locals following him all the way. It had been prime time on the news channel for nearly ninety minutes.

He hung up the mike, took his flashlight off his belt, and turned it on. The torch was a substantial weight in his hand, meant to be used as a weapon if necessary. He didn't think it would be. Santerias were, mostly, nonviolent. He did not approve of them, but he knew that if Mrs. Davis' cat had been taken by them, he would have died at their hands rather quickly and cleanly before being harvested for his other organs. Only kosher butchers killed more humanely. He did not expect any trouble.

Then, of course, there were always those times when he was wrong.

Within four feet of the front door, he could smell the sweet coppery reek of blood and hear the panicked bleating of a lamb.

It was after midnight in Haiti. Delacroix sat comfortably in the dirt, the small creatures of the night crawling over his bare crossed legs as if as unaware of him as he was of them. Their chirps and hums underscored the sound of his barely audible chanting. The air was thick with evening moisture and warm and redolent with the smell of his last offering and the incense he burned.

Because of the time of year and the phase of the moon, he knew that other people in other places would also be making sacrifices, though they prayed to other gods than he did. It scarcely mattered. He had been given such power that the common tie of spilled blood gave him entrance to their ritual, if he wished. He knew every drop they sprinkled, every twig and ash they burned, every syllable they uttered.

He had little care for their petty and feeble attempts to gain favor. They scarcely understood what they did. They were beneath his contempt. Others would deal with them. Delacroix had no need to be concerned for them.

Tonight, however, something stirred. It was not another mambo, though he knew it was inevitable he would someday spar again with the woman who had fought his loa. No, this was different. It came to him on droplets of crimson, riding the back of another sacrifice, far, far away. It brought to him not only the rich scent of freshly spilled blood and homage, but a touch of the man he searched for. Delacroix's back stiffened as it touched him.

So faint was the trace that he had to withdraw from his other thoughts and focus his trance on this single incidence. The vision came to him through the death-dimmed green-gold eyes of a rusty-haired cat.

The man in question wore a uniform and he was police, and, ah, Delacroix had had much dealing with police. He knew their lust for power was universal, and their cruelty, and their corruption. How different could Haiti be from this other spot in the world? And though this man was not the military man Delacroix sought, he had passed him by recently. Perhaps that day, last week. The resonance was unmistakable. Once the loa was in possession, he could use the policeman to backtrack and find the man he sought.

Delacroix began to chant loudly, swaying from side to side, and he fanned his hands out palms up, gesturing to the night and the sacrifices he had made and he felt the loa returning to him, still hungry, still filled with the powerful magic Delacroix had given him. Delacroix felt his body move with the ecstasy of the forces filling him and when it was time, he sent the loa to do his bidding. For a moment, his own spirit soared as well, leaving the empty body to topple over sideways and lie twitching in the dust like a lizard's suddenly detached tail.

They came, like invisible smoke, out of the cat's green-gold eyes, exploding into the eyes and mouth and nose of the policeman as he bent to look, and they took him with no trouble at all. He had been holding the platter with the sacrifice upon it, and dropped it suddenly, stricken, the bleating of the lamb pulsating in time with the pounding of his heart. The loa was well pleased.

Delacroix withdrew before his own heart began a troubled beat and found his flesh cooling like the night, softly, gently, inexorably. He would be stiff in the morning, and perhaps insect bitten, but he would be full of the might of his magic.

He felt his loa take the blood of the lamb and leave the shanty, striding within the body of the policeman. The hunting would be good.

Brand lay curled in a fetal position. It seemed to help, although he could count on the fingers of both hands all his ex-wardmates it *hadn't* helped. He lay willing himself to see when he opened his eyes, the blankets of his bed all skirled around him like some gigantic nest. But he wasn't alone.

Bauer lay curled with him. Breathing with his breath, thinking with his thoughts, and all Brand could do was lie very still, terrified, horrified, at what would happen if he were blind, shut into the darkness with Bauer.

Bauer liked slicing. Maiming. Torturing. He lived somewhere deep inside Brand's mind, and he was imprinted there, behind his eyeballs. When there was nothing to be seen, he liked to show Brand *his* visions. Blood-streaked sights. Torn flesh. The cries of innocents.

Dr. Susan Craig had given him Bauer. Wrapped them together like a ball of yarn, rainbow yarn, whose strands changed color as you pulled them free, never quite sure which color would follow what. Brand's grandmother had always liked to knit with yarn dyed like that, until her heart had attacked her and she'd died. He twisted his fingers now in one of the afghans she'd made for his room. Indigo fading into blue fading into green fading into lime fading into indigo. . . .

Brand knew that Bauer was just waiting for Brand to fade away completely, waiting quietly, coiled away in the corners of his mind and thoughts, hiding in the shadows. As long as Brand could see at all, any point of light, he could wrestle Bauer back. This was still his body, his life.

As long as he could see. They wanted him shut away without light, warned him against it, but they did not understand it was more necessary than air to him.

Brand opened his eyes. As he looked across the room, the door jumped into sharp relief and then blurred abruptly. His heart leaped too. He'd never been able to see the door well without his glasses before. He sat up in bed, his chest thumping with apprehension, as a smudgy cloud lowered itself over everything he tried to view.

"Oh, God." He put his fingers up to his eyes, thinking to claw the veil away, unable to do more than just touch his flesh, unable to save himself, afraid of doing more damage than had already been done. Nothing he could do erased the smudges.

His heart felt as though it dropped away, right through the bottom of him, sinking like a lead anchor, through the bed, through the second-story flooring, the first floor, the house's foundation, the bedrock below it, and on into the center of the world, plunging downward.

Right into hell.

His chest immediately caved in on the vacuum. He couldn't breathe. His throat clenched. He was blind and locked in with Bauer. He was the scum of the earth. He was *evil* beyond imagining.

He was alone.

Brand hugged himself, doubled over. He panted, and his ears dully told him that he whimpered, over and over, "Yellow Dog, Yellow Dog," like it was some kind of mantra which would save him. His face grew damp. His heart returned to thump like a painful drum inside his body, making his pulse roar. He thought it would explode.

His mother knocked on the door.

"Brandon? Brandon, are you all right?"

He stuffed his fist into his mouth, as Bauer fought to answer, something incredibly crude and cruel. He chewed on his knuckles. He couldn't let her know. He found his tongue, forced a voice out.

"What?"

His mother peeked in. "Were you sleeping?" The hallway light was faint, a parchment yellow, but he found himself blinking painfully at it.

"Yeah."

She smiled weakly. "That's good, isn't it?"

If a living nightmare isn't in residence, waiting for night to fall. . . . He heard the relief in her voice. She walked the same tightrope he did, he thought suddenly, and she no more wanted him to unbalance her than vice versa. And part of that delicate act was not to be too involved. What he wanted, he thought, was a hug, but he would not get it from her. She feared he would shatter. And he feared she would refuse if he asked. So he did not.

"Yeah."

"How do your eyes feel?"

"Sore."

One of his sibs poked her head in. "Brandon, your eyes are all swollen! You look like a Mike Tyson fight victim."

"I wish." He grinned feebly. "Think of all that money."

She beamed even as their mother gently nudged her out the door, saying, "His doctor said bed rest today. Now leave him alone."

"But we're hungry."

"I want to make sure Brandon's all right."

He didn't need her hovering over him. He wanted company, but not theirs. He wanted to walk with people who knew him well enough to thump his shoulder but didn't ask him if he was sleeping well. If he was still sane. If he was going to be all right.

Phil appeared in the doorway, too, his bland face a pleasant blur. "Awake, sport?"

He really, really wanted all of them to leave. "Not much. Why don't you take the gang out somewhere? I'll be okay."

"What are you going to eat?"

"I'm not hungry."

"Well. . . ."

He could see a tiny movement of hesitation. Sweat beaded his upper lip. He was going to have another anxiety attack, he could feel his chest closing, like a vise of ice was gripping it, and he did not, DID NOT, want any witnesses. "Order me a pizza."

"I could do that."

Phil added, "I'll leave the money on the sofa table by the door, okay?"

A long pause. His mother repeated. "Okay, honey?"

He balled his hands back into fists. "Right. Gotcha." His voice sounded strained to himself, but they backed slowly away from his door.

"Don't forget to take your medicine," his mother called out faintly, and then she was gone.

He found himself holding his breath, looking at the closed door, as though she would come back, would invade again.

He had to get into the light. Nothing blazed brighter than the mall.

But he couldn't go like this. Brandon pushed himself out of bed. His eyes focused, then lost it again, but he knew his room well enough to get to his bureau. Once within hand-reach of it, even his damaged eyes could see it well enough.

He tore through the clouds and found the drawer he wanted and pulled it up. At the back, stuffed behind clothes which had been thrown in every which way, he found his stash. He took the bandanna out and opened it carefully.

Even to his dimmed sight, he could see the reds and yellows and blues, the black and whites, capsules and tablets. Hands shaking, he picked out what he needed. Horseshoe-shaped, with a hole in the center. Haldol. One made him mellow, dealt with anxieties and depression. Psychoactive. They'd taken him off it when the doctors had decided he wasn't schizophrenic, but they hadn't taken the prescription away, and he'd hidden his remaining tablets, for they had shielded him against Bauer. Today, he decided he needed help to keep Bauer at the gates. Two should do it. He shoved aside the bentyls and the Prozac. Not strong enough. He looked up, saw the vial of Vicodin the ophthalmologist had given him for pain. They had worked admirably so far that day. Again, two. "Better living through chemistry," he muttered and choked them down, following it with half a glass of tepid water left on the nightstand.

He crawled back into his nest and hugged his grandmother's

afghan to his body. He kept his eyes wide open until the first of the drugs overwhelmed him, and then the wave hit, an onslaught which quelled even Bauer, and Brand fell back onto the bed.

He was not used to the Vicodin, he thought. The codeine was giving him hallucinations. He thought he could hear a muttering, a snuffling, a dragging, like something from the graveyard coming after him. He could feel a cold touch sweep over him, blindly searching. He opened his raw eyes wide.

He saw it then, not Bauer, not Yellow Dog, but a thing . . . a thing like an elongated human shadow, a hungry thing, with a sucking mouth, traveling through his house, across his ceiling, searching, questing. He thought to touch it, and then recoiled.

Whatever it was, it was not human. Unlike Bauer, had never been. And was far, far worse.

It responded to his touch, shadow-thing and dove down at him.

Brand screamed until his throat went raw and flailed to leap out of bed, knocking his curtains aside, letting the last of the afternoon sun flood in. . . .

Yellow Dog leaped out of the sunlight, barking, snarling, after the shadow-thing, driving it away.

Brandon snatched up his sunglasses, both grateful and alarmed, and lay still on his bed until the pharmaceuticals began to buzz in his bloodstream. He did not remember Yellow Dog leaving or falling asleep.

He was awake, without remembering he'd awakened, the room smelling of pizza and cheese stringing from his fingers. He looked at himself in the mirror, image sharpening as he leaned toward the glass. "What a buzz! You answered the door and don't even remember it!" The Vicodin and Haldol surged through his bloodstream, an overwhelming sense of well-being and even, hey, how about this, happiness.

There were times when his mother approached all right, catching a glimpse of himself, dark hair and all, like a protegé Quentin Tarantino. The shades were awesome, even if he did have to stand almost chin close to see himself. His pupils looked huge, staring out of puffy lids. Brand giggled slightly, then cleared his throat and sobered. "I had eye surgery today," he told himself. "Keep your shades on."

The house was quiet. This feeling was too good to contain stowed away in his bedroom, with the lights on low, extra cheese and pep-peroni dripping over the crust, munching and wondering what to do.

He wanted to be hip, not good.

He wanted bright lights and action. Even if it hurt. Because noth-ing could touch him now.

Brand sighed.

The phone rang. He wiped grease-glistening fingers on his jeans and picked it up on the second ring. "Speaking."

"Hey, X-man. Feeling better? Your mom wouldn't let me talk to you earlier. Told me not to call on your line."

"No surprise. You're not exactly her favorite person after letting me get canned."

Curtis made a rude noise and said, "Your mom eats it."

"Hey, don't rag on her, all right. She tries, sometimes."

"No kidding? She must have done something right, huh, for you to care. So tell me."

"I've got Tarantino shades."

"Oh, shit. Really? How do they look?"

Brand sat straight up in his bed. The pizza box slid off his lap and landed sloppily on the floor, but it was still cool, it landed pizza side up. "They look great."

"Wear 'em to school tomorrow."

"Can't."

"Why not?"

"Don't think I'm going."

"Still feel bad?"

"No. I feel stoned. I need to make the mall. Okay?"

"Cool." Curtis hung up.

Brand stood up quickly and felt the answering throb in his eye-balls, reminding him. "Whoa—head rush." He put a hand to his brow as if he could check the sensation. He grinned at himself as he climbed out the bedroom window.

Chapter 8

It wasn't dark yet, but nearly, and the concrete peaks of the mall threw long, dark purple shadows across the canyons of the parking lot as Kamryn pulled in and scanned the employee lot over the steering wheel. On the unpopular side of the mall were the freight ramps where, descending into the lower level of the older mall, there were all sorts of nooks and crannies that she hesitated to walk by. The security cameras tended to focus on the front two-thirds of the oval shopping center, protecting the customer rather than the worker. Weather had been no factor in designing the center—what weather?—and so the parking lots swooped around the shops like a Grand Prix street circuit, flat and open to anyone and everyone.

Only the new, upscale stores had garage structures. Built on graded acreage, the mall was single story at the south end and rose three stories toward the grander shops at the northern end.

At the upper level, the new end, the parking garage which twinned Nordstrom's glared with light, except she saw, the third level, which lay plunged in darkness. Someone must have gone through and broken the bulbs again. Probably the skaters, intent on vandalism. It would take a day or two for maintenance to get in there and replace the fixtures. Meanwhile, there was no protection for her at all except alertness. Leaning over, she thumped all the door locks into place, as though that could make some sort of safe house or fortress out of the vehicle. The irony of her actions did not escape her.

She gathered her wallet and climbed out the driver's door, looking across the lot. It wasn't too crowded, which might give her something of a break as it was her night to work the coffee bar, something she normally did not mind, but she did not feel right about tonight. An odd sensation had been crawling over her skin all day, a sensation she would not place and did not like. She had tried several times to call Lyndall to talk things over with her—her friend had a natural psychic sense about things, but the ringing phone had never been answered.

She chafed her fingers lightly over her long sleeves, trying to soothe the healing skin underneath. Maybe it was just her nerves reacting to the laser work. She felt raw, every nerve exposed. Or maybe she just didn't feel like going to work. Sometimes she wondered how other people did it, by rote. Not that Darby had ever worked to take care of her. Darby was only a temporary port in a storm, shelter she'd taken out of desperation, and now that she could think clearly, she was well rid of him.

Kamryn slowed as she approached the concrete stairwell which descended into the back wing of the mall. The store didn't want employees coming in the back door anymore. Hot Flash had posted a new policy that entrances must be made into the mall itself, and then into the store by the front. She hesitated at the top step, looking down into a hole that already lay pooled in darkness, thinking that she was probably the only one who minded.

Her feet refused to make the descent. Kamryn swallowed tightly. For a moment, she thought she could feel the steely hand upon her neck, gripping her, the hard barrel of a gun digging into her flesh just below her opposite ear.

Come on, sis. Come down into the basement with me. I've got a surprise for you.

Her joints locked. She could not move, could not take that first step. It wasn't the basement of her old Pennsylvania home, she knew that. But she couldn't help staring down into the black pool of shadows, and she couldn't help the tremors of fear that began to ripple through her body.

Come on, sis. I've got a surprise for you.

Now, as she had then, she began to pray. *God, get me through this, and I'll change. I swear I will. Just get me through this.*

Those stairs were not these stairs. As she told herself that, her knees bent and she went down a step. Kamryn fought to take a steadying breath. Was this like claustrophobia? Did it have a name, this choking tightness in her chest, this panic that made her ears deaf and her heart explode into her throat and her bowels clench?

Stair-o-phobia.

The thought loosened a squeaky laugh. She put a hand out to catch herself, and jammed a thumb into the hard wall of the stairwell. That brought a curse, hoarse and barely audible, but the sound of her own voice echoed. It pierced the numbness that gripped her. She cleared her throat, stuffing down the air, trying to relax.

There's nothing down here but a turn at the bottom and a door into a universe of shoppers. That's it. That's all.

Kamryn managed another step. She could feel the leading edge of coolness where the shadows lay. It was like plunging into a swimming pool, she told herself. Brisk. Cold. Frightening, but without reason. There was nothing to be afraid of here. She had run from Pennsylvania and even though Darby was not the haven, the guardian, she'd wanted him to be, still she was not living the nightmare any longer.

She plunged down the last four steps, stilt-legged, at breakneck speed, but that was the only way she was going to get down them, at this rate, and she dropped her wallet on the last step and kicked it, skidding, around the corner toward the entrance door. It disappeared in the darkness. Anger replaced the phobia.

"Oh, shit." Kamryn bent over to retrieve it.

"I've got it."

Her choked lungs kept her from screaming. She bolted backward, fetching up against the wall, trapped, caught, nowhere to run. She felt her eyes bulge, her throat paralyzed. Grime-encrusted hands came out of the enveloping darkness, groping toward her, fingers wrapped about the wallet.

"Don't scream. I didn't mean to scare you."

He took a step toward the mall door and the faint illumination cast from it. She saw the disheveled hair, the worn and somewhat dirty clothes, but it took a moment longer to place the face. She knew this man, a transient who'd been hanging about the mall almost as long as she'd been working there.

Kamryn didn't feel much better about touching him. She stared at her wallet.

"I'm sorry. Really. I didn't mean to scare you," he repeated. "Don't yell or anything. Please."

"I'm lucky I can breathe." Kamryn took her wallet back gingerly. "What are you doing down here?"

"Other than scaring people?"

"This is an employee entrance. I *know* you're not working here."

"No," he said dryly. "I'm not working here." He looked behind her, to where the sunlight gleamed across the top of the stairs, as if deciding on something. "I'm trying to avoid somebody."

"What did you do?"

"Nothing."

"Someone's looking for you?"

"I think so."

"Police?"

He hesitated, then shook his head.

"You must have done something."

"Sometimes," he answered slowly, "all you have to do is exist."

She wasn't all that certain that what he was doing was even on that level.

She steeled herself against her gut reaction, answering, "I won't tell anyone you're here, but if you're hiding, this is not the place to do it. Hot Flash has everyone coming in here now."

"Thanks for the tip." He started upward, then turned. "You won't tell anyone—"

"You scared the hell out of me? No." She felt her lips twist in a lopsided smile. "Besides, somebody's already done that to me."

He gave her a saluting nod and continued to the parking lot. She watched him disappear. The panic had ebbed, leaving behind a raw chill. She decided she needed a good, strong cup of coffee and she knew exactly where to get it. Kamryn pressed through the door into the mall, gathering enough wits to think, *Thank God it wasn't Darby.* The thought sent her hurrying down the marble corridor.

"Watch out for Brewster's rottweiler," Curtis warned as they skirted the corner.

"She loose again?"

"Mom says she's going to call Animal Control. Says the dog's gonna kill somebody someday."

Brand took his friend's opinion in silence. He personally liked rottweilers, but like many of the bigger guard dog breeds, they'd been spoiled by bad owners. He was of the opinion no dog was born bad. As they rounded the yard where the dog was kept, he looked through the chain-link. The wind, threatening all day to pick up into Santa Anas, rattled the fencing and the dog came charging from behind the stucco house, barking loudly. To his surprise, he could see her quite well.

Curtis jumped, but Brand halted. She was a beautiful dog, even frothing in anger at their intrusion as she was, heavily muscled, black and tan, with eyes a cinnamon brown. He looked at her, wondering what she saw in him, gawky teenager in cool shades, and something dark and splintery crossed his eyes. *Damnit.*

The dog's barking beat at his senses. He waited to see if the splinters would leave, but they didn't. He clenched his jaw in irritation. Curtis tugged at his arm, indicating they should beat it, but Brand shook his head. His eyes watered a little and he blinked furiously to clear his vision. The dog lunged against the chain-link, spittle flying, ivory teeth clashing. With every bark, a cloud of hatred seemed to be emerging, a thin, smoky substance which enveloped the animal. Brand stood in wonderment.

"What is that?"

"That is one angry dog-bitch. Now let's get out of here," Curtis shouted over the rottweiler's incessant barking.

Froth from her lips splattered the knee of his jeans. She snapped at the air and more spittle went flying.

"Oh, man," Curtis groaned. He wiped his face with the back of his hand. "This is too gross. Come on!"

Brand stayed, rocked back on his heels, transfixed. "You don't see anything else?"

"I see a fence between us, and a house that's gonna spit out some angry broad in about two seconds. Brand-on, please."

Brand put the tip of his forefinger at the edges of his glasses frame and, very carefully, edged them up, just a little, so he could look at the dog. He could see the charcoal smoke had not really dissipated, but had settled about the animal like a cloak, like a big, dark Darth Vader cloak.

"Brand!"

"All right, all right, I'm coming." He let Curtis haul him down the street until the dog's baritone barking faded to nearly nothing. He looked back over his shoulder. The rottweiler stood in the full blast of the last of the setting sun, and she looked like a thunderhead. The clarity with which he'd first seen her fled. Brand stood a moment, dealing with the uncertainty of his life and vision.

"I can't deal with this if you're going to weird out on me," Curtis said.

He didn't know if he could deal with it either. He didn't have that many drugs. The irony of it tugged at the corner of his mouth before he answered.

"I like dogs."

"Not that one. I swear she's a killer."

"Only because she's been taught that way."

"Mom says it's the backyard breeders. You know, cross one bad temperament with another. Anything for money. You end up with mean pups, or scared ones that'll go mean. Anyway, she doesn't trust that one."

"Don't blame her."

Curtis looked him full in the face. "Thought you liked her."

"I do, but—" Brand shrugged. "There was something about her. You know?"

Curtis tried a demented laugh, finishing, "The Shadow knows what evil lurks in the hearts of men. And dogs."

Brand smiled thinly. "Something like that, I guess." They crossed the last intersection approaching the mall and its lesser plazas. "That must be where Nova got Captain Evel from."

"The Shadow?"

"Sure. He can see the alien possessed, right?"

"Yeah, but—"

"They stole him. Plain as anything. I wonder if they can sue."

"Who?"

"The Shadow people. Wonder if there's anybody alive who owns the rights."

"Like I care."

"Your dad's a lawyer. You should." Brand gave Curtis an affectionate shove.

"My dad," said Curtis in a mix of admiration and disgust, "can sue anything that walks." He added, "Anyway, Nova's a cool game."

"It doesn't exactly suck," Brand agreed.

"So, if you could do it, would you?"

"Do what?"

Curtis twisted his face. "See evil."

"If it were possible."

"Let's say it was. Let's say you went to see the Dalai Lama or somebody like that, and they took a sacred crystal and they implanted it in your forehead, right between your eyes, like a third eyeball or something, only nobody else could see it. And whenever you looked through it, you could see all evil."

"You're really into this."

Curtis bumped him. "Just answer me. Would you?"

He didn't want to answer, but he knew Curtis would bug him all the way to the arcade if he didn't. "Hell, no."

"No?"

"No. Everybody's got their dark side—we've all done something. Stomped ants or something. Forget it, Curtis." His voice changed slightly, uncomfortably. "And don't tell me you would. You'd rather have X-ray vision and see through people's clothes."

"You wouldn't do?"

"Absolutely not."

"But you play Captain Evel."

"That's different. I like stomping aliens." They completed their walk arguing over finessing the finer strategies of the game.

Approaching the arcade, Curtis ground to a halt. "Whoop, whoop. Old dude at the doorway."

Brand looked. He saw a tall, dark-haired man in a suit half-blocking the doorway, with papers in his hands. He wore a tie, but had unbuttoned the collar of his shirt and loosened the knot. His skin had been pitted horribly and Brand let his stare slide away.

"Evenin' boys," the man said and let his white, even teeth show in a half-smile.

They stopped warily.

"I'm looking for somebody. Think you might help?"

He had a slight accent, just enough to tell Brand that he wasn't from around southern California, and his tone was a little too casual. He didn't look like a casual person. His spine was ramrod stiff.

"Aren't you a little old to be hanging around arcades?" Curt answered.

The man flushed slightly, but Brand sensed it was not with embarrassment. The man's hands twitched. He held up the pages. "Maybe you can tell me if you've seen him around anywhere?"

"You a cop?"

"No, no. Nothing like that. I'm an attorney. He's inherited some money and the family wants me to find him. You could help him out. He might even be real grateful you did."

Curt bypassed Brand and kicked him lightly in the foot as he went, and disappeared into the arcade. The man stayed, head slightly atilt, eyes locked on Brand.

This was no attorney. Curt had let him know that as he went by. But Brand didn't think he was a cop either. So the curiosity of what he was, and what he wanted, held him. His gaze flickered to the pictures, one a copy of a photo, and the other a drawing. He looked at them briefly through his Quentin Tarantino shades.

Then he shook his head. "Haven't seen him."

The inquirer shook the papers. "You're sure?"

"Listen, like I pay attention to people like that. I've got better things to do." Brand shrugged. "Try a milk carton."

He turned sideways and shifted past into the arcade. Curtis was waiting for him. He snaked his hand out and collared Brand, dragging him into the twilight safety.

"What'd you say to him?"

"Nothing much. Did that look like Mitch to you?"

"No. What do you think?"

"Maybe," Brand said slowly. "Maybe not. What do you think he wants him for?"

"Nothing good," retorted Curtis mournfully. "Nothing good."

Brand looked back over his shoulders where the propped open door showed no one lurking. The man had gone. He straightened his shirt where his friend had collared him. "Did he look funny to you?"

"He looked scary."

Brand was not sure he had repaid his debt to Mitch. He pulled aside, to the pay phone, and placed a call to the Brea police department. He cleared his throat, waiting for the desk to pick up. The faint *beep* which told him the call was being recorded sounded almost before the desk sergeant's voice.

"Brea Police."

"Hi. Um, I'm calling from the mall." Brand let his voice go high and breathy, trying to recapture the tones of his immature self. "There's a guy hanging around here—an old guy—and well, he doesn't seem normal, if you know what I mean."

"Has he been bothering anyone?"

"Well . . . not yet. But he has this picture he keeps showing around, someone he says he wants to find, and he wants one of us to go with him to look."

Curtis twitched a lip at him as their eyes met, and he gave a thumbs up. "We shouldn't go with him, should we? I mean, my mom always said—"

"We'll send somebody over to talk to him," the desk sergeant said. "Can you give me a description?"

Brand repeated the most accurate description of the stranger he could remember. He added, "Uh-oh," and hung up, cutting off the desk sergeant in mid-sentence.

The desk sergeant listened to dead air, and then the dial tone. He thought for a moment, when a faint *beep* reminded him that the call had been monitored. If it had been legitimate, and not a prank, there would be a record. And if it had been some kid fooling with his mind, there was a record of that, too. It was a win-win situation from where he was sitting.

He took a look at the duty board. Nicholas Solis was cruising the afternoon shift, one of the few who hadn't been involved in the high-speed chase and wasn't up to his knees in paperwork. Nick was amiable and streetwise. He put out a call, sending him to check up on things at the gaming center at the mall.

"That ought to take care of him."

Brand pushed his sunglasses into place. "I think so."

Curtis turned away, his interest already riveted on the machines. "Got any more quarters?"

Brand slipped one from his pocket, rolled it through his fingers and produced it, sleight of hand, in midair. His friend snatched it away. Despite the wave he rode, of being stoned, events were eating away at his edge. He did not know sleight of hand—Bauer did.

Oh, my, Grandmother, what quick fingers you have.

The better to slice you with, my dear. And, instead of the silvery coin, he could see a knife blade gripped in his hand.

He would not scream. Or sweat. Or faint. He just simply would *be,* and in that being, Bauer still could not gain the foreground. As long as there was light, as long as he could see, as long as he was not left alone with the dark. Brand did not move for another long minute, staring at the beam of sunlight through the doorway, weak and diluted as it was as the sun set. When he finally turned away, it was fighting the instinct to rub his eyes, as though he could clear them of the smudges. The doctor had warned him of flare, but this was not a flash of light or bright aura. The blurring had begun to sharpen, replaced by this strange phenomenon he could not name.

This was something dark and dreadful.

Nick found himself sitting at the light, coming down out of the Brea hills, waiting for the signal to change. He stank of blood. His driver's side window was down, as if he'd needed to gulp in fresh air. He looked at his hands and found them, still pink and sticky, fingers wrapped tightly about the steering wheel.

"Oh, Jesus." He pried his hands away, the skin burning, as though the dried blood had stuck him like glue to the wheel. He leaned over to the glove box, where he kept those packets of cleansing towels and as he did, he saw what rode in the passenger seat.

"Shit!"

The cat's head seemed to eye him with fogged green orbs, the rusty hairs of his neck serrated and matted even more rusty with dried blood and ganglia. Without conscious thought, he scooped up the object and threw it out his window, then sat sweating by the open portal.

"Dear God in heaven." How had he gotten it—and why?

Nick tore the towelette open and rubbed his hands clean, scrubbing them over and over and over. When he'd finished, he found himself thinking of retrieving the head, bringing it back to the woman who'd owned and loved that cat, but he couldn't bring himself to touch it. Not again. His mouth felt dry as cotton, and his hands shook as he put the window back up.

This was stupid. But he'd gone into that arroyo and done something he couldn't remember, and come back with an object so horrible that it gave him the heaves just to think of it—

Get a grip, Nicky. You've seen worse in South Central.

Yeah, which is why I'm riding *here* tonight.

Nick took a steadying breath.

There was nobody at the light but him, and so he sat through two complete cycles, shaking, trying to remember what had happened. Nothing came to mind. When the dispatcher came over the radio, sending him to the mall, it sounded like a good idea. Bright lights and people, mindless yuppies, shining auras of streetlights over the parking lots.

Nothing like the dark canyon where he seemed to have temporarily lost his mind.

Nick gave a last shudder and when the light turned green, he let the patrol car surge forward in answer.

Chapter 9

Sandy had purple-red hair, finger-waved about her head, large hazel eyes, and a sprinkling of cinnamon freckles over her nose. She also had a navel ring, set off by the trendy crop-top blouse she wore and a short suede leather skirt. She met Kamryn at the espresso bar, her full lips set into a pout.

"Cam-er-on," she greeted. "The freakin' espresso machine is not working a-*gain*. I can't do anything."

Kamryn stifled a sigh as she pulled the hot pink and yellow chef's apron on over her head. "Did you close the valves, Sandy? Did you check them?"

Sandy put a hand on her hip, the Hot Flash bar where one of the front display windows would normally have been, and studied the monster espresso machine that took up half the back counter. "The whole flippin' machine is nothin' but valves. How would I know?"

Kamryn approached the machine, assuming an air of calm. If she said anything to Sandy, she would get a mouth full of attitude back, and sulkiness all evening. Espresso bar duty was hellish enough without having to run it by herself—and Sandy in a sulk was less than nothing. She checked the settings and valves swiftly, found that two had been left open, closed them, and then ran through the last of the check. "Got it. Why don't you weigh the grind, make sure we've got enough for tonight?"

Sandy stepped in and busied herself.

Kamryn opened the refrigerator doors to double-check the

milk, whipping cream, and other perishables. "Looks like we're in business."

"I don't know," Sandy said slowly, her voice muffled as she looked into the various coffee grind containers, "why I just can't seem to get the espresso machine to work."

"It's just temperamental. And it's not that you can't get it to work. You just have trouble getting it started. It's working now," Kamryn said pointedly.

"True. You're just cool with things like that. And, like with the gloves you wear and all." She cast an envious hazel eye on the lacy half-gloves Kamryn wore. They hid the rough pink patches from the laser work. She'd cut the fingers off halfway, like some of the winter mitten styles, and Sandy was one of the girls from Hot Flash who'd commented on them. Sandy measured out some Java Gold beans and poured them into the grinder. "They've got the transfer aps out."

"Oh?" Kamryn had been waiting for the forms. "Where to?"

"Seattle and Palo Alto. I don't know." Sandy shrugged. "The Bay Area is all right, but I wouldn't want to go to Seattle. For one thing, it rains all the time, and for the other—half of everybody there is already from California."

"Sounds all right to me."

"Yeah, but—" Sandy gave her a sideways glance from under a swinging purple tress. "Don't you have a boyfriend or something?"

"Had. The farther away I get, the better."

"Oh." The girl punctuated her understanding with a burst from the grinder. "It won't get busy for another half hour or so, when the theater lets out. I'll watch it if you want to pick up some applications. You have to ask for them . . . 'opportunities are limited,' " she added, mocking the cold tones of the store manager. She poured the freshly ground coffee into the container. "And if you're looking for a new boyfriend, you could always pick up the one from the arcade." She laughed, a high, whining sound.

"The arcade?" Kamryn was halfway around the counter, and stopped.

"You know the one. He's about shoulder high—got a crush on you, girl. In fact, he's watching you now."

Kamryn got an icy feeling up the back of her neck and turned her head slightly, trying to see into the dark mouth of the arcade, several door fronts away. She could see only milling forms, and then one stood out, his pale face accented by sunglasses, ridiculous to see in the gaming den's twilight. She let her breath out.

Sandy added her opinion. "He'll be cute when he grows up."

Kamryn twisted her lips into a smile. "If it's a male, you think it's cute," she returned.

"Hey." The girl shrugged. "Aren't they?" She corrected herself. "I guess not if you're leaving one behind."

Kamryn didn't feel like talking about it. "I'll be right back," she answered, and pushed her way into the clothing store.

"Pull in over there," Snake told Darby. He lay half-coiled in the back seat, one shod foot firmly planted on the back passenger window, the other tucked away under his leg. The parking garage had corners full of dark possibility, and the level they drove on had few cars—no one wanted to walk if they had to, and so the lower levels were packed. Snake took his foot down and straightened in the car seat. He stuck his hand out over the seat.

"Gimme the piece."

Darby opened his mouth as if to protest, then shut his lips firmly. He handed over the .32. Snake closed his fingers around the heavy chrome piece and said, admiringly, "This is going to make some fuckin' noise when it goes off."

Darby looked at it, thinking of Kamryn. Thinking that he had made his choice, and the bitch deserved everything that was coming to her, but even so. . . .

"I promised you, didn't I?" said Snake smoothly, as if reading his mind.

"You did."

"The bitch earned it. You took her in when she was in trouble, protecting her, protecting her brother, and now she's turning her back on us. On the Brotherhood." Snake's eyes were avid on the gun. He held it to his lips and his tongue flicked out in a quick caress, tasting the cold metal. "I ought to put it in her mouth and make her suck it off, just like it was a cock, my cock, and then—*Bam!* Brains all over the place."

"Snake—"

"Shut up." His languor fled, his attention to the exterior, to the parking garage. "Somebody's out there."

"What do you mean—"

Snake threw himself into the front seat of the car. "What the fuck do you think I mean?" He tucked the gun under his thigh. "Get out and go find him."

"He couldn't have heard anything."

"Doesn't matter." Snake showed his teeth, yellow, crooked, too sharp. "If someone else is up here, sneaking around, I want to know about it. Now go get him."

Darby slid out of the car reluctantly. He could see nothing, but he heard the sound as the vehicle *ponged* faintly to remind him that he'd left his keys in the ignition. The scurrying noise could be rats or it could be someone else hugging the shadows. He walked casually toward the garage elevator as if he had heard nothing, had nothing else to do but take the elevator down and enter the mall, all the while listening behind him and to his flank, where shadows pooled the darkest behind cement columns.

Another scrape. Darby whirled, took three leaping steps and came upon the man. As the quarry straightened, Darby swung about, kicking high, and took him in the chest, hard. He could feel it all the way through the heavy lug nut soles of his shoes.

The other fell back with a gasping grunt, collapsing onto the balcony edge of the garage. His face caught the scant illumination from a nearby lamppost.

White scum. Worse than black or brown or yellow scum, because he was white. He could have been somebody.

Darby inhaled tightly and stood over the man, taking in the worn clothing, the long hair, the clean but sun-darkened face. "Homeless scum," he said, and spat, out of the way of the approaching Snake.

"Good job," Snake told him, as he came into the small beacon of light himself, and his tattoos glowed. The butt of the gun showed from his waist where he had tucked it in.

The scum saw it, too, a quick look, and Darby tensed.

"I've got nothing."

"You've got a white skin. That counts for something, don't it, Darby?"

Don't use my name, Darby thought, too late. He sniffed. "He's a disgrace."

"Maybe. Maybe not." Snake walked one way and then the other, sizing up their prey. "Maybe he's just tired of all of them little brown faces and black faces getting what he ought to. Maybe it was all just enough for a fella to quit, instead of fighting back."

Their prey straightened up a little. Darby watched him catch his breath, knowing he could be dangerous now, if he wanted to be. But he wouldn't be. This type survived on being anonymous, like a piece of litter on the beach.

The captive held up his hands. "I haven't done anything, and you haven't done anything. Let's call it square, and I'll be on my way."

Snake dropped a palm onto the handle of the .32. "I don't think so. I think we need your help."

"What kind of help?"

"Directions. You probably know this area pretty well. Darby and me, we don't. We're lookin' for a place called the Hot Flash."

Darby shifted his weight uneasily. He didn't like Snake's tossing around of his name, nor could he see the sense of getting someone else involved. As he rocked from one foot to another, Snake uncannily looked at him, and straight into his eyes, and smiled. As if he was reading his thoughts again.

"I could probably help you with that," the scum replied. "Unless you're planning to rob it."

"Smart man. You're talking about this," and Snake rubbed the butt of the revolver again. "This is just for protection. We're not too far from La Habra, y'know, and there's a lot of gangs in La Habra. Some of them have no reason to like us." Snake's eyes glittered. "No, my bud got a girl works here. We're here to give her a ride home. We're like, her bodyguards."

Darby thought, *Who's he fooling?* but the white scum flexed his shoulders and said, "I can live with that."

"Good. Let's go see if we can find her."

The scumbag looked across the floor of the parking garage, hesitating. Then, "What's in it for me?"

"I don't need a gun," Snake answered, "to do a lot of damage. You're like a scab on the face of the community. I don't think anybody would mind if we picked you off."

Their captive made up his mind quickly. "I get you inside the door, and I'm gone."

*   *   *   *

Snake showed his teeth slightly. The tattoos on his skull rippled. "Oh," he agreed. "You're gone, all right."

Jon Fleming looked at himself inside the Brea security office, catching his reflection on a monitor as his Casio went off, beep-beep, beep-beep. He punched it silent and rechecked the time. Yup, it was just about time for break and to mosey down to the Hot Flash espresso bar. That dark-haired girl should be there, the one who was older, wiser, and prettier than most of the high school bimbos who worked down there selling to the trendies. She liked him, he sensed it instinctively. He'd known it the first time they'd swapped gazes. Now he wanted to be swapping spit with her. No time like the present to go down and make his intentions known.

He smoothed down his collar and hiked his belt. He liked the mall security uniform, it was almost as good as the county's sheriff uniform, although his time in that one had been very short before he'd washed out. He liked the center's winter outfit best. The summer outfit came with a pair of tailored bermuda shorts that, frankly, made Jon look like a mailman. He preferred the power image of the full suit. The mall was the best of both worlds, he'd decided long ago. It had the prestige, the community service, with little of the stress. Not that ugly things couldn't happen in here, like the year some woman was killed in the parking lot by her estranged husband, but that didn't happen on his watch, by God. Not on his watch.

As he approached the door to the tiny cubicle of the security post, it began to swing open with a fraction of a squeak. A man leaned in, nicely suited, though his shirt had been opened at the collar for comfort, a man who was both handsome and ravaged looking at the same time.

Jon instinctively reacted to protect his territory. "Excuse me, sir, but this area is not open to the public—"

"Officer Fleming? I was hoping to have a word with you." He flashed a badge that Jon barely caught a glimpse of, save perhaps the image of the spread eagle. ATF? Had it said ATF on it?

Embarrassed at his failure to recognize the emblem, Jon retreated. "Is there a problem?" His chair hit the back of his knees, and Fleming sat abruptly.

"No, sir, not at all. I was hoping that you could be of assistance to me in locating a suspect."

His help was needed. Jon put his chin out. "I could certainly try."

"Good. Good. I thought you might. But I was hoping to review the perimeter security videos over the last, say, forty-eight hours."

"Review the tapes?"

The agent smiled. "That's the idea, son. Now, I don't want to get anybody in trouble here, this isn't being done officially. Yet."

"You don't have to worry about that. I have the authority. Have a seat." Jon pointed a finger at the extra chair and swung his about, reaching for the tape library. The bank of monitors showed him his profile, lean, decisive. There would be time later to go down and make a good impression at the Hot Flash. He had business here and now.

"This will take a while," he said. "Even skimming it."

"That's all right." The agent unbuckled his jacket and sat back in the chair. "I have time."

The October night had grown chilly, dry, and cold, and the few leaves which had fallen skittered outside over the mall parking lot like scurrying animals. Kamryn caught a hint of the wind and night every time the main entrance to the wing opened, and new customers hurried in. The line at the espresso counter went knee-deep. She found herself barking at Sandy to keep up.

She mopped her forehead once, and found her lacy mittens were almost more damp than her skin. She wanted to strip the gloves off and cool down, but the healing scabs from the lasering made her hands look like pink, scaly freaks. She topped off another cappuccino with steamed milk and smiled at the customer. "Cinnamon sprinkles or chocolate or both?"

"Both, young lady, if you don't mind," said the gentleman. He had gray feathering the wings of his hair, and the woman he was ordering for smiled indulgently as if aware her escort was flirting with Kamryn.

She smothered a sigh and bent her head over the drinks.

"I think it's time for a break," Brand said. The back of his neck itched, and he could feel sweat trickling down his pits inside his shirt. Sweating off the drugs. Not too fast, not too soon, he prayed. He hitched up a shoulder to relax muscles grown tense at the video game. It was too hot inside the arcade, overcompensating for the briskness of the night outside.

"Something cold and wet," Curtis agreed. He stepped away from the main floor of the arcade, and followed the direction Brand stared in. He groaned. "Coffee was not what I had in mind."

"Jerk," returned Brand. "They've got cold drinks, too."

"If you don't mind me saying so, caffeine is the last high you need."

"I mind." Brand repositioned his shades. "I'm wired for sound and I'd like to stay that way." He stepped outside the main arcade entrance and maneuvered his way into the line at the espresso bar which the girl was serving. He could see her name tag from five deep in the line, and read it. Kamryn. He tried it out silently, tasting it, and liked it. She stood, half-shadowed by the espresso bar sign, or maybe it was his sight again, for she was neither wholly in the light nor smudged completely. He lifted his glasses and rubbed gently at his right eye. It felt as though smog was eating away at it. He dropped his shades back into place and waited.

A blast of wind skirled down the marble corridor and he turned to face it. He could not only smell and feel the air, he could see it, thin blue-gray, like the exhaust from a car or the last puff from a smoldering fire. Like some kind of toxic fog, it wafted toward him and he stepped backward instinctively, bumping into Curtis.

Curt shoved him gently aside. "Watch it."

"I am," Brand answered absently. He found himself blinking rapidly, but the smudge through his eyesight stubbornly remained. "Shit."

"What is it? You weirding out on me, X-man?"

"I'm not doing shit," Brand fired back, "and if you don't like it, you can just shove off."

"Hey." Curt lifted his palms in surrender. "Chill out, okay?"

Brand did not respond. He stared down the mall floor, toward the source of the breeze, and saw three people crossing the marble expanse. His newfound vision sharpened for a moment, then blurred again, but not before he'd recognized Mitch through dark fractals splintering his view. Mitch shone silvery, as though he attracted what light his vision could pick up. The other two he did not know and he paused, waiting for them to draw closer.

"That's Mitch, isn't it?"

"Think so."

"Who's that with him?"

Curtis grabbed his elbow and started to pull him away from the coffee stand, saying, "I don't think those guys like us."

Brand identified their shaven skulls. "Skinheads," he muttered. What was Mitch doing with skinheads? They wore jackboots, and their progress was anything but quiet. It discomfited him to see Mitch elbow to elbow with them.

Curt let out a low, breathy whistle. "Can you see that, Brand? Can you see the tattoos on that guy?"

He could, for a cystalline, if dark, moment. The guy wore his shirt open and short-sleeved, and the skin artwork moved over him as if it were alive. Brand brought a hand up to rub his eyes and rid them of the stain. The inkwork reminded him of something, but he could not quite grasp it, except to stand and stare in thought.

The low, gentle murmurs of customers waiting in line were shattered by the fall of a coffee mug to the marble below. Brand whirled around and saw Kamryn, face as pale as ice, staring. She pushed behind her assistant as if she thought to flee the stand. One of the skinheads moved out, flanking her.

"Where do you think you're going, Kamryn?"

She stood her ground, one hand tugging absently at her apron. "Don't bother me."

"Oh. I get it. Don't freaking bother *you*." The young one, the one with dull brown hair, what there was of it, let his lip curl. "You stole my bike and sold it."

"You gave it to me. I needed the money." Her voice shook a little, but her face, her stance, stayed dead calm.

Brand felt his knees wobble slightly in sympathy. People, muttering, moved away. Kamryn watched them go and called out, "Someone call Security. Please."

The tattooed one flexed his biceps. "Now the bitch says please."

Her eyes shut for a long second. "Darby," she said. "I won't go with you."

"That hog was a classic."

"I know." Something like a smile flickered briefly over her mouth. "I got good money for it." She tugged the apron off over her head.

The ruffled edges of it caught on her mittens and one of them came off as well, exposing pinkish, raw skin.

Darby stared.

Her hand fluttered away as though it had a life of its own, hid in the wrappings of the apron.

"Where's my name, Kamryn? What happened to our ring tattoo?"

"Gone. Just like me. And I'm not coming back. I don't know how you found me . . . Lyndall, I suppose. But I'll just go farther next time. Now why don't you leave before Snake talks you into doing something stupid?"

Darby protested, "Snake don't tell me what to do," but it was punctuated by Snake's hissing laughter.

Brand thought it was funny. Before he could stifle the impulse, he laughed, too. Aloud. Loud enough that Mitch looked at him. Looked sharply at them and then down at Snake's belt buckle. Brand followed the glance, saw that the belt buckle looked bulky and warped somehow . . . the butt of a gun.

The sucker had a gun tucked inside the front of his jeans. He stopped laughing abruptly.

"Come on!" Darby started forward, grabbing at her. She twisted away and kicked him, trying for his balls and missing, catching him in the long, lean thigh muscles. He let out a blistering curse and doubled anyway.

Brand lurched forward to help Kamryn. Curt caught at his elbow, bumping him, and his glasses came off. They hit the floor with an explosion of plastic, and it seemed that time came to a halt, everyone moving with slow, exaggerated gestures.

The tattooed skinhead reached for his gun. Mitch moved then, striking at the pistol, and Brand realized why he had been standing there, why he had stayed with them, why he now lunged for the weapon, lightning moving among the stormy clouds of darkness in Brand's vision. They grappled and the pistol fell. It slid across the marble as if across ice. It came to a rest at Darby's boots. He scooped it up.

Brand unfroze his own feet and shook off Curt. He threw himself through the thickening air, forever it took, forever and a day, through fog and blazing sunlight, through the dappling of light and shadow, the figures etched crystal clear and then blurred almost beyond recognition.

He hit the skinhead's wrist as Darby leveled the pistol, saying, "I'm not taking no for an answer, bitch."

The gun fired. Kamryn jerked with a scream and went to her knees, scrambling across the tiles. Brand could hear other screams of panic, and the glass behind the espresso's neon sign shattered into a thousand diamonds, cascading downward.

Brand tottered off balance and went down on his hip point. He could see Kamryn scrambling, knew she hadn't been hit, she was moving too well.

The gun shouted again. Someone screamed sharply and went down, the other girl at the counter with the waved purple hair, her eyes opened and glazed, staring nowhere. Brand looked into her face. He thought he saw . . . but how could he . . . he thought he saw a fine white steam coming out of her half-open mouth, and her nostrils, and even—Jesus, even her eyes. He shrank back.

Real time came back with a thundering in his ears. Someone grabbed him by the ankles and yanked him away from Darby and the line of fire, flipped him onto his feet. Mitch stared down at him.

"Run," he said. "Get in the arcade." He left Brand standing and started for Darby, and Snake tackled him.

"Holy shit," Curtis said, and they hugged each other and ran like they'd been tied together for a three-legged race for the safety of the arcade, which had gone abruptly dark, the store lights turned off, only the machine faces gleaming like obscene stars. He stepped on someone already hugging the floor.

Curtis couldn't stop talking. "What did you do that for? What did you think you were doing? Did you make him shoot that girl? Was she dead? You looked at her, Brand, right in the face . . . was she dead? He could have killed all of us, he could have—"

"Shut up!" Brand shouted in his face, and his friend went still. Mitch fought with both men, and he watched for a moment, appraising the action. Mitch looked like he could handle himself.

He went down on one knee, yanking Curtis down with him. Where was Kamryn? What was she doing? He peered around the base of the arcade machine.

She came toward him.

"Kamryn!" He held his hand out.

On her hands and knees, she looked up, ebony hair wispy about her face, eyes wide with desperation. The struggle of the three men behind her framed her. She saw him and reached for him.

Like the snake for which he was inked, and named, the skinhead wrapped himself around Mitch, bearing him down. Darby lunged free of the tangle, pistol still in his hand, barrel waving about wildly.

Brand sucked in his breath, took her hand, and pulled her into the cloak of the arcade room. Curtis bolted to his feet.

"What are you doing—"

His voice cracked, breaking off high and sharp. As Brand turned to look at him, he realized the pistol had spoken at the same time.

Simultaneously.

Exploding high and sharp.

Curtis toppled over.

He flopped against the base of the arcade machine like a rag doll. "Brandon," he exhaled fearfully, voice bubbling out, weak and thin, white with foggy condensation like that girl's had been. A crimson flower blossomed down the front of his shirt.

Brand let out a tiny sound. It might have been a sob. It might have been a gasp. The girl moved against his knees, and they both looked up, toward the doorway, where Darby stood, pistol in hand.

Nick wheeled into the south end of the mall as the dispatcher's voice crackled urgently, "All units, we have a report of shots fired at the Brea Mall. All units, shots fired at the Brea Mall."

His pulse quickened.

He reached for the mike. "I'm already here, send backup."

"Roger that, Solis. Unit 5 is already on the scene, backup requested."

He could see people running from the southwest entrance and guided the patrol car down onto the lower level of the center. He could feel the adrenaline begin to surge, a fire in the blood, and his senses leaped to embrace it with a fervor that surprised even him. Nick got out of the car, ran his hand down his left hip to make sure his nightstick was in place, his holster thumping heavily on his right as he shut the car door.

Someone screamed, "Officer, at the arcade, bullets everywhere—"

A teen put his face in Nick's, blotchy with acne, sheet-pale between the eruptions. "Some guy shot up the espresso bar at the Hot

Flash. There's a chick with blood all over her . . . now he's in the video room."

He could smell the blood and fear on them. His nostrils flared, and something primitive reared in him. He was like a wolf, a god-damn wolf, his senses were so keen, and he knew what he wanted, what he hunted for lay within—*what he hunted?* The realization frightened him.

And a second self, shunted aside, the police self thought, *Dear God, in the arcade, the kids, like shooting fish in a barrel, who went insane here, what am I up against, will I get home again if I go in there—don't go in alone.*

He'd never been afraid like this. Not of himself or what he would face. Not in the South Central riots where the very sky seemed to burn, not when the hoods were calling in and ambushing policemen, not when he'd been caught and earned the scars on his face. Never had he been terrified to do his job, to work alone.

But he was not alone. There was something that rode with him, coiled inside him, and it took over now, propelling him toward the disaster.

Rembrandt felt something icy lance through him, and he straightened in his chair, alerted. He knew the feeling, though it took him a moment to place it. He had been touched by the uninvited, the dead, a frosty assessment—he knew the feeling from something that had happened at the funeral home months ago. New Orleans, that black woman who'd stared him in the face and flung holy water over him—and something else.

Something cold and unforgiving and hungry.

It passed him now like a bullet ricocheting by. It left a chill behind. Stunned, he leaned toward the live monitors, thinking that he had let the tapes lull him while something was taking place in real time. He saw shapes struggling.

"What was that?"

The security man stopped the tape. "Ah, nothing, I guess. I mean . . . I don't see anything." He never resembled Kato Kaelin in stumbling confusion more than he did at this point.

Rembrandt stood up, leaning over the console, pointing at the live monitors. "What the hell is going on there?"

The phone began to ring sharply in the security office, despite the blockout Fleming had put on it. Someone was using the emergency code. He grabbed it up and his face immediately grayed under his tan.

"Oh, hell." He kicked his chair out from under him. "Shots fired."

It looked more to Rembrandt like a fight, but then he saw a man separate himself out, and he was carrying a weapon as he headed down the mall. He let the wanna-be sprint out the door ahead of him and followed, the Glock in his shoulder holster a comforting bulge.

Beyond the young man Kamryn had called Darby, who stood disheveled and wild-faced, Brandon could see Mitch was in a fight for his life, and losing. But his predicament seemed that much more urgent. Curtis lay collapsed at his side, either already dead or bleeding to death. Kamryn hugged his knees, trying to disappear into the pooled shadows. And this skinhead guy, this freak with a gun, stared at both of them, trying to decide which one to shoot first.

And then there was this business of his eyesight which had finally begun to focus normally, but was hampered by what he could only call the lava lamp syndrome . . . great blobs of darkness which blotted out and then revealed whatever he looked at. It made him want to puke that the first thing he could see clearly, really clearly, was the barrel of that freaking gun.

"Trying to make a decision?" he asked, getting to his feet, feeling Kamryn's hand first tighten, then give up and go slack, releasing him. He stepped into a pool of illumination from the mall. "Which one of us to shoot first? Why waste bullets, I say. Take us both out with one shot."

"Get—get away, kid. I got no quarrel with you. I just want the bitch."

"Well, you're not getting her. Because you just took out another kid, and he's probably the best friend I have in the whole world. He means more to me than anything I have waiting at home, and if he's gone, I might as well go, too. So long as you're running around pulling triggers, you better get me, too." He felt calm inside, dead calm, and maybe it was the pills talking, and maybe it wasn't. There was a limit, he thought. A limit to the shit which he was willing to take, and he'd just passed it.

Kamryn murmured softly, "Get out of his way."

He did not answer her, but waved his fingers at her, signaling. *Stay cool, stay down.*

"I wasn't supposed to do it," the skinhead muttered. Darby ran his free hand over his sweating head, and flung drops all over when he shook his palm. "He was supposed to do it."

Mitch landed with a heavy grunt, punctuating Darby's words, and Snake kicked him in the ribs with his jackbooted feet, once, twice, hard, to make sure he was going to stay down this time. Brand could see that Mitch breathed, and that was about all. He wet lips gone inexplicably dry.

Snake ordered, "Gimme the gun."

Darby narrowed his eyes at him. "No."

"C'mon, we've got to do it and get the hell out of here."

Darby hesitated.

Nick kept his back in the shadows, out of sight, watching the punk with the gun. He didn't know how to use one, wasn't comfortable holding it, wasn't blasting at anything that moved. He could probably be talked out of it once he saw Nick in position. His policeman's gut told him that, but it was a tiny voice compared to the other inside of him who wanted—what? Blood awash on the white marble flooring, a tidal wave of crimson, copper-tanged and warm, powerful. . . .

Nick shook his head, trying to clear it.

He watched the two fighters grapple, and the shaggy man go down, and stay down. The compulsion to get him, the true quarry, flooded him. This was the one he'd come for.

Nick knew he'd never seen the man before in his life.

His job was to get the others out of harm's way. *To serve and to protect.* He inched closer.

No, he'd come for the downed man. The fallen warrior. He must be brought back, to be tortured and die slowly. . . .

Nick swallowed hard. What was he doing there, arguing with himself like a, like a man possessed? His heart felt as though it had swollen and filled his entire chest cavity, throbbing with every beat, heavy as an anchor, he could not breathe for the pressure his heart exerted on his chest, his lungs. He fought to keep thinking, and realized that, the longer he waited, the closer he came to losing a final battle.

He moved closer to the scene when a kid stepped out of the arcade, and moved into the line of fire between them. Nick tried to inhale, to shove enough air into his lungs to call out.

He listened to the exchange as the tattooed perp moved in, and wanted his piece back.

He could wait no longer. He stepped forward.

"Put the gun down. This is Brea police."

Brand was beyond fear, but he whirled about, startled, and saw the uniform, the man's stern face above the police-issue gun and collar, and an immense cloud of soot hanging over him, about him, smothering him. More than sight, it was sound, dry mutterings in a language he could not understand, even if he were to hear it distinctly; it was touch, icy cold and beslimed, like carrion. It was feeling, ravenous, empty hunger and, even more, it was *evil.*

It would gladly slaughter him and anyone else standing before it.

Brand saw all that crystal clear, and it sank to the core of him, to that center which even drugs could not protect, and he felt a sudden urge to scream and pee his pants, the realization scared him so badly. This thing, like a funnel cloud of destruction, was going to suck him up, all of them, and it would be a worse thing than dying. Involuntarily, even though he knew the skinhead stood behind him with a gun, he took a rapid step backward.

"Don't move, son."

It looked human. Brand squinted slightly, he could see the white knuckles of the fingers the cop wrapped about the gun, see the struggle of the man holding it. He *was* human. He stood in the vortex of all that awfulness, and he fought to stay human.

Brand swallowed.

Suddenly the gun barrel swung, the cop fired, marble shattered, Mitch twitched as the shards showered about him, and the cop shouted, "I said, don't move!" His voice bellowed like thunder. "Put your gun down, and the three of you move over there."

He motioned to Mitch, Darby, and Snake where to put themselves.

Brand did not dare even look to see what Mitch was doing. But he could see the cop cared, cared intensely, his white-rimmed eyes kept flickering to where Mitch probably lay.

Snake muttered, "Fuck *this.*"

Brand heard him and dropped like a ton of bricks. His knee joints just went, like water, and he fell.

A calm, collected voice, unheard before, but familiar to Brand, rang out.

"Officer, I have them in a crossfire. You have backup."

Brand looked up as Darby let out a howl of pain and disappointment. The gun flash exploded near his eyes as he screamed, "This is for you, Kamryn, you bitch," bullet whistling into the arcade. Kids screamed. Brand could hear them shift and tumble, and he could not tell if she had been hit.

"Son of a bitch!" cried Brand. Darby swung wildly in response, and the gun roared a second time. The policeman went down.

Snake hit the deck by Brandon, slid past on the marble, momentum taking him to the open door of a storefront which stood abandoned. He kicked a hard boot, the glass front shattered, and with its shattering, another pistol shot, and Darby collapsed. His face slammed into the marble a hand's width away from Brand who watched as his tongue slammed forward in a rush of bloody vomit. Brand turned away.

He did not want to see what he had done, what he had caused, but it was either look one way or the other. The policeman lay, panting, his leg a bloodied mess, his face gray and sweating. His eyes rolled wildly and he tried to gesture, tried to get up. Coming down the stairs from the second story, Brand saw the man who'd fired the shot that got Darby.

It was the suited man with the ruined face who'd been asking after Mitch in the arcade. He stood beyond Hot Flash, where the wings of the mall intersected, in an FBI shooting stance, and as the building quieted, he took his supporting hand down and lowered the gun.

He walked up to where Snake crouched by the abandoned building and kicked him in the jaw. Snake's head snapped back and he lolled unconscious on the glass-covered tiles. Brand heard someone sob. It sounded womanish. He thought it might be Kamryn. How had Darby missed at such close range?

He scooted away from Darby, who must surely be dead, from the tide of blood and vomit which rose about his slack body, and got shakily to his feet. He looked for Mitch and saw—nothing. No one lay there.

He turned back to the cop as the security man and the suited man came up. What could he say? What could he do? Something sour burned at the back of his throat. *What, smart-ass, cat finally got your tongue?*

"Oh, God, I'm sorry."

"Not . . . your . . . fault. Protect . . . and serve." The wounded man gasped for breath.

Brand wanted to touch him, to hold his hand tightly, to take the pain away, but he couldn't. He watched in horror as every gasping mouthful released flames of soot. He jumped back, lest they touch him. The vortex about the cop grew more and more vast until it reached the immense ceiling above them.

As the policeman bled to death, this *thing* had a life. Brand stood frozen, holding his breath, afraid he might breathe it in.

The cop reached for Brand and caught him by the ankle, dragging him close. Brand recoiled. The policeman stared into his eyes.

"My name . . . is Nicholas Solis. I have a wife. Tell her—" He gasped again.

The ruined man, who had been trotting the perimeter, came up. He got to one knee. "It's a thigh wound, and it's deep, officer, but you should be all right." He ripped at the torn uniform trouser, tearing a strip off, and tied a pressure bandage on, quickly, efficiently. Brand thought, *Whoever he is, he's done this kind of thing before.* The ruined face glared at Security, who stood absolutely dumbfounded, tousled blond hair and tanned face slack. "Get paramedics down here, Fleming."

"No good," protested Solis weakly. He arched his back. The cords of his neck stood out. "Pain." He managed to put a hand on his chest.

"That's just adrenaline pumping. You get a hold of yourself, son, and you'll be fine."

The ruined man laid a hand over the pale other one. He frowned. "I think he's having a heart attack." He leaned over, as if thinking of CPR.

"Don't touch him!" Brand blurted. He could feel the shadowy cyclone, whirling, casting, searching. It pulsed, as if throbbing with the struggling heartbeat of Nicholas Solis. It raced, then ebbed, slower, slower. It drew near the ruined man, even as it abandoned the police officer. "Can't you see it?"

They locked eyes.

"See what, son? This man needs CPR."

"Can't you see— Can't you—can't you tell?"

The dark thing spread out like ebony wings over the ruined man.

"Why don't you tell me, son? This man is dying."

Brand looked at Nicholas Solis. The policeman looked back at him, a sudden calm expression on his face. He knew. Maybe he even understood. Brand swallowed down a tight, dry throat. "There's nothing you can do. He's hollow inside. There's nothing there but that black stuff—"

"What black stuff?" The voice of the suited man had been soothing. Now it coarsened with impatience.

Solis put his head back, kicked once, and stopped breathing. Every orifice of his body gouted black flame. It spumed out of him and Brand put his arm up to keep it from striking his face, inhaling the last of it himself.

The ruined man got up without concern. Leaning over the body, he said, "Why don't you tell me where your friend went? What did he have to do with all this?"

"He's not my friend!"

"You recognized his picture, didn't you? And you protected him. That's something you do for a friend. What was he doing with these two?"

"He didn't do anything! And I don't know where he went." Brand kicked loose as the fingers holding his ankle convulsed.

Nicholas Solis, whoever he was, whatever had happened to him, whatever had possessed him, was dead, and had died trying to tell Brand that he loved someone.

It didn't matter. Curtis, dead. The skinhead dead. The policeman, dead. The funny, harmless little bimbo from the coffee stand, dead.

And it wasn't enough for what hung over them. It rumbled over them as though life itself offended it, the joy of life and warmth to be destroyed. The KillJoy.

The ruined man gestured. "I think maybe you'd better come with me. I have questions to ask."

Brand shrugged. "I don't have any answers to give." He could feel the hunger watching them, tasting them. It drew close to the ruined man. It wafted across Snake's quiet form, circled, then brushed it again. Hunting for a new home.

"Now I know you didn't mean to get that policeman shot, boy, but you've got some explaining to do."

Snake twitched and writhed on the floor. Brand could see that thing injecting itself into him, sucked in through the tattoos, inhaled through the eyes, ears, nose and mouth. Snake coiled and recoiled, like a reptile constrictor seeking a victim.

That broke Brand's nerve.

Brand bolted, and he could hear the ruined man cuss behind him, then say, "Let him go." He bulled through the arcade where a dozen teenage boys jostled him, and hid him, and let him bolt out the back door into the night.

He ran all the way home. Nothing was darker than that which clouded his vision and awaited an opening to come in, that hunger which he had only left behind momentarily.

Chapter 10

"Phil, it wasn't his fault."

The dweeb and his mother arguing, muted by the distance of a bedroom between them and him, still distinct because of the anger in their voices. He lay in bed, cold, very cold, in pain, his ears still ringing from the shouting. He was grounded, of course, but that hardly mattered. They'd been home, waiting, when he came running in, and the shouting had barely begun when the police called, to ID him, and to request an interview in the morning.

He had not even had a chance to tell them about the worst thing, about Curtis. Not that either of them had been in a mood to listen. No. It was blaming time and until that was settled, there would be no listening, no discussion.

"It was his fault he was at the arcade. He had no business leaving. He's playing you for a fool, Lucille. He got us out of the house and as soon as we were gone, boom—he was at the arcade. Every time he ditches school, he's at that arcade. While you try to decide between being a mother and being his best friend, he's running around, doing everything he wants. He's a bad example for all the kids—"

"For God's sake. He had surgery. He was in pain. I should never have left him alone."

"The boy's fourteen. He's old enough to stay home alone while the rest of us have a life, too. You shouldn't have to worry about him."

"That's not fair. You don't know what he's been through."

Phil's tone rumbled, a thunderhead voicing an ominous future. "I know what he's put you through."

"I've got a call in for the therapist. God knows what this will do to him—"

"Lucy, you've got to stop handling him with kid gloves. He's responsible for his actions!"

"He was in a shooting!"

"Yes. He saw a shooting. And the police want to see him in the morning."

"No police. You heard him, he won't talk to them, no matter what. Maybe the therapist could interview him . . ." her voice dwindled.

A pause. Then Phil's baritone. "I'm taking him down there tomorrow morning. He's not a child, Lucy, and you've got to let him face the consequences of his actions."

"His actions? So he's responsible for some—idiot—who went in and shot up the mall because of his ex-girlfriend? I don't think so! And I don't think you're trying to understand what's happening here."

Brand rolled over. He was clammy, and his pajama bottoms stuck to his legs. He kicked free of his twisted sheets and tried to fasten his pillows to the sides of his head to muffle the argument. He would never, never sleep at this rate, and he had to sleep, had to, because sleep would sometimes shut Bauer out of his mind, until that last, inevitable nightmare. His thoughts rattled around in his skull like a desperate, starving creature in a cage. He had to stop thinking and only sleep would bring that. He thought of hitting his stash again. Three Haldol would put him out for a day or so. Blessed numbness. Only, he wouldn't be in control then, and he had to be. Had to keep beating Bauer down.

His phone rang sharply, two, three, four times. Only Curtis ever called. He stared at it, with no intention of answering it ever again. It rang two more times, then stopped.

Then his mother's bedroom phone rang, trilled softly twice before it was picked up.

"Hello? June, how are you? Yes, he's here—how is Curtis? Oh, God. Oh my God. In shock, I don't think Brand even knew, he didn't say anything. Is there anything I can do? In the morning. Yes. June, I . . . there aren't words . . . I'm so very, very sorry. Call me if you need anything. Day or night. Tomorrow. Yes."

Voices paused.

"God, Phil. That was Curtis' mother. He was killed in the cross fire! Brandon didn't even . . . he didn't even say anything. Do you think he knows? How could he not tell me?"

"He and Curtis have been joined at the elbow for the last year. How could he not know? You're taking too much bullshit from him. He's probably waiting to tell you, to pull some ultimate sympathy card! You've got to stop letting him slide through life."

"Phil!"

Phil's baritone mumbled something which Brand could not hear through the pillows. Then his mother's high, clear voice again.

"I don't . . . I don't want to put him through it, but you're right. Curtis' death makes a difference. Surely he'll want to help find who did it. He must have seen something. I have to work tomorrow—"

"I said I'd take him down."

"Yes, I know, but . . . the therapist says I need to be there at times like this. He says that Brand doesn't trust me, but I can't do this. I can't. Phil . . ."

"That's why you married me." The deep voice softened. "To help you through the tough stuff."

"What am I going to do?"

"That's what we have to figure out, together."

Their voices lost their clarity, dropping into a comfortable, lulling murmur. They were still discussing him, he knew it, but the edge had come off his thoughts, finally, and he no longer cared.

He heard little more, his eyes drooped, but never quite closed, seeing Curtis in his mind's eyes. The dead skinhead. The cop.

And the nothingness, the void, the awful thing which had shadowed all of them. The hunger of the KillJoy. The evil. He'd seen it in the cop. What had it been?

He knew what it wasn't. It wasn't good. It wasn't benevolent. It wasn't anything he ever wanted to see again. As he began to fall into sleep, he wondered what the difference was between it, and the void between his thoughts and his dreams.

Had he seen Death itself?

And as the paralysis of sleep claimed his body, twisted and unhappy, sheets wrapped about him like pythons, Brand fled the mall again, his throat stretched in a scream which he could not let out, loss he could not howl, and the thing followed him.

He tried, but could not wake, could not forestall the fatigue he fell into. The blanket of drugs were now wiped out of his system by the adrenaline rush of all the fear, all the terror he'd been through, leaving him almost comatose. The rest he'd prayed for was now his prison.

Bauer had been prowling through his thoughts, drawn by the blood and carnage earlier, disgusting Brand with his reaction to the events, and now the thing which pursued Brand attracted him strongly. Behind the flickering of his eyelids, played against the theater of his sleeping mind, Bauer hunted as much for the phenomenon as it searched for Brand.

He had to keep them apart. They were separate evils, but they called to one another, power to power, and if they joined—he had no chance. He would be overwhelmed. He did not want to see evil, hear it, taste it, smell it, but he would do all that and more, as long as it did not possess him. As long as the KillJoy did not creep within and take up residence as Bauer had. Anything that gave him some chance of remaining himself, wrestling with demons.

And in his dreams he was, as he usually was, alone, hoping for Yellow Dog to appear and guide him, to keep him away from both Bauer and the thing that devoured. He raced fleet-footed down the slipstreams of his mind, calling for Yellow Dog in the dark corridors, searching for that beam of gold.

He saw a glimmer. Brand altered his course. Around a corner it was, sharp and slippery, like a knife it would cut if he did not make the turn, but he saw the yellow dog, lips curled in a doggish grin, feathery tail waving.

It was a golden retriever he dreamed of, a heroic dog, and he did not know where he'd gotten the image from, for they'd never owned a dog, but he'd seen his like in commercials and on dog food packages, and so he knew what it was.

Yellow Dog tossed his head, brown eyes gleaming, soft golden-red ear flaps moving, the ruff at his throat swelling as he barked his doggy greeting. Brand put his hand down. He touched—he could swear he touched—the silky softness of his fur, the warmth of life coursing through the canine body, so real, so very real, this dream ghost dog. Yellow Dog bent his body, bringing his chops around so he could lick at Brand's wrist, wet but still warm, alive, happy dog pup.

The moment of joyous reunion was replaced as Brand could sense the snuffling of the hungry thing hunting him.

"Take me away," he said to Yellow Dog. "Hide me. Please."

The retriever let out a low woof, and bounded away, his tail flagging behind him, urging Brand to follow. He sprinted after. He would not be able to catch up to Yellow Dog again, he never did in his dreams, but the guide would take him on until morning, chasing safety. The dog knew the turns of his mind better than he did.

Then Brand stumbled. He saw the dog's hindquarters bunch, launching him into the air—over something—what? Brand's heart thumped in panic as he slid across the darkened corridor of his dream, slid across slick icy marble, hit a fault and fell.

His body jolted to a stop. Brand lay, gasping for a moment, looking upward, waiting for Yellow Dog to come back and get him out of the pit, how, he didn't know, but somehow—

A hazy golden aura lit the edge of the pit, something looked down at him. Brand got to his feet, extended his hand, breathing gratitude.

But it was not Yellow Dog who looked at him. It was Mitch, and for a mumbling second, Brand thought—I'm in the Dumpster again, trapped, and Mitch is helping me out. There was even the faint metallic click as something Mitch wore around his neck swung forward, hitting the rim of the trash bin.

Brand accidentally touched it as it did so. A shock zapped through his fingertips and he snatched his hand back, but not before reaching the awareness that he had touched something else, awakened something else.

Two in the morning in New Orleans. Mother Jubal had told her client to come when the tide changed, and so she had, seeking her love potion and her reading, murmuring, "Madame Jubal, I pray this works," and she making polite, soothing noises back, looking into her crystal after stoppering up the potion she'd cooked and wrapping it in a clean cloth to give to the woman.

Outside her shop on the back side of Pirates' Alley, a cab sat waiting, its lights on, engine idling. The white woman sitting on the edge of her chair opposite Jubal had tiny lights about her eyes and her mouth, knife-edge lines of unhappiness. The white woman was not one of Mother's congregation, and so she did not do what she would have done for one of her many children, but instead she worked by means more acceptable to her client. She put her palm over the crystal, feeling its coolness against her warmth. Unseasonably warm still, for Nawlins, and the touch of the crystal felt as good as the perpetually blowing air conditioner at the back of the candy counter beyond the curtains.

She could see the blurred image of her client reversed in the crystal, and concentrated, bringing up new images and sights. The woman sat so tensely on the edge of her chair that her butt might be made of porcelain, but she began to relax as Jubilation spoke, and the corners of her mouth slowly crept into a half-smile. She tucked the handkerchief-wrapped perfume bottle into her purse, and hesitated for a moment, then brought out her wallet.

Mother shook her head. "Now don't you be doing that. You've already paid me."

"But it's so little—"

"Little enough to see you smile. Now you run on. You've got fine things waiting to happen to you." Jubal reached for the midnight blue swatch of velvet she used to cover her crystal.

The white woman stood, a pale splinter in the dimness of the room, and the crystal reflected that splinter, then suddenly, the image shattered into a spidery picture of darkness and light.

Jubal hastily covered the crystal, walked the woman to the door of the candy shop, the store smelling of brown sugar pralines, and let her out to the waiting cab. She watched behind the door, looking out through the grille to make sure her client entered the vehicle safely, then bolted the door.

The cloth, so hastily spread over the ball, had slipped and fallen to the tabletop as if some unseen force had pushed it aside.

Mother sat down firmly to draw the crystal toward her. Arrayed in its depths rested a silver amulet, fingers grasping it.

"So this is the way it is," she told herself, and looked closer.

She did not see what she expected—a boy pushing his way into manhood, sable brown hair waved across his forehead, a sprinkling of freckles across his nose and cheekbones, eyes bloodshot with worrying (or sorrowing, perhaps, she thought), and shadowed by dark purple bruising beneath. The fringes of his hair were plastered wetly to his light forehead. Had he been running? And if he had, from what?

Mother had barely asked herself the question, when she felt the answer, the fear, the terror welling up in this child as if he were a newly dug spring. Dark water geysered upward from below, swamping him near to drowning.

She wrapped her hands firmly about the crystal ball.

"You come here to Mother Jubal," she instructed the man-child. "You come here and I'll help you. I know the loa, and it knows me. You come to me. I know what to do."

She exuded more confidence than she felt, but she knew she was the only hope.

The boy's face looked out at hers, and his eyes widened, as if he both saw and heard her. "You see," she said, and threw her power at the loa following him.

She surprised the spirit and it withdrew abruptly, and Mother Jubal laughed at her triumph, small though it be. Next time would be harder, and the time after that, harder still.

But she took her joy where she found it, and let it fill the room.

The astonished boy met her glance for a second longer, and then power recoiled spitefully, a last bitter blow from the loa. A sharp sound cracked through the air, and the crystal split into three shards between her palms.

"You remember," Mother coaxed the now empty crystal. "You remember me, child."

She let go, and the seeing glass fell hollowly upon the tabletop.

Chapter 11

"How the hell did you get caught in the middle of that?"

Rembrandt sat back in the rental car seat, looking at the stars through the sunroof, his laptop resting on the passenger bucket seat, his phone connected through the system, and listened. It was early morning on the East Coast and Bayliss was up—did the man ever sleep? Up and angry. Idly, he tracked a star which was not a star, but a satellite, visible even through the L.A. Basin's murky night sky, and wondered if it was the com satellite he had hacked into to make his call. He listened to Bayliss thunder about making preparations, ordering supplies, finding a wilderness camp, building a voting bloc, laying a foundation, the need for secrecy intensifying . . .

Rembrandt interrupted mildly, "I found our man."

"Found. Not have." Bayliss stopped rambling, became instantly alert.

"Not yet. I will. First, I have to make sure that things here are tied up."

"Were you identified as a shooter?"

"No. I managed to convince the security man that I was under-cover and wished to remain so. He was more than eager to take whatever credit he could."

"Those malls are up to their knees in monitors—"

"It's been handled."

"Witnesses."

"They'll be taken care of." Rembrandt watched as an owl flew overhead, low, silent, a shadow coasting by.

"What does our man have to do with it?"

"He was there. I'm unsure of his role yet, but he was in the thick of it."

"Damn. Local yokels spot him?"

"He bailed."

"Anyone deal with you?"

"Just Security." *And the kid,* Rembrandt thought, but he would have a handle on that shortly, too. As far as Security was concerned, he would have an accident soon, but not too soon, nothing spectacular, just a run-of-the-mill traffic fatality. "Everything's been arranged."

"Good. I can't brook much further delay. I need my shipment, Rembrandt."

"Yes, sir," Rembrandt answered, and heard the line go dead. He reached over to his keyboard, typed in a string, entered it, got a response, entered a series of codes, then backed out.

He hung up his phone. Initiating action and taking responsibility for the reaction, that's what his job consisted of.

He did it well.

He ran his tongue over his teeth, probing for an uneven spot, thinking. What to do with the kid? It might be best to proceed slowly there . . . the kid might help him find Christiansen. Also, there would be family involved. Best to avoid additional entanglements. He could handle the kid alone, and he would be solitary now; his friend had died in the incident.

Perhaps suicide might be appropriate after Rembrandt had learned what he wanted to know. It afforded a solution which, although painful for the family, would not involve a great deal more of tidying up. Yes, suicide was a definite option. He must not forget that. Sometimes he did, in the fervor of the moment.

He had been accused occasionally of enjoying his work.

He secured the laptop under the car seat, deciding where he would begin picking up the threads of finding the boy, without disturbing people who might ask questions later. After a long moment, he withdrew the laptop again, opened it, activated the modem, and began to search for the local school district's private records. After hacking into the Defense Department systems, the effort was surprisingly simple.

He would begin checking absenteeism records, and he had the name of the other victim. A correlation would soon come up, Rembrandt was certain. They had been friends, those two, and undoubtedly shared the same vices beyond the arcade. Truancy, detention, sooner or later, he would have a record with possibilities.

He would find the boy.

She was hyperventilating, she knew she was hyperventilating, and it was all she could do to stay conscious. Maybe passing out would be better. Kamryn leaned over the steering wheel of her car, feeling her heart thump through her chest like some kind of weird machine. She looked out over the small city park, the Brea plunge, a great empty swimming pool until next summer, the streets of bungalows, built in the '30s, the city traffic humming sporadically down Brea Boulevard, and tried to catch her breath. She had bolted from the mall and just driven, then she'd found herself here, and the park was quiet, slumbering. She knew the police department was a shout away and for now, the park was safe. She was alive, and it was awful, and it was a relief, and it was frightening. So much blood. Poor Sandy. And the kid in the arcade. And the cop. She wanted to feel sorry for Darby, too, poor, unhappy, stupid Darby, but couldn't.

Someone was singing an off-key song, a litany really, a chant: "Oh, God, oh, God, oh, God."

Kamryn took a deep breath and realized that someone was herself.

She pushed her bangs from her face, found it sopping wet with tears, and twisting the rearview mirror, took a look at herself.

"Oh, God," she said one last time.

She looked awful. Some women looked radiant when they cried. Not her. Her eyes swelled until they were beady, piggy little eyes, and her face went blotchy, and her nose ballooned up until she resembled a clown.

The mirror in her hands gave a tiny ping and something metallic fell out of it, hit the car mats, and rolled out of sight. The mirror instantly lost all firmness in her hand and when she let go, it dangled weakly from its post, completely vertical.

"Oh, shit."

She leaned over and felt the car mats for the screw, brushed her fingertips over the nap of the fabric, forward, backward, as elusive as finding a fallen contact lens. On her side, scrunched over and awkward, under the car seat, she bumped the hardness of her gun, and paused. If she had had the gun with her, perhaps none of this would have happened. It was not enough to carry it in the car. She should have had it in her purse, under the counter, something, anything—

Who would have thought Darby could have killed her?

Kamryn sat up, and leaned her chin against the steering wheel again. She let out a shuddery, hiccuping sigh.

Come on, Sis. I've got something to show you downstairs.

Tears began to cascade down her face again.

"Dear sweet God. Mom, Dad, I'm so sorry. I'm so sorry. I let you down, I let you all down. I just thought—" Kamryn swallowed tightly. "I just thought, one step at a time. Just get away, get clean—" She scrubbed at her arms despite the pain of the raw skin. Even in the dark, she could see the faint outlines. Almost gone, but not quite. And now she was afraid to go back.

Darby was dead, but Snake, who had worshiped Darby for some peculiar reason, would be looking for her. Kamryn dried her face against her sleeve. It had been Darby who'd done the shooting, so Snake would probably be questioned and then freed. He would not rest until he had her. There were secrets to protect, and then he would be getting even for what had happened to Darby.

There would be questions she did not want to answer. They might find the gun and take it from her. They were sure to turn up the false social security number she'd given to work at Hot Flash. They might even discover her name was not her name. They would be all over her about the shooting, and Darby, and Darby's background. There would be press, too. Cameras in her face. Stupid questions.

She couldn't go back. She could only go forward. Somehow.

But she had to find a starting place. How? Where? She couldn't sit in the park all night. The police patrol would notice her eventually, stop, check out the car, ask other questions.

Her nose began to run. Kamryn searched through her small purse until she found a worn tissue, not used, but carried around in the purse until it had gotten dirty and wrinkled. Mommie Kleenex, she'd called it when she was young. Mom.

She began to cry again. She blew her nose hastily, then found a corner and blotted at her eyes.

She had to stop this. Toughen up. Do what had to be done. She closed her eyes. There was no going back.

Someone rapped sharply on the driver's side glass. Kamryn stifled a scream and looked into the face peering down at her.

Snake sat in the chair, admiring his tattoos as he flexed his forearm and made the patterns ripple. He kept his mind clean and clear of anything except the skin art, so that he would not forget the objective he had picked up that night.

He would hunt Kamryn down and kill her for betraying Darby, and before she could betray the Brotherhood. It was his sole reason for breathing, his destiny. In that way, he would keep himself and the organization pure. He had always been very careful to keep everything simple, uncomplicated, direct. He had no record because of it and he knew, that even though they were talking to him about that night's happenings, they were running his prints looking for a clue as to his past. The weapon wasn't traceable and neither was he, not without eyewitnesses.

A voice intruded on his meditation and Snake lifted his chin to stare at the speaker.

". . . I said, we had a cop killed here tonight. Does that make any difference to you?"

The cop had a lot of red to his brown hair, under the station lights, and Snake wondered if he'd been a potato-digging Irishman. He wondered if the burrito cop and he had known each other. He closed his eyes and opened them again slowly.

"I had a friend who got shot. I don't see the bitch in here anywhere. Why aren't you asking her questions?"

"What makes you think we aren't?"

Snake tilted his head to one side and looked at the cop.

The lieutenant cleared his throat and adjusted his nameplate slightly. Graham, it read. Lieutenant Peter Graham. Snake let the name roll down his gullet, held it inside like he was doing a toke, let it live inside of him, and didn't let it go. Then, slowly, he exhaled. He wouldn't forget Lieutenant Peter Graham.

"Let's talk about the gun."

"We already talked about the gun."

"You told me it was Darby's."

"Yeah. I had taken it from him, but he took it back inside the mall." Snake inhaled deeply again. "And the rest is history." He looked at his hands. "You tested me. I'm clean."

"You didn't pull the trigger," Graham returned. "That doesn't make you clean."

Snake wrapped his ankle about the chair leg. "I have a suit," he answered. "In Costa Mesa. Do I need one at this point?"

"You agreed to talk to us, to give a statement."

"Which you got. So. Now, do I need my lawyer?"

Graham's ruddy complexion began to darken again, when a fellow officer came out of the adjoining wing and approached from the rear, leaning over him. Snake half-closed his eyes and watched the other's mouth, knowing they were talking about him.

The computer hadn't pulled anything up. He stood.

Graham watched him, his mouth tightening as the other policeman finished informing him.

"You're free to go. But I advise you to stay close in case we have any more questions."

"Cool," said Snake and turned to leave.

Brand awoke, suddenly, sharply, crusty with dried sweat and as stiff as if he'd been pounded on. He lay in the night and blinked once or twice, then reached quickly, out of habit, for his glasses. They weren't there, of course. His hand brushed the touch-sensitive lamp on the nightstand and it glowed.

Brand didn't know what woke him, but the readout on the clock told him it was 4:30 a.m. He rubbed his eyes carefully. Shadows were cast in sharp relief on the far wall. His heart did a doubled-up beat that hurt in his chest, then steadied. God, he could see! He could see!

But what was he seeing? Were they shadows, or the KillJoy looming over him, waiting, even though Yellow Dog and the other, that black woman, had chased him off? Had it filled Snake and then had enough left over to come looking for him? Because it had been looking for him, sifting through his dreams. That hadn't just been a memory of the massacre. That had been real. As real as anything which had been happening to him lately.

He shifted in his bed and tried to make a nest in the crumpled covers, punched his pillow with his head and lay back down, balled up, wary.

Something tap-tapped on his bedroom window. Brand sprang upright in his bed, eyes wide, throat tight. His head froze to his shoulders, it wouldn't turn to let him look to his right at the second-story window. Slowly, aching inch by inch, he cranked his head about on his neck. His muscles grew tighter and tighter until he thought his head was simply going to shatter at the neckbones and fall off. Fall off rather than let him look at the windowpane to see who or what tapped for him there. *Don't look. Whatever you do, don't look.* It could be the KillJoy coming for him. Or the ghost of Curtis. Or the ruined man.

Brand looked.

Chapter 12

Light from the nightstand caught it full in the face, reflecting a silvery moon back at Brand, a moon fractured by an ink-dark splinter down the center. The disk looked like nothing human. Now he wished that he could not see, that his vision had not sharpened, returned, giving him the ability to see it. Eyes widened, he stared at the creature and it stared back at him. A tiny slit opened near the bottom of the silvery reflection and mouthed at him. A hoarse, whispery voice it had.

"Brand. Let me in."

The shock that the thing knew his name kept Brand from taking a breath. He sat, his head twisted at an angle to his body, aching, turning blue for the lack of air, unable to move. He would die like this, he thought. Frightened to death. Had Bauer somehow gotten outside as well, to attack him from both within and without? It did not look like his mind's image of Bauer, the computer-generated photo of a serial killer which Susan Craig had shown him over and over and over again.

But who said his attacker had to play by the rules and show himself as he really was? Who knew what forms the KillJoy could take?

The thing moved, a shadowy limb became recognizable as an arm, a hand, and it rapped gently on the windowpane.

"Brand X, let me in."

No! He managed a tiny squeak of protest. It was like sticking a pin in a balloon . . . suddenly, the blockage in his throat leaked out, explosively and he began to gasp for much-needed air.

The onslaught of air unfroze his thoughts, his jaw, his lungs. He blinked rapidly and the moonish face at the window suddenly took on proportions. Longish hair and trimmed beard framed it—it was human, looking in at him, someone human, despite the chasm down the center of its face and it was—

"Mitch!" His voice hissed out of him.

"That's right, buddy. Let me in." Mitch leaned on the window, voice pitched low, no one could hear him but Brand.

Brand, who'd made the trip in and out that window more times than he could count, knew it took someone fairly athletic to be kneeling on the eaves. Thought, which had been frozen, thawed at the speed of light. Was it really Mitch? How had he gotten here? What did he want? Why had he been with those two skinheads, and *Why had he let Curtis get killed?*

As if he could read his thoughts, Mitch said, "I let you down, I know that. I thought I could take them before they did anything. I'm in trouble and I've got nowhere to go but here. Let me in."

There were questions now. There would be tons more of them if the man were found in his room. It might even bring the ruined man, and Brand instinctively wanted nothing to do with him. And just who had Mitch been, anyway, that he thought he could handle two men with a gun?

Suddenly furious, Brand leaned forward. "No way."

"I need your help."

Brand rubbed at his sleep-ridden eyes. The silvery illumination which shone around Mitch lessened slightly, as did the chasm which cleaved Mitch's face almost in two. *I'm seeing things again,* thought Brandon. Not Mitch, he's here, but the way he looks. . . .

Maybe he was going crazy again, and Mitch was just part of it. He shook his head emphatically. "Mitch doesn't know where I live."

"I tracked you home weeks ago, making sure you didn't get trash-canned again. Brand, I've got nowhere else to go."

He couldn't stand the begging tone of the other, but was he even real? Brand leaned so close his breath steamed the glass pane. "You're in trouble, I'm in trouble. And if I get caught with you here, I'm in worse trouble. You're on your own."

"Just for the rest of the night, and the day. I'll hit the road when it gets dark again. Hell, if there's room, I'll sleep in your closet."

"What do you mean, if there's room?"

As urgent as his expression had been, Mitch grinned. "I was a kid once."

Brand said wryly, "You'd die in there."

"I know what old socks smell like." Mitch put his palm against the windowpane. "I need your help."

He couldn't stand crouched outside the window much longer. Brand decided that the scream of a falling man would attract more attention than letting him in. He moved to the window to unlock it.

Mitch came in swiftly and silently. He helped Brand tug the screen back into place before locking the window back down.

He tracked a broken fingernail down the screen's framework, looking at the wear. "You ought to put a door in."

"Then think of the visitors I'd get." Brand sat down on his bed Indian-style. "There's cold pizza in the box," and he pointed at his bureau where he'd tossed the remains of dinner. The meal seemed so long ago, it was ancient history, because of everything that had happened since, but he knew the slices would still be good, and that Mitch was probably hungry.

"Don't mind if I do." His guest grabbed up the box, sat down, and began to eat. He held the slice by the crust and devoured each slice in two or three bites. Once inside, with full lighting on him, he looked near normal. The shining aura had retreated to a slight glare, or haze, and the chasm looked more like an irritating interruption. Brand watched him eat, thinking of the darkness of the hungry thing, the KillJoy. His eyes blurred suddenly, aching, throbbing, and he shut them tightly in fear.

Suddenly, he was glad he'd let Mitch in. He didn't want to be alone in the night, blinded, vulnerable. He found himself sitting with his arms folded tightly about his rib cage, hugging himself. He waited until Mitch was finished before telling him the bad news.

"You can stay here until morning, but the dweeb's going to take me down to police headquarters after that."

Mitch, who had been busy chowing down, grew suddenly alert. "Why?"

"Because they want to talk to me. About . . . Curtis . . . and everything."

"About me."

"Probably. The ruined man was hanging around, showing pictures, and asking questions."

"Pictures?"

"Yeah." Brand tilted his head. "Was that you in uniform?"

"Don't know. Didn't see the picture. And," Mitch looked at him steadily, "it's better you don't know, either."

"Who was he, anyway?"

"Who?"

"The ruined man."

Mitch found a half-filled glass of soda and drank it down, made a grimace as if it were horrible tasting, which it probably was, warm and gone flat. "Don't know," he repeated. "Haven't seen him."

"He knows you. He shot the skinhead. I think he's probably FBI or something."

"Think so?"

"Yeah. Anyway, even if you don't know who he is, you probably know someone's looking for you."

"What I do and don't know is not open to discussion." Mitch looked around the room. "Could you tell if someone's gone through your things?"

"Of course I could!"

"And?"

"Everything's right where I dropped it."

"All right. I'm good for the rest of the night. What about later?"

Brand thought. "There's a studio over the garage. A loft. The dweeb was going to make it into a studio, but he's never done it. I have a key."

"What are the chances anyone would go in there?"

"Practically none. Only the dweeb would ever go in there, and he's going to be busy with me."

"But you have a key."

Brand shrugged. "Never leave home without one."

"Then I should probably go in while it's still dark."

Brand tried not to let his disappointment show. He slid a hand under the top mattress and fished around until he found a key. He tossed it. "Here."

Mitch caught it in midair, a silvery object disappearing into his hand. Without looking at Brand again, he said, "It's been a long night. I think I'll just bunk down in here anyway, if you don't mind."

Relieved, Brand threw him a blanket, too, and added, "Just lie down anywhere."

Mitch found the comforter Brand had kicked off and straightened it, then folded it. He lay down and pulled the blanket over himself, then looked up to meet Brand's amused look. "I'm old," he said. "I need more padding than you do."

Brand reached out. "I'll get the light."

The glaring white light in Kamryn's eyes flicked away, and she could almost see the policeman as he leaned close. "Are you all right, miss?"

Middle of the night, and she'd been crying, and she was hiding out in the city park. Kamryn smiled. "Of course. I was just . . . my mirror broke." She pointed. "I was at my boyfriend's, and we had an argument, and I was driving home and the damn screw broke, or something."

"Would you open the car door for me, ma'am?"

Hesitantly, after another look at him to make sure he wore a patrol uniform, Kamryn unlocked the door and swung it open. Flashlight in hand, the man leaned inside and aimed it at the mirror which now hung limply in the middle of the front windshield.

"Shouldn't drive around with it like that," he commented as he straightened back up.

"I know, I know. But it just happened. I thought if I found the screw. . . ." Her voice trailed off.

"You're headed home, then?"

"Yes, sir."

He had no expression on his face. Did he know she was lying? Did he care? Would he be looking for her because of the shooting?

He reached for his pocket. "I'd like to see your registration and license, please."

Her heart sank. A ticket! She couldn't believe it. She fished her registration out of the glove box, then pulled her purse onto her lap and rummaged around until she found her wallet. As she shifted her weight, the back of her heel struck the butt of the gun.

Shit! Could he see it from where he stood? They'd haul her in for that. Carefully, she nudged the gun farther back under her seat, as she pulled out her license. The address was no good, but she didn't care about that. By the time they backtracked it, she'd be gone. She passed everything over.

He balanced it on the citation pad as he began to write. "This is what we call a 'fix-it' ticket. You have thirty days to get the mirror replaced before we actually issue a citation. Just bring the car in to the station so we can see everything's in order."

"That's all?"

He smiled briefly. "That's all. Just bring it in, let anyone look at the mirror, and we tear the ticket up. Okay?"

"All right. Thank you."

He handed her the citation and her license and registration back. "I wouldn't hang around here too long. It's pretty late, and there's been some gang activity in the area. And don't you let that boyfriend of yours bother you, okay? You shouldn't even be driving if you're too upset."

Kamryn tried a brave smile, let it fade from her trembling lips. "I won't. And, thank you."

He stepped back so she could close and lock her car door. With him watching, she pulled out of the little park's lot, and headed for the streets. If only she had somewhere to go.

An hour after dawn began to lighten the streets of the Quarter, Mother packed up to leave the candy shop. Her sister and her sister's daughters were already busy in the candy kitchen, cooking up bubbling pots of brown sugar syrup to make pralines and chopping pecans on marble cutting boards to add to the candy just before it set. They sang as they worked, and their voices and the rich smell of the brown sugar filled the air. They nodded at Mother as she walked through, past the glass candy counters and gondolas. Her youngest niece was cleaning the interiors, whisking them out quickly and efficiently, getting ready to restock them with fresh dipped chocolates and turtles and pralines.

Though the sign of the door was marked both Candy Kettle and Madame Jubal, there was no sign of her place at the back of the sweet shop. Only those who knew her, knew how to find her, or had been directed to her, looked for Madame Jubal. She liked it that way.

Her sister, putting the cash drawer into the register at the front, looked up. Geneva was too young to remember their mother well, but she was the spitting image of her, Mother thought. Just the spitting image. She smiled, but there was a little worry frown between her eyebrows. "Mornin', Mother. Late night?"

"Sure was, Geneva. I've shut down the shop for the mornin'. Just let the answerin' machine catch my messages, all right?"

"All right. Trouble brewin'?"

Mother paused by the front door. She could not put a finger on what it was about the boy which bothered her, or why she had seen him through the amulet, or why the crystal ball had shattered. Stranger things had happened to her. But perhaps her sister had put a finger on it. Trouble brewing. She smiled widely. "Always brewin', Geneva, always. Just like the candy syrup in the pot. The Good Lord above is always workin' on something for us. I'll see you later."

Despite the earliness of the hour, despite the relative coolness of the day, the sun smote her like a hammer as she stepped out into it. Mother paused on the sidewalk and cast her eyes down from the glare. There was a breeze in the day, a goodly one, and as she looked down, she caught sight of a crow's feather. The wind caught it up, set it down on its quill end, and it revolved in a flurry, trapped. Mother watched the feather spin, knowing Aido Wedo had sent her a message, a sign, but one which she was not sure she could read.

Then she looked around, and leaves and debris from the night swept about her in a bigger, wider circle, faster, more furiously, so that the island of calm in which she and the feather stood was like standing in the eye of a hurricane.

Hurricane. Mother took a deep breath and stared down the alley-street, past the wrought-iron balconies and toward Jackson Square. Chalk artists were already out, sketching their livelihood onto the walkway. October neared the end of the hurricane season and few reached any strength this late. Hugo had, though, up the Atlantic coast. Any 'cane getting a start this late might well stay in the gulf waters, swinging toward Louisiana or Texas. Might. Might not.

The wind flurry died as quickly as it had come up. Mother hugged her purse under her elbow. She would have to do some thinking about the sign when she came back, after a short nap.

The sign and the boy. She had to work on bringing him to her, him and the wearer of the amulet. They would need her before they were through.

As for the 'cane, that would be a work of nature, and it would do what it would do, uncaring of the good or evil of its destruction. That was the way of the wide world, and why men prayed to gods. Mother took another deep breath, smelled the sea and the morning, and started the day's journey.

Chapter 13

"You're sure you're not too upset over this?" the dweeb asked, for about the fourth time, over cereal.

Brand looked at him. The dweeb had carefully blown-dry, caramel-colored hair, with wings of graying blond at the temples, glasses, and a clean-shaven face with a sincere expression. He looked like a banker (which he was) and someone who could say, "Thank you for banking with us" while he foreclosed on the mortgage (which he had also done). There was not a visible shred in him of the frustrated artist, although that was supposedly why they had a loft/studio over the garage. Brand had not known the dweeb to visit it since they bought the house and moved in. The loft had originally been advertised as a "maid's apartment" or "granny room" as it had a half bath and a very small kitchenette, although the kitchenette was not currently hooked up. Why run gas to a stove top never used? Why call it an artist's loft if there was no visible artist?

As for being asked if it upset him, he'd already been told he had no choice. Short of going into a coma (and he'd already done that, thank you very much, Dr. Susan Craig, and didn't particularly want to do it again), he knew he was going. He didn't want to, but he had not yet figured out an escape route.

Brand put his spoon in his mouth carefully before answering, "No. Another day off school is what every kid wants." The house had cleared of the other children, only they three sat at the breakfast table.

"Don't talk with your mouth full," his mother said, without looking at him.

Brand grinned. Milk slid out of the corner of his mouth and he grabbed up a wadded paper napkin. If he were younger, he'd consider barfing in the dweeb's car on the way to the station. He could pass it off as nerves. But, as he wasn't younger, there was a line of irritation he could walk, and it was a fine one.

In despair, his mother said, "Brand, don't do that. You look like a drooling idiot."

"Lucy."

"Honestly, what am I going to do?"

"You don't believe me."

"Brandon, honey, how can I? What do you expect? They told you what could happen. You wouldn't wear the solar shields they sent with you, you went to the arcade, you're telling me you see things, you're lying . . . it's just like it's happening all over again—"

"Lucy," the dweeb repeated again in a low warning.

Flushed, she looked away, then down at her wrist. "I'm going to be late. You'll take him to the therapist later?"

"I've got the whole day off work."

She stood, brushed a kiss across the dweeb's receding forehead, and left without glancing back.

That left the two of them staring across the table at each other. Brand lowered his gaze and paid serious attention to finishing his cereal and wondering how he could shake loose.

"You look like that surgery's really taken hold. No glasses?"

"Yeah." That, at least, had been a relief. But his failure to explain the side effects to his mother left him isolated. Even as he thought about it, a charcoal-gray smudge drifted cloudlike across the dweeb's banker countenance and floated away.

"I'd like to try RK sometime," the dweeb mused, as he scraped his cereal bowl clean. "I've worn glasses since I was a kid. It gets tiresome. Someday I'd like to buy myself a pair of those Italian wraparound sunglasses. . . ." His voice trailed off.

Brand pitied his mother. It looked like the dweeb was about to enter the "driving a convertible, bald-headed with groovy sunglasses" phase. He decided not to aggravate his stepfather overly much. "Sounds cool."

The dweeb blinked as if bringing Brand back into focus. He checked his watch. "Your therapist should be in now. Want to give him a call before we go see the police or after?"

Oh, please, Br'er Dweeb, don't throw me in the Brea police department patch. Brand sighed. He thought of Mitch hiding in the loft. A talk with down-to-earth, understanding Mitch would do him far more good than his twitchy psychotherapist who, Brand was fairly sure, got into psychology with the hopes of analyzing himself. Although Brand had to admit, he had not yet told Mitch of what he'd seen happen, there was an adult who might be inclined to listen and judge later.

Brand pushed his bowl away, resigned. "Let's just do it."

His stepfather made no move to stand. He did, however, carefully dab at the corners of his thin-lipped mouth with his napkin. "There's something else we have to discuss. Your mother is having almost as much difficulty with this as you are, so I agreed to tell you. But I don't want you to think she's avoiding this."

Oh, no, not Mom. Brand pushed back in his chair. "What is it?"

"They're holding the funeral for Curtis tomorrow morning. I'll be taking you there."

His stomach did a flipflop, and the milk and cereal went sour immediately. "I don't want to go."

"I know it's not pleasant, but you were his best friend. His family would feel better seeing you there."

He didn't want to see Curtis laid out, whiter than marble, eyes closed, sleeping the sleep of the dead. "I don't care. I'm not going."

"Brand, we don't ask much of you. Taking out the trash now and then, your turn with the dishes, good grades in school—and now this. Death is something we all have to deal with." The dweeb smiled slightly. "After all, none of us are getting out alive."

"Well, Curtis got out a hell of a lot sooner than he expected!" Brand threw his napkin on the table, felt like he was going to lose his breakfast as well. "You can't force me."

"Actually, we can. You need to function within certain limits of normalcy, Brandon, or your mother is obligated to hospitalize you again so that you receive help. That's part of the agreement with the social services department and the hospital after the fiasco with Susan Craig. Your mental well-being is being monitored. As of right now, your behavior is borderline."

"So that's it. Go or you'll send me back to the loony bin."

"That's the general idea. Stay in school, try to be a member of this family and normal society, or we'll see you get additional help adjusting."

"Since when is being a member of this family being normal?"

"Don't push it."

Brand stood up. "I'm not pushing, I'm shoving. Mom keeps trying to marry a solution to her problems, you married a pair of nice boobs and a great pair of legs fifteen years younger than you are—and the rest of us bounce around like we're in a Pachinko machine. I'll go, but I'll tell you this—this game can be played both ways. Forcing me to go just might push me over the brink, and you two will be responsible."

"Don't threaten me." Now Phil stood, to his full adult height.

"That's not a threat, it's a promise." His mouth tasted sour. Brand swallowed it down. "I want to talk to the police now."

The Brea Police Department was not at all like Los Angeles. He remembered Parker Center in all its glory. For a few days there, he had an entourage close to that of O. J. Simpson during the trial days: his mother, his then-stepfather, two or three social workers, the attorneys and their team, the hospital representative and their attorneys and someone who had been related to Susan Craig and represented her estate, and then, of course, there had been the media. His face had been hidden whenever it was shown on television, but the cameras had been there, right in his face, every time they went to be interviewed at the police center or at court. The then-husband had caved under the pressure, partly because he had wanted to sell Brand's story to the tabloids and to trash TV.

His mother had been by his side then, fighting like a female bear over her wounded cub. He thought now, as they pulled into the parking lot, that it was probably only because such interviews and appearances would have ruined their settlement against the hospital and Craig's estate. He didn't know how much it was, but it came in regular increments, and after the first one which had bought their current home, he saw little difference in their lifestyle except that she met the current dweeb while setting up bank arrangements. As far as his mother was concerned, it was over, done with, finished. Gone with the wind and the second husband. It might never have happened except that she had a new home, a new husband, and had to take her son to regular therapy appointments. The exceptions were a little like speed bumps in her road of destiny, he thought. He was more like a Botts dot, one of those hard and round lane markers that let people know when they veered on the highway. A minor, sometimes helpful, inconvenience.

His life, of course, had never been the same. The therapist was good only to vent to about the inconveniences of what the shrink called a "blended family." Brand privately thought that if he ever shared what really went on in his head, let Bauer get hold of the shrink and show him just how blended things could get, the man would probably pee his pants just before turning him in to the psych ward.

Phil leaned back into the car. "Are you coming?"

Brand realized that they had been stopped for some time. He felt his face grow warm having been caught daydreaming. "Can't wait."

He had resorted to wearing the eye gear the surgeon had given him, his new shades lost. Even as he looked at the humble Brea police building, hacienda style as so much of the area was, it swam in and out of focus. He wondered what normalcy would be for him and when, if, he would reach it. Brand tilted his head back and looked up. Dark, smoky clouds drifted over the building, gathering, building like a massive storm front. Behind it was a typical late October day: dry, windswept, slight smoggish tint to the air, not a wisp of a cloud in sight. Even the sky looked faded. But not where he directed his gaze. The sight made him stumble on the walkway.

Phil said impatiently, "Thought you couldn't wait for this."

Brand tightened his lips, then realized he might look like the dweeb when *he* did that, and instead twisted the corner of his mouth. If he had anything to do with it, anything at all, no one was going to be happy with the outcome of this interview.

They gave him a private room and it was clean, cheerful, and laid back. Brand let himself slouch down into a chair across from two suited policemen, while a uniformed cop stood in the background, near the window. The older man placed a tape recorder on the table and his partner a file of papers and a notebook. Phil took the other chair, straight-backed, with a flip of his suit jacket coat.

"Our understanding is that this is just to ask a few questions."

One of the plainclothesmen smiled at the dweeb while the second took a pair of folded sunglasses out of his pocket and slid them across the interview table toward Brand. "I think these belong to you."

Being nice to the kid. Brand looked at the glasses. "Maybe," he said. "They look like a pair that I lost."

Phil sat up even straighter. "How could you lose them so soon? Your mother just bought them for you yesterday."

Brand reached out and curled his fingers around the glasses. If the police had tried to take prints from them, they'd all been cleaned off. There was a scratch across the top of the right lens, high, and crooked, like a lightning bolt. "It happens," he answered, before picking up the glasses and dropping them in his lap. He looked at the officer across from him. "If he keeps interrupting, this is going to take twice as long."

A stir ran through the room. The two suited cops sort of leaned toward one another as if in silent communication, and the uniform by the window twitched a little.

Then the policeman opposite Brand looked at Phil and said, "If you don't mind, sir, I'll ask you to be quiet. We'd like to get this statement in the boy's own words, as much as possible. If you have any objection, we understand, and the questioning can be stopped. Then we'll have to get a court order and do this officially."

"There's no need for that! We said we'd cooperate."

"Sir."

Phil stopped talking with a familiar grind of his teeth, and his thin mouth stretched out like an unhappy rubber band.

The policeman opposite Brand was the oldest person in the room, and he wore a dark blue suit with a blue and white striped shirt and a dark blue tie with a Snoopy Joe Cool policeman on it. He was tanned, and crow's feet webbed out from his eyes all the way to the bottom of his cheekbones. He wore a wedding ring that had been put on when he was a lot younger and thinner. It looked almost embedded in his finger. But he was not a heavy guy, and Brand got the impression that this man might have been a soccer coach or maybe even Pop Warner football . . . something wholesome, to be by his kids.

The other guy was Hispanic, cool olive skin and luxurious dark hair and warm brown eyes. He'd lost one earlobe somehow, and he was the one taking notes, and occasionally his hand would sneak up and tug on that ear. Maybe he'd pulled it off during a particularly difficult case.

The older man said, "I'm Officer Leopold and this is Officer Ramos. That's Patrolman Katz."

The uniform gave a curt nod.

Brand thought of Nicholas Solis in his uniform. "Anyone tell the wife his last words?"

Another ripple ran through the room.

"What last words?" repeated Leopold.

"I told the guys who showed up last night. It was like he knew he was dying, only it was just his leg that was trashed. Anyway, he told me his name and said, 'Tell my wife I love her.' Didn't anybody get that?"

Katz said hoarsely, "I'll tell her."

Ramos shifted in his chair. He slid a piece of paper out from under his notebook, marked something on it, and quietly slid it back.

The report, Brand thought. That's the report from last night. And somebody is going to get their ass chewed.

"Thank you, Brandon, for letting us know."

"Brand," he corrected. "I like to be called Brand."

"Okay. Why don't you tell us what happened, as far as you know."

"These guys came in, skinheads. I was in the arcade with Curtis and—"

"Curtis. The boy who was killed."

"Yeah. My ex-friend. Anyway, we were going to head over to the espresso bar at the Hot Flash when these guys came in the mall entrance."

"Know any of them? Ever seen the skinheads before? Can you describe them?"

"I didn't know them, I never saw them before, and the dead one wore blue jeans, Doc Martens, suspenders over his T-shirt, and real short hair. He was kind of blond, I guess. Didn't see his eyes until he was dead. They were blue then. The other guy, he wore heavy boots, too, and jeans, and his shirt was opened all the way, and his sleeves were rolled way high, to show off his tattoos. His head was shaved."

"Anyone else?"

He meant Mitch. Brand did not want to name him, but knew there were probably others who had seen him. "Yeah. They were flanking this homeless guy who scrounges around the mall. I don't think he was with them, exactly."

"Can you describe him?"

"Scruffy. Long hair. Beard. I don't know. I was watching the skinhead with the tattoos."

"What makes you think," Leopold prompted, "that the third man was not 'with' them?"

"He just didn't act like it. And when stuff started happening, he tackled one of them."

"What stuff?"

"When the young one . . . the one called Darby . . . grabbed the gun from the other guy's pants."

"The one with the tattoo had the gun?"

"Yes." Brand stared at Leopold. "Does he have a name?"

"Snake."

Brand did not attempt to hide his shudder. "And the scruffy guy tried to stop it, but he couldn't, and Curtis and I were like caught in the middle, because Darby wanted the girl at the espresso bar, and the gun went off and Curtis—he sort of turned around and fell back into the arcade and then the cop came."

He let his voice go high and trembly, and jumbled his words together. "And I was still out there in between and then Darby started shooting, and the cop went down, and Darby got shot, and he fell and he was holding onto me, and all this blood and vomit came out of his mouth—"

He halted.

Leopold looked at Ramos and Ramos returned the look.

Leopold reached forward and pushed a button on the tape recorder. "I think we have all we need."

"But that's not all that happened—"

"Our concern here is identifying Darby as the shooter. You've done that. We have witnesses from the dress shop who saw most of the incident."

"That's . . . that's all?"

"Yes. For now."

"Aren't you going to arrest me for leaving Curtis?"

"No, son. I don't think you meant to leave him, and even if you hadn't, there was nothing you could have done."

Brand looked at the dweeb and breathed heavily. "He told me—"

"I did what?" Phil half came out of his chair.

Brand looked back at Leopold. "He told me I could be arrested. That I had to come in today. I couldn't sleep all night. He got shot, and I couldn't do anything about it—" He let his voice rise high, and break.

Leopold stared at Phil. "I think you need to take the boy home and get him settled. He's been through a lot, and he needs help to deal with it."

Phil had gone pale. "His mother and I—"

"I'm sure you have, sir," Ramos answered smoothly. He stood and offered his hand. "Thank you for coming down today."

Phil did not say another word as they left and walked down the rows of cars in the lot. Brand took a last look. There were officers walking in and out of the building, and none of them seemed to notice the cloud boiling overhead, or the strings that reached down and touched them from time to time, strings that wrapped around and around their uniforms, their souls.

Death touched them all.

Brand shuddered. He no more trusted the police than he did Snake. If they had wanted the truth from him, they would not have let him go. If they had been interested. If they had not been shadow eaten.

Chapter 14

Black and white TV. Cary Grant wooing Myrna Loy with patter about the man who has the power. What power? The power of voodoo. Who do? He does, the man who has the power. What power? Kamryn blinked, focusing slowly on the classic movie, having fallen asleep to a late evening infomercial and now waking up to Grant and Loy at their most witty and handsomest. She looked at the program guide. *The Bachelor and the Bobby-Soxer.* Shirley Temple had the sidekick role as younger sister. The movie was older than her mother.

Kamryn rubbed her eyes. A cheap hotel bedspread with a waffle weave seemed imprinted permanently in her cheek. She yawned.

If anyone here had been interested in the shooting, she hadn't noticed it. She'd checked in, paid cash, and crashed in the room sometime after Tony Little ranted and raved about washboard abdomens for the one hundredth time. She'd paid for two nights, not knowing if she was going to sleep at all, or if she'd sleep the day through.

Kamryn levered herself up, reaching for her duffel bag and rummaging through it for some decent clothes. She always carried the bag, and as luck would have it, there was also a basketful of dirty laundry in the car's trunk because she had thought about going to the laundromat after work. The thought of chores and a regular day rattled her. How could anything go back to normal? After a shooting. After a murder.

She showered and changed, and left the room long enough to go to the news racks at the front of the hotel office and buy a local paper. The shooting had made front-page news, along with the latest international blowup. She went back to the room and read the story without looking at the pictures. Some of the detail was the way she remembered it, most was logical conjecture, and there was a good deal left out.

She paused when a teen's half-awful, half-sincere school ID picture interrupted the column despite her efforts not to look at any of the victims. This was not her boy, it was his constant companion, although she did not know how her boy, as she thought of him, had not gotten killed as well. He had tried to save her, putting himself in the line of fire. It had been his best friend, instead, who'd caught the bullet.

Too upset to finish the story, Kamryn shoved the paper aside. She dropped her face into her hands and dug her fingers into her hair. She had a long list of amends to make, and now this added to the weighty length of it. How was she ever going to make up for all of this?

It made no difference. She had promised, had bartered her life for it. If it cost her her life doing it, then she could only hope it was better than costing her soul. God, maybe it would have been easier if You had just let me go in that basement along with Mom and Dad.

She opened her eyes and pulled the paper toward her again, unable to think of anything else. Before she had descended into that bloody basement in her Pennsylvania home, she had fallen into a pit of hatred and violence. Perhaps her mother and father had deserved to die. Perhaps none of this would have happened if she had taken just one step differently, long ago. It wasn't just the steps she'd taken, but those her parents and her brother had. Was she responsible for all of them? Logic told her no. Hope told her that she was no longer responsible even for those she had taken in the past. Just the new path, the new road.

She ran her fingertip along the newspaper fold. She would have to leave. Snake would be looking for her, to finish what Darby had begun, knowing instinctively that she had not only turned her back on Darby, but on the entire movement. She knew too much, she was dangerous to all of them. She could not stay.

But she could delay a day or two to say good-bye. She creased the paper where it told of the funeral arrangements for the dead. She owed the boys this much.

Rembrandt stayed at the Ritz Carlton. He sat on his balcony, drinking a glass of fresh squeezed orange juice, into which he had sprinkled, but not emptied, vodka from the room's minibar. He liked his juice relatively pure and natural. The day was crisp and a little overcast, but the marine layer would burn off before noon. He sat back, a copy of the county's conservative newspaper across his lap, and watched the tide on the beach below. Its teal phosphorescence boiled pleasantly onto beige sand, and the tiered walkways from the rear of the elegant resort hotel led people down to walk romantically entwined along the water's edge. Brilliantly red bougainvillea bloomed extravagantly along the atria and pathways and stone walls of the hotel, edged by iceplant and grass upon the grounds. The view refreshed his eyes as much as the juice did his throat.

Sucking orange pulp from between his teeth, he finally scooted himself closer to the glass-topped table and looked at his laptop screen, scrolling through the files it displayed. "Let's see what I can find, boy."

He had managed to cull a list of five names from school district records. He had had more, but had tossed most of the Latino surnames, though in this county he knew he stood a chance of being wrong, as the intermarriages and cultural interlacings of the population were myriad. Orange County had long ago lost its staid white only face and now wore the melting pot mask that the entire nation was famed for. He knew he might have to backtrack if he were wrong on the surname of the boy he sought.

He looked from the screen to the paper one last time. "Gotcha." With a brilliant red felt tip, he encircled the notice in the paper. Curtis Reynolds, fourteen, memorial services the day following at Brea Evergreen United Methodist, eleven o'clock. The picture was not good, but he recognized the companion to the one he sought. The boy ought to be there as well, belonging to one of the four names left on the screen, staring him in the face.

"You just hang out, son. I'll find you. You don't have to have a name. I just need to get my hands on you. And I will."

Rembrandt could find him sooner, if he wished, driving from

southern Orange County and the pleasant atmosphere of the beach, crisscrossing north to Brea at the other end of the county, but then there was still the matter of isolating him from his family and whatever police surveillance might be upon him. The funeral, however, posed opportunities. Vast opportunities. There would be plainclothesmen there, as well, but he could deal with that. Like riding a good cutting horse, he could separate the calf from the herd.

Rembrandt closed his files and shut down his laptop, and sat back once more in his chair. He poured another glass of iced juice from his carafe, saluted the surf, and proceeded to enjoy his day of leisure. There would not be many more of them once the base camps were set up and basic training had begun. There would be logistics and intelligence to work out, but the program would not be fully operational until Christiansen was located. First the boy, then the Marine sergeant. Tomorrow the hunt began in earnest.

He looked and felt ridiculous. They had dressed him in black jeans, one of Phil's old navy sweaters, and a dark banker's tie, too long, its length buttoned away inside his shirt where it tickled him around the navel. All of this could have been done in the relatively private confines of the home, but no, they were doing it here in the church parking lot. The dweeb solemnly tied the knot and then tugged it into perfection, murmuring, "You ought to learn how to do this someday."

"Why? So I can be like you?" *More than half dead less than halfway through life?* Brand stared into Phil's eyes.

His stepfather's mouth thinned again, but he said nothing, merely took him by the shoulders and spun him around so his mother could look at him. She pressed a handkerchief to her lips.

"Don't make a scene, Mom."

She put her back to the car and looked around at the multitude of other vehicles. "I have no intention of doing so." She scanned with the practiced eye of one used to dodging the media and commented, almost disappointed, "No one's here."

"There's a hostage situation in a mini-mart in Stanton," Phil told her. "And there's a baby getting a heart and lung transplant at Loma Linda."

And Curtis' death was obviously old news. Brand took a deep breath. The church was nestled deep between housing and a golf course. He looked at the groomed fairways of the course, wondering if it used to be a cemetery at one time, so suspiciously close to the sanctuary. The trees which edged the course and made a natural hazard also framed the back and side of the church. Watered by the golf course, they were a deep, dark green despite the fact that the rainy season had yet to hit the area. Their soothing color attracted him.

"Brandon, I want you to take your glasses off the minute you get inside."

He pushed his shades into better position on his nose. The lightning bolt etch mark floated just above the vision of his right eye, sort of like a pointer. He shrugged inside the stiff collar of the new dress shirt and felt the tie uncomfortably hug his neck.

"Brandon, did you hear what I said?"

"Yeah."

Her eyes narrowed, but she turned away. Phil said, "We'll be right behind you."

Cutting off escape, Brand thought. He took another deep breath and crossed the parking lot to the big, wooden double doors which had been flung open to the crisp October day. He passed through, noticing their surfaces, carved with the symbols of Christianity and the promised afterlife.

He could hear bagpipes playing "Amazing Grace" and it struck him funny. Fartbags, Curt had always called them. Scottish sphincters. He used to play his armpit and drone in imitation. Brand did not think Curtis would have been happy to have bagpipes played at his funeral, but it was not something they'd ever discussed.

Nobody his age ever discussed funerals. Kids weren't supposed to die. He remembered the rash of car accidents last summer, when sixteen- and seventeen-year-olds were flying out of smashed cars at an incredible rate, by the dozens it seemed. It had been shocking, but it was something everyone knew wouldn't happen to them. Till the next time somebody went cruising and missed a tight turn at, oh, say, eighty miles an hour, aluminum beer cans soaring clear just ahead of bodies. Just another hazard of the California lifestyle.

But here they were, freshmen in high school, confined to campus during hours, when the drivers, the juniors and seniors, cruised away for decent food, screeching back seconds before the final tardy bells. They had counted the hours until Curtis would get his learner's permit. He would have turned fifteen and a half first, barely a year away.

A year to freedom. The first rites of passage. A year that would make their miserable existence gain hope, become bearable even. A year closer to manhood.

They'd never thought about ducking bullets.

He'd barely set foot inside the chapel when Mrs. Reynolds descended on him. She wore a black jacket dress, with a thin white pinstripe, and it was new, because she preferred jeans. He didn't think he'd ever seen Curt's mom in a dress before. He could see why. Her legs didn't look like they were meant for the public to view. Her face was puffy and her eyes bloodshot from crying, and his father stood in the corner, gray around the mouth, his dark eyes sunk in his face, saying nothing.

Curt had been the only boy.

Before he could duck, Mrs. Reynolds wrapped her chubby arms around him. "Oh, Brandon," she whispered hoarsely as she hugged him tightly. "You must go see him. He looks so . . . natural. We decided to leave the coffin lid open so everyone could say good-bye."

She knocked his glasses nearly off his face, and he stared down the row of double pews at the white and gold coffin at the front, where the altar was, and smelled the heavy perfume of the flowers.

Half the school was here, it seemed, and their heads all turned and a whisper started through the chapel that he could almost hear. Bzzz, bzzz, bzzz . . . the shooting . . . bzzz, bzzz.

He shrugged out of June Reynolds' death grip. He retrieved his shades and tucked them inside his shirt pocket, as promised. The inside of the chapel seemed to glow in matching whites and golds, like candlelight, and he stood for a moment, bedazzled. The sharpness of his newly created vision wavered, then darkened, then lightened. He fished around for courage to step down the aisle toward the coffin and found himself empty inside.

He had spent most of the night talking with Mitch. That had kept the darkness and Bauer away for a while, but Mitch wasn't here, and he did not like taking drugs, so he hadn't hit his stash again. He hadn't induced a chemical calm, he had no pharmaceutical well from which to draw safe emotions. How do you manufacture something out of nothing? Where could he find the backbone to go say good-bye to Curtis?

Mrs. Reynolds seemed to sense how difficult it was. She reached for his hand. "I'll walk down with you."

"No! I mean, that's all right." Brand cleared his throat. He put a hand up to the tie knot and tugged at it, trying to loosen it a bit. He could hear his mother and Mrs. Reynolds hugging and talking in a muted tone.

The coffin beckoned him. He slid a foot forward and started toward it.

His face felt chilled and clammy, and his hands began to sweat. He turned suddenly, looked back through the tiny lobby of the chapel, and saw signs for restrooms. Just in time. He pushed hurriedly past Phil and his mother. She made a sound of protest, but Phil said, "Let him go. He looks pretty pale."

He made it to the tiny bathroom and threw up in the stall toilet, until he was dry heaving, his throat burning. He flushed, then went to the sink and washed his face. The water felt tepid and smelled stagnant, like old pond water. He wondered where they pumped it up from. He stood there over the sink a long time, running water now and then, splashing it on his face.

"It's not a good thing to see, is it, son?"

Brand froze. He raised his eyes, caught only a corner of the speaker's visage in the mirror. A vertical fraction of a face, sharply contoured, skin ravaged by old scars, eyes coal dark. The ruined man.

"They're waiting for you now. Any minute now, someone's going to come in after you. So you better get yourself straight."

Brand stared at the splinter of the man's face. So soft-spoken, so hard behind the words. "What do you want?"

"Why, I want to get the men who got Curtis killed. Don't you?"

"I don't know what you mean. The skinhead's dead."

"Ah. But there's more to the story than that, isn't there, son? You know it, and I know it. I should think you'd want to tell me . . . to get justice for Curtis. Someday you'll be crossing over, too, and he's going to look you in the face. He's going to wonder why you didn't stand up for him. He's going to wonder why being your friend got him killed. You know, he was still dying when you ran. The paramedics tried working on him, but it was too late."

"You shut up! He was dead! I know he was. I saw it in his eyes—" Just like Darby. It wasn't like the eyes stopped glistening or anything, they just stopped . . . reacting to life. There was nothing, no one, no soul, to see.

"You ran, and I don't blame you. You saw a terrible thing happen. But you should have heard the machine. A high-pitched whine, and then the paramedics would yell 'Clear' and then his body would flop when it got all those volts. They did it again and again. Once they thought they got his ticker jump-started. But it didn't keep. No, sir, they worked real hard on him, but there was nothing they could do."

"My being there wouldn't have made a difference."

"Wouldn't it now? Well, that's something you'll never know."

"Leave me alone," Brand said softly, but it was as if the ruined man couldn't hear him.

"You and I need to talk, son. Or else the guilt is going to eat you up inside."

Brand wiped his hands dry. "You stay away from me."

The ruined man held up a hand. "I'm ready when you're ready. But don't you forget we've got things to talk about."

Brand started to turn around and confront him.

The bathroom went dark. "Shit!" Brand stood, his heart in his throat, thinking he'd gone blind. The bathroom door opened and he saw the silhouette of the ruined man slipping out.

Brand grabbed the door before it eased shut and slapped his palm against the wall and found the light switch. He turned it on before leaning out. The lobby was empty except for Phil and his mother standing in the chapel doorway. She turned, as if alerted by his very presence, and waved.

"They're waiting for you," she mouthed, and took him by the elbow.

He took her hand off his arm. Her fingers were chill, and she gave him a look that, just for a moment, he imagined hurt lay in. Brand turned toward the coffin and began to drift toward it.

Drift, because he could not feel his feet touch the carpet runner. Drift, because there seemed to be no time, no heartbeat, no sound.

The church had swelled to overflowing, people crowded the side aisles along the wings, but he could not hear them breathe, they might as well be the dead themselves who waited to welcome Curtis into their ranks. He thought he recognized faces from his school as he floated closer toward the coffin, teachers, counselors, students, past and present. Where had they all been when he and Curtis were being taunted, snubbed, trash-canned?

A handful of people were still making their way past the casket as he drew near. They parted to let him close.

If he couldn't hear their voices, their breathing, their steps, it was because his pulse thundered in his ears. Every breath he took sounded as though some immense bellows must be sucking in the air and releasing it. With each inch he came closer to the coffin and seeing over its gilt-edged rim, his body reminded him that it was he who lived and Curtis who did not. Every part of his body except for his guts, which had disappeared, leaving an ice cold cavern in their absence.

He put out a trembling hand and touched the rim. Like a ship docking and throwing out an anchor line, it steadied him and he pulled himself closer. Curtis' face became visible, no longer eclipsed by the coffin's side.

Brand held his breath. It was and was not his friend. Curt had never worn suits, never intended to, but they had him laid out in navy blue. His hair was freshly washed and someone must have lightened it, because it was a true blond now, not the dirty blond he remembered so well. And he'd never known Curtis to be without a pimple or two; smooth peach makeup hid the red blotches. Now his face looked serene, both older and younger than the friend Brand had known, childlike, peacefully asleep in the coffin, but with a newfound maturity in the suit and the solemn expression of his face.

But it wasn't Curtis. Not the one he knew. Curtis was always laughing, talking, or eating, his expression in constant motion, his hair uncombed, his skin outraged by an excess of hormones, his eyes open and defiant. Curt, the coward, the brave fool, the scholar, the delinquent, the kidder, the loyal best friend, Curt . . . *the dead*.

Brand found himself wondering where the bullet holes were and how much damage they'd done.

"It's good luck if you kiss them good-bye," a girlish whisper said in his ear.

He flinched, caught a glimpse of Curt's mother in the corner of his vision, and bit his tongue on his reply. As he shied away from the edge of the coffin, he looked up and saw darkness dripping from the rotunda ceiling overhead. It flowed down the back of the altar and geysered up from the pulpits, charcoal fog, and it was hungry and cold. It fell, like rain, with a plink and plunk, onto the casket.

It did not pool like water, but gathered, like smoke or fog and as Brand stared in absolute horror, the coffin filled with it. The KillJoy snaked along the white satin lining and smothered Curtis' torso.

"Shit," Brand murmured. He hoped he had imagined it, stoned as he'd been, afraid as he'd been. He hoped that perhaps Bauer had thrown him a curve and that nothing was what he'd seen, what he'd imagined.

The darkness inundated the chapel. The large crucifix hanging on the wall deterred it not at all, and as Brand stared aghast, Jesus disappeared from sight altogether.

Mrs. Reynolds' grief-pale face bobbed through the dark air toward him, like a hot air balloon. "Brandon, are you all right?"

"No." His knees went like water and the only thing holding him on his feet was that he leaned on the corner of the casket, gripping it tightly with both hands. "You need to get out of here, Mrs. Reynolds. Now. You need to get everybody out." He could feel its overpowering appetite. He knew that if he turned and looked, he would see it tasting the people sitting unaware in the pews, licking at their faces, nibbling at their eyes. But he would not, could not, turn and look. He watched as the KillJoy enveloped Curt's body altogether, until nothing was left but his ghostly, powdered face.

It was real. He could see it. Any hope that it had come out of the codeine and Haldol vanished. He'd been stoned, but he had seen a true thing. It had existence, and he was aware of it, and he didn't know what to do. He had a margin of safety, that he did know. Although it had chased him through his dreams, Brand thought it could be nothing personal. It hungered as a shark hungered. If he stayed out of its waters, he would be safe. He stared at Curt's placid face.

And then the eyes popped open. They were opaque and filmed,

gummy and still, and they looked right into his. The jaw cracked open, issuing misty dark words.

"I know you," the corpse said. "Brandon, Brand, Brand X, the X-man. I come for you, too."

Brand let out a yell that tore through the hushed quiet of the church. He pelted through the side door.

Chapter 15

Kamryn found a quiet corner of the chapel near the exit doors and waited. She observed as the building filled, watched the faces of the young so shocked and curious to be there, and the old, so tired, so worried. She found herself humming lightly to the music being piped in. She thought of her aunt who, in the last decade of her long life, had refused to go to any funeral, even of her best friend, even of her husband, as if fearing a preview of her future.

She would like to have told her aunt not to worry, but she couldn't have then and even now was not entirely sure. Simply being in the church almost overwhelmed her. She had never seen God, but she was not certain that she hadn't felt His Presence, or at least that of one of his angels. It left her feeling tremulous as she stood in the sanctuary, tremulous and on the verge of some vast emotional experience she could not quite understand.

She saw the boy start to enter the chapel, then push back and hurriedly leave. Kamryn thought of going after him but held back, thinking his parents surely would, but they did not either. After many long minutes, after several more hymns during which the crowd grew so thick she thought of leaving rather than be trapped in the multitude, the boy came back. He went down the center aisle so quickly that Kamryn had barely a glance at his sheet-white face. The music had changed to "Morning has broken, like the first day. . . ."

She wished that she had not stayed in the back, but had gone to the front so she could join him, that he didn't have to make the walk alone. The dead boy's mother hurried to catch up, but he seemed oblivious. The few mourners already at the casket moved aside to give him clearance.

Kamryn folded her hands tightly, trying to send him courage in her thoughts, understanding what he must be feeling. There had always been for her, as young as she was, at her great-aunt's services, and then her grandfather's, and then her parents', a sense of unrecognition. It was as if, when she faced the living, that whatever it was in the other person that she greeted, that she recognized, was intangible and left when life departed. It was more than warmth and animation . . . it was . . . oh, she couldn't explain it . . . but she knew as the boy stood over the open coffin and looked down, that he would be searching for the familiar in his friend, that which had always leaped out to greet him, and was now missing.

The dead boy's mother moved up and said something. The boy reacted as if shocked, and then stood and looked around the room wildly. Kamryn felt a chill touch her. Despite her long-sleeved dress, despite the warm-winded October day outside, with the sunlight streaming in the open doors, an icy feeling permeated the chapel. The faint tattoo scars prickled in her skin. She hugged herself, her purse with its gun-hard bulge digging into her rib cage.

She decided to leave and quietly ducked out, and had her key in the car door when she heard the agonizing cry. It was primal and drove the very hairs up on the back of her neck, a primitive wail of loss and fear, a raw file of sound against her nerves. Emotions cascaded over her and gooseflesh raised on her arms. *Come on, Sis. Come down into the basement. I've got a surprise for you.* Her throat closed slightly and she could feel her pulse ticking wildly in the hollow of her neck. Death and grief. Before the echo of the boy's cry faded, she had turned back as if she could do something. Then she saw the man waiting in the grove where the golf course met the churchyard, waiting as if he knew someone would come his way.

At first, she thought it might be a driver for the mortuary, but he wasn't dressed right, and he had an attitude to his body posture. Kamryn slid quickly into her car and fought the desire to hide further, watching, as the side doors flew open and the boy bolted out, head down, running for his life.

He barged right into the waiting man. There was a brief struggle, and then the man picked up the boy, right off his feet, Kamryn's boy, and hauled him toward the grove where a car waited. He threw his captive into the car, got in, and started up, heading down a service road to the back of the church, into the golf course.

Kamryn's jaw dropped as she tried to decide what she'd just seen, when people boiled out of the building, and began to fill the parking lot. A woman in a blue-dotted swiss suit cried, "Brandon! Brand! Come back here!"

A tall man joined her and added his shout to hers. "Brandon! Come right back here, young man!"

Brandon. Her boy. She should tell them what she'd seen, but she'd also watched their strained, cold faces in the church. Whatever fate Brandon had awaiting him was not much different back here.

Kamryn started her car and backed out slowly, until she hit the gravel service road the first car had taken. No one paid any attention to her.

Brand sat in the front seat, nursing a sore wrist, shoulder up against the door panel so he could be as far away from the ruined man as possible. He watched the groomed fairways pass by and become undeveloped land, eucalyptus and pepper trees brushing the car window as he drove through, toward the foothills, toward the canyons.

"Well, now," said the ruined man in that faintly accented drawl of his. "I didn't think it would be this easy."

"Congratulations."

The ruined man smiled broadly. "Sounds like you had some of the sauce knocked out of you, son."

"I'm not your son."

"Well, let's trade names then. I'm Rembrandt and you're . . ."

"Brand," he answered reluctantly. He did not want to look at the man, but he did. His eyes were smudged again, and he blinked several times to clear them, but nothing helped. He finally closed them in frustration.

"If I were you," Rembrandt said, and the road swerved away from them, shifting Brand into a door handle, "I'd want to stay awake and alert. My life might depend on it."

Brand opened his eyes to stare out the front window. They were on a firebreak road now, and the tires sent puffs of dirt out behind them like smoke signals. He said wearily, "If you think I'm scared, I'm not. You just want to ask me some questions."

Rembrandt's smile disappeared as if it had never been, and he jerked the steering wheel to a hard right, bringing the car to a stop, headed into a small copse of pepper and oak trees. The car filled with the smell of dirt and freshly-bruised grass.

"You're not as smart as you think you are, son. Because I do intend to ask you questions, and I intend on killing you if I don't get some answers."

Brand snapped his head around. "What the hell are you talking about?"

Rembrandt shoved the car door open, fishing something out of its pocket. "Your quarter's finished. Game time over. I get some answers or you're as dead as your little buddy back there, and I'll tell you something else. The way he died will be easy compared to the way you're going to die."

Words dried up in Brand's throat as he watched Rembrandt get out of the car carrying a rope. Massaging it through his hands, the ruined man went to several trees before finding one he liked, and throwing the end of the rope over a convenient tree limb. At the re-alization, Brand kicked his feet over the center console, ready to bail out the driver's door, but Rembrandt moved amazingly fast. He snatched the door open and buried his fist in Brand's collar, lifting Brand out of the seat. He manhandled Brand across the ground until his back hit the rough bark of the tree, and the limb and rope shad-owed his face as he looked at the ruined man.

"Don't mistake me, son."

"Who are you?"

"You don't really want to know that, because right now you have a choice. If I told you, you wouldn't." Rembrandt removed his hand from Brand's collar, giving him breathing room, and quickly fash-ioned a slip noose.

"We don't know each other very well, you and I, but I know you've got a quick tongue. So I'm going to save you some valuable time." He pulled the noose over Brand's head. "I want to know what you know about Mitch Christiansen. Where's his crib, how long has he been hanging out at the mall, and who else might know anything about him."

Brand felt the stiff bristles of the rope cut into his throat as it settled into place. "I—I don't—"

Rembrandt jerked the noose tight. "I said I was going to save you some valuable time." He tied the rope around the tree and left, coming back with weathered wooden crates in his hands, bee boxes. He stacked them on top of each other, next to Brandon. He pointed at them. "I'll ask you one more time, and then I'll make you stand up there, and then I'll make you jump. You'll hang the way they did a couple hundred years ago, before the hangman's knot was invented. Do you know how the knot works? It breaks your neck when your weight hits the rope. Takes only minutes to strangle and die that way. This way could take hours. But you'll still be dead before anybody finds you."

Brand tried to gather his thoughts as Bauer barged in, thinking of the time he hog-tied one of his victims around the neck and every time the child grew weary and dropped his legs, the noose got tighter and tighter. Bauer appreciated the image. The remembrance made Brand sick. Sweat popped out on his forehead as he fought for composure.

Rembrandt let out a sigh. "You're tough to convince. Well, son, I've been doing some research. I pulled up your school records. I know you've been in and out of psychiatric care. This is going to look like suicide. Isn't anybody going to come looking for me. I've got nothing to lose here, and you've got everything."

"Just a minute!" The rope cut into his neck. "I met him a couple of weeks ago. He's been hanging around the mall and plaza for a couple of months, though. He doesn't make friends. I don't think anybody else knows him. And I don't really know him. Just Mitch, that's all he told me." His voice sounded strange to his own ears. "That's all I know. Everything."

"Everything?"

"I swear!"

"Get up on those boxes."

His vision swam. Perspiration cascaded down his face and the wind dried it, but he could taste the salt of his fear on his lips. "What?"

"You heard me. Get up on those boxes."

Brand climbed onto the wooden crates. They creaked under his weight. They were empty, abandoned, and the thought lanced through him that at least they were empty of bees. He balanced gingerly on his feet.

"He never took you to his crib."

Brand wet his mouth again. "We just used to say hi around the parking lot."

"Where?"

"Behind the arcade, in the storage areas outside Hot Flash and the other stores."

Rembrandt ran his fingers across the rope. "Who'd he talk to besides you?"

"No . . . nobody. He kept to himself. The mall cops ran him off a couple of times. If he stayed anywhere, it was probably behind the plaza across the street."

"But you don't know that."

"No." Brand tried to swallow again and found his mouth dry of spit. He could stand here until doomsday and not work up a drop. He wondered if Rembrandt could tell that he was lying.

Rembrandt wrapped his hand in the rope. "Thank you, son," and began to take up the slack.

Brand felt the noose tighten. The air whooshed out of him, leaving him without protest. He clawed at the noose. He was being hanged anyway! The air grew dim in front of his face.

"Stop it! Hold it right there!"

Rembrandt turned, and behind his lanky form, Brand could make out a blurred figure with a determined feminine voice. And she was pointing a gun.

"I mean it!" Kamryn called. She twitched the gun aside, fired twice, puncturing both rear tires of Rembrandt's car. "Brand, quit fooling around. Get yourself free and get over here."

He tore a nail to a bloody quick getting the slipknot to budge, then pulled his head out of the loop and jumped toward Kamryn, shying away from Rembrandt.

"Get in my car." She pointed an elbow toward the firebreak.

"Wh–where?" His breath choked up in his throat.

"Back there, behind the curve." She eyed Rembrandt over the barrel of her gun. "Hurry up!" She started to walk backward.

Rembrandt had been holding his hands out at his sides and moved, ever so slightly, dusting off his suit jacket. "I did not think about you, ma'am. I see now I should have given you more consideration."

"Forget me. It's the gun you're giving credit." She stumbled over a knot of grass, but Brand was there, reaching for an arm, steering her. She looked briefly at him. "I told you to run."

"I'm not leaving you alone with him." Still white-faced, still determined.

"Okay. Can you drive?"

"I'm only fourteen."

"Screw that. Can you drive?"

"Sure. As long as I don't have to parallel park."

They were bracketed together like a three-legged race at a picnic. Rembrandt was slowly walking toward them, cautiously, a step to every three or four of theirs.

Kamryn took a deep breath. "Run," she ordered and shook him off. Rembrandt let out a bellow and charged. She fired into the ground, and he plunged to a halt in astonishment.

She turned and took to her heels after Brand. He already had the car in gear as she grabbed the open passenger door and jumped in.

They'd switched drivers and reached the open road before she spoke. "I was at the church. I heard you scream."

Brand was looking out the rolled-down window, his sable hair tousled and swept back from his forehead. He made a wry face. "The whole world heard me scream."

"Why?"

"Just did. It gave me the creeps, seeing Curtis like that, y'know." He shut his mouth firmly, looking back out the window.

If he didn't want to talk, she couldn't force him. But she had things she wanted to say. "I want you to know that I know what you did."

Sharply, "When?"

"At the mall. I know you tried to protect me."

"I guess you didn't need all that much protection."

"Maybe. But I'm sorry for your friend, Brandon."

"He wasn't trying to protect you."

"I know. He was just . . . there."

"In the way." Brand rubbed his nose briskly. "I suppose you're taking me to the police."

Kamryn shifted weight. She had the gun secured under her thigh.

"No, I don't think so. Maybe that's a decision you should go home and make."

"I don't have a home," he said bleakly.

"You have to go somewhere."

"Yeah." He chafed at his throat lightly, where the rope had bitten into tender flesh. "I have to go away from here."

"Brand, you have family. You can't just run like that."

"They'll put me back in the psycho ward. You were listening to Rembrandt. You heard him. I have a rep." He looked at her, hazel eyes reflecting his misery. "You don't know. I can't stay here. I can't tell you everything, but It knows me, knows my name—I can't stay."

The desperation in his voice struck a chord in her. She knew what it was like, and she knew she couldn't stay, either. "You won't get far on foot."

"I don't know where to go either. Mitch would know. And I've got to tell him about Rembrandt."

"Mitch," Kamryn repeated with a faint smile. "And you wouldn't know where he is."

"He's in the loft above my garage, but we can't get in there until after dark. If I know my mom and the dweeb, they're talking to the police right about now, shifting the responsibility for finding me. Then they'll round up my siblings and head out to dinner. We'll park around the block and come in through the backyard."

"I'm going with you?"

"You volunteered, didn't you?"

Kamryn guessed she had.

Chapter 16

Rembrandt watched the bumper of the car disappear in a cloud of dust and dried grass as it pulled around the curve of the road. He waited a moment to be sure that the young woman hadn't changed her mind and decided to come back with her firepower, but the air cleared of the engine's drone.

He turned and surveyed the damage to the car's tires. He had only one standard spare in the trunk, but she'd known that. He wasn't going anywhere unless he wished to ruin the tire rims. It wasn't his car. He got in and fired up the vehicle, then pulled back down the road. By the time he reached a main street and a filling station, he had Bayliss on the cell phone.

"I want two agents."

"Street ready?"

"I want the best we've got."

Bayliss did not ask why. He said only, "We don't have expendables at this point."

Because of the systems they had routed the calls through, and because of the scrambling, there was a slight delay between each phrasing. It made it difficult to read the nuances of Bayliss' voice, but Rembrandt caught that last.

"Christiansen's made me."

"That is not good news."

"No. But I'm close enough to be breathing down his neck. I need our best."

"I'll have them sent out by jet. Where to?"

"John Wayne Airport. Page me with their ETA. And, sir—"

"Yes?"

"I apologize for the difficulty."

A long pause. Then, "You're the best man I've got. There is no one more loyal, more serving. Not even that voodoo priest could give me a better right hand."

"Thank you, sir."

"Just find Christiansen. My timetable is losing flexibility."

"I understand."

Rembrandt hung up. A spark burned in his chest, as it always did, when he thought of what they were trying to accomplish, just as it did whenever he saw the flag being raised or heard the anthem being played. This was a time of trials and bold decisions. Judgment would come later, generations later.

He was prepared.

He stowed the cell phone in his briefcase as the sound of air wrenches filled the air, making normal conversation nearly impossible. He had paid the attendants well, but not too well, for new tires and a quick transfer. He had his own personal timetable now. The quarry would be running again, and easier to track.

This time he would have the woman and the boy with him. He did not know if Military Intelligence was also still tracking Christiansen or if the local police would be looking for him, but he knew what they did not. Christiansen would take them along, for the camouflage they offered. He would be right behind.

"No," said Mitch flatly. "It wouldn't be right."

"I have the car," returned Kamryn. She sat cross-legged on the dusty floor, showing a good deal of leg, unaware of it, flexing chopsticks in her hand. The loft smelled of lo mein and pork fried rice. "And we all have to leave."

"Brand doesn't have to."

She flipped a look toward Brand, her dark hair feathering about her face as she did so, wings of ebony accenting her movement. "Rembrandt tried to kill him."

"If I move on, Rembrandt will come after me. I can guarantee that." Having a name, at last, for the shadowy adversary helped. It made his flight and fight more concrete instead of abstract.

Brand whispered hoarsely, "I have to leave more than either of you." He had not eaten much and now pushed his lo mein noodles aimlessly about his paper plate. She wondered if his throat hurt, or if the rope burns had only chafed his skin. It did not matter. He had been close enough to hanging. She would not feel much like eating either, but her last good meal had been yesterday.

"You have family."

"They won't protect me. They never have. If you won't take me, I'll hitchhike out. As far as I can get. I can't stay!"

"Brand, I can't take anybody with me. You've met Rembrandt. This is the first time I've known his name, but he's been on my heels for months, and he doesn't take prisoners. I don't know how much longer I can stay two jumps ahead of him, and if and when he catches up, I can't keep either of you safe."

"I didn't ask you to," Kamryn said brusquely. "I can take care of myself. You're not taking my car and leaving without me."

They studied each other. To Brand's surprise, these two seemed to know each other almost as well as he knew Mitch. When told who they were going to meet, Kamryn had stopped at a mini-mart as well as for Chinese take-out, and bought razors and scissors. She had insisted on cutting his hair and making him shave before they ate, and she'd worked quickly, paring him down to a civilized look. His skin showed one or two small cuts where the razors had bitten lightly.

"The shooting's over," he commented. "You're not even front-page news."

"Snake will come after me and probably others. They won't let it go until I'm as dead as Darby." Kamryn put down her plate and chopsticks. She hesitated a moment, then rolled up her sleeves. Like the lower half of Mitch's face, her skin was too tender, too pink . . . and the tattoos imprinted up and down her arms were faded, but still visible. "I've been having them lasered. It takes about ten treatments, but that's only skin-deep. I won't tell you why I did it in the first place, but I'm not that person anymore."

Brand stirred. He reached forward tentatively, then pulled his hand away. "It must hurt."

"It hurts worse having them." She shuddered slightly and let her sleeves fall back into place.

Mitch's gaze stayed on her face. "You know too much."

"About what?" Brand looked back and forth.

"About the skinheads."

Brand curled a lip. "They're thugs."

"That, and more. They're organized. They have cash sources of money, weapons, and publications, paper printed and electronic. Hatred is an easy culture to spread." Mitch raised his eyes and rocked back on his hips, forgetting the plate of Chinese food in his lap. "You're right. You can't stay here."

"And it *is* my car."

"We might have to exchange the car."

"I've got some money." She put her chin forward defiantly. The color of her eyes deepened.

"I'm thinking of backtracking up toward Seattle. Rembrandt's already been up there. It might throw him off."

"No," interrupted Brand. "That's the wrong way."

"You're not going," Mitch responded, without looking at him. "You've got family and it's time you took the responsibility for getting along with them. It's not a one-way street."

"You don't understand—"

"No, you don't understand. I can't take you with me."

Brand mumbled something. Both Mitch and Kamryn said, with irritation, "What?"

"Nothing." He folded his plate up and squashed it until the food ran out of it in dribbles before shoving it into a trash sack. "You can't leave here until I do or the police will be all over you."

"In about two hours, most of the West Coast will be sound asleep."

Brand hunched down and folded his arms. "I'll wait."

Kamryn asked, "What will you need?"

"I have most of my things in a duffel. No ID. Very little money. What about you?"

"I have," she said firmly, "clothes, my car, money. And my gun. I've got everything I need."

"ID?"

"Several."

Mitch's eyes widened slightly, but he did not comment on that. "We should take the 5 up to Sacramento and on up. There's a lot of agricultural traffic, nobody will notice us one way or the other."

"We won't get out of the area before dawn if we try to exchange the car here."

"No. We'd better wait until we hit Sacramento. You've got ownership, registration?"

"All the papers."

"Okay."

Brand tried to listen, but his throat hurt and the little food he had gotten down hit his stomach like a nice, warm ball, and lulled him. He lay down on one of the blankets he'd given Mitch to use and curled up, puppy style. They were just like his parents, they wouldn't listen, and he didn't want to tell them everything or they'd be the first to drop him off at the lunatic ward. He had plans of his own to develop, to either go with them or get out as well. He still had a set of Curtis' keys. Maybe Mrs. Reynolds' spare car key was on it. He could drive, as long as it was in forward. He didn't have much practice backing up. He had forty bucks for gas. He could get maybe all the way to Phoenix on that. . . .

He sleepily asked himself, *Why Phoenix?* Because that was the way he had to go. And because it sounded great. Mystical. Anything was possible in Phoenix. He fell deeper. Sleep cushioned him.

Yellow Dog came to greet him, tail waving enthusiastically, chops grinning. He pricked his ears forward alertly and Brandon checked behind him to see if he'd brought anybody with him. Could Yellow Dog sense Mitch and Kamryn?

But he stood alone in that netherworld, an ambiguous landscape around him, nothing distinct but himself and the dog, young dog, old pup. Brand chucked him behind the ears, and the dog pressed his ribs against his knee. The dog was always so real, warm and silky, his nose damp and cold, and Yellow Dog slobbered at his hand as if to prove the point. What had happened to him, Brand wondered, that the dog had been exiled to the realm of dreams and nothingness?

Why didn't you go to dog heaven, huh, boy?

Yellow Dog looked upward with eager brown eyes. He shook himself all over and bounded a step away. He hunkered down on his forelegs, haunches up in the air, canine language for, "Let's romp!"

Brand stepped after him. Yellow Dog let out a tenor bark and trotted off, stopping now and then to make sure he was being followed. Brand told him all that had happened, Yellow Dog bumping into his legs now and then in that herding way dogs have, listening with his doggish sensibility to every word Brand said. It was strange and delightful to be with the creature without the threat of Bauer or the other. They trotted side by side down an unknown road, toward an unknowable destiny, as if they were making their way down to the park or the beach for a session with a Frisbee.

Brand slipped on something wet and slick, and went to one knee. He put a hand in it as he braced himself to get back to his feet. It glistened blackly in the sepia lighting, but he could smell it: warm blood. Yellow Dog pivoted on one paw and whined anxiously.

Brand put out the hand to show him, "Look, blood," and stopped, aghast.

The dog's throat gaped open at the golden ruff, and the blood dripped steadily, quickly, from the wound. Yellow Dog shook his head as if worried and hurt.

Brand stumbled up to his feet. He tried to pull a length off his shirt, but the fabric wouldn't tear, and it had to; he had to bind the wound or the dog would bleed to death. Yellow Dog danced away from him when he reached and tried to seal the lips of the gash together, to stop the flow.

"No!" cried Brand. He lunged at the dog, trying to catch him, slipped and fell again in a slick, warm coppery-smelling puddle.

The dog trotted off a length, and turned. He let out a low woof as if to urge him upward and onward.

Brand felt his face grow warm and his eyes sting. "No, come back, come back!"

He got up again and ran after the golden retriever. Yellow Dog stopped once, and Brand could see the bitter slashes on his face. They appeared as if someone invisible sliced at him: down his muzzle, one ear in rags, on his flank. Blood everywhere. Brand whirled, looking for the assailant. He kicked at thin air and screamed at the dog.

"Run! Run!" but the animal took the assault as if it were an expected, inevitable act.

"Jesus," Brand pled. "He's killing you! Run."

The dog seemed weary. His eyes lost their gleam. He panted heavily, as animals in pain and fear do. For a second he leaned against Brand's kneecap, and he could feel the shuddering, the awful agony in the dog's body.

He barked again and trotted wobbily away, drawing Brand after him. Brand wiped his face on his sleeve, sobbing like a baby. All that blood. Even Curtis hadn't bled like that. He staggered after, barely seeing Yellow Dog, being led farther and farther. . . .

The dog toppled. Brand caught up and knelt down next to him. He stripped his shirt off and tried to bind the pup's throat and chest, but there was little he could do. The feathery tail thumped several times as if acknowledging what Brand attempted.

"Is this what happened? Who would do something like this? Oh, God . . . God, make it stop bleeding. . . ."

"Sssshust, boy."

Brand looked up. The black woman leaned over him. She had come out of nowhere, exuding the same kind of goodness that Yellow Dog had, like standing in the basking warmth of the sun on an Indian summer day. "You can't help him now. Not yet. But he feels your love, he does, child. He feels it."

"He's in pain! You've got to do something."

"He feels your pain. Let him go, if you can. Just let him go."

Yellow Dog grew insubstantial between his hands as Brand tried to hold pressure on the wounds, his flesh disappearing, until there was nothing left but a congealing pool of blood and slickness on his fingers.

Brand's nose ran. He sniffed sharply. "Is he dead? Is he gone?"

"No, child. He'll be back when you need him. He has a job to do. He has to bring you to me. When that's done, when that's over, he'll be free."

"It's not fair. He's just a dog. He's never done anything to anybody."

"He's a thread in the cloth, child, just like you and me."

"What do you know?" He swallowed back his tears.

"I tol' you to remember."

"Mother," answered Brand.

"Mother Jubilation," she repeated firmly. "In New Orleans. I know a lot o' what you need to know. You look for me in the Quarter, do you hear? And come quick. And you bring your friends with you. I can't help you if you're scattered all over the face of creation."

"In New Orleans," Brand repeated. "In the Quarter." He suddenly added, "Why do you smell like incense and candy?"

She laughed, flashing good strong white teeth, her bosom heaving.

"You know when you get here! Come quick, child. It's your only hope."

"You know about the KillJoy, don't you?"

"That's what you named it, did you? You're a clever one. Don't out-clever yourself, now. Naming something gives it power. Calls it."

"They won't bring me."

"Then you bring them. You tell the white boy, the soldier, I gave him his charm." The black woman began to fade, her handsome face and snapping black eyes all he could see of her now. "Mother Jubilation," she repeated one last time. "Now wake up."

He was left with nothing but a shirt dripping with the brave dog's blood. Brand hugged it to his chest and let himself cry, alone, not knowing how to go ahead or back without his guide.

"Wake up, Brand."

His face felt wet and chill. Someone stroked it. He sobbed in his waking, still crying. He blinked his eyes. A blurred Kamryn reached out and wiped his cheeks again. He shook the tears from his face and dug at his eyes. The clarity came back, but he could not depend on it. The fear of that chilled him further.

"Brand, it's all right. Wake up."

His nose throbbed and he wiped it on the cuff of his shirt.

"You were dreaming."

Her face looked unhappy, as if she shared with him.

He took the napkin from her and scrubbed at his face, hard, ashamed that Mitch had seen him like that, embarrassed that she had. "Leave me alone."

Mitch passed him a dry napkin, emblazoned with a red Chinese dragon. "Here."

He took it because he had to, and blew nosily. Kamryn's mouth twitched, and he stared away from her.

She put her hand on his shoulder. "It's good to get it all out. I cried like a baby about . . . about Darby, in spite of everything."

"I don't cry," he said stubbornly. And he didn't, not usually. He could not afford to. Even through sorrow-swollen eyes, he could see that Mitch and Kamryn had cleaned up, and Mitch's duffel waited by the loft doorway. They were ready to go. He did not know how long he had slept, and wondered if they were going to leave without waking him. He could not let them.

"Rembrandt had my school records. He knows where I live. He won't let me go again."

"You tell Rembrandt I've gone south, to Baja. He'll follow," Mitch explained patiently. He tied the strap on his duffel.

"You can't leave without me. I have to—we have to—go to New Orleans."

Mitch's head snapped up.

"Why New Orleans?" Kamryn offered him the damp towel to wipe his face.

"We have to, that's all." He cleansed his face in desperation. Mitch was shining all silvery again, except for that shard of ink which seemed to cleave him in two, and even Kamryn had smudges floating across her, like storm clouds, and he knew he was going to lose his sight and be left behind, alone. Alone with Bauer and the KillJoy. "I saw it," he started, and stopped. They would think he was raving. He put his face in his hands. "You won't believe me."

"Does this have anything to do with what Rembrandt was talking about? Your . . . record?" asked Kamryn gently. She sat down next to him, knees touching.

"Record?" repeated Mitch.

"Psychiatric record," Brand told them bitterly. "I'm certifiable, okay? You leave me, and my dear mom will just have me stowed away again. But what I'm seeing is there, it has to be, it's just that nobody else can see it—"

"See what?"

Brand turned desperately to Mitch. "You've got to believe me."

"I have to understand you first. What are you seeing?"

"It's usually in my dreams. I have bad dreams, really bad dreams. I was diagnosed as having fragmented sleep patterns and depression and a couple of other psychobabble disorders. You need regular REM sleep for your brain to process everything okay, only I don't. Didn't. I've been hospitalized for it a couple of times. They wired me, gave me drugs . . ."

"Everyone has nightmares."

"Yeah, right." Brand thought of telling her about Susan Craig and the permanent houseguest she'd imprinted into him, and changed his mind. She would never understand that. "Only now I'm having them awake."

"Schizophrenia."

"Thanks," Brand said dryly. "I need all the help I can get. No, not schizo. At least, not yet. They tell me that's an organic brain dysfunction and usually appears in the teen years. Look what I've got to look forward to."

Mitch cleared his throat. "You're carrying a heavy load."

"I don't want pity. I deal with it. I see a therapist and I take melatonin to help me sleep, and I can handle it. I just don't want to have to go back to a ward. But this is different. This is something I can see, and no one else can, and it creates death. It's like a . . . a black hole or something, and it's hungry and that's the only thing that can feed it. I saw it at the mall. And it came to the church today—"

"Brandon," soothed Kamryn.

He swung on her. "It knows my name. It's real, only I don't know what it is or how to fight it or why it wants me. And the black woman, she said to come to New Orleans—"

Sharply, from Mitch. "Black woman? What black woman?"

He looked over. "She says her name is Mother Jubilation. I dreamed about her. Look I know this is crazy—"

"You saw her in your dream?"

"She knows what the dark thing is."

Mitch straightened. He picked up his duffel. "It's getting late."

Kamryn stared over her shoulder. "You're not going to leave him like this."

"You think I'm crazy."

"No. But I can't take you with me."

Brand stood up. His legs felt like pins and needles, half-numb, half-pain. He stared at Mitch, at the open throat of his shirt, at the black cord lying against his tanned neck. "She gave you that charm. Mother said to 'tell the white boy I gave him his charm.' "

"You know what he's talking about?"

Mitch shifted his duffel from one hand to the next, reaching for the threshold, but Brand had already seen it in his eyes. Realization, and denial.

"Tell her!"

Mitch shrugged, turning to Kamryn. "He's seen me wearing it around."

"Did she give it to you? Do you know what he's talking about?"

"We can't go to New Orleans," he told her flatly. "No way."

Brand closed his eyes. Giving it a name gave it strength. Calling the name would call it near. He took a breath. "KillJoy."

Kamryn bore down on Mitch. "I won't leave him behind if they're going to put him in an institution—"

"Maybe that's where he belongs. Maybe that's the only place they can help him—"

"KillJoy."

The loft grew cold. The wind began whistling in along the cracks in the unfinished walls, skirling along the bare floors. He could feel the chilling as the temperature began to drop rapidly.

Kamryn and Mitch stopped arguing.

"What are you doing?"

"Seeing," said Brand tightly, "is believing." He took the doorknob from Mitch's hand and flung the portal open. "And maybe I'm the only one who can see it, but you've got to feel it! You've got to! It's like being in a cemetery or a morgue. It's cold and empty and hungry. It makes you feel like you want to kill somebody to stomp out the warmth."

A blast of air drove him back, almost into Kamryn's arms, and it was a raw October wind, a Santa Ana, but this had come from no desert. It smelled faintly of carrion and embalming fluid, and Brand knew he had called it from its temporary resting place within Curtis. It rushed into the loft as if filling a vacuum and Kamryn let out a faint cry as it grazed over her with its shadowy touch.

"Holy Christ," Mitch said. He put a hand to his charm, still tucked inside his shirt, and balled his fist around it.

Brand did not wait for an invitation. He bolted down the garage stairs, and he could hear Mitch and Kamryn clattering down behind him.

Mitch passed him on the back lawn and threw his duffel over the fence, then cupped his hands for Brand. "Go, go," he said.

He tossed Brand over the block wall fence as if he were a rag doll. Kamryn came scrambling over the top on his heels and Mitch thumped down last.

"How fast can it move?" he asked.

"I don't know. I've never had it chasing me before. I think it . . . I think we might be able to outrun it."

Kamryn had her car keys out and loped away from them. Mitch

found his duffel in a rosebush, bit out a curse as a thorn pricked him, and grabbed Brand by the elbow.

"I'm coming."

"Damn straight you are. At least until I find out what's going on here."

Kamryn hit the Porters' garage cans and vaulted over their gate. Not silent, but not incredibly noisy either. Mitch boosted him up and pushed the duffel into his hands.

Their eyes met in the moonlight.

"You know the black lady, too."

"Maybe."

"Why?"

Mitch's jaw flexed. "It's better not to know."

"All right." Brand threw his legs over and hit the ground lightly. Kamryn already had the car started.

They all squeezed into the front seat. Mitch bucked shoulders with Brand, said, "To hell with it," picked him up and threw him into the back.

Brand dusted himself off with dignity. "Okay. You can ride shotgun."

Kamryn pulled away. She watched in the rearview mirror as if expecting to see what Brand had told her she couldn't. "How long before it follows?"

"I don't know!" Brand swiveled around on the car seat. A vortex of incredible, icy darkness filled his vision, his eyes feeling as well as seeing the terror. Even as they retreated, it sensed him, drawn toward him. It would follow. God, what had he done? Let it leave his family alone, half-dead though he thought they were. Nobody deserved this. Nobody. Brand buried his face in his hands, unable to watch.

PART TWO

Chapter 17

Rembrandt was on the phone before he had fully entered the darkened recess of his suite, cradling his laptop in one arm, the card key to the room in his other hand. He hooked a foot around a chair leg and dragged it to him as he sat down, waiting for the various satellite connections to be made and redirected, tapping in strings of commands whenever necessary. Only the computer screen's glow illuminated the room, an eerie greenish flickering. It steadied when the final connection went through.

Bayliss answered, deeper-voiced than usual, but crisp and curt. "Speak to me."

"The crib is clean," Rembrandt told him.

"Shit. You searched the entire area?"

"Every nook and cranny. There's no place he could have secured your goods."

"Then he has to have stashed it somewhere."

"He's never abandoned the crib before." Rembrandt paused. "I found a box with his medals and service ribbons."

"You surprised him, then. It *has* to be stashed," Bayliss repeated, "unless he carries it on his person."

"I agree with you, sir."

"What are your plans now?"

"I can go back to the boy, but that might entail some cleaning up later."

"You're the best at what you do, but the more cleaning up you do, the more risk you run."

"Yes, sir." Rembrandt had plans, but he could tell that Bayliss was also thinking, and he wanted to let his boss play it out. After his failures, he needed to know where he stood with Bayliss, and what, if any, reservations had now arisen about his service. He needed to draw the other man out. Something stirred in the room, a current, like fingers caressing the nape of his neck. It smelled briskly of the ocean—and something else. Something feral, something human, richly-scented sweat. Rembrandt said, "I'm open to suggestions," and turned very quietly in the chair, eyes now adjusted to the dark, searching his room.

"Option one is that I pull you, and bring you back to base camp, where I need you badly right about now. We have SALUTE reports coming in which you need to review." Bayliss cleared his throat, as if admitting need bothered him emotionally. SALUTE reports came from intelligence, referring to the operations of clandestine groups: size/number, activity, location, unit, time, and equipment. They had groups to keep track of, and ensure that their own newly burgeoning operations had not yet been detected.

"I can make the next flight out," Rembrandt answered. He saw nothing in the room, though the corners pooled inky-dense and revealed nothing. Then, he found the source of the current.

The heavy, brocade drapes at the balcony were slightly open, edges of the gauze sheer behind them rippling with the night sea breeze. The balcony glass door showed the barest of cracks where it should have been securely sealed and locked.

His safe place was safe no longer. Security had been seriously breached. His invader might still be here, trapped on the balcony overlooking cliffs that sheared away to the sand below.

Rembrandt instantly ceased to listen to the nuances in what Bayliss said. He stood up, interrupting. "Sir, I've been on the road all evening. You keep talking, but I'm taking the phone into the bathroom. I've got to take a leak."

Bayliss stopped cold as if offended by Rembrandt's unusual lack of courtesy and by his crudeness, both extremely out of character. Then he said, "Are we being tapped? Is this still a secure connection?"

"No, sir, not exactly, but along those lines." Rembrandt smiled, in spite of his tension, admiring the quickness of the other's mind. Bayliss was sharp. It was one of the first things which had drawn

Rembrandt to his employment. Rembrandt tolerated no fools, either under him or over him. He rose from his chair and crossed the carpeting.

"Call me back," ordered Bayliss, and disconnected.

Rembrandt continued to talk smoothly. "I think you need to cancel those flights into John Wayne. I'm going to grab some sleep, get a decent meal, and then drop in on the local police, see what I can find out." He threw open the bathroom door, placing the cell phone on the sink. "I'm putting you on speakerphone, sir. I need both hands to handle this." He stripped off his jacket and snugged his shoulder holster tightly, readying for an assault.

He snapped on the switches. White light flared like a beacon, cutting through the room, dazzling light he kept at his back as he wedged himself through the balcony doors.

The October night was filled with the scent of salt and sweat. He lost the element of surprise with his charge onto the balcony; it scarcely mattered. He knew after the first blow that the two had come not to spy on him, but to kill him. Rembrandt caught glimpses of ebon skin, moon-white teeth in a rictus smile, open-throated island shirts and fists like hammers. He ducked and rolled and fought back, slamming into the balcony glass-topped table which skidded with a screech across the decking.

He regretted not having pulled his gun first. Their numbers and their intensity surprised him. He took a blow to the gut and doubled over, breathing through his mouth roughly. He did not try to straighten as his assailant approached confidently. He charged headfirst, driving into the assassin's torso. His opponent fell back with a grunt and then windmilled, the small of his back against the balcony's edge. Rembrandt thrust his right arm straight out, slamming the heel of his hand into the young man's dark chin. His head snapped back and he went over the balcony wall, silently, arms and legs flailing. Rembrandt watched him slam into the rocks and sand a hundred feet below. High tide would take his body out.

His partner flinched, then looked back at Rembrandt. He, too, was a young man, rock-hard muscles showing in the biceps revealed by his short-sleeved shirt. He had already taken one solid hit from Rembrandt, blood that looked purple in the pale moonlight trickled from one nostril.

Rembrandt did not know how much time he had before the scuffling on the balcony alerted someone. The suites on either side were empty, but there were people above and below. The evening was late, the sky pitch-dark, the moon a pale, pale sliver. He readied to defend himself, curling his hands into position.

They were not American. They did not dress American, smell American, or fight American. If he had to guess, he would say Haitian, but he did not want to have to guess.

"You can go back to Delacroix," he said softly. "If you leave now."

His assailant's eyes widened in recognition, but he did not answer. He took several breaths, preparing to move in.

Rembrandt shifted his weight, giving himself the reach and experience advantage. His opponent moved nearly imperceptibly also; still Rembrandt did not expect what happened next.

He kicked up, his foot thudding harshly into Rembrandt's chest and then into his neck. He staggered back, shaking his head, reeling out of range, ears ringing, his breath stuffed in his throat. The assailant made a sound of pleasure and closed in.

Rembrandt grabbed a patio chair and slid it between them, fighting to get his breath back, eyes blurred. He coughed once or twice, then got a deep swallow of air. He threw up an arm to block the next kick, grabbed the leg and tossed the fighter onto his back. He followed up with a punishing blow of his own. He only had time for one, then his opponent was up on his feet again, circling warily.

Adrenaline surged through Rembrandt. Adrenaline and the knowledge that he could die this time, he had met his match. Not in cleverness perhaps, but in speed and decisiveness. They closed, knees, hands, and elbows flying, trading vicious blows that could break ribs and sever carotids if landed properly. Rembrandt pulled himself back, breathing harshly, night air ripping through his bruised throat.

His opponent fought like a soldier, a well-trained and conditioned soldier, one who knew no fear, who would never hesitate to fight, for whom retreat and detente were not an option, one whose body was a finely-tuned weapon which knew no pain. He felt a grudging admiration for the assassin. Rembrandt put the table between them momentarily, watching the whites of the other's eyes, gauging the strength he had left. He had heard bone crack when they'd closed. It could have been him, but he thought it was the other. The pumping rush of adrenaline masked pain; he might not know until later, much later.

If he lived.

"How did Delacroix find me?"

His opponent flexed, broad muscles rippling under his tropical shirt. "You were kissed," he said, "by the loa. Delacroix knows where you are."

Rembrandt hunched uneasily. Little of what the other said made sense, but he thought warily of voodoo, and then shook it off. He was not superstitious, he had no time for the spiritual, he placed his trust in research and planning. If they were trailing Christiansen, then they would have crossed paths with him also. He had thought his unknown shadow to be MI, trailing the AWOL Marine. Perhaps it had been this pair from Delacroix.

He sucked in a painful breath. Decision time. He knew that, in all likelihood, he would get no more information than that which he had guessed. If he had time, he might be able to torture more answers, but he did not have time.

Rembrandt took a step back, felt the balcony ledge grind into his pelvis. In the wan light, his assailant saw also and smiled widely, white teeth cutting across his face. "You are mine, now." He moved close for the kill.

Rembrandt pulled his gun as his assailant drove into him. They met, body to body, and he pulled the trigger three times in quick succession, feeling the other jerk with every muffled report.

"Think again," Rembrandt said, and twisted to one side, his free hand wrapped in the other's collar. He levered him over the balcony and let him drop.

Again, there was no sound, no scream. But this time it was because the man was dead before he left his feet.

Rembrandt wiped the gun clean on his shirttail and tossed it as well, leaving the tide to obscure the rest of the details of what had happened.

He went back into his room, packed his bags, cleaned the sliding glass door, shower, and sink, and whatever else he might have touched. He returned to the balcony a last time, cleaned the chairs and the table quickly, then withdrew.

He made a last sweep to see if he'd left anything of gravity in the room. There would be hairs, fibers, but he doubted if anyone would do that thorough a sweep. It might be days before anyone local connected the bodies below with a balcony above. By then, the maids would have changed linens and vacuumed several times over.

Rembrandt decided to delay a while longer calling Bayliss. He used the express checkout after first opening and then altering the electronic clock which stamped the paperwork fed into it. He took the back way out, through the gardens and pathways and into the underground garage.

As he pulled the rental car out of its space, he tried to gauge what Bayliss' reaction would be to the attack. There would be some surprise. There might be enough concern to curtail plans which had been months coming to fruition. Rembrandt decided that Bayliss could wait an hour or so while he determined his options. He decided to make that determination outside the boy's house.

The freeways were relatively clear on a cooling fall evening. He found the housing tract, upper middle class and newer, but old enough to have mature pepper trees and eucalyptus shading its boulevards, not far from the Brea Mall. It fit the boy's pattern. The high school was farther north, up the 57 freeway, but not so far he could not hitchhike back down to the arcade whenever he wished. Rembrandt did not know if the environs had caused Brandon's trouble or if Brandon had already been a troubled kid, and the environs drew him naturally, but the pattern had been laid out.

When he took the boy this time, no one would question his disappearance or his ultimate fate. Rembrandt parked his car, carefully away from the corner, watching the house on a slant, knowing that the boy must come home eventually. He had nowhere else to go.

Rembrandt watched as a Brea squad car slowly slid past the house on its frontal street, not stopping, but observing. The parents must have put out a report on the missing child. The cops were checking the neighborhood, as he was, reading the same human behavior he did.

He checked his watch. It was later than he thought. He knew Bayliss would begin to edge toward unhappiness by now. Rembrandt pursed his lips, debating with himself over his final course of action, when the evening breeze grew chill, very chill, and he looked out the car windshield in surprise.

Tree leaves shivered and danced in frenzy, their edges growing frost-rimed, and blackening. Rembrandt lowered his car window to look closer, as his breath had suddenly fogged up the inside, so much warmer than outside. He leaned his head out, and saw the tiny snowflake pattern of jackfrost across the asphalt, over the boulevards, leading straight to the boy's house.

Or, more accurately, to the built-over garage in back. Rembrandt rubbed his eyes as the cold wind dried them, rubbed his eyes and wondered if he had slept, if he had been unaware of some happening, as a finely-iced wave rolled toward and then over the garage.

He saw nothing else, but sat next to his rolled-down window and shivered. He had not been this cold since his survival training days when, stripped down to the bare essentials and a compass, he had been told to find his way back through an unforgiving wilderness. He'd done it, though three of his companions had died of hypothermia that night.

He breathed in deeply, and immediately coughed, for the autumn wind bearing the frost also carried a scent, foul and fetid. He coughed harshly several times, put a hand to his rib cage, just now finding out that it was his own bone he'd heard crack hours ago, and tried not to cough anymore, though his lungs fought that smell with all their might. It coated the back of his throat and Rembrandt finally spat outside the car, trying to rid himself of the nastiness.

It was then he saw the three sprinting down the back of the garage staircase, running like gazelles ahead of the hunt, across the backyard and fence. Rembrandt hurriedly started his car and backed it up, cautiously, quietly, along the block, until he could see the adjacent street, on a diagonal.

A silvery Honda pulled away, the girl driving, and it shot away toward the freeway. Rembrandt watched it for a second or two, patiently, then followed after.

Once on the freeway, he stayed as far behind as he could and still keep it in sight. Down the 57 to the 91 toward Riverside, San Bernardino and the east. Traffic in southern California was always there on the highways, though sparse in the dead of night, so he found it not too difficult to keep three or four cars between them. He drove with his left hand pressed to his left rib cage, feeling the bone grate, wondering when he could get a corset, though that was old-fashioned now. Ribs were left to heal on their own, but he could not leave that to chance, he was too active. He drove with one eye on the economy Honda, watching the girl skillfully negotiate the traffic lanes, and the other eye on any other cars which looked as if they might be following.

When the 91 ended, the Honda unerringly went to the 10, just outside Riverside, the 10 freeway to Palm Springs and beyond, across the desert. Rembrandt kept an eye on his gas gauge. He would lose them when he stopped for a fill-up and he would have to stop soon. His full-sized rental car did not have the economy capacity of the Honda.

He wondered where they headed. Not west, to the ocean, or south to Baja, or north, but east. To Phoenix—or beyond.

Then Rembrandt smiled, peeling his lips back from his teeth, remembering what had brought the police to the boy's house, what had brought him to the boy's home. The fugitive invariably traveled in circles.

Christiansen was headed back to New Orleans. Whether he knew it or not, consciously yet, that was his inevitable destination.

He had to have stashed the goods there, perhaps even before he had delivered his corporal's body to the funeral home. And, if Christiansen was the Marine Rembrandt thought he was, he had to realize that only by recovering the powder could he possibly hope to negotiate for his life, for the girl's, for the boy's.

He was wrong, of course, but that did not matter. Whether the decision had already been made or would be made in Phoenix or Tucson or Denver or in New Mexico, the course would be charted.

Rembrandt could pick them off any time he wanted.

His grin widened.

"Gotcha," he said.

Chapter 18

DAY ONE

NWS 0630 AM EST
BULLETIN
National Hurricane Center

A SYSTEM APPROACHING THE LESSER ANTILLES HAS
ORGANIZED ENOUGH TO QUALIFY AS A TROPICAL STORM,
NAMED TS YOLANDA. AS LATE IN THE SEASON AS IT IS,
THIS DISTURBANCE IS GATHERING STRENGTH AS IT
LEAVES THE COAST OF AFRICA, PROCEEDING IN A WEST-
ERLY/NORTH WESTERLY DIRECTION. SUSTAINED WINDS OF
55 MPH HAVE BEEN MEASURED. THE STORM IS EXPECTED
TO PICK UP STRENGTH AS IT PASSES INTO CARIBBEAN
WATERS.
PLEASE CONTINUE TO MONITOR THESE CHANNELS AS
WE UPDATE THE STORM'S PROGRESS.

Rembrandt read his laptop screen, then tapped a few keys to take
him out of the weather news and into the stock market and headlines, far more current than those on the newspapers lying about
him. Airport noise hummed busily, but he had not yet been paged
and his flight to Albuquerque would not be called for another hour.
He reached for the paper cup of coffee and sipped it as he pulled up
the headlines.

* * *

THE DOW DROPS STEADILY AS INDICATORS THE FED IS
CONSIDERING AN INTEREST RATE HIKE AFFECTS TRADING.

A fairly decent brew of domestic coffee blends eased down his
throat, fulfilling an intense need for the taste and caffeine. He continued to scan the immediate online. news.

SENATOR HANOVER BAYLISS URGES A NO VOTE ON THE
$400 MILLION RENEWAL OF THE 1995 DISARMAMENT
PACKAGE, STATING THAT SENDING MORE MONEY TO THE
FORMER SOVIET UNION REPUBLICS WHERE CORRUPTION
IS RIFE IS UTTER FOOLISHNESS. SENATOR BAYLISS, MEM-
BER OF THE ARMS COMMITTEE AND THE BANKING COM-
MISSION AMONG SEVERAL OTHER IMPORTANT POSITIONS,
CALLS FOR SENSIBILITY. MONIES BEING FUNNELED TO
THE UKRAINE AND OTHER AREAS TO DISMANTLE REMAIN-
ING MISSILES, ARMAMENTS, AND MISSILE SITES IS A BUR-
DEN THE AMERICAN PUBLIC SHOULD NO LONGER CARRY.
BAYLISS STATES THAT FISCAL RESPONSIBILITY FOR PRO-
GRAMS AT HOME IS MORE IMPORTANT. FURTHERMORE,
THE SENATOR VOWS THAT THE NATION CANNOT WAIT
UNTIL THE NEXT ELECTION FOR CONGRESS AND THE
PRESIDENT TO COME TO THEIR SENSES, THAT PARTISAN
POLITICS IS DESTROYING THE FABRIC OF THE COUNTRY.

The computer screen filled with a three-quarter profile of Bayliss,
his leonine hair curled back from his dynamic, square-jawed face, his
hand gesturing. The computer-generated image was nothing less
than compelling.

Rembrandt's mouth curled. Bayliss was giving them hell again.
The senator would be heard.

One way or another.

The airport paging system came on. "Flight 213 from Albuquerque
now arriving Gate 5B."

Rembrandt checked his watch. Twenty minutes early. Good. It
would give him time to debrief the recruits before their turnaround
flight. They had work to do.

Chapter 19

The International Terminal at Acapulco had been given a new wash of bright white paint, disguising the oldness of its stucco walls. Its large, cavernlike terminal reflected more of a whitewashed warehouse than it did a jet-set airport, guarded by Federales, some not old enough to shave as they cradled their rifles slung over their shoulders. It was old under its new coat, old and not extremely well built, unlike the Haitian airport which, although old, had been built by the French. Only the X-ray machines, their plastic arches and conveyor belts were relatively new, as embarking passengers waited in staggered lines to pass through them.

Customs, on the other side of the terminal, seemed lax. A stream of passengers heading for cruise lines chatted and passed through in endless streams until the crowd finally thinned out. A tired woman, her uniform creased with the tropical heat that permeated Acapulco even at that time of the year, opened a passport and readied her stamp.

She paused, glancing at the two passengers. "Professor Delacroix?"

"Of Haiti," the gentleman said quietly, in English, though it was liltingly accented.

She thumbed through the passport until she came to the visa, folded over and stapled to the inside back cover. The tension in her shoulders relaxed abruptly. "You are here," she noted, also in accented English, though hers was Latino in origin rather than Franco, "to study our Day of the Dead."

"Yes. This has long been my wish, despite political difficulties. I am here at last!" He smiled, giving warmth to his sharp, lean features, his brown skin glowing with the heat of the building despite the fans moving raggedly in alcoves overhead. "And this is my assistant from the United States, Alexander Stark." He shrugged a shoulder to let the unmoving man at his back be seen more clearly.

She fingered the second passport, also with a stapled visa, then briskly stamped them both. "Do you have anything to declare?"

The professor shook his head, but laughed and said, "When I leave, I may have a suitcase full of your masks and dolls. Is there a duty on them?"

"Read these papers. It depends on the value, and if they are antiques or not." Rather impatiently now, she shoved brochures into the passports, her eyes already moving on to the next passengers in line, having dismissed these two.

The man designated as Stark moved to pick up the two suitcases, lifting them as if their weight was inconsequential. Delacroix said, "Follow me," and walked through the terminal toward the signs marked AUTOBUS. He did not wait to see if he were followed, as if it were unthinkable for Stark to do anything else.

Outside, in the warm, moist air, jitneys and buses of various worn-out facades waited for incoming passengers. They sat at the edge of broken tarmac lanes, pastureland edged with bananas and other palms lying fallow beyond the modest lanes heading into Acapulco proper. Delacroix removed his panama hat and wiped his forehead. Stark made no movement of comfort, whether to ease the burden of the suitcases or to dry his brow.

"Put the suitcases down," Delacroix said mildly. "We have a moment."

Stark did as he was bid. Delacroix appraised him, looking for signs of infirmity from his mortal wounding, but he saw none. The man had healed well, exceptionally well, and his skills were proving invaluable. Stark would take Delacroix into the States, and guided by the loa, he would track the men who had betrayed him and desecrated his powers, and take his revenge. It would be all the sweeter knowing he was turning their own weapon against them. Surely the legba who was the gateway for all things spiritual had blessed him with this man, just as Delacroix had been blessed with the loa of his vengeance. It was fitting that his visa gave him permission to study the festivals known as the Days of the Dead.

Calmly, to Stark, Delacroix noted. "I have done as you told me. Does this mean all arrangements will be followed? A boat will be waiting to take us to Baja and then into the States?"

Stark looked at him, flat, expressionless eyes like those of a shark in the water, calmly seeking its destiny of being a killing, feeding machine. He nodded.

"Good," answered Delacroix. He spotted a bus pulling up, in a little better condition than the others, its routing card reading "Acapulco Princess." There was some slight hope of comfort in that the windows remained closed. It must have air-conditioning that functioned. He motioned to his bags. "Here is our transport."

Stark silently picked up the suitcases and followed to the bus.

Junior, called that because he wasn't, rode alone because he liked it that way. He worked weekdays in a lock factory in Anaheim and weekends he rebuilt classic hogs in his old lady's living room, because the garage was full of bodies and fenders and tires and he didn't like working in the driveway because the old bikes he built were worth somethin' and he didn't want the neighbors to know. Octobers called him to the mountains in Big Bear, where the mostly German founding fathers threw one helluva Oktoberfest shindig, although Junior had to admit it wasn't like in the old days. In the old days, one hundred, two hundred bikers came up the mountain and drank their beer and owned the roads, because the San Berdu police couldn't get up the hill in time to stop them. Now, the policia maintained a presence in the resort community and bikers were tolerated, but their meets just weren't the same.

But it got Junior out from under the glare of his bike bitch and above the smog line, and the beer was still just as good as it always had been, and so the ride down the road was just as sweet even though he had to wear a helmet now. His long hair fuzzed under the helmet, and his kinky beard caught bugs in the wind, and he didn't mind it. Hell, this was living.

But he'd overstayed his welcome in Big Bear. He'd found a woman and forgot about the weekend and now it was midweek, and word was his old lady had been calling for him, and maybe he'd even lost his job for not showing up. Unlike the old days, Junior now had rent to worry about, and bills, and he'd woken up from a five-day drug and beer binge with his skull caving in and his buddies pounding on his cabin door.

Junior wasn't stupid, and now he was headed down Highway 38, the back way, through Redlands and San Berdu, in the middle of the night, and he realized he might not be welcome at home when he got there. So he peeled his hog off toward Beaumont, naked and alone on Highway 10, a slight detour toward the east, and he found a gas station with a lone attendant. He parked his bike by the garage bay, which didn't look like it had been used by a real mechanic in some time, and approached the attendant cautiously, looking for surveillance cameras. There was one, but its eye was still, and the swivel base was broken, and Junior determined it was a fake.

He dismounted and sauntered over to the booth, pulling on his leather vest to straighten it over his paunchy stomach, a well-earned beergut, he reflected, and smiled at the attendant.

"I wonder if you could help me."

The attendant, a thin, wiry man who was not American, and probably was Indian or Pakistani or one of those funny-lookin' foreigners, eyed him nervously. "Yes, please? All pumps are open."

"Naw, naw, I don't need gas." Junior put a finger to the corner of his eyelid and dragged it down. "I got somethin' in my eye. It feels pretty sharp. Think I got some glass in it, blew up from the road. Take a look, will ya, and see what you can see? I don't want to mess with it, if it is glass. I'll just call 911."

The attendant squinted out through the barred window. "Please, I see nothing."

"Naw, you gotta look closer. Lissen, this is real painful, y'know? I don't want to go blind or nothing. See, it's right . . . here."

The attendant danced on one foot and then the other, then came out of his booth to lean closer. "I still don't see anything."

Junior's finger had pretty well made the eye bloodshot and tearing, and he smiled. "Maybe this will help." He took his helmet off.

The attendant peered very close again, and Junior head-butted him with all his power.

The man dropped like a wet sack of cement. His head made the sound of a ripe melon as it hit the drive.

Junior shook himself. "You still got it." He reached down, grabbed the foreigner by his twiglike ankles, and dragged him back inside the booth. The cash drawer was crammed full. It looked like someone had not made the day's deposit.

"Jackpot. Just like Vegas." Junior gave a sigh of contentment and began to roll the bills into a wad, taking care not to touch anything metal or plastic. He used his leather vest like a potholder, opening and closing bins.

A car pulled in before Junior had finished. He watched it circle the pumps, then back into the one it wanted, a Honda, a Jap car, ruining American economy, and Junior sucked at a tooth. He looked at the switches inside the booth. He could shut down the pumps if he wanted, denying the car fuel. Or he could just wait it out.

A guy got out of the passenger side, walked across the way, slid a twenty in the cash window, said, "Pump seven," and left without a second look.

Junior took the twenty and added it to his wad. Like taking candy from a baby. The attendant at his feet groaned. Junior gave him a tap in the temple from his Doc Martens, and silence rewarded him.

He leaned his elbows on the counter, watching the man fill the gas tank, and the woman who drove got out. She was a looker, though a trifle thin for his liking, the more cushion for the pushin' was his motto, but she looked familiar. She had an attitude. The guy didn't want to check the water, but he could hear her voice clearly in the booth.

"If I'm driving to Phoenix, I want the water checked. We're here, let's do it." No nonsense, all attitude, but the other finally did what she wanted.

A small portable TV on the booth counter caught his attention. The color picture wavered every now and then as the local news portion of *Headline News* came on.

"In Brea today (*Yesterday,* thought Junior, *don't these freaks know it's the middle of the night?*), police from all over the county and even Los Angeles came to the funeral of Brea police officer Nick Solis. Solis, who had transferred to the Orange County city department only a few years ago, was shot Tuesday while answering the call for a domestic violence situation at the Brea Mall. An estranged boyfriend pulled a gun and shot two innocent bystanders while terrorizing his ex-girlfriend. Officer Solis was then himself shot when he attempted to intervene. However, local authorities credit Solis with shielding public areas with his own body, preventing further deaths. A commendation will be issued posthumously. Solis is survived by a widow who is expecting their first child. This channel would like viewers to know that donations for the welfare of Mrs. Solis and her unborn child can be sent to a trust fund at Brea Bank of America—"

Junior looked away. Policemen rode their motorcycles like they had broomsticks up their asses. The scene of the funeral no longer interested him. The man and woman were discussing something he could not hear, until her voice rose. She looked aside, saw him watching, ducked her chin down, and he could no longer hear them.

Junior sighed. The newscaster added, "In news which is related, one of the bystanders who fled his best friend's funeral, is reported missing tonight. The parents of young Brandon Dennis ask for your help in locating their son. Fourteen-year-old Brandon was on the site when the gunman accidentally shot and killed Curtis Reynolds. At his funeral, also held on Thursday, Brandon bolted out of services and disappeared. His mother pleads for anyone who knows of his whereabouts to contact her through the Brea police. Brandon has a history of depression requiring medical and psychiatric attention. Again, anyone with any information as to Brandon's whereabouts is asked to contact the Brea Police Department. Locally, temperatures drop a bit lower tonight, weatherwise and there is a chance of—"

Junior blinked as the slender bitch turned and came to the booth. "Change, please."

He looked at her. He'd emptied the cash drawer. "Isn't any."

"He gave you a twenty. That car doesn't hold more than fourteen gallons of gas. Now I know I have change coming."

He looked at the board, where the readout told him the gallons and the total. She had $3.20 coming back. She flipped her head, dark hair winging around her face and neck, short, not the way he liked it, but there was something about the broad.

He dug in his jeans and pulled out three bills and then fingered two dimes out of the rear of the cash drawer. He dropped it into the cash window. She scooped it out.

"Thank you," she said with sarcasm and walked back toward the car.

"Come again," Junior called. He had her placed in his mind now, all legs and cool expression. He watched them pack the car back up and pull out. He dug some more change out of the drawer, wiped it as clean as he could, then went to the pay phone.

He had to feed in nearly two dollars to get the number he dialed. He watched in the dark fall evening as the car's rear lights faded, heading toward the 10 eastbound.

"Yeah."

"It's me, Junior. Tell Darby I just saw that biker bitch of his, and she wasn't with him." Junior chewed on a strand of his kinky beard, and listened as the other end of the phone told him the sad story of Darby's death. "Shit, man, you're kidding! I just saw a tape of the cop's funeral on HNN. God's nuts, I've been out of it this week. I didn't know. That's too damn bad about Darby. Well, she's headed toward Phoenix, driving an '86 Honda, silver, with a guy in the passenger seat. She gave me a mouth fulla bad attitude. Thought Darby should know what she's up to. Guess he's too gone to care now. Well, I gotta get the hell out of here before my old lady comes gunning for me." Junior hung up, feeling good. Buddies had done him a favor, waking him up to his situation on the mountain, and now he'd returned it, down the line. Too bad about Darby. If he'd known that, he'd a hit on the bitch, even though she wasn't his type.

He hesitated at the side of his bike. That little TV wasn't such a bad piece of shit. He oughta take it home, too. He walked back to the booth. To his surprise, the foreign dude was on his feet, back to the counter, shaking.

Too bad, because that meant Junior would have to finish him off. A second look at his ugly mug was one look too many. He put his hands up, palms out. "Just give me the set, man, and I'm gone."

"No. You rob me, I lose the money, my job. No. This too much." The gas station attendant pulled out a black automatic, his hand wavering from the weight of the gun.

"Whoa, now. I think we can settle this. Just put the gun down, and let me walk back to my bike, and leave. Or," and Junior smiled crookedly. "I'll have to tell somebody it was your idea to be robbed and we was gonna split the money."

"No!" The gun barrel waggled furiously. "No, I'm a good man. Good. You're the bad man."

Junior eased a step closer. "You sure about that, little buddy? You've seen enough real cops on TV. They're going to ask a lot of questions, a lot. By the time they're finished, you won't have a job, anyway. Ever seen the inside of a jail? They'll eat you up for lunch."

He took another step. "Besides, you haven't got the balls to shoot me. Now, give me the TV, and I'll be out of here. If you like, I'll even tie you up, loose like, so it'll look good."

"You no take anything more!"

Junior was close enough to grab the man by the neck. His hand and arm shot out, like a cobra striking, lightning fast.

The gunfire was faster. It reverberated through the tiny booth. Junior felt his chest grow hot and fiery and damp. He looked down in astonishment, then slowly went to his knees on the pavement.

"I am American citizen," the man said, his voice growing thin and high. "I know my rights! You a bad man."

Junior heard sucking and bubbling when he tried to breathe. His vision narrowed, and he had the sensation of racing his bike, hell-bent for leather, down the side of a mountain.

"You not take anything anymore."

He was gone.

Snake hung up as the line flattened to a dial tone. He put a palm to his bald head, where he could feel the heat of his tattoos, as though he wore a living, breathing snakeskin. He had been restless all day, with the need to get out, to be moving, searching . . . something inside driving him. Now he knew why. Now he knew where.

He knew where she was headed.

Chapter 20

Mitch caught her yawning just outside Indio. It was one of those endless yawns that seemed to go on forever as if she were trying to swallow the moon, and tears came to the corners of her eyes.

He waited until she had finished, then mildly said, "Pull over and let me drive."

Kamryn sniffed and blinked several times, shaking off the yawn. "In a minute. I've got somewhere to go first." She aimed the Honda for an off-ramp.

"We don't need gas."

"No. Darby and I biked out here sometimes. We need to pick something up, and this is probably the best place to get it in this direction." She took a hand off the wheel and dabbed at her eyes. The sky had begun to lighten ever so slightly. Dawn must be about a half hour away. Traffic was light, but it would be getting heavier as early morning workers started their commute.

"If this trip is long enough, you'll have to explain to me about that."

Kamryn looked at him. He had dozed for a while, head against the passenger side window, which had left a tiny mark on his temple and a shadowy crease down toward his jawline, like a sexy scar, as if he'd been a sword fighter sometime in his past. "Explain what?"

"About you and Darby."

"Mmmm. I'm not sure I know you well enough for that."

Mitch smiled crookedly, as though the creased side of his face were still asleep. "There is that."

She turned down a side street. A car delivering the morning papers crept in front of them, its headlights a yellowy streak. The houses were seedy, sidewalkless, fenceless, in most cases even garageless. She watched as the newspaper deliverer made a sporadic throw or two before pulling away.

"I guess not too many people out here are interested in the news."

"I guess not too many people out here even know how to read," she said shortly. She found the house she wanted, with a perpetual YARD SALE hand-lettered sign, faded and tattered, nailed to the front tree. Junk was piled all over the front lawn. It looked as though the inhabitants had either been thrown out, or that the yard sale was never picked over and cleaned up.

She stopped the car. Mitch frowned.

"The kid needs clothes," she said. "He looks like a junior Perry Como in that outfit. Besides, he needs to be comfortable."

He looked in the back seat, where Brand was sprawled, snoring lightly, his eyes twitching under faintly blue-veined lids. "Think you can find anything?"

"Sure." She swung the car door open and paused. "I had a brother once, know my sizes pretty well. How about you?" She looked him up and down, amused as faint color came to clean-shaven cheeks that had formerly been hidden behind his beard. "32-32?"

"32-34," he corrected. "Levis. If you can get longs."

"Never know until I look." She leaned back in and pulled her revolver halfway out. "Use this if there's trouble."

Mitch looked down at it. "Jesus," he said. "I thought you said a gun. That thing's a cannon."

"The intimidation factor is almost better than the ammo." Kamryn grinned. "Be right back."

It took her about ten minutes to find the boy two pairs of jeans, one flannel shirt and one T-shirt, with Earthworm Jim in his mighty spacesuit emblazoned across the front. She also found briefs which were still in their package, and a single pair of Levis, well worn, in Mitch's size. She stuffed a ten in the coffee can sitting at the base of the pepper tree and hurried across the lawn, as waking householders and their dogs began to prepare for morning.

She went to the passenger door as Mitch scooted over, got in, and buckled her seat belt.

"Back to the highway?"

"Take two rights here, and straight on till morning." She yawned again as she folded the clothes into a neat stack on her lap.

He guided the car through the residential streets and back toward the highway. As if refusing to be impressed, he asked, "What about shoes, socks, toothbrushes?"

Kamryn gave him a look. "We'll find swap meets. The great cash society of the United States. Even if I had found a toothbrush back there, *I* wouldn't have wanted to use it."

"No argument there." Mitch twisted his head, waiting for a signal change. "Coffee and doughnuts?"

She was hungry. She also wanted to use a restroom, but she shook her head. "Not yet. We've got another three, four hours to Phoenix. Let's get closer to the border."

"You've been this way once or twice."

Noncommittal observance, but she knew that whatever she answered, he would file away, a piece of the puzzle he had made of her, a puzzle which he would try to put together. That gave her a funny feeling, that someone cared enough to wonder about her, and worried her because she did not want to let her personal life jeopardize their flight. "Once or twice," she agreed. "Skinheads are big in Arizona. Our—their—printing plant is outside Phoenix."

Flatly. "Hate literature."

She looked down the highway, crossing gently rolling desert, as the road moved away from irrigated, agricultural Indio. "Hate literature," she repeated. "Always a big business." She rubbed her arms gently, as if she could brush away the remnants of her tattoos. "Always." A third yawn caught her up.

Amused, Mitch told her to grab some sleep. She put her head back on the car seat and tried.

She had had a brother. Lanky and wiry, dark-haired and hazel-eyed, who had liked jeans best when they were soft and faded and had straight legs. Blue jeans and plaid shirts, rolled up at the elbow . . . covered in blood.

Come down to the basement, Sis. I've got a surprise for you.

Kamryn caught her breath and held it, trying not to see what she saw behind the darkness of her closed eyes. Held her breath until it went away. But she could not sleep, so she feigned it, listening to the sound of the car tires on the asphalt, catching pebbles and the grooving meant to keep desert rains from flooding the road.

Somehow, she fell asleep anyway.

Brand woke, with a crook in his neck from being jammed up against the car door, and an urgent fullness in his bladder. Mitch had a hand over the front seat and shook his knee again. "Rest stop," he said. "And breakfast."

Brand sat up, wedged his body upright against the other door, trying to fully wake. The car was streaming with light, brilliant, clean, painfully so, and he slipped a hand inside his shirt pocket. He still had his shades. He put them on, but not before seeing Mitch, aglow as if he were radioactive, except for that chasm down the center of his being, and Kamryn, asleep in her bucket seat, curled up like a kitten, dark smudges drifting across her like clouds of woe.

Fear and sunlight struck him like a physical blow, and something in the pit of his stomach churned. Would his sight never be normal again? Had it gotten better? The focus had, no doubt of that, he would never need glasses again—but if all the world were reduced to brilliant flares and despairing pitch, what would it matter?

Or could it be worse, far worse? Did the inky veils mean that the KillJoy had touched her, marked her for its own . . . was he seeing the aura of death to come? Had Mitch been so marked and then escaped it in the mall? Was that why he sparkled except for that fractal of darkness? Death delayed, all but defeated . . . death retreating to its normal mortality?

If that were it, if that was what he saw, then at least he'd been forewarned. Kamryn was in terrible, crucial danger.

He would have to do anything he could to protect her.

Mitch looked at him closely. "You awake?"

"Pretty much." His mouth felt like glue. His breath carried the scent of Chinese spices and garlic. He didn't want to breathe and smell himself.

Mitch handed him a stack of clothes. "Why don't you go in first, and change. Some of these places even have showers."

Faintly surprised, Brand took the clothing. He doubted the showers, but headed for the concrete block building anyway, knowing that if anyone knew, Mitch would. They were in the desert, and off to the side of the sparsely landscaped rest stop, several Indians sat at the edge of spread-out blankets, goods for sale catching the glint of the sun. Beyond, the highway rolled with traffic. An arrowhead of bikers drew close, riding bikes with the long forks, their seats slanted for long-distance comfort, the man in front wearing one of those Nazi helms instead of a proper motorcycle helmet. They were moving at a near blur, like a hundred miles an hour. As if sensing his stare, the biker glanced over as he sped by, his face a pale streak clouded with darkness.

Light mirrored off the riders, cold light. It struck his eyes like an icicle spear, with the feeling of the KillJoy. Brand stepped hastily behind the corner of the building, and watched. He shuddered in his tracks as the phalanx passed and the glare washed over him. For a moment he stood dazzled, blinking despite his glasses. Someone honked, and he stirred. The feeling had gone. He put up a shaky hand to make sure his shades still rested on his nose, that his head still sat on his shoulders. The car horn sounded again, a musical blast, and the crowded rest stop bustled with activity.

Inside the parking lot, a catering truck was doing a brisk business with a lineup of trucks and tractor-trailer rigs. He could smell the hot coffee and frying eggs. His body reminded him of essentials and he broke into a jog.

No shower, but he washed at the sink. Someone had left behind a mini-tube of toothpaste and he'd scrubbed his mouth with his finger. All in all, in jeans which fit pretty decently, and an Earthworm Jim shirt that was nothing less than cool, he felt a lot better when he left the restroom. He'd wanted to trash his other clothes, but instead rolled them into a tight bundle and brought them out with him.

Mitch was carrying a cardboard food box away from the catering truck as Brand fell into step. He dropped the toothpaste tube into the corner of the box. "Goodies," he said.

Mitch canted an eyebrow. "We could all use that." He nodded. "Fried egg sandwich on toast, coffee, cream, and sugar."

Brand laughed as he looked into the container. "And tea and yogurt for Kamryn."

"She told me she's on a diet."

"Aren't they all?" Brand dipped a hand and brought up the slightly greasy, waxed paper bundle. He unfolded a corner and began to wolf

down the sandwich. It was fresh, sizzling, the egg cooked in real but-
ter—he'd developed tastebuds for that a long time ago and could
never understand how people couldn't tell the difference—and had
his breakfast half-eaten before they were back to the car.

Kamryn sat on the fender. She'd changed, too, into cords and a
denim shirt. She smiled as she lifted the yogurt cup. "Pineapple and
coconut. My favorite."

"Good. Check the expiration date." Mitch sat the box down,
popped the lid on his coffee, and chugged it.

"That's the beauty of yogurt," she answered. "You can hardly tell
the difference." She found a plastic spoon and began to eat, delicately, like a cat lapping at cream.

His sandwich had fogged up his shades before he finished the last
corner. He looked at the empty waxed paper wrapper, then back at
the catering truck. "Seconds?"

Mitch wiped a bit of yolk from his lips. He looked at Kamryn, and
she shrugged. "Better hurry. He's pulling out in about ten minutes."

Brand put his hand out and Mitch slapped a five into it. As soon
as the bill touched his palm, he sprinted to the truck.

He came back with a thick, chunky bundle, and two and a half
dollars change. He gave it to Mitch who solemnly passed it to
Kamryn.

"What is that?"

"A chorizo and bean burrito. This ought to stick to my ribs." Brand
stretched his mouth for the first bite. The glorious, hot Mexican
sausage exploded warmth and spices into his mouth, cooled by sour
cream and refried beans.

Kamryn looked away, but her shoulders shook a little. Mitch said
to her, "He's a growing boy."

"He's going to be an exploding boy, at this rate," she answered.

Brand would have complained, but the burrito took his attention.
Mitch finished his breakfast and strolled over to the bathrooms. The
catering truck pulled out with a "La Cucaracha" playing horn, and
most of the other truckers left as well.

The air was tight, tight and dry in his nostrils and his chest. As he
looked around the barrel of his burrito, he spotted the glint of Indian
jewelry and trinkets again. He swallowed and pointed. "Can I go
look?"

"Sure." Kamryn had a small jar in her hand, and she appeared to be rubbing cream into her skin. Brand walked away, wondering how much of what he thought was beautiful about her was natural and how much applied. He fought the instinct to tell her that it wouldn't matter, that if what he'd seen were true, she wouldn't live long enough to wrinkle.

He choked back the mean-spirited thought and strolled along the rest stop. Bauer had awakened, for that had been his style. "You're a shit, Bauer," he muttered under his breath. "A real shit."

He finished his coffee and tossed it in the trash can. A third of the burrito was left. He wrapped it carefully in its paper and foil, intent on saving it.

Instead, he gave it to the hollow-faced Indian boy perched at the edge of his mother's blanket. Then, hands free, he shoved them into his jeans pockets and looked over her goods. For the most part, the jewelry and dolls and hats were disappointing, no different from anything he could see at a swap meet or in the stores, although the prices were a little cheaper. He smiled at the woman who leaned forward, gently hawking her goods.

He came to a dead halt as her waving hand flowed over a line of charms and amulets, all on black cord, their silvery facets cut and molded in a variety of ways. One was damn near a dead ringer to the amulet he'd seen Mitch wearing. He squatted down to look closer at it. His ever-present sunglasses cut down on the glare of silver metal, and the crooked etch in the lens echoed a bolt carved in the amulet.

"You like?" she said softly. "Ten dollars, please."

He shook his head. "I haven't got any money. These are nice, though. Do you know what that one means?"

"No, no. I don't make those. Those are made by the tribal shaman. I make these others."

He stabbed a finger at the twin to Mitch's amulet. "And you don't know anything about this one? I mean, like if it's good luck or to chase away bad spirits, or anything?"

"No, I'm sorry. They are good magic, that is all I know. You like? Seven-fifty. You were nice to my son."

Brand straightened. "No, I can't, this time. Good luck to you, though." He backed away. As he left, the boy was sharing his breakfast with his mother.

Mitch and Kamryn were waiting in the car. He got in the back. "Hey, Mitch. She's got an amulet just like the one you wear."

Kamryn's head turned. "You wear jewelry. I never would have figured."

"It's just something someone gave me." He stared at Brand. "Couldn't be the same."

"It is, I swear it. Take it out and show Kamryn."

"I don't think so. Listen, you ready to hit the road again? No stops between here and Phoenix."

"Yeah, I'm ready." He rolled the window down to let the fresh morning air into the car. The Honda moved forward across the parking lot, slowed behind a line of semis getting back onto the highway. The car crept along.

Someone pounded on the back window. Brand turned, and saw the Indian boy, something clutched in his fist. As soon as the boy saw him looking, he dashed around the car and ran to the window.

He shoved his fist in and dropped the object in Brand's lap. "For kindness," he said. "My mother sends." He sprinted away across the parking lot, laughing as semis honked at his impudent path.

Brand looked and saw, through the tangle of wrapped black cord, the twin to Mitch's talisman.

"What is it?"

"Nothing," he told Kamryn, and poked the item deep into his pocket. "A dolphin on a string."

"We sell those in our shop," she mused. "They cost us next to nothing, but they're popular. We always sell out."

Mitch said nothing, but Brand looked at the rearview mirror and saw Mitch watching him, a slight frown between his eyes. He bit his cheek and moved away, to the corner of the seat, where he could not see Mitch's eyes. He might tell Mitch what he had later, but now was not the time. All he had to do was figure out how to get Kamryn to wear it. If it helped Mitch, perhaps it might save her.

Chapter 21

The Bell Ranger lifted him over the sparsely-treed mountains and dropped into the foothills, where drought-tolerant pines and a few aspens lined the edge of the valley and the growing encampment. The northern mountains of New Mexico's landscape found rain scarce, but greenery did hold the range up to the timberline and then broke into what was best described as high desert foliage. Rembrandt stirred impatiently, leaning out of his seat, straining against the harness, looking at what had only been planned a few short years ago. Excitement flooded away the fatigue of a few short hours' sleep and the flight to Albuquerque and the subsequent copter tour here. He had not seen the camp yet, and his first glimpse was exceedingly promising.

Camp Second Hope, it had been named, hidden behind a maze of corporate blinds that he doubted anyone without inside knowledge could ever pierce, even with the aid of computer tracking. Ostensibly, it was a nonprofit religious institution, a wilderness survival camp designated for juveniles in trouble. Because it was religious, it could be hidden fairly benevolently for several years before it would attract attention. By then, it would be too late. This was the second of the camps to go online. There was one in eastern Oregon, a third in Michigan, and a fourth in West Virginia, not too far in striking distance from Quantico, Virginia.

Secure measures had been taken against satellite surveillance, the spies in the sky, sweeps through camouflage by nature and by intent. Rembrandt found himself picking out huts, training ranges, and ammo dumps only after intense scrutiny, as the helicopter drew nearer to the landing field. As good as the cameras in the sky were, as intent in focus as the lenses shot, he did not think the true scope of the grounds could be discerned. It would take an onsite visit to determine the exact nature of the camp. He knew bureaucracy. If they kept their noses clean, if they had handpicked their troops as well as they thought they had, by the time anyone thought to investigate them, it would not matter.

He had the other camps to visit, but if they were set up as well as this one, the future held only great expectations.

The pilot tapped him on the shoulder. "I'm taking you down, sir."

The corner of Rembrandt's mouth twitched at the statement of the obvious, but he said nothing, counting it to courtesy. The two men sitting in the back of the chopper had not spoken a word since leaving Phoenix, and that was as it should be. They had been in the air nearly thirty-six hours, sent out and brought back on his command. They had no questions or, more likely, if they did, they did not voice them. If they were disappointed at the abort of their mission, they did not show it.

Rembrandt spotted a welcoming committee at the edge of the pad. The chopper settled down, and he cracked the hatch, and was out and hurrying before the pilot could finish his warning about the blades. He knew choppers. Damn, he'd nearly cut his teeth on the aircraft. He could remember the days when they'd been called whirlybirds. Rembrandt straightened up, the current from the blades still whipping around him, and felt his thinning hair stand nearly on end.

Josey Meales strode up to meet him, snapping off a salute which Rembrandt returned. Josey took his suitcase, but not the laptop computer. A man's computer was his lifeline and coded to him and him alone.

Josey was in his early forties, and looked as if he had once been a military man, despite his shortness in height. He wore khaki with his pants tucked into his jackboots. The boots shone, but they also looked comfortable, well-broken in. Gray hair was sprinkled liberally at his temples and there was a palm-sized balding spot at the back of his head, but there probably wasn't a man in camp who was fitter or faster.

"Pleased to see you again."

Not many, reflected Rembrandt, could or would say that to him. He nodded brusquely. "Same here, Josey. I need to get up to speed on happenings as soon as possible, and then you and I need to reestablish my mission."

"Right this way." Josey indicated a path off the landing field with the suitcase, despite its weight, as if it were no more than an empty briefcase. "I wonder if I might ask a favor of you, sir."

Rembrandt looked at him. Josey did not often offer more than was required of him. "What is it?"

"It's noon, sir. The trainees are gathering at the mess hall. I wonder if you might say a few words to them. They know you're arriving and although you won't be here long, I think it would be important to them. They've been working hard and making a lot of progress. I'd like to think we could reward them with about five minutes of your time."

If the request had come from anybody other than Josey Meales, Rembrandt would have suspected brown-nosing, but this man did not curry favors by words, but by deeds, hard work in the field. He'd been hired by that ethic as well as ideology. Rembrandt checked his watch. It would take more than five minutes to handle the request, but he had time.

"Josey, I'd be pleased."

The commander smiled. "Thank you, sir. Let me show you to your quarters where you can freshen up and secure your equipment, and then I'll inform the mess sergeant."

Rembrandt followed, stretching his long legs to keep up with Josey's brisk march. The trainees he'd seen at the field's edge were given no time to watch him, they were already engaged in tenting camouflage nets over the Bell Ranger and staking them down against the ever-present wind. The two men he'd brought back with him fell out at Josey's orders and dog-trotted back to their barracks.

Josey had more than comfortable quarters set up for him. There was a hot meal platter waiting, its savory smells filling the suite. Meales had also laid out fresh clothes and an encrypted bulletin from Bayliss. Rembrandt closed the door behind him with gratitude, but also with a slight bit of worry. Josey was this camp's commandant. He did not need to be acting as Rembrandt's aide-de-camp. He would have to remind Josey that his efforts were better turned elsewhere and that he could, for the time being, take care of himself.

He took a stinging hot shower for two minutes to awaken himself, then sat down and ate. Steak with bernaise, fresh asparagus spears, orange slices with Spanish onion salad, and a cup of sorbet, along with a carafe of newly brewed coffee. He doubted the trainees in the mess were having much less of a meal. These people had been culled as the premium of troopers, they deserved and got nothing less than the best.

He'd barely set down his fork when a tap came at the door.

"Enter."

The door opened. A young woman saluted and informed him, "I've come to escort you to mess. The lunch hour is over, but you're expected." She wore a minimum of makeup, but needed none to accent her high cheekbones and rich, full mouth. Her glossy dark hair was bound back in a French braid, and she looked at him without looking at him, respectfully.

Rembrandt caressed his lips with the fine linen napkin and stood. "Lead the way and I'll follow."

"Ten-*hut!*"

Chairs scraped as fifty recruits sprang to their feet. They wore cammies, only their faces distinguishing them above their collars. Rembrandt scanned the room, seeing an egalitarian reflection of race and gender in the young faces looking back at him. His escort peeled off and joined an end table.

Josey had a modest podium and speaker set next to him at the head table. Rembrandt saluted back and told them they were at ease. He did not sit at the podium until they had settled, the chairs noisy in the confines of the mess hall. The cooks and cooks' helpers leaned out over the kitchen, listening, wiping their hands on their white aprons.

"Commander Meales has asked me to say a few words to you. First of all, let me tell you that I feel privileged to be here today. Although my stay here is scheduled to be very short this visit, and I have not been able to take a tour of the camp, I have already seen results of your hard work. All of us enlisted in this effort would be proud. I am proud of all of you.

"We have come together because we felt that, if an opportunity to save our country was to come, we would have to make it ourselves. We have evolved from a fiercely independent, self-ruling country to a land of sheep led by media and image, style not substance. Results of the recent election left us no choice but to join together in an effort to save what remains of our nation's original principles."

Rembrandt paused, to gauge the effect of his words. Faces rapt with attention watched him. "We can no longer afford to leave our material, spiritual, physical, and ecological rescue in the hands of those committed to lining their wallets, to being guided by pork barrel politics and shiny images on television. The partisan mind of our governing branches is hell-bent on destruction. We cannot afford to make war on ourselves, while supporting foreign nations which despise and cheat us. It is painfully apparent we have to take action ourselves. We have to pull ourselves up by our own bootstraps, before it is too late.

"All of you chosen here are training for elite jobs of position, to be in readiness for what must come. You have months of difficult training yet ahead, but you must not falter. Some of you will go out in the field as Seals, ATF, FBI, Department of the Treasury, the Pentagon, wherever you will be needed. Others will stay behind, forming task forces for covert operations. No one of us is more valuable than the others; we are all in this together. We are of a common mind to do what needs to be done. We will turn this tide and though it seems a thankless job now, future generations will remember our names as we remember those of Jefferson, Adams, Washington. Welcome, ladies and gentlemen, to the next American Revolution." Rembrandt paused and then saluted the trainees.

The mess hall vibrated with the sound of their applause. He met their enthusiasm with a solemn face, looking over the crowd, knowing that, in the weeks ahead, there would be defectors from these ranks. And, in all likelihood, despite careful screening, there would be agents, gathering information, already debating what to tell their intelligence operations about just what this group had planned. That was the way of these things. It was inevitable.

Which was why he could afford to stand here and bask in their approval. The sooner he had recovered the chemical compounds Christiansen had stolen, the sooner this front would become impenetrable, defectionless, undefeatable. The voodoo priest had promised Bayliss soldiers without pain, without doubt, without betrayal. What the superstitious world had once called zombies had nothing to do with the raising of the dead to do one's bidding. Delacroix had discovered a chemical compound which was even more powerful than legend. What Rembrandt had nearly had his hands on was a powerful psychoactive drug which channeled free will into one will, tireless, loyal until death.

The chain of conspiracy was only as strong as its weakest link. The drug promised by Delacroix would eliminate any weakness. If Rembrandt had to go to hell and back to retrieve the drug from Christiansen, to ensure the success of this endeavor, he would.

Meales, who had a sense of timing, bellowed, "*Dis*-missed!"

Geneva came in quietly, not intending to disturb Mother, but although she said nothing, she brought a freshly dipped turtle with her, and the smell of a newly-minted piece of candy filled the air as she entered the back room. Mother sat back in her chair with a sigh, then looked around with a grateful smile at her sister.

"Sometimes," she noted, "the smell of a good chocolate and caramel turtle is a heap better than incense."

Geneva handed over the patty, still cooling on a hand-sized sheet of waxed paper. "You're working too hard, Mother."

"I have to. I haven't much time. You, Geneva, need to shut the shop and pack up the girls." Mother pinched off a bit, pecans and caramel and milk chocolate, and savored it.

"Why?"

"Things are stirrin'."

"You've never had any trouble taking care of matters before."

"You know, girl, there are two sides to every coin. I fear that this man is the other side of me."

Geneva wiped her hands carefully on her bakery apron. "D'you think so?"

"It appears like it to me. I can take care of myself, but you and the girls need to be gone."

"The shop—"

"Can be shut a week or two."

"And what will you be doin'?"

"They have to come here." Mother stretched her neck and straightened her necklaces around her throat. The lemon boa around her wrist raised its delicate head, then settled again when she stroked and murmured to it. "Do all white children have such thick skulls?"

"Mmmm-hmmm." Geneva began to clear the round table in front of Mother. She pinched out candle flames, renewed incense sticks in their holders, set out new herbs, her hands efficiently whisking through the religious objects Mother studied. "But you won't give up on 'em, girl. I know you."

"Do you know?"

"A-course I do. You raised me when Mama took sick, and Papa left. You took me under your wing like a mother hen, and I've never seen you let a chick go by without takin' it in, just the same."

"Do you think Mama had the power?"

Geneva paused, put one hand on her hip as she tilted her head to the side to think. "She must have. How could she have named us so—you Madre and me Geneva? You always mothering everythin' and me always the peacemaker, always trying to settle the troubles you couldn't. But you should know that."

"Sometimes I think I know nothin' anymore." Mother rubbed the deep crease between her eyes. "I remember Granma better than you, child. Oh, if she didn't have the true power, then she had the meanness to scare the bejesus out of you!"

Geneva laughed sharply. "Didn't that woman! No wonder Papa left." She paused. "Do you ever look for him?"

"I looked, but Damballah does not let me see. Maybe it's because I'm not mambo enough—because I have a foot in this world and a foot in the other. I don't practice one religion or t'other, but both. Is that right of me?"

Geneva patted Mother on the shoulder. "Whether it's right or not, it's *you*. I don't see you ever being any different than you are." She headed back to the candy kitchen and shop front, pausing at the door. "We'll go. Tomorrow. But. . . . if you needed help, Mother, would you ask me?"

"I would, Geneva."

Her sister nodded, then stepped through.

Mother waited until the door shut firmly, finishing, "If I thought it would do any good." She stroked the ivory-and-lemon-yellow-patterned reptile. "If it would be any help at all." She stared down at the corn-grain drawing she had done on the tabletop, and lit the new candles her sister had laid out for her. She did not know if the boy was coming her way or not, bringing the others, but she could see that trouble was on their heels, very close. If they were not moving, they would soon be swallowed up.

And she had sensed the moment Delacroix had stepped onto North American soil, like a trembling deep in her soul.

She had no answers, but she had a heap of questions, including wondering what that mambo was doing. Why was he sendin' a curse after the others? How could she shelter them from it?

She had never regretted the path she'd taken, not the one her mother would have chosen for her, not the one her granma had chosen and trained her for . . . but a middle road, her own. She had chosen the Christian church, as well as the chants and charms and superstitions, the gris-gris bags to be tied to the thigh to bring a lover home, the cursing and uncursing. She was neither deacon nor mambo, but both, and she prayed in both voices, and saw miracles with two sets of eyes, and had become convinced in her lifetime that the great God above all, the Bon Dieu, was all one and the same.

She had never doubted her ability to face down anything the dark side might raise. She was a force of her own, and she had felt the goodness of Bon Dieu, and knew it was right.

Until now.

Now a mambo came who had been trained in the discipline of true vodun. She had already tasted his power, and it was considerable. Had she made a fatal mistake which she no longer had the time to rectify? Would she be strong enough to vanquish this foe?

As she stared into the drawing, she could feel the power emanating outward, the aura, but all it would do was knit closer to itself and spin, a hard, brilliant knot of energy. Spinning and spinning and spinning.

Chapter 22

The desert outside Phoenix was not a desert. It rippled in carpets of green, grain and vegetable and fruit, piped in through irrigation networks which lay at the edges of the field, doling out water like the precious commodity it was. Brand watched the scenery in vague disappointment, not knowing what he'd expected, not seeing anything he had. Crossing the last of California had been flat and uninteresting—the painted rocks and sands only meant a reddish tinge instead of dirt-color beyond the fields, and to watch any of it was like sticking his face in an oven. His eyes rejected the reflected heat and light, flinched from the ribbony highway, until he finally sat back in the car seat and watched nothing. The backs of Mitch's and Kamryn's heads. The dashboard. Anything he could to ignore the sun and light.

He'd been excited at first when Kamryn pointed out the fields, knowing they were close to Phoenix, and seeing them had been like looking at the Emerald City of Oz—much better farther away—and now he laid his temple against the car's glass, bored by row after row of broccoli despite the skyscrapers on the horizon. Even the greenery did nothing to soothe the assault of the daylight on his pupils. He felt like one of *The Lost Boys*, that near-classic movie, morphing into a vampire almost without his knowledge or consent.

He put a hand into his jeans pocket and wrapped his fingers around the amulet. Cool to his touch, the metal warmed only slightly as he held it, counterpoint to the pain of his eyes. He wondered if he still looked slightly like a racoon, or if the puffiness around his eyes had finally gone down. He thought of his mother, lying on her bed after a rough day at work, with brewed tea bags, chilled in the refrigerator, over her closed eyelids. It always looked weird, especially when she used the square bags with the paper tags, but she swore by it. He wondered if he should try that. He'd left his eyedrops behind and hoped it wouldn't be a big mistake. He needed the light. He craved it. The thought of shunning it indefinitely rode him uneasily.

Day-o, day-o. Daylight come and me wanna go home—

Shut up, Bauer, Brand said voicelessly. Bauer, of course, preferred the dark for what he liked to call his wet work. Daylight for stalking, nighttime for pleasure. Bauer went silent, but Brand would feel him, watching Kamryn through his eyes. Bauer tolerated daylight because it was better to see the victim by, but he also hated it because it exposed him and his activity, putting him at greater risk. He'd been caught in the daylight, caught and sentenced to death. He'd escaped later.

Brand sighed and closed his eyes, putting him toe to toe with Bauer, shutting the other off from watching his friends. As long as he could feel the sunlight streaming in through the car windows, as long as he could somehow even *sense* it, Brand could bask in its protection, like a cat in a window-focused ray. Bauer wasn't happy. He wanted to watch Kamryn. He liked her long, slim, angular looks, boyish in a way. He liked boys, young boys, young girls . . . liked them best when torturing them, vise grips on tiny, raised nipples, their torsos slick with blood, his ears filled with childish cries of anguish. Wet work. Brand pushed back, hard, shoving Bauer aside in his thoughts, images, thinking of sunlight streaming in, fiery, yellow-white light burning out his soul, his mind's eye, cleansing it. Bauer retreated, but Brand knew it was only temporary. He felt sick to his stomach.

Please, God, don't leave me blind and alone with him, he prayed silently, unaware his lips moved slightly and his breath made tiny whispery noises.

Kamryn moved her head. "Asleep again," she reported to Mitch. "I thought he said he had problems sleeping."

"He has bad dreams. He's probably exhausted, though, after the last couple of days. Don't blame him. The view's putting me to sleep, too." He checked the rearview mirror, put his hand to it, trying to adjust it.

"Don't touch that! It's hanging on by a stripped screw and a bobby pin."

Mitch grinned as he looked at her. "Did you buy this as is or was it a fixer upper?"

"Laugh, but it's paid for." Kamryn crossed her legs and looked out over the farmlands. "And it's taking you where you want to go."

"We'll be in Phoenix in another forty-five minutes. What did you have in mind?"

"Swapping this baby over as soon as I can. My California plate is like a spotlight, even though there will be a lot of them over here. I have . . . friends . . . who might be able to help. Then I thought we'd get a room. He's had plenty of rest, but I feel as bad as you look. I thought we'd drive down to Tucson after dark, then get as far as we can into New Mexico."

His hand flexed on the steering wheel. He drove with his left arm on the door's rest, his hand free. "Texas is going to be a two-day drive. Taking the 10 across is cutting through the heart."

"I know," Kamryn answered. "No place else to go."

"Enough money in that belt of yours to buy air fare?"

Reflexively, her hand went to the flat of her stomach and the canvas money belt. "You know, I told Brand I'd help him get to New Orleans, but this money is for the future. I won't have one without it. I don't intend to bankroll this with my last cent."

"You don't."

"No."

"How'd you meet Brand, anyway? Get roped into this?"

"I never met him, really. He was just this geeky teenager down at the mall . . . staring at me. He tried to help me out once, a streak of the Lone Ranger, I guess. Then, when Darby came—well, you saw him . . . he would have taken a bullet for me. For me," she repeated softly, in wonderment. "What makes a kid like that? Willing to sacrifice his life for a stranger?"

Mitch's hands tightened on the wheel again. White knuckles, then loosened. "What makes a kid the other way?"

"That's easy, I suppose. Hatred. Self-hatred. Bad role models. Low self-esteem. Then something comes along, a thought, something that strikes a note, a Pied Piper, something that looks better, at least an escape, maybe. Only it's not. It sucks you in before you notice it's a trap of its own. Then it builds."

Mitch was watching her, she felt, but she did not want him to see her face. She had talked too much, too long, but to stop now would tip him off.

"Is that what drew you in?"

"Sort of, and not exactly."

"I don't see you doing it just for a boyfriend."

"No," she answered softly. "It was in the family. The boyfriends came later. And I'm not a skinhead. Not anymore."

"No," he agreed. "Now you're an avenging angel, dashing in to rescue Brand."

"What about you? Why do you have somebody like Rembrandt asking about you?"

"It's personal."

"It's more than personal, it's deadly. Forget what Brand saw, or thinks he saw, or made us think we saw. He could be psychotic or it could be a flashback from the drugs. Rembrandt is flesh and blood, and he's a killer."

"You're better off not knowing."

"You can't fight what you don't know about."

"I don't know what he is." Mitch licked his lips as if they'd gone dry. "At first, I thought military police."

"He acts like government. Military intelligence?"

"Maybe."

"And why you?"

"I'm AWOL."

"Really? From what?"

"The USMC."

"Well, semper fi." Kamryn looked at him appraisingly. "I can't see you as a jarhead."

"I wasn't a jarhead." He shut his mouth, the lines across his jaw tightened, worked. "I was a Marine."

"Still are, is my guess. You must have done something big. Get the base commander's daughter pregnant?"

He looked across the desert, north, to where low-lying mountains just edged the horizon. Dusty, dun-colored mountains. Somewhere beyond them lay the fantastic canyons and gorges of the Grand Canyon. He felt about to tumble into its depths. He did not want to answer any more questions. "You don't need to know any more."

"Yeah, well, I don't need to know any less either." Kamryn let out a short laugh. "I never would have guessed. Only The Shadow knows the secrets which lie in the hearts of men. Or something like that."

He caught sight of the road sign, and said, with a touch of relief in his tone, "Sixteen miles and we're in."

The fields were broken now by squares of commerce, scattered, dusty gas stations and abandoned homesteads, and an occasional bar. She stared at one as they passed, motorcycles lined up outside, haughty, road-faring bikes, monsters of the road. A group of jacketed riders lounged around the doorway of the concrete block building, cold beers in their hands, watching her pass by even as she watched them being left behind, raising uneasy thoughts in her, but as she twisted back to look, the bar was too far from the road and too far behind to tell. She shook it off.

"Ever been to Phoenix?" she asked of Mitch.

"No."

"Well, 10 goes through the southern quarter. Just follow it on in. We'll stay in Tempe, just outside the major part of the city. It's cheaper there. No one should notice us."

"What about Brand?"

Kamryn looked back. "What do you mean?"

"Any chance they'll be looking for him out here?"

"Possibly. L.A. has a pretty wide sphere. We'll have to catch the evening news on that, and do whatever we have to."

"Meaning?"

She gave a half smile. "Meaning we have to get a more expensive motel, with TV. And at least one of us might have to get a haircut and a dye job."

He ran his hand through his hair. "I don't have much more to lose."

"We all," she contradicted gently, "have a lot to lose if they catch us now."

The same recruit who'd escorted him to the mess came to Rembrandt's room several hours later, interrupting his review of the SALUTE reports while he was confirming his feeling that intelligence operations by the Aryan Nations and other groups had been stepped up, equaling only the recent surge in the latter part of 1994 through 1995. They were watching each other, they were, circling warily, looking for that terrorist strike or demonstration which could be capitalized upon. There was, gratifyingly, no mention of his own operations, however. Their build-up had yet to be noticed, as they had planned, giving them a definite advantage. Rembrandt looked up, prepared to be annoyed at the disturbance, but the truth was that she was easy on the eyes, a lot easier than the damned reports, and he ended up scowling to hide her effect on him.

"Recruit Reynolds."

She saluted smartly. "Commander Meales sent me, with a request that you come to the computer room. He says you might be interested in a report he's running for you."

That would be on the Honda's license plate, tracking the girl down. He folded his reading glasses quickly. "Ah. Thank you." He stood and took a few minutes to return the report to the desk safe in his room, then joined the trainee at the door. "After you."

Crossing the squad between buildings, her alarm watch went off. Without hesitation, she reached out, took his wrist and said, "Come with me, sir."

She ducked in under the extended eaves of one of the buildings and waited, motionless, until her watch pealed again. He noticed that all activity between the buildings did the same, and out on the field. He could only think of one thing that would precipitate the actions.

She counted to ten before stepping out from the sheltering eave and apologized.

"Quite all right, Reynolds. We avoiding a sweep?"

"Yes, sir. We appear to be on the northern edge of a rather broad look-see. The commander thinks the main objective is Los Alamos and Roswell."

"Ours?"

"We don't know yet." She smiled grimly. "But we will."

Rembrandt followed after first looking upward, though he could not possibly see the spy satellite which was taking camera surveillance of the area, not with his bare eye, and not in the daytime. He had been in his quarters all afternoon and had not noticed, but calculated that every seventeen minutes or so, or whatever the orbit of the cameras might be, all activity would halt, the personnel of the camp either taking shelter or hitting the ground in their cammies to avoid being identified by the photo reconn. If they were on the fringe of the sweep, such evasive action could be successful for months.

If he were a betting man, he would gamble that Bayliss had not yet heard of this minor complication. Meales would know that the base had been located where it had because of such logistics. The commander might even lose his command and be transferred to another camp, and Second Hope abandoned. Josey had worked hard for this promotion, it would not sit well with him to be moved.

It would not sit well with Bayliss to know that they might have been detected. It mattered little if it were domestic or foreign, at this point. Later, perhaps.

Not that he needed to have Meales indebted to him, but it would not hurt to pull Josey's bacon out of the fire. It was possible he could trace the computer connect to the satellite and reroute the camera angles. It would take some time, time he did not have until Christiansen was brought in, but Rembrandt thought he could do it. Meales might even have hackers working who had already traced part of the signal. They should have the facilities to do it.

Even though he had helped to design the communications and computer areas, he was still awed to see the design at work. Reynolds led him into the building, its interior a good fifteen degrees cooler than outside to keep the equipment at its optimum. Inside, he noticed personnel wearing their long-sleeved uniforms against the chill. The recruit motioned him into a lab, where activity seemed constant yet constrained. Everyone he saw wore headsets, free-roaming, and one or two carried computer notepads, etching as they talked. A phone rang in the corner cubicle, and a fax immediately started to pick up the signal.

The cubicles were set apart, each area a pod of activity, sometimes working on a clear plexiglass board. He recognized a map of Washington, D.C., on one of them as he passed it by, a recruit busily sketching in information as his headset fed it to him. Rembrandt's head turned slightly as he passed it, keeping it in view. The vice president, he decided. They were charting the movements of the vice president. The president was in Canada for the weekend, at a minor summit.

Even more importantly, he could see the recruits, as a second joined the first, charting the movement of the Secret Service detail escorting the vice president. They did not notice as Rembrandt passed, engrossed in their work.

"This is Recruit Trinh, sir. He's been assigned to your request."

"Thank you, Reynolds."

"A pleasure, sir." She smiled fully, her sensuous mouth curving into a bow. "Just send for me when you want to return to quarters."

He was not to move about unescorted. That surprised Rembrandt briefly, but he nodded acquiescence.

Trinh sat in a cubicle dominated by three computers and several external modem hookups in addition to the internal modems of the computer models. His area was messy in a familiar way. The recruit made ready to stand, but Rembrandt pulled up a chair and sat down, saying, "At ease, son. What have you got?"

Trinh reached for a stack of paper with a fine-boned hand. He was Vietnamese, unless Rembrandt missed his guess, probably brought into Camp Pendleton with thousands of others in the mid-1970s and relocated from there. "I checked out California DMV on the license plate you gave me. I've been working all afternoon on it."

This was nothing Rembrandt couldn't have done himself, but he had not had the time. Regardless, getting into the motor vehicle records should not have taken the bulk of the afternoon. "Recruit, I don't know the particulars of your background, but this was not a project requiring the effort—"

"Sir." Trinh looked at him intently, dark eyes narrowing. "Meaning no disrespect, sir, but she left a paper trail I've been several hours following."

"I see." Rembrandt sat back. "Let me see what you've pulled up."

"First, I have the latest registration records. There is a change of address about eight weeks ago. The current address is a dummy, but the state doesn't know that yet."

"But we do."

Trinh nodded with satisfaction. "Yes, sir, we do. The prior registration is an address in Costa Mesa, Orange County, but it, too, was fairly recent. It shows the car was bought and registered there about ten months ago. The car was used and I checked out the former owners, but I don't see anything too interesting about them." He passed over several sheets of paper, printouts of previous registration information.

"What about her?"

"Kamryn Talent? Well, that's the thing. First of all, there is a city police inquiry on the record of the dummy address, but no follow-up."

Rembrandt scanned the hard copy. "Brea P.D. That's possible. She was witness to a shooting several days ago." So now the police department was also aware the address had been a fake. He was glad he'd listened to his instincts and let the girl and kid go. He could strike in Arizona or New Mexico and dispose of the bodies where they would never be found. If he'd done the job in Orange County, the alert would have gone up instantly. He did not like attracting attention.

"Okay." Trinh shuffled more paper from the stack at his elbow. "But there is also a state inquiry, plus two Orange County sheriffs' flags on the authentic Costa Mesa address."

"Really?" Rembrandt checked the printouts as Trinh fed them over. If she had lived with the boyfriend previously, then the skinhead had drawn attention he probably wasn't even aware that he'd drawn. They'd been watched, and didn't even know it. Interesting, and logical, but not particularly illuminating. But it was obvious Trinh had done more.

"What else can you tell me?"

"First, I checked out the residential address. The primary occupant, male, is deceased—" Trinh paused. "The shooting, right?"

"Right."

"Okay. Well, he has—had—local skinhead connections, but nothing too significant. So I went back to the girl since she was the object of the original search." Trinh paused. "I'm right, aren't I, sir? It wasn't the car."

"No, it wasn't the car."

"Good." Trinh smiled briefly, a fleeting expression that passed quickly over his Asian features. "I decided to check on the driver's license, since I'd already been into DMV. It was fairly new, too, predating the car purchase by only a few weeks."

"Totally new, or from out of state?"

"Totally new. Although," and Trinh paused, looking at his own hard copies, "I don't find any notation that she turned in an out of state license. I find that unusual. She's twenty-three. She should have been driving for at least six or seven years."

It was unusual. Trinh had the same instincts Rembrandt had. "Go on."

"So, I checked birth records as given on the driver's license and in the taxation records. I couldn't find a Kamryn Talent in California for birth, although there have been state disability fund installments for about six months or so from employment checks, in addition to state withholding."

"And you did a national search on the birth?"

"Yes, sir. I used our own databases which seem to be fairly complete and then I tapped into the IRS briefly—that was a quick connect, sir and I had to get out faster than I wanted to, unable to locate an adult record—but I did locate Kamryn Talent in Oregon."

"Oregon." He wouldn't have thought that. She had an inflection to her voice which he had not placed, but she had not struck him as Oregonian.

"But that's the end of it, sir. The skinhead association bothered me, so I kept checking. Death records, this time." Trinh's face blazed with triumph. "There is no Kamryn Talent alive in the United States at this time, sir. She died in 1974 after a very short infancy."

"The birth certificate is fake."

"As far as I can trace."

Trinh passed him the remainder of the hard copy.

"Let me commend you on an excellent job." Rembrandt looked down, reading what he'd already been told.

His question had been answered, but a more vital one raised. There was no Kamryn Talent. The thorn in his side should not exist, but she did. And, for some reason, she had false papers. An identity which had been well-provided, and one which he could assume had come courtesy of the Aryan Brotherhood.

But why? Who in the hell was she?

"What do you suggest, sir?"

"Run a scan on news articles, give me an eighteen-month parameter, with anyone matching her gender, age, and general physical description. Let's see what comes up."

Trinh frowned in concentration. "All right. Anything else?"

This was an unusual trio. He had not been able to understand what brought them together, or what, if any, bonds would hold them together. He thought he knew Christiansen. Now he had to learn what he could about potential allies.

He leaned forward intently. "Let's see what you can help me pull up on the boy. I have some indication of psychiatric problems. I want anything you can pull up."

Chapter 23

Delacroix took a room in a hotel which would not have existed except for the sport fishing in the area, and although he surmised it was not luxurious by American standards from the complaints he heard as he passed through the lobby, it was far grander than almost any establishment he had ever seen in Haiti. Perhaps Port-au-Prince or the president's palace might have more elegant buildings. Perhaps. He had never been to the city or to the capital. Yet. He felt in his heart that there would come a day when he would be summoned. Yes. Summoned and dined and asked his opinion, and offered respect due his position. That day was coming.

But first, he had to pass through this day and night, and the others immediately before him. He would rest in the afternoon and, in the early evening, they could cross the territory overland, and into Arizona. He did not expect trouble. The border guards would have no reason to look for him, no expectation to deny him. He was, after all, traveling in the guise of a professor, a man simply after knowledge and learning.

And didn't Americans think that they had an obligation to educate the rest of the world? Their own arrogance would be their downfall.

He sat down in a comfortable, cushioned wicker chair by a veranda which looked down on the Bay of Cortez with its bluer than blue waters, and opened a chilled bottle of fruit juice which he had purchased on the way to the room.

Stark brought in the bags and set them down.

Delacroix turned around at his entrance. He pulled a second bottle of juice from the pocket of his jacket and tossed it onto the twin bed nearest Stark.

"Drink," he said. "You must be thirsty."

Stark stared at the glass bottle for a moment as if not recognizing it, then picked it up, twisted the cap off, and drained the bottle in three long gulps.

Delacroix smiled. "Yes. I thought you might be." He swung around in the chair, looking at the ocean again. "My assistants will be here shortly. You might as well rest while you can. We have a long night ahead of us."

Stark took off his safari jacket. His skin showed a faint pinkness from being in the sun at the helm of the boat. He laid the jacket out carefully, stretched out next to it, and closed his eyes.

In a moment, perhaps two, his breathing had deepened into a cat-like purr, and he was asleep.

Like the American arrogance that they had much to show the rest of the world, Delacroix would turn this, too, back on them. Stark was his, wholly, despite the years of training and, in fact, the training was what made him an invaluable tool. He knew more than weaponry. Without him, Delacroix might have wasted months and gutted his precious financial resources obtaining the correct paperwork and transportation. His loa rode a man who had found the trail he sought, but it made little difference if Delacroix could not follow after. The loa might capture, might kill, but it would not retrieve the sacred powders. For that, Delacroix trusted only himself. It was Stark who paved the way, like Judas himself, showing the priest the soft underbelly of the American system.

He had never doubted that he could bend Stark to his will, but there had been a time when he was not certain if Stark's body would heal, if it would allow him to follow the new set of his mind and spirit. The man had been abandoned for dead, on the threshold, and it had taken much from Delacroix to keep him from passing. There had been severe bleeding, and infection and fever. Weeks of weakness and listlessness had culminated in a body which was only a shadow of what it had been. He did not know if he had a tool he could use or not until the day Stark had risen from his cot in the hut, and come to the altar where Delacroix sat meditating and said, "I must run."

Delacroix had heard him approach in the silence and, without turning, answered, "You cannot leave without my willing it."

"I do not wish to leave. I must run."

And so Delacroix had given in to the strange request and let the stranger run. Stark did so, gone for hours, staggering back pale and deluged with sweat, falling into his cot, unmoving for hours until that day when he did not fall upon returning.

Then he came to Delacroix and said, "I must lift weights."

Delacroix had laughed at that. "Work in the fields. Carry the sheep and goats and pigs. Carry the bails if you wish to lift weight."

And so Stark had done that, all summer, in the fields of the two or three villages which huddled close to the hills where Delacroix tended his church and shrines. He grew tanned and strong and returned to Delacroix at sundown every day, where he said little, but listened to Delacroix as he talked of and to his gods.

As was fitting of Delacroix's position, he explained to Stark the importance of vodun, how it had strengthened the slaves of Haiti, how it had given them the power to rise up and make of themselves an independent nation, though troubled, and how it would aid them yet again. How the United Nations and the Protestant churches were trying to bury voodoo, but how it would triumph. How even the president's palace sat on ground which had been hallowed by its rituals, and although forgotten, would be brought down again and rise again in vodun pride.

How he, Delacroix, and even he, Stark, might have a part in this. All of this, and more, he spoke of in the evenings, in his soft, lilting island French patois, and Stark not only understood, but absorbed every word until it came time to plan these days, and then Stark had begun speaking back to him, in American, but they two understood each other perfectly. Stark, then, as now, confined his speech to only what was absolutely necessary. Then, as now, he had a complete and deep comprehension of what it was Delacroix hoped to achieve.

This, Delacroix told himself, this was what could be achieved with the powers given to himself. Without the touch of the god, the powders were little, without the understanding of the spiritual, the binding of the physical to a purpose was a binding which was brittle, which could not be trusted or would not last. The consecration of flesh to body to will to god was all.

A soft knock sounded on his door. Delacroix dropped his feet to the rug and crossed the room. Stark did not stir in his sleep, but his breathing lightened a little, and the priest knew he was listening on some level, as a soldier would, determining if there were peril.

Genet stood outside, his cocoa face rippling with sweat from the heat of the fishing village. At his heel waited Covarubia. Both men inclined their heads in respect.

"Only two of you," Delacroix noted, as he let them in.

"We are sorry," Genet pleaded. "The others did not return from California. We have not heard from them."

"I am sorry as well. Come in, sit. Rest in the breeze. We will talk about our plans this evening, but keep your voices low. Stark is resting."

Genet flashed the sleeping man a suspicious look, one which Delacroix caught with some surprise. He did not show it, however. He would remedy matters later, for Genet could not be allowed to ruin his plans with petty jealousies. Genet would be reminded that he did as he did not for Delacroix the man, but for Delacroix the high priest, the mambo, and for the dark face of Damballah and for other gods whose names when mentioned would make Genet tremble.

"We must assume they are dead. We will proceed without them."

"My brother!" Genet protested. "Take Covarubia with you, but let me go to California to find him. Anything could have happened. He needs me."

"If he is alive, he will return home. If not, the legba has swallowed him . . . he has passed through the spirit gate, he is no longer someone you can help. Only I can help him now."

Genet's face paled beneath its rich coloring. "He is my brother," he repeated, and his large hands moved restlessly. "I can't leave him behind."

"He is already gone, or already safe. Those were his instructions if he could not make it here. He understood this . . . now you must understand it also."

Covarubia sat cross-legged on the second bed. He commented, "Rich men must sleep here."

"Rich men or soft men," Delacroix agreed. "Do you have trouble with this?" he added, looking into Genet's eyes, brown eyes flecked richly with green, the features of his face reflecting his heritage of mixed blood.

Genet's mouth twisted, but he said nothing else, giving a brusque nod.

"Good. You two may rest if you wish, or leave to find food and drinks. I must do what I must do." Delacroix slipped off his jacket and his shoes, opened the veranda door, and pushed the small table and chair aside. He sat down, facing the serene view of the sea.

Genet left. Covarubia's snoring twinned that of Stark. Delacroix closed his eyes, seeking commune with the loa he had sent into the world so many months ago seeking his vengeance. It was not his own loa, or he would not have survived its passage for that length of time, but it drew on him and he could feel the tug on himself grow threadier and threadier. This loa had been summoned from its place in the world beyond, and it wished to return, thirsty and eager to do its work so that it could.

It grasped him, cool and unearthly. It sensed the beginning of the end of its hunt. It told him of the chase and where its horse, the possessed human which carried it, had brought it, and Delacroix was well pleased. He urged it to feed, to keep its strength, and informed it of his coming.

It promised to eat.

"We should have followed her."

"Shut up, butt-munch," Snake said, and drained the last of his beer from his mug. The dust in his throat stayed there, raspy and harsh. He had not been able to swallow well for days. It did not matter what he did. "If she'd seen us, she would have taken off."

His companion snickered. "Butt-munch. Mutt-munch, that's more like it!"

The object of the derision straightened, his young face reddening roughly. "It's Mott. Not mutt, not butt."

"Might as well be, for all the thinking you do," Snake muttered. "Go get me another beer."

Mott's chin jutted out belligerently, but he grabbed the glass mug from Snake and left, his Doc Marten boots clomping loudly. He pushed his slim, hipless body through the growing crowd in the bar, disappearing into interior darkness, until even his white T-shirt could not be seen.

Snake turned back to Fleer. "Got any questions?"

Fleer shrugged. He had trimmed his blond surfer hair until all that was left was an inch-long fuzz on his crown, and the iron eagle tattoo on his left forearm blazed with the newness of fresh, black ink, its edges still a little pink-red from the needles. "Mott's an idiot."

"So are you," Snake said.

"But a smart idiot." Fleer looked at him with his southern California baby blue eyes, so innocent, so deceptive. He'd personally helped Snake stomp some homos into the sand at Dana Point not two months ago. "I'm cool if you're cool."

"Right." Snake drew his lips back. "That's the way it should be."

He had wanted to follow the bitch right into Phoenix, but having come this far, he thought he knew where she was headed. She might have left Darby, but she had not run to the police. The news dudes had been speculating for days about her noncooperation with the police investigation and her disappearance. Snake had found the information vaguely surprising, but useful. She had drifted into the Costa Mesa community of skinheads via Arizona. It seemed logical that, in trouble, she would go back.

New papers, new identity. That meant Snake knew exactly where she was headed.

She'd had passengers in the car, so she would have to stow them somewhere while she did her business. When she was alone, when she was in the midst of the print shop operation, he would do her. He did not anticipate much reaction to the deed. Better a dead mistake than a live one.

Mott came back out and shoved his beer in his hand. Snake took it, blew off the foam, and downed it. He'd drunk enough that his bladder gave him urgent signals, but he did not feel as if he'd had enough. The road dust clotted his throat, knotting there, like something living.

He coughed. Thrust the glass back again. "Get me another."

Mott had not yet chilled out, but he took it, and disappeared.

Fleer said, "Snake."

"What?"

"Don't ride him too much. His dad has a lot of bucks in the movement."

Striking like a cobra, Snake had Fleer by the suspenders and back up against the wall of the building. "Don't tell me what to do. Ever."

"Right."

"Don't tell me anything about the brothers. I *know*. While you guys were still crawling on your surfboards and skateboards, I was kicking in skulls."

"Right."

"When you guys were just sittin' up in your high chairs, realizing that the blacks and the browns were giving you the shaft, I was running 'em down in the street."

"Right."

"When you busted your first cherry, I was papering high school lockers, spreading the truth."

"Right."

"Don't forget it." Snake let him go. Fleer did not move.

He had only decided to flex his shoulders when Mott came back a second time. He traded glances with Mott but said nothing.

Snake drained the glass, then said, "I'm going to the head. Then we're leaving."

"Right," said Fleer again.

Snake marched through them, but he could feel their eyes on him as he went into the cool, inky darkness of the bar. He found the head as much by its smell as by the flaking signs on the eaves.

What light it had came in from a high overhead window. The fixture bulb had either burned out or been broken. One of the urinals leaked through a cracked basin. Snake unzipped and took a stance.

He was uneasy, for reasons that escaped him, and he did not like it. He knew part of it came from Darby's woman. She needed to be taken care of, and that would cause problems among the brothers. For reasons he had been told he did not need to know, she had been taken in and passed along, given papers and money. She knew people and things he did not know, and she had importance to someone in the hierarchy.

But he'd already decided his course with her. She would die, and he would explain later. He did not expect to have to face any consequences. She had left the Brotherhood, she had inside information, she was dangerous. It was all that simple. It should not bother him, and it didn't actually, although it was like an itch somewhere he couldn't quite scratch—and he sure as hell couldn't ask anyone else to scratch it for him.

But there was another uncomfortable feeling sliding around on its belly inside of him, one that almost seemed like it was not part of

him, but was. He knew it was there, although it seemed every time
he tried to focus his attention on it, it would slip and slither away. He
could imagine its track in his mind, like silvery snail snot, and it
rubbed him wrong wherever it touched.

And it was an itchy itch. It crawled around his throat, knotting it,
like he'd swallowed some kind of hair ball, choking him. Then there
were the feelers it sent into his skull, aching, throbbing, creepy shots
that iced through and he would have scratched them away, if he
could have, if he could have reached them.

But Snake knew they lay more than skin-deep, under bone and muscle and maybe even thought, like a spiderweb which had grown in him,
and something skittered along the strands, itching and twanging at
him. He did not like it, and the more he thought on it, the stronger he
could feel it.

He could feel it growing now, and the warm bleary feeling of the
beer coursing through him began to chill. The itchy thing began
to uncoil, growing larger and larger, pushing his own thoughts of
himself out of the way. The stream of urine he pissed into the broken porcelain basin felt cold as ice water. He felt his eyes roll back
into his skull, and found himself looking at his brain from the inside out.

And then he felt nothing.

Delacroix opened his eyes, looking upon the Sea of Cortez. It was
very blue, darkening as the sky darkened, as though it drew night into
its very depths. He gave a pleased smile.

"Hey, buddy. You tryin' something or what?"
Snake felt himself come awake, as if he'd been standing unconscious, blinking, his eyes narrowing in the dim confines of the bathroom. He stood with his feet spread, his dick in his hands, and did
not know how long he'd been standing there. He tucked himself in
and zipped up. "Shut up, asswipe," he said, and brushed by the other
biker as he went out the door.

Mott and Fleer had edged inside and had their elbows on the
counter. Both hurriedly finished their drinks and slid a couple of dollars over the counter as they saw him emerge.

Mott opened his mouth as if to say something, then shut it, twisting thin lips. Fleer merely stared at him with icy blue eyes. Snake wiped the back of his mouth on his bare arm. "Let's get out of here."

Somewhere near the door, a battered brown cowboy boot jutted out insolently from a crowded table. Snake tripped, stumbling violently into the door jamb, where he caught himself. Raucous laughter followed him. He swung around. He could feel sweat springing up through the pores of his naked head.

"Somethin' funny?"

The owner of the cowboy boot dragged his feet back in under his chair. "Yeah. You. Tattooed man."

Snake knew the bar. Knew the drinkers. Knew the type who was welcome and who was not.

And whether Cowboy knew it or not, he didn't care. He stared down. "Listen, beaner. You're in the wrong place at the right time."

Cowboy straightened in his chair, his brown face weathered by the harshness of the Arizona sun. He maybe even had a touch of Navajo in his broad cheekbones. "Shove it up your ass, freak."

Snake could feel the rush. He flexed his biceps. This, *this,* was what would scratch the itch which had been driving him crazy. He knew what he wanted, and it wasn't an apology. "Come on, cucaracha. Let's talk about it outside."

Cowboy leaped to his feet, his sudden movement scraping his chair across the floor. One of his buddies grabbed for his arm, muttering, "It's not worth it, man."

Cowboy shook him off. "You and me, skinhead."

Snake, grinning, followed him out into the blazing afternoon sun. He did not care if Cowboy's friends followed them out or not. He did not care if Cowboy carried a knife or a gun. He beckoned to Mott and Fleer.

"Get your butts on the bikes."

They did as they were told. Bodies crowded the doorway and Snake could hear the noise of their voices, like bees buzzing in his ears. He cupped his hand. He waved to burrito boy. "Come a little closer."

Cowboy made a move to a hip pocket. Snake could hear chain being drawn out, its links clinking. He struck cobra fast. So fast that Cowboy never had a chance to pull his weapon free.

A stomp, a knee, and he drove his fingertips into the base of the throat. Cowboy dropped to his knees, choking, spitting out blood. Crimson gushed from his nose and his lips. He toppled into the dirt.

Over that quickly. Snake grinned downward.

"Don't mess with the big boys. You ain't good enough."

He got on his bike and the three of them pulled away. Damn, but it felt *good*.

Chapter 24

NWS BULLETIN
National Hurricane Center 0600 am EDT TS Yolanda

TS YOLANDA IS CONTINUING IN A WEST, NORTH WEST-
ERLY DIRECTION, GAINING STRENGTH AND BECOMING
ORGANIZED. ABOUT TEN AM EDT, TS YOLANDA WILL POS-
SIBLY BE UPGRADED TO A FORCE 1 OR 2 HURRICANE IF
WINDS CONTINUE TO BUILD. STORM WARNINGS ARE IS-
SUED TO THE OUTLYING ISLANDS OF THE CHAIN. WIND
GUSTS OF UP TO 70 MPH HAVE BEEN MEASURED. ANTICI-
PATED RAINFALL 4–6 INCHES.
PLEASE CONTINUE TO MONITOR THIS CHANNEL FOR
UPDATES ON TS YOLANDA.

Kamryn woke, flashes of light playing fiercely upon her face and
the cracked ceiling of the motel room, and thought of St. Elmo's fire.
It wasn't, of course. It took her another second or two to realize it
came from the TV, and Brand sat cross-legged in front of it, an inky
silhouette lit by the TV in the dark of the room. She could not tell
what time it was, though it must have been early. She had slept in
one of the two sagging king-sized beds, Mitch and Brand in the
other. Blackout drapes hung solidly across the motel window, shutting out the world, but Brand sat watching the weather channel.

She rubbed at the corner of her eyelid and sat up, drawing the
sheet around her. She watched him for a second, engrossed in read-

ing the storm warning as it scrolled across the screen, a fine classical music piece playing in muted accompaniment. Then it cut to
scenes of recent hurricanes and typhoon destruction. A young man
with a distinctive New England accent stood in front of a weather
map and began to speak, oddly muffled, until she realized he had the
sound down incredibly low.

Kamryn swung her feet out. He heard her and swiveled about on
his hips, bringing his fingers up to his mouth. He pointed at the
mound of tousled blankets that was Mitch on the other bed. She nodded and came over, sitting quietly next to him. One of her kneecaps
popped, the one that always did, and it sounded like a champagne
cork going off.

Startled, Brand kept his hand over his mouth to catch his laugh.
She shook her head.

"How long have you been up?"

"Early. I slept too much yesterday. And," and he tilted his head
slightly, the eerie reflection from the TV screen intensifying the dusting of freckles across his face, "I'm hungry."

"So what else is new?"

He shrugged. Mitch snored rhythmically and the two of them listened to it in companionable silence for a moment. Then Kamryn realized she was smiling, like a fool, when Brand asked, "What is it?"

She shook her head. "He sounds like an old dog we had. A big old
farm dog."

"Memories, huh."

"Sure." She paused. "You ever have a dog?"

"No." He looked back at the TV as if fascinated by the scenarios
of destruction. "Not exactly."

"Well, you should. They're great. I wouldn't be without one, yard
duty and all. Every boy should have a dog."

"I guess they thought I was already busy with my psychosis."

"You seem pretty normal to me."

"Other than seeing things."

"Even that."

He looked back and forth. "You didn't like me watching you at the
mall."

"Well, you gotta admit, that got a little creepy." She watched his
face. So young. So unmarked. No sun lines, no tattoos. No lies.

"I didn't mean it to. I just thought you were, well, pretty."

"Thanks."

"And you thought I was, well, you know, creepy."

She grinned. "Something like that."

"But you're here now."

"You're worth it."

He was silent.

She nudged him. "Come on, Brand. You're worth it, aren't you?"

"Maybe not."

"After what you've been through? You're saner than most of the adults I know."

"It's not that. Do you cook?"

She had, once. Memories of a big kitchen which served as family room, birthday hall, diner, flooded her. "I grew up helping my mom."

"I peel potatoes and stuff. Ever peel a perfectly good spud and then you get to the inside, all brown and rotten?"

She nodded.

"Well, maybe that's how I am, but you don't know it. Only you kind of do, because you thought I was a jerk."

What could he have done? Ditched school? Borrowed ahead on his allowance and squandered it? God, didn't he realize there were kids his age shooting other kids for their jackets, their shoes? What could he have done compared to what she'd been through? "Brand." She laid a hand on his shoulder, felt the muscles flinch under her touch. "I know we're all leaning on you, some of us harder than others. I know what it's like. But you're tougher than you think you are. You're not going to cave in."

"Did you?"

She could feel her face change. "You know I did. I'd like to think it was only skin-deep, but . . ." She took her hand from Brand's shoulder. "I'm not you. And I'm here to tell you, there's a second chance. If you fall from grace, there's a second chance."

She took a deep breath. Kamryn got back to her feet. "Shower?"

"Already." His subdued voice sounded a little relieved.

"Okay. I'll be out in a couple of minutes if Mitch wakes up. There's a Denny's a couple of miles up—they'll be open."

"Okay." He shoved his hand in one pocket and opened his mouth as if he thought of saying something, then he blushed slightly and looked down at his feet, back to the TV set, anywhere but at her.

Kamryn looked down and saw that her sheet had slipped, revealing one satiny bra cup and cleavage. She drew it back up, pretending she hadn't seen him blushing.

He reared back. In a coarse and cunning voice, he began to recite. "Bitch. Juice box, cunt, hairy clit—" He broke off, choking, stammering, his face crimson, mortified. "That wasn't me. God. That wasn't me."

If it wasn't him, then who was it? Her own face had warmed with shock. She swallowed. "It's all right, Brand. I have a second cousin who had Tourette's—do you know what that is? He'd get tics and twitches. Sometimes he'd rattle off until the air turned blue. It wasn't anything he meant to do. And I've been called worse."

And called others worse, far worse. Brand mumbled again, ducked his face down, unable to look at her.

She gathered up the rest of her sheet like the train of a bridal gown. "If that's all the rotten you get, I guess I can take it." He stood, she reminded herself, over that terrible abyss which separated boy from man. He wouldn't answer back.

By the time she was done showering and had dressed, Brand had found CNN. Flickering light from the screen bounced and reflected off his sunglasses. Odd, to see him wearing them in the darkness of the room. She wondered if he used them to hide behind, still embarrassed.

"Your eyes still bothering you?"

"A little." He took his glasses off and rubbed gently at them. The puffiness had nearly disappeared. "They feel kind of dry and scratchy."

"We'll pick up some eyedrops today if we can. Nothing medicated—the kind contact wearers use. They should help."

"Okay."

"Any news?" Kamryn chewed on her lower lip.

"Yeah, but we were just a blip. 'Two witnesses to L.A. area shooting disappear—boy feared to be suicidal, ex-girlfriend involved said to be avoiding police and media attention.' "

"Any photos?"

"Me. My junior high ID picture. It sucks." His voice had began to loosen up. He sounded like the old Brand.

She smiled in spite of her own tension. "Anyone able to recognize you off that?"

"Not even my mom."

"That bad, huh."

"Worse." He settled his glasses back on his face. "They're not talking about Mitch at all."

"Probably don't have him ID'd. He left the scene before I did." Kamryn let out a soft sigh. "Seems unreal, like it never happened."

Brand tilted his head back a little to look at her more fully. "There's a hurricane coming up the gulf. Forecasters say it's headed toward Louisiana."

Hairs raised on her arms and the back of her neck. "How bad?"

"It's building. Do you think it's going to bother us?"

She shrugged. "Those things sometimes just fall apart. How many hurricanes hit that area? One every two or three years? What are our odds? I'm more worried about people."

"Rembrandt."

"Our number one priority. Come on, why don't you see if you can get Mitch up? I'm going out for a paper."

She came back to some sort of argument between the two that stopped the moment she opened the room door. She could hear the muffled percussion of their voices out in the parking lot, so she knew something had been going on, and she looked at the two who stood close-lipped.

"What's going on?"

Brand, sulky. "Nothin'."

Mitch, only a little less, "It's handled."

"If it's handled, what is all the fuss about?"

"No fuss," Mitch said, and opened the door. "After you."

She scanned the room. "Got everything? We're not coming back."

Mitch said, "All the suitcases are packed and my tux is in the car."

She ignored the sarcasm, turned around, and went to the Honda. Brand climbed in without a word and sat stonily, his nose to the glass. Mitch got in the driver's side.

"Where we headed?"

"Thirty-eighth and Indian School. There's a Denny's on the corner." She folded the local news and tucked it under her leg.

"Anything?"

"No. As Brand put it earlier, we're just a blip. The world is onto much more important things."

"Good." He put the car into reverse out of the parking lot, then into forward and headed out.

She wondered if they'd been arguing about Brand's burst of obscenity. She decided not to mention it, that Brand would be better off if she just let it go. The sun was just rising above the cityscape, still very early in the day. "We should make it into New Mexico today."

"If we ever get on the road."

"Bellies come first. Then I want to see about getting another car."

"Right."

The atmosphere fell into silence as Mitch headed the five miles north and located the restaurant. They found a table and sat. The mild, accented voice of the cook as he talked to the waitresses carried through the nearly empty room. She watched him work, thinning dark hair combed back, dark mustache over a sensitive mouth, and a shy manner even though he talked to the girls as if he'd known them for years. He had a southern courtly charm and gentleness. She wondered how he'd come to Arizona.

She ordered an omelette and listened as Mitch and Brand both ordered the combo special for the day which included everything but the kitchen sink. She ordered cranberry juice, Brand milk, and Mitch got seconds on coffee before the waitress said, "Anything else?"

Kamryn tucked a wing of dark hair behind her ear. "Where's the cook from? I haven't heard an accent like that in a long time."

"Parkersburg, West Virginia." The waitress scratched her chin with the eraser end of her pencil. "He's a doll, isn't he? Ron only works here weekends. That do it for you?"

They nodded and she left to turn in their order.

West Virginia. She thought she'd recognized it, just down the Ohio River from Pennsylvania. A neighbor's voice. A wave of homesickness tinged through her.

No one said anything else until the breakfasts came, and Brand tucked into his as if he hadn't seen food in weeks. Mitch watched him for a moment, then smiled to himself and began eating as well.

Kamryn did not like the silence. She took a forkful of the well-stuffed omelette before asking, "What's going on?"

Mitch put down his fork with a sigh. He glared a second at Brand, then looked back at her. "You said you had friends who would help with the car problem."

"I do. South of here, along the highway to Tucson."

"I don't think we need to avail ourselves of their services, if they're the friends I think they are."

She considered him. "And if they are?"

"I repeat. We don't need them."

"I'm not asking you to approve or disapprove of them, Mitch. I'm just there to use them."

He shoved hash browns around a bit, staining their edges with golden yolks. "There could be problems because of the Darby situation."

"Not likely. As Brand would say, he was just a blip on the screen. Their concern will be with me, and if there's one thing I don't mind doing, it's using them. That's all they're good for." She stabbed her omelette viciously.

Unasked for, Bran added, "We need a four-by."

That startled Kamryn. "Whatever for?"

He looked at her. He'd taken off his shades and his eyes had cleared, staring at her with innocence. "To get into New Orleans."

"The last I heard," Mitch commented, "Lousiana had roads like everyone else."

"Hurricane's coming." Brand swallowed half a pancake, chased it with a gulp of milk, and finished, under a white mustache, "That part of the state will be washed out."

"This true?"

Kamryn shrugged at Mitch. "Possibly. It's five, six days away. We should make New Orleans in four. Maybe even three if we can get a tradeoff this morning."

"You're insisting on this?"

"Yes. I am. Rembrandt knows the car is an older Honda Accord. If he was quick enough, he even got the license number. I don't know who *your* friends are, but I don't want to take the chance they can track us."

Brand leveled his fork at Mitch. "She's got a point there."

Kamryn turned her attention back to the omelette. "I think the point is, we've all got lousy friends, present company excepted."

Mitch did not answer, but the lines by the sides of his mouth deepened as he ate. The waitress sailed by and Kamryn snagged another milk for Brand.

"He's a growing boy."

The waitress smiled, and Brand changed color again.

South and east of Phoenix, along the 10, the desert was far more intrusive. Brand grew quiet and Kamryn got the impression that he hid behind his shades. The eyedrops they'd bought seemed to have helped only temporarily. Mitch had grabbed up a summer T-shirt on sale, proclaiming Pete's Wicked Ale with roguish lettering, and changed into it. Traffic had been crowded and thinned as they went south.

About a half hour out of Phoenix, she took him off the highway and into a developing industrial neighborhood. Homes were sparse. She pointed at a warehouse type building, set off by itself, worn and uninteresting. Four or five cars sat outside it, parked with careless abandon.

"In there."

Mitch headed the Honda in by the side, where aluminum garage doors were closed. "What's in there? Body shop?"

"Print shop," Kamryn waited until they got out of the car. Midday sun rippled down on them, at least in the 80s, maybe better. "You won't like what you read. I suggest you keep your eyes, hands and opinions to yourself."

Mitch nodded. Brand started to ask, "What—" but Mitch wagged a finger at him.

Brand shut his mouth. Defensively, he shoved his glasses firmly onto his face.

She went around to the front office doors, where the windows were shuttered off, and knocked. Someone came to the intercom and scratchily asked, "Who is it?"

"Kamryn Talent. I need to speak to Viktor."

The intercom snapped off. She crossed her arms across her chest, waiting. She wore long sleeves again, cotton shirt unbuttoned at the cuffs, but it felt to her as if her tattoos had begun to crawl under the fabric. She rubbed one forearm.

The door opened. Viktor stood there, wiry, nerdy, heavy black glasses, his thin and continually disapproving mouth drawn to one side, dirty blond hair combed from deep on the side of his head to the other, hiding near baldness. "Kamryn! How are you?"

"I need your help again."

His pale blue gaze darted to one side of her and then the other, taking in Brand and Mitch.

"They're friends."

He drew the door open. "Of course they are."

As they entered the office, the sounds of printing presses and the hum of computers and other office equipment could be heard. Viktor smiled, but on him the expression was more one of contempt than humor. "Did you hear about last week? We got an entire printing into Cracker Jack boxes."

"No. Not yet. You're clever, Viktor."

He wagged his head humbly. "We try." He beckoned her into the warehouse plant. "Come with me and we'll talk."

She strode after, weaving her way through stacks of printing supplies and bundles of pamphlets and flyers, already printed, getting ready to be sent out. An occasional loose sheet, smeared or crumbled, floated along the cement flooring. Behind her, she thought she heard Brand stumble and then his muffled, "What kind of crap is *this?*" and she could only hope that Viktor, several strides in front of her and next to the presses, had not heard as well.

She heard what it was he'd seen. A single sheet flyer, crudely drawn, hand-lettered "Mexican bitches born pregnant, carry dozens of fertile eggs to make brown babies to steal your tax money!" It got worse. She'd seen it many times. High schools and junior highs got papered with this sort of propaganda several times a year. Childish images purported to show a pregnant Mexican teenager, her belly bulging with child, and then went into biology that was racially inflammatory and physiologically impossible. Cockroaches, maybe, humans, never.

She hadn't thought that once. Kamryn licked her lips as if sensing something distasteful and followed Viktor into rear offices beyond the printing area. Unlike the clutter of the vast warehouse, his office was impeccably clean and straight.

"Sit. Tell me." Viktor made a steeple of pencil thin fingers.

"You know about Darby." Mitch and Brand filed in behind her, but there were no chairs for them. She heard them flank her chair.

"A little. You are a heartbreaker, eh?"

"I didn't intend to be. He was a baby, Viktor. A mean, abusive baby. He jeopardized the movement by coming after me publicly." Kamryn paused, trying to gauge the effect of her words on Viktor's pale, emotionless face. "I left rather than talk to the police."

"Under the circumstances, I don't see how you could have done anything else. What do you need from me?"

Either he was satisfied or well aware of his ranking in the organization. "A trade on my car. It's in good condition, but the California plates and registration—" she spread her hands.

"Could be a problem. I understand."

"I'd like something with offroad capabilities. A Jeep or Suburban—"

"A BMW, eh? I'll have to see what I can do."

Brand, blurting out, "BMW!"

Viktor looked across her shoulder. "BMW—Big Mormon Wagon. It's a joke in Arizona." His attention returned to Kamryn. "How soon do you need it?"

"Today. Now."

"You challenge me, Kamryn. I might be able to handle it. It won't be new, of course."

"As long as it's in excellent working condition."

"Naturally. You're headed—?"

"North," she answered. "Wyoming or Montana."

"Ah. Give me a minute." He stood and retreated to an inner office, shutting the door behind him.

She knew the inner office was soundproof. She craned her neck and mouthed to Brand, "Shut up."

He pinched his lips together and gave an embarrassed shrug.

They said nothing to each other in the five minutes or so that Viktor was gone. He came back, his spare mouth stretched wide.

"Jeep Cherokee, four years old, twenty-three thousand miles. It's a gas guzzler, but comfortable."

"Hard or soft top?"

"Hard. Winters are harsh in Wyoming."

"What do I owe you?"

"Nothing. I'll take the paperwork and keys to the Honda." He did not sit, but beckoned. "Come sit. The driver will bring the vehicle in, we'll make the exchange, and you'll be on your way."

Mitch traded a look with her as if disbelieving how easy it was. Kamryn got to her feet to follow after Viktor.

The lounge was in one of the garages to the side, not as insulated or cool as the warehouse, two tables with benches, and several broken-down sofas. The door to the bathroom stood open and she could hear the toilet running. Viktor stayed in the doorway as they filed past.

Brand immediately went to a decrepit-looking TV. Mitch stopped at a lunch table, where a deck of cards had been folded in mid-hand. Kamryn hesitated, then said, "Thank you, Viktor."

He blinked. "Later." He shoved her into the room, then shut the heavy fire door. She heard the lock click, and then a bolt being thrown. Mitch leaped to his feet.

"Son of a bitch!"

Kamryn jogged the door handle frantically. "We're locked in."

Mitch scanned the garage. "No way from here. Unless—" He glanced straight up at the revolving ceiling fan. "Unless you're mincemeat."

Kamryn sagged. "I knew it seemed too easy."

"Nice friends."

"Thanks."

Brand said, "Now will someone explain to me all the crap on that flyer?"

From Mitch, "Lies. Twisted lies."

"A touch of truth, with a lot of lies."

Mitch looked at Kamryn. "How can you say that?"

"The only thing that's true is that a woman is born with a hundred or so ovum. A kernel of truth with layers and layers of inflammatory lies." Kamryn sat down. "This might not be as bad as it looks. He could just want to keep us secure."

"He locked us up for our own good?" Mitch had been pacing, studying the converted garage. He stopped to glare at her.

"There's a lot of stuff being printed out there that is important and secret to the organization. He might trust me, but not the two of you."

Brand said, as if still a little dazed, "I used to find crap like that stuffed into my locker. I couldn't wait to throw it away."

"But it still got there. And even if it only got hammered into one or two of your classmates . . ." Kamryn stopped. She did not want to think of it anymore. She sat down and put her face in her hands.

"How long are we going to have to wait?" Brand said to Mitch.

Mitch's answer, flatly, "Until they've done whatever it is they're doing."

Hours passed. The bare coolness of the converted room had evaporated, the air stiffling as the heat outside built up. The john ran until Brand had jiggled the handle at least a hundred times and Mitch lost at solitaire forty times in a row before discovering he wasn't playing with a full deck, before the door knob turned again.

The door opened with a current of cool air, and a figure stood at the threshold, bare arms bulging, tattoos rippling, bald head shiny with the heat.

"Hello, biker bitch," greeted Snake.

Chapter 25

Brand had been half-drowsy in front of the TV set, which had been able to receive only one channel all afternoon, one of the home shopping channels, which was better than nothing at all, when the door banged open and Kamryn gasped.

Cold shot through him. As he leaped to his feet, responding to the sound of Kamryn's voice, his glasses fell and he juggled them in midair.

But nothing could stop the arctic blast he saw and felt, glasses or no glasses, not Mitch leaping to his feet and hurling himself across the garage floor toward Snake—he saw the black-and-yellow-diamond patterns of the inking on his skin rippling as if something reptilian blocked the doorway, something cloaked in a greater darkness.

It reached toward Kamryn, enveloping, stifling. It bore the KillJoy's touch. Brand screamed, "Kamryn!" His voice crackled and tore out of his throat. He jammed his glasses into his pocket and shot forward to protect her.

Mitch was already there. He lunged at Snake, who fended him off with a forearm, shoving Mitch back into the garage. Bodies behind Snake pushed forward eagerly. There seemed to be a small army.

Kamryn grabbed for him. "Mitch, don't. They want me!"

Mitch shook her off. He took a stride toward Snake, his hands curled, then swung about, bringing up his foot, his booted foot. The sole cracked into Snake's jaw, snapping his head back. Snake sagged into the arms behind him, still on his feet.

He shook his head and growled softly. "Mott."

A skinhead answered his call. Mitch blocked the first block, slid off the second, grabbed the kid, and slammed him head first into a wall.

Mitch balanced himself for the next one. "Brand, get Kamryn."

Brand took a step forward, forcing himself, afraid. He could feel the chill, the slimy chill, as it settled around her. Dead, she was dying and didn't know it, and he could do nothing! She pushed him back with her hand. She shoved something into his palm.

"Run," she said, looking upward swiftly.

Toward the cooling fan in the ceiling. They'd looked at it one or two more times during the day, then decided against it. She squared at the door.

He looked at the palm of his hand. The car keys. He dug them deep into the pocket of his jeans.

She took up a martial arts stance as Snake straightened, still shaking his head. Shark eyes fastened on Mitch.

"Let's finish it," Snake suggested.

Mitch flexed his shoulders and readied himself.

Brand started running, hit the lunch table, and then jumped onto the bathroom door. He hit and clambered up it, perched on top. He could hear the grunts and thuds behind him as he carefully stood and then his fingertips grasped the metal rafter that ran across the loft. He took a breath and jumped, launching himself high enough so that he could throw his arms about the beam. He caught it, and the bathroom door jerked out from under him, his legs waving.

A jostle of bodies underneath reached for him. Brand kicked up and wrapped his legs around the beam, breathing hard, his rib cage aching as if he'd been slammed into something. Below, he could see Mitch, fists flying, holding off Snake. Kamryn kicked once, and whirled. Her opponent staggered back and came on again. The inky smudge that threatened to swallow her stayed with her.

Brand gulped and pulled himself along the rafter as one of the skinheads began to climb up the bathroom door, taking his route upward.

He swung himself upward onto the wide beam as soon as a diagonal strut crossed it, giving him another handhold. He looked up. The fan was directly overhead. He looked into its silvery gleam, heard its blade swish-swish-swishing.

The diagonal strut carried him right to it. He shinnied up even as his pursuer got onto the main rafter, swung his feet up onto it and began to cautiously walk after him.

Mitch took a fall, rolled, and got back up, dodging Snake. He took a hit in the flank from behind. Kamryn ducked, but could not avoid a capturing embrace.

Brand swallowed hard. It was up to him. He looked up at the flickering sky. The light hurt his eyes. His glasses bulged in his jeans pocket, along with the car keys.

He would have to try to kick the fan out of place. He steadied himself with a deep breath, then swung his hips out and kicked, feet up, as hard as he could. Expecting his feet to be sliced off at the ankles. Expecting pain. Expecting failure.

He did not expect to miss the fan entirely, but he did, and crashed into the housing where it had been welded into the ceiling. The welds popped and the dome fixture gapped open.

Brand grabbed himself up and slid out through that bulging gap, the fan still swoop-swooping a finger's length from the top of his head.

Brilliant light flooded him, painful light, flashes of white and silvery stabbings. Brand blinked and shielded his face, sliding down across the rooftop. He found a rain gutter and skidded halfway down it before letting himself fall to the pavement. The Honda sat in front of him.

He got in. The car started immediately and he looked at the stick shift. He wasn't good in reverse, but he had no choice—he had to get a run on the corrugated garage door that stood between him and the others.

He pushed in the clutch and jammed the shifter into position. The transmission ground a little and then a hop, and he was in reverse, racing backward. Brand could see figures running around the corner of the building, headed his way from the front.

He jammed it into forward and put the accelerator to the floor.

The garage door crumbled on impact. It threw him forward, chin onto the steering wheel, his neck whipping and the car hopping to a stop, halfway through, sheet metal lying over it like a hood.

Kamryn came sliding under the door. She got to her feet, her lip bloodied, her hair flying. Brand leaned over and unlocked it. She threw herself in.

"Go, go, go!"

"Where's Mitch!"

"He's coming! You scattered everybody! Just put it in reverse and go!"

Flustered, he ground the gears but good. Protesting, the Honda backed up, tearing out of what had once been a warehouse-sized garage door. Paint scrapings and sparks flew everywhere. As the wreckage flopped, Mitch exploded through the jagged tears.

Kamryn had a back door open for him. He threw himself in, feet hanging out and she screamed again, "Go!"

Brand found first gear and forward. He saw a line of men running at him, and another car beginning to back out. He put the accelerator pedal to the floor. He shifted when Kamryn screamed at him to.

The Honda lurched forward as if it had been launched. Mitch slid on the back seat. Kamryn cried, "Hang on!"

Brand could not keep the car from careening across the parking lot. It seemed to have a mind of its own, the steering wheel alive in his sweating hands. He glanced off the moving car, sending it jolting into the front of the building. Figures scattered. He saw gun barrels everywhere. The car careened to the left. He oversteered back to the right, hit a parked pickup, saw a corner of the Honda's bumper go flying.

He took a turn veering. A small herd of motorcycles lay in his path. The Honda flew through them as if it were in a demolition derby. Classic bikes crunched and crashed in their wake.

Mitch got his door shut with a grunt. Kamryn shoved herself down in the passenger seat as Brand took the Honda speeding and bucking onto the main street.

"We've got pursuit." Mitch's voice, flat and amused, from the back.

"Brand's got 'em." Kamryn dabbed at her bleeding mouth with the back of her hand.

Brand didn't feel any such thing, as the Honda wove back and forth down the main street.

He looked at the speedometer. Eighty-eight miles an hour.

He found the highway on ramp and hit it, going south, at seventy, having slowed down to make the curve.

Kamryn said, "Next rest stop pull over and let me drive. In the meantime, step on it until you redline it."

"Redline."

She pointed a shaking hand at the dash tachometer. "Don't push it past that. Just drive it straight. Don't slow down unless we hit traffic." She took a deep breath. It sounded strained.

"You all right?"

"Yes. Just drive."

He wanted to look at her, didn't dare, had to know if the inky cloud had gone, saw her out of the corner of his eye as he sped down the highway.

The chill had faded. But he could still see a darkness crowning her brow, a veil across her beautiful, bruising face. But it receded slightly as he took his glance.

He hit ninety and kept it there.

"Remind me," said Mitch, "to give you some driving lessons."

They were all breathing hard. Kamryn disagreed. "I think he did fine. He even took evasive action when they started shooting at us."

Brand's mouth had gone dry. "Evasive action? I couldn't steer straight!"

Mitch started laughing. After a moment, Kamryn joined him.

Brand said, "I don't think that's funny." Kamryn laughed harder.

"Well, I don't."

"Oh, God." She wiped a tear from her eye. "Just drive, Brand. Just drive." She stretched both hands out, one toward Brand and the other toward the back seat. "My heroes."

Brand tried not to jump as she patted his thigh. He could feel the chill of her touch through his jeans. He brushed her hand off, stammering something about needing his glasses and pulled them out, feeling like a jerk.

The needle pricks of sunlight into his eyeballs subsided as he slipped the familiar shades on. He stared ahead at the road.

"Will they follow?"

Kamryn settled back into her seat. "We talked about Wyoming. Maybe we threw them off."

But Brand was shaking his head in answer to Mitch's idle question. He had felt the KillJoy. It had tasted Kamryn, and him. It wanted Kamryn. It wanted him. It would follow. There was no safety in taking the highway, no matter where it led.

If not the skinheads, then Rembrandt. If not Rembrandt, then chance.

Whatever form Death could take, it would.

He felt that more sincerely in his heart than he had ever felt anything.

But he could not voice it to them. Fear would not let him.

Snake looked at the rippled and twisted fork of his motorcycle. A classic bike, gone, like that. It could be fixed, but it would take time and loving care. Time he didn't have.

That itch crawled around inside his skull. Snake put his hands up to his dome, dug his fingernails in until he drew blood, wanted to rake his nails through his naked skin until the pain drove out the itch. He wanted them, all three of them, and the urge filled his chest like a deep, angry shout until he lifted his chin to the burning Arizona sky and let it out a bellow.

Fleer dropped his handlebars, startled. The chrome piece hit with a dull *twang* and bounced into place next to the wreckage.

The force of his voice had squeezed his eyes nearly shut. Snake dropped his chin and opened his eyes wide, saw the others standing around the parking lot, staring at him.

He whirled. Viktor stood there, watching.

"Give me your keys!"

"They got my car, too."

"Not those keys. I want the keys to the SHO. I want that bitch, the boy, the other."

"I can send out a patrol," Viktor said slowly. "As soon as we know which direction they're headed."

Crawly feelings inside him turned him again, away from Viktor, south by southeast. "I know which way they're going," said Snake flatly. "Now give me the fucking keys!"

Viktor tossed them. They flew, sparkling through the air, like the American-built high-performance Ford they fit. Snake snatched them in midflight.

Mott had his bike up, crippled but ridable. Snake knew where Viktor stored his prize vehicle. He swung aboard behind Mott.

"Move it!"

Mott kicked the gear shift, and the bike jumped away. Fleer ran alongside.

"What about me?"

"Kiss my ass," Snake screamed back over the roar of the engine, and swung, knocking Fleer right out of his baby blue eyes.

He wanted nothing but the road between him and his quarry.

They ate blue corn tacos in Tucson while Mitch worried at the fender, pulling crumpled metal away from the tire. He kicked at the bumper until the Honda shuddered all over as he tried to straighten that out as well. He eyed the makeshift repair work critically in the restaurant parking lot lights before deciding he'd done as well as he could.

"It's a wonder it looks as good as it does." He took the last taco from the cardboard carrier, its purple-black soft shell oozing meat and lettuce.

"I don't think the patrol will be looking for us as a hit and run. Viktor doesn't like to attract attention."

Brand chugged down the last of his drink. The evening had begun to cool rapidly, a breeze rising off the arrid countryside. Kamryn checked a map she'd bought at the last filling station. "I'll drive until we hit the summit at Dragoon. Then you can take it into Lordsberg."

Mitch nodded.

"When do I drive again?"

They looked at Brand. He put up a hand. "Do I have two heads or something?"

Kamryn folded up the map and threw it at him. "Navigate, smart-ass."

He caught it. "All right. But I have to ride shotgun to do it."

Mitch had driven the last several hours. "Fine with me." He rested his soft drink cup over a swollen right hand. "I'll ice my knuckles."

They loaded the car back up. Heading out of Tucson, Kamryn dropped the speed down to the state limit.

"Bor-ring."

"But legal. We don't want to attract any more attention."

Mitch pitched a piece of ice from the backseat. It clipped Brand in the ear. Brand batted it away. "Okay, okay. I'll shut up." He lay the map across his lap. "How about some music?"

"Be my guest."

He managed to find one station that wasn't golden oldies or country western, but as they headed out of Tucson and into the night, its
broadcast grew weaker and more and more staticky. Soon there was
nothing but two-lane highway and desert and darkness. An occasional glint of feral eyes from the side of the road as a coyote bolted
past or a jackrabbit threw up its ears from cover were the only signs
of life.

Brand felt himself going cross-eyed as the night grew older and
older. The beams of the headlight seemed to weaken against the des-
olation of the countryside.

He was yawning when he saw it. The edge of the headlight beam
barely caught it. Brand sat up straight and leaned forward.

A yellow dog, trotting along the rim of the road.

He choked down a breath. The animal reacted as if it heard the
car motor—he had to be hallucinating, it couldn't be his dog—and it
swung off the highway shoulder, onto the road.

It continued trotting as the Honda sped down upon it.

"Kamryn—" He flung out a hand to stop her.

The dog swerved into the full blast of the headlights and paused,
wavering, blinded.

"The dog!"

"What dog?"

He shoved the steering wheel. The car flinched to the left, but
there came a heavy thud and a yelp. Kamryn hit the brakes, and they
skidded into the night.

"You hit him!" cried Brand.

Chapter 26

The Honda skewed to a halt, its rear tires off the road in the bordering ditch. Its headlights canted into the sky. Brand sat for a frozen moment. Kamryn pounded a hand on the steering wheel.

"Oh, my God."

Her voice thawed him. Mitch, tossed from the backseat and wedged onto the floor, began to swear. "Son of a bitch—"

Brand clawed at his seat belt, freeing himself. As ditches go, it was minor, but enough to have the Honda in an awkward position. Tearing fingernails, Brand got the door open and levered himself out before Mitch finished turning the air blue in a way that would do a Marine drill instructor proud. He could smell the engine heat and burned rubber from the tires. The desert air smelled sharp and clear under it, and sounded terribly still. He pounded down the highway, following the skid marks, his heart drumming in his chest.

Either be dead or be alive. But don't be lying there shattered—I can't help! I can't put you back together! His heart throbbed in his mouth. Visions of a mangled dog filled him.

A golden dog. A retriever. Visions of the guide which had temporarily abandoned him in his dreams, but for which he would do anything. Cross any bridge. Face any darkness. Do anything he could, but please, God, oh, please, don't let there be blood and jagged bones. Just let it be a little hurt. Just let it be dazed and alive.

In the dark gray nothingness of the desert, something moved and groaned off the road. Brand angled toward it, crying, "I'm coming! I'm coming!" as if his voice could soothe the injured animal.

It rose out of the road dust and opposite ditch, shoulders humped, emerging from the shadows and into the dim reflection of the headlights though they shone the other direction. It rose and rose and rose until it stood taller than him, and shook all over.

The man said, "White men are bad drivers. White women are worse." As Brand slid to a halt, he leaned over, and dusted off his denims, jeans and jacket vigorously, his long hair tied back from his shoulders, his unmistakably Amerindian face weathered with years.

"But I—I saw—"

The Indian grunted. He swiped a last time at his left elbow. "You saw too late. Ran me off the road!"

He had seen a dog. He knew that. He *knew* it even as he knew his name. Brand stammered. "B–but you—but you—"

"Will be stiff in morning, but all right. No thanks to white woman." The man narrowed his eyes and looked closely at him. "Or were you driving?"

"No. I—I thought you were—"

"Hurt? No. I am old and wise, but I have good reflexes." The Indian straightened his shoulders, looking past Brand, and he could hear the other two approaching.

Brand did not understand. "You can't be . . . I saw a dog . . . I saw—"

"I am Chiricahua. Apache." The Indian looked fiercely at him, at all three of them. "Are you afraid? You should be. Once, all white men in this part of the country feared the Apache."

"It depends on how much to drink they've had," Mitch answered dryly.

"Mitch!" Kamryn sounded shocked.

Mitch pointed his chin at the ditch. A damp and crumpled paper bag lay in the dirt, and a small wet patch was rapidly being absorbed by the dust.

"A beer," said the man. "For the road."

"Did I run you down—or did you fall down?" Kamryn got out, her voice still quavery.

"Ha!" The Apache laughed sharply and then laughed again. "Does it matter? No one is hurt." He put his hand out, fierce look fading. "I am of the Mescalero Apache tribe. Call me Yellow Dog."

Brand lost all feeling in his legs. His head swam. His vision narrowed to a single spot, filled by the other's face. He thought he got out a sound, a peep, before crashing.

"So the boy is all right?"

"Just tired. He's had a rough couple of days."

Brand could hear Mitch talking, sounding as though he were an underwater attraction at Sea World, his voice burbling through the nothingness which held Brand. If he held his breath, he could surface, he thought. He did. His ears popped. His cheeks bulged. Someone thumped him on the chest.

"Breathe, boy, breathe!"

He caught a whiff of sage and a faint smell of beer as he came up gasping. He lay in the car. A golden haze of light floated in the backseat, light that did not come from the interior dome in the roof. Brand blinked once or twice, as if he had just caught an October moon in the vehicle. Yellow Dog smiled back at him, even older looking than he had seemed standing in the night.

Kamryn asked, "Is he all right?"

"I think so," the Mescalero replied. "Are you?"

"What . . . what are you doing here?" Brand stared at the fourth passenger.

"Kamryn thought it polite to give me a ride home, since she ran me off the road."

The Honda bounced and jolted. Brand looked out the window. They had left the highway. Cactus and downed fences and shrubs lined a dirt road. Clouds of fine dust drifted after them, motes shining like silver as he turned his head to the rear window. "We must be miles from 10."

"It would have been a long walk."

"What," Mitch put in, "were you doing out here?"

"Coyote scared my mule. He threw me. I walk home. Sooner or later, I'd get there. Maybe sleep in the ditch, let the mail truck pick me up." Yellow Dog watched Brand as he spoke. He wore a yellow-and-blue-plaid shirt that looked as if it had been pounded against many a stone in the river. His dark face was seamed with age, but fine-boned, and his hands moved as he spoke, small, wiry hands. His hair had a few pewter-gray strands in it, but otherwise were as black as they must have been in Yellow Dog's youth.

Brand observed, "Even a mule wouldn't take you too far."

"No. But I don't like to drive when I drink." Yellow Dog brushed another patch of grit from his denim jacket. He leaned forward between the two front seats. "There's my house now."

Two window patches gleamed in the night like opening eyes. Fencing surrounded it, except for the road's entrance, and a Ford Explorer and an Escort sat parked in the front yard. The compact had seen better years, but the Explorer looked fairly new. There was a patch of garden to the rear, and a stucco garage that sat alone. Also a corral and small shed. A mule stood outside the corral, his head resting on a fence pole, bareback, but wearing a bridle. There were shadows of other outbuildings not entirely visible from the front drive.

Yellow Dog swung his door open. "You come in," he said. "It is too late to drive much farther. The boy is not well, and you—" he looked down at Mitch's hands. "Could use some ice."

"I don't think—" Kamryn stopped as Yellow Dog tilted his head, watching her.

"You are far from the road. No one will bother you here. I live alone now, except for the mule, but my house is big."

Brand could almost hear Mitch and Kamryn thinking. He had his hand in his pocket and could feel the amulet between the tips of his fingers. He blurted out, "I'd like to stay a while."

"Good." Yellow Dog nodded. "Boy and I have things to talk about." He paused, looked at the bashed-up fender of the car. "Maybe you'd drive better in the daylight."

Kamryn's ears turned faintly pink and she ducked her head as she followed after their host.

The house was cool, even after the stifling heat of the day, but as Brand passed through the threshold, he noticed the thickness of the walls. It was not adobe, but concrete block and stucco, stacked in double-thickness. The insulation against heat and cold must be incredible. Nothing inside was what he expected. The furniture was well-upholstered, green-and-blue plaid, with burnished pine arms and feet. There was an immense television in one corner.

"I have a dish," Yellow Dog remarked when he saw Brand staring at it. He took off his denim jacket and lay it over the back of the chair. "I would not live like this if I stayed on the reservation."

Mitch sat down in an upholstered rocker. "What do you do?"

"Construction foreman. Tucson and the area are growing. Big resort. People like hot, dry weather. I'm like a turtle. I stay in this shell if I get the chance. Winters aren't bad here, so it works out."

"Aren't you supposed to live up north?"

Yellow Dog looked at Kamryn as he solemnly fixed her a ginger ale and then handed it to her. "Four Corners?"

"Something like that."

"That is Navajo. I'm Apache."

"Oh. I . . . I'm sorry."

"Good." Swiftly, Yellow Dog fixed three more ginger ales and passed them around.

Brand didn't particularly like ginger ale. He wrinkled his nose as he took his drink. Yellow Dog said, "Drink it. Ginger is good for the digestion."

He sat down on the couch between Kamryn and Brand, ignoring the drink in front of him, and put his hands on the worn knees of his jeans. "Now tell me why you are driving in the middle of the night like there is a devil wind behind you."

"I don't think so." Mitch stared at him levelly.

"Then it is your loss. The Apache have been here for centuries. Think we care what you do? It won't bother me. I will still be here tomorrow, and the day after."

Kamryn rubbed her arms uneasily. "Not," she answered. "If the people I'm leaving behind have anything to say about it."

He took her slim wrist and pushed up the sleeve of her shirt, baring the faded but still legible tattoos. He looked for a moment then said, "You are not like them. They hate everyone."

She gently removed her arm from his hold. "If they come after us here, if they think you know something, they won't leave you alive after they find out what they know." Kamryn massaged an eyebrow. "And you have no idea what I'm like."

Yellow Dog tapped his cheekbone, under one coffee-colored eye. "I see. I know." He smiled, breaking his solemn words. "I am called Yellow Dog because I am cousin to the coyote—the coyote who is one of our gods. He is fast, quick, the trickster. The dog is almost as fast, but he is loyal. His motives are never in doubt. He is not a god, but he is good to have on one's side. We are fast and quick also. The ones who seek you will have a hard time finding me." Yellow Dog beckoned as if the outside world, the desert, would hide him.

Mitch drained his glass and set it down. "I think we'd better be going."

"You will not meet many friends along the road," Yellow Dog said to him. "I would not turn down one now."

"I don't know that you're a friend, and I don't know that, if you are a friend, I want to involve you in any of this."

"You are a soldier. You like to face problems," and Yellow Dog suddenly smacked a fist into the palm of his hand. Kamryn jumped at the sound. "Head on." He dropped his hands back to his knees. "The sidewinder travels sideways across the sand. He is sometimes very difficult to see and avoid his attack."

"A sidewinder's a snake, right?" Brand asked.

"Yes."

"How did you know he's a soldier?"

Yellow Dog merely smiled widely while Mitch said, with irritation, "It's just a figure of speech. He's referring to how I attack situations."

"And your bruised knuckles," the Mescalero added.

Brand looked at Mitch. "I just want to stay the night. Just five or six hours of sleep. I don't want to run into any *snakes*."

"I have the room," Yellow Dog added.

Without looking at Mitch, Kamryn sighed. "It sounds all right to me."

"And me."

The lines along Mitch's jaws moved as if he ground his teeth. "Just till morning."

"Good. It is settled. I will go fix your rooms. You will sleep on the floor, but the blankets are very soft. They're Navajo," he added, with a huff of a laugh, and he got up and left.

Brand dreamed of Yellow Dog, for the first time in days, and the canine's feathery tail wagged in greeting, but he did not come close. Brand held out his hand, entreating, but the dog moved away through nebulous clouds of his imagination. Brand tried to coax him back and failed.

Then a calloused hand closed on his shoulder, waking him.

Yellow Dog the Apache looked down at him, moonlight barely

touching his rugged face. "Come with me," he said, very quietly, not waking Mitch.

Brand got up from the sleeping pad and followed after the silent footsteps of the Indian, uncertain why he should follow, and uncertain why he should refuse.

In the living room, moonlight from the kitchen windows flooded the house with soft light. The stars hung like crystal in the desert sky. Brand stared at it a moment, drinking in the beauty.

"You don't see this in the city."

Yellow Dog held out a blanket, like a cloak and dropped it around his shoulder. "Come with me. You and I need to talk. Then sleep will come easier."

He opened a side door through the kitchen and stepped outside, barefoot, also wearing a blanket. Brand went after him, and their feet crunched on cold sand. Their breath fogged slightly on the air. Yellow Dog went to a small building and put his hand on the door.

"I get it! This is a sweat lodge, for medicine dreams and stuff."

Yellow Dog opened the door. "Actually, it's a portable sauna. But you're right, it's good for sweat and my arthritis." He stepped inside, the warmth enveloping him.

Feeling more than a little foolish, Brand stepped inside and sat on the opposite bench. Yellow Dog closed the door. There was a tiny light inside, with an amber hue, and a basket of artificial coals in an alcove on the floor glowed as they burned. Yellow Dog poured a dipper of water over them. An obliging hiss and cloud of steam arose.

Brand watched him. He snugged into the blanket, its colors grayed out. "What did you want to talk about?"

"What you saw on the road."

"How could I have seen what I saw?"

"And what was it you think you saw?"

"A dog. A big golden retriever, trotting by the side of the road. That *was* you, wasn't it?"

Yellow Dog did not answer directly. "Do you have a dog at home?"

"No."

"But you had great regard for this dog. When you thought it had been hit, you came to help. You cried for mercy for it. Would you do this for just any creature?"

"I thought I saw a dog on the road."

"It could have been a coyote."

"I know the difference." Brand looked at the basket of glowing coals. "There are a lot left in Orange County. You can see them trotting along the golf courses, or out by the trailer parks, or along the freeway. They almost look like dogs, but they're not. I know the difference."

"And this was not just any dog."

"No."

Yellow Dog dipped more water over the coals and then spread his hands to receive the steaming cloud. "Would you believe me if I said I was the dog you saw?"

He hesitated. "Yes."

Yellow Dog shook his head. "Your spirit answered before your mouth. I will not tell you if it was me or not. You must decide for yourself. But I will tell you of the meaning of your imaginary dog. A dog is loyal. He made his choice before the gods to be with man, to help him, to guide him, even if it meant his pride. The color yellow, in my world, is a color of the spirit, of the goodness of the spirit, and of guidance. If you believe in such an animal, only good can come of it."

"He helps me," Brand whispered, his throat suddenly tight. "I need to help him."

"The three of you were strangers not long ago." Yellow Dog suddenly changed subjects.

"Yes." Brand looked up. "How did you know?"

"Satellite television. Your face was on the news yesterday. A horrible picture. A skinhead was killed after he shot many people. She wears the skin of a skinhead." Yellow Dog grinned suddenly, as if enjoying the play on words.

"There's more."

"I thought there might be. I ask myself, why don't these three trust their white man police."

"I see things."

"This I also know." Yellow Dog moved his hand through the air, stirring up a rippling current of heat. "On the road."

"Everywhere. I think it's . . . I think it's Death. It's all over Kamryn. I can't let it take her. I can't!"

"Death is a dark god, but a natural one. He will come for all of us, boy. It does not help to fear him."

"Well, maybe it's not Death. Maybe it's evil. I don't know, all I know is, I can see it . . . it knows my name . . . it wants me, it wants Kamryn and maybe even Mitch. And in my dreams, the dog took me to a woman, a black woman, in New Orleans, who told me she could help us."

"Help you what?"

"Get rid of the KillJoy."

Yellow Dog stopped moving. His eyes glittered in the slight illumination. "Is that its name?"

"It's what I call it."

"Then you must not. You have the truth of it, and you will bring it to you by naming it." Yellow Dog shifted on the redwood bench of the sauna. "Do you know the woman? Is she named?"

"She calls herself Mother. Mother Jubilation."

Yellow Dog poured a third dipper of water, and this time he dispersed the cloud with an eagle feather which he seemed to have produced from out of thin air. He looked into the steam. "Her way is not my way, but those who walk the spirit walk cross paths. I do not know her, but I know of the medicine she uses. Do you trust her?"

"Yellow Dog . . . ah . . . my imaginary dog led me to her."

"Then you must trust her also." Yellow Dog dug deep into the pockets of his jeans. He pulled out a faded blue bandanna. It was knotted in the middle. Laboriously, he undid the knot and opened it up. A wrinkled bit of root lay there, hardly bigger than the tip of Brand's little finger. "Do you know what this is?"

Brand shook his head.

"This is peyote. Mescal."

"Drugs."

"That is right. It only takes a very small piece, chewed." Yellow Dog knotted the peyote button back into the bandanna. Brand watched, faintly surprised, for he had thought Yellow Dog was going to use it.

He pressed the bandanna into Brand's hand. "Now you must listen and remember. The spirit walk for the living is dangerous if you do not have inner strength and peace. Before you take the peyote, you must be cleansed. You must be alone. Your mind must be calm. You must be like a lake in the desert, without wind, rain, or tide. You must not take more than a pinch, like so, of the button, or you will be horribly ill. Your body could die while your spirit walks.

"And above all, you must be ready to look into yourself and face whatever it is you see there. If you need to spirit walk, you must be ready to accept the truth, to fight the evil, to banish the darkness. All colors of the world are in the spirit world, even black. It is the absence of color, warmth, truth, love, hope, that is the enemy. You remember this."

Brand clutched the bandanna tightly, then he put it in his free pocket. "How did . . . how did you know about us? I mean, really about us, not just what you saw on television."

"I felt a trembling many months ago when this spirit came upon the land. In my dreams, I called it the Devourer. Although I searched for it, it was not for me to see, only feel. Yet there was never any doubt in my mind that I would meet the warrior who would fight it, who would send it back to its own lands."

Yellow Dog had already called Mitch a warrior. Brand pulled his blanket tighter about him, chill tremors running through him despite the glow of the sauna cabinet. "We're trying to outrun it."

A vigorous shake of the head greeted his hope. "It must be faced and fought."

"But how?"

"I cannot tell you how the battle will be won. But you must know your enemy. That is the key. The spirit weakens . . ."

"Then we won't have to fight it!"

"No. It weakens, then it must kill to be strong, and it will be strong until it does what it has been sent here to do. It will kill whoever and whatever it has to in order to remain strong."

"Like Curtis. Like the others."

"Whatever it must do, it will," repeated Yellow Dog firmly.

"What can I do?"

"It is tracking you."

Brand could not contain a shudder. "I think so."

"You must draw it near even as you must stay away until you are ready to fight it."

"How do I do that?"

Yellow Dog shrugged. "That, I cannot tell you. But you will do it, Brand the X. You will do it."

He thought of the amulet and brought it out. "Can this help?"

"This was made by a wise man. It carries symbols of power and medicine. It might be of some use." Yellow Dog rubbed a finger across it. "Couldn't hurt." He stood. "Enough steam for the night. You need to rest for the morning."

Brand found his eyelids incredibly heavy as he recrossed the yard, trailing Yellow Dog's footsteps. He stopped by the back door.

"But you didn't tell me," he murmured.

"Tell you what?"

"If you were a dog or not."

Yellow Dog laughed. He laughed and threw back his head, looking at the slip of a moon in the sky, and let out a howl. Brand jumped, and then from the wasteland around him, coyotes answered.

Yellow Dog let him in the house. "I'll never tell," he said, chuckling.

In the morning, Yellow Dog was gone and so was their battered Honda. Keys to the Explorer lay on the coffee table, along with its registration, and Kamryn's gun. Her baskets of clothes stood in the corner. An inviting scent led Brand to the kitchen where a huge platter of scrambled eggs and bacon waited for them in the oven, still fairly warm.

Brand opened the back door, just to check and see if Yellow Dog had gone back out to the sauna to warm up his bones in the chill morning.

Nothing met his eyes but piles of rock and stone and brush.

Chapter 27

Delacroix stepped across the border at Aqua Prieto, mildly astonished at how easy it had been. Just beyond the walkway, a weakness struck him, made him stop and put his hand up, to catch his breath in the brisk morning air. The moment lingered, and he considered it, knew that the soul of the land itself was protesting him. He slipped a hand inside the pocket of his jacket, took out a packet, and scattered its contents upon the ground in a pattern which might have seemed random, but was not. The colored corn grains lay there until a mild wind diffused them further.

The weakness gripping him eased, bit by bit, until it faded, leaving a hollowness behind. That hollowness, he knew, came from the loa. He must urge it to feed again or else he and it would be too drained to do what they had come together for. He lifted his head. Stark and the other two stood impassively watching him, waiting.

"I am ready."

Stark had arranged for a van to transport him to El Paso. From there, he would rest and determine the flight of those he pursued. They were fleeing eastward, steadily, along a road marked as Highway 10. He had had Stark study the maps with him earlier, but in his heart, he felt he knew which way they would go.

Toward New Orleans. It could be no other place, for there lay his challenger who alone could stop him. She must sense him already. If not, she would before the end of the day. If she had sensed him, she would be calling for his prey to join her, for her strength lay in togetherness, in the bonds, and in the gathering.

His did not. He could attack them anywhere, but he would not. Not until that which was his was returned and to find it, to have it gathered up and presented back to him, he must look his enemy in the face.

The loa would herd them. He, Delacroix, would find out what was needed and obtain what he was owed.

Then they were the loa's. Whatever he would do with them, he would do. Then Delacroix would send him back.

Not before.

As if sensing his weakness, Stark took his arm and guided him to the waiting vehicle. Delacroix let him, then paused at the curb in the street. He put his hand on Stark's muscular forearm, and gripped, gripped tightly until the man's face paled beyond pale.

He would not have Stark think that his infirmity was physical.

He released his grip and stepped into the van. "Between here and New Orleans, a large city. All roads leading in from the west, going to the east. What would be the name of such a city?"

Stark looked at him. Thought a moment. Said flatly, "El Paso."

"Drive us there."

He nodded.

NWS UPDATE HURRICANE YOLANDA 0900 EDT

HURRICANE YOLANDA IS NOW GRADED A FORCE 2 STORM, WITH SUSTAINED WINDS OF OVER 100 MPH, PRO-CEEDING NORTH, NORTH-EASTERLY, HEADED TOWARD THE GULF STATES. PROJECTED PASSAGE OF THE HURRI-CANE INDICATES THE GULF OF MEXICO'S UNSEASONABLY WARM WATERS MAY CONTINUE TO FEED ITS STRENGTH. AT ITS PRESENT RATE OF SPEED, LANDFALL IS EXPECTED IN THREE DAYS. WATCHES AND WARNINGS WILL BE IS-SUED AS ITS DIRECTION STABILIZES. ALL RESIDENTS FROM GALVESTON, TEXAS, TO ALCONTE, FLORIDA, ARE ADVISED TO BEGIN EVACUATION PROCEDURES AND STAY TUNED FOR FURTHER ADVISORIES.

Mother sat in her quiet room. The candy store was dark and shut down. True to her promise, Geneva had taken the girls and gone. Mother stared at the crystal shards in the palm of her hand, rolled them carefully back and forth, wary of their jagged edges, watching them cast prisms of colors on the walls of the meditation room. She had felt the intrusion of the mambo on American soil, growing closer, ever closer.

He would come to her, in the wake of the others, as much a force of nature as the storm that approached. They would all come together, she thought, the natural and the supernatural. The mambo would not expect that, perhaps, and she wondered if she could somehow use that to her advantage.

New Orleans had begun to prepare for Yolanda. The levees and canals were being sandbagged, and the pumping stations were being manned with extra shifts. The storm surge, which would come twenty-four hours before landfall of the actual hurricane, would be expected to be twelve to sixteen feet above those levees, if Yolanda came in directly. The wave would be devastating to a city already technically under sea level. The parishes below the city were being urged already to evacuate, for the 10 was their chief way up and out, through the bottleneck of New Orleans, and roads would be at a standstill if all parishes tried to leave at once.

Today evacuation was voluntary. Tomorrow, if Yolanda continued to forge a path toward them, it would not be. The emergency planners allowed for forty-eight hours to bring the population out. Already she could feel the sheer strength of the human will to hold the city together, to protect the lower parishes and bayous of the state, to shelter their fellow man. Race and religion would be forgotten in a few desperate hours to survive. All would be human, accepted, shared.

A quartz splinter slipped, slicing her palm, and blood welled up slowly. Mother dropped the other fragments and looked at her hand, pain forgotten. She drew a mirror to her and let the drops fall onto it and run into whatever pattern they would run before they thickened.

When the blood stopped dripping and not before, she looked into the hand mirror. She did not like what she saw.

"Hurry, boy. Hurry!"

Midday, Lordsberg, New Mexico, they bought a loaf of bread and a pound of bologna and sat in the city park where Mitch showed them how to make fried bologna sandwiches, hot and juicy, on a small briquette barbecue. Kamryn wrinkled her nose and ate one before retreating to her nonfat yogurt. Brand ate half a loaf before shouting, "Who was that masked man?" for the seventh time that day and running off to catch a Frisbee, snatching it from the jaws of a black and white border collie.

The boy and the dog's master exchanged friendly words. The plump-sided woman sat, gratefully, and let Brand run around with the dog. Mitch and Kamryn watched him from their end of the park.

"That boy needs a dog," Mitch commented.

"He's never had one."

"See?"

"That boy," Kamryn answered softly, "needs a lot of things. A decent family would help."

"And you're expert."

"No." She tossed her empty carton into a trash can. "Wish I was. Wish I knew what I was doing here."

"You're here because you can't go back."

Her head snapped around and she stared at Mitch for a quick heartbeat or two, then she visibly forced herself to relax.

"Back there? No. Not that I would want to anyway. Do you know what a relief it is?"

"What is?" Mitch finished the last sandwich and began to clean up wrappers.

"It's a relief to look someone in the face and not have a chant of ethnic slurs and labels run through my head. Not to have to peg them as to what I think of them and how I should treat them and what kind of payback I need to plan for them. Just to see *people,* ordinary people." She reached for a sweatshirt and tied it over her shoulders, loosely, despite the clear sunshine.

"You were brainwashed."

"I suppose. When it's something you grow up with, you don't know what other people do, how other people react, and then you're in school, high school maybe, and you realize that someone is twisted. Really twisted. Scum of the earth. Problem is—you don't know if it's you or them."

"You must have decided it was you."

"Eventually."

"You make it sound easy." Mitch perched on the corner of the weather-beaten picnic table.

"Easy?"

"Everyone should come to their senses that way."

She shook her head. "It's never easy. And it didn't just happen that way. There were . . . other circumstances. No. Deciding to change my life was far from easy. What do radio psychologists call it? Leaving the comfort zone. Even beaten, abused wives will stay rather than leave the comfort zone when that's all they know."

"If it was a family thing, where is your family?"

"Around." Kamryn picked at the knot she had tied in the sweatshirt sleeves. "What about your family? Was being in the service a tradition?"

"Yes, more or less. I didn't do it right. I was supposed to go to college first, so I could be an officer."

"And you didn't."

"No." Mitch scratched his jaw. "I didn't like school. I tried to tell my dad he was lucky I hung in for my high school diploma. He didn't see it that way. I played professional soccer for about four years, until I discovered I wasn't really good enough, then I enlisted and went to see the world."

"And?"

"Dad was right. Being an officer is better. Or maybe not better, but easier. I know a lot of fine noncoms, most of whom wouldn't put up with the bullshit J.G.s try to give them."

"It was a career?"

"Maybe. It's hard to stay in now, with all the demobilization and downgrading. I was in for nine years. Now they would probably hang me if they could catch me."

Kamryn looked across the park, saw Brand still playing a lusty game of Frisbee catch with the border collie. She smiled in spite of the seriousness of their conversation.

"What made you leave?"

"Oh, no." He shook his head.

"After what we've been through, you won't tell me."

He stared into her eyes and said, "Damn straight."

"Don't give me that."

"All right. Then how about this . . . I'll show you mine if you show me yours."

She stood up by the edge of the table. "What do you mean?"

"I mean that there's a lot you haven't told me about yourself. I mean that there aren't too many ex-girlfriends of skinheads who could walk into an operation like that print shop and expect preferential treatment, and be shocked when they don't get it, and not shocked when one of their thug assassins comes after her."

"You know why Snake wants me."

"Yeah. That's true. What I don't know is why Viktor didn't whack him upside the head and tell him to forget it. Viktor didn't, so I'm figuring that whatever importance you had to them, all of a sudden it's just as important you're dead."

Kamryn sucked in her lower lip and chewed on it for a second. Then she answered, "What you don't know about me doesn't affect what's happening here. It's incidental. It doesn't have anything to do with Brand."

"It could get us all killed."

"It won't! I won't let it, if it comes to that. What about you? I don't buy the theory that Rembrandt will leave me and Brand alone if he decides we don't know anything. He tried to hang Brand to get some answers and I'm willing to bet that even if the kid had told him what he wanted to know, that noose would have stayed around his neck."

Mitch watched her face. Then he nodded. "All right. You're probably right on that one. I owe you this—when the time comes, I'll tell you what I can. But until I get some pieces of the puzzle together, you're better off not knowing. Fair enough?"

A breeze had picked up. It rattled through the bare branches of trees at the park's edge, and the evergreens swayed. It had a raw, dry edge to it. Kamryn resisted hugging herself against it. "Fair enough."

Brand came running up, cheeks blazing, his sunglasses a dark slash across his face. "I'm thirsty!"

"Let's buy some drinks and hit the road," Mitch suggested. "There's a mini-mart on the corner."

A Halloween cutout of Elvira and her gravity-defying cleavage dominated the store and an aisle-wide display of beer. Kamryn left Mitch and Brand to make fools of themselves over the vampire cult actress and her plunging neckline while she bought a six-pack of cold soda. A small TV set behind the counter was running local cable news as she waited her turn in a small line.

"... from Tucson today comes the shocking story of a famed local tribesman who was severely beaten and left for dead on the construction site of the fabulous new Elysian resort grounds. Yellow Dog was unable to identify his assailants and this afternoon lies in critical condition—"

"Shit, no," Brand said breathlessly at her elbow. "No!"

She put her hand on his shoulder. "Quiet." She could feel his emotion tremble through him, wondering how he could bear it, hoping he would stay quiet so she could listen.

"Praised as a wise man as well as an astute and honest businessman, the Chiricahua Apache spearheaded many local drives for the destitute, regardless of their race. Authorities tonight have impounded a car he was reported to have been driving, though his employees say it was not his vehicle. Authorities are looking for a recreational vehicle he was said to drive. More later. Weather tonight, rain squalls coming in over the mountains, light to moderate, as the evening temperature drops, chance of snow flurries, not expected to hold—"

"That'll be three fifty, ma'am."

Kamryn looked at the counterman. "Oh. Right." She counted out the change. She shoved the six-pack into Brand's hands, staring into a face numb of expression and said, as if she were talking to a child, "Get in the car."

Stricken behind the sunglasses, he finally nodded and shuffled away.

She followed.

The Honda.

Their fingerprints in the car. *Her* fingerprints in the car.

"What is it?"

"They got Yellow Dog." Emotion cracked Brand's voice. He stopped in the midst of another word, unable to speak at all.

"What?"

"It's on the news. They caught him and beat the crap out of him. He might live. He might not."

"Shit." Mitch started the Explorer's engine.

"My fault," Brand mumbled.

"It's nobody's fault! It was his, his—he took the freaking car. He should have left well enough alone. Should have left us alone." Her own voice sounded distraught to her ears.

Mitch wheeled down the street. "He knew what he was doing. If he hadn't done it, I was going to."

She looked at him. "Leaving us alone?"

"For a while. Until I caught up with Snake." Mitch's mouth pulled downward. "But Yellow Dog took off first." He cleared his throat. "What do we do now?"

"We have to make El Paso. If we have to drive all night." Across state lines. Sometimes highway patrol departments took a while to coordinate cooperation. Sometimes they didn't. She had decisions to make.

"No problem." Mitch scanned the skies. "Barring bad weather."

"Whatever it takes." She belted herself, and hugged her stomach tightly, feeling the money belt beneath her hands. Whatever it took.

"It's all here, sir." Purple bruises lingered under Trinh's eyes, testimony to his fatigue, but his expression was one of pride as he handed hard copy files to Rembrandt.

Rembrandt opened the first one, paged through, his reading speed quick, then slowing, as he became engrossed in the information. He looked up once. "You're certain it's the same boy."

"According to the databases. There's a printout of his photo ID for social services."

Rembrandt curled a corner of the report back, saw the photo, gray-scanned, but he recognized Brandon Dennis. "That's him." He continued reading. "This is remarkable, recruit." He looked up and steadied his gaze into Trinh's almond eyes. "This is to remain confidential."

"Yes, sir."

Rembrandt put aside the file, intending to read it more fully, his mind working rapidly. He picked up a file on the young woman.

Trinh had matched three possibilities, but he had circled one set of newsclippings in red. Rembrandt scanned them and he concurred with the match the recruit had made. He ran his finger under the headline. "My, my. I knew she was good with a gun, but who would have thought she'd pack an ax."

The lurid copy read: BROTHER, SISTER, WANTED IN HATE CRIME DEATH OF PARENTS, SIBLINGS, AND NEIGHBORING

FAMILIES. Brother captured, but sister still free. Bodies hacked to pieces in frenzy, authorities say they have never seen anything like the carnage. . . .

"My, my," repeated Rembrandt. "What have we got here?"

He looked up. "Dismissed, recruit, and excellent work. Would you mind telling Commander Meales that I'd like to have words with him as soon as is convenient?"

Trinh snapped off a salute. "Affirmative."

Josey came in after dinner. Rembrandt had already read the boy's file three times and the girl's file twice. He sat with the laptop in front of him, making plans.

"Nice of you to come," he said.

Josey flushed, difficult to do under his naturally olive coloring.

Rembrandt moved his chair around. "Please sit, Josey. I have something to discuss with you."

Meales pulled up a chair and did as requested, his spine ramrod stiff.

"We have a chance to save each other's butts."

The flush under Josey's late afternoon shadow grew deeper. "I'm not aware, sir, that there is a problem."

"I have a problem of which you are very much aware." Rembrandt tilted his chair back slightly. He balanced his chin on the palm of his hand, elbow on his desk, watching Meales. He could feel the ruined landscape of his complexion under his fingers.

"Christiansen."

"Bingo. He has been elusive, but I'm closing in on him. The services of recruit Trinh have been invaluable."

Meales returned, "You were speaking of our collective asses."

"Yes, I was. You were instrumental in picking this area for a camp and its location was based partially on your recommendation. But I don't recall that you've ever notified Bayliss that you're on the edge of a sweep. A regular, around-the-clock sweep."

"No, sir." Josey had gone white around the nostrils.

"We're in agreement, then."

"Yes, but—shit, Rembrandt. I didn't know myself until the place was half-built—"

"Better late than never."

Josey shifted uncomfortably. "The budget wouldn't have allowed relocation. Not yet."

"And you wanted your command."

Meales flinched, looked away. When he looked back, his eyes had lost some of their confidence.

"I think I can solve your problem, Josey, and I think you can help me solve mine."

"How?"

"Satellites have been known to fall out of the sky. I pride myself on the expertise I have gained. Do you know yet whether it's one of ours?"

"No. We haven't been able to crack it yet."

Rembrandt straightened in his chair. "Leave that to me, then. This is what I need you to do for me." He handed the commander a printout.

Josey scanned it. "Compile a video, build an isolation chamber, program a virtual reality presentation— This will take time."

"I want it ready yesterday. You have VR simulators for training. I don't need much time on a conversion, we're talking stripping in some videos from news footage. What you need to pay attention to is the speed of the animation frames on the virtual reality programs, inserting new frames at this synaptic speed. You have recruits out there who can do it. Use whatever manpower you have."

"Subliminal programming." Understanding dawned on Josey's face.

"Yes. And if my subject confirms what I think he will, Bayliss will be pleased. Very pleased. He won't need drugs to build an army. The late Dr. Susan Craig has already found a way."

Rembrandt slept lightly. He heard the soft knock on his door, was on his feet and at the entrance before the third soft rap.

"What is it?"

Recruit Trinh stood, swaying with tiredness, caught in half-yawn. He snapped his mouth shut. "Sir."

"Come in, son. You've been working hard."

"Yes, sir." A burst of a smile lit the taciturn Asian face. "But it was worth it, sir! I asked for permission to report to you."

Rembrandt settled himself in his desk chair and crossed his legs, pulling at the hem of his pajama bottoms. "It must be important to wake me."

"Yes, sir! I put flags out on your subjects in case any further inquiries were being made. I was woken up this evening by the graveyard shift with the news."

"Which is?" Rembrandt was aware his slight southern drawl made his tone sound more patient than it really was. It gave him an edge on occasions like this when his temper preceded his diplomacy.

"We have a fingerprint match inquiry on Kamryn Talent, lifted from the silver Honda accord registered to her, found as part of a crime scene investigation just outside Tucson."

"Bodies?"

"A local Indian spokesman, critical but improving, found beaten inside the vehicle. Our three are missing, and so is the Indian's four-wheeler."

Rembrandt drummed his fingers in thought. "That doesn't sound like our crew's M.O."

"No, sir. Tucson police reports, not released to the news media, suggests that skinhead and neo-Nazi graffiti were also found on the site, suggesting a hate crime."

Rembrandt moved his head in denial. "No. No, that's not our girl. She's running. She doesn't have time to stop and fucking spray paint the place! No. Unless . . ."

"Sir?"

He met Trinh's tired eyes. "Nothing. Not yet, anyway. How soon did the flag come up?"

"Within the hour."

"Good. I want you to get into the system, if you can, and intercept any inquiry for fingerprint match from the FBI. I don't want anybody else to know our beauty's a fugitive. But I want you to request the Pennsylvanian prints and see if you can get a match on what Tucson's circulating. Can you do that?"

"Yes, sir, if the commander gives me time—"

"He'll give you the time. Do you have a description, license plate, VIN for the four-wheeler?"

"It's a 1994 Ford Explorer, forest green, Arizona plates—I've got it."

"Good. I want you to send that to Texas highway patrol, El Paso division. I want you to send it as an official request from the Bureau of ATF, that the girl is wanted on arms violations, is a suspected member of the Order." Rembrandt named a neo-Nazi militia group which had been somewhat dormant after a turbulent 1980s and which was now beginning to recover from the last siege of FBI and Department of Justice actions. The Texans were unlikely to question that. "And she may be on the run from California with an underage hostage and a companion. Ask that they be held, matter of national security, local bureaus to be kept out of the matter, I'll be jetting in from Albuquerque to pick them up when apprehended. They'll be traveling on the 10. They should be easy to ID and pick up. Can you do that?"

"I can try."

"Trying is not doing. I asked you if you can handle that, recruit. Because if you can't, I have to find somebody who can."

Trinh blinked rapidly two or three times. "I can do it, sir."

"Good. We'll let those good old boys be our hunting dogs, flush our quarry right into our line of fire. Now, go report to Commander Meales and carry a request for a chopper, immediate transportation to Albuquerque."

"You'll need the Lear."

"Yes, Trinh, I will. Please convey that also. And remind Meales that I intend to be bringing back prisoners."

Chapter 28

Rain pounded the windshield. The wipers of the Explorer made a slight tocking sound as they went back and forth monotonously. The headlights could barely pierce the curtain of night and bad weather. They had driven until midnight, when snow and ice had made the pass through Deming temporarily unpassable, the New Mexico highway patrol pulling traffic over until the roads could be scraped clear. A few cars had shot through, daring the bad conditions, but the patrol had managed to keep most of them back. They had sat in the Explorer, cold, even Mitch shivering, for three hours until finally waved on. Now he had little sense of where they could be.

Brand's ears felt the pressure of a steady grade through the rugged, barren mountains. He swallowed every few minutes trying to ease the pounding of his head. From his spot in the backseat, it looked as though Kamryn had gone to sleep, her head bent from her neck in an awkward angle, temple pressed to the side window. Brand couldn't sleep, his thoughts tumbling over and over.

Why hadn't he seen the darkness over Yellow Dog? Why couldn't he have warned him? Why hadn't his eyes, his damn eyes, *seen* the disaster coming? He could have done something. He could have saved the old man. It wouldn't have been all his fault.

But he hadn't seen it. Nothing. No smudges or patches or bolts of darkness anywhere about the wise man. And even if he had seen it, Brand thought, staring into the storm miserably, would Yellow Dog have believed him?

Why not? He had not asked questions about the other.

Brand was not used to being believed. He was, after all, Brand X, the stuff nobody wanted, the X-man.

It didn't matter! If he had only seen the peril, he could have saved Yellow Dog. His friend would not now be lying in a hospital somewhere, fighting for his life. If only.

He felt useless.

He should have done something.

Something flashed in the headlights. "Damn!" Mitch veered the car. Brand caught the barest glimpse of eyes—silvery, shining orbs, a leaping body through the beams, then nothing.

"Damn deer."

"Was that what it was?"

"Mule deer. Didn't you see its ears?"

"No." Brand leaned closer. "Wouldn't it be scared of the car?"

"Headlights blind 'em. They only know to run. It wouldn't be out in this weather, but it's rutting season."

Sex, thought Brand, sagging back into the bench seat. It drove everybody crazy. There were few deer in the Los Angeles basin. He couldn't remember having seen one in the wild before.

Mitch went back to his tuneless humming, which the windshield wipers nearly drowned out.

Had Yellow Dog leaped into the path of the skinheads, just like the deer, blinded for the moment, unaware of the danger? He didn't think so. Yellow Dog had been around. He knew things that Brand could not figure out how he knew.

Mitch had intended to take the Honda as a decoy. Yellow Dog had done it instead. He knew what he might be facing, how dangerous they could be. But why the skinheads?

So Brand would be free to bring the KillJoy *after them.* Yellow Dog had told him he had to do it. He would do it, somehow. Lure the KillJoy to New Orleans.

And so Yellow Dog had taken the lesser danger, so he could take the greater. He'd decoyed the skinheads to give them time. To give Brand time. That was the only thing that made any sense.

Thoughts clicked into place. The pounding in his head disappeared as he made a half-yawn and his ears popped gently. The answer was worse than the questions.

Yellow Dog's sacrifice would be in vain if Brand did not do what he had been left free to do.

Mitch had spent most of his waiting time in Deming reading the road maps.

"Where are we now?"

"Just outside Las Cruces. Then, in this weather, a little less than an hour to El Paso."

Brand tried to imagine it as he looked through the car windows.

El Paso. *Come get me, KillJoy. I'm in El Paso. Looking for me? Come and get me if you dare.* He thought of how he'd first seen it at the mall, inky gusts of nothingness, black flames from the dead policeman's mouth and nostril. How it had come into the chapel over Curtis' body, a dripping, oozing blackness.

Something stirred. Brand turned his thoughts away quickly, shaken, for it had grabbed for him, striking cobra fast. Not thinking of it would be like not thinking of the word rhinoceros. Brand squeezed his eyes shut, and let Bauer distract him.

Kamryn woke with a jerk, breathing hard, her inner eye still filled with a vision and a voice. *Come on, Sis, I've got a surprise for you. . . .* She stared out the windshield, uncomprehending for a moment, then saw the sleet whirling down, white and gray against the headlights, the Explorer making slow but steady progress against it.

"Good thing we've got a four-by."

Mitch turned. The corner of his mouth went up. "You're awake."

"Just. I'd ask for a pit stop, but this doesn't look like a good time."

"We stop in this, we might not get started again easily."

"Tired of driving? I'll take over."

"I thought we agreed not to stop."

"I can make a change on the fly. I just scoot over, sit on your lap, take control, and you scoot out from under me."

"While I admit," Mitch said slowly, "the idea of your sitting on my lap has its merits, I don't think so."

"Has its merits? Oh, yes. I'm sure you'd appreciate that."

"Damn straight I would. It's been a long time since anybody offered to get close to me. You lose a lot when you're homeless. You lose yourself, your identity, your sexuality."

Kamryn found herself staring at him. "Do you?"

"It would be hard not to. Suddenly, you're not a man anymore, not human. You're . . . homeless. Maybe a homeless man or a homeless woman, but not in a sensual way, just a gender label. No one would think of looking me in the eyes. What sex there is on the streets is generally rape."

"But you wouldn't—"

"No. Never. But that doesn't mean I didn't miss what I was missing."

"Of course not." Kamryn brushed her hair from her forehead. "Is that what you saw in your boyfriend? Some kind of sexual identity?"

"I don't think I want to answer that."

"Sex or power?"

"Power," she said shortly. "The sex tends to be rather proprietary. Sometimes even violent. An aside. It's power." Feeling warm, she leaned forward and adjusted the defroster setting on the dash. "What about you? Did you leave a girl behind when you went AWOL?"

"No. When I enlisted. She waited for me. Then we were engaged for two years."

"Then . . ."

"She decided that a Marine staff sergeant wasn't what she wanted out of life. She married someone else."

"Who?"

"A banker."

"A banker does it with interest," Kamryn quoted.

"Oh, jeez." Brand rose out of the back seat. "Give me a break. Am I going to have to listen to this?"

She'd forgotten they weren't alone.

"Virgins have delicate ears," Mitch said, laughing.

"Who's a virgin!"

"You are," Mitch told him and reached back to thump him.

Aggrieved, Brand replied, "It's not my fault."

Kamryn put her hands up. "Okay, that's it. That's enough."

Brand looked at her seriously. "One can never have too much sex."

"I don't want to talk about it."

"You did, two minutes ago."

"That was then, this is now."

"How am I ever going to learn anything?"

Kamryn closed her mouth firmly, refusing to say another word.

* * * *

The hotel was a huge structure, U-shaped and two-storied, occupying vaster grounds than even the presidential palace, rainswept and new looking. Delacroix took the stairs to their rooms, and leaned across the railing.

"Nice place," he observed, his accented English dry with irony, as he faced the chain-link fencing topped with razor wire that encircled the hotel. To protect the guests and their vehicles, he'd been told. "This El Paso."

No one answered him. Stark opened a room door and held it for him. He entered, to a faint smell of disinfectant and lemon. The room was in cheerful colors, quilted spreads neatly arranged across the beds. Carpeting bent rose-beige fibers under his tread. Drapes matched the splendor of the quilted coverings. The bathroom porcelain was uncracked and as white as eggshell. This America, to take both crime and prosperity so casually.

He pulled up an upholstered chair to sit by the window. "Pull the drapes," he told Stark. "And leave me."

Stark hesitated, then did as he was told, going to join his fellows in the next room.

Delacroix bent his head over his hands.

Moments later, how long he could not be sure, it might even have been hours, tires squealed in the parking lot below. A door slammed, followed by another. Then the outdoor stairs trembled with the sounds of ascent.

He had left the door unlocked. Delacroix lifted his head. Footfalls rang the length of the hotel, then stopped outside his door.

It crashed open. A man stepped inside, blinking at the dimness of the room. He flexed, and his arms looked like two mighty constrictors at his side, skin rippling in inked tattoos.

"I've been waiting," Delacroix said.

Snake came to a halt, Mott on his heels, his head crawling and pounding until he thought it would explode, squeezing his eyeballs and brains out of his skull. He had walked, as he had driven for the last six hours, out of a kind of animal instinct, not thinking, not slowing even when snow had threatened the high desert roads. He had not eaten since leaving California, but it did not matter. His flesh crackled with fever. He could feel sweat running down his face like tears, and he could smell the rank smell of his body.

He had navigated by the thing curled up inside the bones of his head, by the itching and the crawling and the yearning. It did not stop until he stopped, here, inside this hotel room.

He wiped the sweat from his face, looking into the dim interior of the room and saw a nigger waiting for him.

A protest burst from his lips, shattering the silence.

The man, dressed in ivory linens, like a suit from the tropics, got to his feet. "You will not address me like that," he said, his voice heavily accented.

"And a frigging foreign nigger, too." Snake clenched his teeth. The cords in his neck bulged, as if bars in a cage for the words, but he got them out, anyway.

Mott shuffled his feet uncertainly. "He ain't the girl, Snake. Let's get out of here. Viktor's going to be pissed about the car."

"Come in and close the door," the black man ordered softly. "You are attracting attention."

"No fucking way," Mott began, but something hard poked him in the back of the rib cage, just shy of a kidney.

"Do what the man say."

Mott looked over his shoulder. Two more black faces stared back at him. A white man stood just behind him, and he carried the gun. Snake staggered forward as if obeying an unseen force, like a marionette pulled by strings, and Mott followed him into the room.

"Sit and tell me who you are chasing."

"I. Don't. Take. Orders. From. You." Snake forced each word out.

"Au contraire, mes amis. You do. I am Delacroix, and I am the master of the most important part of you."

Snake shrugged, fighting invisible chains, until his face glowed red with the effort.

Mott looked uneasily from side to side.

"I. Don't. Take. Orders. From. No. Nig—"

Delacroix waggled his fingers. "That is enough. Look in the mirror and tell me what you see."

Snake ground his heel into the carpet, turning in a slow movement, inch by inch, until he faced himself in the mirror over the bureau. He saw himself, shirt rolled at the arms, baring his muscular limbs and tattoos. He saw his face, sweat-soaked and burning with effort. His tattoos writhed and moved like something alive. He clenched his fists.

Behind him, also visible in the mirror, Delacroix's sharp, calm face. He began to chant softly.

That itchy thing began to claw at him from inside.

Snake tried to shake it off, but he couldn't. It was inside him, inside. He ripped at his shirt, tearing it open, felt it coil in his throat. He put his thick, knobby hands at his throat, squeezing, squeezing, as if he could smash it.

He drove himself to his knees in wheezing agony. Then, as he looked back in the mirror, dizzied, defeated, he saw it.

An inky darkness began to pour out of him, out of his hands, his throat, his ears, his eyes, his mouth, his nostrils, streaming out of him, covering him, blanketing him, a second skin.

Until the only thing he could see in the mirror was himself, brown-hued, with black and yellow tattoos upon his skin.

He opened his mouth to scream, but the other white man was on him, muffling his horror with his forearm, gagging him.

"See what you are," Delacroix said calmly, "and know my orders. Release him, Stark."

Snake stood crouching on the floor. He raised his hands in front of his eyes, staring at them, stared at his mirror image.

"You are mine. What is done is done. Tell me who the quarry is."

"Biker bitch. Kamryn. Some kid. Man. Homeless. Scum."

Delacroix considered this, as if there had been a right and wrong to the answer, then nodded, pleased.

"Where are they now?"

"Coming." Snake gargled a word, then spit it out. "To El Paso."

Mott looked around the room in desperation, afraid.

Delacroix looked at him. "You must feed," he remarked to Snake. "Take him. This room has a lovely closet. Put the body in it."

Mott's mouth opened and shut like a fish on the hook. He took a step away from Snake.

He was not quick enough.

Chapter 29

"Take us through town and on into the airport." Kamryn put down the map, frowning. "Be careful. We don't want any tickets." They had gone from barren desert to a bustling commute through a major city. Cars jostled them from every side. The night had been long, and was finally gone.

"I am careful."

She followed the state trooper as he dropped off, then looked back. "Well, he was staring at something."

Mitch flexed his neck. "A ticket is a ticket. What are they going to do, throw us in jail?"

"Just remember: there's justice, and then there's Texas justice."

"What's that supposed to mean?"

"It means," Mitch answered Brand when Kamryn didn't, "that Texans have their own way of doing things."

"Well, duh. But what does it mean—" Brand stopped. "Are we flying out of El Paso?"

Kamryn, her tone short. "No."

"But then, why are we going to the airport?"

"We're going to park the Explorer in one of those long-term parking lots and then we're going to rent another four-wheeler."

"Because of what happened to Yellow Dog."

Mitch looked at Kamryn. "You think they might have a fix on the car?"

"Could. Why take chances?"

"Makes sense to me." Mitch eyed Brand in the rearview mirror. "Okay?"

"Sure." Brand had hoped for a moment that the other two had decided on a quicker route. The moment passed with an icy swiftness. He did not know if Yellow Dog had made it through the night. They had long since passed out of the range where his condition was featured on the local news, having put the entire state of New Mexico between them. The only thing he knew was that the KillJoy had drawn close.

Very close.

The orange-red of dawn bled out of the sky quickly, leaving it a dazzling blue. Brand let out a sigh and reached for his sunglasses. The lightning bolt etching had lengthened a bit, scratched across the face of the lens. The light did not seem to bother his eyes as much as it had, but as he watched Kamryn, he feared for her.

Darkness made an aura about her, a saturnine glow that was as far from an angelic halo as it could be. His pulse quickened at the recognition of what he saw. He was failing Kamryn, losing her, watching her slip away before his very eyes. He fingered the amulet in his pocket. Yellow Dog had not known if it would help.

But he had not thought it would hurt either.

Brand knotted his fingers in the black cord necklace, thinking to draw it out of his pocket and give it to her now, without delay.

Mitch informed them, "There's another trooper on my tail, approaching slowly."

Kamryn slid down in her seat. "Get down, Brand."

He ducked down. "What's happening?"

"Nothing. I'm not even sure if he's giving us a look over."

The heavy traffic sound of the major thruway traversing El Paso surrounded them. Mitch said nothing further, but the car moved in a smooth lane change.

"What's happening?" Kamryn's voice, squeezed, tense.

"Nothing. He's taking the off-ramp, leaving us. Probably wondering what doughnuts to have with his coffee."

Brand moved. Kamryn hissed, "Stay down!"

Mitch braked suddenly. The amulet, as he drew it out of his pocket, slid underneath the driver's seat. The charm was gone, as surely as if it had jumped from his hand. Brand patted around, looking for it, unable to find it. Then, the coolness of the metal answered his search.

He put it back in his pocket.

"What is it?"

"Gridlock," explained Mitch patiently. "Texas style." The Explorer moved in inches, until he veered sharply left and then began a moderate acceleration. "We should be at the airport in another ten minutes."

Kamryn got up and Brand followed suit. He could hear the overhead scream of jets as they circled the city outskirts. He'd never been on a plane. He watched their path with a certain envy. As they found the thruway exit to the airport, Brand saw another state trooper approach quietly from the right rear, then drop back. He opened his mouth to say something, then decided not to. Kamryn was about to jump out of her skin. Why worry her further? The trooper got no closer and then turned off approaching Airway Boulevard.

They hiked in from the parking lot rather than take the shuttle. Kamryn threw the last of her belongings in a Dumpster.

"We travel light," Mitch said ruefully.

"Clothes are replaceable." She wore a short jacket and stopped in the parking lot aisle long enough to tuck her revolver into her waistband at the small of her back. "Just give me the necessities." She did not meet Mitch's eyes when she looked up.

In a wing of the main terminal, they sat down to hot drinks and doughnuts. Brand had hot chocolate and three twists. Kamryn had picked hot cider and a plain glazed doughnut. Mitch took coffee, black, and a fist-sized apple fritter. They ate with sugary satisfaction. Kamryn stood.

"You guys wait here. I'll go rent the car."

Mitch got seconds on his coffee and Brand kicked back, listening to the sounds of a nearby passenger's CD player, Hootie and the Blowfish. Mitch blotted his coffee cup on the front page of the paper, Senator Haywood Bayliss celebrating the disarmament package defeat.

American Airlines announced that their 11:30 a.m. flight, connecting to Dallas/Ft. Worth and on to New Orleans would be their last flight of the day to that region because of the gulf states' hurricane watch. Brand found a quarter and wandered off to the arcade bordering the coffee shop and gift shop, the enveloping darkness and neon lit machines comforting.

Kamryn found him blazing a trail among the current high point holders on NOVA. She took him by the elbow and pulled him away.

"Where's Mitch?"

"He's gone to get the car. A red Cherokee. It's a hike, according to the rental counter, so he won't be back for about twenty minutes. I want you to watch for him."

"Sure. Where are you going to be?"

Kamryn looked at the flight departure monitor. She looked back at Brand. "I won't be here."

"Why?"

"I have to leave. The two of you will be fine without me." She had a small duffel in her hands, imprinted with the logo of the rental car agency. "Take this, give it to Mitch. He'll know what to do with it."

Brand stood shock-still, the bag pushed into his chest. "I don't get it."

"There's nothing to get. This is where we part ways. I can't—" She looked out the bank of windows toward the parking lot, and back again. "I can't do this anymore." She let go of the bag, turned heel, and started to walk away. Her footsteps clicked on the marble tiles.

Brand quick-stepped to catch up. "What do you mean, you can't do this anymore?"

The two of them were walking against a tide of people coming out of the terminal arm where the gates were. He saw their direction.

"You bought a ticket. You're flying out."

"That's right."

"Leaving us."

"With a car. There's two hundred dollars in the bag and," she lowered her voice, "the gun."

"I don't want it."

People were beginning to stare at the two of them.

"I have to go. My plane's boarding. Brand—you can't bring that bag through with you."

"No. You're not going anywhere without me. You can't. You don't know what you're up against—I should have told Yellow Dog, and I didn't, and it's my fault they tried to kill him—"

She tried to outrun him. He kept pace. "You've got to listen. I'm not crazy. I'm not!"

"Brand!"

"Kamryn, don't go!" He grabbed for her arm. The duffel fell, spilled open, gun sliding and money flying, all under the belted x-ray counter. Airport security and the uniformed woman manning the x-ray machine looked down in total surprise.

"Shit!" Kamryn bent over, kicked the money and gun back in the duffel. She locked her arm with Brand's and stepped away from the x-ray threshold.

Security put his hand on his holster, and stepped with them.

Very quietly, Kamryn said, "It's time to run again."

"Not without you."

They turned and sprinted. A sharp whistle cut across the air behind them, echoing through the terminal. Kamryn angled into the crowds. Her arm tore loose from Brand's, but he could see her dark hair, among the passengers. She cut across a wave, headed toward a wing which was labeled: NO ACCESS. Maintenance only.

He followed.

He couldn't protect her if she left. Couldn't watch her cool beauty, couldn't laugh at her quirky sense of humor, couldn't be without her.

He cut across the flow of disembarking passengers and trailed across the forbidden wing. The corridor turned a sharp corner, but he could hear her rushing footfalls.

"Kamryn!"

She halted. Turned around slowly.

"Brand, I know you don't understand, and now I definitely don't have time to explain it to you. We're both in trouble here, now, and neither of us can afford to be caught. So you just go back that direction, and I'll go this way. Find Mitch. Get to New Orleans. Do what you have to do." She backed carefully toward an emergency exit door off the corridor.

"Not without you."

Looking skyward, she said again, "I can't do this!" When she looked down, she froze.

"Please, Kamryn. Come with us."

"Now, son." A deep, pleasantly southern voice cut across Brand, from his rear, and the hair rose on the back of his neck.

"Son, I don't think you want to go anywhere with that woman. She's nothing but trouble. I have airport security with me. Put the bag down, turn around, and let's make this as pleasant as possible. Where's the other one?"

"Gone," Kamryn and Brand got out in unison. They looked at each other. Brand recognized the voice, saw the look on Kamryn's face.

The ruined man had caught up with him.

"Well, now. That matters a little, but it doesn't ruin my entire day." Rembrandt drew even with Brand. Impeccably suited as always, he wore a pleased expression. "If I have the two of you, I think it'll be possible to find him later. Don't you?"

Kamryn put her hand in the duffel. "I wouldn't count on that. Brand, step away from him and come with me."

Rembrandt raised an eyebrow as he guessed what Kamryn had in the duffel. "After all the trouble I went to to find you." He tilted his head slightly, still amiable. "You won't be walking out, little lady. The state troopers have been looking for the three of you and your car. They were most cooperative in letting me know you were here at the airport. Cooperative of you, too. I had just flown in about an hour ago. Put the bag down."

"No. Brand." Her eyes pleaded. "Come with me."

"This is a heck of a note, isn't it, son? First she doesn't want you, then she does."

Brand took a sideways step, uncertain. He knew Rembrandt wanted him. Kamryn was extraneous here. She had to get away, to find Mitch, to tell him—

"Kamryn, go on."

She moved back a fraction, stood with her back to the emergency exit door. She could feel it, she must! She stayed there, watching them.

Rembrandt smiled. "Maybe she'd respond better if you called her by her real name, son."

Kamryn grayed. The duffel shook in her hands. "Brand, don't listen to him."

"She didn't tell you, did she? Well, I've had occasion to do a little background check on this little lady. Her name isn't Kamryn Talent. In fact, she's no lady. She's an ax murderer wanted in the Commonwealth of Pennsylvania. She'd been on the run for about a year and a half now—"

Brand's words strangled in his throat.

"Isn't that so, Amelinda? Amelinda Terhuven. A nice old-fashioned name, Amelinda." Rembrandt reached for something in the pocket flap of his jacket.

"Nooo!" Brand screamed and lunged at Rembrandt. He knocked the black object out of his hand. It skidded along the tiles to Kamryn. She stooped and picked it up, throwing it in the duffel. Without standing, she backed out of the emergency exit door.

Alarms went off everywhere. Rembrandt shook Brand off, into the arms of a security officer and dashed out onto the tarmac.

A taxiing plane narrowly missed him. He looked, and could not see which way the young woman had gone.

"No sign of her, sir," confirmed security at his side.

"It doesn't matter," Rembrandt said grimly, looking down the runway, listening to the fury of departing jets. "I've got the boy."

Chapter 30

"Where's Brand?"

"Rembrandt's got him." Kamryn brushed her hair back. Tears streaked her face. She tried to wipe them, her eyes kept flowing. "Drive, damnit! Just drive before the troopers spot us."

He maneuvered away from the terminal, merging in with the traffic. "Then we were being watched."

"They caught up with us. They must have had the airport cordoned off the minute we pulled into the parking lot. This is my fault. I tried—I tried to leave."

"Leave?"

"It's an airport, for Christ's sake. I tried to take a flight out, leave you and Brand behind. I can't take a chance of being caught. You wouldn't understand."

His mouth thinned. "What I don't understand is how Rembrandt ended up with Brand."

"He did it! Trying to protect me again. Rembrandt thought he had us cornered. He threw me Rembrandt's gun and I took off."

"It's in the bag?"

"Along with mine. I tried to give it to Brand, told him to find you. He made a scene. We got caught at the x-ray gate. Shit! What a mess I keep making of things."

"Give me the gun."

"What?"

"I might need it. You've got yours. Let me see what Rembrandt was packing."

She picked up the duffel, reached in and rummaged around. She brought out the hard black object Brand had thrown her. "I don't— Mitch, it's a pager. Brand threw me a pager."

She held it out on her palm. He looked at it, reached out and took it, clipping it onto his waist band.

Kamryn tried to compose herself. She wiped her face dry again. "Mitch, God, who is he? How does he have the power to show up, and everybody toes the line? He had the state troopers looking for us. Airport security. Who does he tell these people he is?"

"I don't know who he is, but I do know what he wants. Ultimately." He made a turn back onto Airway Boulevard, leading back to the 10.

"Where are we going?" Kamryn could not stop shaking. She hugged herself tightly. Her teeth chattered.

"New Orleans. What he wants is in New Orleans, and that's where he's going to have to meet us if he wants it."

"What about the KillJoy?"

"That's another story. But it started in New Orleans, too. I have to go full circle." He took the on-ramp marked East and merged into thinning traffic.

"And leave Brand?"

"For now. If Rembrandt wants his goods, he's going to have to make a trade."

"But how's he—how's he going to know that? How are you going to get hold of him? How's he going to find us?"

"Easy. He's a smart man." Mitch tapped his belt. "He'll probably page us."

Rembrandt sat in the President's Lounge. The plush surroundings nearly muffled the sound of the airport. He checked his watch. "She's no saint, son, or she would have come back for you."

Brand sat with his hands cuffed, resting on one knee. Loose shackles around his ankles kept him from running. A bump was rising on one cheekbone and his glasses were gone, irretrievably shattered. He kept his eyes narrowed against the glare of the fluorescent lighting, but the pain was not as it had been the past few days. He would rather have had the pain, and the glasses, all of it, instead of the darkness which patched in and out, like an incandescent bulb going out, like a TV screen fading into oblivion.

If Rembrandt thought he was Brand's worst nightmare, he had another think coming. The fact was obvious that if the agent were going to kill him, he would have. No, he was bait, and Brand knew it. He did not answer.

"I have to wait anyway," the ruined man continued pleasantly. "We need to refuel and file a new flight plan before we can get out of here. But I would say they're not coming to get you. No, it doesn't look like rescue is imminent. You're expendable."

Brand felt like a scab that Rembrandt enjoyed picking and probing. He turned to look fully at the man. "And you're a son of a bitch."

"Probably. Probably. But have I ever lied to you?"

"I don't know you well enough to know if you have. And that doesn't change anything. What good is the truth if all you talk about is evil."

"I suppose you prefer Lizzie Borden."

"Whatever it was, she didn't do it!"

"Son, I'm afraid she did. We've matched fingerprints from the crime scene in Pennsylvania with those out of the Honda which the Arizona state police were kind enough to put online. for us. It's her all right."

"Then the truth lies." Brand kicked at the small teakwood table in front of him. There was an answering echo of a heavy thud.

Rembrandt's face went chill. He put up a hand, signaling for quiet. There were only the two of them sitting in the airport's executive lounge. Rembrandt put a hand out to the remote and muted the television set, although neither of them had really been watching the hockey game.

No other sound followed. It was, perhaps, too silent.

Brand felt a twinge of hope bloom in him. They'd been in the lounge for the last hour and a half, after security had escorted them there. Rembrandt had left twice to consult with his pilot, leaving one of the security force at the door, in case Brand had thought of shuffling to freedom. No one else even knew he was there, so it had been beyond hope to think Kamryn and Mitch could find him. He watched as Rembrandt rose smoothly to his feet, put his hand inside his coat pocket, and strode to the doorway.

"On the other hand," Rembrandt told him, "perhaps I was wrong."

He jerked the door open. The threshold stood empty. The security guard who had been placed there was gone, no sign of any occupant anywhere. Rembrandt backed in, shut the door, and locked it. He studied the interior of the lounge. No windows. No other entrances or exits. Brand followed his reconn.

Rembrandt came to him and hoisted him onto his feet. He bent down and undid the shackles. "I want you to stay with me, twinkle toes."

"Where are we going?"

"Somewhere a little more public. The Lear should just about be ready for us." Rembrandt pulled his automatic. Brand stared at its flat black surface. He wondered what it was he'd grabbed earlier and tossed at Kamryn, if it hadn't been a gun.

The ruined man linked elbows with him. He smiled down at Brand. "Now, son, I know you may feel this is your opportunity, but I wouldn't want to bet your life on it. You stay with me, and we'll get through this together. Understand?"

Brand pressed his lips together.

Rembrandt had been listening to the door again. Now he turned, and his eyes bored into Brand's.

"I could shoot you right here, right now, and put up with a hell of a lot less trouble."

"Then do it."

"No. You see, I don't want to. You and me, we're a lot alike. We're survivors. You might be expendable to Christiansen and the girl, but you're not to me. You have quality, son, a rare commodity."

Brand did not want to listen, but he could not look away from the other's compelling face. And then, behind Rembrandt's head, something peculiar began happening to the door.

White crystal had begun to form on its surface as the surface grew horribly cold. Brand could feel the drop in temperature down to his bones. Jackfrost formed before his stare, growing in streaks and flakes over the door. Brand clenched his jaws to keep his teeth from chattering and his breath hazed the air.

Rembrandt whipped around in amazement. Then, fog began to drift in through the minute cracks in the door jam.

A black fog.

Brand reared back.

Rembrandt had hold of him and braced himself. He clicked the safety off his pistol and raised it by his temple, in readiness to level and shoot.

The doorknob rattled.

The two of them stared at it.

Then the door burst open and the KillJoy walked in.

Brand forgot to breathe. He knew the man who strode in despite the cloak of darkness he wore, despite the fact that his skin now mirrored that cloak, despite the fact that he barely resembled a man at all. His sable and black skin rippled like snakehide, yellow diamonds brilliant scales upon the dark. He exuded the KillJoy; it issued through his every pore, and looking into his eyes was looking into black flame. Brand realized he wasn't breathing, couldn't breathe, and thought his heart might stop as well.

"Stop right there."

Snake hesitated in midstride, then came to a halt. He curled his lips back in greeting and inky clouds carried his voice.

"Your ass is mine."

Brand choked. The reflex started his lungs pumping again, his heartbeat skittering in his chest like a frightened, caged animal. This was the familiar, contemptible Snake as well as the KillJoy.

In the corridor behind, where white frost took on a blackish tint, he could see a man waiting, a black man in a tropical sand-colored suit, shirt open at the collar, a sharp-faced man with glass-hard eyes, a professorial type with the stare of an assassin. The corridor wall of windows looking out on the runways framed him. The sky looked a brilliant blue. Immense white planes rolled ponderously past. The black man stood with otherworldly stillness and took in the scene with keenness, then looked into Brand.

Into, and beyond. Brand saw the same kind of radiance about him as he had observed in Snake, but different. It did not overwhelm him, it was him, a negative aura that was like night to Mother Jubilation's day. He did not know why he thought of Mother as the balance to him, but it seemed natural. Like yin and yang. This man was not the KillJoy. . . . He was, quite probably, its master.

He wanted to shout at Rembrandt. *Kill him, and Snake will die,* but his throat stayed frozen. His lips trembled as he tried to force the words out. He could not turn away from the other's eyes. Impaled on them, like one of Vlad Dracula's victims. Why could he see the other that way? Why couldn't Rembrandt?

Two other men, young men, dark as their leader, stepped in to flank him, protective.

Light flooded the airport corridor as a plane moved past, letting the sunlight flood in, glittering, overwhelming.

Flare hit him. His eyes burst with the aura, white-blue, bedazzling. He jerked his head back with a muffled cry, seeing nothing but the painful flash.

It broke the other's hold on him. He craned his face toward Rembrandt, to his ear.

"Shoot him!"

Rembrandt jumped. Snake gave a snarl, no longer hesitant, and charged them.

Rembrandt let go. Brand dropped like a sack of wet cement. The ruined man had been holding him on his feet, and he hadn't even known it. His vision whited out, Brand crawled aside as the gun fired. Blurred vision overrode the flaring. Snake staggered and his chest blossomed red, but he shook and like an angry bull, dropped his head, and came on.

"No!" Brand cried. "The other one. Shoot the other one!"

The pistol spat. Brand saw bodies repel, hit the corridor floor, slide out of view. Tears welled up in his eyes, further blurring the images. Flare throbbed, then began to subside.

Rembrandt had no time. Snake hit him and the building seemed to shake. Rembrandt seemed to evaporate away from him, switched hands on the pistol, and came up swinging.

They grappled. Rembrandt wore an expression of slight surprise, as if Snake should no longer be on his feet. They sparred, Snake nailing Rembrandt with punches that drove grunts out of him. Brand thought he saw the KillJoy's master kneel down, examining the two bodies in the corridor.

Snake slipped in a trail of his own blood and crashed to the floor. He rose, rose on a cloud, his feet flailing, arms dangling, a broken marionette. He rose superhumanly and then rotated upright. He laughed.

Rembrandt brought up his gun. He emptied it into Snake.

Snake danced and quivered with each shot, dancing backward,

staggering forward. Brand could smell the hot coppery blood flowering from him. He made a noise, a guttural growling deep in his throat, flexed his fists and came on again.

Rembrandt clipped off one last shot.

Snake's head exploded.

He dropped and did not move.

Brand felt sick. Rembrandt, breathing hard, blood trickling from his nose and mouth, reached down for him, yanked him onto his feet. "Let's go before that thing gets up one more time."

They reached the threshold of the lounge, the corridor empty except for slashes of blood. Rembrandt paused, looking side to side, calculating.

Brand looked back.

He wished he had not. The KillJoy geysered from Snake's body, spouts of darkness, coalescing, coming after them.

Coming after *him*.

Brand wanted to close his eyes, could not. Horror held him in fascination. The KillJoy spread out, bat-winged, immense, enfolding.

It reached out for them.

He felt its icy touch graze him. His heart did a double-beat, then warmth flooded him. He opened his eyes. The KillJoy was gone.

Rembrandt ejected the empty clip. He slammed Brand up against the wall and held him there with an elbow while he put in a full clip. Brand could see one of the bodies slumped up against the other end of the corridor at the end of a blood smear.

He did not see the master.

Security flooded the corridor from both ends. Rembrandt put up his hand with the gun and then carefully slipped it back inside his suit coat.

"The perps are down."

Brand stayed against the wall as if glued to it. Security swarmed the body, then waved Rembrandt off.

"Your plane is ready, sir."

"Good. I'll fax you a statement. They tried to free my prisoner. One of your men is down, as well. Check the emergency stairwells." Rembrandt took Brand's elbow. "One step at a time, son."

The wind came up across the tarmac as they stepped out. The

Lear waited, door down, engines idling. Rembrandt hustled Brand across the open ground and up the stairs.

He sat Brand down, went up front to say a word or two to the pilot, came back and pulled the door shut and secured it, before returning to the plush bench seats in the main cabin. He unbuttoned his suit jacket and sat with a sigh.

"Well, son, looks like we made it." He smiled at Brand.

The KillJoy looked out of the black depths of his eyes.

Brand screamed, but no one else heard him over the jet engines.

Chapter 31

BULLETIN
HURRICANE YOLANDA LOCAL ACTION STATEMENT
NATIONAL WEATHER SERVICE NEW ORLEANS, LA
1200 PM CDT

   YOLANDA A POWERFUL AND DANGEROUS HURRICANE
RATED FORCE 4 PACKING 150 MPH WINDS STRONGER
THAN PAST HURRICANES ELENA, FREDERIC, AND ELOISE,
RATED WITH OPAL.
   HURRICANE WARNINGS IN EFFECT FROM THE MOUTH
OF THE MISSISSIPPI RIVER TO INCLUDE COASTAL MISSIS-
SIPPI . . . LOWER ST. BERNARD PARISH AND LOWER
PLAQUEMINES PARISH IN LOUISIANA, ALSO FROM MOUTH
OF THE MISSISSIPPI RIVER TO EAST OF MORGAN CITY . . .
THIS INCLUDES THE METROPOLITAN NEW ORLEANS
AREA.
   THIS BULLETIN APPLIES PRIMARILY TO THE FOLLOW-
ING PARISHES IN LOUISIANA . . .
   ASCENSION . . . ASSUMPTION . . . EAST BATON ROUGE . . .
EAST FELICIANA . . . IBERVILLE . . . JEFFERSON . . .
LAFOURCHE . . . LIVINGSTON . . . ORLEANS . . . ST. HE-
LENA . . . ST JAMES . . . ST JOHN THE BAPTIST . . . ST. TAM-
MANY . . . TANGIPAHOA . . . TERREBONE . . .
WASHINGTON . . . WEST BATON ROUGE . . . WEST FELI-
CIANA.

ALSO THE FOLLOWING COUNTIES IN MISSISSIPPI:
HANCOCK . . . HARRISON . . . JACKSON AND PEARL RIVER
CRITICAL INFORMATION SUMMARY
LOCATION . . . AT 1030 CDT HURRICANE YOLANDA WAS
NEAR 28.1N AND 88.2W OR ABOUT 275 MILES SOUTH
SOUTHWEST OF PENSACOLA.
INTENSITY . . . MAXIMUM SUSTAINED WINDS ARE 150
MPH. YOLANDA IS A DANGEROUS SAFFIR SIMPSON CATE-
GORY 4 HURRICANE. SOME FLUCTUATION IN STRENGTH
MAY OCCUR BEFORE LANDFALL.
MOVEMENT . . . YOLANDA IS MOVING NORTH NORTH-
EAST AT 19 MPH, EXPECTED TO BRING THE CENTER OF
YOLANDA INLAND TOMORROW AFTERNOON OR EARLY
EVENING.
TIDES . . . RUNNING 2 FEET ABOVE NORMAL ALONG THE
SOUTHEAST LOUISIANA AND MISSISSIPPI COASTS. TIDES
COULD RISE 3 TO 5 FEET ABOVE NORMAL IN LAKES
PONTCHARTRAIN AND MAUREPAS, ALONG THE COASTAL
AREAS OF ORLEANS . . . ST. BERNARD AND PLAQUEMINE
PARISH. ALONG THE MISSISSIPPI COAST, TIDES 6–7 FEET
ABOVE NORMAL. AS THE HURRICANE MOVES CLOSER,
THESE TIDES ARE EXPECTED TO BECOME MUCH HIGHER,
AS HIGH AS 12 TO 15 FEET ABOVE NORMAL.
EVACUATIONS . . . EVACUATIONS HAVE BEEN CAR-
RIED OUT IN THE COASTAL LOCATIONS OF SOUTHEAST
LOUISIANA AND OUTSIDE THE HURRICANE PROTECTION
LEVEES. MANDATORY EVACUATIONS HAVE BEEN OR-
DERED IN LOWER PARISHES. MISSISSIPPI EMERGENCY
MANAGEMENT SHELTERS ARE OPEN, WITH EVACUATIONS
REQUESTED. MOBILE HOME RESIDENTS ALONG THE MIS-
SISSIPPI COAST ARE BEING URGED TO SEEK SHELTER IN
SUBSTANTIAL BUILDINGS DUE TO GALE FORCE WINDS.
RAINFALL . . . FLASH FLOOD WATCH IS IN EFFECT 3–5
INCHES EXPECTED IN THE EARLY MORNING HOURS AS
YOLANDA PREPARES TO MOVE INLAND. FURTHER RAIN IN-
TENSITY EXPECTED TO INCREASE. LISTEN TO YOUR EMER-
GENCY PREPAREDNESS CHANNELS FOR FURTHER UPDATES.

LOCAL ACTION STATEMENT WILL BE ISSUED AROUND 300 PM CDT.

The ticket agent nervously punched in the request, her hands shaking, trying not to look at the two men facing her over the counter.

"This is the last flight in."

"I understand that," the professor said, in his soft, lilting voice. "But it is most important that I gain a ticket for myself and my aide."

Perhaps not a professor, she thought. Perhaps she had guessed wrong about his demeanor. "Are you a doctor?"

He paused. "Yes," he admitted, almost reluctantly. "With the UN. I thought perhaps I could help. I am used to . . . how would you say it? . . . working under extreme conditions."

The man at his elbow shifted weight.

The ticket agent found two seats. She hurriedly reserved them and cleared her system to print. "I'm so sorry it's taking me so long. I'm really rattled. We had some trouble here this morning."

"We understand," the doctor said soothingly.

"A shooting, can you imagine? The next terminal over. Three dead. Not terrorists, though, thank God."

"Yes," murmured the passenger. "A tragedy."

The printer chucked out the tickets. Hands still shaking, she separated them and put them in folders. "Two tickets to New Orleans," she said, and handed them over. "Mr. Delacroix, Mr. Stark. Have a safe flight."

Delacroix smiled. "We hope to."

Mother Jubilation could hear a lonely saxophone. Its player, like herself, had chosen to stay in the city despite the evacuations. The storm surge had begun to rise, Yolanda already beginning to take a toll, despite the fact landfall was a little more than twenty-four hours away. New Orleans was a city that depended on her canals and pumping systems against flooding. Yolanda would overwhelm them. Even now the city had begun to sink under the tremendous rising tide. Rainfall would worsen the situation. But she could not leave. This was her destiny. She waited for the boy and the white soldier and what troubled them. Mother gathered up her stones and knuckle-bones, shook them and played them out again.

They would tell her nothing. They had told her once, at dawn that morning, of a fearful danger. Now silence.

She cleared them from the table. She drew a pottery jar of corn-meal to her and dipped her hand into it. Letting it slide, grain by grain from her fist, she drew the sign of legba on the table, the supreme loa, the gatekeeper.

Open the signs for me, she prayed over the corn grain symbol. Open the signs for me.

All was still, except for the patter of rain which had fallen sporadically all morning. It would stop and start until tomorrow morning, then it would fall in torrential amounts, wind-driven, streets flooding, levees groaning. Jackson Square was empty of all its sidewalk chalk artists, its vendor wagons, its tourists, its lovers, its jazz musicians. Even the pigeons had gone and the great bronze statue of Jackson on horseback was curiously alone. The white church which graced the west side of the square had its renovated doors sand-bagged. The east side of the square facing the brewery/mall was bagged as well. The narrow and roguish streets leading down to Pirate's Alley and her small shop were all barricaded, waiting for the inevitable.

A well-worn deck of tarot cards sat by the rim of her table. Card by card, they began a gentle slide over the edge. No hand touched them. The tabletop had not moved, but the cards fell until every one of them landed on the floor.

Mother watched them.

She thought of standing to see how they fell, in what pattern, if any, which face up and face down, but before she could, they rose.

They gained the air in twos, like winged things, and began to fly about the room, high under the ceiling. They picked up speed with altitude and they made a terrible rattling as they flapped, like cards pinched in a bicycle spoke. Around and around they went, faster, faster, until Mother's eyes hurt to see them.

Their orbit grew tighter, nearer. Noisier. They spun about the table, eye height, faster, faster until they could not maintain their course. One by one they exploded out of the circle, shooting across the room and dashing to the floor until the last card, which fell into her lap and lay wiggling, breathing like a spent animal, until it quieted.

Mother reached down and picked up The Tower of Destruction.

Her children were in danger, great danger, all of them, all, even the ones she had sent away to what she hoped would be safety. Mother rocked on her chair, back and forth, and chanted her prayer of hope and protection for them, whatever good it would do any of them.

Brand could not see from where he sat on the floor of the helicopter. He kept his face buried in his hands where the pilot could not see his bloodshot eyes, could not laugh at the fear he knew showed in them. He sat in abject misery. He did not care that Rembrandt seemed in control of the thing. He wasn't. Brand could hear it in his voice from time to time. See it in a facial tic or an off-color laugh.

It did not matter if Rembrandt stayed in charge or if the KillJoy gained total control. Either way, he was screwed.

The pilot began speaking and the chopper dipped down, down. They were arriving, wherever they were. Rembrandt pulled his feet in under him, preparatory to standing.

The chopper settled with a hard bump, and then the rotors began to slow. Rembrandt had him on his feet and out the door, ducking his head down to avoid the blades.

A uniformed man met them, a man not much taller than Brand who traded salutes with Rembrandt. He was compact, all muscle, and his olive complexion looked as though he shaved twice a day to keep the beard down. He appraised Brand as Rembrandt asked,

"Everything ready?"

"Yes, sir, it is. You have some messages waiting in your quarters, as well."

"Good." Rembrandt smiled at Brand. "First things first. Where are we putting him, Josey?"

"I've sealed off a compartment in the unfinished dorm, next to the com control. This way."

Brand had little time to take in the sight of what appeared to be a military base, complete with a patrol of joggers going past them, shouting in cadence. There was activity and noise, from the routine to the sound of planks being dropped in place and the whine of drills and air hammers.

He put his cuffed hands up, shading his face a little. Rembrandt pushed and prodded him in the right direction until they stood in a building which matched the officer's description. Rembrandt disappeared behind a narrow door, was gone a minute, then came back.

"Excellent job, Josey."

"Thank you, sir. Permission to withdraw, sir. I have other details to take care of."

"Did you get those Orleans P.D. uniforms I called for?"

"Yes, sir, we did. We're instructing a patrol now."

"Good." Rembrandt pulled out the handcuff key.

"What are you going to do with me?"

Something glittered in Rembrandt's eyes. "Whatever I have to. Right now, you're the key. You're the key that unlocks Christiansen and gives me what I want. Whatever it takes, it takes."

He guided Brand to the door and opened it for him. Inside, a pool of darkness. No light, any place, anywhere. Ceiling, floor and walls blended into total insulation. Brand's mouth went dry. The officer waiting to be dismissed stood stiffly, not looking into the chamber.

"What is this?"

"Your cell. You'll be alone in there, son, alone with your thoughts." Rembrandt put a finger to his mouth as if quieting himself. He tapped his lips twice. "Well, I told you I didn't lie to you. You won't be quite alone. You see, Brand, thanks to the wonders of technology, I didn't just dig up Amelinda's background. I found yours. I know all about Dr. Susan Craig and Georg Bauer and the excellent groundwork she must have done on your mind. So I'm not putting you into solitary alone. No. I've arranged a little refresher course for you."

"I'm not going in there!"

"You don't have any choice."

Brand dug in his heels. "Don't let him do this to me! You can't do this!" He tried to face the officer. "He's crazy. Look in his eyes. He's possessed. You can't do this to me!"

Rembrandt laughed, then stopped as the sound came out eerily cracked. He stopped so quickly his teeth clicked together and Josey stirred uneasily.

"Sir—"

"Commander, if there's any doubt at all who you should listen to, I'll relieve you of duty, right here, right now. Susan Craig has created a cunning creature, a sociopath, who will say anything, do anything, manipulate anyone he can. Let's see if we can make a straight arrow out of him."

Brand dropped to the floor, dead weight, clawing at the frame of the door. Rembrandt let out a growl as he struggled to get him back on his feet, lifting him. "He tried to hang me once! Don't believe him—he's not who he says he is, he never is! Look in his eyes!"

"Sir—" Josey again, questioning.

"You can't make omelettes without breaking eggs." Rembrandt hauled Brand to his feet, held him limply. He shook, like a dog shedding water, and Brand could feel the KillJoy within him. They were fighting each other, fighting for control.

The KillJoy was still not in charge. Rembrandt was, but Brand realized he did not know which was worse.

Both would kill if they wanted to.

"Give me a hand, Commander."

The officer hesitated, then took Brand's other arm.

They shoved Brand inside and slammed the door.

For an eerie moment, he thought the world had left him. Then he collapsed, letting his legs fold under him. The concrete slab felt icy, as hostile as the darkness around him. But at least it was solid. He sat up and crossed his legs. His eyes strained, trying to adjust to the unrelenting shadow of the room.

Blinded, he dared not move. He did not know if Rembrandt still stood outside the room or if he still held the KillJoy in check. Brand could not see his hand in front of his face, would have no warning when death came.

Alone in the dark.

Old feelings began to crowd him, the panic, the closed-in fear. The walls would crush him, the ceiling fall. He panted in fear. Helpless, without control, there was no exit, no light, no protection.

He would die here, suffocated by his memories. Brand tried to regulate his breathing. Was there even air in here? He could not detect a current.

He'd been buried alive and alone. He would be sealed in and left to die. If anyone came to rescue him, it would be too late.

He shut his eyes as if he could lie to himself, but he knew the difference. The darkness was too complete, too overwhelming.

He was no good. He must be. He'd failed Yellow Dog, gotten him nearly killed. Kamryn, Curtis, Mitch, his father (wherever he'd disappeared to), his mother, the list went on and on. Not living up to his potential. Getting in everyone's way. Seeing things.

Crazy.

Psychotic.

Brand X, the stuff nobody wanted. Who could blame them? He'd let them all down. He had never been the boy who'd done the expected, what they wanted. He tried, he just didn't know how. Life seemed so absurd.

You're absurd, Jerkoid. Just *breathe*.

He concentrated on that. In, out. In, out. For how long? Minutes? Hours?

Seconds?

Colors pierced his eyelids. He opened them.

Soundlessly, a projection filled the space in front of him. It gave dimension to the wall. A fighter plane zoomed down on a landscape. The little illumination the projection gave bloomed with a spectacular display. Other planes winged close and out, some breaking away in flames. His hands itched for the trac ball controls of an arcade. It was a flight simulator, on a bombing run. Brand watched it curiously, taken in with the gamelike quality of it, then became aware of a crawling sensation behind his eyeballs, like an itch.

Or an assault.

He closed his eyes again, then opened them, watching the virtual reality program through a web of his fingers. Flash, flash, flash—the colored animation playing out before him moved with a strobelike effect. There was enough light in the program that he could see the dark that streaked it, the cloudy smears of his own vision overlaying it.

Death here. The evil touch of the KillJoy. He could *see* it. He thought for a moment he would welcome the final collapse of his sight. Then remembered it would leave him trapped forever in his mind, at Bauer's mercy.

A thing which had no mercy.

For a flash of a second, a bloody knife. A still photo of a face, a sullen man.

He was not even sure he'd seen it. Then he knew. He wasn't, because the images were being flashed too quickly for normal eyes to focus. But the brain caught the messages, saw them, retained them. Subliminal programming.

Rembrandt knew of Susan Craig. The imprinting. Bauer, the serial killer.

He was doing the same thing to Brand all over again. He must be. Hidden in those animated simulator frames had to be images of Bauer. The bloody knives and visegrips. The crime scenes. The victims. Had to be. Had to be. Feeding Bauer. Giving him the strength to overcome Brand finally.

Brand covered his face.

He cowered. He couldn't go through this again.

Alone.

Don't worry, kid. You still got me. Bauer laughed coarsely. He forced Brand's chin up, watched the project for another minutes or so. *That's old stuff. Boring. We don't like to be bored, do we, kid?*

Georg's cruel voice echoed inside the hollows of his mind.

"Get out!" Brand concentrated, and shoved. Bauer wouldn't budge. He stayed, firmly planted in Brand's thoughts. He couldn't stop thinking, couldn't stop hearing Georg, couldn't run without a guide through his dark place.

Yellow Dog!

He squeezed his eyes tight, calling the canine to him, imagining the golden retriever, his silky, wavy coat shining in the night. He fought to build the image the way he loved to see the creature.

Yellow, bright yellow, like molten gold. A spirit color. All spirits, all colors, like the rainbow, Yellow Dog the Mescalero had told him. The dog was more than yellow. He had a pink tongue that lolled in doggy laughter over sharp ivory teeth, coal black nose that he liked to put in the palm of Brand's hand, and eyes, warm, brown eyes.

Dog!

Brand had him, saw him. Yellow Dog tossed his head and whined uneasily. He barked once, low and demanding. *Follow.*

Brand could not move.

The dog came to him, whining, pressed against his leg, warm, real.

He dug his fingers into the coat, sensuous, alive. He roughed him up, both hands, massaging and stroking the dog's flanks. Yellow Dog threw his head back and licked his face, hot, wet kisses. Tail thumping he moved around and through Brand's arms, wiggling with joy.

Then he stopped. Pricked an ear. Looked off into the nothingness. Let out an anxious whuff.

Brand looked, too. Could see nothing.

Hackles rose on the back of Yellow Dog's neck. Brand rubbed his hand along them. The dog turned his head, poked his nose at him, went back to alert. He whined.

Nice doggy, Bauer said. He was a presence, unseen but felt, a force, an invisible being who lurked in the recesses.

But the dog saw him. Yellow Dog backed up against his knees. Brand put a hand on the dog's head. He rubbed an ear. *Go away, Bauer.*

The dog jerked free from under his hand, dragged out, nails scuffling. Brand grabbed for him, heard the dog yelp as the unseen tore him away.

Dangled Yellow Dog in front of him.

We know what happens now, don't we, kid?

The sinking feeling in the pit of his stomach. Bauer liked to carve things up. Yellow Dog could not save him this time, could not take him away, could not show him the way out of his own mind. He coiled into himself, rolled up like a ball, shoved his hands in his pockets. He did not want to see or hear or feel ever again.

He touched the amulet. Touched the bandanna with the peyote knotted into it in the other. Grasped each with a hand.

Heard Kamryn's voice. *You're tougher than you think you are.* She knew the dark side. He didn't believe what Rembrandt said about her, but even if there had been a kernel of truth in it, he knew there had to be a story he hadn't heard. What she'd said at the airport . . . could have been aimed at her as well as him. She knew the dark and bitter side of things.

Or not. Maybe he was Brand X, the stuff nobody wants.

Only I want me.

He wanted himself. He wanted to keep that spark burning. He had to be better than Bauer. He knew that! He might not be good, but he was better than that. He hadn't lost the colors of the spirit yet. He couldn't lose himself. He couldn't. There would be nothing left. He didn't want to explode and phzzt out like some arcade character.

That was the death that mattered, losing himself, his mind, to Susan Craig or Bauer or Rembrandt or the KillJoy. Or, like his mom and her dweebish husbands, to bills and mortgages and a relentless pursuit of some kind of mundane happiness.

He knew what mattered. Long hours in the psych ward had shown him the way as surely as Yellow Dog ever had. The schizophrenic, the catatonic, the psychotic, those locked behind the bars of Alzheimer's, the walking dead, those cut off from their minds as surely as the truly dead had shown him the truth.

Wherever Curtis had gone, he hadn't been there in that casket, KillJoy or no KillJoy. Not in that wooden box. Not among those satin pillows. Not trapped. Freed.

Not wrapped in a straitjacket, not kept in a rubber room, not tranquilized out of his mind. He was still here. Rembrandt himself had given him that recognition. He'd *survived*.

He had kept Bauer all these years, kept him at arm's length. He had done it and the realization of it filled him now. He *had* done it.

He was not Bauer. For all the imprinting and programming Susan Craig had fed him, he was not Bauer. Never would be, not unless he gave up.

Yellow Dog squirmed and yelped anxiously in midair, tossed in invisible, tormenting hands.

No! He screamed at Bauer. *Not again!*

The dog fell. He tucked tail and ran.

Brand alone with Bauer. He put up his hands, ready to defend himself, his self, all that he had in this world, all that he had been given, all that God seemed to have decreed he would be left with.

It's just you and me, sweet cheeks. Did I tell you how I like to do little boys?

They closed in the darkness.

Chapter 32

Rembrandt and Josey looked in on the boy. He slept, loose-limbed and slightly curled on his left side, his face smooth. The eyelid twitches signaling REM sleep were not visible. Nothing suggested that he was even still alive except for his light, rhythmic breathing.

"Damn."

"We've lost him."

"Probably." Rembrandt paced.

"It's not been twenty-four hours." If Meales had been restless the past night, Rembrandt had been relentless. The hollows of his face had sunken, the craters of his scarring sharp and savage, the eyes burning with a kind of manic fervor.

"Doesn't matter. Looks like he's completely disassociated. Classic brainwashing tells us to break them down, then build them up. He was a tough kid. He had an edge. It shouldn't have happened." Rembrandt took a deep breath, released it quickly, repeating, "Doesn't matter. I need bait, I still have it. As long as he's breathing, I can maneuver Christiansen into place. Get the Lear ready."

"Where?"

"New Orleans."

"Sir, there's no way I can get clearance for that! Yolanda is just off the coast. She'll be making landfall—" he checked his watch. "Less than eight hours after I get you in there."

"Just get me in there. Tell them I'm an advance member of FEMA. Set me down at Baton Rouge, if that's what it takes, and get me a ve-

hicle. Do it now!" Rembrandt pressed, as Meales hesitated. "Do you
want to be explaining to Bayliss?"

"No, sir."

"Then get me there. I'll find a way to do what I have to."

Meales saluted and left. Rembrandt watched him go, a hard glitter in his eyes.

Nothing would keep him and the boy from New Orleans.

Nothing.

It might even be easier if the boy were more dead than alive.

The rain in Louisiana was different from Texas, which was different from California, which was different from home. Kamryn sat at
the slightly greasy window of the small hotel room and watched the
waters pelting against it, knowing it was still hours before dawn. The
room was cheesy by any comparison and the neon lights of Baton
Rouge blinked on abandoned streets. She hugged her knees to her
chin. She wondered where Brand was in the night, where Rembrandt
had taken him, if he was even still alive. She wondered if she would
feel it if he weren't, like some kind of surrogate mother, then decided
that she probably would not, no matter what their connection. She
had never known when her own parents had gone. So much for psychic bonds.

She had to believe there was hope for Brand, that Mitch had been
right. Rembrandt had a use for him, therefore he would still be alive.

But what if Mitch were wrong?

She had come to rely on him, she realized, taciturn and unbend-
ing. Brand had been quicksilver, humor and dry wit, a teenage tum-
bleweed, moving here, prickling there. Mitch had always been there,
silent, unmoving, unruffled. He had driven Texas in the face of a
storm watch and never flinched. If she closed her eyes, she could almost see him, imagine him in his Marine dress blues, an icon. Semper fi. Had any motto ever fit a man better?

He was nearly the exact opposite of anyone she had ever known.
She had left the bed they'd been sharing, together but apart, because
the feeling of him next to her had unsettled her. She, who had told
him truly that sex with Darby had never been a matter of loving and
sharing, sensed that if she'd gone to him, laid her cheek on his chest,

listened to the steady beat of his heart, she might have discovered something new and wonderful.

She did not have time for that. Both Brand and Mitch were asking things of her she could not give. Not now. Perhaps not ever. Her presence with them endangered them. She ought not to be here, except that she had failed in saying good-bye.

Kamryn laid her head on the windowpane, the better to hear the rain, to feel the drive of it against the glass, to lull her to sleep. Whatever the morrow brought, she had to try to be ready for it.

A roll of thunder. An attempt of the rain to break through sodden clouds, to break the leaden oppression of a coming spring rain. Levin bolt and crash and drum, but no rain yet. She'd come home early from her friend's house, leaving a planned overnight, unhappy with the attitude of the girls she'd grown up with, who'd been her schoolmates, who now looked at her askance. Their heads, and their lives, were empty lies. She left them behind for what would be the last time, she told herself, a life that she would not be going back to.

The house stood on its forty acres, white sideboards with dark green trim, the laurel bush shading its eastern corner, the curving driveway filled with dad's truck, mom's car, her brother's car and now hers. All older and serviceable except for dad's new truck, his pride and joy. The moon had risen, a young, full moon, casting shadows across the drive.

The house had been dark and she wondered if they'd lost power again. Passing the Vanderowen home, she remembered their property had been dark also.

A hazard of living in the country.

She approached the open door. Came to a stop, looking at it, like a mouth, waiting to swallow.

Mom would never leave the door open. She did not like insects in the house, and in springtime the air was full of them, clouds of them, rising from new-plowed ground and freshly-bloomed flowers. Amelinda put a hand out. Touched the door framed in night.

Brought her hand away slick and sticky. She rubbed it dry on her hip.

"Sis!"

A flashlight beam caught her in the face, the light as powerful as a slap, and she took a step back. Beyond the circle of the beam's focus, she caught sight of Eric's face. He had tattooed himself anew, this time a swastika on the crown of his forehead, where the hairline, if he had left any, would meet it. He looked a little as if the inking had splattered, splotching him from head to toe.

"Sis! You're home early. Come down to the basement. I've got a surprise for you!"

He took her arm. He, the older, the stronger, the leader, the protector. He'd kept her safe from bullies on the playground, took her away when dad and mom screamed at each other about the bills, the lost pension when the unions had gone affirmative action; he who had first helped her realize why the world had gone bad, why they were angry, the lost majority. He who had gone in search of the truth, shared it with them all, eliciting Mom's silence and Father's grumbling agreement. He who had not been afraid to commit himself wholly to the movement.

Who stood there now, his iron grip on her arm, guiding her to the basement to show her—what?

She breathed hard in fear. He smelled of blood, oddly, and she could not understand why. Step by step, he took care to make sure she did not slip . . . *Why was the basement dark? Why were the steps treacherous, wet and slippery?*

"I have a surprise for you."

"A surprise."

"I did it.

"For you."

The last argument with her parents had sent her away for the night, but she'd come back early, finding the outside world even more condemning than home. They, at least, shared her burgeoning beliefs. They hated the way the world had gone wrong. They hated everything, even her, sometimes, but it was home.

Her feet touched the basement floor. Eric moved, and white light flooded the basement.

She blinked in amazement. There was no power outtage. The moment dazzled her.

Then she looked. And saw.

Crimson, not black, splattered Eric. Splashed against the basement wall. Led into the room built below. Lying in a pool of red, a white arm, very white, very pale, from elbow to fingers.

A severed arm.

She caught her breath to scream. She knew that arm, those work-worn fingers, that ancient thin-banded gold watch.

Eric drew her close, kept her from breathing, from screaming.

"Sis. I have a surprise for you."

He put the flashlight on the shelf, exchanging it for the bloody ax laid there. Walked her across the basement, stepped over the severed arm as if it did not exist.

She knew then the only truth that would matter to her. *She was going to die.* Then and there, at her brother's hand, just as their mother had.

"Wh—where's Dad?"

He held her very close, just as he used to when he was twelve and she eight, and they were trick or treating, and he had been pledged to keep her safe from cars and the night and bigger kids. He spoke softly into her ear, tickling the faint buzz of hair she had kept.

"He got mad," Eric said. "He found out what I did last week, and he got mad." Forlornly, "He never really understood the movement."

"Last week? When you went to Tucson?"

His fingers tightened and she could feel the excitement in them. "We derailed the Sunset Express. We did it. For the movement."

She had always understood that there would be things which had to be done, domestic terrorism, institutions which could be changed only by violence just as they themselves existed in violence, but this? Attacking Amtrak for no particular reason except to do it?

"Eric—"

He recoiled from her. Had heard it in her voice, or seen it in her eyes. Unacceptance. Rejection.

"Amelinda," he answered sadly. He raised the ax.

She began to pray then. It would not help, but it did not matter. It was her final refuge. She alone had put out the manger scene for Christmas, had left the house and trudged across the snow and blackfrost to the Vanderowens to catch a ride to church, to sing, to see the wonders at Christmas and Easter and any Sunday she could manage. She alone in the house had ever seemed to care about the soul and of all the souls in that house ensnared by Eric's philosophies, she had been the last to fall.

She asked to live. She asked for the chance to undo all that she had done, for in the end, all Eric's manifesto had come to was simply death and bedamning.

He raised the ax high, higher, as if knowing he would need a tremendous swing to cleave her head from her neck. Above him the bloody ax head raised. Raised until it touched the wires which hung above.

She asked for forgiveness and promised to repay it somehow.

Eric took a deep breath and stabbed the ax head backward, at the pinnacle of his swing. It bit deep into the wires and into the beam which held them. His blue eyes bulged. His tongue fell forward out of his mouth and his hands fastened convulsively about the ax handle, and his booted feet danced frantically on the damp basement floor.

An aura flashed outward, yellow and white and pale blue, flashed about her, separating her, keeping her from the electrocution. When it was over, Eric's hands slipped from the ax handle and he fell to the basement floor.

She groped across the workshop until she found the flashlight.

He breathed. He had not died, but she was free. She stumbled across his prostrate form, looked in the print shop which had been her father's pride and joy and saw the shambles there, the blood-washed walls and computers, copiers and printers, and what was left of her father in his coveralls.

She put her hand in her mouth to muffle her sobbing. She made her way to the laundry room where she saw the rest of her mother.

Eric groaned. She backed out of the laundry room and to the stairs. His body lay between her and the steps. He smelled of burned, singed hair and ozone, the bitter bit of a lightning-struck tree. The soles of his shoes were curled and smoking.

She stepped across him.

He put up a hand and caught her ankle.

Amelinda dropped the flashlight. It went bouncing down the steps. She fell on her stomach and tried to crawl up the steps, wet and sticky as they were, clawing at them, escaping.

He pulled her down a step. She kicked, heard her foot thud home, stood, and put her hands up. Felt along the beam, along the fried wiring, until she found the ax.

She ran her hands down its handle and prised it out of the beam.

Eric jerked her feet out from under her, his strength returning, fueled by pain and anger. He bellowed like a bull.

She remembered screaming, terrified and horrified. Raising the ax. Hitting him. Splitting open flesh and muscle and the arm which grabbed her went limp.

She screamed all the way upstairs and out into the yard. She screamed, thinly, the way a wounded deer in the sparse woods along the road screams when it's injured, frightened, but still alive. Her hands shook so she could barely get her car keys in the ignition. She drove out of control to the Vanderowens, the car sliding off the road and birm and into and out of the rainwater ditch, tires spinning.

She ran into their house, the front door thrown open, and stumbled to the wall, hands searching, blood-covered hands leaving prints searching frantically for the light switch.

Then she went from room to room, finding the family butchered there, including Claude Vanderowen, her brother's best friend, his skull freshly tattooed, now seeping a crimson pool into his mattress.

And she went to her car and sat, afraid. Looked at her clothes, splattered, and her shoes, and her car, and the tattoos upon her arms.

And, God forgive her, she ran screaming into the night to hide. When the rain finally came, it came heavy enough to wash her scent from the ground and groves, and flood out the small bridge leading to their road, and she was long gone.

But she was still screaming.

She woke, throat aching, her face wet. She put her hands to the cords of her neck and stroked them. They throbbed with a need that was almost sexual, the need to scream again, the need for release.

Kamryn uncurled. She crept across the room and knelt by Mitch's side of the bed. She put her hands upon his face.

He woke instantly. He put his hand on hers, and then stroked her face, and felt the dampness there.

"I need to tell you my name," she said. "I need to tell you who I am, and I need you to hold me and tell me it's all right anyway."

The tears came again as he reached for her and lifted her into the bed, cradling her next to his warm body, raising the sheet and tucking her along his flesh, and then holding her close.

"Tell me," he said softly.

So she did, haltingly, and never felt him pull away. Instead, he held her closer, comforting her, stroking her hair and temple. When she'd finished talking, he put her head upon his chest, and plied his fingers upon the nape of her neck, gently massaging her.

"Don't tell me it doesn't matter," she said slowly.

"I won't."

They were silent for a while, maybe twenty minutes, then Kamryn said, "Tell me what to do."

"I can't."

"I should go back."

"From what you tell me, they'll free your brother if you don't show up as a witness. If the grand jury is still looking for you, it means the evidence isn't strong enough without your statement."

"They'll never believe me."

"You don't know until you try." He ran his hand down her arm, captured her wrist. "These were only skin deep. The rest of the truth goes all the way to the heart."

"I'm afraid."

He tilted her face until she could peer up at him. The edge of dawn had crept into the room, lightening it so that she could see him, the warmth in his eyes. "Brand is right. You are beautiful."

She became aware that a tension lay in his muscled body, that his rib cage rose and fell with a growing intensity, that an awareness of his closeness caught her breath. "No."

"Yes." He kissed her brow, brushing her hair back from her face. With both hands, he raised her so that she lay upon his chest, her face to his, and he kissed her eyebrows and then her eyelids when she closed them as he drew near. The feel of his fingers gently untangling her hair, combing through, sent a shiver down her spine.

"Let me make love to you."

She shook her head. "Not because of what we're going to face today. Not because of that."

"No." His voice thickened. "Because I need you tomorrow, and the day after tomorrow. And now."

The power of his voice opened her eyes. "I can't promise you any-thing—"

"I didn't ask. I'm tired of being alone. I'd like to be together, with you." He kissed her, roughly, closing her mouth against protests, tongue caressing, then probing her lips. He kissed her until they were both breathless. He slid his hands down her back, inside her panties, cupped her buttocks, drawing her close to him until she could feel his urgent need.

He took his lips from hers. "Will you?"

She took the last of his clothes off, then hers, and lay back down beside him. She ran her hand over his thighs, his legs taut, then cupped his testicles and carefully lowered her mouth over his hard penis. She took him in her mouth, tasting him, feeling him respond, his skin like velvet, his cock rigid. He did not move though she could feel him quiver.

She stroked her tongue over him one last time, then moved in the bed again, next to him. He reached for her breast, gently, strong hands with incredible feathery touches that made her tremble until he put his mouth to her nipples. He teased her with his lips and teeth. It made her throb and she wanted him then, hard and full and fast, but Mitch murmured, "No. Not yet."

He held her and stroked her, kissed the hollow of her throat down the fullness of her breasts to the tiny indent of her navel until she cried for him. When he entered her, and she rocked with him, mov-ing to his movement, seeking pleasure with his seeking, it was like nothing she had ever felt before. It was not a crude thrusting until fulfillment, it was an embrace that touched all of her, intimately. He murmured loving words to her, even as he gasped when she came, and then he followed. They lay entwined in fragrant warmth, and when he left her, he got a towel and gently cleaned her, then took her in his arms, and held her until she dropped off to sleep, the light of the day on his face.

Then the beeper went off.

Chapter 33

The sky was gray, dark gray, and the rain pelted across the lake in wind-pounding sheets and gusts. Glimpses of its misty banks were revealed by breaks between trees, and bare-kneed cypresses, and brush. Driving against the beginning fury of the hurricane seemed to take forever. Kamryn checked her watch several times. "We told him two hours," she shouted over the howling of the wind and the drone of the engine. "We're never going to make it."

"He'll wait."

"How do you know? How did you even know he'd trade for Brand?"

Mitch steered as a limb trailing Spanish oak rolled off the highway. The Jeep's rear wheel caught part of it and bucked accordingly. "No secrets. Okay?"

"You won't do anything foolish."

"He doesn't want me. He wants something I've got. Giving it to him—that would be foolish. But he's got to think I'm going to give it to him."

The Jeep veered again. Mitch kept both hands firmly on the wheel. He downshifted.

"These winds are seventy miles an hour. They're going to double by the time Yolanda makes landfall, according to the radio."

He nodded. The road, except for whipping rain and debris, was nearly empty. No one going their way, a few going out. The radio had been warning that anyone not in an evacuation center already had better be prepared to sit tight and wait it out, that travel was becoming too dangerous.

Kamryn wrapped her hands in her seat belt, trying to combat the constant jostling. "You know he's going to kill us. In this weather, he can make almost anything look like an accident."

"I know he's going to try." Mitch shifted. The car's transmission downgraded obediently. "How good a shot are you?"

"In this wind? There's no telling. It's going to affect the bullets. Accuracy is nearly impossible."

"He'll have the same problem unless he's using something with rapid fire—if he is, he's going to be spraying a target anyway. If he's not . . ." Mitch shrugged. "I'll take whatever chances we can get."

"We only have the one revolver."

"With any luck, we won't even need that." Mitch squinted through the frantic wipers, then hit the brakes, squealing across the road, and came to a halt.

Despite the seat belt, Kamryn practically stood on her toes. She stared aghast out the windshield at what Mitch had avoided. A gator, its thick tail lashing back and forth, half walking, half wind-driven, crossed the highway. It must have measured a good ten feet from snout to tail tip. It moved belly first into the rain-filled ditch and disappeared through high brush on the other side of the road.

The aluminum signpost that marked Metairie, Lake Pontchartrain Causeway swayed back and forth dramatically, then uprooted and tumbled down the banks after the reptile.

"We're nearly there. Now I want you to stay in the Jeep. No matter what happens. Understand?"

She nodded.

"If we get separated, what are you going to do?"

"Try and find that woman Brand talked about. Mother Jubilation. Pirate's Alley, near Jackson Square, in the French Quarter," she recited.

"It'll be flooding. It's only a few blocks from the Mississippi."

She looked at him. "I'll get through—but what makes you think she stayed? She'd be crazy. The radio said that area would be ten, twelve feet under the tide."

"She's waiting for us. She'll be there."

The highway swung in a long, low curve and the woodlands gave way to flatlands, dotted with houses, then neighborhoods, the skyline of New Orleans and the football stadium with its golden dome barely recognizable under the gray skies and heavy rain.

The New Orleans P.D. had the road barricaded, their emergency vehicles across the lanes, their lights flashing. They wore heavy yellow rain slickers, marked with N.O.P.D. and under it stenciled, Emergency Management.

They flagged Mitch down. Even with their slickers and their plastic hooded hats, they were drenched. They shone a flashlight into the Jeep.

"Sir, we're turning back all traffic. You are advised to turn around on 10 and head for evacuation centers as indicated by hurricane markers."

"We need to get in."

The policeman shook his head at Mitch. "Sorry, sir, but we can't allow that."

Kamryn leaned over. "My mother called. She's blind. She can't get out on her own!"

"I'm sorry, ma'am. Hopefully one of our workers or one of her neighbors has stepped in to help. We're losing a levee and pumping station and it's only going to get worse. No one in. It's for your own safety." He had his hat tied on, but the wind caught the bill of it and it seemed for a moment that not even the tie would hold the hat on. He put up his hand.

"A work of art," said Mitch suddenly.

The policeman blinked. He shone the beam on first Mitch's face and then Kamryn's.

"All right, sir. You'll have to follow me in." He turned, said something to the three officers standing at the barricade, then went and got into one of the emergency vehicles blocking the roadway. He wheeled it out of formation and beckoned for them to follow.

"Son of a bitch." Mitch sucked on a tooth and aimed the Jeep after. "He's already got his men in place."

"How did he do it?"

"Who knows? With all the activity, it's possible they just stepped in and took over key positions. No one is going to have time to ask questions, check ID."

"How many do you suppose he has?"

"I couldn't guess. It's less ambitious, but more efficient if he only uses a handful or so. Harder to get caught. But he might have a whole damn army in here, patrolling the streets."

"Just for us?"

"Maybe. Maybe not. And maybe," Mitch watched the escort ahead closely, "he's planning something a little more."

"Like what?"

"He hasn't done anything, since the beginning, that I've expected. If he's with the government, he's with a part of the government that has its own agenda."

"CIA?"

"Something like that. Maybe even . . . private." They drove past the HOME OF THE NEW ORLEANS SAINTS, its parking lot bare, its golden dome dulled by ceaseless wind and rain.

"Why you?"

"I was part of a patrol on a covert mission. We were dropped in to Haiti. We were told that we were supposed to take in a money man, make contact with a local dignitary, and make an exchange."

"Bribery?"

"A trade-off. Yes. We were supposed to be smoothing the way for Aristide to stay in control. We brought in someone, all right, an agent named Stark. He had to have been Special Forces. The dignitary turned out to be a local voodoo priest, someone very powerful—"

"Voodoo? You're kidding me."

"Not now." The Jeep fought him, water in the streets spraying off its wheels, the escort in front of them churning through and leaving a wake. The streets had begun to hold water, their surfaces dark and slick, mirroring the buildings. "I didn't believe it either, then. Stark was picking up some kind of drug the priest had made, and he was dropping off test subjects—us—for a project. Only, things went wrong. One of my men had a bad feeling. We shot our way out. I lost several of the patrol and Stark. We left the money behind. Got the drugs."

"Heroin?"

"No. I don't know what it is. Brown—my corporal who made it back and then committed suicide—he told me it was zombie powder."

"What?"

"This stuff must be real. Men like Stark aren't sent in on a whim.

Chances are it's some sort of psychoactive drug that brainwashes extremely effectively. I don't think it creates the undead, but it's possible it does something equally terrible to the living. I saw that man's disciples. They were blind in their devotion to him."

"But why? Why would you want such a thing?"

"I don't know. I don't want to know. But you can bet Rembrandt and whoever pulls his strings have a truckload of plans. They've been on my heels since April."

"The others?"

The escort emergency vehicle signaled right. Mitch prepared to pull over behind it. They were the only ones in the Coach Royale parking lot. Canal Street ran straight down to the Mississippi where it was lost in the rain and tide.

"I'm the only one left. And they're right. I do have it. I'm going to trade it for Brand."

"And you have it stashed somewhere in New Orleans."

"Indeed I do. My corporal came from here. I brought his body back. And when I stood watch over his casket, I saw things I still don't believe. Some of them were supernatural, some of them initiated by Rembrandt. I couldn't tell you which scared me the most." He put the Jeep in park, left the engine idling.

She studied him, realization in her expression. "All this time, it's been you. You, not Brand."

"I don't know. I've never seen the KillJoy and I don't know why Mother called Brand. But I do know that you're right—it's my fight. That's why I came."

A man came to the glass lobby doors and looked out, nonchalant, one hand in pants pocket, suit impeccable, brilliantly-colored tie a slash that stood out against the gray, constant rain.

"There he is," Kamryn said. She undid her seat belt, ready to slide into the driver's seat.

"Across the street is the French Quarter. Her shop has to be only blocks away. Drive it if you can. If you can't—"

"I'll do whatever it takes."

He nodded. Started to open the door, then hesitated.

Kamryn smiled slightly, bent over, and brushed his cheek with her lips.

Mitch grinned then, and got out of the car.

* * *

If I, if we, get out of this alive, I'll go back. I swear, Kamryn thought. She'd go back and do whatever she could to put her brother away, even if it meant exposing her father's involvement in the intelligence network of the Brotherhood. Even if it meant she could not prove herself innocent, for she had been part of the family, and she had not been, totally. Eric had thought their father only shallowly linked to the organization, despite the small print shop in the basement, despite everything. Kamryn knew better. Newspaper reports about the murders had speculated that it was all Eric and her and when her parents had discovered it, they'd turned on them and murdered them.

Kamryn did not know why Eric had done what he'd done. Knowing now what she didn't know then, she suspected that the movement had attracted Eric not because of its philosophies but because of its violence. And that had led to a downward spiral for her brother. When she saw him again, face-to-face, if they let her, she would ask. *Why?* Maybe she would get an answer.

And if she did not? Kamryn stared through the downpour, watching Mitch slowly put up his hands, approaching the elegant French-styled hotel. Then, perhaps, there was always the future. That would have to be good enough. It was all any of them ever got, after all.

For now, her future was measured in minutes, perhaps even less. She watched as Rembrandt came outside, shadowed by a N.O.P.D.-marked figure who shaded him with a black umbrella. The umbrella immediately turned inside out and shredded as Rembrandt stood. He had Brand with him, and motioned Mitch to take the boy.

Something was wrong with Brand. Drunk or drugged, he seemed limp as a rag doll. Rembrandt and Mitch exchanged angry words. She had no hope of hearing them through the wind, but she could see the look on Mitch's face. Then, the four of them got into the emergency vehicle, the N.O.P.D. officer driving.

She eased the Jeep forward to follow.

They crossed Canal Street and went into the French Quarter, that famous section of New Orleans, narrow streets, two-storied buildings with their balconies wrapped by wrought iron. There were peep shows and blues bars and art galleries and souvenir shops. Water already flowed through the cobblestones and brick, splashing over the curb and washing back. It would not be long before the tide from the gulf and the river would be licking at the sandbagged doorfronts.

The emergency vehicle took them through the French Quarter and into streets less famous, less traveled, more dilapidated. They were traveling, she realized, back toward Metairie.

They stopped on a street with a church/mortuary and churchyard, bordering an old cemetery. She could see the whitewashed above-ground graves called ovens, and the mausoleums, with their stone cherubs and angels overlooking the burial sites. Spanish oaks buckled the sidewalk, and magnolias shuddered in the wind. Whatever resistance might have been met at the locked doors of the mortuary were overcome as the dark oak-stained doors swung open. She got out of the Jeep, put her gun in her waistband at the small of her back, and followed the four of them inside Shepherd's. The rain was, as it had been all day, in a deluge, warm heavy drops without end. The air felt hot and steamy.

Rembrandt noted Kamryn's arrival with a slight bow. "I wondered when the lady would join us."

Kamryn's attention riveted on Brand. The boy stood pale, listless, as if he could barely hold himself upright, his eyes blank and unfocused. "What have you done to him?"

"Nothing, dear girl. It's congenital, I fear. Events have conspired to collapse his mind. But I will still give him to you when I get what I want. Perhaps treatment will bring him out of it. Perhaps not. Nothing in life is certain." To the officer shadowing him, he added. "Watch her. She usually carries a gun. I have not had the occasion to watch her use it, but experience suggests that she can."

"Yes, sir." A young, stoic face watched her carefully.

Mitch had been helping to keep Brand upright. He set him down on a settee.

He faced Rembrandt. "I get what you want, and the three of us walk out of here."

"Correct." The ruined man smiled, the crags and pits on his face shifting with his expression. "You are free to go."

Without warning, Mitch swung on the N.O.P.D. officer. Three brutal chops of the hand, and the young man fell with a groan. Mitch shoved him under the settee with his foot.

Rembrandt had not moved, smile frozen in place.

"Just to even the odds a bit," Mitch said.

Rembrandt inclined his head.

Mitch looked at Kamryn. "It's in the chapel. I'll be right back."

She put a hand to her gun and drew it out carefully. Rembrandt waved both hands at her amiably. "You have nothing to fear from me."

She knew better. ·

The chapel's swinging doors swung back and Mitch emerged, carrying an urn, Uncle Godfrey inscribed on its side.

Rembrandt looked at him. "Show me," he said.

Mitch worked at the lid, pulled it off, reached in and extracted a string of packets, six in all, filled with ivory powder. He dropped them back in the urn and replaced the lid.

The various doors of the mortuary began to tremble in their thresholds, wood clattering. Startled, Mitch looked up and then around. The chapel doors started swinging to and fro under their own volition. The heavily polished floors started to creak. A chill permeated the building.

Rembrandt continued to smile, his expression expanding until it became grotesque. He reached for the urn, his back to the chapel.

Mitch grabbed Brand, hauling him onto his feet as if he were weightless. "Get out of here, Kamryn. *Now!*"

"What is it?"

"I don't know."

Rembrandt ducked over suddenly, reached into the downed officer's slicker and pulled out an automatic rifle, cocking it as he came up. He tilted his head, looking at Kamryn.

"Give me the urn and put the gun down."

Around them, the building moaned and wood creaked and walls swayed. Kamryn glanced to the side. Had the hurricane hit already?

"Do it!" Rembrandt snapped.

She looked at Mitch and Brand in dismay. The barrel of the rifle swung over to them, targeting them.

"Do it now."

He had his back squarely to the chapel. She saw a flash of motion through the tiny, stained-glass window. She gripped the gun tighter and said, "Let them get out of the building first."

"No!"

The doors burst open, catching Rembrandt in the spine. The rifle jerked upward, let out a burst of fire. Plaster rained on them and the building suddenly quieted. Mitch leaped and grabbed the rifle. He caught Rembrandt and clipped him in the jaw with the butt of the weapon. Rembrandt staggered back. Mitch slugged him again. The ruined man went down.

A black woman stood in the open chapel doors. She shook her head. "He does not learn, does he?"

"Was it you this time?" Mitch leaned over Rembrandt, patting him down for more weapons. He found a 9mm in his inner coat pocket, emptied the clip, and dropped it. The N.O.P.D. officer groaned.

"Yes, it was I. But we must get out of here quickly before the hurricane does more than make an old building rattle." The woman leaned over Brand. She spread her hand and touched her fingers to his forehead. "Wake up, child. You are here. You have found me."

Mitch had taken Rembrandt's belt and was busy securing his ankles. "Kamryn, this is Mother. Mother, this is Kamryn."

She looked over her shoulder. "A pleasure, child." She wore a swirl of yellow and red and blue, a many-pocketed apron over her dress. She dipped her free hand into a pocket and pulled out a small, stoppered vial. She shook it, then pulled out the cork and waved it under Brand's nose.

The boy jerked and gasped. His eyes fluttered open. They batted once or twice before he coughed and a blush flooded his face.

"Get up," Mother coaxed. "We're not done yet!"

Brand saw Mitch taking in the last notch on the belt around Rembrandt. "Don't touch him!"

Mitch straightened.

"He's the KillJoy!" Brand stood, staggered a step as if his legs had gone to sleep, and reached out to hold onto Mother for safety. "Get away from him, Mitch! He's carrying the KillJoy!"

Mother said, "This way, and quickly." She did not wait. Half carrying Brand, she turned and went out through the chapel.

Mitch grabbed up the urn and Kamryn left with him as Rembrandt began to moan loudly, and his heels started thumping on the floor.

They ran past the churchyard. Gravemarkers began to shake in the ground. They started to topple. The ground churned. Over it all, Yolanda howled and poured.

"What's happening?" Mitch called to Mother Jubilation.

She shook her head, braids flying. "I don't know. We can't fight him here. We let him in, he can stand on this ground."

Beyond the cemetery wall, an oven burst open, its plaster crumbling. Kamryn caught a glimpse of something stirring inside, something rotten and determined to emerge. She screamed and ran after the others.

Mother opened the doors to a battered station wagon.

"What about the Jeep?"

"The front is watched."

"Rembrandt had us followed," Mitch said to Kamryn. He climbed in, helped Mother slide Brand in. All doors slammed shut and she started the vehicle.

Kamryn turned for a last look. It smacked the glass at her face, half-flesh, half-skull, grinning in at her, as the car jolted into motion. She screamed. The corpse left a gory smear as it slipped down the window.

Mother pulled away with a screech of tires as the wrought-iron fencing went down about the churchyard. Graves collapsed into the ground and rotting limbs bubbled up.

She took them through side streets, careening through a rising tide of water and debris, back into the French Quarter. They left the station wagon in a torrential gutter and waded toward a storefront where the storm surge had begun to batter the sandbags. She opened the candy store's door and helped Brand over the barricade. Mitch swung Kamryn over, handing her the urn.

They paused, clothes sodden and dripping, in the center of the candy store while Mother locked the door and barred it, moving a huge sheet of plywood into place over the glass.

"Somehow," Mitch said, "this isn't the way I imagined your shop."

Mother laughed, a warm, booming sound. "I practice my voodoo in the back," she said, and came up, patting Brand on the cheek.

Brand did not look comforted. "He's coming. I can feel him."

"It does not matter," Mother told him. "I'm ready for him, child." She crossed the shop, opened another door, and held back beaded curtains. They crowded past her. The electricity flickered, then went out. Mother looked up as the howling wind grew louder.

A match flared. "Never mind it," the wielder said. "I will light candles."

They stopped and stared at the man sitting at the end of the room, his dark face shadowed by the candlelight, another man standing at his elbow.

Mitch lost all color as he stared at the second man who stood motionless as a statue.

"Stark." Mitch got out.

"And it is I, Delacroix."

Chapter 34

"You were left for dead."

"You should have made sure." Stark braced himself.

"If I'd known then what I know now, I'd have killed you myself." Mitch bit off his words angrily. "We're the only ones left, you and I."

"Soon it will be only me."

Mother's nostrils flared as she pushed her way to the fore of the group, bristling with outrage, the whites of her eyes gleaming. "How did you get in here?"

Delacroix inclined his head. He pointed a slender hand at Stark. "My man here has abilities in a great many things." His voice remained calm, lilting, but there was steel in it. He looked at Mitch and the urn. "I believe you have something that belongs to me."

Mitch hugged the urn tighter. "The world doesn't need a perfect soldier. It doesn't need a perfect war! I lost my patrol for this. My men, my *friends,* paid for it with their blood, and if you want it, you'll have to get it over my dead body."

Stark moved, peeling his lips away from his teeth in an uneven, fierce grin. Delacroix put a hand on his sleeve, staying him a moment. He narrowed his gaze on Mitch. "By Damballah and Aido Wido and other names which I shall not utter here, I made it. It is sacred to them."

Mother shook with the intensity of her retort. "The Bon Dieu holds nothing sacred that makes slaves of men!"

They looked into each other's faces, the woman and the man. Delacroix spoke softly.

"You have come a long way, woman. You have left many sacred ways behind. You are neither one nor the other—how can you think to stop me?"

Delacroix got to his feet. "The loa answers to me. He will take that which is mine, and my vengeance, whether you wish it or not. I cursed the Americans who came to my island and treated me with bad faith. I cursed those who gave the orders to do so. And, finally, I cursed the man who planned all of this. Give me the powder, and I will release him back to his place. He will bother you no more. Only I can do this."

Brand rubbed at his eyes and then put his chin up defiantly. "No way. You'll use it again. I can see it—it's written all over you. You don't have the KillJoy in you now, but it came from you. I can see it!"

Delacroix twitched a couple of fingers, as if flinging something into the air. Stark responded, lunging at Mitch from across the room. They fell on the table, crashing through it. They hit the floor and the whole building shook. An unearthly noise howled down and Mother looked up to the ceiling. Stark and Mitch thrashed, flesh thudding, while Kamryn let out cries of despair, but over it all, Mother heard the sound of something greater and more fearsome. She grabbed for Brand, anchoring him. The wood and bricks and beams of the building groaned, then screamed. Brand struggled a second in Mothers' arms, his ears filling with pressure, and then, with a *Boom!*, the roof exploded from above, disintegrating into splinters and shingles that flew into the hurricane. Kamryn shielded her face and ducked away from the destruction.

Rain poured in, funneled off neighboring eaves. It drenched Delacroix as Mitch threw Stark off him and rose into a crouch, hands and feet ready. Delacroix hissed something in French to Stark and pulled a long knife from his sleeve.

Kamryn drew her gun and fired, three quick shots, without thinking. Crimson splotched the ivory linen suit. Delacroix staggered back to the wall, and sagged. He coughed. Pink foam flew out, stained his lips, and dribbled down the front of the suit. She stood in shock, wind-blasted and rain-drenched. "God. What have I done?"

Mitch held out his hand to her. "Kamryn. Give me the gun."

"No." She looked back at Delacroix, his rich brown face growing paler before her very eyes.

"What indeed?" he said weakly and wheezed, more pink spattering his chin. "Now the loa has no master." His eyelids flickered and his eyeballs rolled whitely back into their sockets. The last breath gurgled out of him.

Brand struggled in Mother's arms, gasping, choking. "It's not true!"

The back door blew open. Kamryn jumped, startled, the barrel of the gun wavering. Stark shoved Mitch aside and leaped for it, disappearing into the storm. Curtains of wind and rain hid him immediately.

"Let him go."

Mitch paused in the threshold. "My men—"

"Let him go. If he belonged to Delacroix, he is dead already." Mother took a deep breath. "Now comes the worse of it."

"Worse?" Kamryn stared at Delacroix's body. Her hand shook. Mitch took the gun from her and put his arm around her.

"The loa," Mother said. "The KillJoy. We must destroy that which cannot be destroyed." She rummaged through the ruins of her shop, picking up items. She sifted through them with quick, brown fingers, filling her apron pockets. "Come with me. Hurry."

The streets ran with water like rivers around their knees. They held onto one another, forging step by step through the Quarter. Yolanda descended on them with all her fury. Signs swung on their iron holders and then twisted away, flung up into the gray and disappearing on the wind. Trees groaned, then slowly toppled, their roots jutting into the air, ripping up walkways and curbs. Lesser trees shattered into long, deadly spears.

She led them to Jackson Square, nearer the storm surge. Waves broke onto the park as if it were the shoreline, waves from the Mississippi, churned up destructively. Jackson, riding his bronze horse, looked as if he forded a raging river.

"There!" Mother pointed at the white beauty of a building, rising out of the flooded parkway and gray hurricane mists, St. Catherine's. Sandbags bulged against the water. Mother helped them climb onto the homemade levee braced against the wide double doors. She laid her palms on the locks and spoke a few words.

After a moment, the brightly polished lock plate and knobs moved and clicked open. Mitch handed Kamryn down into the cathedral's interior, Mother after her, and Brand last, then jumped down into the cathedral, his boots ringing on the floor. Together, they put shoulders to the door and sealed it behind them once again. The banshee wind shrieked in disappointment.

Kamryn shuddered. She pushed her wet hair from her eyes. She tried a smile at Brand.

He looked solemnly back. Then he reached into his pocket and withdrew something. She saw a silver and turquoise amulet on a black cord, nearly a twin to the one Mitch wore.

Brand held it out. "I got it for you. I want you to wear it."

"After all we've been through. After I lost you at the airport?"

He extended it further.

Touched, she took it from him and put it around her neck.

Mother clucked. "Children, we must hurry." She lifted her rain-cleansed brown face to the crucifix over the altar. "The choir loft. When the flood breaks in, we should still be above water."

Chairs had been removed from part of the loft. They sat on soft red carpeting. Mother spread out her many-colored skirts as she knelt and began to light thick, heavy based candles of white and red.

"It comes," she said. "And it must be fought, but we won't win by the flesh."

"What do you mean?"

She looked at Mitch. "The loa is a spirit. It influences the physical world, but its mortality lies in the world of souls. That is how we must face it."

Mitch shook his head. "Not good enough, Mother. Rembrandt will kill us first. You're not going to have time to go looking for some demon soul."

"There is more than one way to fight a war."

Mitch looked keenly at Mother. "I only know what I know. This is my fight. I want the rest of you out of here." He broke away, stood up.

Kamryn put up her hand. "You can't ask him to do that."

"I have not asked. He has volunteered."

Brand looked from Mother to Mitch and back again. "How will you do it?"

"I will send his soul on a journey. Even without fighting the loa, it will be treacherous." Mother reached into her apron and took out a small kit. She opened it. Inside lay a syringe and a packet.

"Heroin," said Mitch, looking at it.

"You use it?"

"No. But on the street . . ." his voice faltered.

"This is not a street drug. It has not been cut. It is pure."

"Jesus. You've been carrying that around in an apron?" He shook his head, disbelieving.

"White boy," she admonished. "Who would steal it from me?"

He did not answer, looked down, could not meet her eyes.

"I chose the cathedral. It should hold the flesh back while the loa hesitates to cross this threshold."

"But if it doesn't," Brand persisted. "What happens then? Mitch will be unconscious, right?"

"Mitch will be dying," Mother corrected. "On the verge between one world and the next."

"Who keeps Rembrandt away from us?"

"I do," Kamryn said grimly.

"Bullets won't stop him."

Brand went to the balcony wall and looked over. The great building groaned under the force of the wind. The noise seemed incredible. Water began to dribble in through the cathedral doors, along the flooring and the carpeting, a steady red-brown stream that looked almost as if the building bled.

Mother took a spoon from her pocket, and foil, and laid the syringe out. "Will you do it?" she asked, as she began to prepare the dosage. "They sometimes call it chasing the dragon. But you know the dragon is real."

Mitch swallowed tightly. "Do I have a choice?"

Brand could not watch. He could see the shining that was Mother, the darkness which fractured Mitch, and the dark clouds which surrounded Kamryn. He did not want to see more.

He did not remember how Rembrandt had brought him to New Orleans or how Kamryn, Mitch, and Mother had found him. He only knew he was here.

And so was the KillJoy.

Mother said to him, "What is it, child?"

He knew, as if he could see through the mahogany of the doors. "It's Rembrandt. He's trying to come in." The front doors boomed. A panel bulged, but held. A human yodeling howl pierced that of the wind. Rembrandt, screaming threats and venting his frustration.

"He'll find a way in," said Kamryn, her voice trembling.

"Sooner or later," Mother agreed. She rolled up Mitch's sleeve, and tied the arm with a band. Mitch looked at the needle as Brand stared at Mitch. "What if he doesn't find his guide? What if he doesn't win?"

Mother looked at him, her brown eyes mild and full of wisdom. "Then, child, we die here. And later, many others."

Brand closed his eyes tightly, shutting himself in with the darkness. And Bauer. And he could feel the edge of the KillJoy now, like a dagger, slicing into his mind. His thoughts. He shoved a hand into his jeans and withdrew the bandanna. He peeled it open. It was wet, but deep within its knots, the peyote button had stayed dry and knobby. He turned and looked at Mitch, shining silver bright, with only a fractal of darkness down him. He did not look at death—he looked at souls. Mitch would not understand the darkness. He would be lost. But Brand had a guide. The golden retriever waited for him.

The KillJoy waited for him.

"Mitch. Don't do it. It's me. I'm the one."

Mother looked at him. "Child," she responded softly, needle in hand. Then she paused. Considering.

"It has to be me," he said pointedly to her.

Mitch looked him in the eyes. "You fight your way and I'll fight mine."

"Exactly. But I have to be alone," he said, remembering Yellow Dog's voice and advice, the Apache wisdom given him. "And I won't use that. Deal?"

Before Mitch could answer, the cathedral doors exploded. Smoke and ashes filled the air, and Rembrandt vaulted in through them, and stood, water swirling about his legs, his eyes glittering as he found the four of them, illuminated by candlelight in the choir loft. He held a searchlight in one hand.

"Well, now, sonny. Where have you led me?" He picked out Brand's face. "Give me what I came for, and we can all forget this happened. This is wild weather. We can hide a lot of unfortunate incidents."

Mitch pushed the syringe away carefully and undid the elastic band with a snap. "Kamryn, take Brand and get him away from here." He took a candle and went halfway down the loft staircase.

Kamryn pulled Brand close to her, her hands gripping his shoulders tightly. Mother stayed on her knees. She began to take twists of herbs and branches out of her pockets, muttering under her breath, laying out patterns. "Take the boy," she said. "We'll hold him as long as we can."

Rembrandt laughed, an eerie sound, that rose and fell like the hurricane's voice, piercing throughout the cathedral. "I have the area cordoned off. You can't get out of here unless I give the signal. I've planned too hard and too long to let this—" he stopped, shuddered, contorted, grimaced.

Brand watched, horrified, as black flame gouted from his streaming eyes, and Rembrandt hunched in desperation, fighting that other which drove him. He let out a roar which was more animal than human, and clawed at his jacket, his shirt, ripping them open as if the loa would burst forth.

Then, suddenly, silence. Rembrandt took a deep shuddering breath. He looked up. He had dropped the searchlight. It swirled away, bobbing up and down in the floodwaters seeping along the cathedral pews. The ruined man stared back into the loft where he knew his quarry stood, watching him.

"I've planned too long to let this slip away," he finished hoarsely. "Come to me, son, and bring me that powder."

Brand could feel himself aching to respond, those long hours closeted away, programmed, working inside him. He shuffled a foot forward, then dragged himself to a halt. "No."

"Now, boy. Just who do you trust here? Surely not him." Rembrandt looked scathingly at Mitch. "Who lied to you across country? Did he ever tell you just who he was? That he was responsible for leading an entire patrol into death?"

"You gave those orders," Mitch said.

Rembrandt laughed without humor. "And I'll give them again, if I get the chance. But I know what I'm fighting for. Do you? And what about that pretty girl at your back, Brandon? I told you about her before." He turned his scarred and pitted face up toward the balcony, drawing closer.

"She took an ax and split her father's skull like a cord of wood. Imagine that. Then she turned around and did it to her mother, just like Lizzie Borden."

Brand could feel Kamryn's hand grow cold, could feel it right through his rain-soaked shirt. "Don't listen to him," she said, her voice quavering.

He found it hard to breathe. Harder to think.

"Women!" Rembrandt cried. "You can't trust any of them. Your mother. Is she looking for you? Seen any pictures of yourself on TV lately, Brandon? Think maybe she just gave a sigh of relief and hoped you killed yourself somewhere so that, finally, she wouldn't have to worry about you anymore. Could get on with her life? And what about the good doctor? Lies, liars, all. All of 'em, son. All liars but me. With me, you know what you're gonna get."

He held out his hand to the balcony.

"She didn't do it!" Words burst out of him, gusts of air, exhalations emptying him so that he could breathe in new air, fresh air.

Rembrandt withdrew his hand. "Trust her, do you? And what about her? Should she trust you? Does she know what goes on in your mind? Does she know what that psychologist buried in your boyish thoughts? The rapist and mutilator that looks out of your eyes? He like to watch you, girl?"

Kamryn made a muffled sound behind him. Brand could feel her shift away from him.

Mitch had descended another few steps closer. He pulled the string of packets out of his shirt, and held the candle close under them. The dampened packets took fire fitfully, hissed as they smoldered. "Forget them, Rembrandt. Your fight is with me." He threw the candles and packets onto the altar platform. The clothes draped over the benches caught with a yellow flame that filled the cathedral with light.

Rembrandt charged with a roar.

Mother turned on her heel, pushing at Kamryn and Brand. "Run! Now!"

Her touch seemed to break the bonds which had frozen Brand to the balcony. He sprinted across the loft to the door in the rear. A stumble or two behind, Kamryn followed.

He clawed at the knob. The door swung up, into darkness, and then Kamryn held up another of Mother's candles. Its light fell upon a hallway. "Go, go, go, go!" she cried softly.

He ran. He raced down a labyrinth of alcoves and rooms and then into a twisting corner where he narrowly missed a last niche. He forced himself past the door and Kamryn followed after. She held up the candle. Organ pipes filled the room. It was immense, and he thought of Christmas music, and the sound the cathedral must give out. She shut the door and locked it, and pulled chairs and equipment in front of it to brace it. She pulled her gun out of her waistband. The syringe rattled in her shirt pocket.

They looked at one another. Brand swallowed. "I'm not like that. Not really."

She set the candle stump on a speaker. Then she faced him, and rubbed her arms. "We're all like that, Brand. Sometimes. Filled with hate. But we have to try to be better." She touched the symbol at her throat, the charm he'd given her. "But you know that, don't you?"

He nodded.

"Do whatever you have to do. He has to get through Mitch first. Then Mother. Then me."

He nodded again and lay down. The storm raged over them. He could hear the building creak around them. Smell a faint scent of smoke and ash. They didn't have long.

He picked off a piece of the button, scraping and twisting it away with a broken fingernail, and put the rest back in the bandanna. He chewed it swiftly. There should be calm and quiet, but he could not help that.

Suddenly, the sky went quiet.

Brand blinked.

Then, he understood. The eye of the hurricane was passing. For a few moments, all was still. He closed his eyes.

To pass through, he had to know himself. He did. He knew himself, and he knew Bauer, who was part of himself, like it or not. He stepped onto a rainbow bridge and waited for the golden retriever.

The dog came, whining and unsure. Brand went to one knee and called him. He wrapped his arms around his ruff, and hugged the creature. As he did, he touched something. He looked closely. Yellow Dog wore a collar, though he never had before. A tag hung from it. "Cody," Brand read.

The dog looked up. Licked his fingers, pulling the tag away from him.

The dog had belonged to someone. Someone else had named him. "Cody," Brand repeated. Yellow Dog went down and rolled at his feet.

"Help me find the KillJoy."

Cody got up, shook, and pressed against his knees. Brand laid his hand on the dog's head. "Help me."

The dog stepped forward.

He did not know what to expect. A spirit walk, Yellow Dog had called it. You must know and expect to go in search of yourself.

An extension of what he'd already gone through at Rembrandt's hands.

Come here, sweet cheeks. I've been waiting for you.

No.

Are we going to kill someone? It's been a long time, too long.

No .

Killing the KillJoy is the only thing we can do.

No. It's the only thing you can do. I am not you. You are part of me, but I Am Not You.

It grew very cold.

Cody whined in distress and his doggish form became insubstantial. Brand held him a last time.

Go. I don't need you anymore. You're free. You have guided me to where I need to be.

The dog looked into his eyes. Brand smiled. There was nothing of darkness in those beautiful dog eyes. Absolutely nothing.

Go on, he urged, pushing Cody away. He turned his face and saw an opening in the darkness. It grew larger and larger. He pointed Cody toward it. Go on!

The dog bounded into the tunnel. He stopped, turned about, tail wagging hesitantly. He glowed as golden as the sun.

Go on! I can do this without you. I—I love you, old dog! Now go on!

Cody let out a joyous bark, and turned, racing down the tunnel. It swallowed him.

Darkness.

He stood alone.

It's just you and me, kid.

No. It's just me. You're only a part of me.

Brand took a step forward. The nebulous nothing about him swirled, grew colder. The KillJoy was very, very near.

You go for it, and I go for you, kid. You can't take us both on. Do it the easy way. Bring me in. Put me in charge.

No.

The darkness burst open with color, and in its midst stood a thing which devoured, a black hole, waiting for him. It stood over a shining light which he knew must be Mitch.

Mitch who had tried his best, and was now about to be eaten.

"It's me you want," Brand said softly, stepping forward. "Really."

Rembrandt broke through the doors. He got to his feet with a growl that had nothing human in it and looked up, as if scenting them by their warmth and their blood. Kamryn stood, sighting down her revolver.

"Stop right there, Rembrandt."

The ruined man took a step forward. Kamryn fired. It knocked him down. He got up so fast, she had trouble targeting him again.

"Don't do it!"

His eyes flashed. The suit jacket flew open, and she could see the hole she'd put in him. He was battered and bruised and torn and rent . . . and she tried not to think of Mitch, of Mother . . of how he'd gotten this far. Not he. It.

Inky fog began to roll out of it.

"Dear God." And then Kamryn knew she was seeing the KillJoy.

She fired her remaining rounds. Rembrandt dropped.

Behind him, in the backstairs of the cathedral, she could smell smoke clearly. Kamryn shuddered. The gun fell from her hands. She grabbed Brand's shoulders and dragged him out of the pipe room, his heels scuffing across the floor, his body totally limp. Her shoulders ached as she kicked the door shut between them and . . . *it*. She took a deep breath. She had to do this. She kept pulling Brand down the hallway.

Something let out a gargling howl.

She hadn't killed it.

"Oh, God. Oh, God, oh, God. Hurry!"

She could hear it shambling after her in the shadows. Crawling, dragging.

A dense, dark mist began to roll up the corridor and coalesce by the stairwell. Kamryn kicked open the door behind her, finding renewed strength. She put her hand to her shirt pocket.

What was left of Rembrandt reared on its hind legs and charged after them. She struck with the hypodermic, plunging it into his neck, all that heroin. Pure, unadulterated.

She prayed.

Brand stared into the nothingness of the loa and knew it would consume him. It had no color. The colors of life, of the spirit, Yellow Dog had talked to him about. As if nothing of life and its colors were in themselves good or bad.

Only the nothingness, the evil, the spiritless.

He threw back his hands.

Come and get me. You can't do it. I won't give it to you, all the colors that make me up. The good and the bad. They're me. They're MINE. I won't die for you!

The loa took him.

Kamryn fell over Brand's still body, tumbled down hard. Her vision flooded with tears. She grasped him, twisted his limp form away from the lump of flesh that had been Rembrandt. His ruined face bled darkness.

Kamryn got him up, somehow. Half over her shoulder, half in a fireman's carry, she dragged Brand down the hallway. She fell through the choir loft door, choking, the air a smoldering gray. Rain from a roof giving way to the storm had put the fire out. Mother reached up to help her. Blood glistened on her battered face, but her expression shone.

The two women struggled to get Brand down into the balcony. The fog pursued them, rushed them, then, suddenly, vanished.

Mother smiled widely. "Oh, child. He's done it."

Mitch lay across the top of the stairs. Kamryn left Brand in Mother's arms and ran to him, swollen with what she felt and had never been able to say.

Mitch groaned. She knelt by him and helped him sit up. He held his head. She kissed his face, all over, until he asked her to stop.

"It hurts."

She kissed him again. "This hurts?"

"Yes." Mitch gave a crooked smile. "But it probably won't tomorrow. If we have a tomorrow."

Solemnly, Mother took Brand's still body in her arms. She began to sing to him.

Mitch absorbed that in silence.

Mother stopped singing. She let out a little sob from deep in her throat and shook her head.

Kamryn cried, "Brand!"

Mitch crawled to Brand's body and dropped his fist, like a hammer, onto the rib cage. "Come on, Brand! You get to ride shotgun!" He leaned over and started pumping.

Kamryn knelt over Brand's face. She looked at Mitch, then leaned down and began resuscitation.

Curtis waited for him, with that slaphappy grin on his face, and a bright tunnel at his back. Yellow Dog let out a woof, beckoning Brand onward. He was halfway after Cody and his best friend when he heard the call. He turned slowly. He hesitated, and with that hesitation, he knew he would have to go back.

He didn't mind, he guessed. He looked down the tunnel one last time.

Curtis yelled, *Be seeing you later, X-man!*

Cody let out a farewell bark.

Brand nodded.

He went back.

His chest hurt. He blinked and groaned, then coughed and said. "I'm going to hurl."

"He's back."

Mitch sat back, breathing heavily.

Kamryn started to cry. Mother put her arm around her shoulders and said soothing things to her.

"I was dead?"

"Damn straight."

"Cool." He sat up. "Did you have to pound on me?"

"It worked."

Brand stared across the loft as if he could see the wreckage of

Rembrandt's body beyond. Overhead, the wind began to cry again, thinly, weakly, as if the worst was over.

He shut his eyes. Inside, was nothing but silence. Bauer was gone. He was alone.

He opened his eyes. He was not alone.

The stained glass windows of the cathedral flooded with sudden light. They struck every corner, even into the organ alcove. The moment shone briefly before Yolanda asserted herself again. Brand reached out as if he could touch the rainbow colors.

There was no darkness anywhere.

No matter where he looked.

He'd done it.

Epilogue

The chopper escort loomed low over New Orleans' International Airport. The President of the United States sat by the open door, looking out at the devastation. The Governor of Louisiana sat next to him, pointing out the various areas still flooded, the roofless homes, the massive loss of trees and utilities, their wires snagged and brought down by fallen limbs. Behind them, Secret Service choppers and the press followed. All touched down, the sky streaked with fading clouds and a sun trying its best to dry out the drenched city and parishes.

Senator Bayliss stood first, framed in the side of the chopper. Scorning the hands of aides and emergency workers, he jumped down to the tarmac, then turned to help out the governor and the president. Camera flashes and camcorder lights blazed on the trio as they walked to the waiting motorcade, which would take them to view the destruction wreaked by Hurricane Yolanda.

The press tumbled out of their choppers and flooded across the tarmac to catch the entourage, lenses focusing and film winding. Bayliss strode next to a frail-looking president. A remnant of the wind caught his leonine gray-blond mane and whipped it back from his broad, intelligent forehead. Bayliss appeared to ignore it as he gave an arm of support to the president. If he thought of the picture it represented, of the symbolism, the senator did not show it.

The N.O.P.D. mingled with the suited Secret Service, jostling each other to protect the group. No one, it was said later, knew exactly where he came from. But he came out of the thick of the various protectors, still wearing a yellow rain slicker, dropped his hood and grabbed Bayliss, spinning him around on the tarmac.

Later, it would be said that his target was the president, and that Bayliss had tried to protect him, although video shows that to be inconclusive. All that is known is that he got to the senator first, barehanded, and ripped his throat out. The attacker went down then, under an avalanche of gunfire and tackled by Secret Service men. He broke his neck hitting the airport tarmac, but others would say he already looked like a dead man, preternaturally pale and bloated, like a floater, a body that has been in water for a while.

The autopsy was inconclusive as to cause of death. Either the broken neck or the water in the lungs could have caused the demise. The attacker was identified as one Alexander Stark, a freelance mercenary, whose recent whereabouts could not be confirmed by the Secret Service or the CIA.

Bayliss bled to death in the ambulance speeding him to the only serviceable hospital in the area, in Baton Rouge.

"When were they born?"

Brand did not wait for an answer, but loped after the slim young woman who was showing him the way to an outside shed, redwood-sided, like the stone and paneled home, and tucked up against it in a huge backyard. She wore a faded plaid shirt tucked into her jeans, her malt brown hair swinging free to her shoulders. He watched her walking in front, then something even more important than teenage beauty distracted him. He could hear the soft grunts of pups under her gentle voice.

"About the end of February. We don't expect them to have their eyes open for a few days yet, but we're already socializing them."

Amelinda brought up the rear. "Are they warm enough out here?"

"Oh, yes. This has a sliding door attachment to our den. They stay in the whelping box at night. We bring them in. Later on, their mom will bring them in through the dog door. They're just now getting their legs. They scoot around on their stomachs." The young woman came to a stop, calling. "Jennifer! I've got someone to see your babies."

The dog who came out of the shed did so stepping carefully about the wiggling bodies which surrounded her. Her teats hung below her, full with milk, and her golden hair had a faint auburn cast to it. She paid little attention to the visitors, but thrust her muzzle into her handler's palm. Her feathered tail glided back and forth in welcome.

"Don't rush her or the pups," Karen guided, but Brand had already gotten to his knees at the edge of the papers and blankets which lined the shed floor. She added in surprise, "Look! He's already got his eyes open."

Brand let the sight of the nine young retrievers fill his eyes, their fat-tummied bodies squirming around in search of their mother and their littermates. They were light yellow in color, and short-haired, with no hint of the wavy, silken hair which would grow in later, although their paws seemed twice as big as they needed to be. He looked at the pup with the open eyes. The creature seemed to be the most precocious one of the bunch. He already knew how to get his legs under his well-fed body and swim to where he wanted to be. Now, his littermates realized mom had left them, and although only a few steps away, were grunting and whining anxiously in search of her.

Only this one crept in search of Brand.

Jennifer shifted weight to swing her head around, sniffing at Amelinda, then carefully at Brand.

He held his hand out. She nosed his fingers thoroughly, then swiped a quick lick across them, and gave her attention back to Karen.

In the meantime, the pup was at his knees, worrying at the denim.

"Can I pick him up?"

"Carefully. Make sure you've both hands under him. If Jennifer frets, just show her the pup and put him back down gently."

"What color are his eyes?"

"Now, sort of a black-blue. As they get older, they turn a warm brown, just like they're supposed to." Karen smiled, her freckled face rippling. To Amelinda, she said, "This his first dog?"

"Pretty much."

"Goldens are great dogs for teens."

Brand carefully lifted the pup to his face, and looked, knowing he would not see anything more spectacular than a fuzzy-faced pup, barely two weeks old, scarcely used to looking at anything from his canine point of view.

Two vivid brown eyes looked back at him, knowing eyes, welcoming eyes, eyes full of life and all its intensity, full of love and loyalty and happiness. Brand sucked his breath in sharply.

"Brandon, what's wrong?"

The eyes faded to puppy newness, but the knowing in them remained. He pulled the pup close and tucked its warm body under his chin. "Nothing."

Amelinda watched him. She swung a wing of dark hair behind her ear. "Sure?"

"Positive."

She hesitated a moment, then asked, "Do you want him?"

"Do I!"

"You have your contract with us. Homework, chores . . . all that family stuff."

"I know." He did not look at her, afraid she would see the plea in his face, afraid she would deny him, his heart accelerating, even though they had had this discussion, he and Mitch and Amelinda, and this agreement. He'd been waiting months for this litter to be born, days until the dog breeders had said they would allow visitors.

Amelinda gave her hand to Karen. "I think you just sold a dog."

"That one? Are you sure? Don't you want to look at any of the others? Both mom and dad are champions."

"No," Brand answered tightly. His voice squeaked a little, in that way changing voices sometimes did. Or perhaps it was a voice full of emotion. He did not look up, his face pressed closely to the golden pup's flank, his fingers gently stroking an ear flap. As for the pup, he had contentedly gone to sleep at Brand's throat.

"Well," Karen remarked, shaking out a royal blue woven puppy collar. "That's what we're here for. You can visit him, after school, if you want. He won't be ready to go for another six weeks."

"Great."

"Got a name?"

"Yeah," answered Brand. "Dakota."

"Good choice." Karen slipped her fingers under Brand's chin to fasten the collar on the pup. "Named for anybody in particular?"

"I used to know a golden retriever," Brand said. "Cody. This is close, but different. A new life, a new name. That's the way it ought to be."

"Sounds good to me." Karen shook hands with Amelinda again. "Looks like our dog has got a boy."